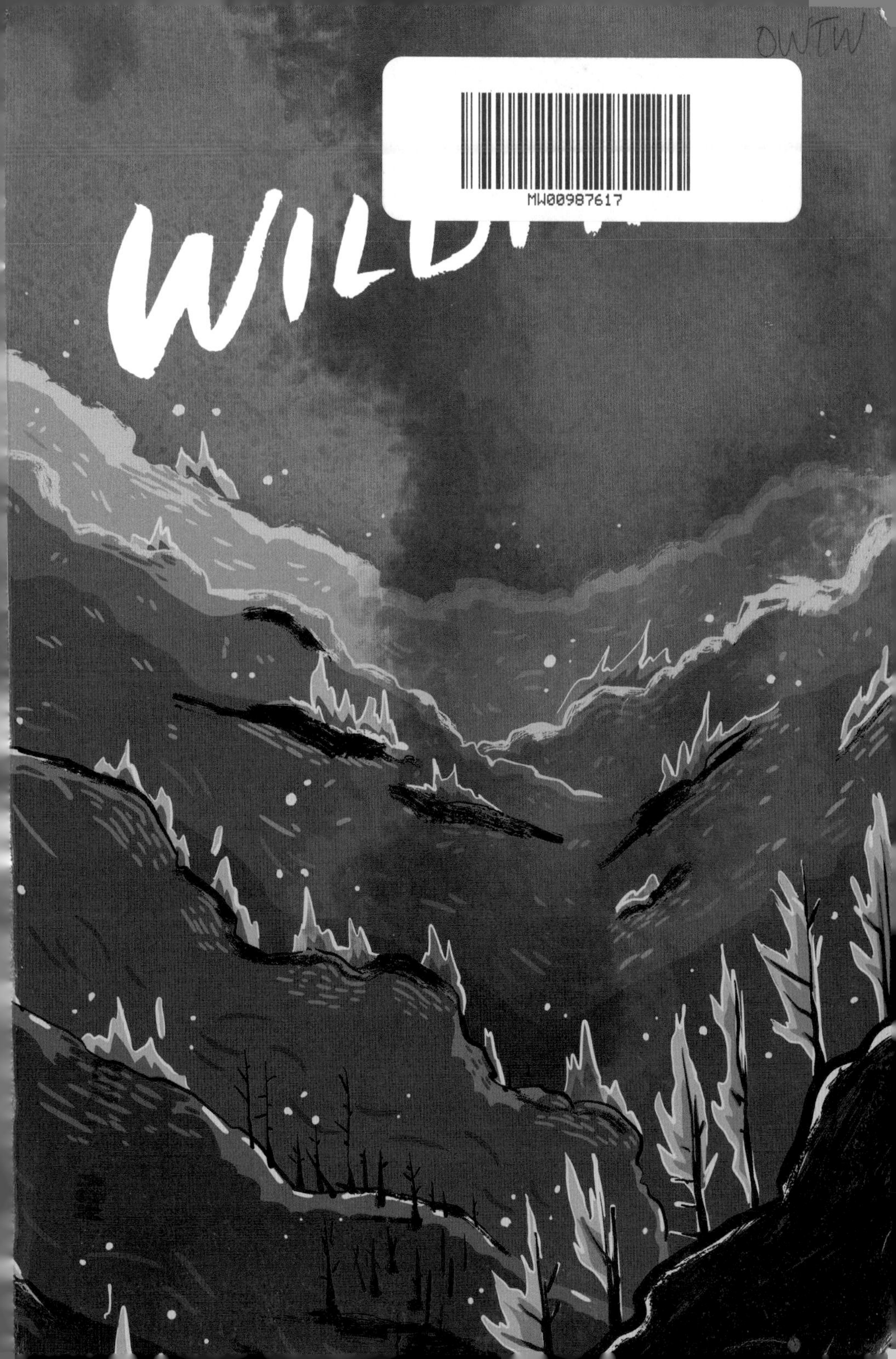

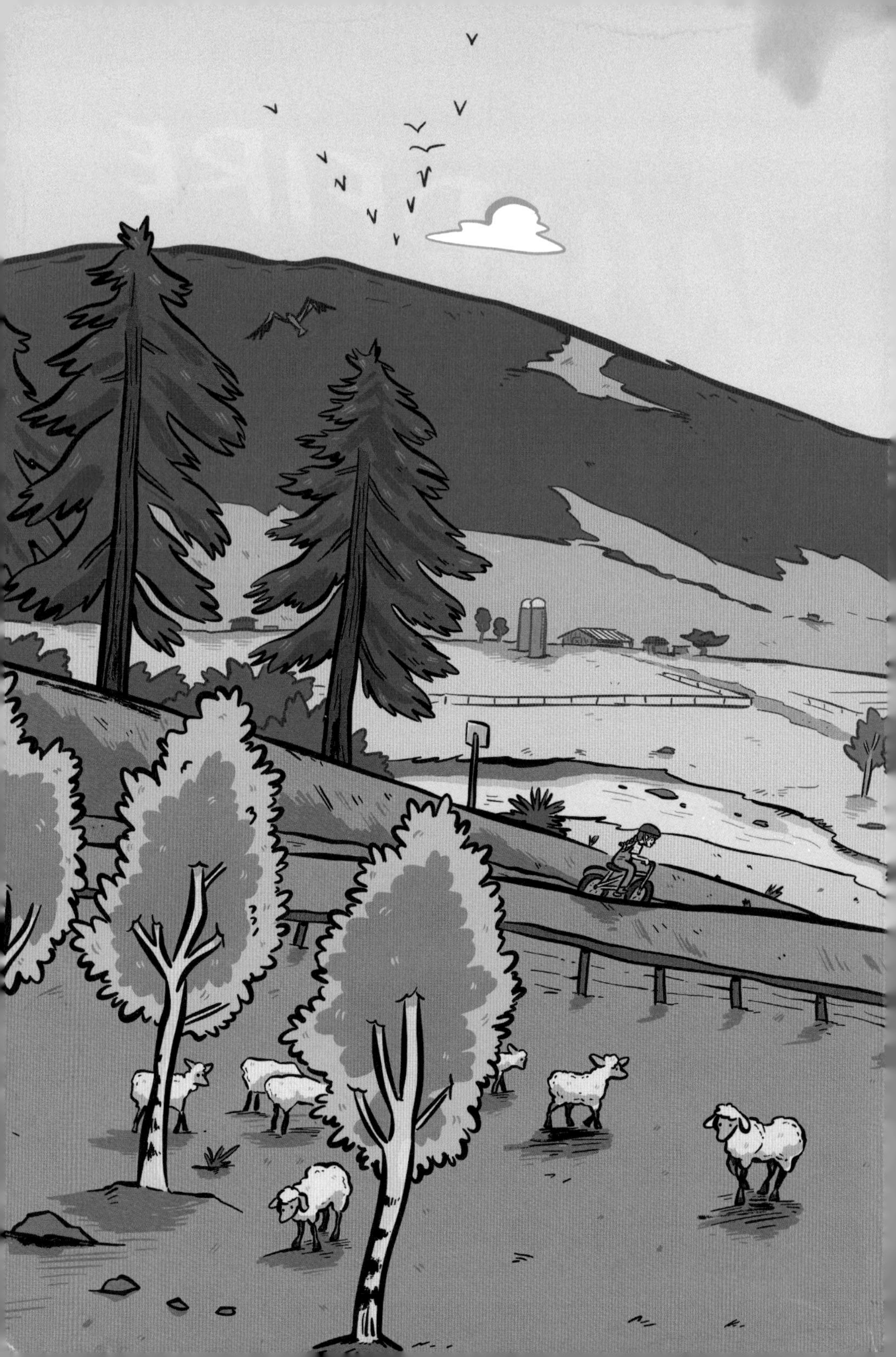

WILDFIRE

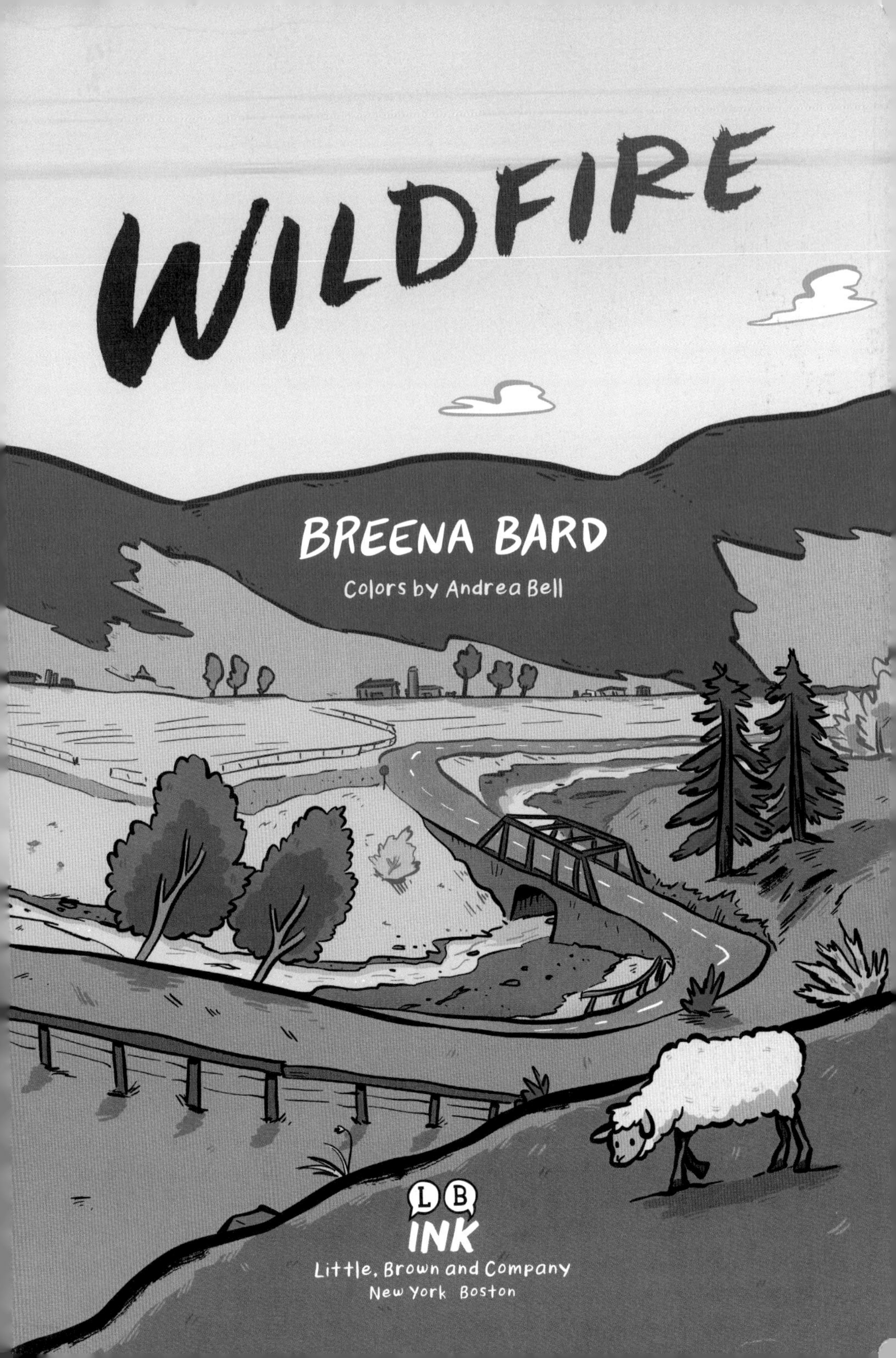

BREENA BARD

Colors by Andrea Bell

LB INK

Little, Brown and Company

New York Boston

ABOUT THIS BOOK

This book was edited by Andrea Colvin and designed by Carolyn Bull and Ann Dwyer.
The production was supervised by Bernadette Flinn, and the production editor was Jake Regier.
The text was set in Buzzerbeater Regular.

Little, Brown Ink
Hachette Book Group
1290 Avenue of the Americas, New York, NY 10104
Visit us at LBYR.com

First Edition: September 2023

Little, Brown Ink is an imprint of Little, Brown and Company.
The Little, Brown Ink name and logo are trademarks of Hachette Book Group, Inc.

Little, Brown and Company books may be purchased in bulk for business, educational,
or promotional use. For information, please contact your local bookseller or the
Hachette Book Group Special Markets Department at special.markets@hbgusa.com.

Library of Congress Cataloging-in-Publication Data
Names: Bard, Breena, author, illustrator.
Title: Wildfire / Breena Bard.
Description: First edition. | New York : Little, Brown and Company, 2023. | Audience: Ages 8–14.
Summary: "After her home burns down, Julianna moves to a new town to start over
but learns that the boy who started the fire goes to her new school." —Provided by publisher.
Identifiers: LCCN 2022021667 | ISBN 9780316277686 (hardcover) | ISBN 9780316277655
(trade paperback) | ISBN 9780316277846 (ebook)
Subjects: CYAC: Graphic novels. | Wildfires—Fiction. | Climatic changes—Fiction. |
Protest movements—Fiction. | LCGFT: Graphic novels.
Classification: LCC PZ7.7.B355 Wi 2023 | DDC 741.5/973—dc23/eng/20220602
LC record available at https://lccn.loc.gov/2022021667

ISBNs: 978-0-316-27768-6 (hardcover), 978-0-316-27765-5 (paperback), 978-0-316-27784-6
(ebook), 978-0-316-38464-3 (ebook), 978-0-316-38484-1 (ebook)

PRINTED IN GERMANY

MOHN

Hardcover: 10 9 8 7 6 5 4 3 2 1
Paperback: 10 9 8 7 6 5 4 3 2 1

For Harvey and Helen

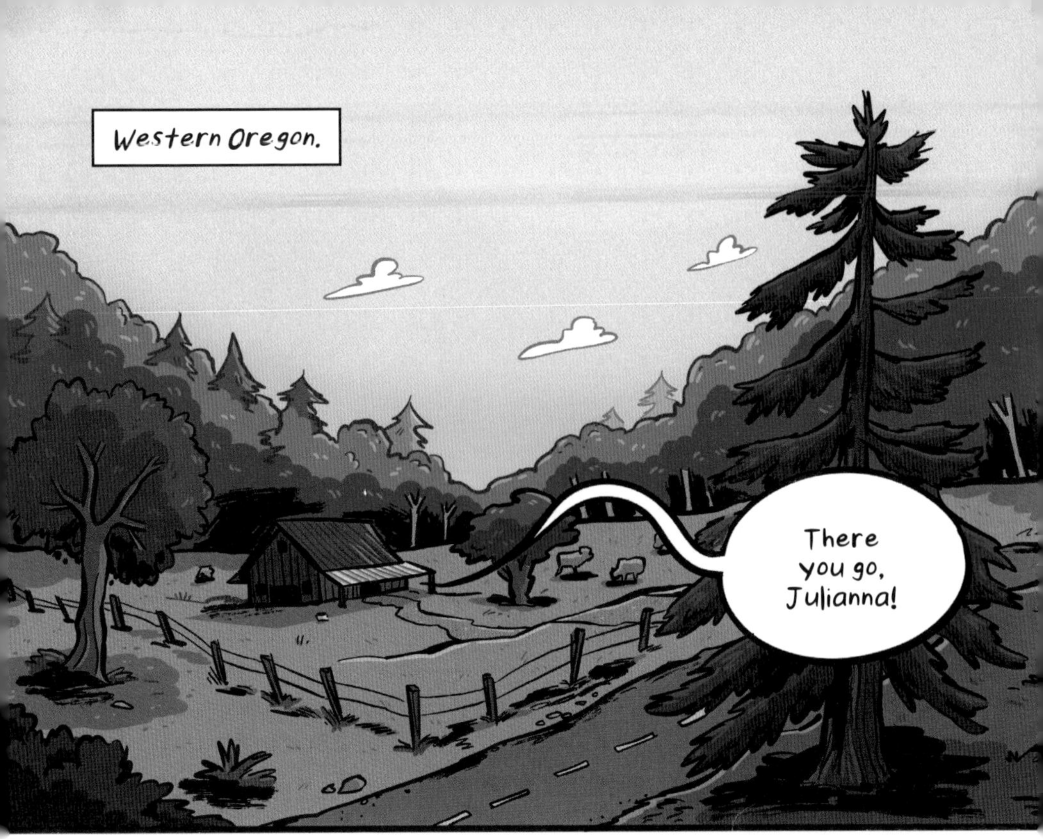
Western Oregon.
There you go, Julianna!

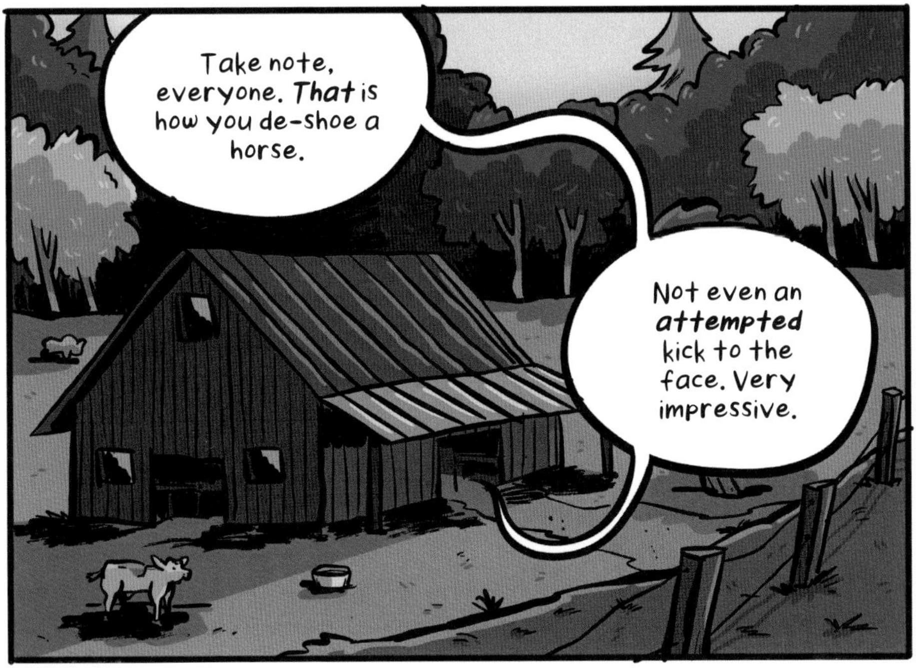
Take note, everyone. *That* is how you de-shoe a horse.
Not even an ***attempted*** kick to the face. Very impressive.

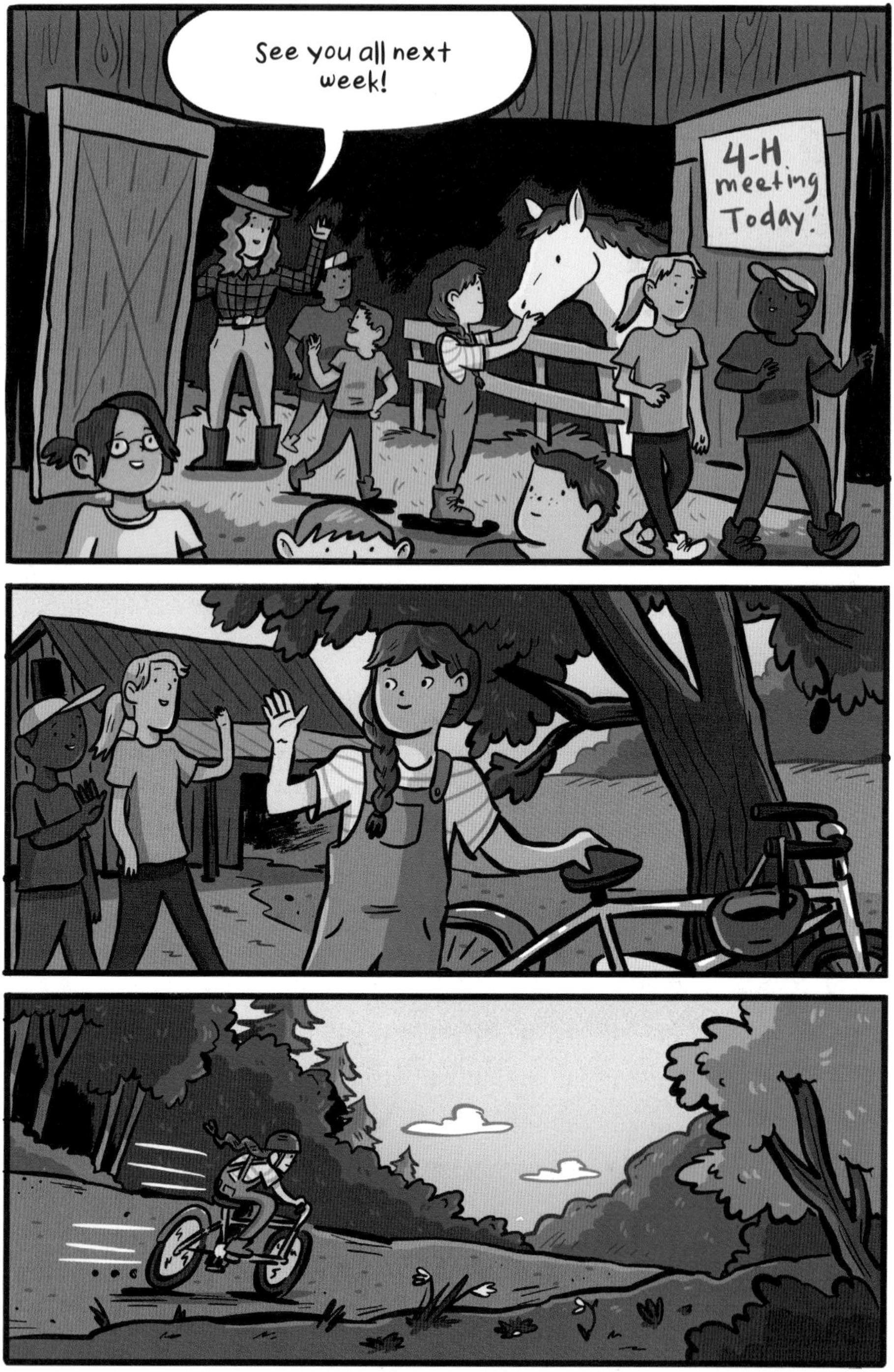
See you all next week!
4-H meeting Today!

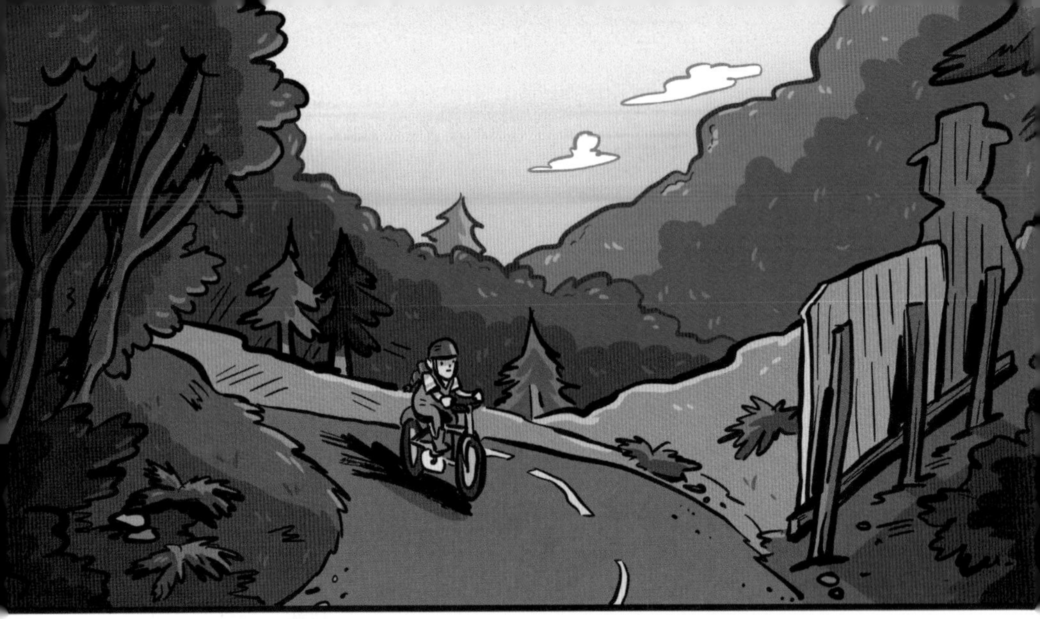

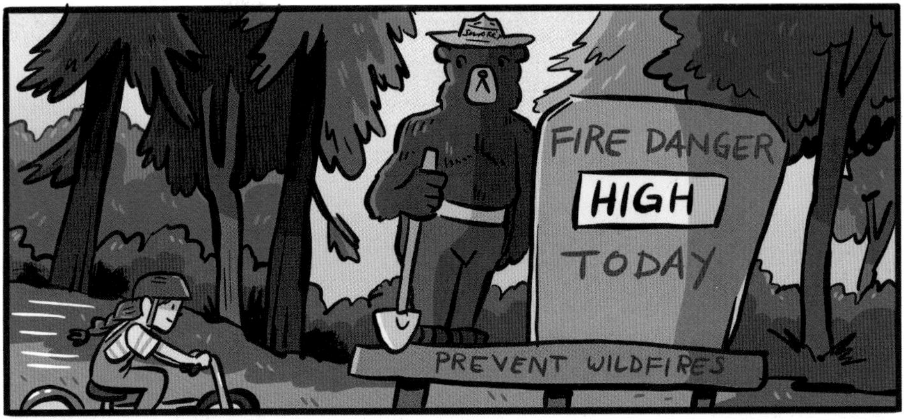
FIRE DANGER
HIGH
TODAY
PREVENT WILDFIRES

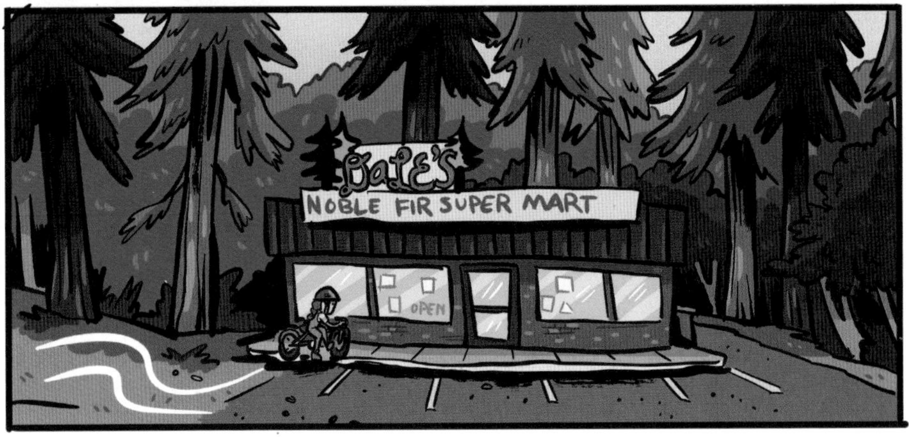
DALE'S
NOBLE FIR SUPER MART
OPEN

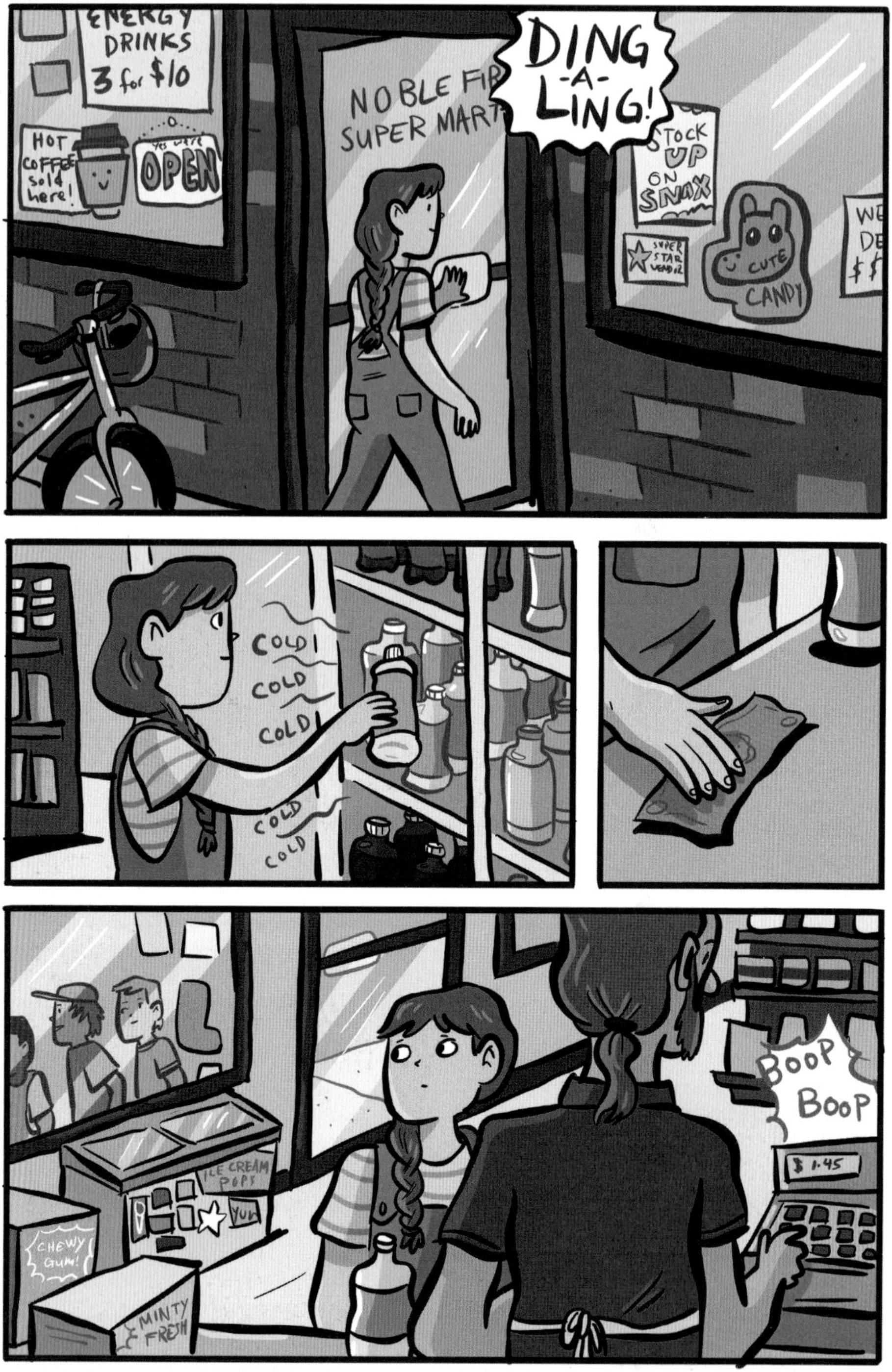
ENERGY DRINKS 3 for $10
HOT COFFEE sold here!
OPEN
NOBLE FIR SUPER MART
DING-A-LING!
STOCK UP ON SNAX
SUPER STAR VENDOR
CUTE CANDY
COLD!
COLD
COLD
COLD
COLD
ICE CREAM POPS
YUM
CHEWY GUM!
MINTY FRESH
BOOP BOOP
$ 1.45

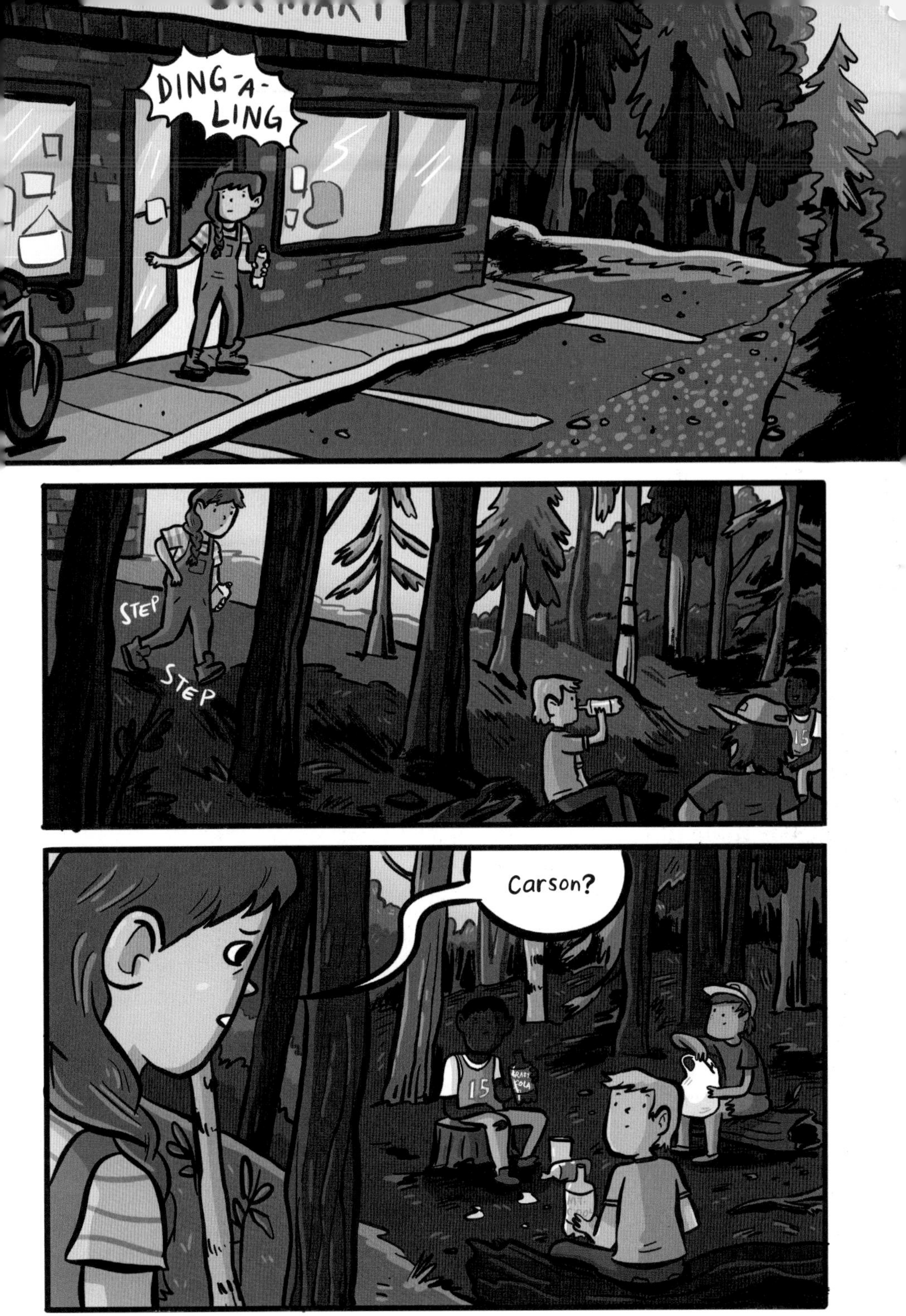
DING-A-LING
STEP
STEP
Carson?

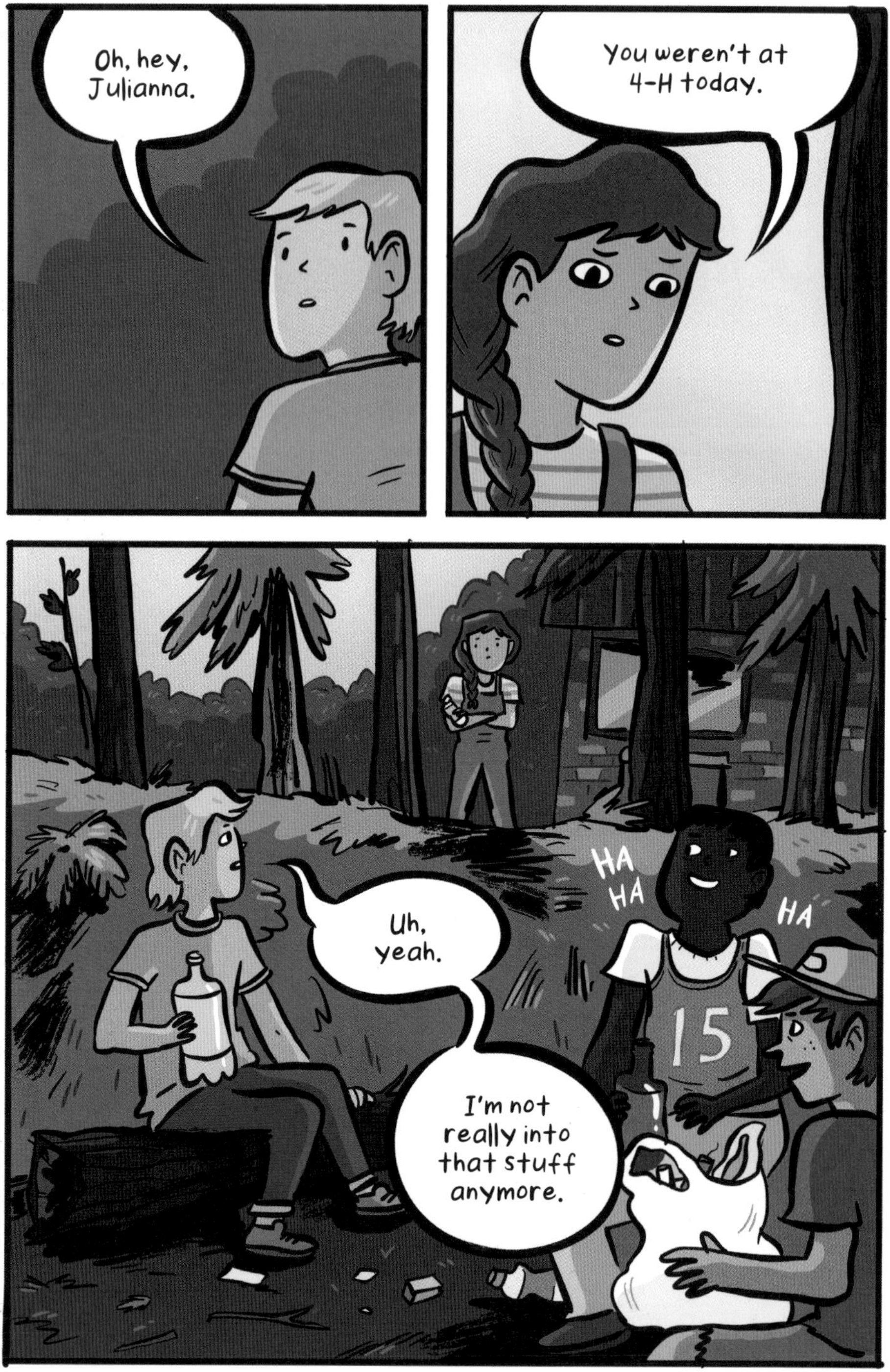
Oh, hey, Julianna.
You weren't at 4-H today.
HA HA
HA
Uh, yeah.
I'm not really into that stuff anymore.
15

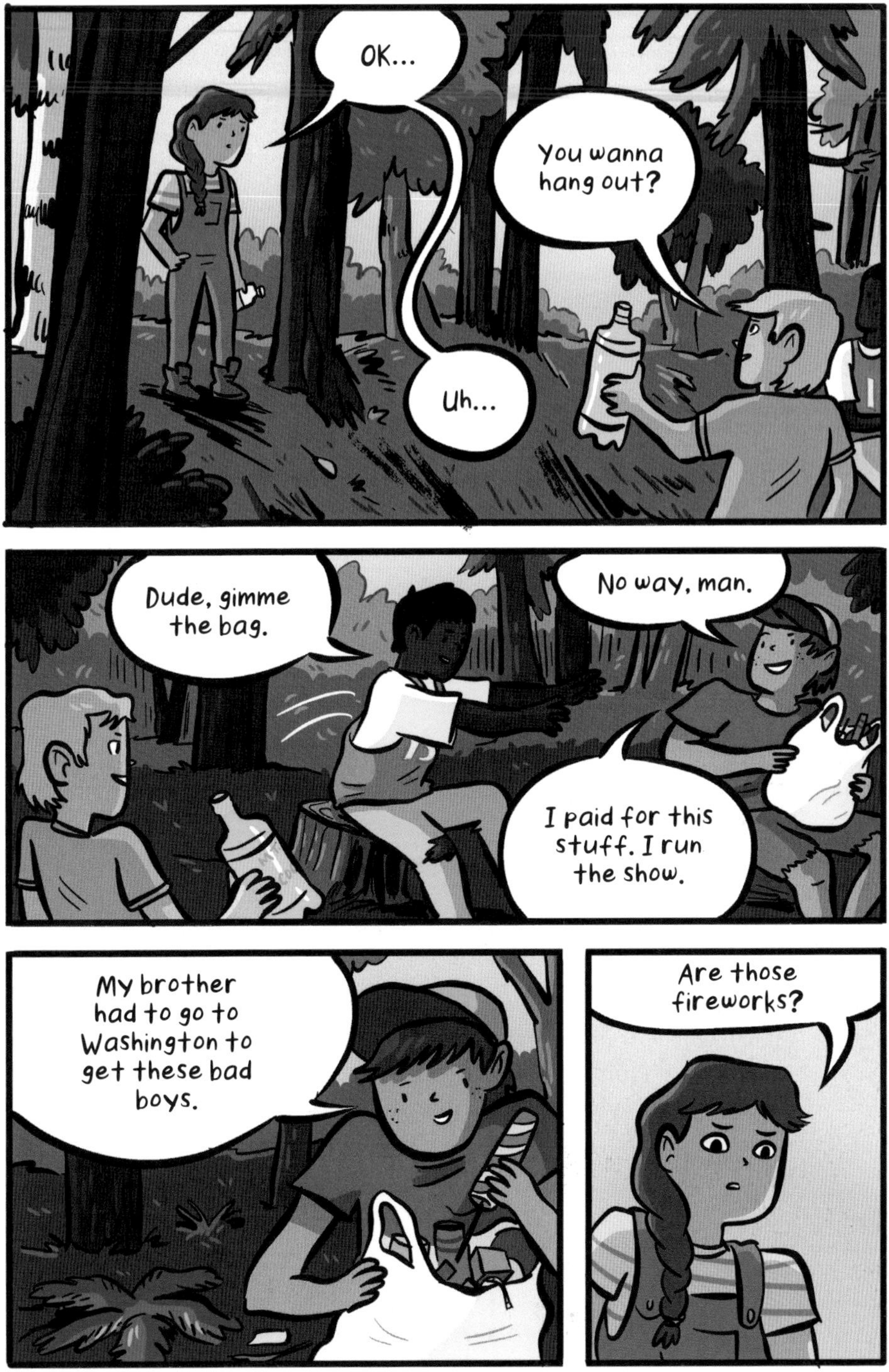
OK...
You wanna hang out?
Uh...
Dude, gimme the bag.
No way, man.
I paid for this stuff. I run the show.
My brother had to go to Washington to get these bad boys.
Are those fireworks?

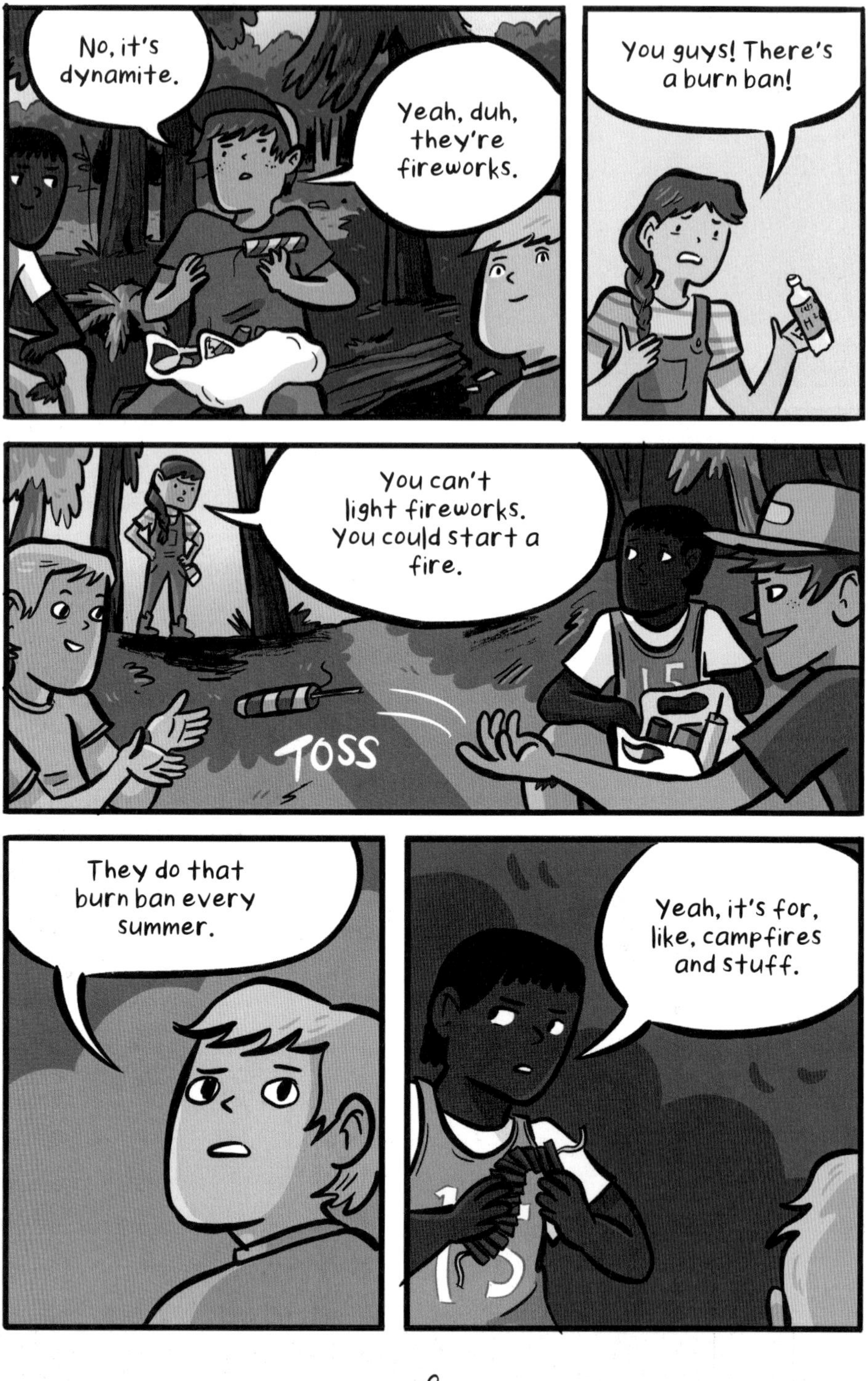
No, it's dynamite.
Yeah, duh, they're fireworks.
You guys! There's a burn ban!
You can't light fireworks. You could start a fire.
TOSS
They do that burn ban every summer.
Yeah, it's for, like, campfires and stuff.

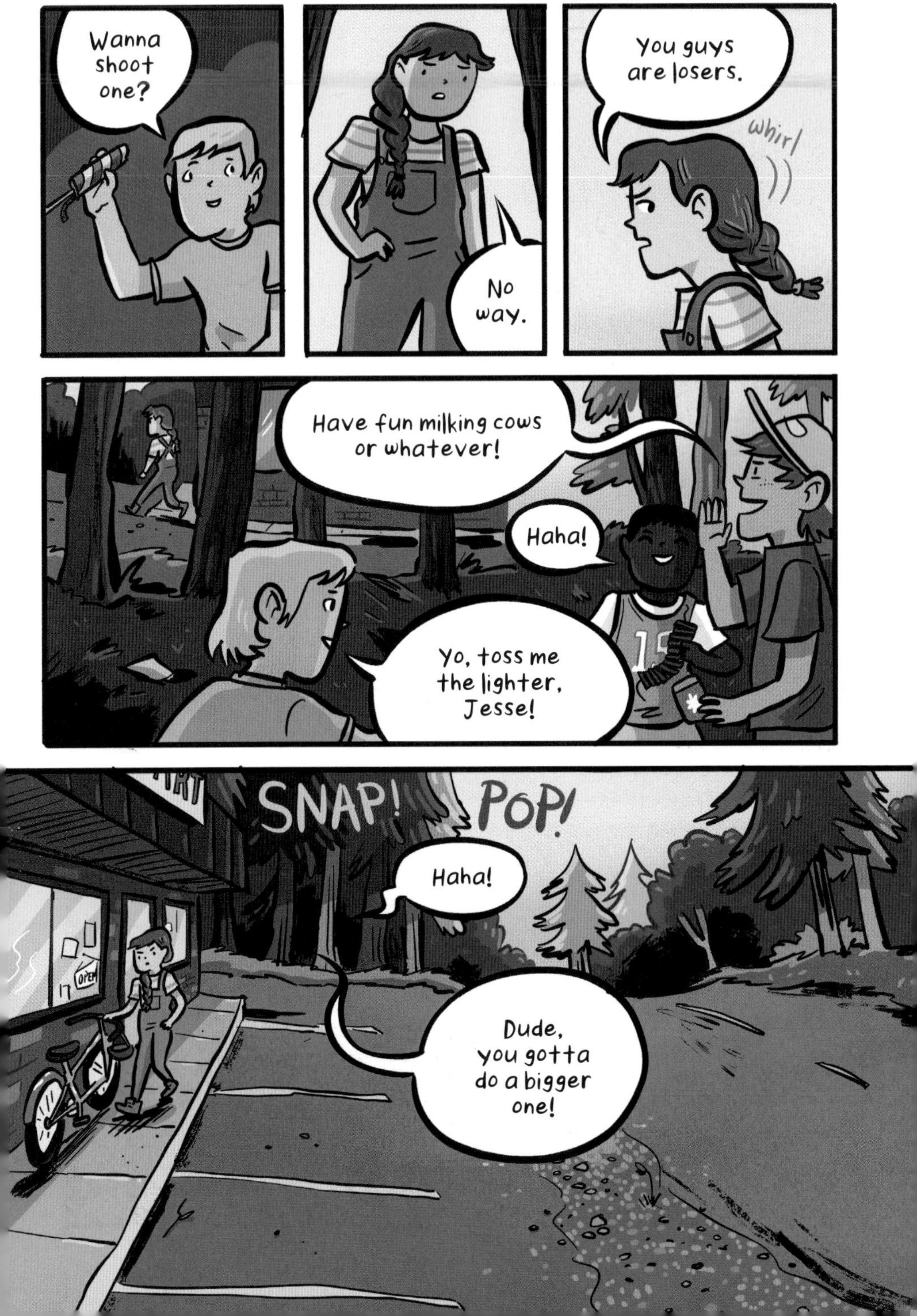
Wanna shoot one?
No way.
You guys are losers.
whirl
Have fun milking cows or whatever!
Haha!
Yo, toss me the lighter, Jesse!
SNAP! POP!
Haha!
Dude, you gotta do a bigger one!
OPEN

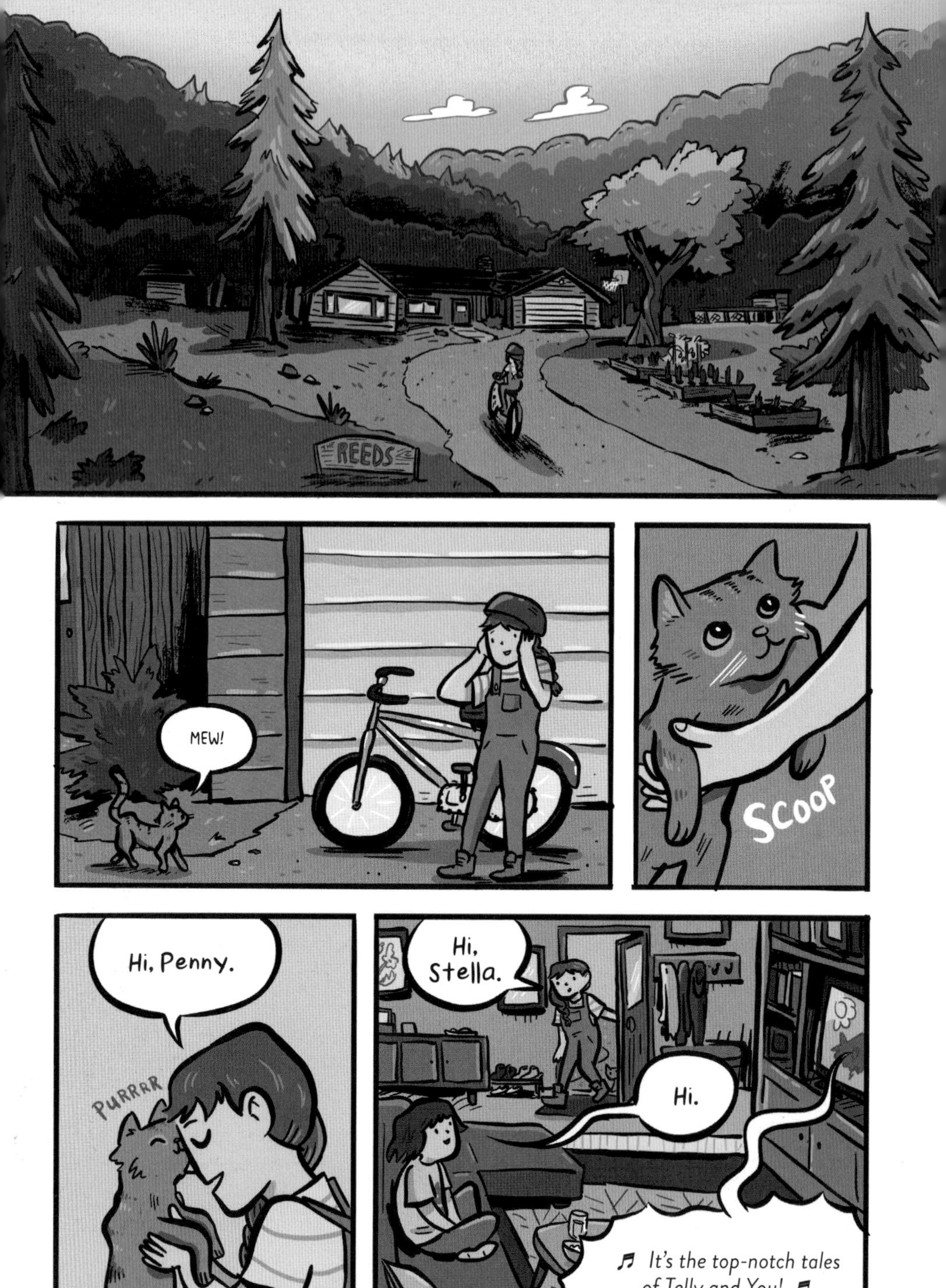
REEDS
MEW!
SCOOP
Hi, Penny.
PURRRR
Hi, Stella.
Hi.
♬ It's the top-notch tales of Telly and You! ♬

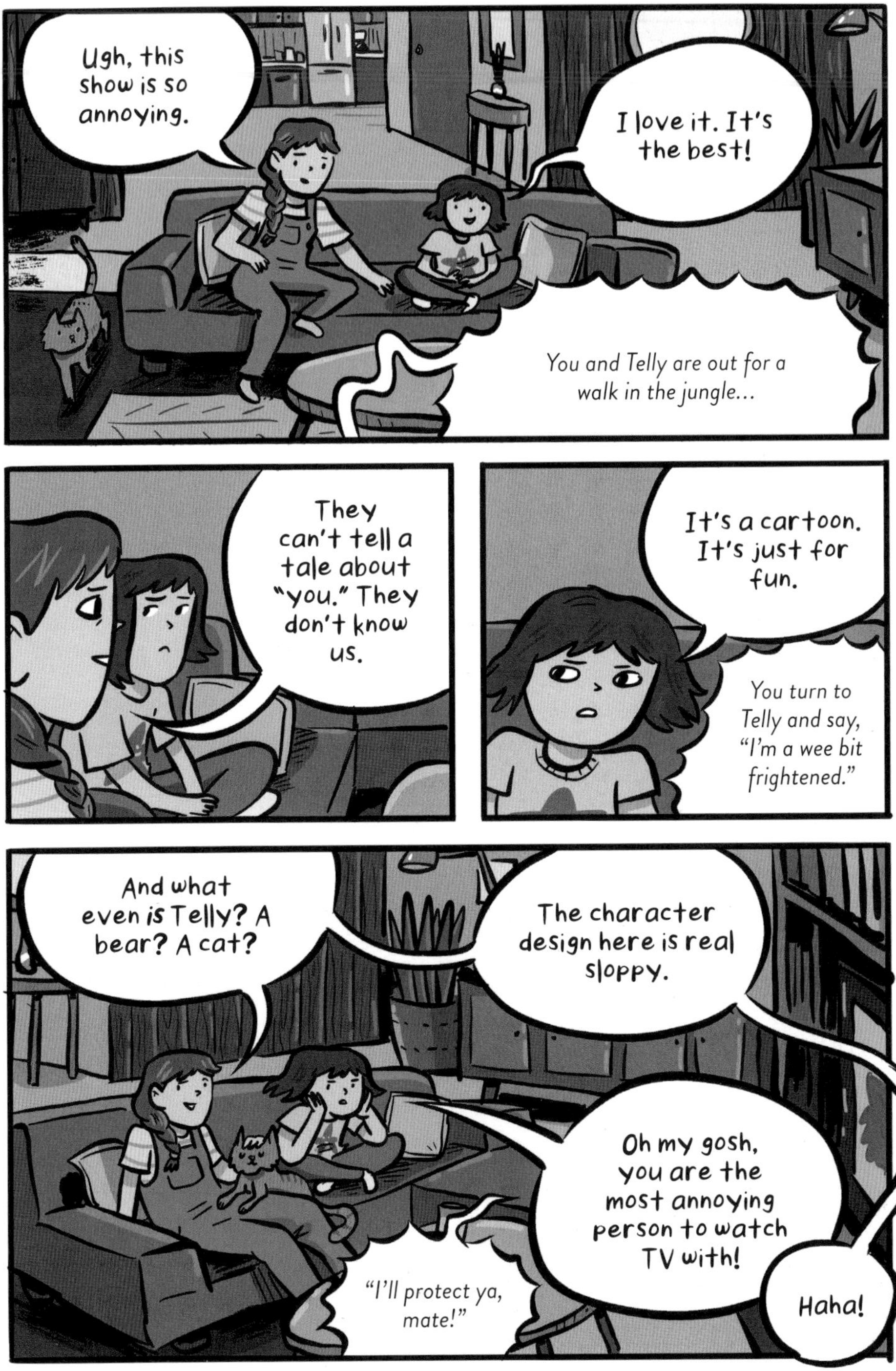
Ugh, this show is so annoying.
I love it. It's the best!
You and Telly are out for a walk in the jungle...
They can't tell a tale about "you." They don't know us.
It's a cartoon. It's just for fun.
You turn to Telly and say, "I'm a wee bit frightened."
And what even is Telly? A bear? A cat?
The character design here is real sloppy.
Oh my gosh, you are the most annoying person to watch TV with!
"I'll protect ya, mate!"
Haha!

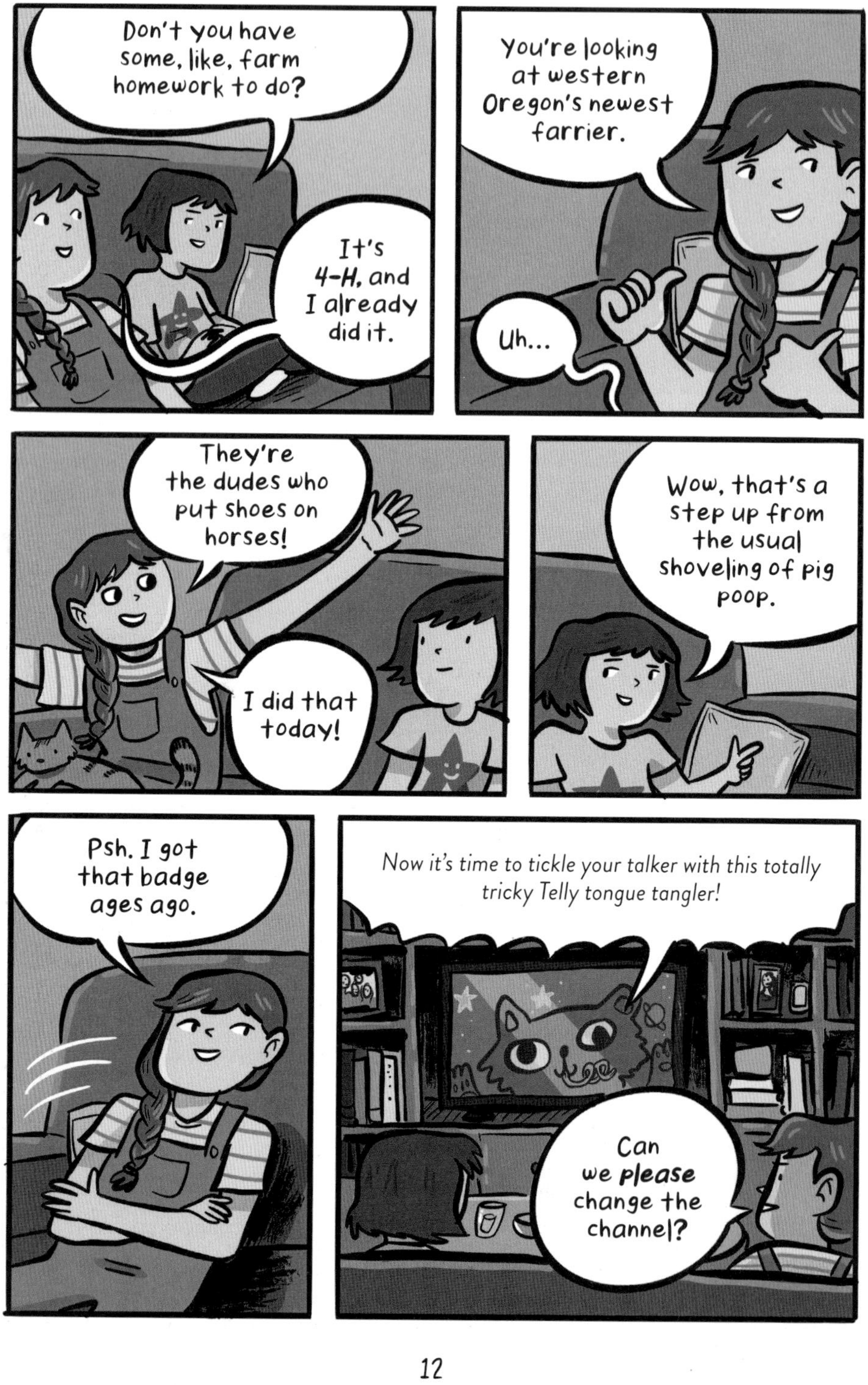
Don't you have some, like, farm homework to do?
It's 4-H, and I already did it.
You're looking at western Oregon's newest farrier.
Uh...
They're the dudes who put shoes on horses!
I did that today!
Wow, that's a step up from the usual shoveling of pig poop.
Psh. I got that badge ages ago.
Now it's time to tickle your talker with this totally tricky Telly tongue tangler!
Can we **please** change the channel?

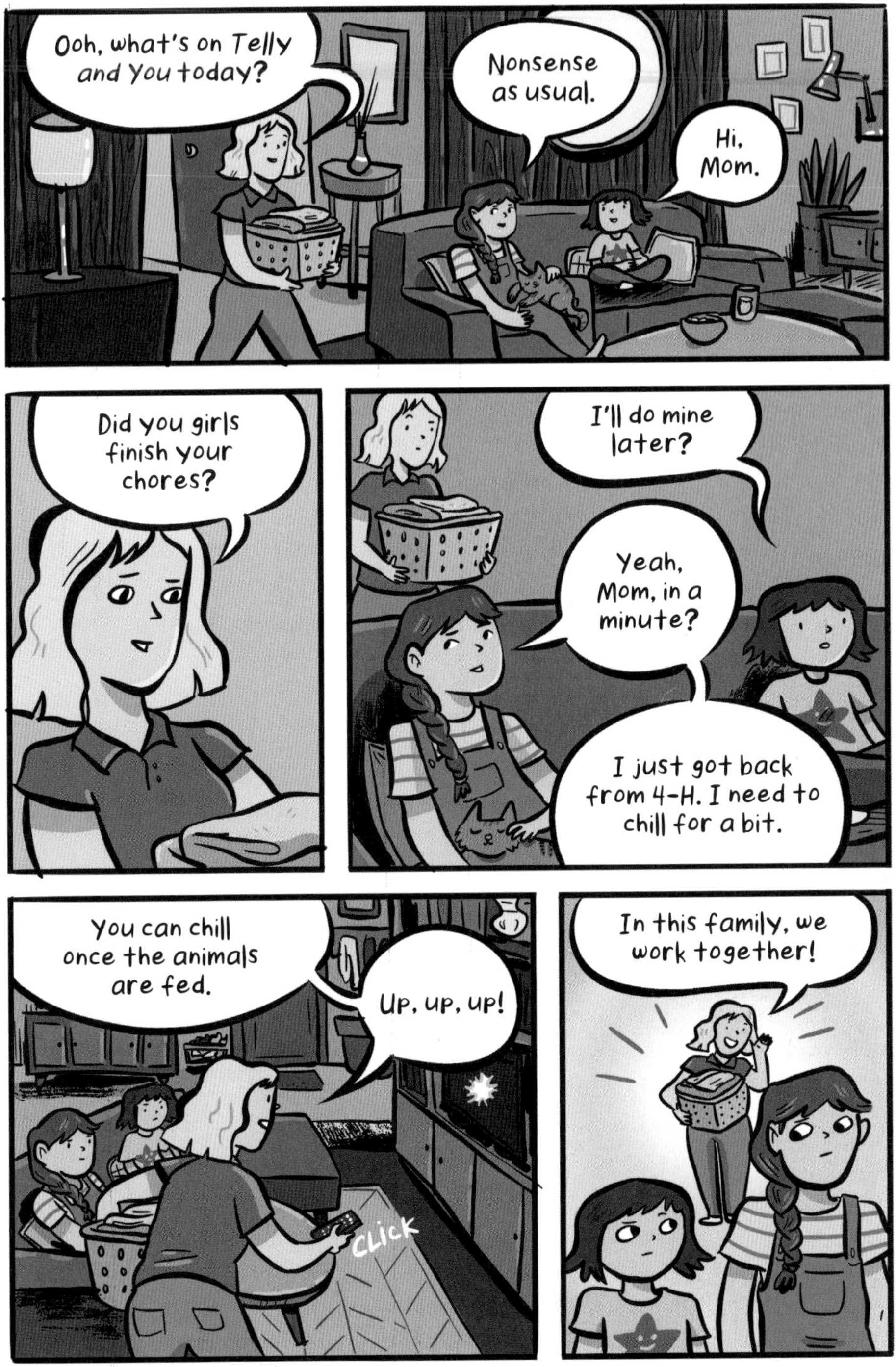
Ooh, what's on Telly and You today?
Nonsense as usual.
Hi, Mom.
Did you girls finish your chores?
I'll do mine later?
Yeah, Mom, in a minute?
I just got back from 4-H. I need to chill for a bit.
You can chill once the animals are fed.
Up, up, up!
CLICK
In this family, we work together!

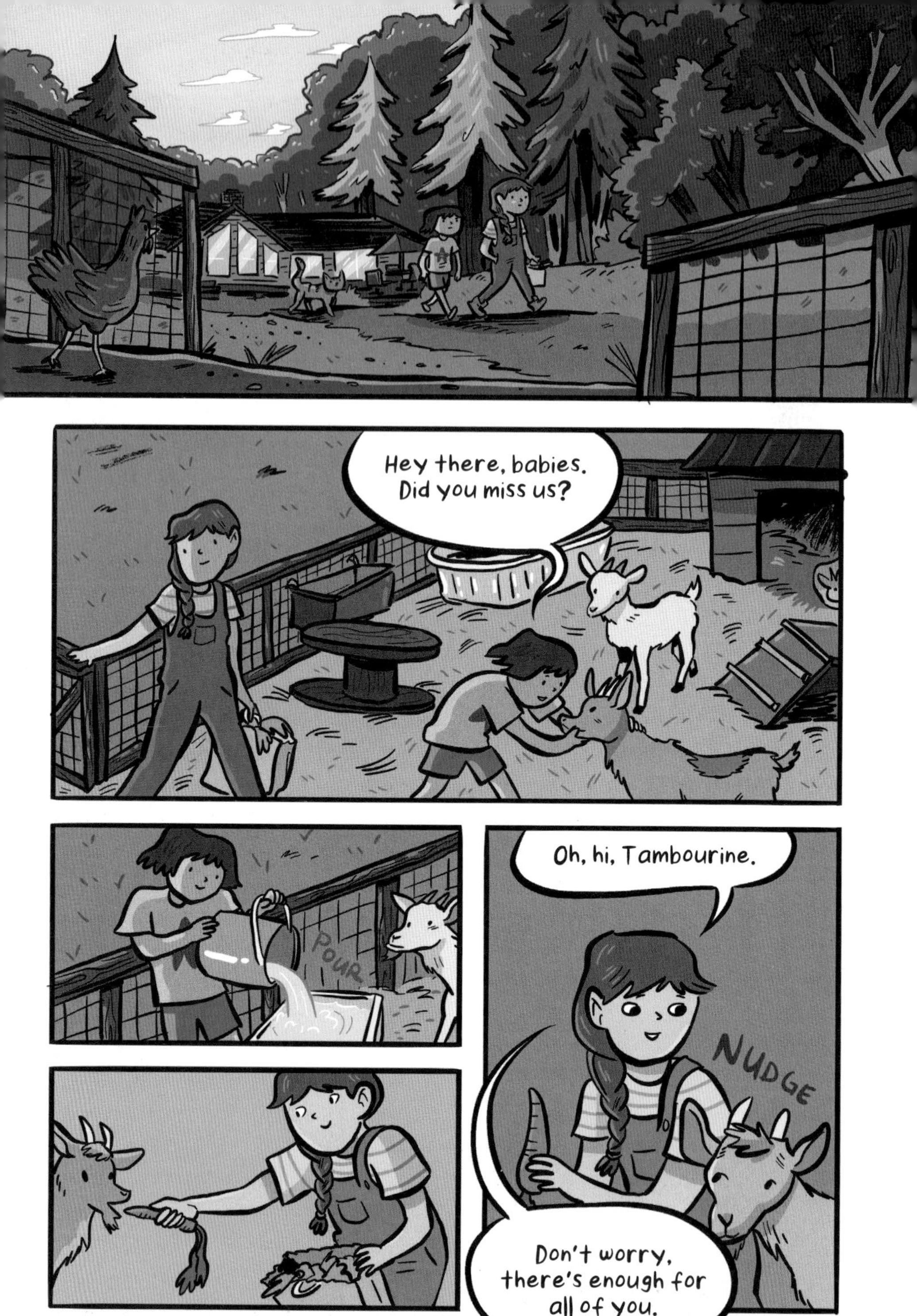
Hey there, babies. Did you miss us?
POUR
Oh, hi, Tambourine.
NUDGE
Don't worry, there's enough for all of you.

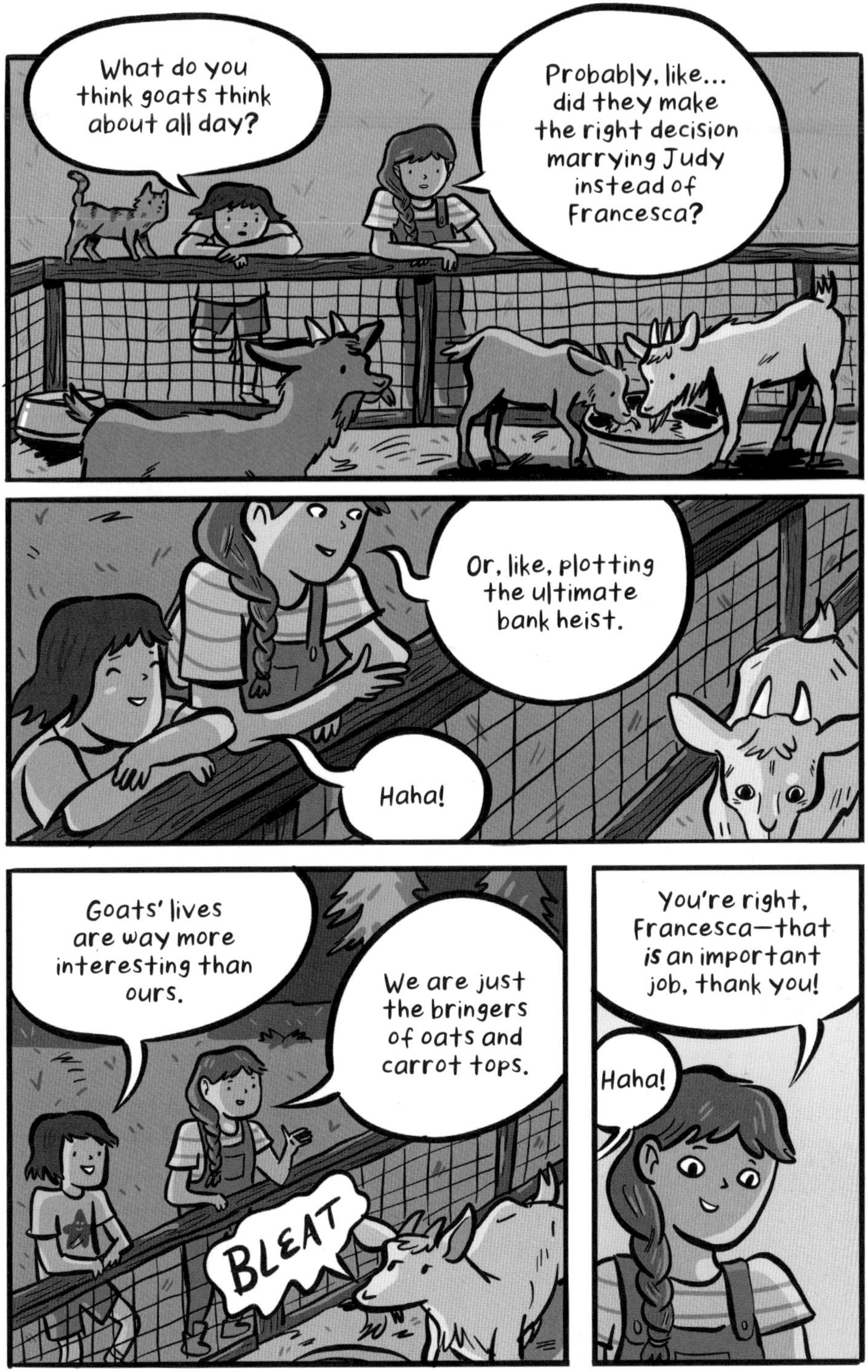
What do you think goats think about all day?
Probably, like... did they make the right decision marrying Judy instead of Francesca?
Or, like, plotting the ultimate bank heist.
Haha!
Goats' lives are way more interesting than ours.
We are just the bringers of oats and carrot tops.
BLEAT
You're right, Francesca—that *is* an important job, thank you!
Haha!

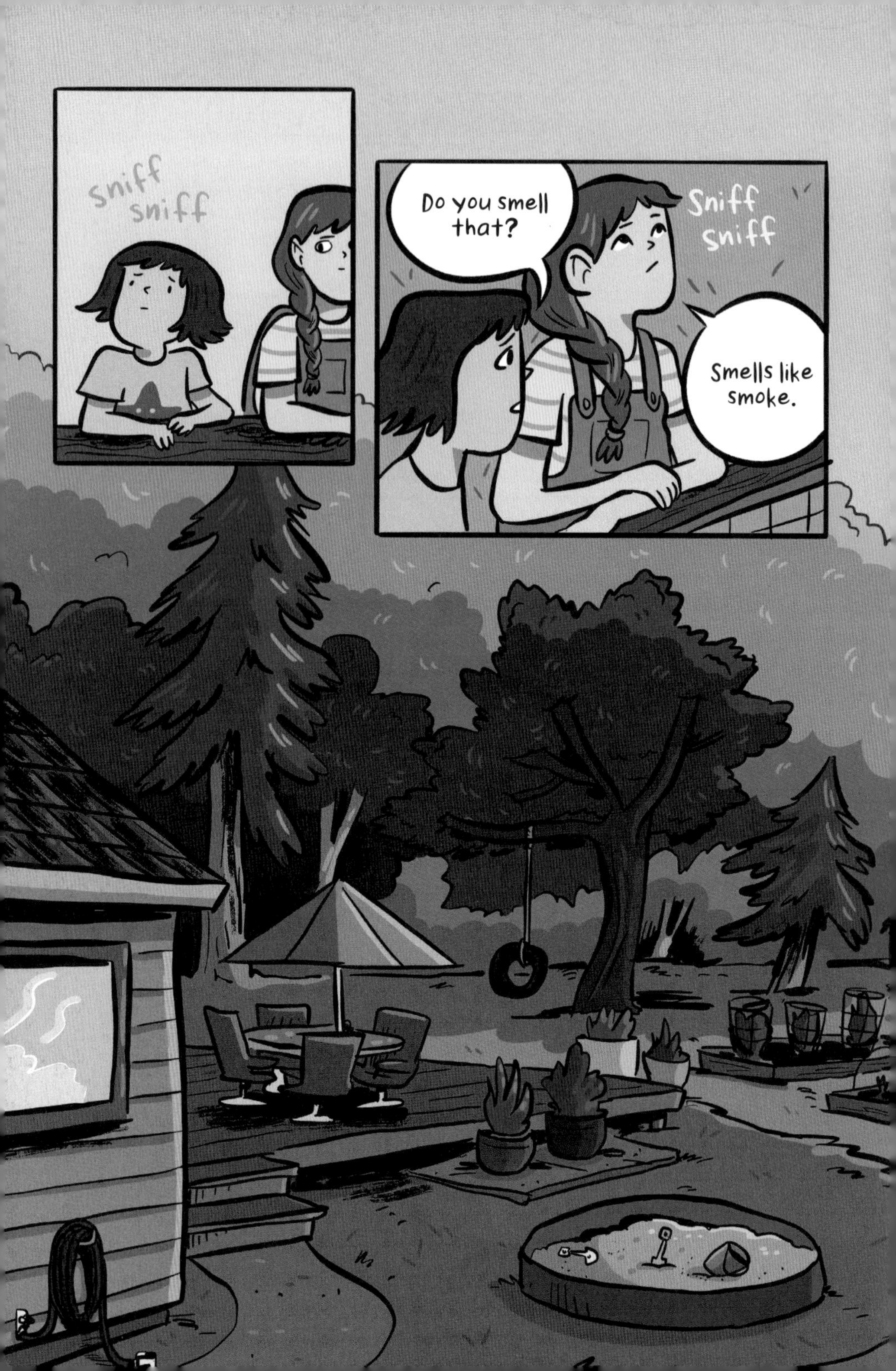
sniff sniff
Do you smell that?
Sniff sniff
Smells like smoke.

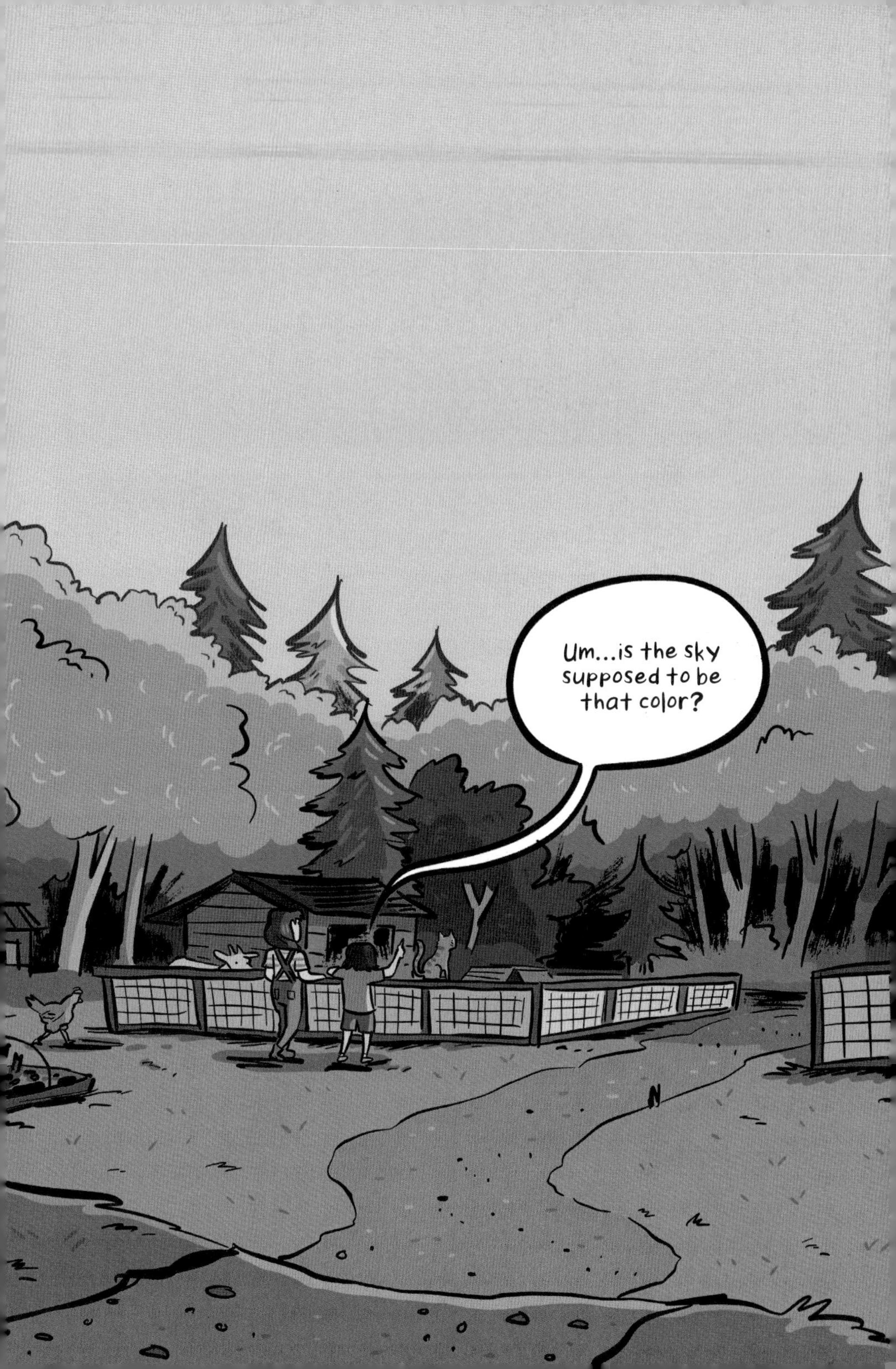
Um...is the sky supposed to be that color?

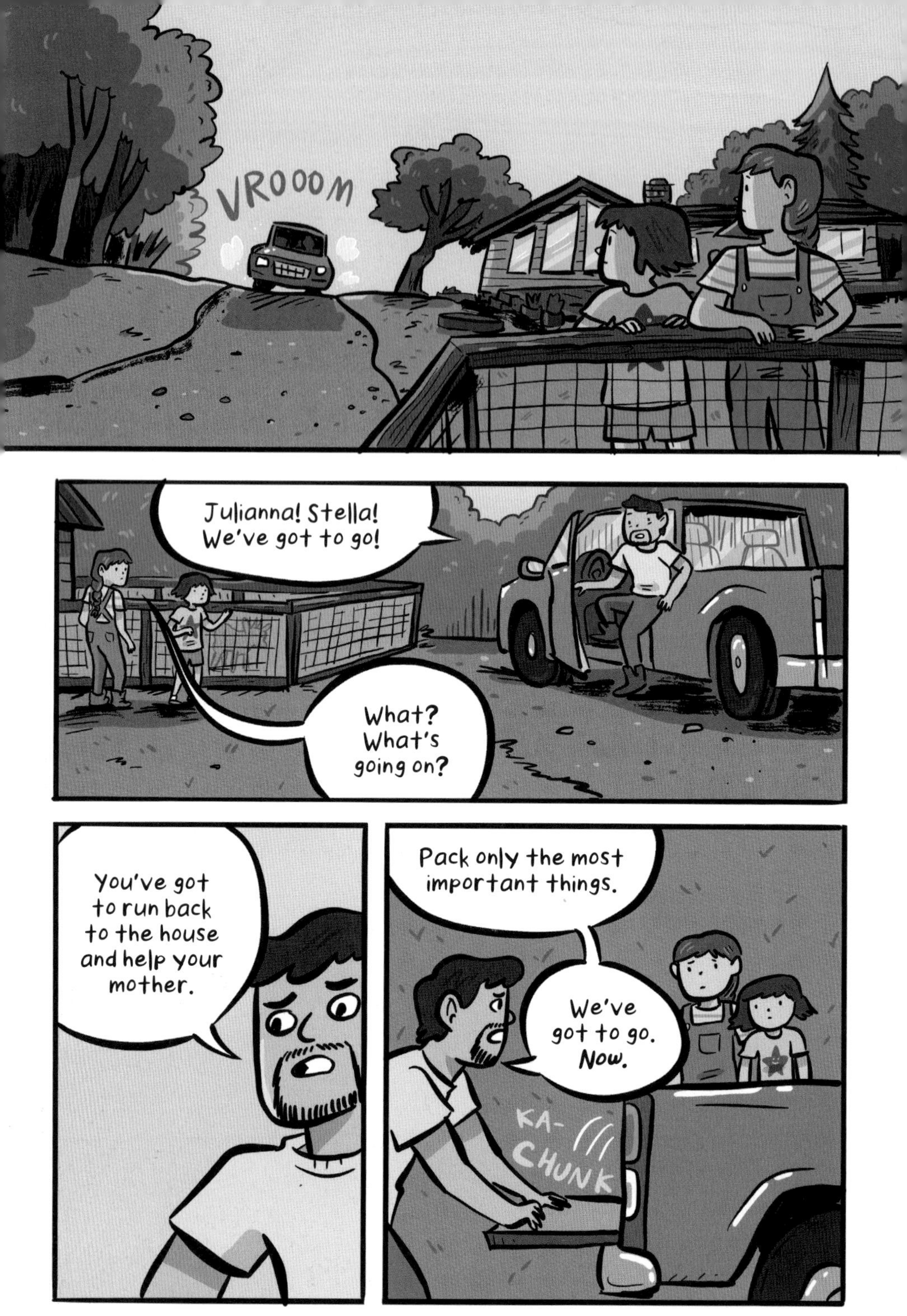
VROOOM
Julianna! Stella! We've got to go!
What? What's going on?
You've got to run back to the house and help your mother.
Pack only the most important things.
We've got to go. Now.
KA-CHUNK

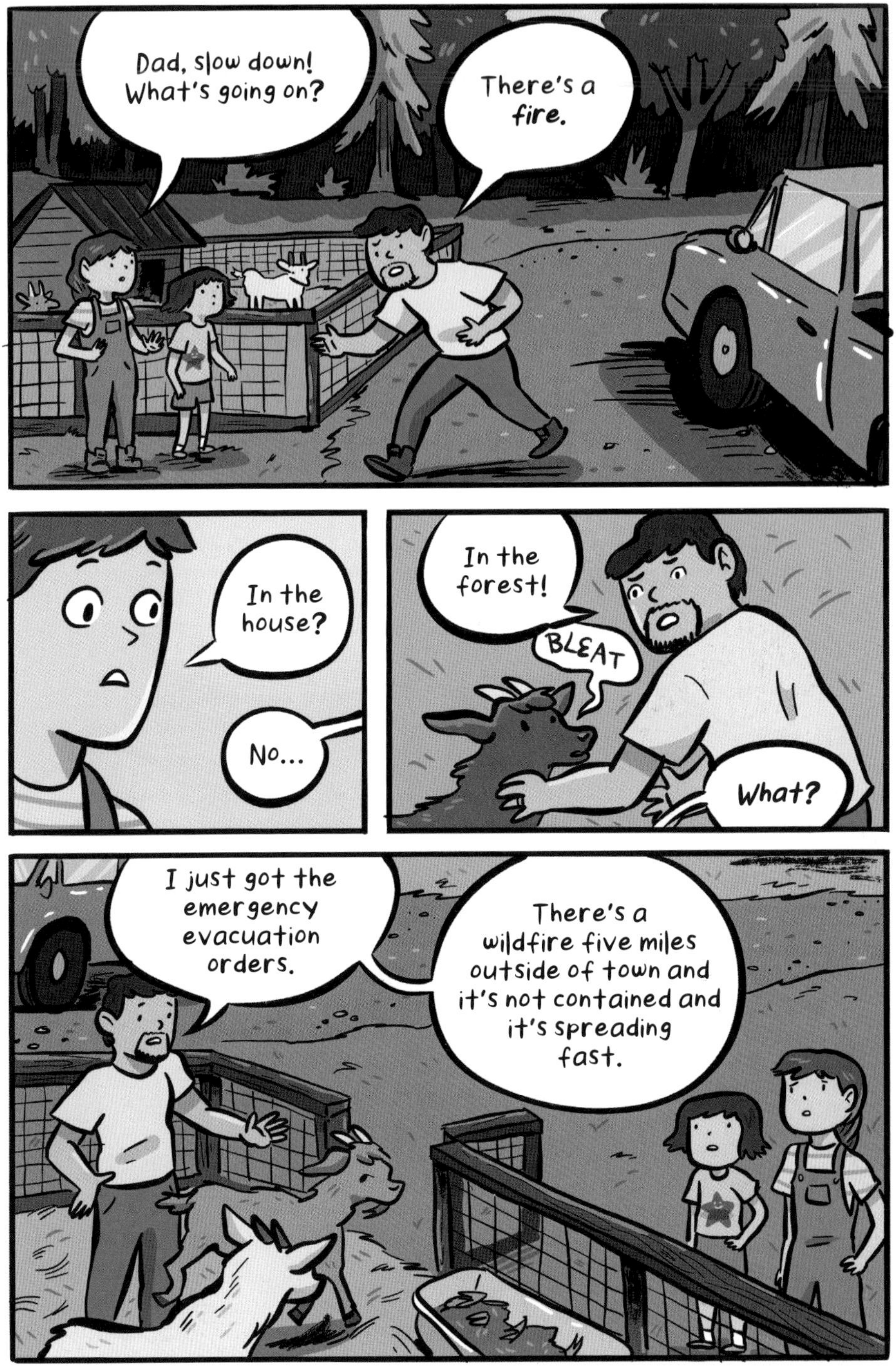

Dad, slow down! What's going on?
There's a *fire.*
In the house?
No...
In the forest!
BLEAT
What?
I just got the emergency evacuation orders.
There's a wildfire five miles outside of town and it's not contained and it's spreading fast.

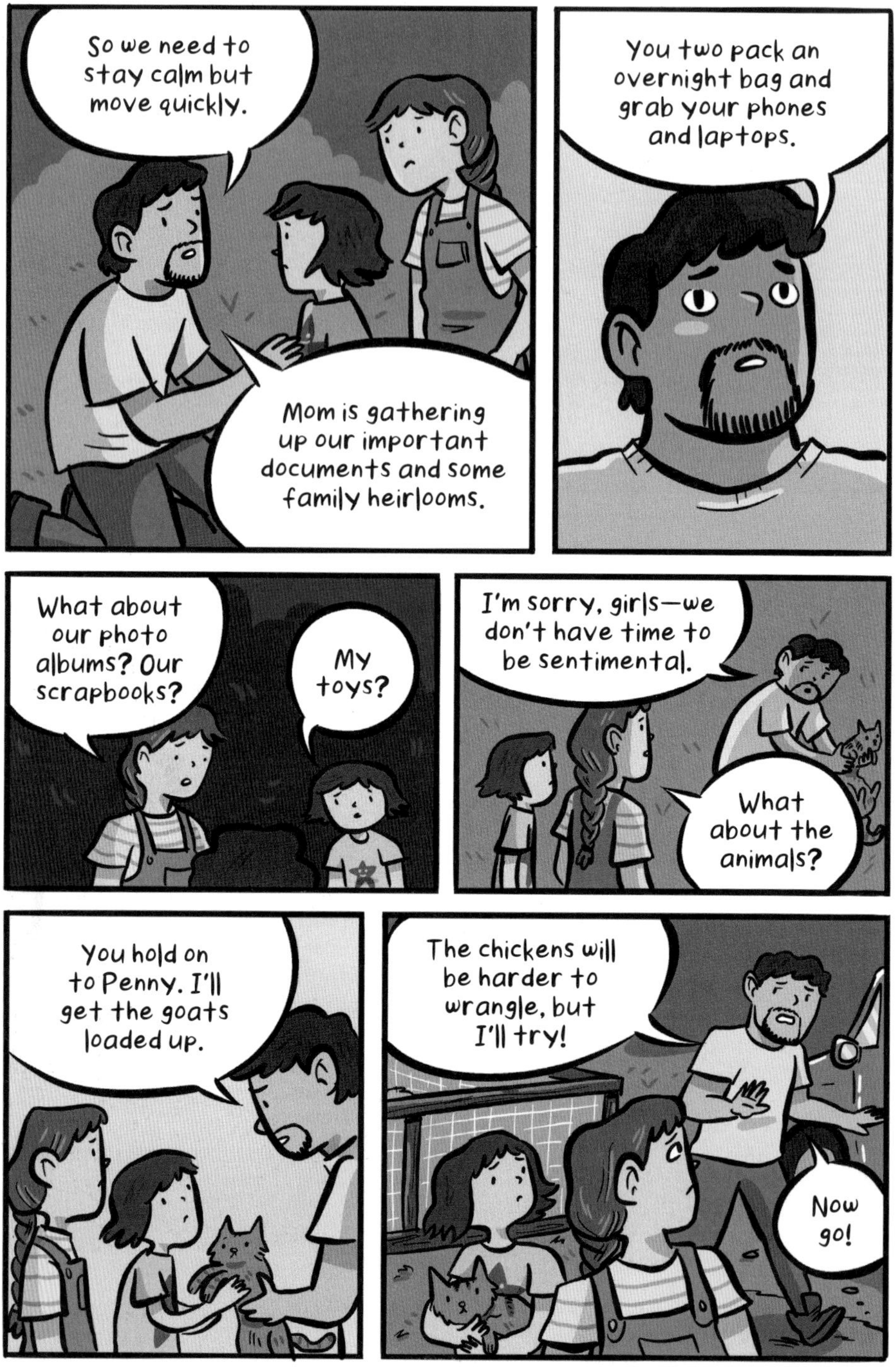
So we need to stay calm but move quickly.
Mom is gathering up our important documents and some family heirlooms.
You two pack an overnight bag and grab your phones and laptops.
What about our photo albums? Our scrapbooks?
My toys?
I'm sorry, girls—we don't have time to be sentimental.
What about the animals?
You hold on to Penny. I'll get the goats loaded up.
The chickens will be harder to wrangle, but I'll try!
Now go!

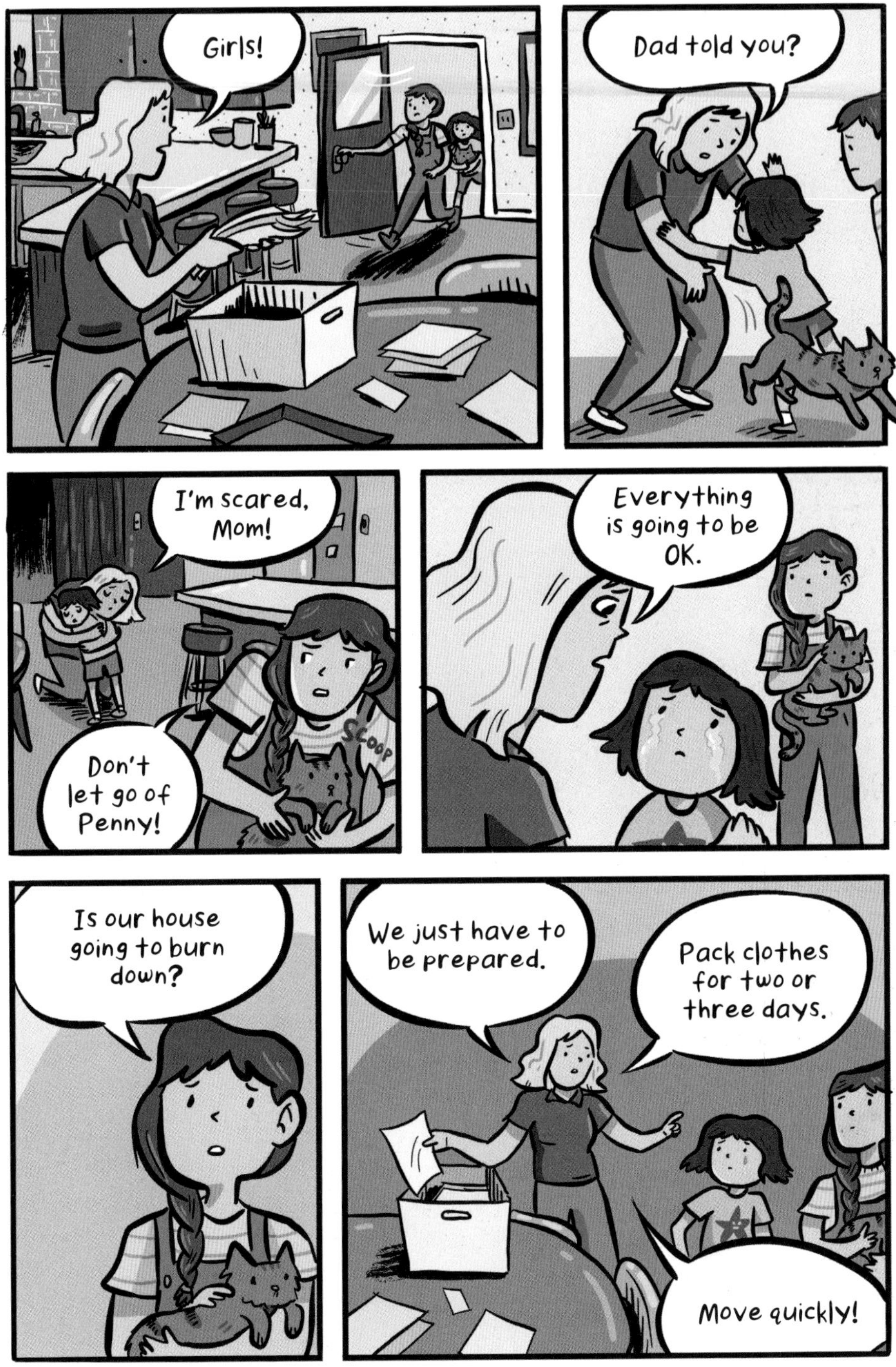
Girls!
Dad told you?
I'm scared, Mom!
SCOOP
Don't let go of Penny!
Everything is going to be OK.
Is our house going to burn down?
We just have to be prepared.
Pack clothes for two or three days.
Move quickly!

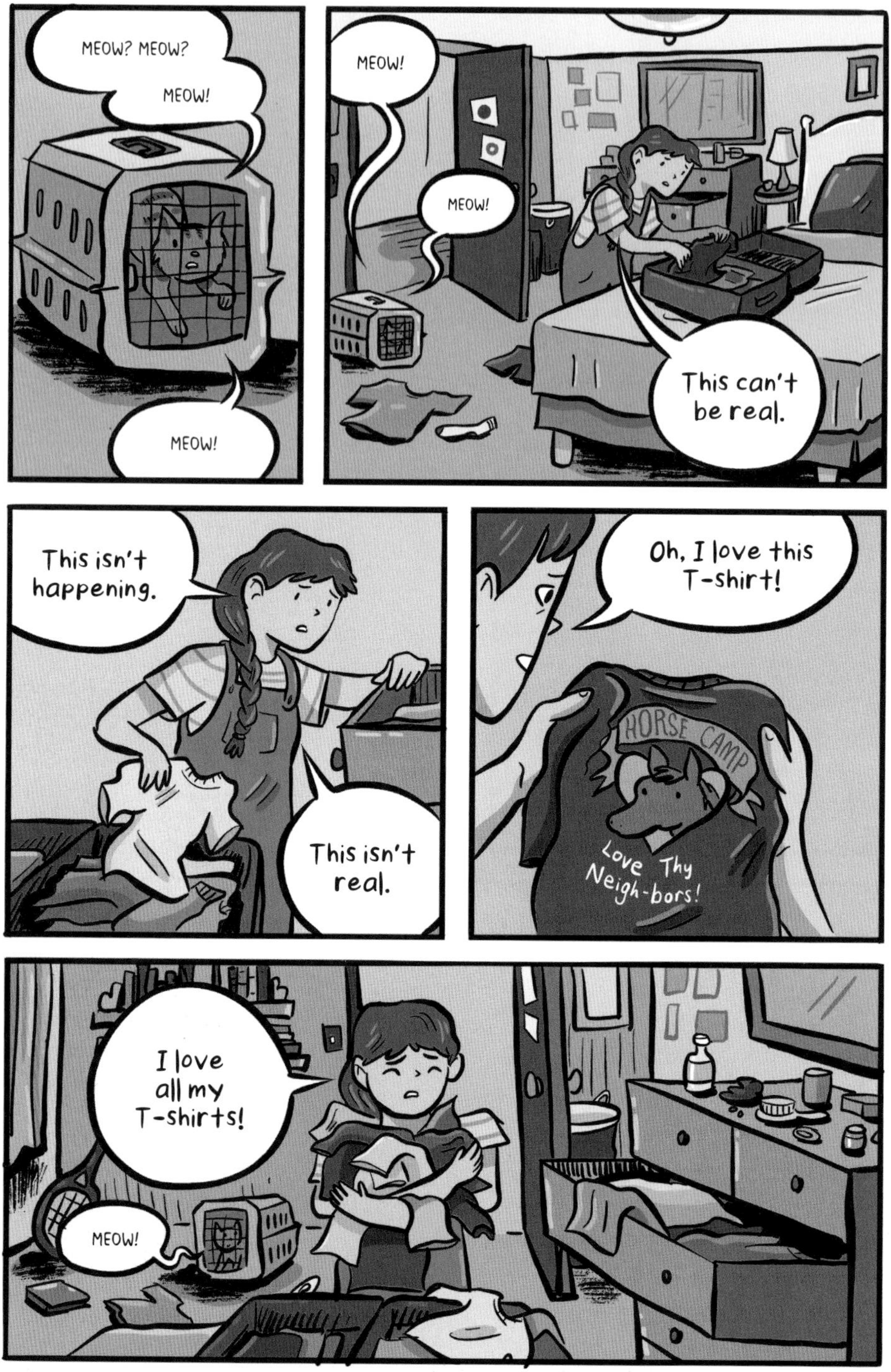

MEOW? MEOW?
MEOW!
MEOW!
MEOW!
MEOW!
This can't be real.
This isn't happening.
This isn't real.
Oh, I love this T-shirt!
HORSE CAMP
Love Thy Neigh-bors!
I love all my T-shirts!
MEOW!

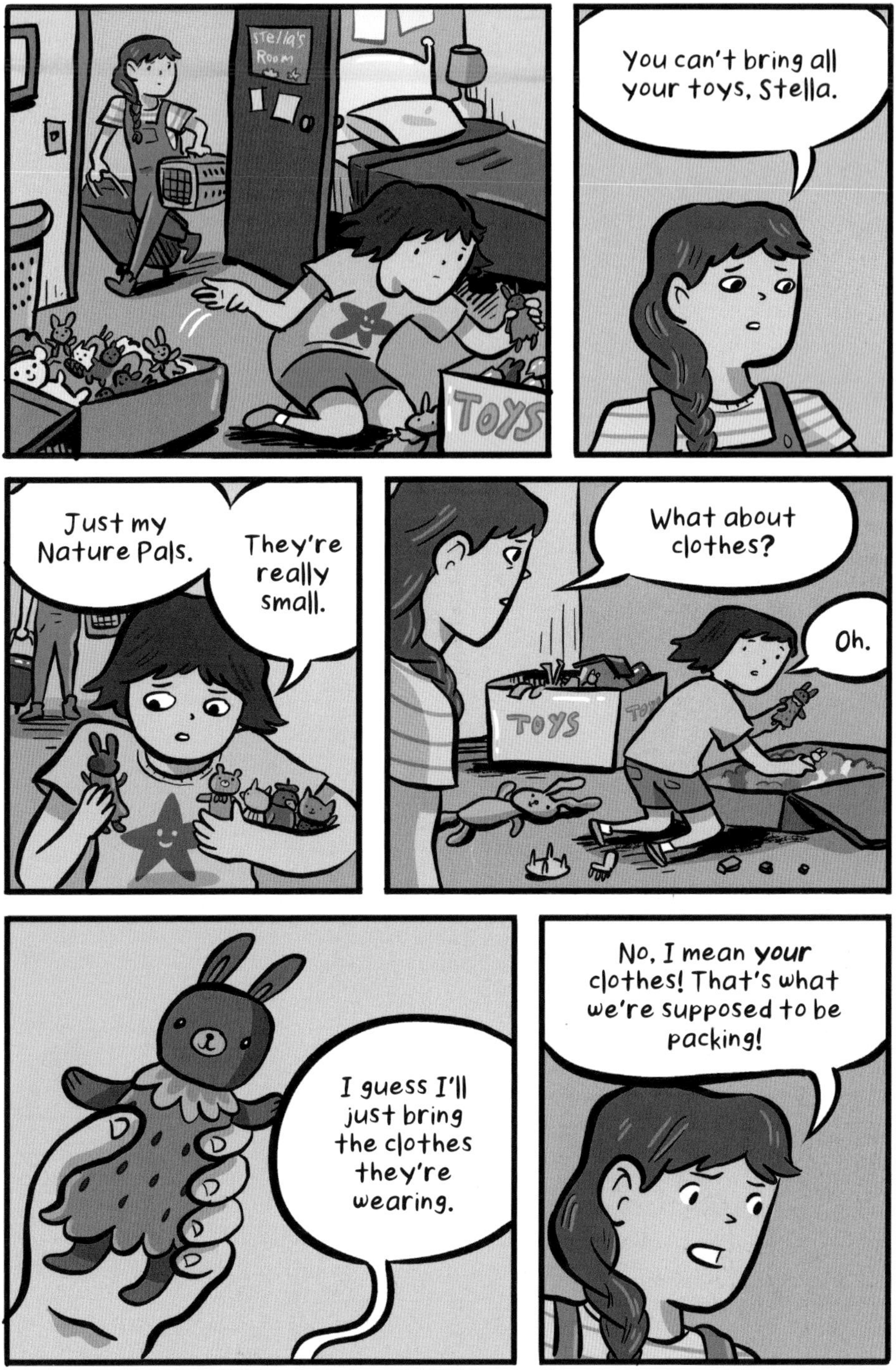

Stella's Room
You can't bring all your toys, Stella.
TOYS
Just my Nature Pals.
They're really small.
What about clothes?
TOYS
Oh.
I guess I'll just bring the clothes they're wearing.
No, I mean **your** clothes! That's what we're supposed to be packing!

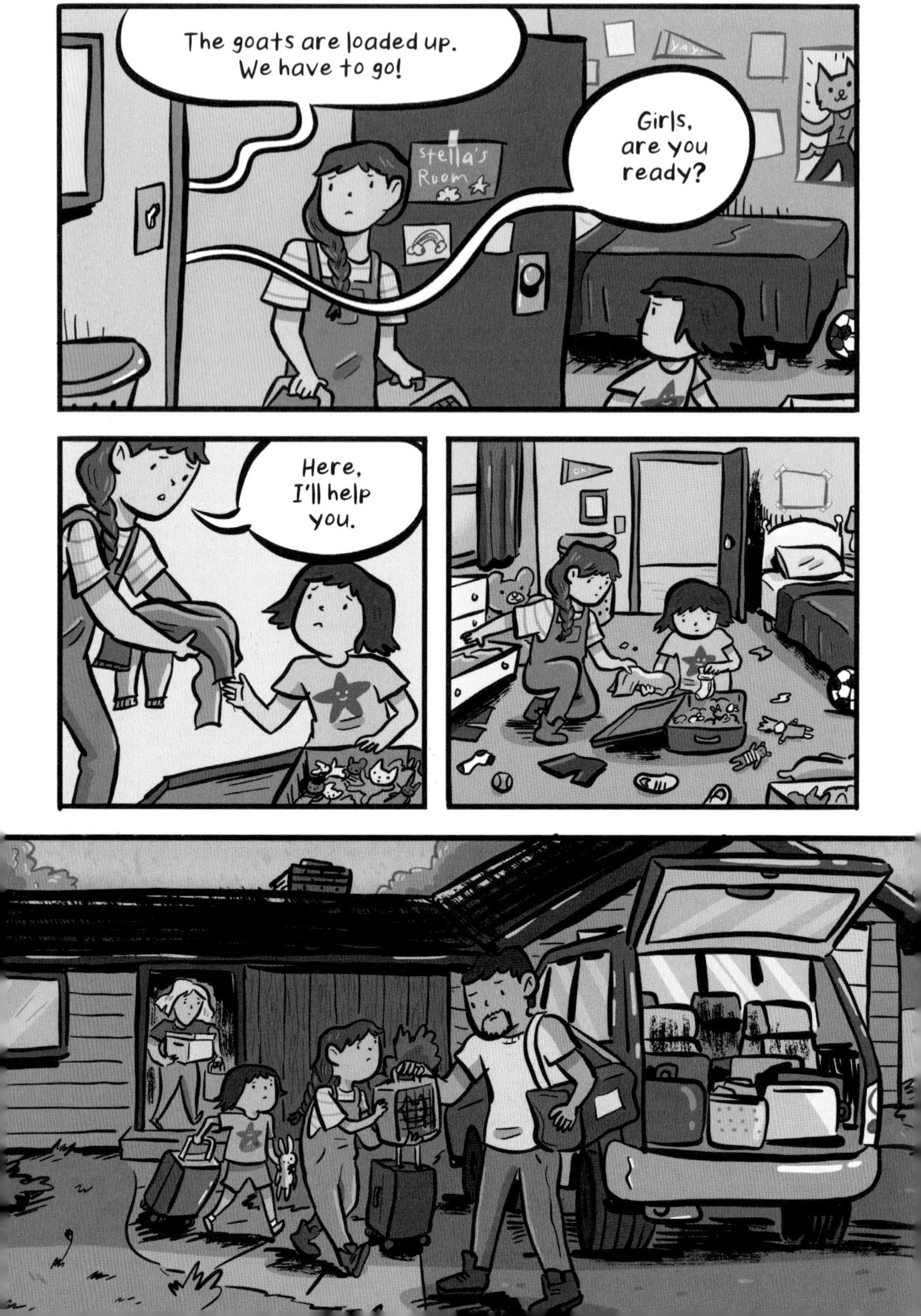
The goats are loaded up. We have to go!
Stella's Room
Girls, are you ready?
Here, I'll help you.

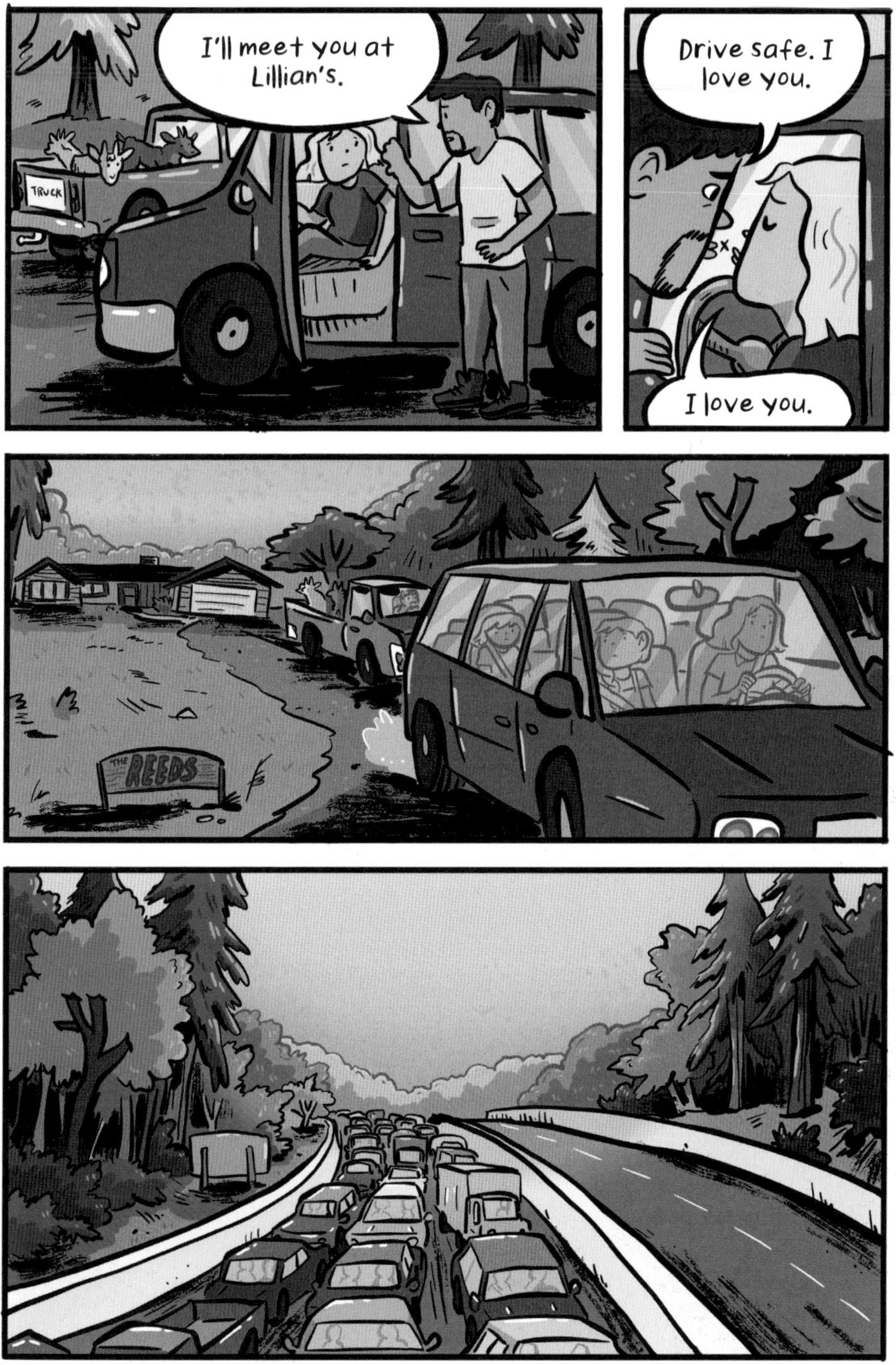
I'll meet you at Lillian's.
TRUCK
Drive safe. I love you.
I love you.
THE REEDS

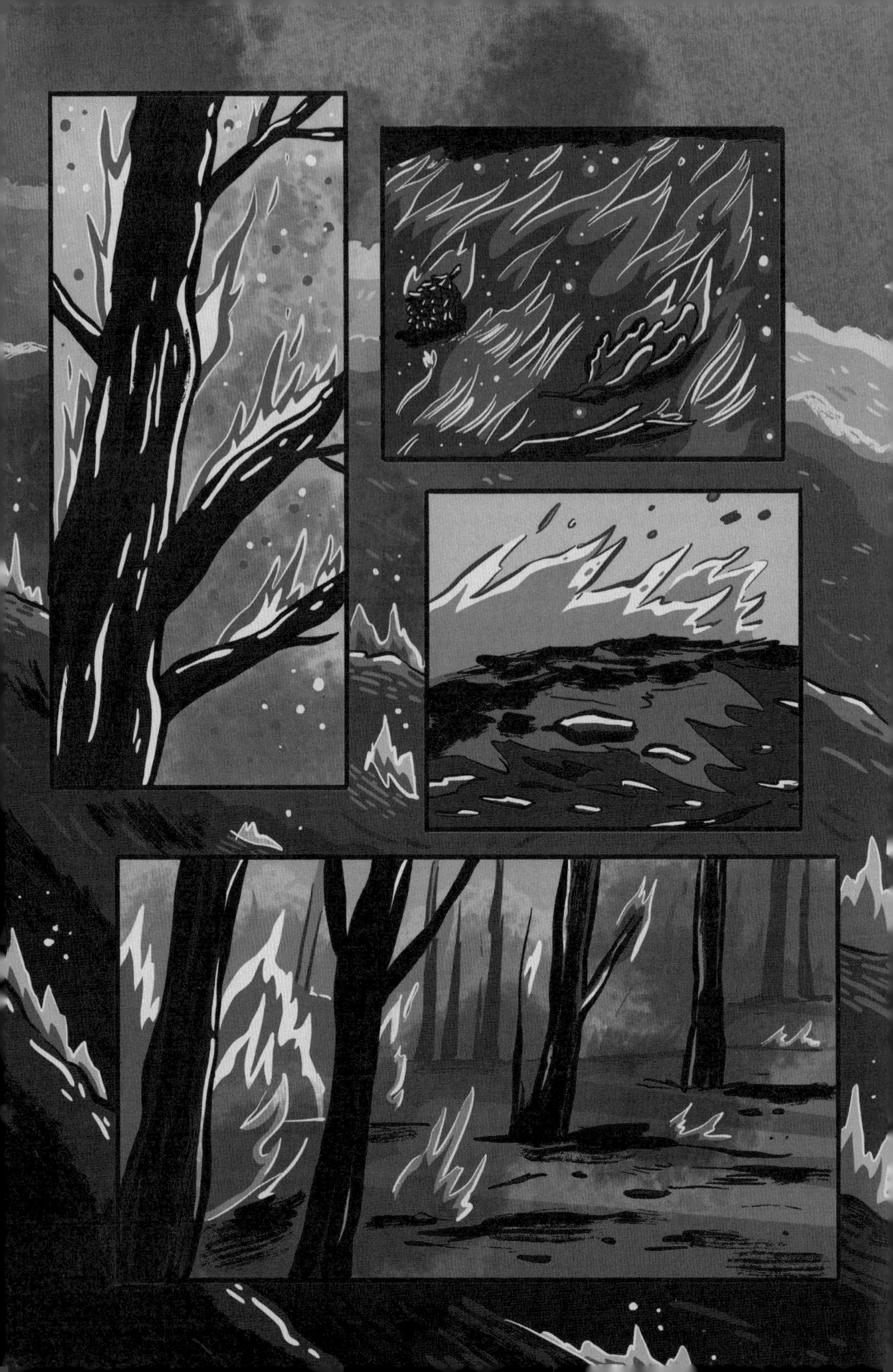

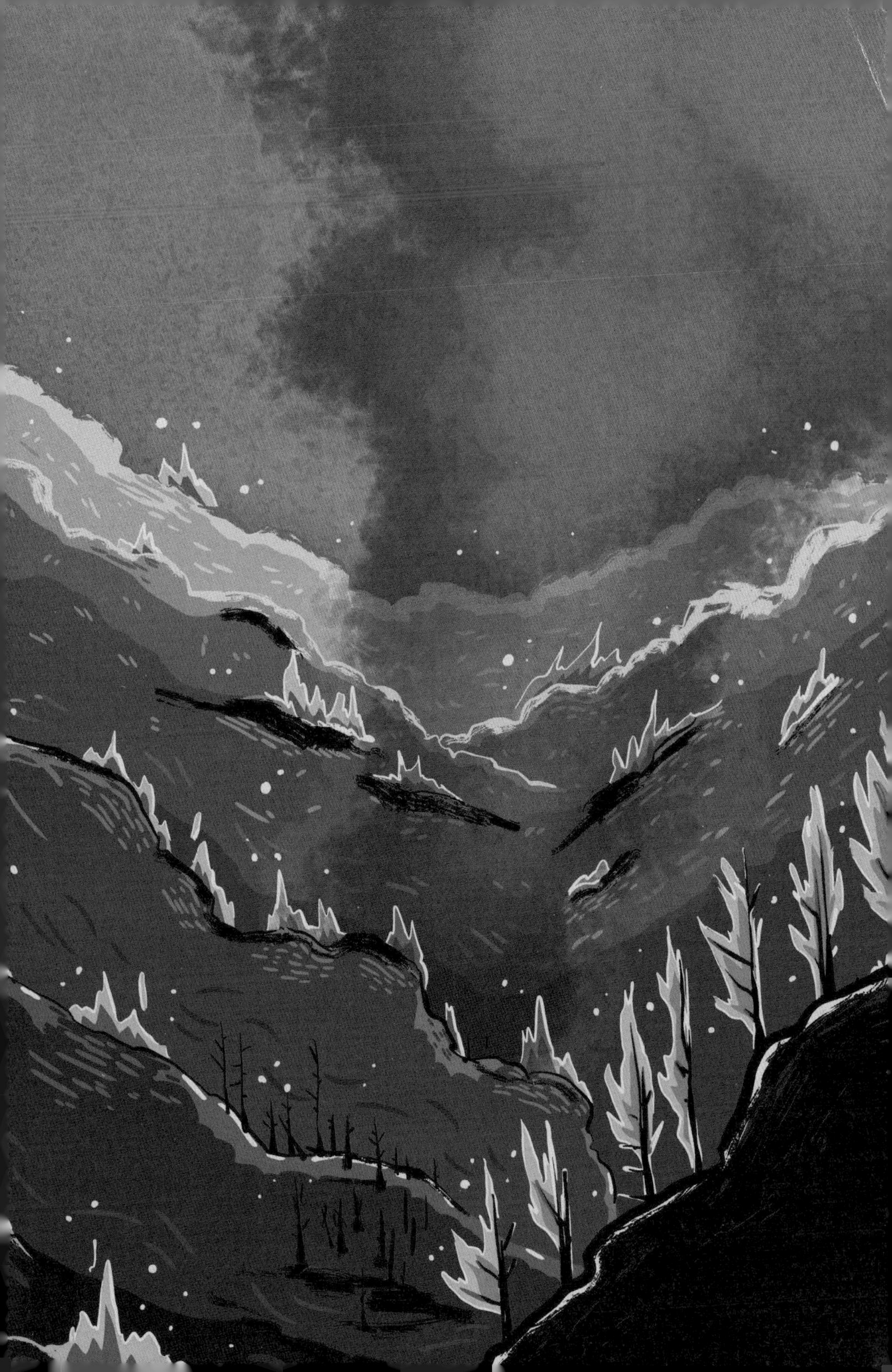

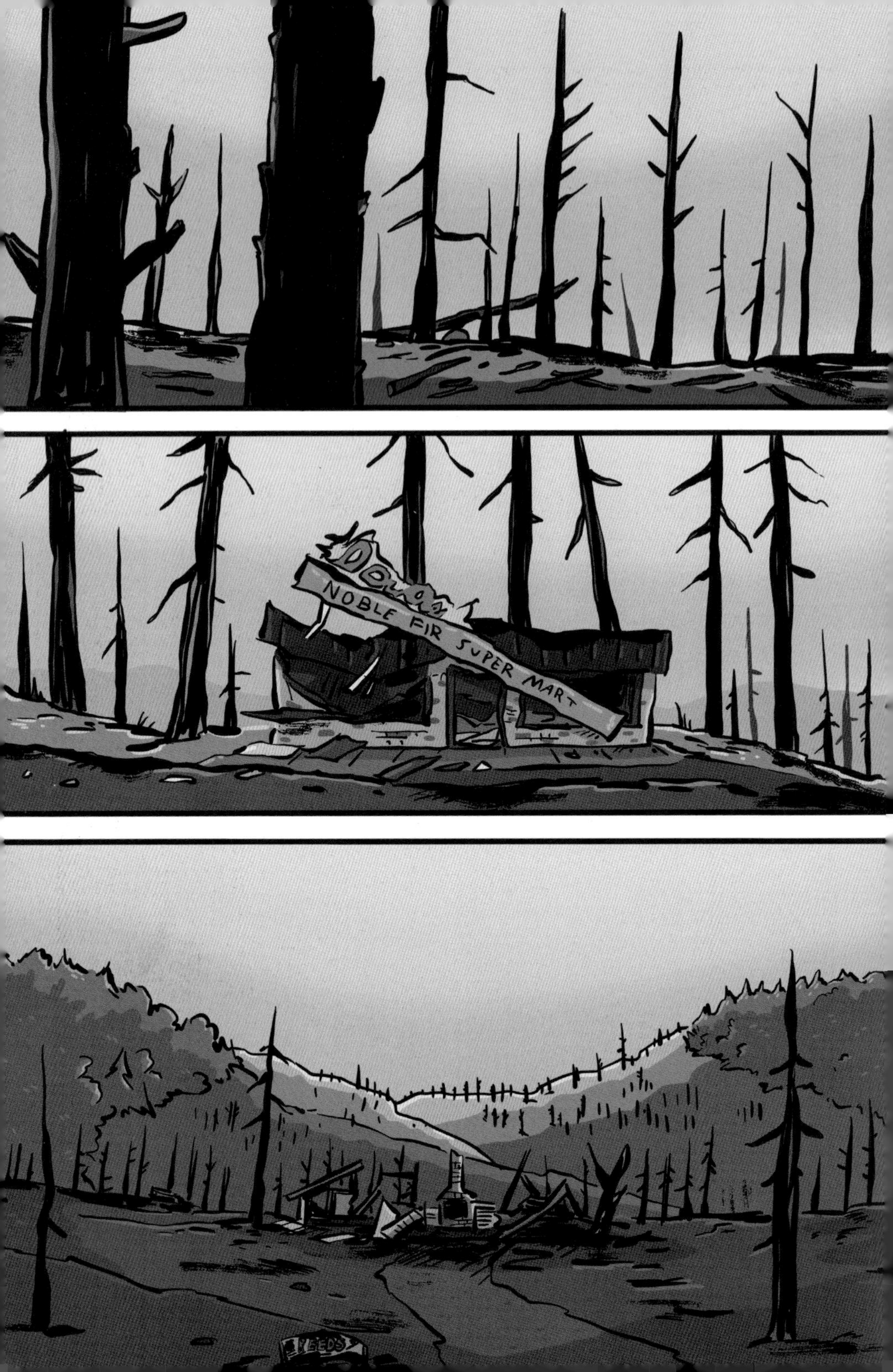
NOBLE FIR SUPER MART

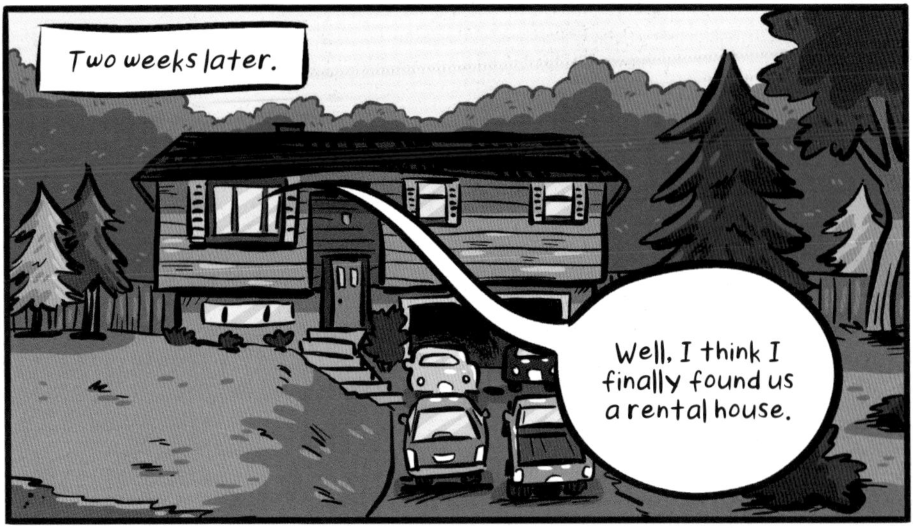
Two weeks later.
Well, I think I finally found us a rental house.

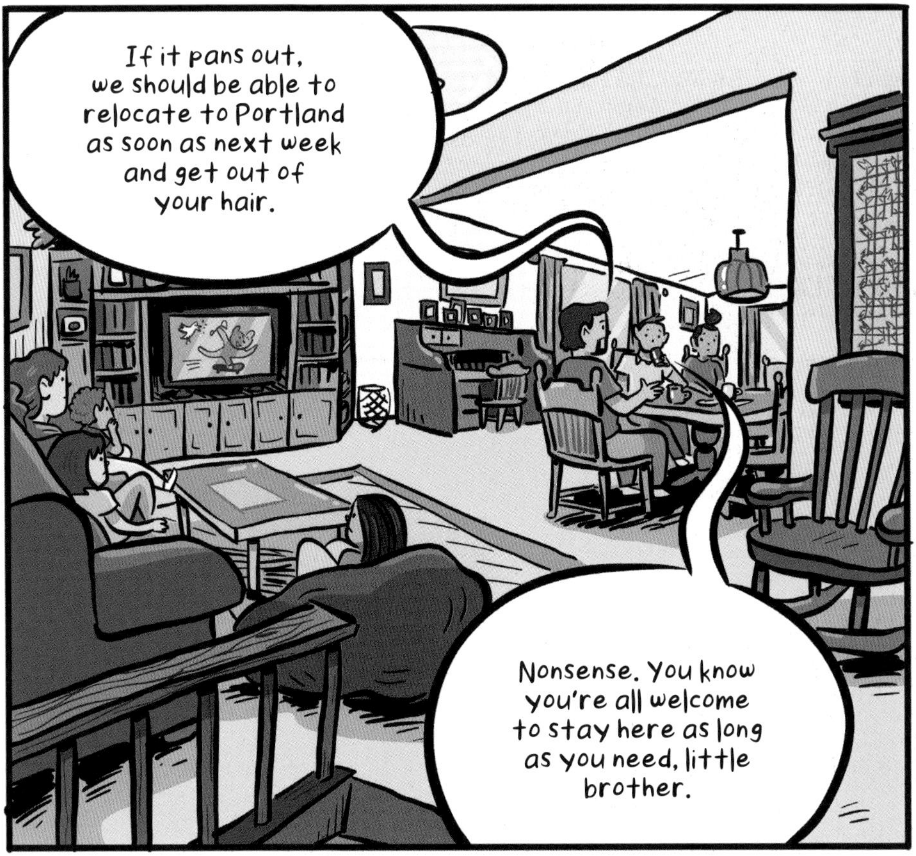
If it pans out, we should be able to relocate to Portland as soon as next week and get out of your hair.
Nonsense. You know you're all welcome to stay here as long as you need, little brother.

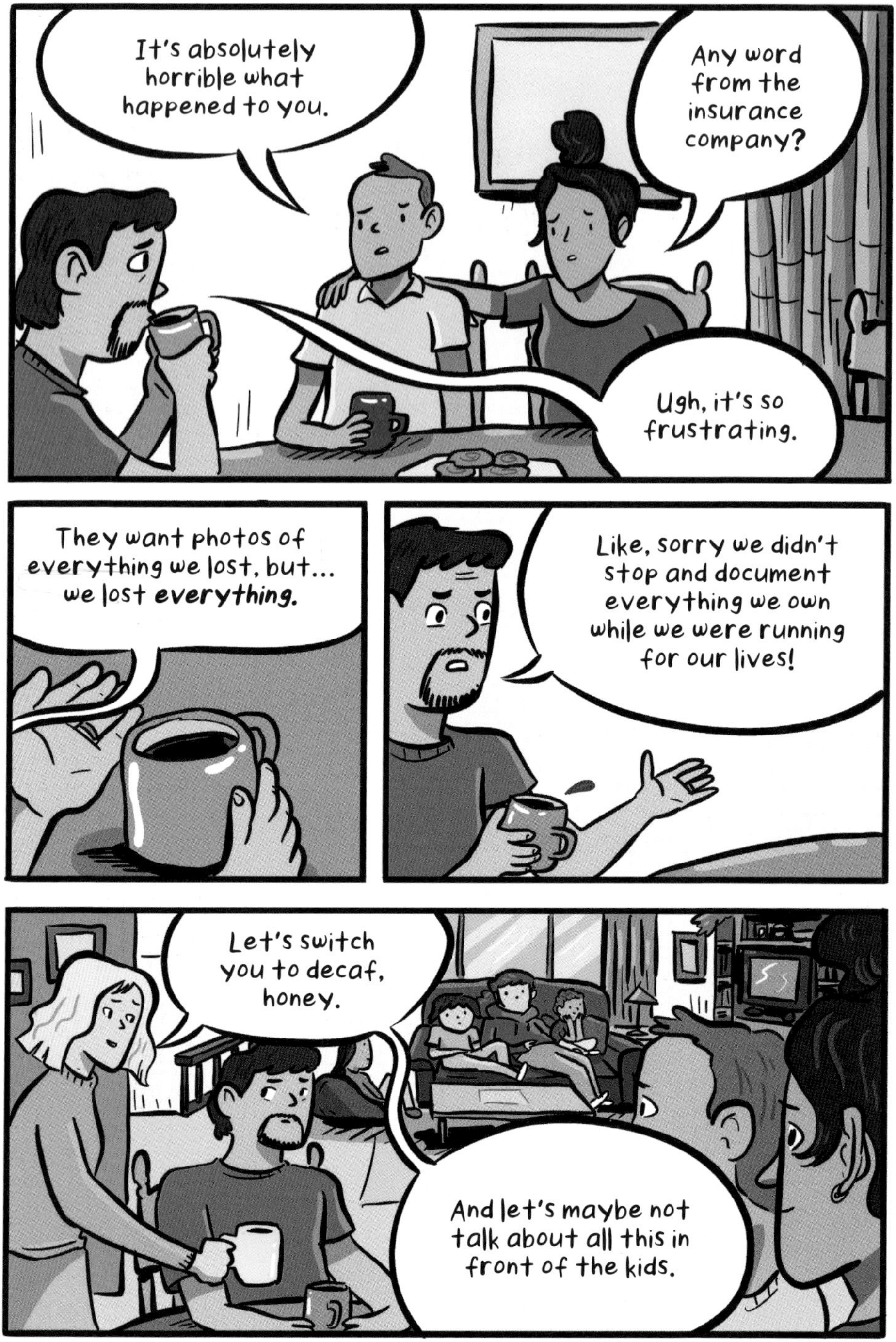
It's absolutely horrible what happened to you.
Any word from the insurance company?
Ugh, it's so frustrating.
They want photos of everything we lost, but... we lost **everything.**
Like, sorry we didn't stop and document everything we own while we were running for our lives!
Let's switch you to decaf, honey.
And let's maybe not talk about all this in front of the kids.

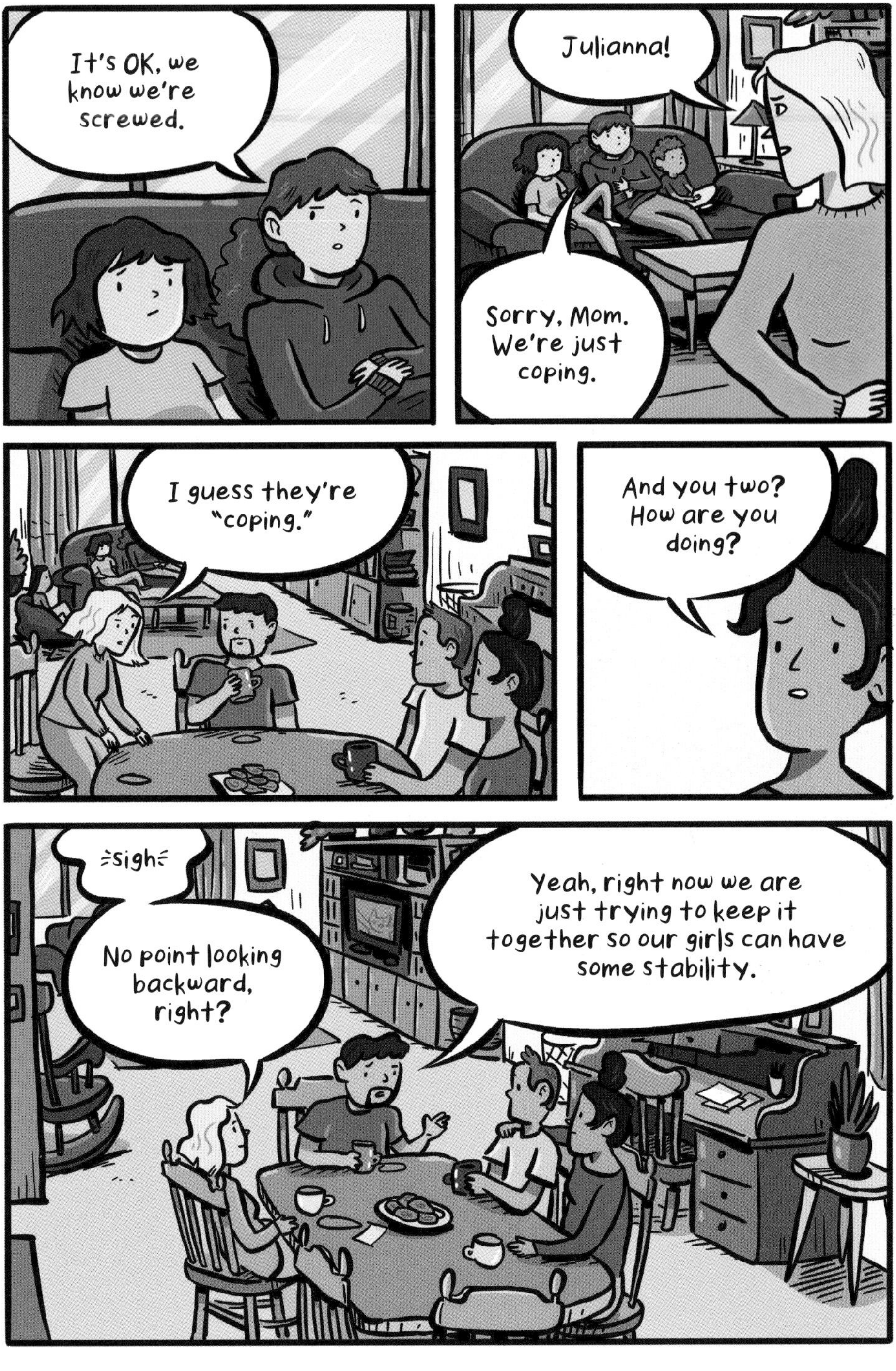
It's OK, we know we're screwed.
Julianna!
Sorry, Mom. We're just coping.
I guess they're "coping."
And you two? How are you doing?
sigh
No point looking backward, right?
Yeah, right now we are just trying to keep it together so our girls can have some stability.

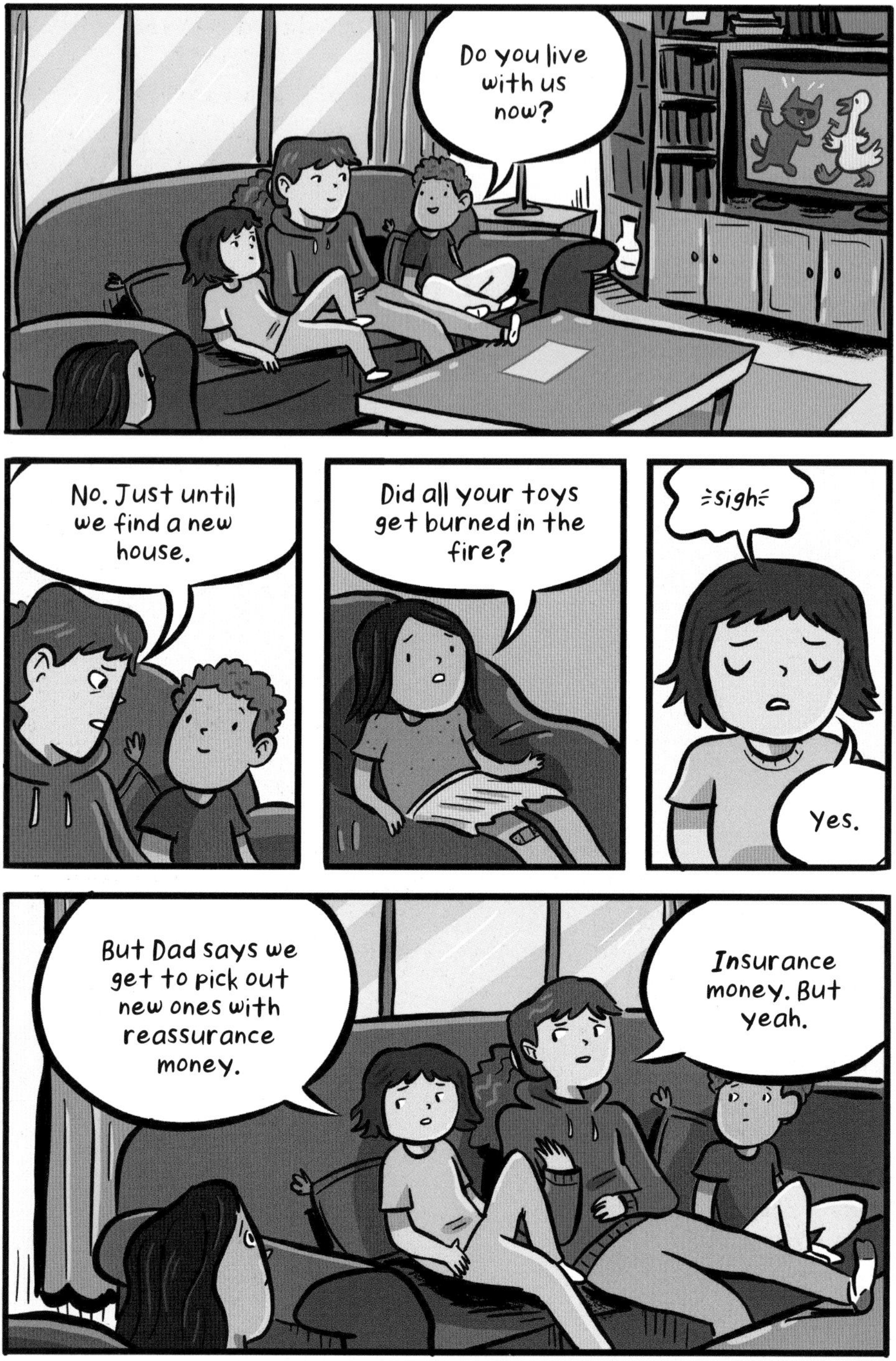
Do you live with us now?
No. Just until we find a new house.
Did all your toys get burned in the fire?
sigh
Yes.
But Dad says we get to pick out new ones with reassurance money.
Insurance money. But yeah.

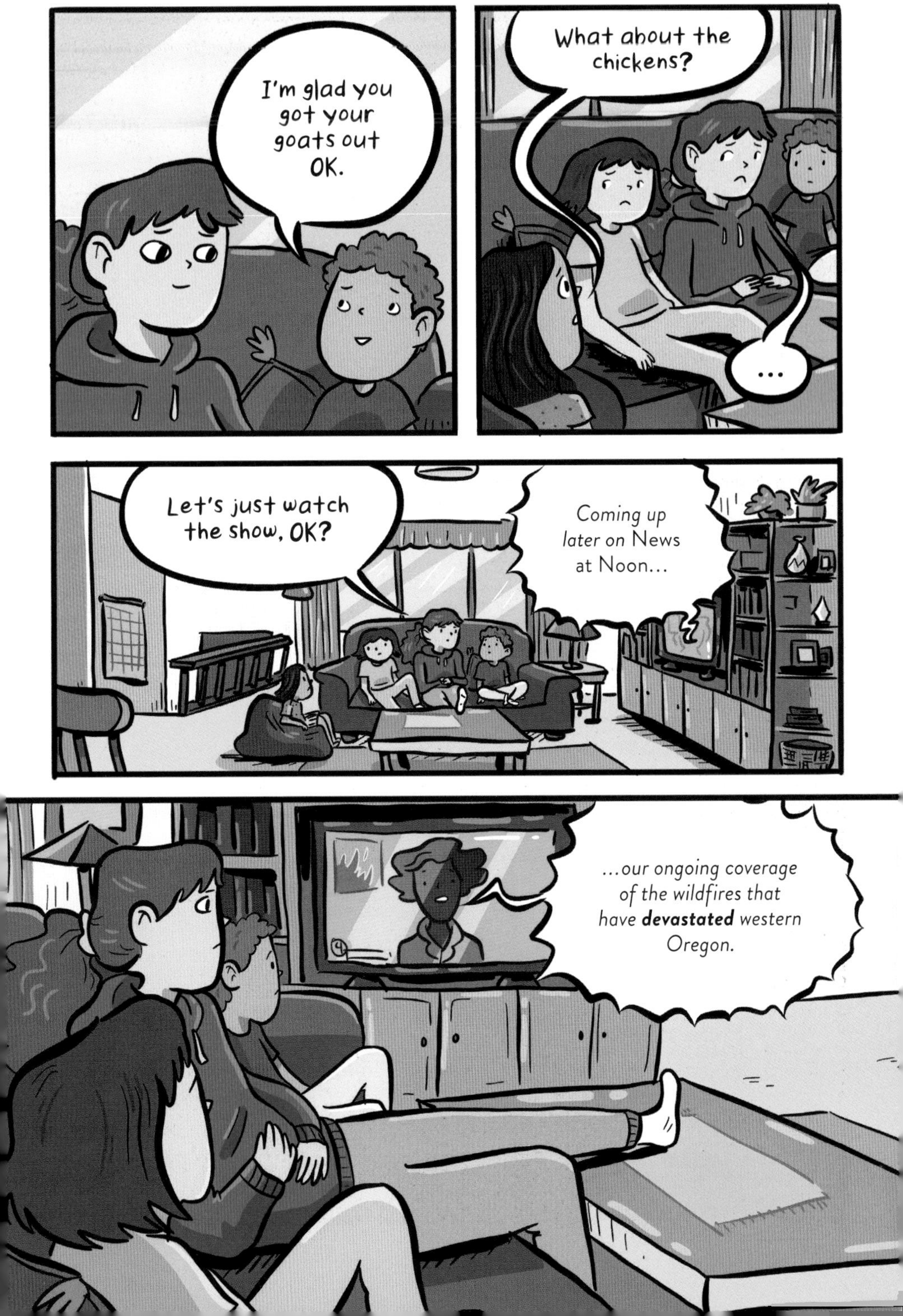

I'm glad you got your goats out OK.
What about the chickens?
...
Let's just watch the show, OK?
Coming up later on News at Noon...
...our ongoing coverage of the wildfires that have **devastated** western Oregon.

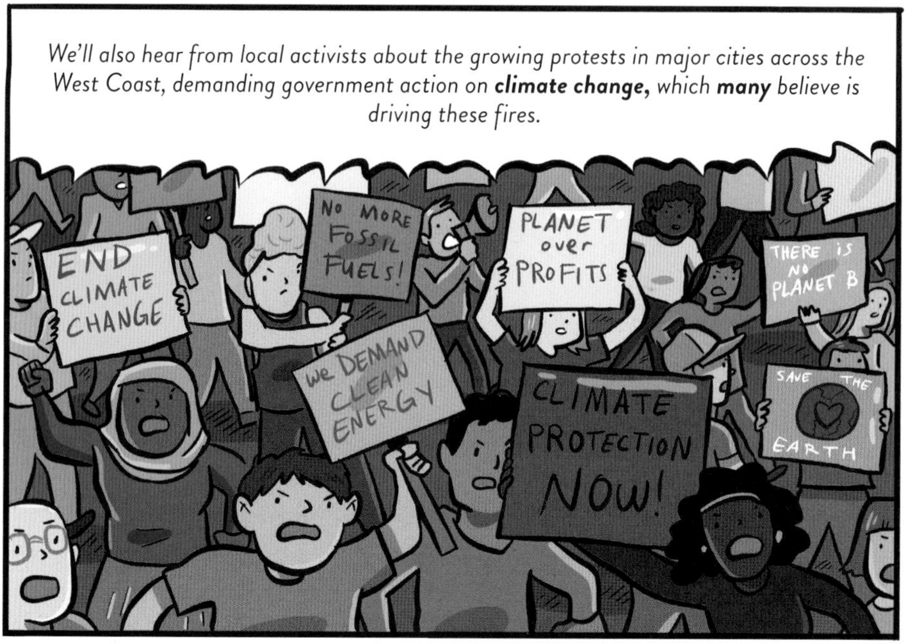
We'll also hear from local activists about the growing protests in major cities across the West Coast, demanding government action on **climate change,** which **many** believe is driving these fires.
END CLIMATE CHANGE
NO MORE FOSSIL FUELS!
PLANET over PROFITS
THERE is NO PLANET B
WE DEMAND CLEAN ENERGY
CLIMATE PROTECTION NOW!
SAVE THE EARTH

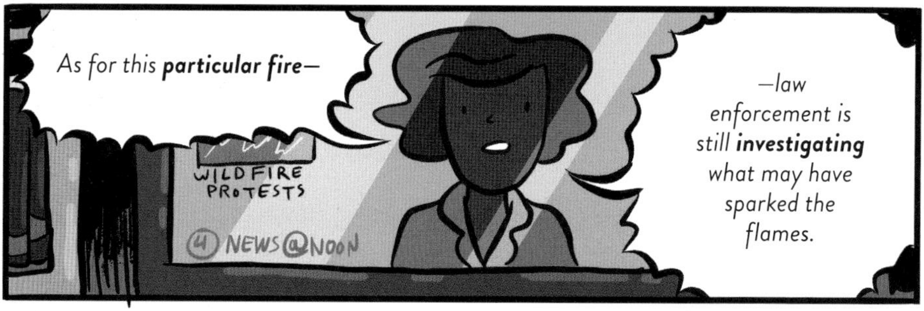
As for this **particular fire**—
WILDFIRE PROTESTS
4 NEWS@NOON
—law enforcement is still **investigating** what may have sparked the flames.

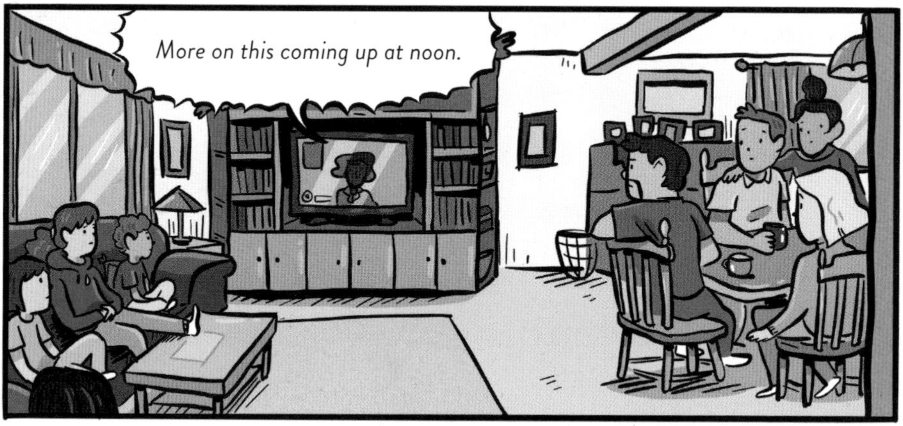
More on this coming up at noon.

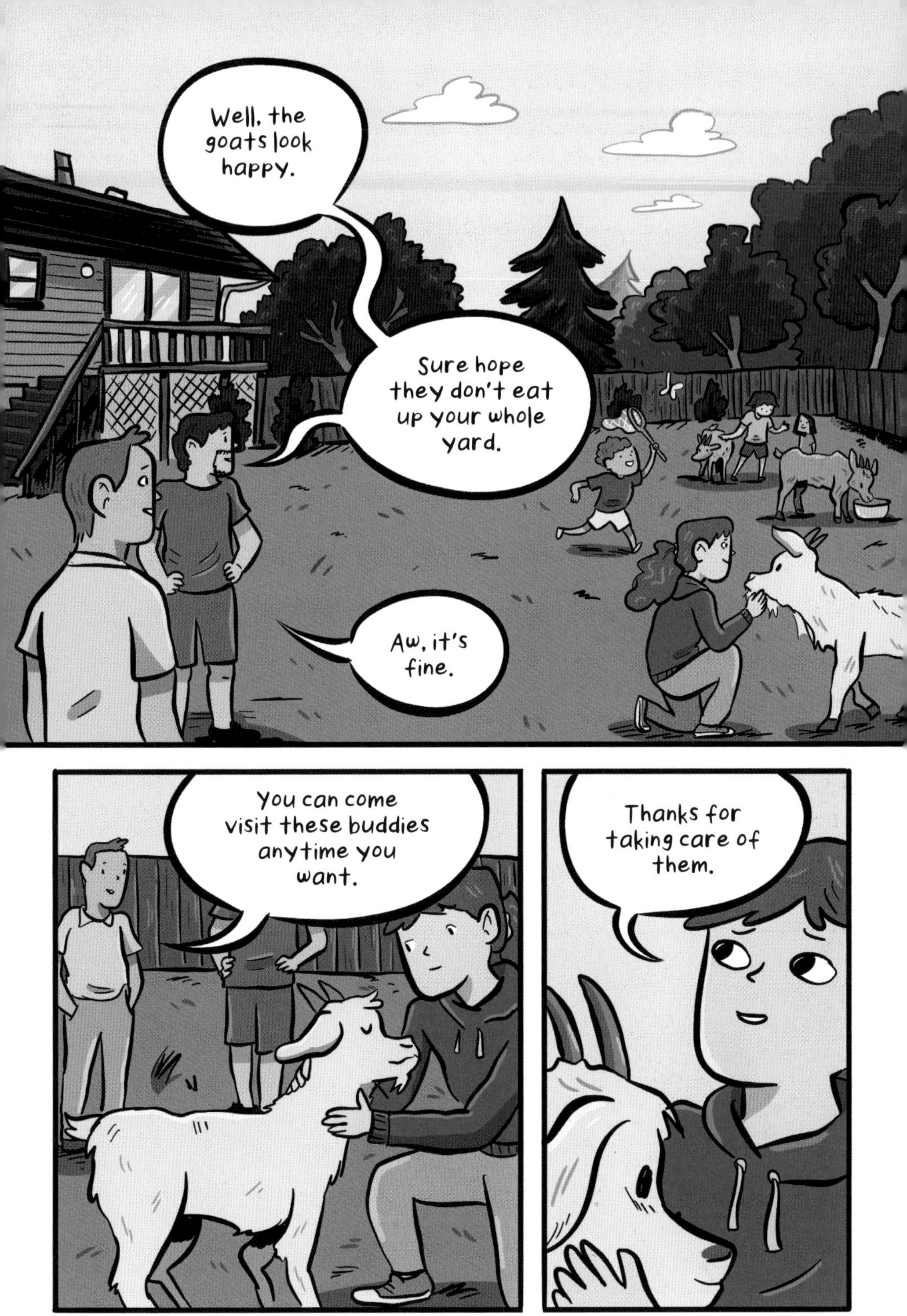
Well, the goats look happy.
Sure hope they don't eat up your whole yard.
Aw, it's fine.
You can come visit these buddies anytime you want.
Thanks for taking care of them.

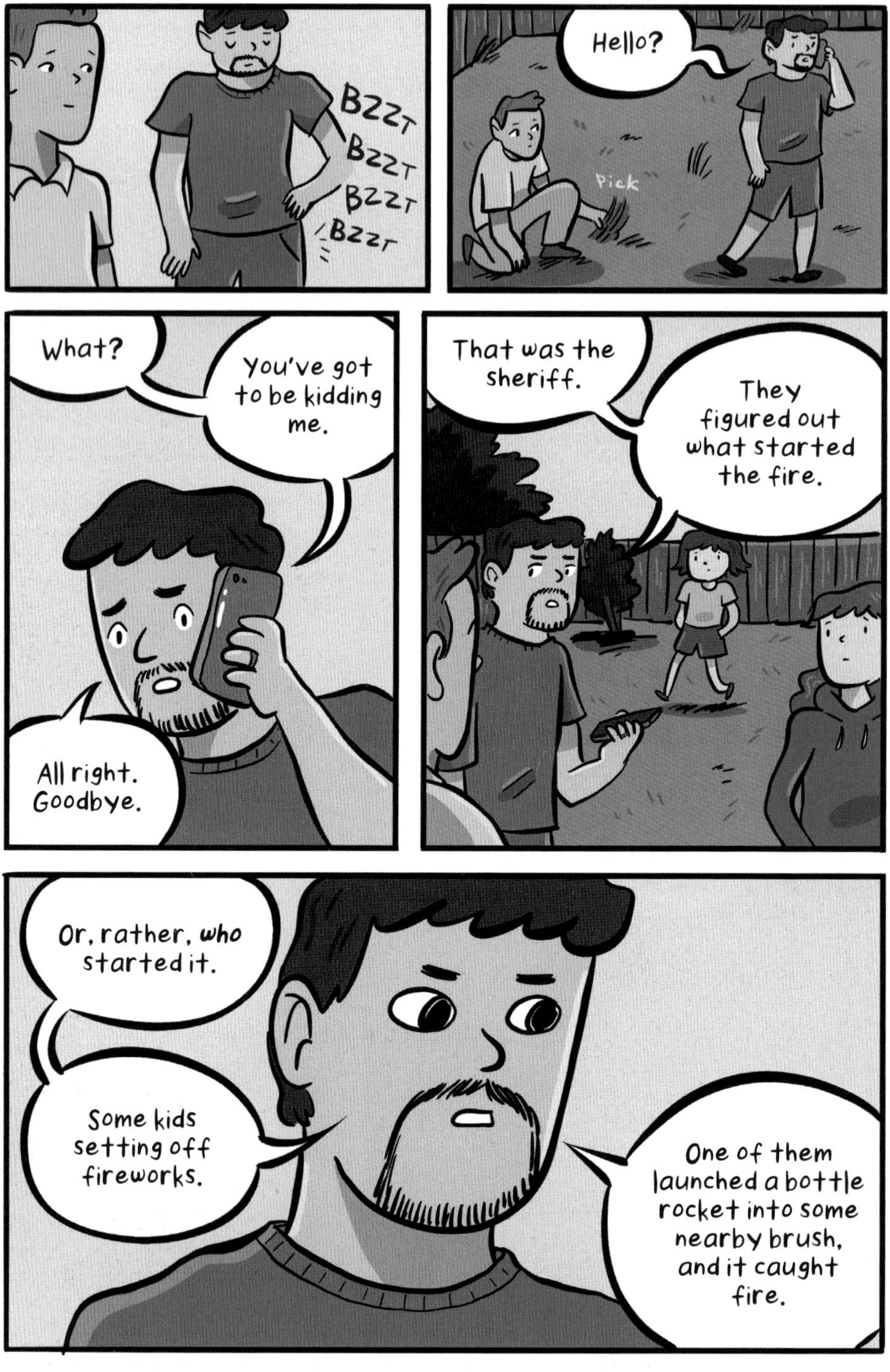
BZZT
BZZT
BZZT
BZZT
Hello?
Pick
What?
You've got to be kidding me.
All right. Goodbye.
That was the sheriff.
They figured out what started the fire.
Or, rather, who started it.
Some kids setting off fireworks.
One of them launched a bottle rocket into some nearby brush, and it caught fire.

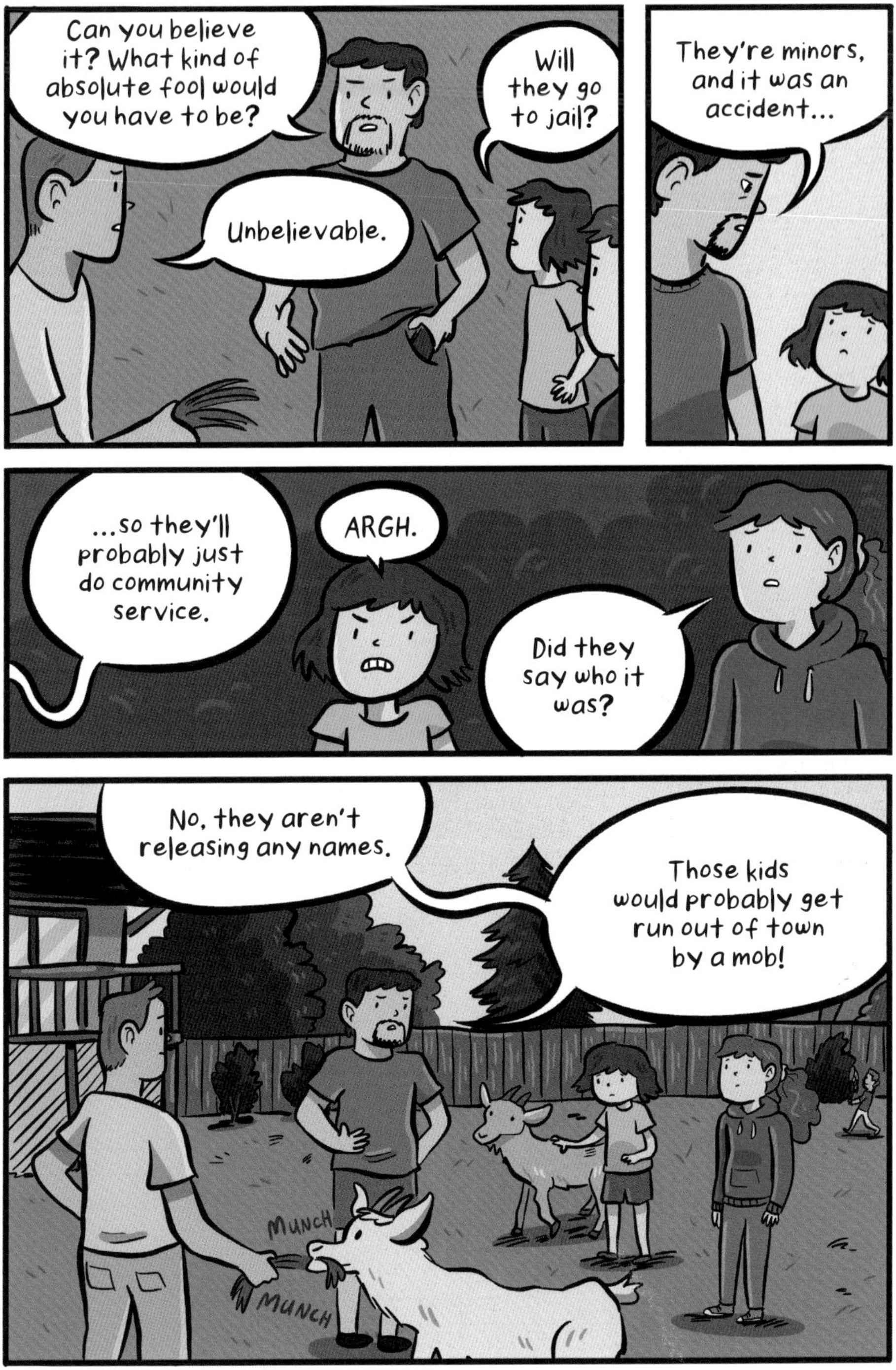
Can you believe it? What kind of absolute fool would you have to be?
Unbelievable.
Will they go to jail?
They're minors, and it was an accident...
...so they'll probably just do community service.
ARGH.
Did they say who it was?
No, they aren't releasing any names.
Those kids would probably get run out of town by a mob!
MUNCH
MUNCH

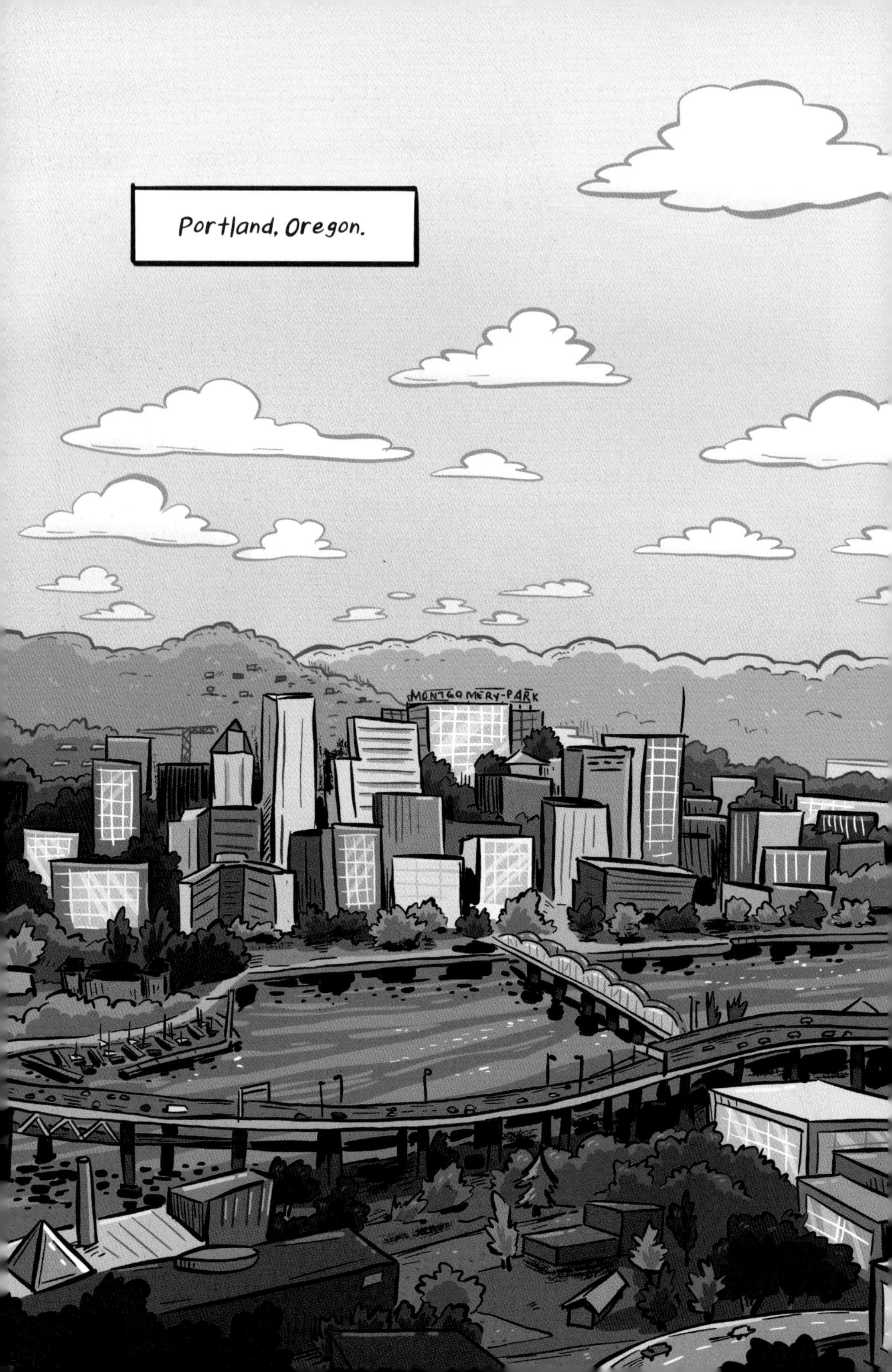

Portland, Oregon.
MONTGOMERY-PARK

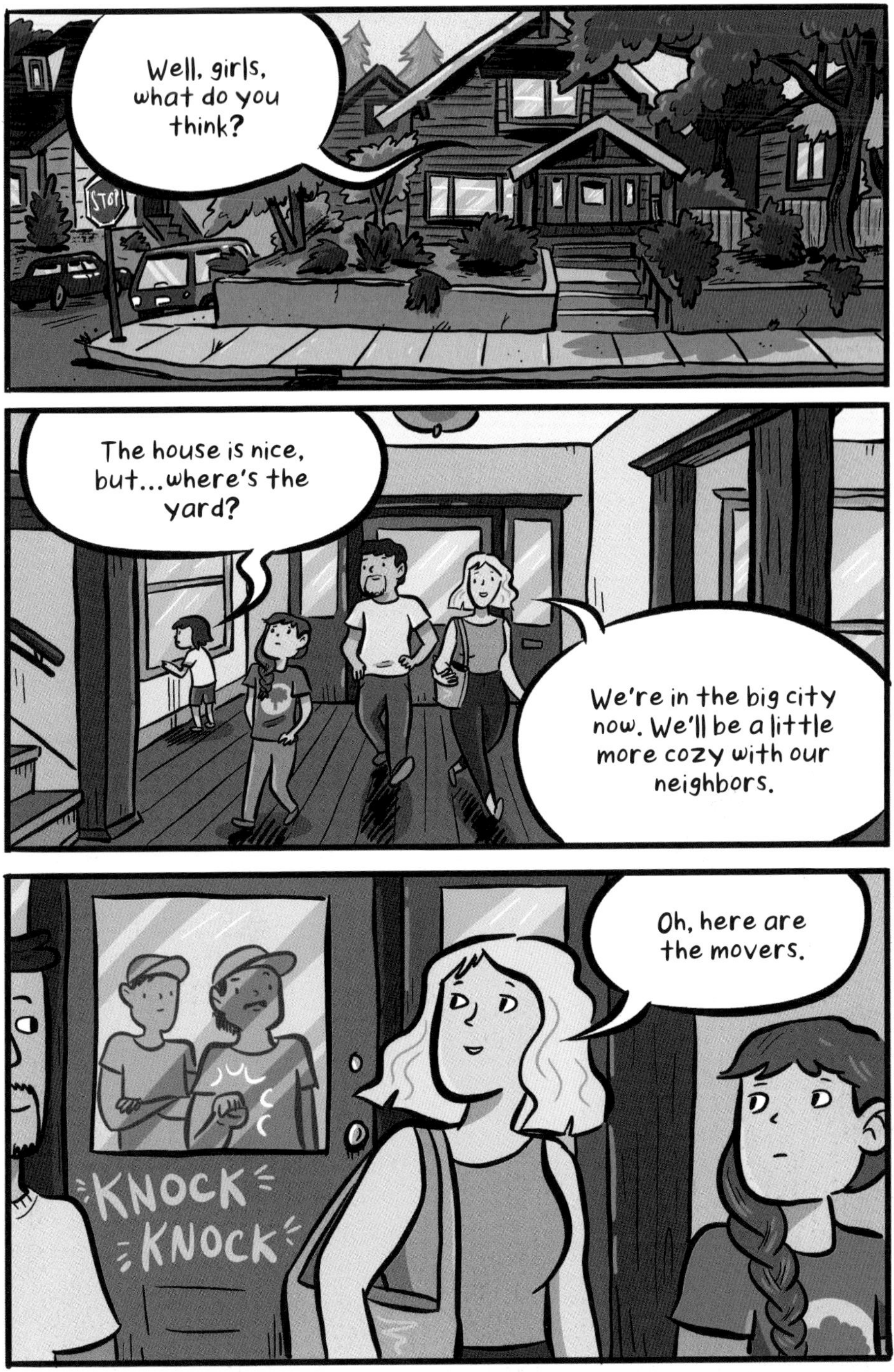
Well, girls, what do you think?
The house is nice, but...where's the yard?
We're in the big city now. We'll be a little more cozy with our neighbors.
Oh, here are the movers.
KNOCK KNOCK

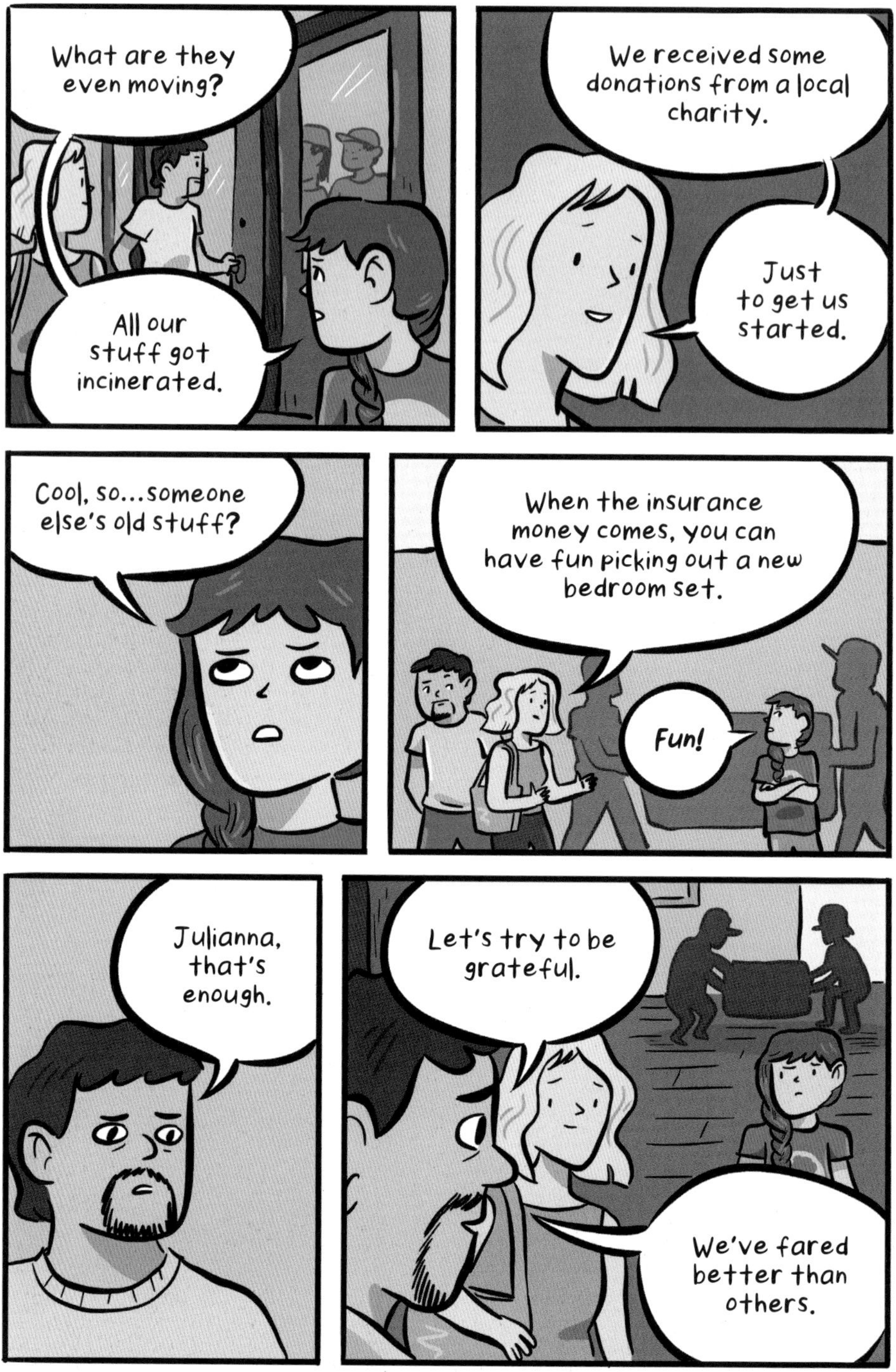
What are they even moving?
All our stuff got incinerated.
We received some donations from a local charity.
Just to get us started.
Cool, so...someone else's old stuff?
When the insurance money comes, you can have fun picking out a new bedroom set.
Fun!
Julianna, that's enough.
Let's try to be grateful.
We've fared better than others.

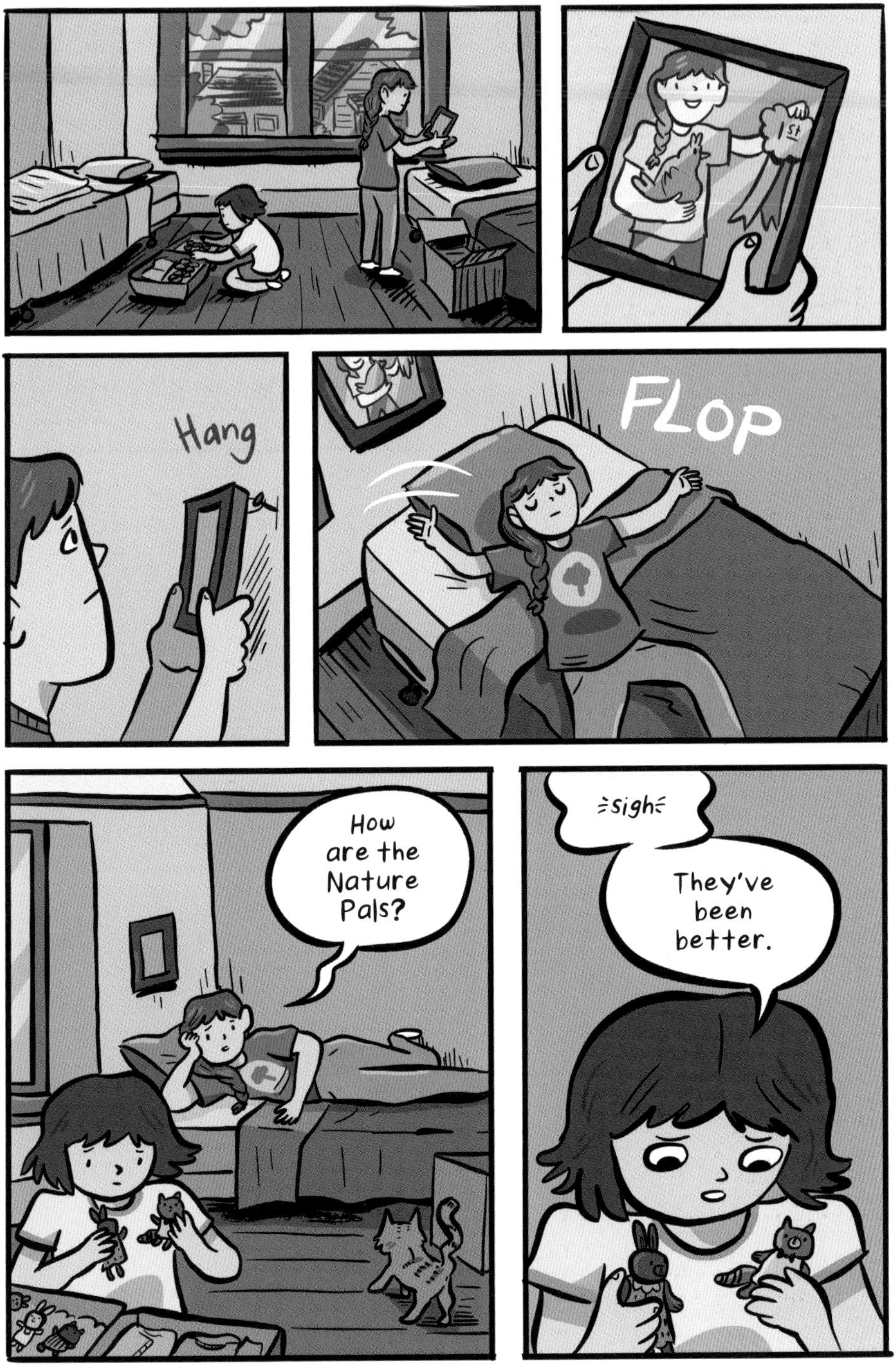
Hang
FLOP
How are the Nature Pals?
sigh
They've been better.

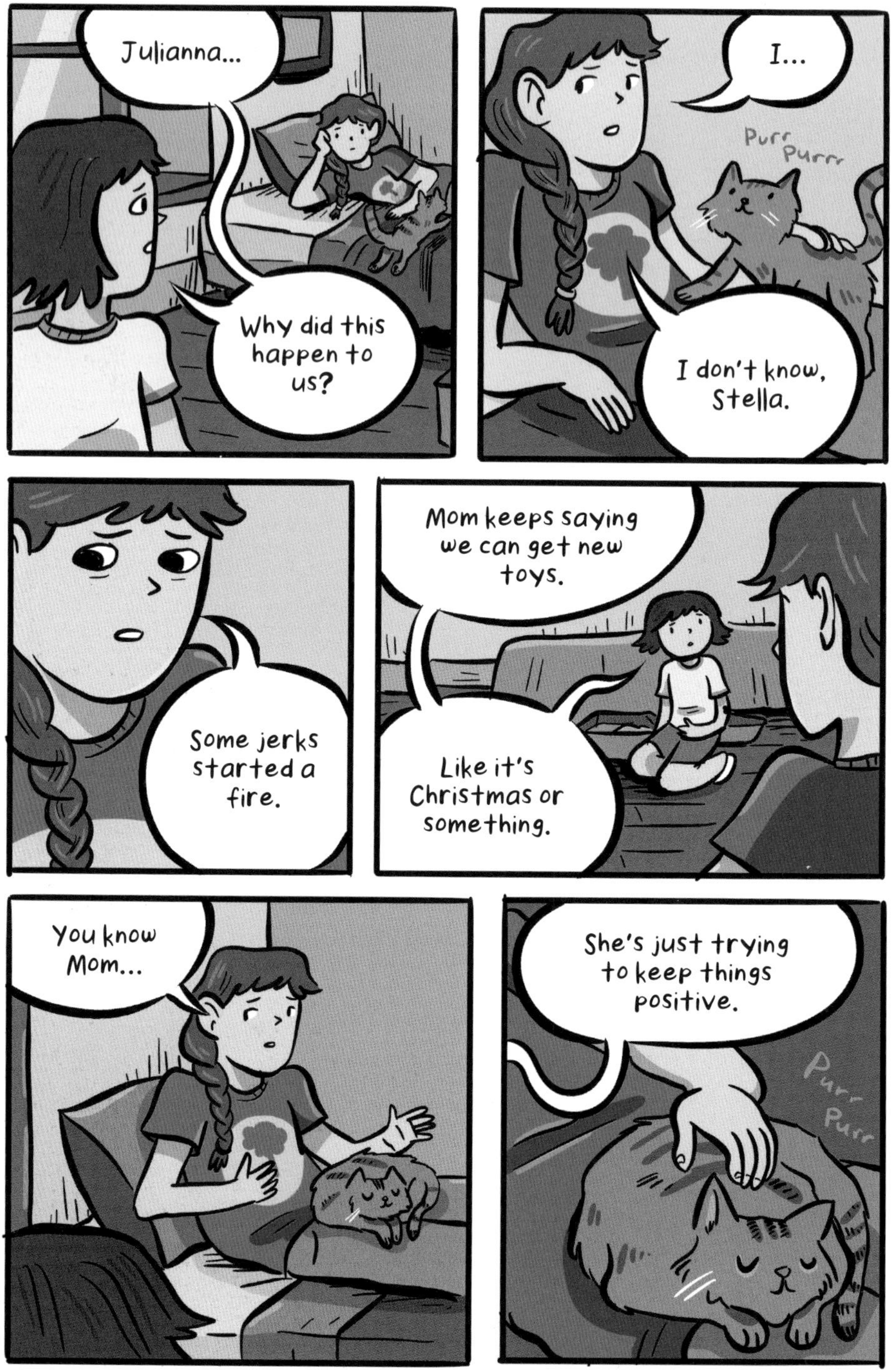
Julianna...
Why did this happen to us?
I...
Purr Purrr
I don't know, Stella.
Some jerks started a fire.
Mom keeps saying we can get new toys.
Like it's Christmas or something.
You know Mom...
She's just trying to keep things positive.
Purr Purr

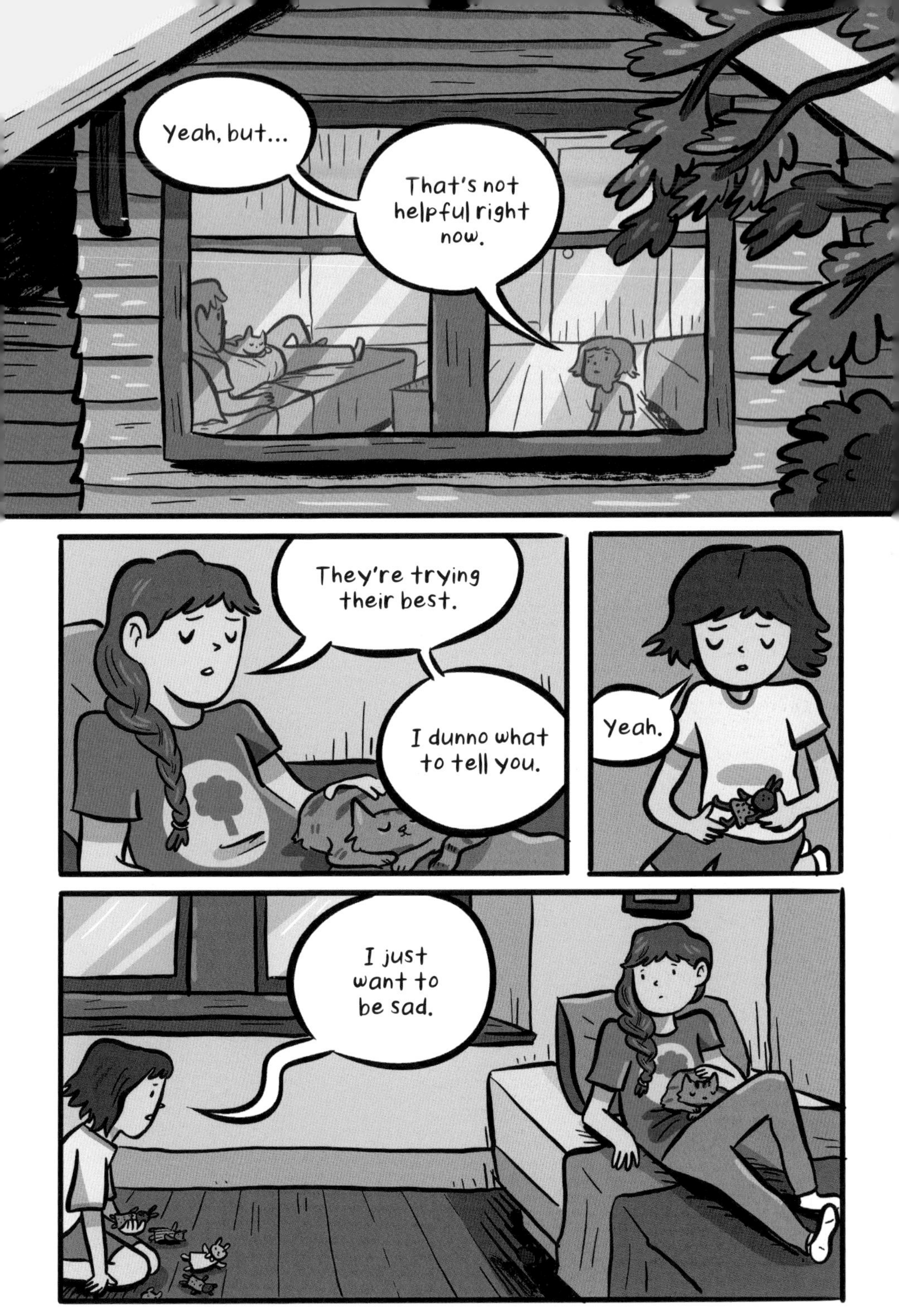
Yeah, but...
That's not helpful right now.
They're trying their best.
I dunno what to tell you.
Yeah.
I just want to be sad.

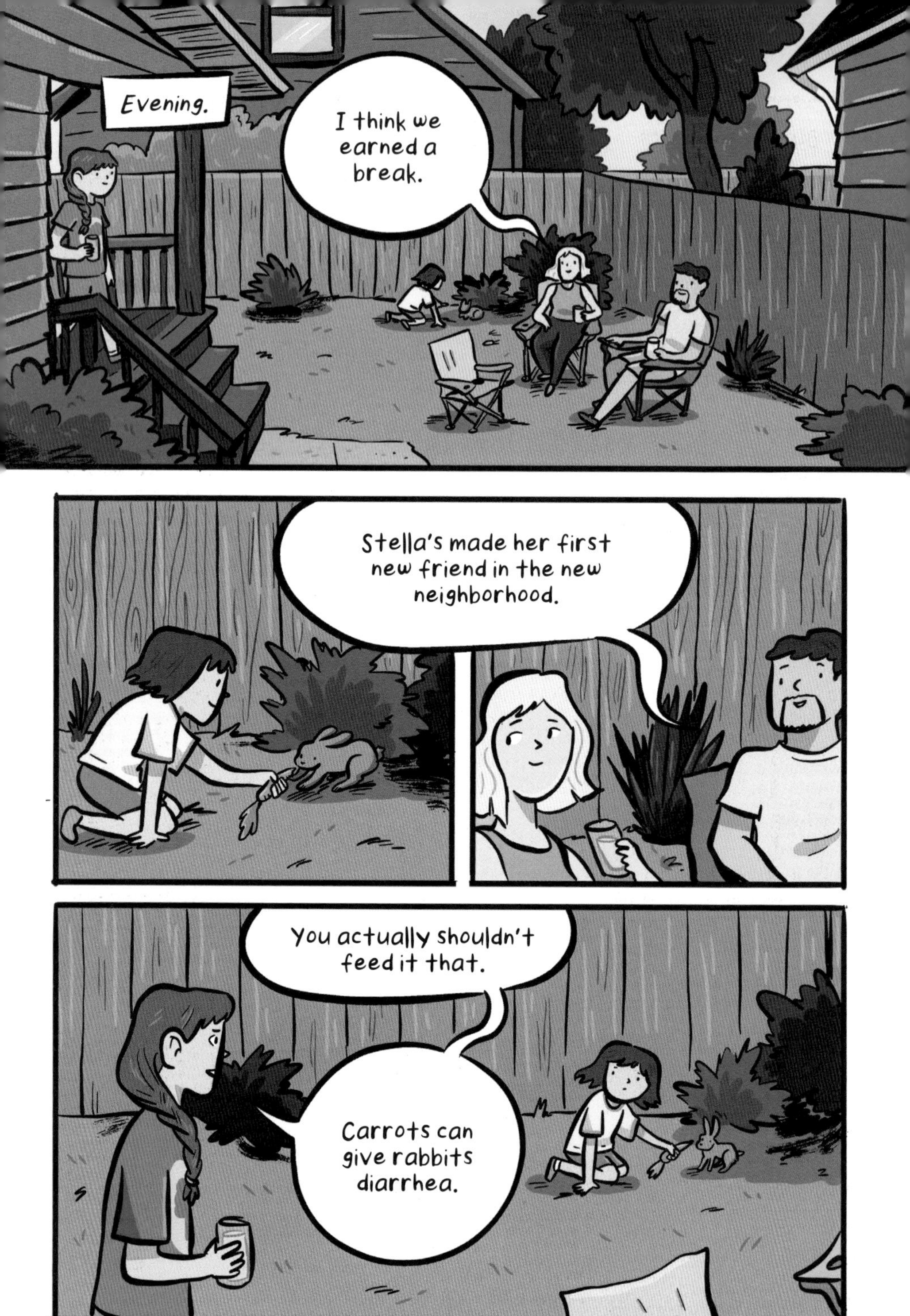
Evening.
I think we earned a break.
Stella's made her first new friend in the new neighborhood.
You actually shouldn't feed it that.
Carrots can give rabbits diarrhea.

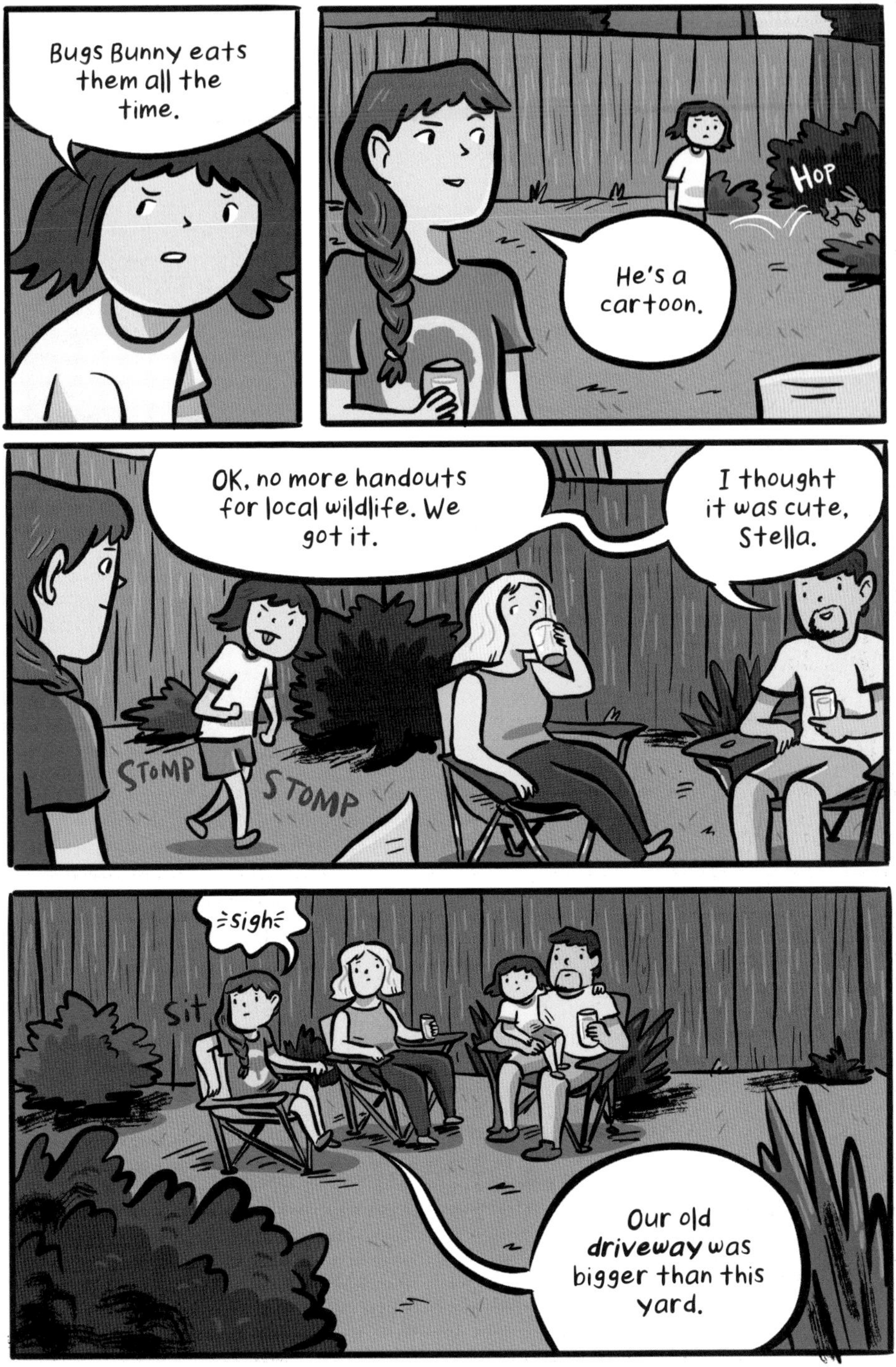
Bugs Bunny eats them all the time.
HOP
He's a cartoon.
OK, no more handouts for local wildlife. We got it.
I thought it was cute, Stella.
STOMP
STOMP
sigh
Sit
Our old driveway was bigger than this yard.

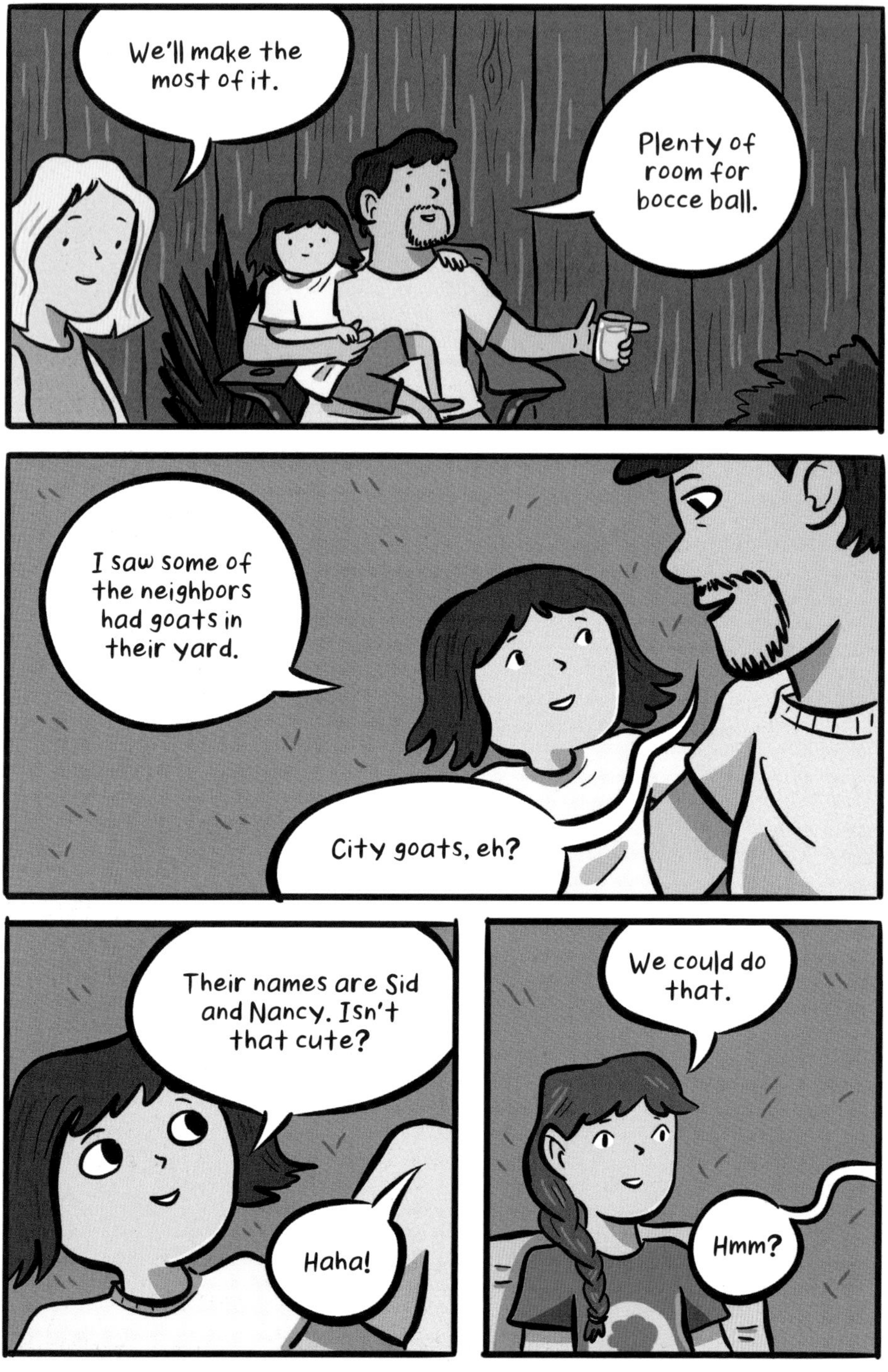
We'll make the most of it.
Plenty of room for bocce ball.
I saw some of the neighbors had goats in their yard.
City goats, eh?
Their names are Sid and Nancy. Isn't that cute?
Haha!
We could do that.
Hmm?

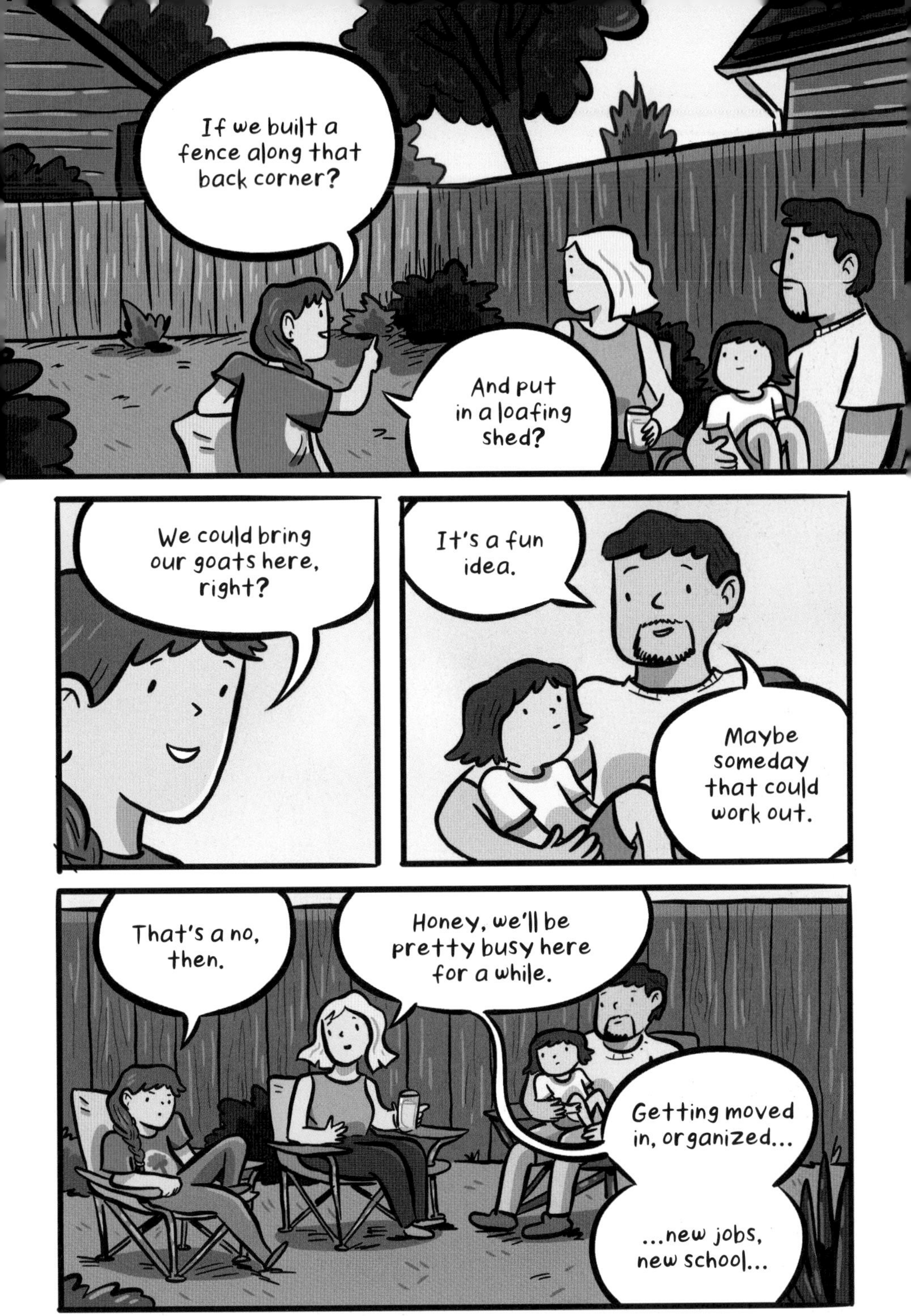

If we built a fence along that back corner?
And put in a loafing shed?
We could bring our goats here, right?
It's a fun idea.
Maybe someday that could work out.
That's a no, then.
Honey, we'll be pretty busy here for a while.
Getting moved in, organized...
...new jobs, new school...

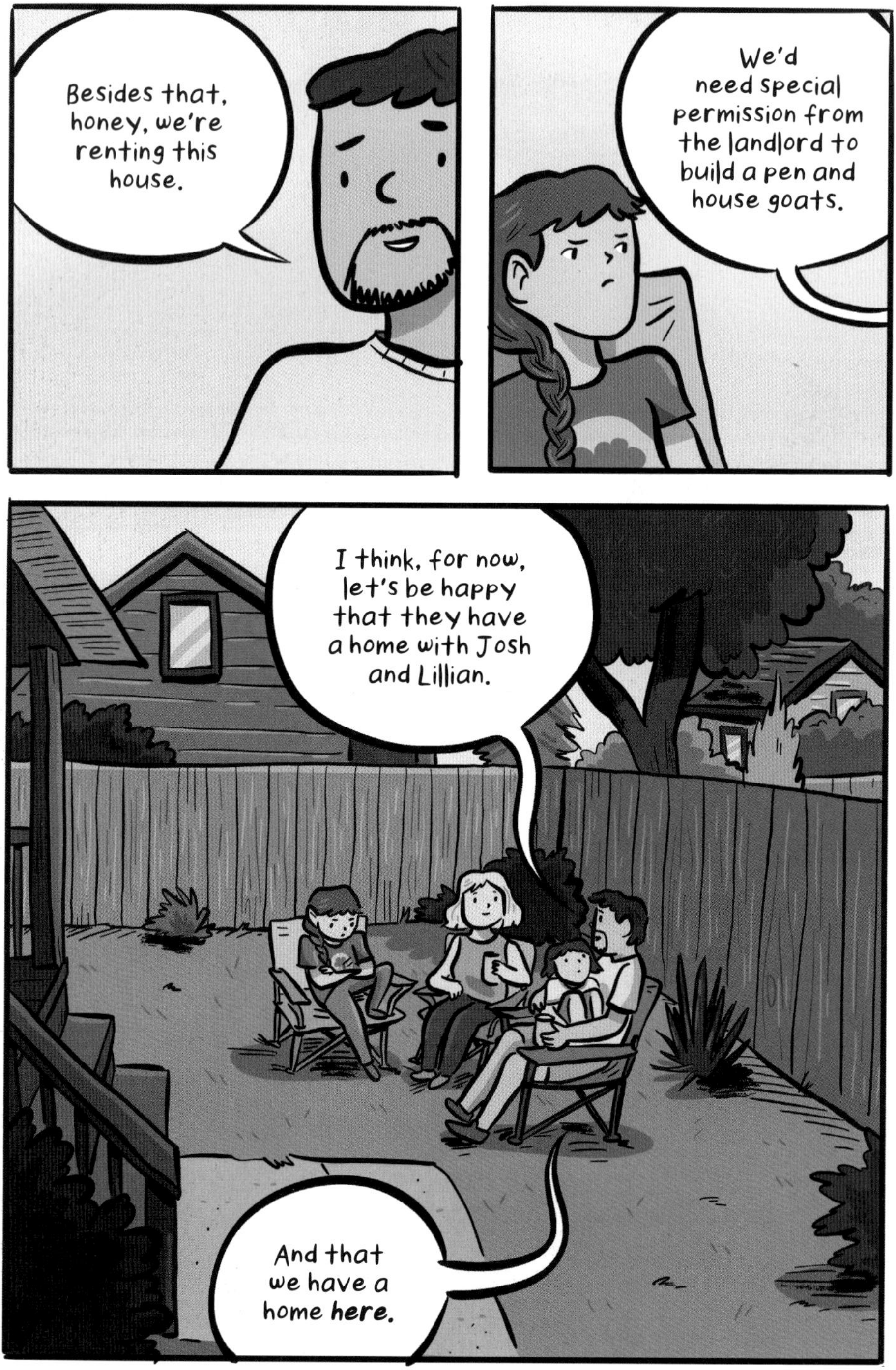
Besides that, honey, we're renting this house.
We'd need special permission from the landlord to build a pen and house goats.
I think, for now, let's be happy that they have a home with Josh and Lillian.
And that we have a home **here.**

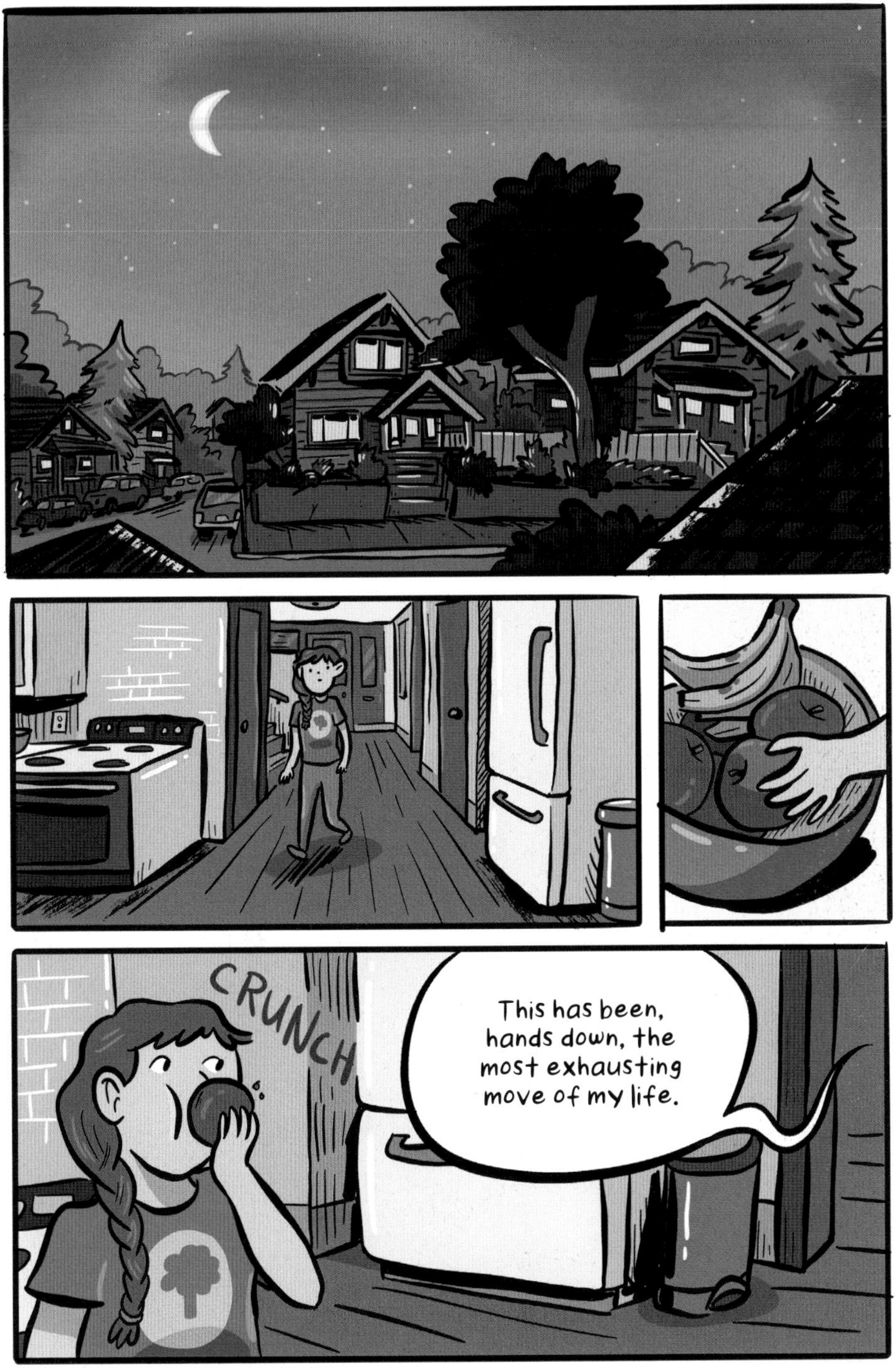
CRUNCH
This has been, hands down, the most exhausting move of my life.

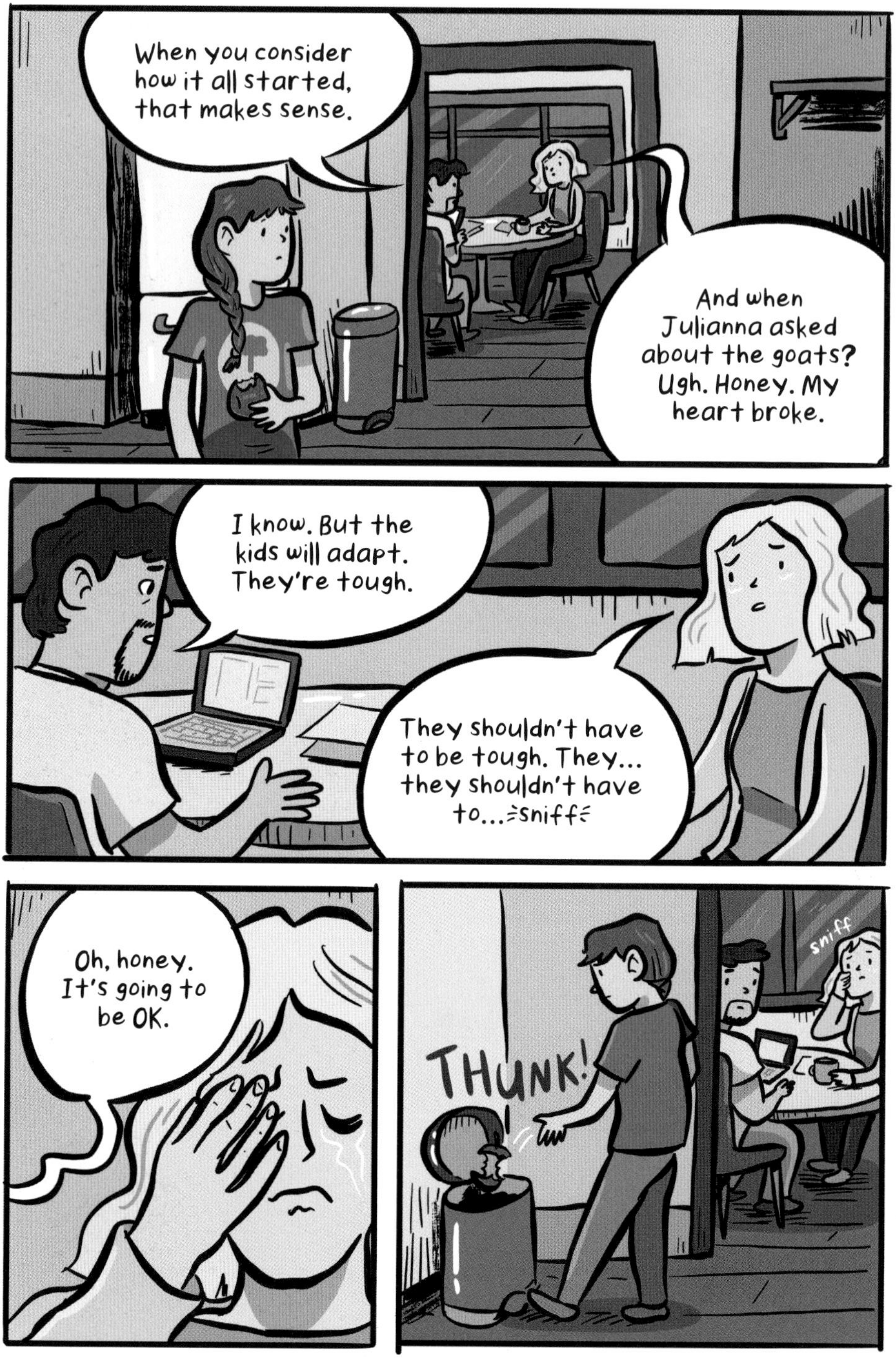

When you consider how it all started, that makes sense.
And when Julianna asked about the goats? Ugh. Honey. My heart broke.
I know. But the kids will adapt. They're tough.
They shouldn't have to be tough. They... they shouldn't have to... sniff
Oh, honey. It's going to be OK.
THUNK!
sniff

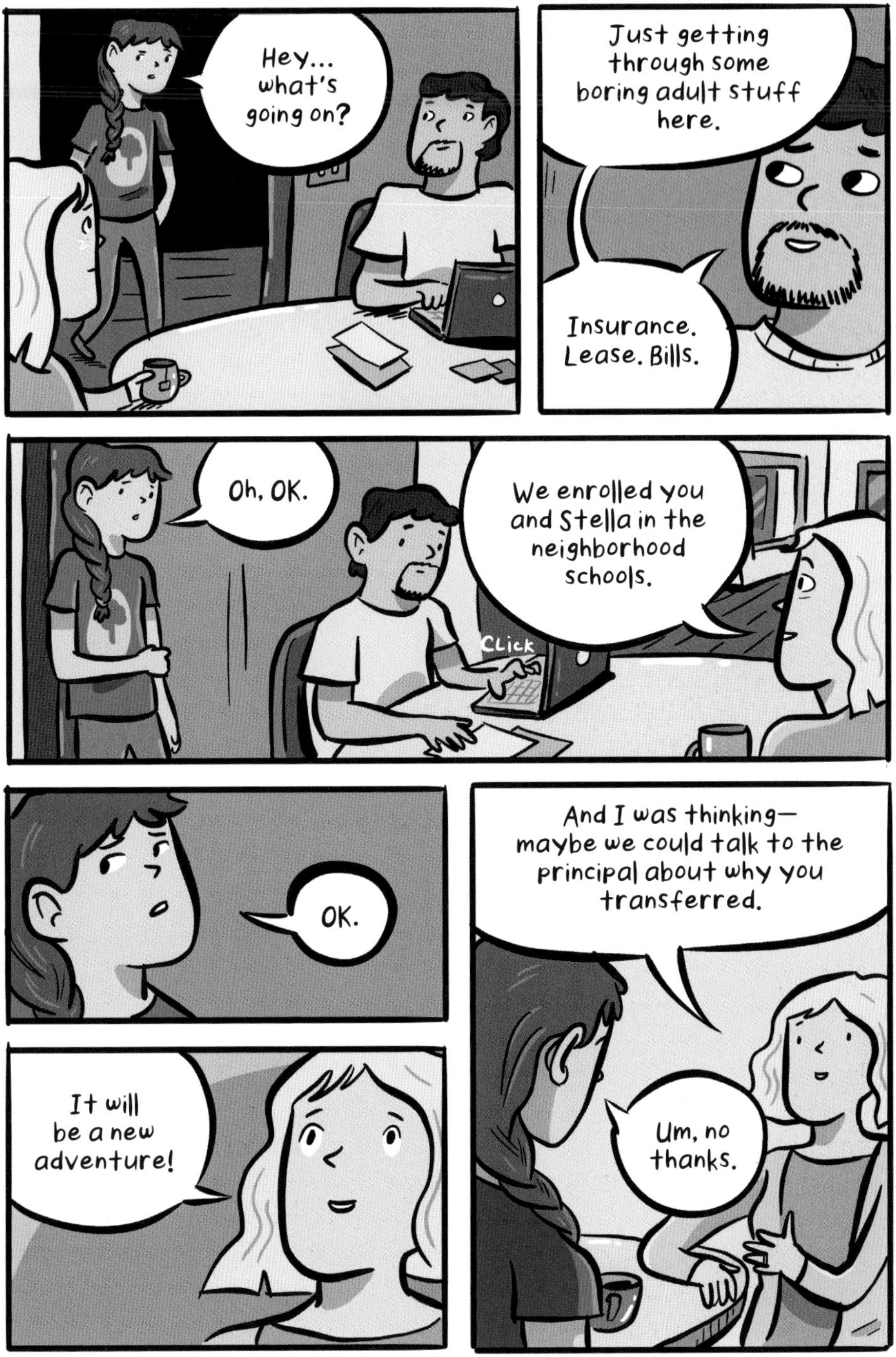
Hey... what's going on?
Just getting through some boring adult stuff here.
Insurance. Lease. Bills.
Oh, OK.
We enrolled you and Stella in the neighborhood schools.
CLICK
OK.
It will be a new adventure!
And I was thinking— maybe we could talk to the principal about why you transferred.
Um, no thanks.

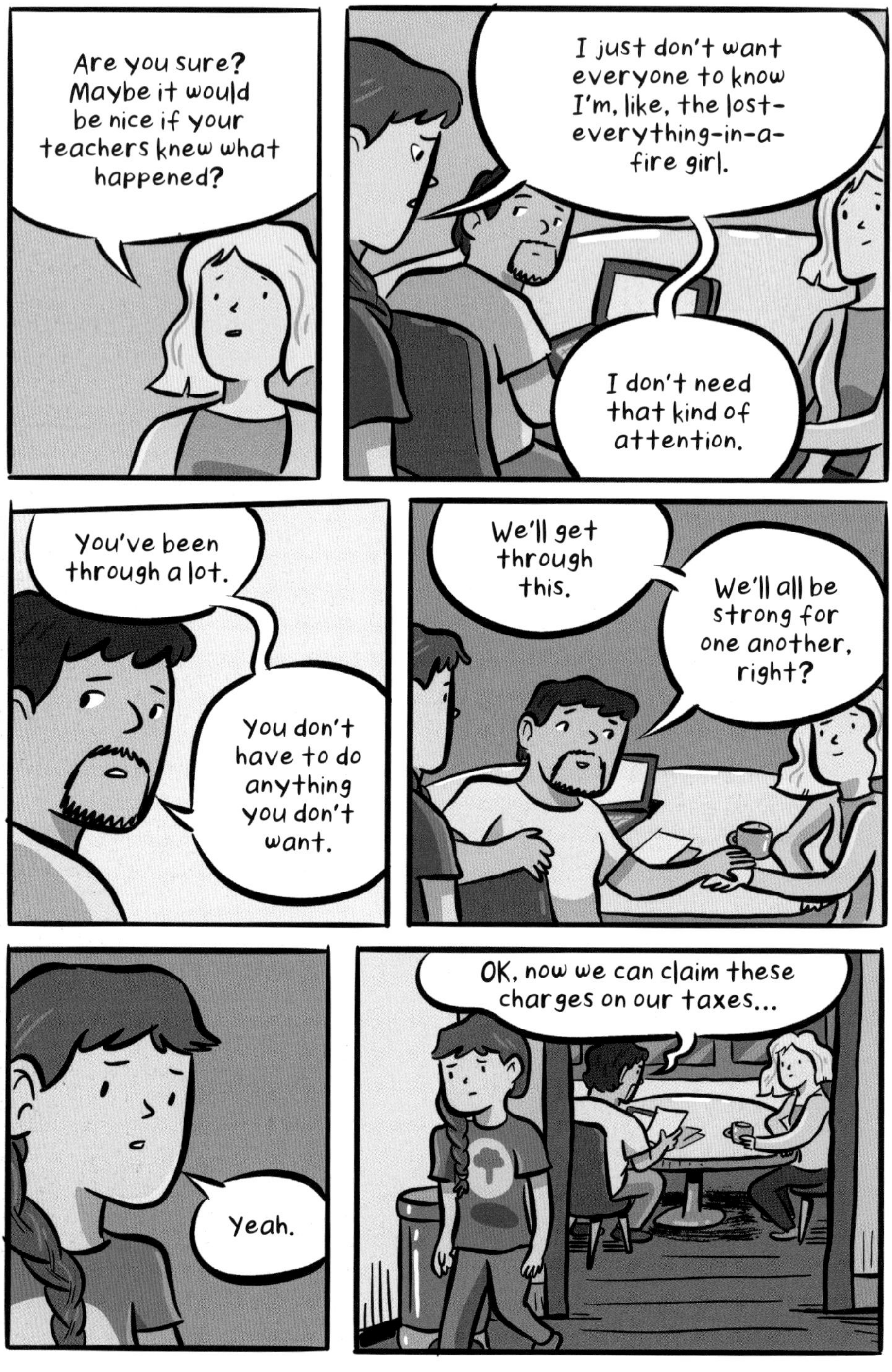
Are you sure? Maybe it would be nice if your teachers knew what happened?
I just don't want everyone to know I'm, like, the lost-everything-in-a-fire girl.
I don't need that kind of attention.
You've been through a lot.
You don't have to do anything you don't want.
We'll get through this.
We'll all be strong for one another, right?
Yeah.
OK, now we can claim these charges on our taxes...

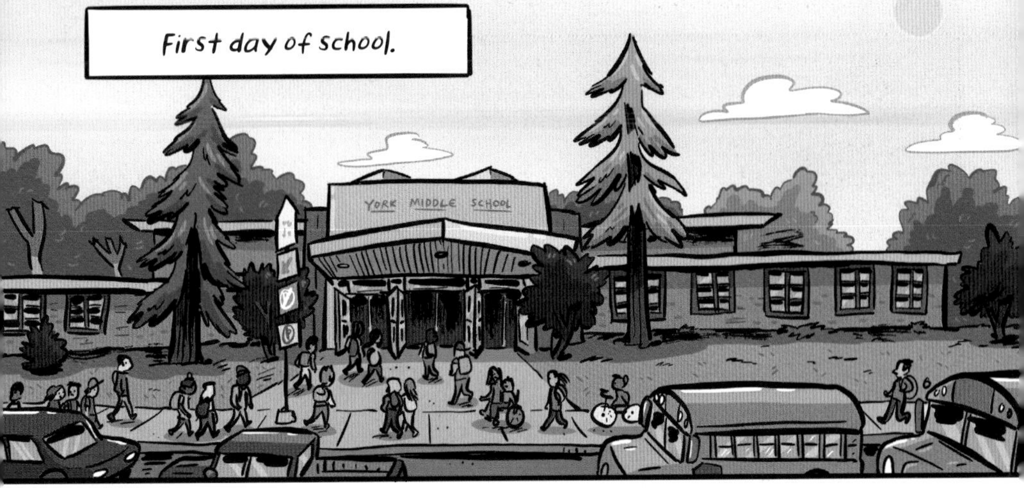
First day of school.
YORK MIDDLE SCHOOL

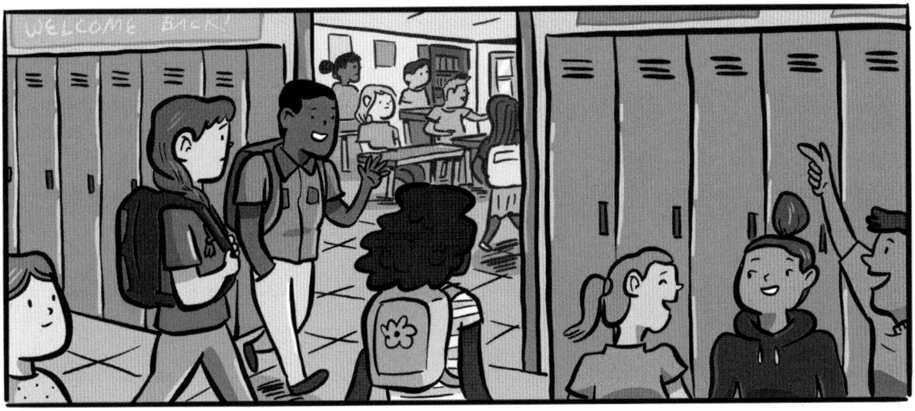
WELCOME BACK!

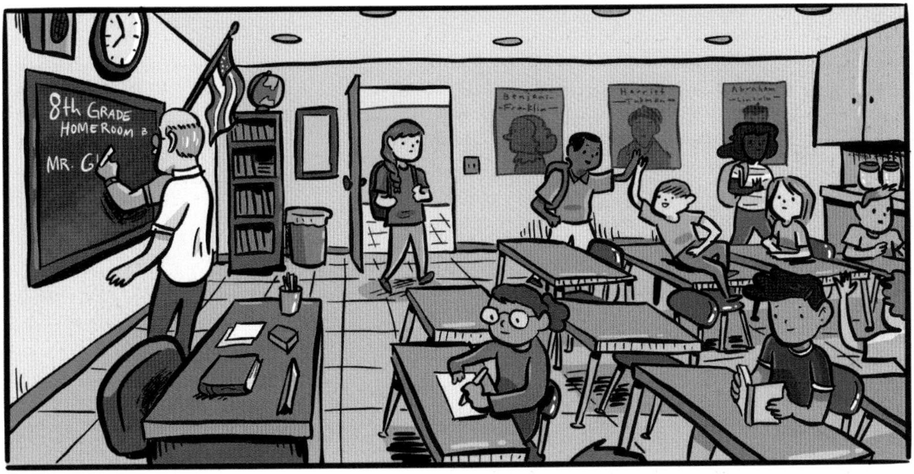
8th GRADE
HOMEROOM B
MR. G

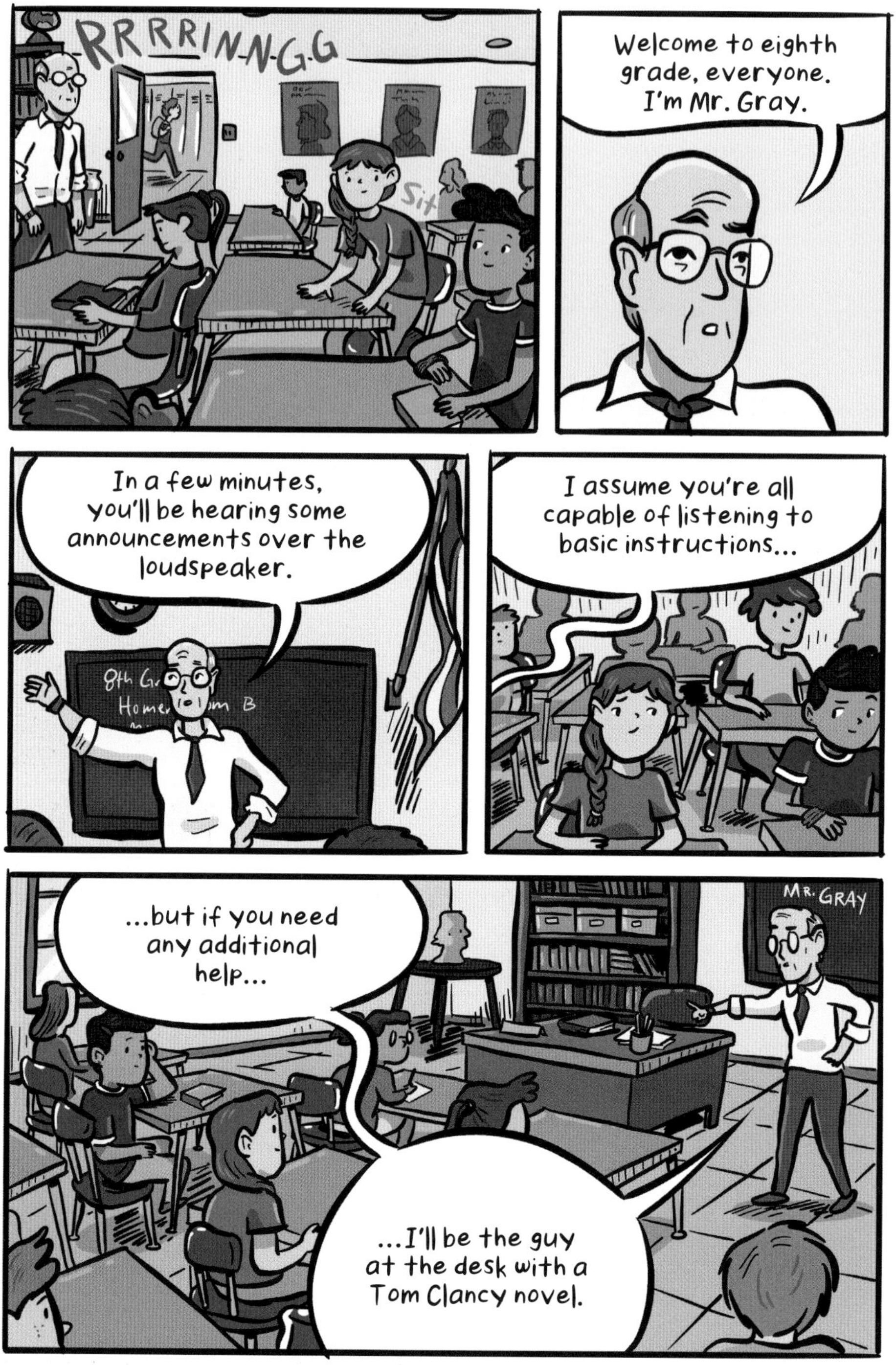
RRRRINNGG
Sit
Welcome to eighth grade, everyone. I'm Mr. Gray.
In a few minutes, you'll be hearing some announcements over the loudspeaker.
I assume you're all capable of listening to basic instructions...
MR. GRAY
...but if you need any additional help...
...I'll be the guy at the desk with a Tom Clancy novel.

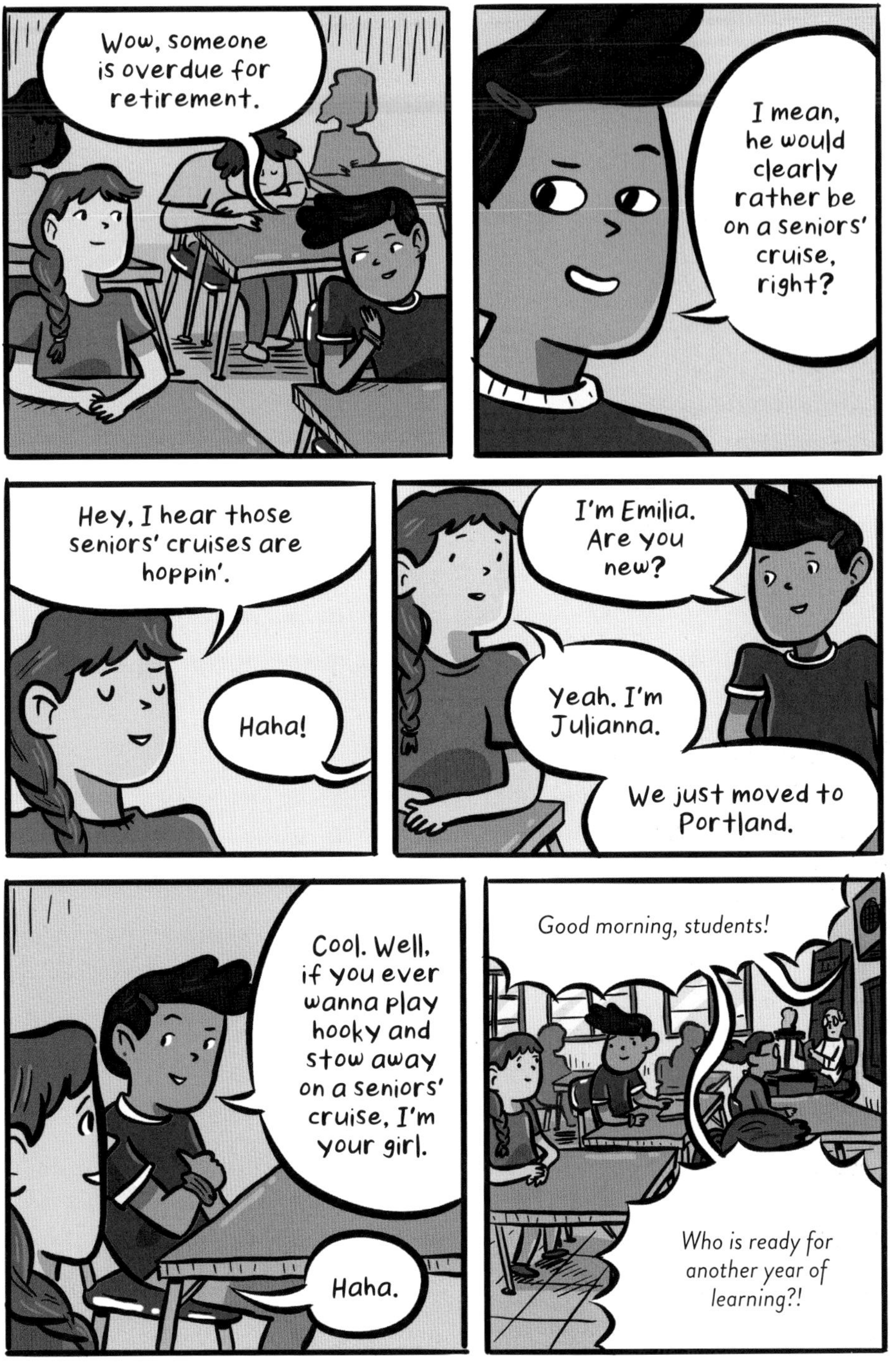
Wow, someone is overdue for retirement.
I mean, he would clearly rather be on a seniors' cruise, right?
Hey, I hear those seniors' cruises are hoppin'.
Haha!
I'm Emilia. Are you new?
Yeah. I'm Julianna.
We just moved to Portland.
Cool. Well, if you ever wanna play hooky and stow away on a seniors' cruise, I'm your girl.
Haha.
Good morning, students!
Who is ready for another year of learning?!

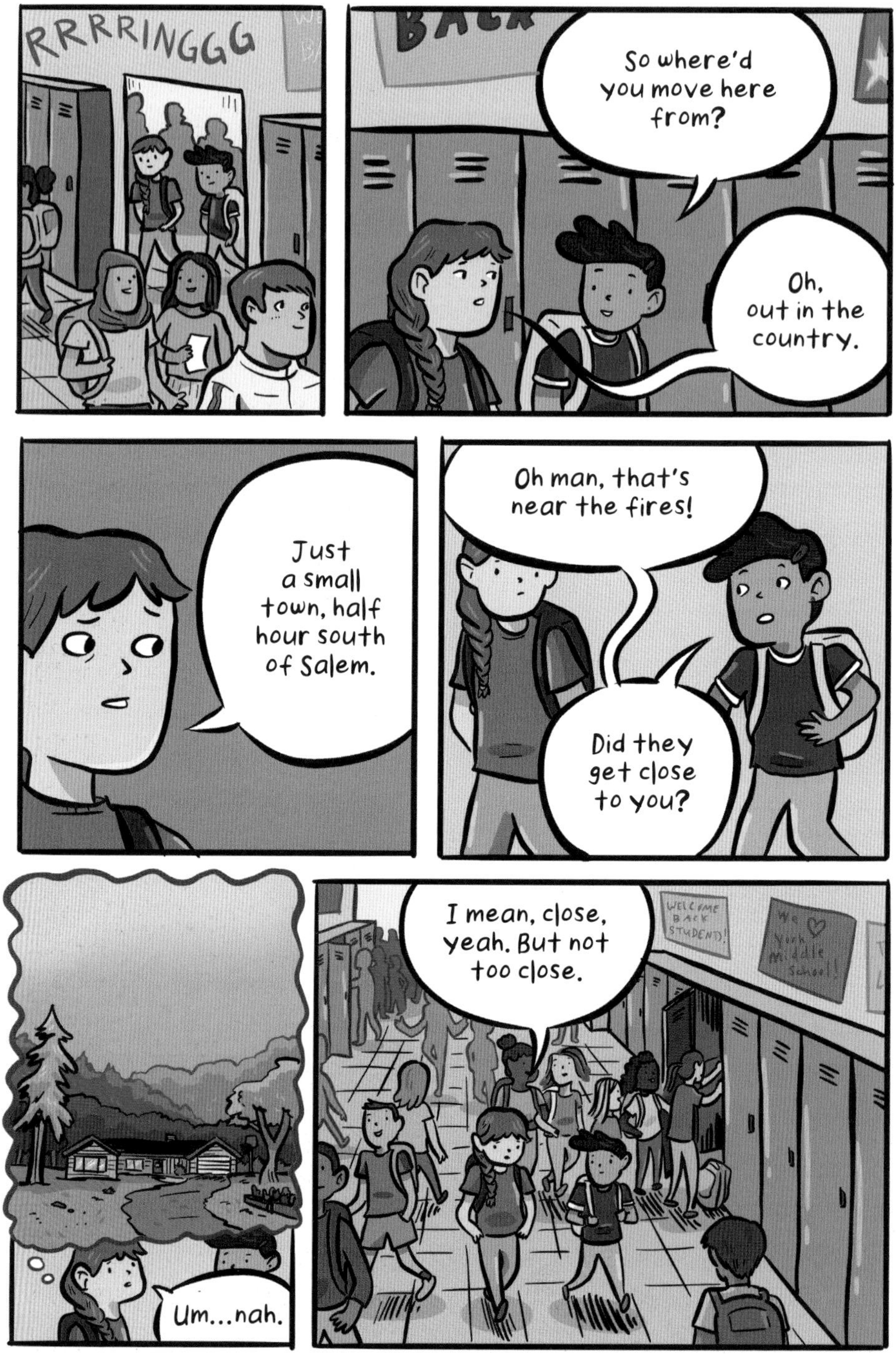
RRRRINGGG
So where'd you move here from?
Oh, out in the country.
Just a small town, half hour south of Salem.
Oh man, that's near the fires!
Did they get close to you?
Um...nah.
I mean, close, yeah. But not too close.
WELCOME BACK STUDENTS!
We ♥ York Middle School!

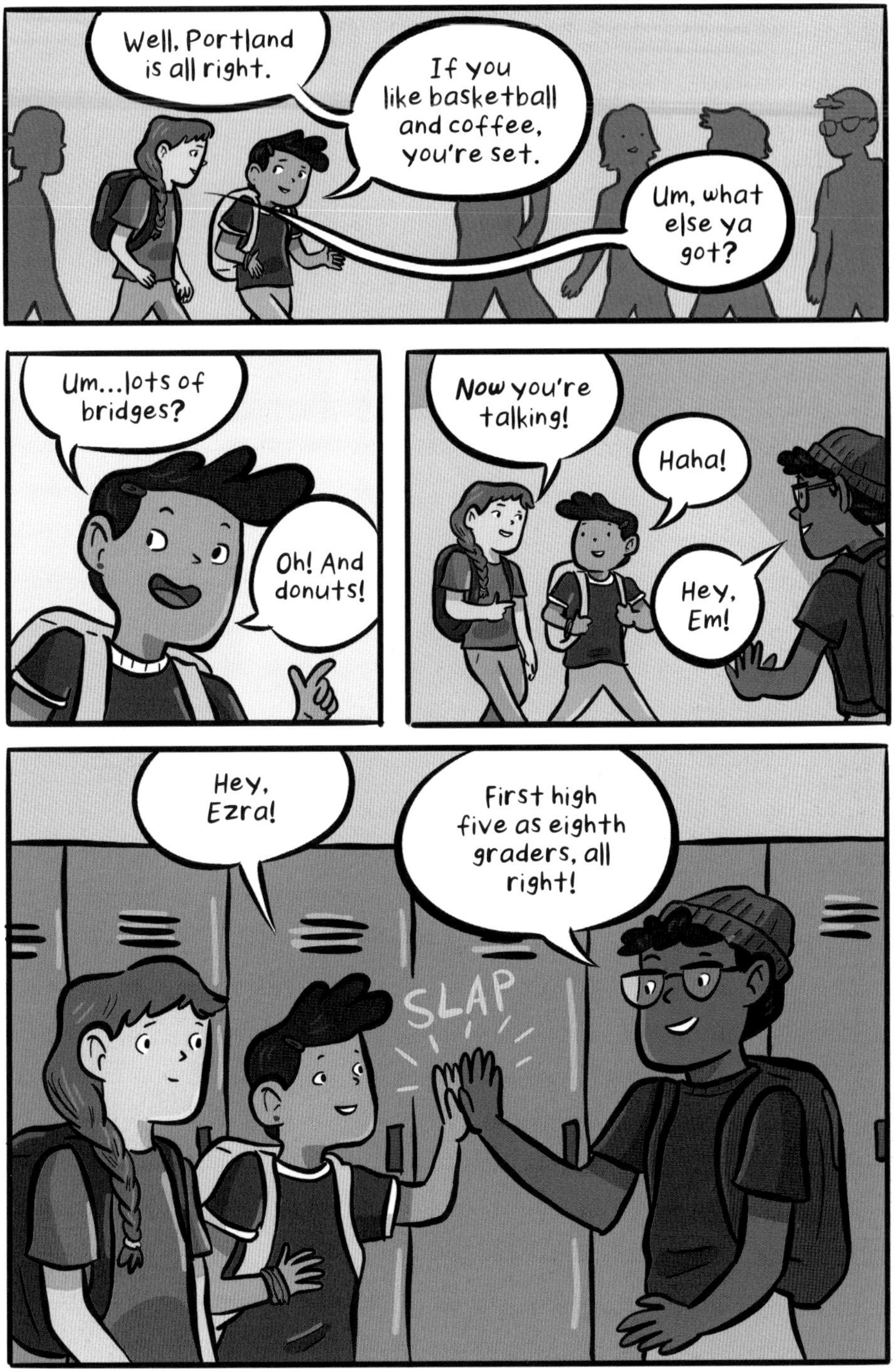
Well, Portland is all right.
If you like basketball and coffee, you're set.
Um, what else ya got?
Um...lots of bridges?
Oh! And donuts!
Now you're talking!
Haha!
Hey, Em!
Hey, Ezra!
First high five as eighth graders, all right!
SLAP

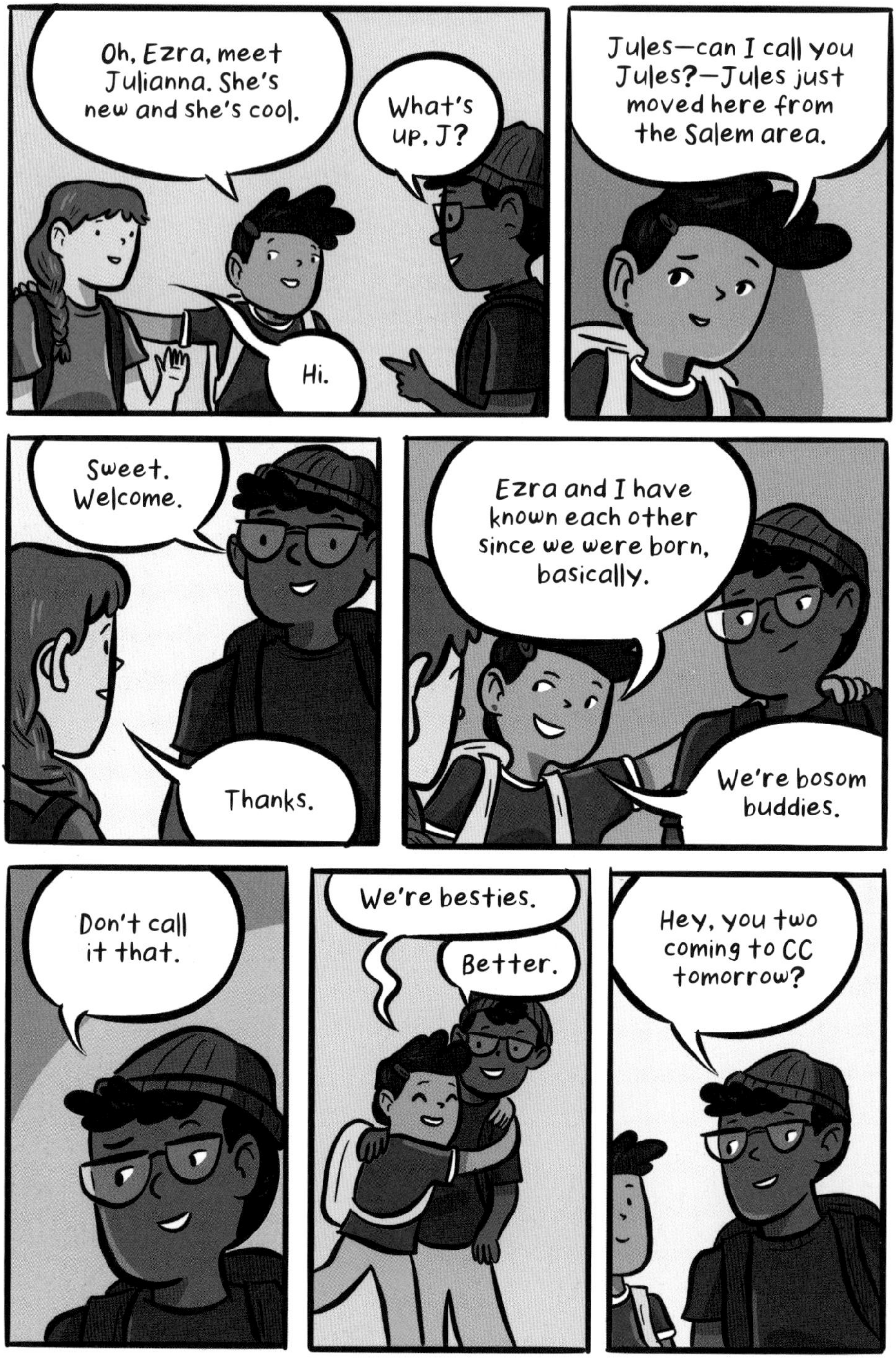
Oh, Ezra, meet Julianna. She's new and she's cool.
What's up, J?
Hi.
Jules—can I call you Jules?—Jules just moved here from the Salem area.
Sweet. Welcome.
Thanks.
Ezra and I have known each other since we were born, basically.
We're bosom buddies.
Don't call it that.
We're besties.
Better.
Hey, you two coming to CC tomorrow?

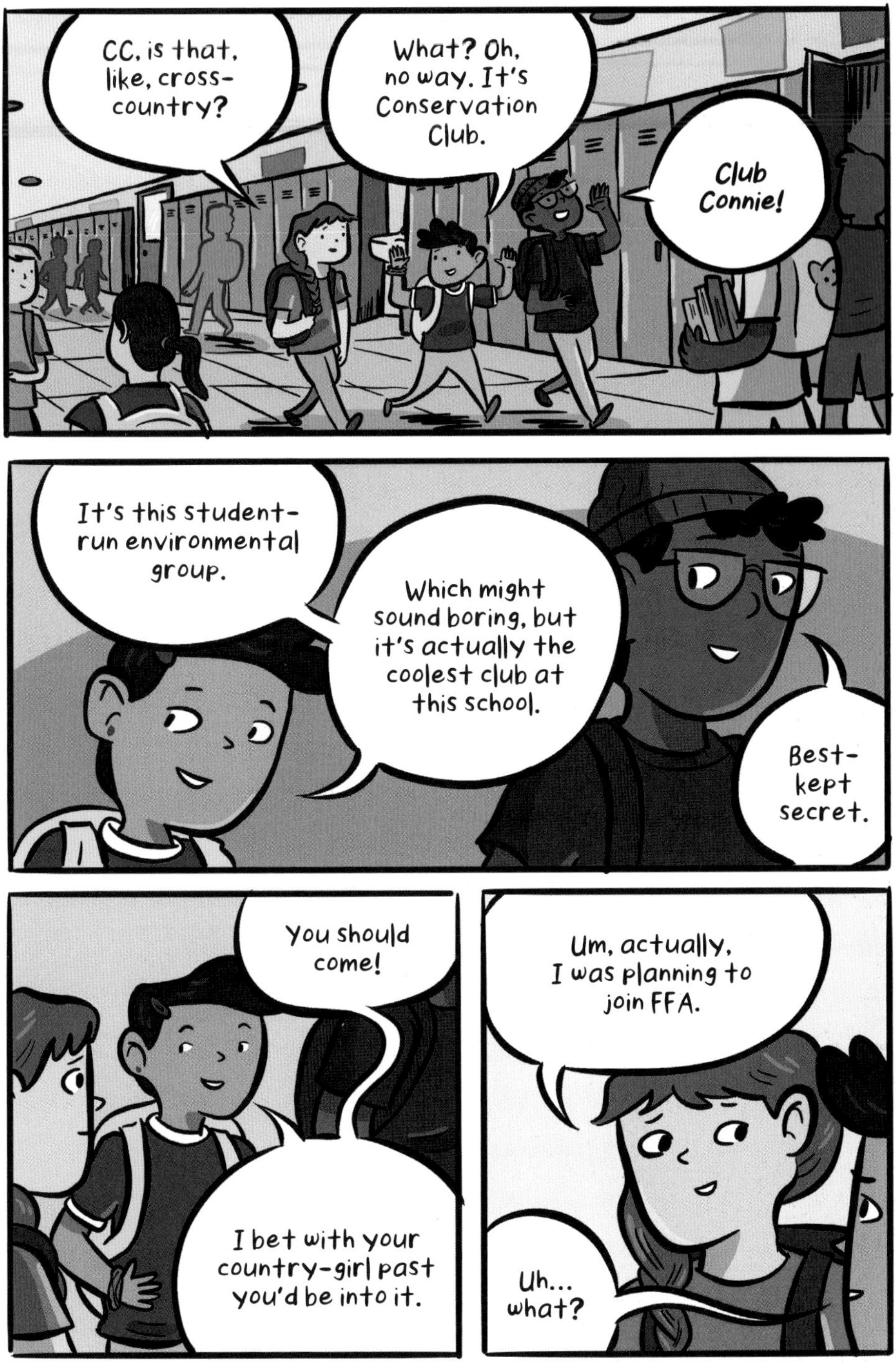
CC, is that, like, cross-country?
What? Oh, no way. It's Conservation Club.
Club Connie!
It's this student-run environmental group.
Which might sound boring, but it's actually the coolest club at this school.
Best-kept secret.
You should come!
I bet with your country-girl past you'd be into it.
Um, actually, I was planning to join FFA.
Uh... what?

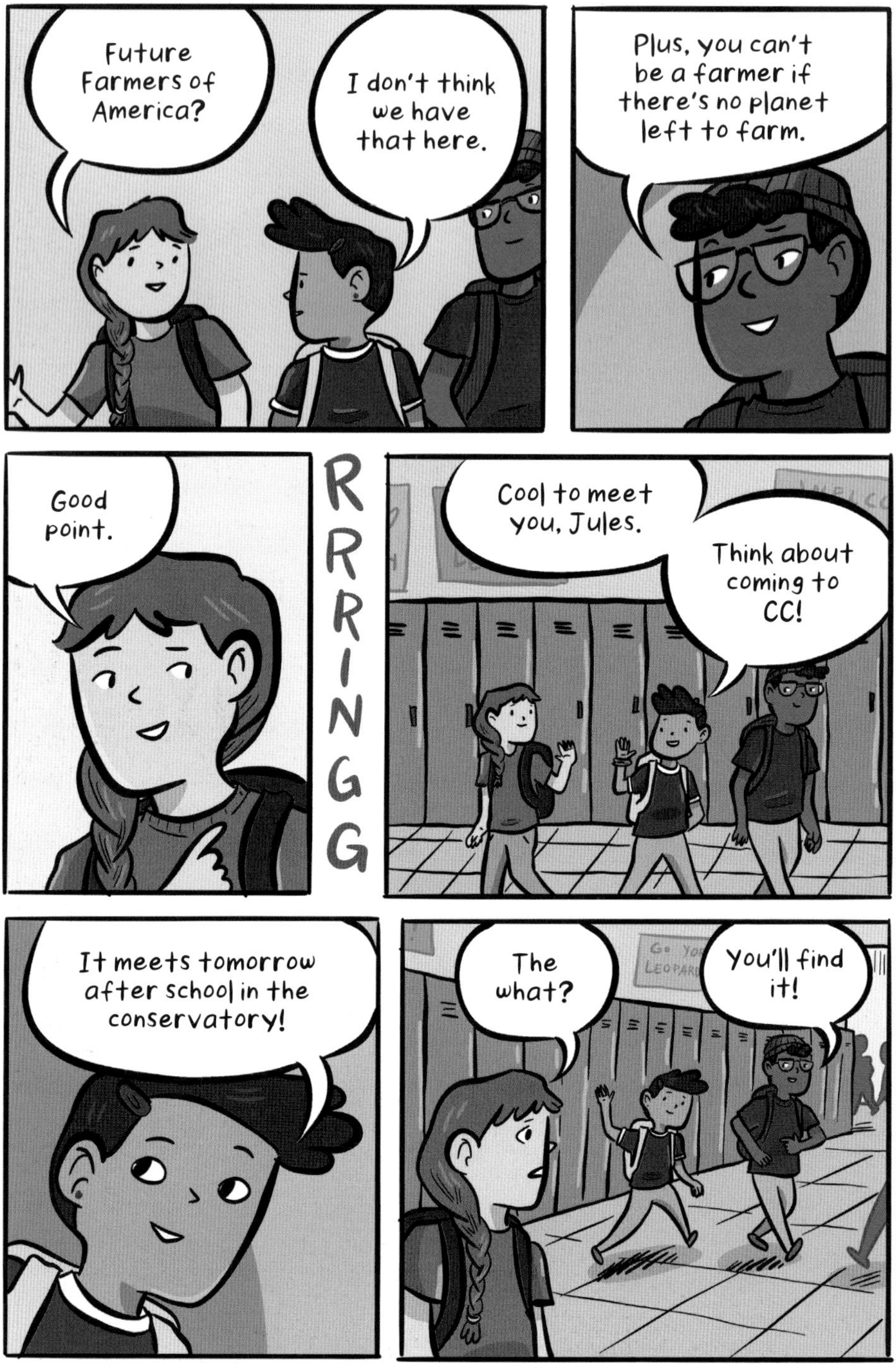
Future Farmers of America?
I don't think we have that here.
Plus, you can't be a farmer if there's no planet left to farm.
Good point.
RRRINGG
Cool to meet you, Jules.
Think about coming to CC!
It meets tomorrow after school in the conservatory!
The what?
You'll find it!

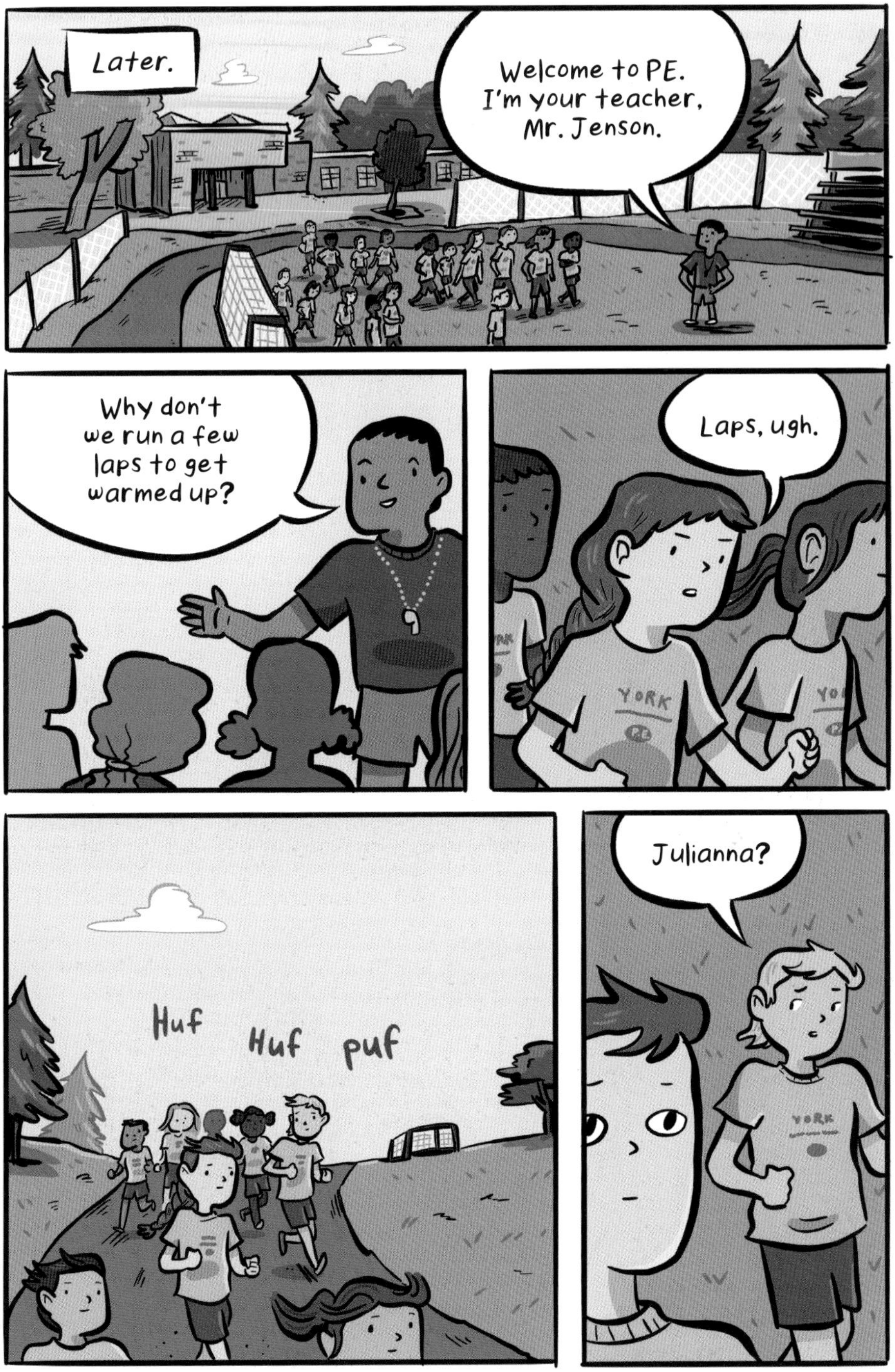
Later.
Welcome to PE. I'm your teacher, Mr. Jenson.
Why don't we run a few laps to get warmed up?
Laps, ugh.
YORK
PE
Huf
Huf puf
Julianna?
YORK

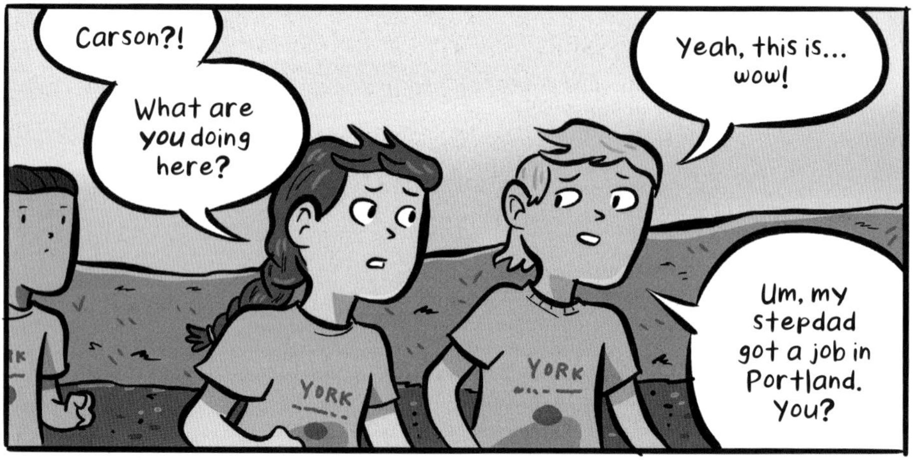
Carson?!
What are you doing here?
Yeah, this is... wow!
Um, my stepdad got a job in Portland. You?

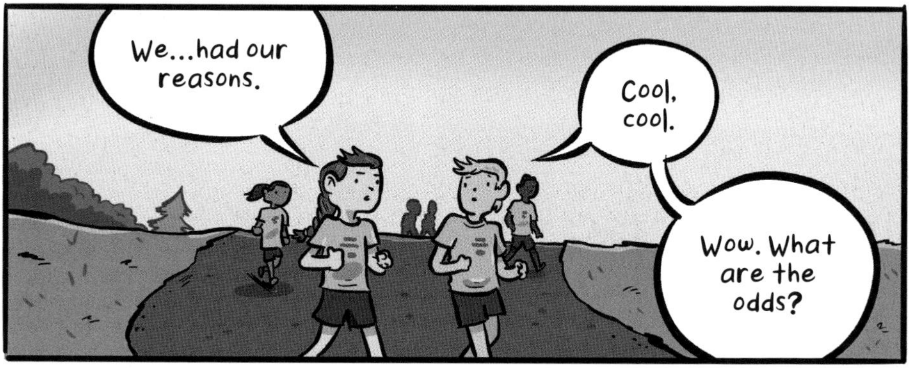
We...had our reasons.
Cool, cool.
Wow. What are the odds?

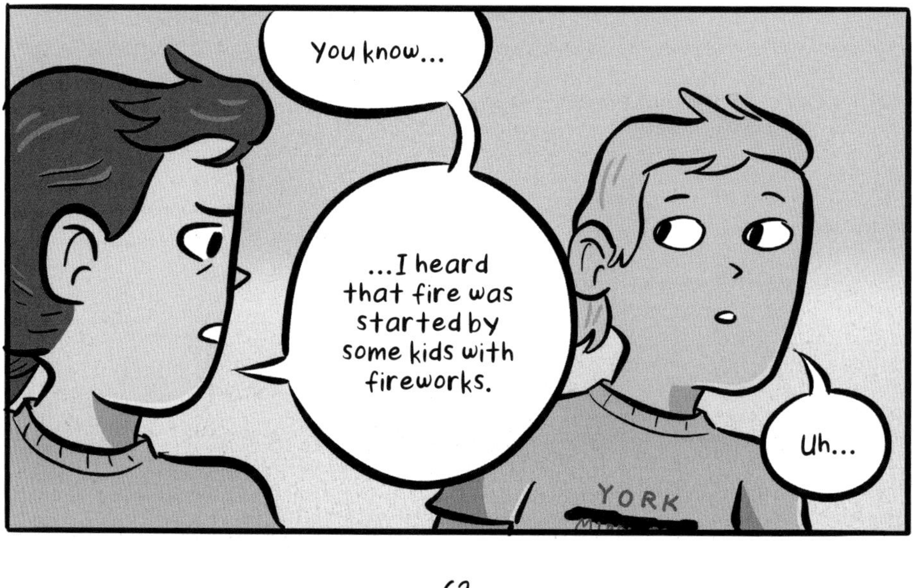
You know...
...I heard that fire was started by some kids with fireworks.
Uh...
YORK

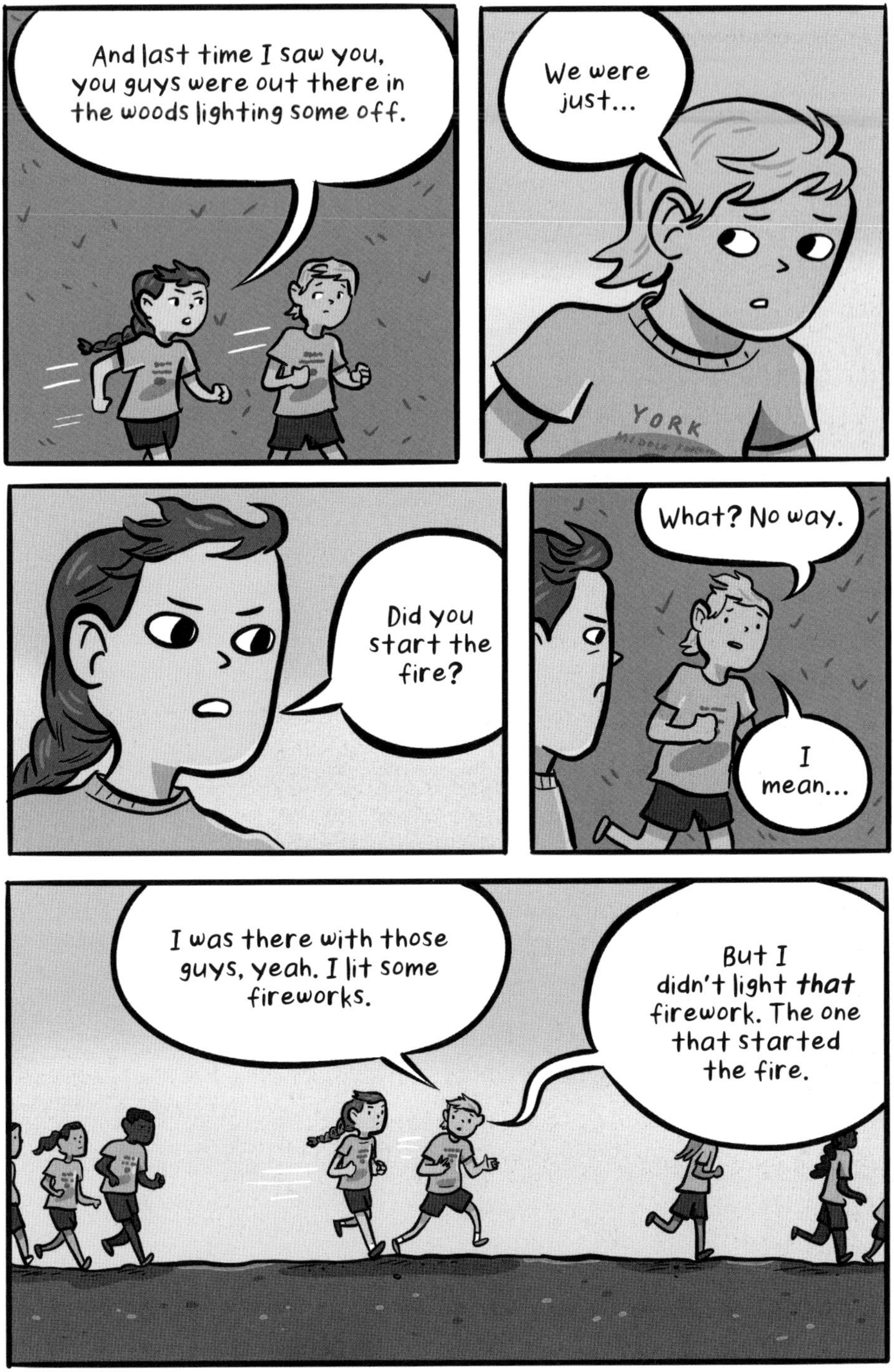
And last time I saw you, you guys were out there in the woods lighting some off.
We were just...
Did you start the fire?
What? No way.
I mean...
YORK
I was there with those guys, yeah. I lit some fireworks.
But I didn't light *that* firework. The one that started the fire.

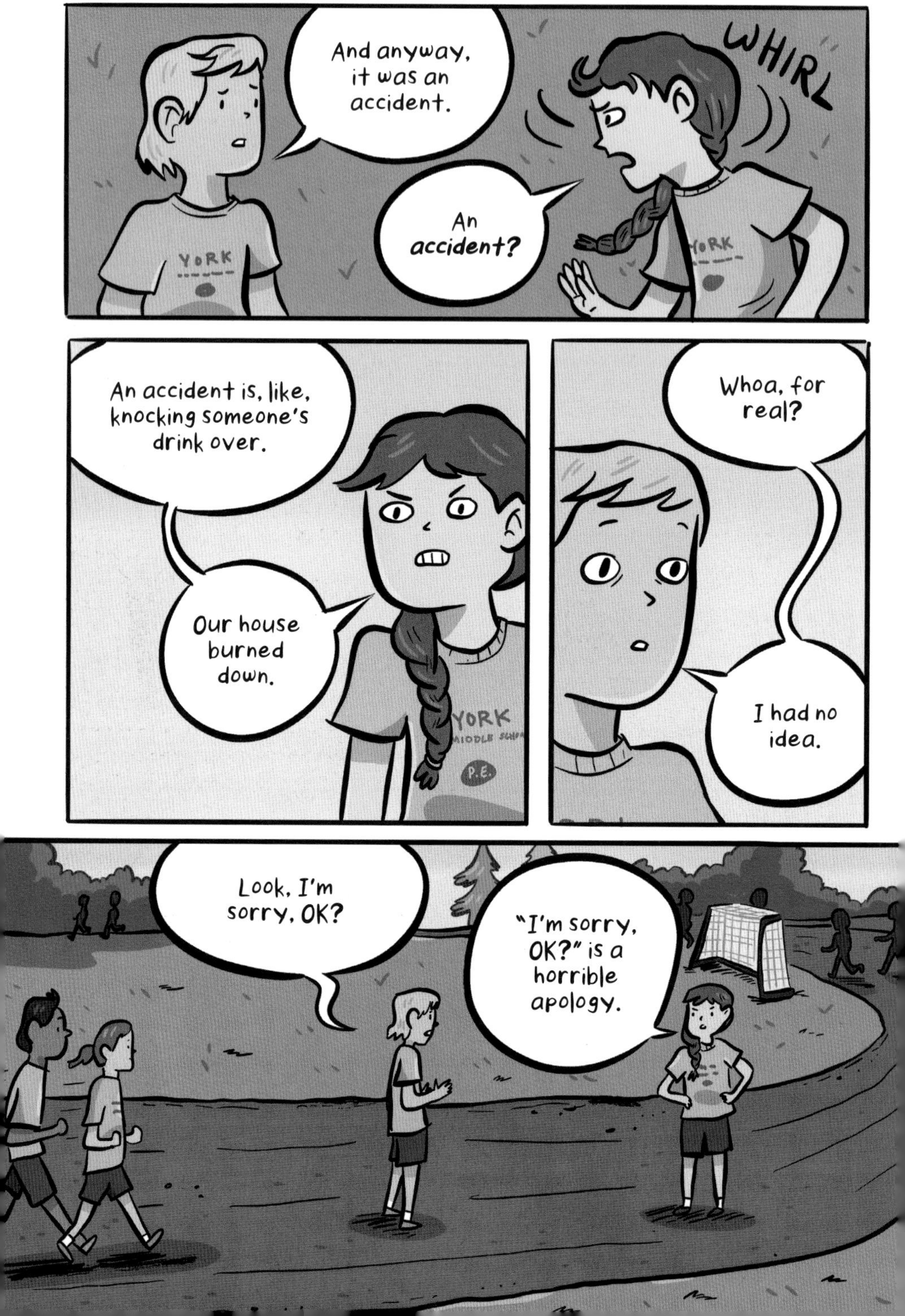
And anyway, it was an accident.
WHIRL
An accident?
An accident is, like, knocking someone's drink over.
Our house burned down.
Whoa, for real?
I had no idea.
Look, I'm sorry, OK?
"I'm sorry, OK?" is a horrible apology.

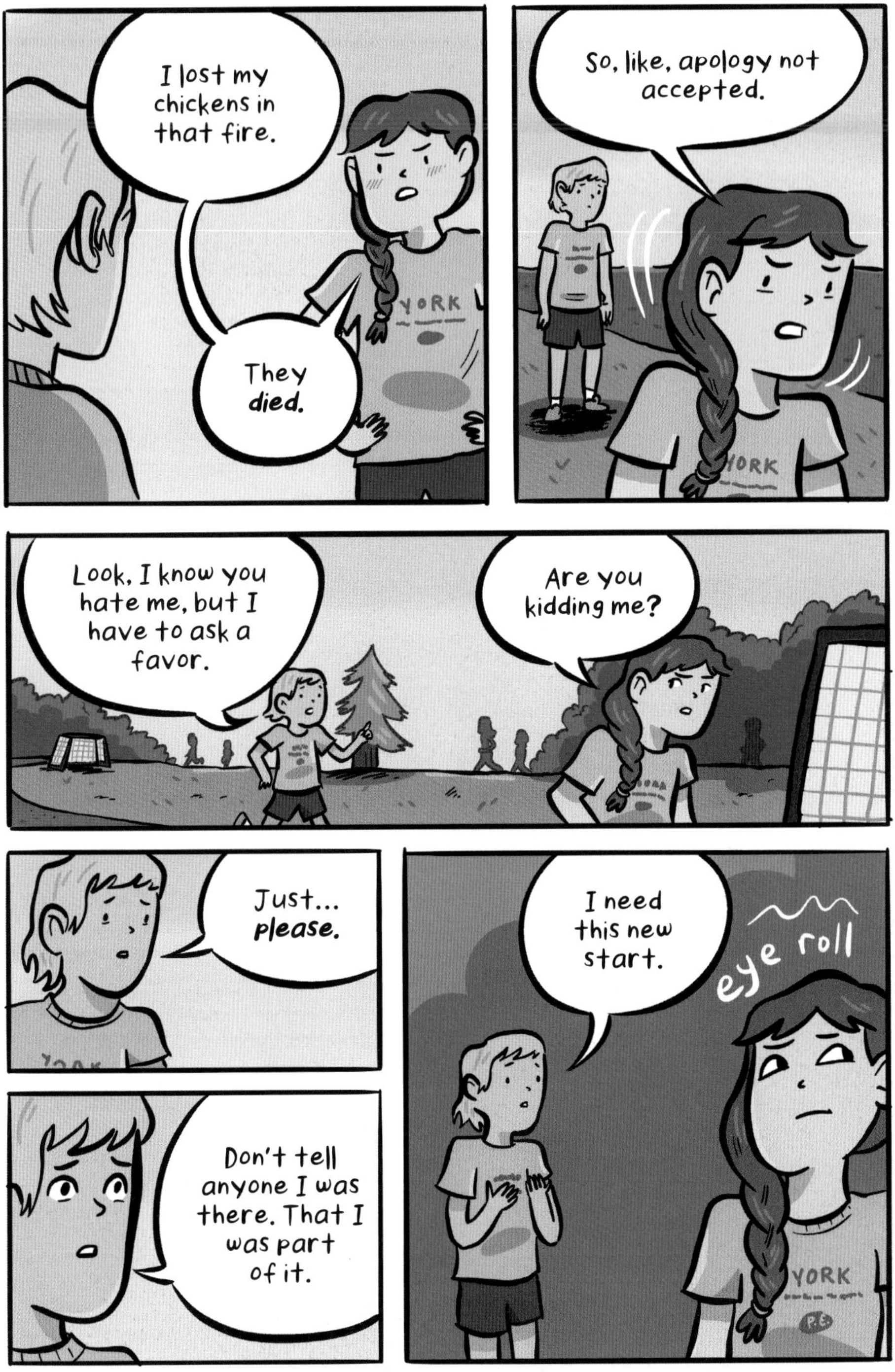
I lost my chickens in that fire.
They *died.*
So, like, apology not accepted.
YORK
Look, I know you hate me, but I have to ask a favor.
Are you kidding me?
Just... **please.**
Don't tell anyone I was there. That I was part of it.
I need this new start.
eye roll
YORK

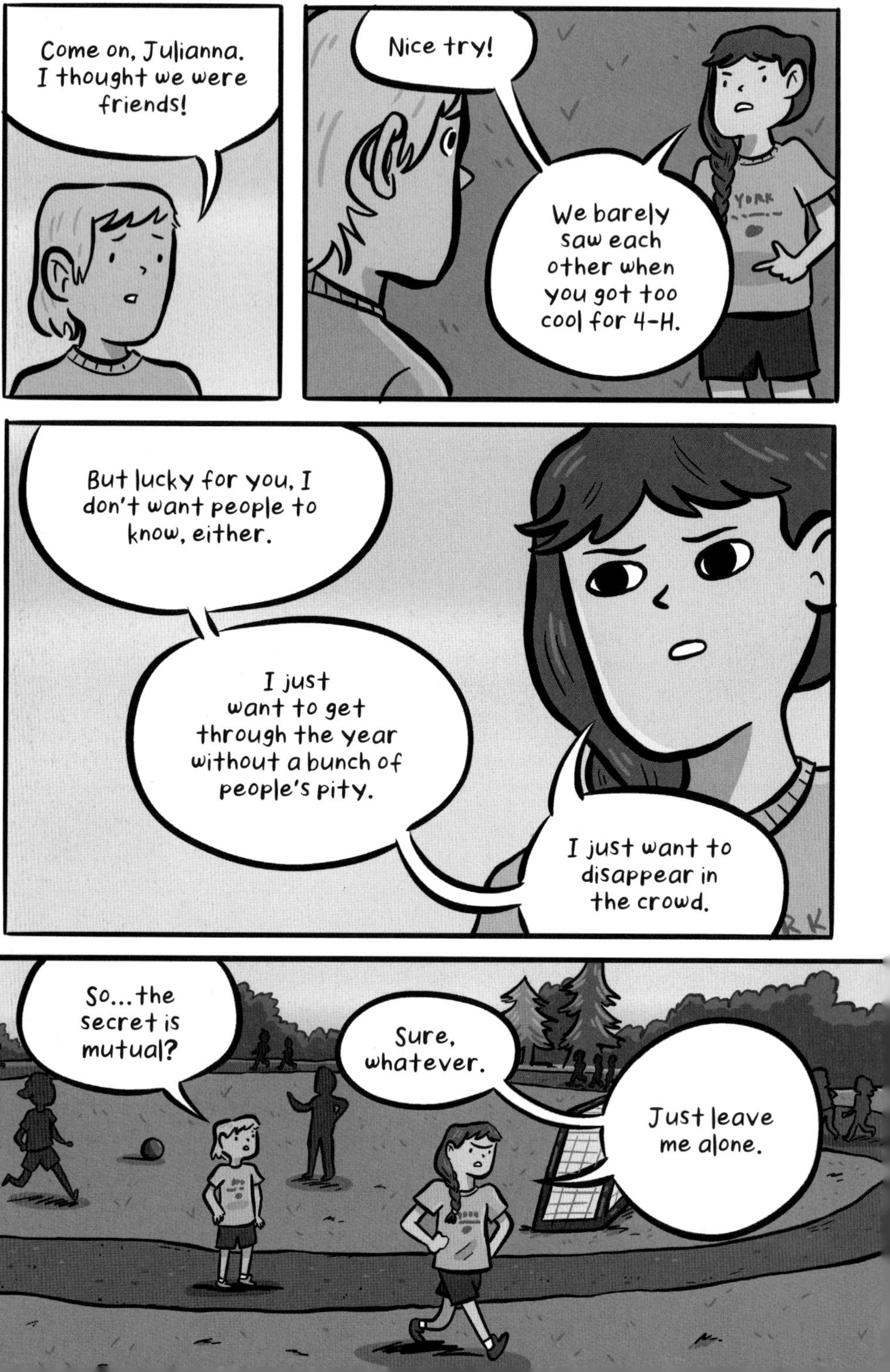
Come on, Julianna. I thought we were friends!
Nice try!
We barely saw each other when you got too cool for 4-H.
YORK
But lucky for you, I don't want people to know, either.
I just want to get through the year without a bunch of people's pity.
I just want to disappear in the crowd.
So... the secret is mutual?
Sure, whatever.
Just leave me alone.

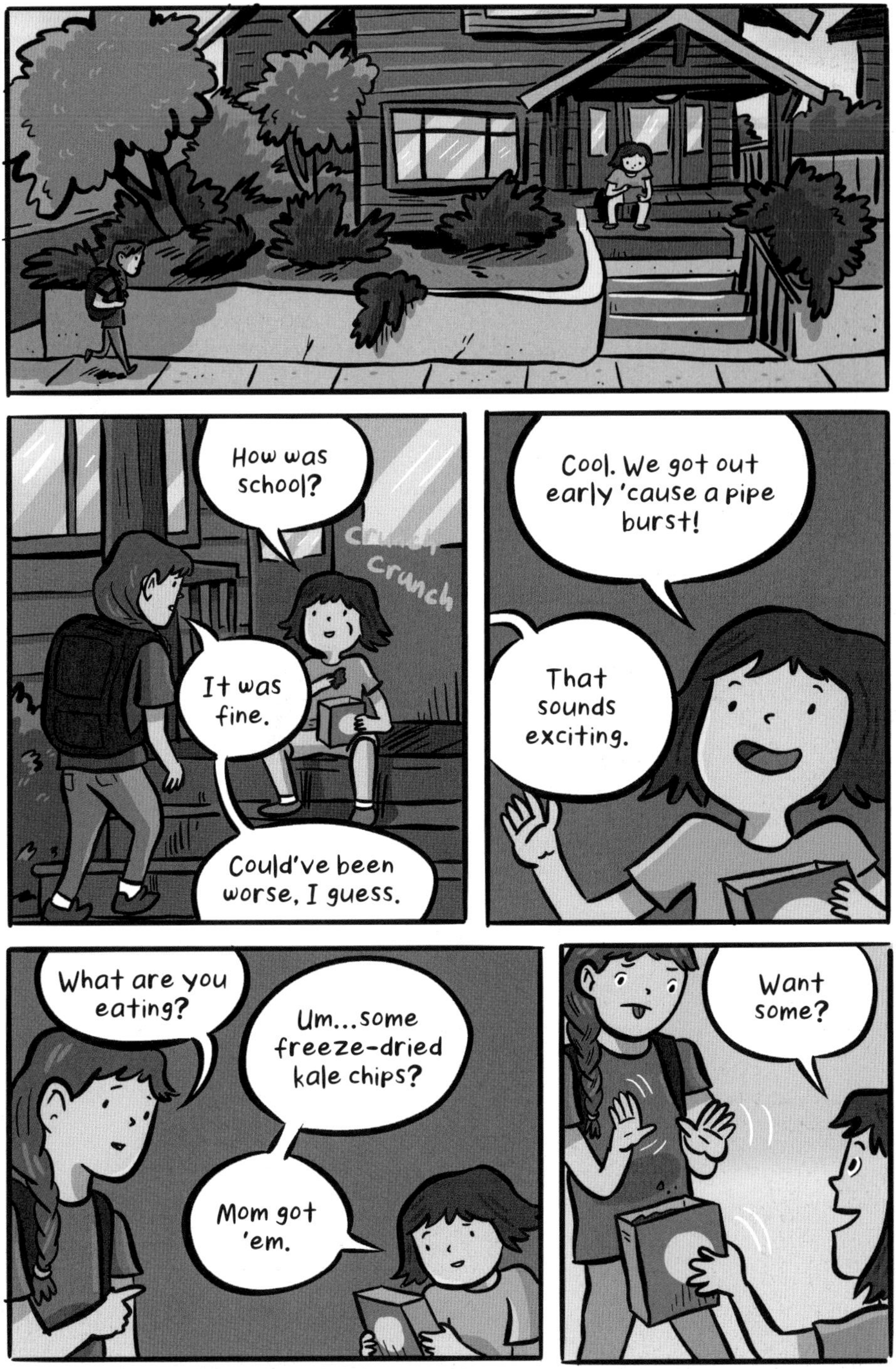
How was school?
crunch
It was fine.
Could've been worse, I guess.
Cool. We got out early 'cause a pipe burst!
That sounds exciting.
What are you eating?
Um...some freeze-dried kale chips?
Mom got 'em.
Want some?

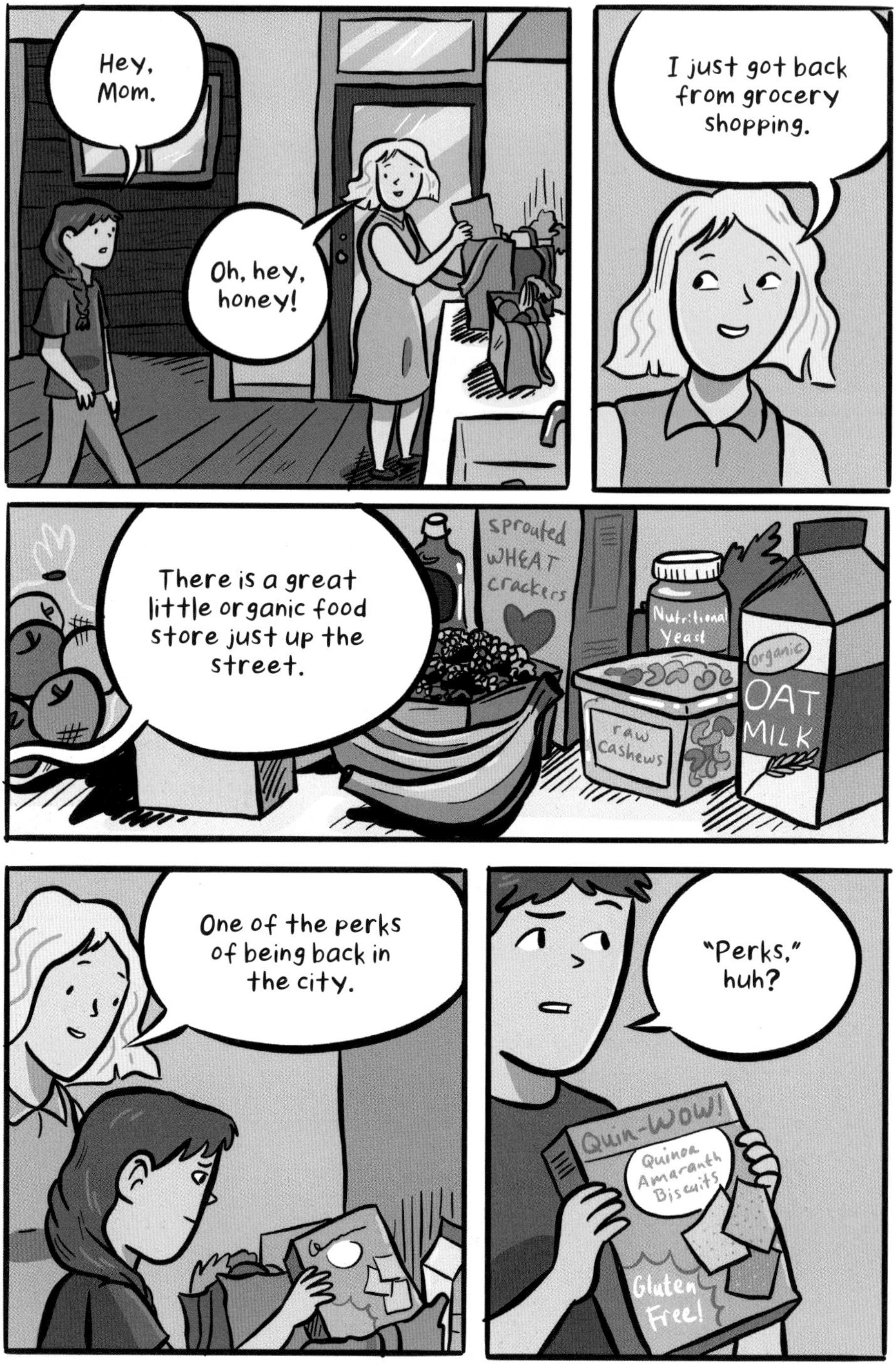
Hey, Mom.
Oh, hey, honey!
I just got back from grocery shopping.
There is a great little organic food store just up the street.
Sprouted WHEAT crackers
Nutritional Yeast
raw Cashews
organic
OAT MILK
One of the perks of being back in the city.
"Perks," huh?
Quin-WOW!
Quinoa Amaranth Biscuits
Gluten Free!

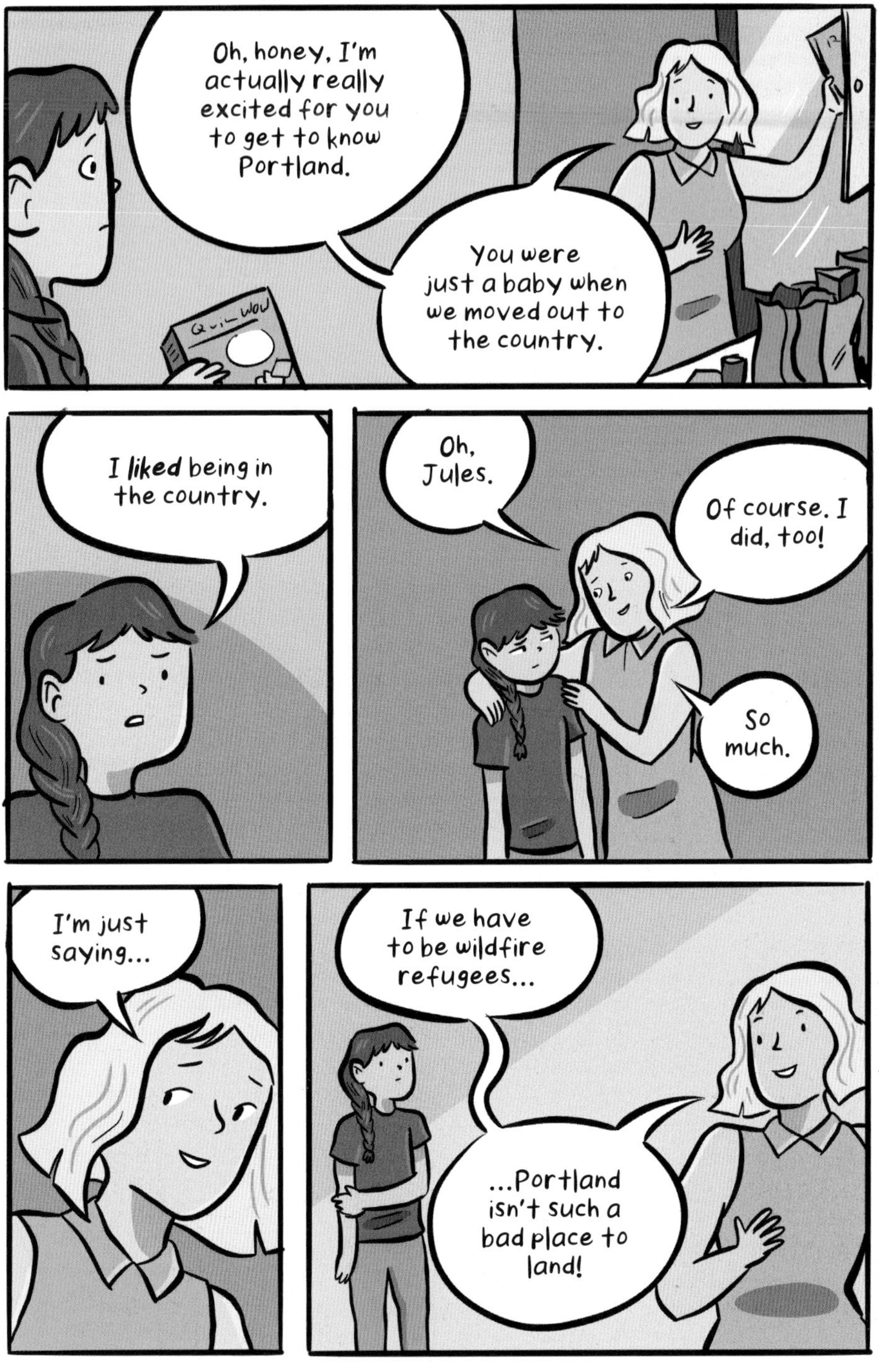
Oh, honey, I'm actually really excited for you to get to know Portland.
You were just a baby when we moved out to the country.
QUIL WOW
I *liked* being in the country.
Oh, Jules.
Of course. I did, too!
So much.
I'm just saying...
If we have to be wildfire refugees...
...Portland isn't such a bad place to land!

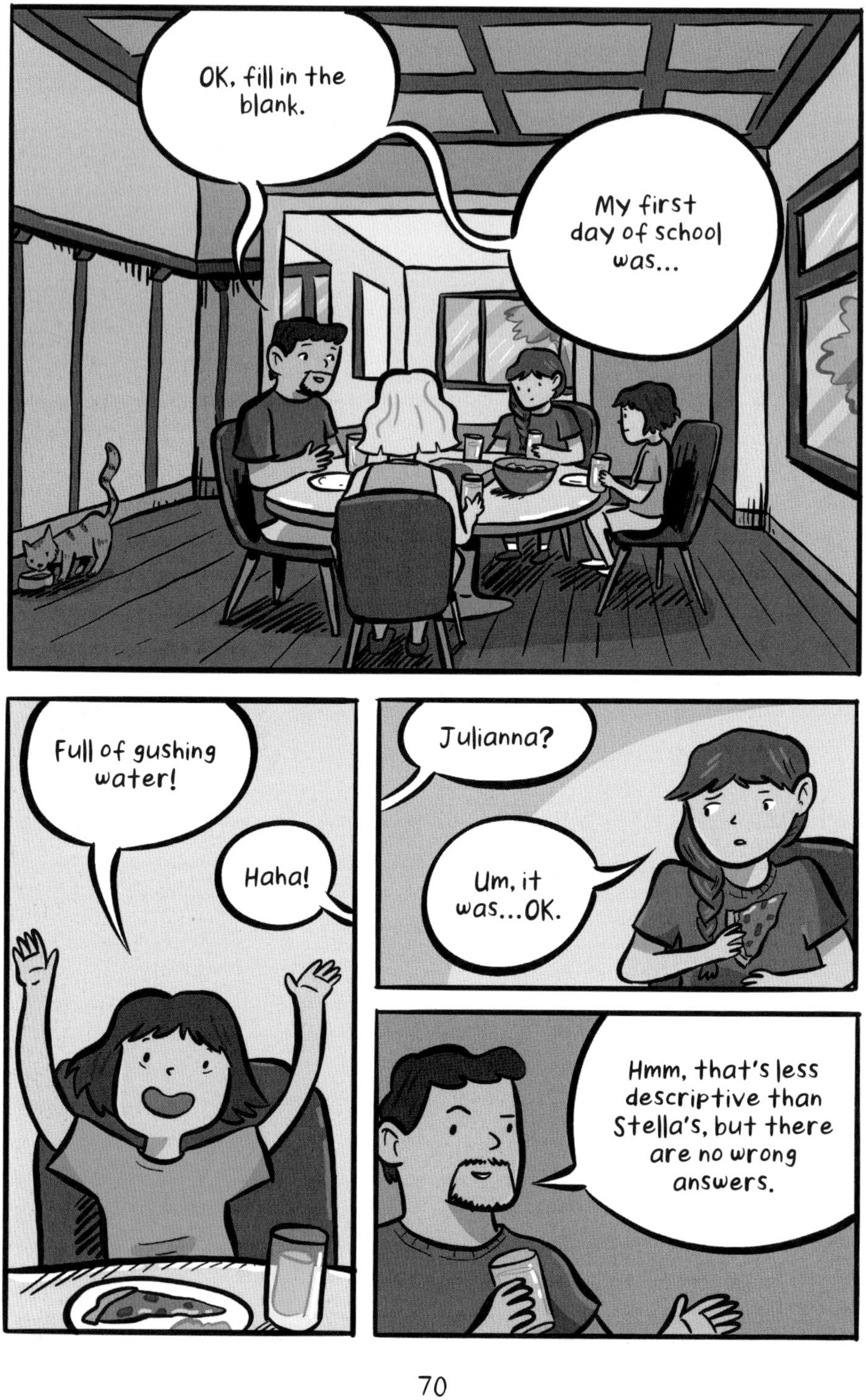
OK, fill in the blank.
My first day of school was...
Full of gushing water!
Haha!
Julianna?
Um, it was...OK.
Hmm, that's less descriptive than Stella's, but there are no wrong answers.

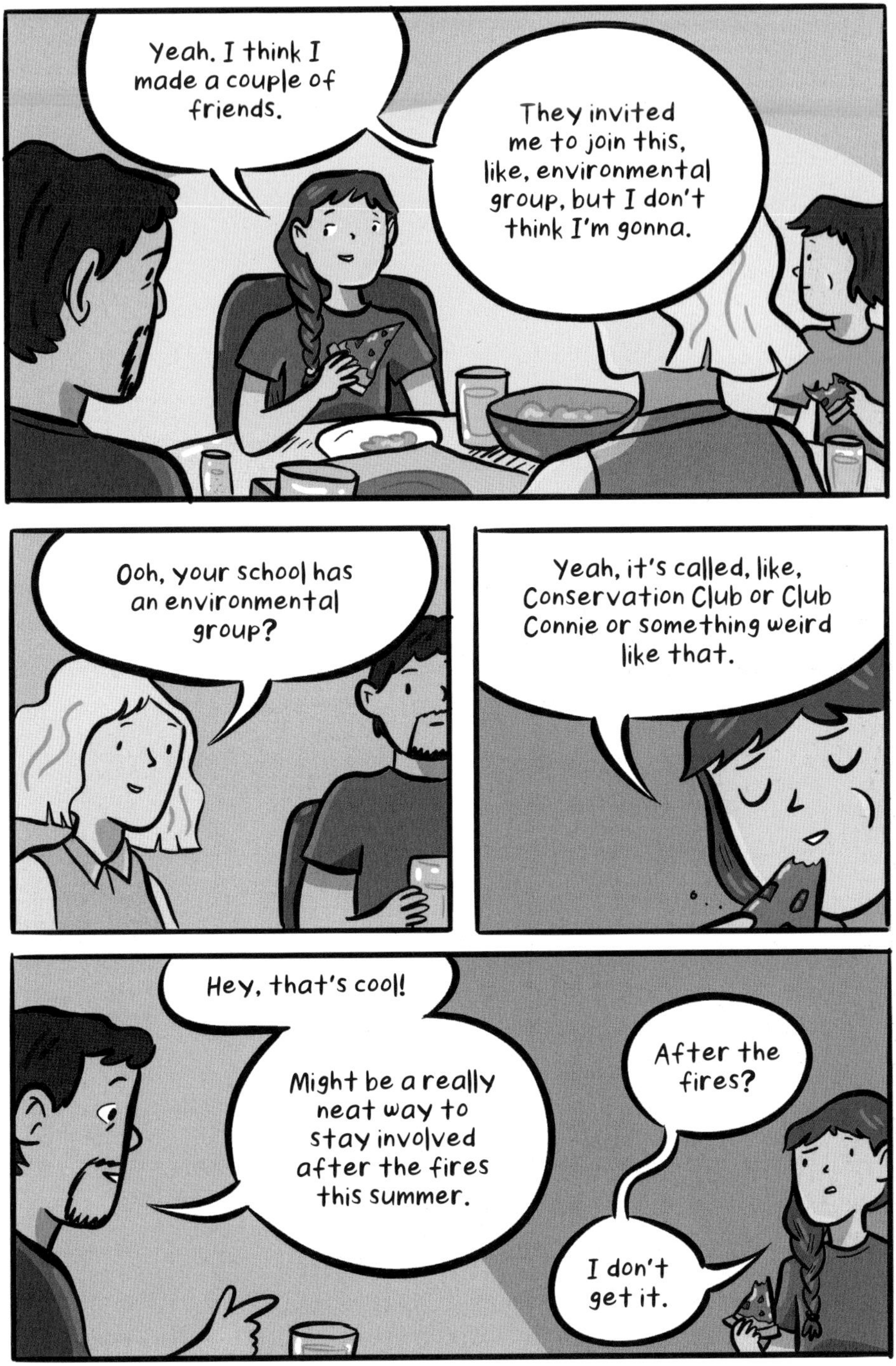
Yeah. I think I made a couple of friends.
They invited me to join this, like, environmental group, but I don't think I'm gonna.
Ooh, your school has an environmental group?
Yeah, it's called, like, Conservation Club or Club Connie or something weird like that.
Hey, that's cool!
Might be a really neat way to stay involved after the fires this summer.
After the fires?
I don't get it.

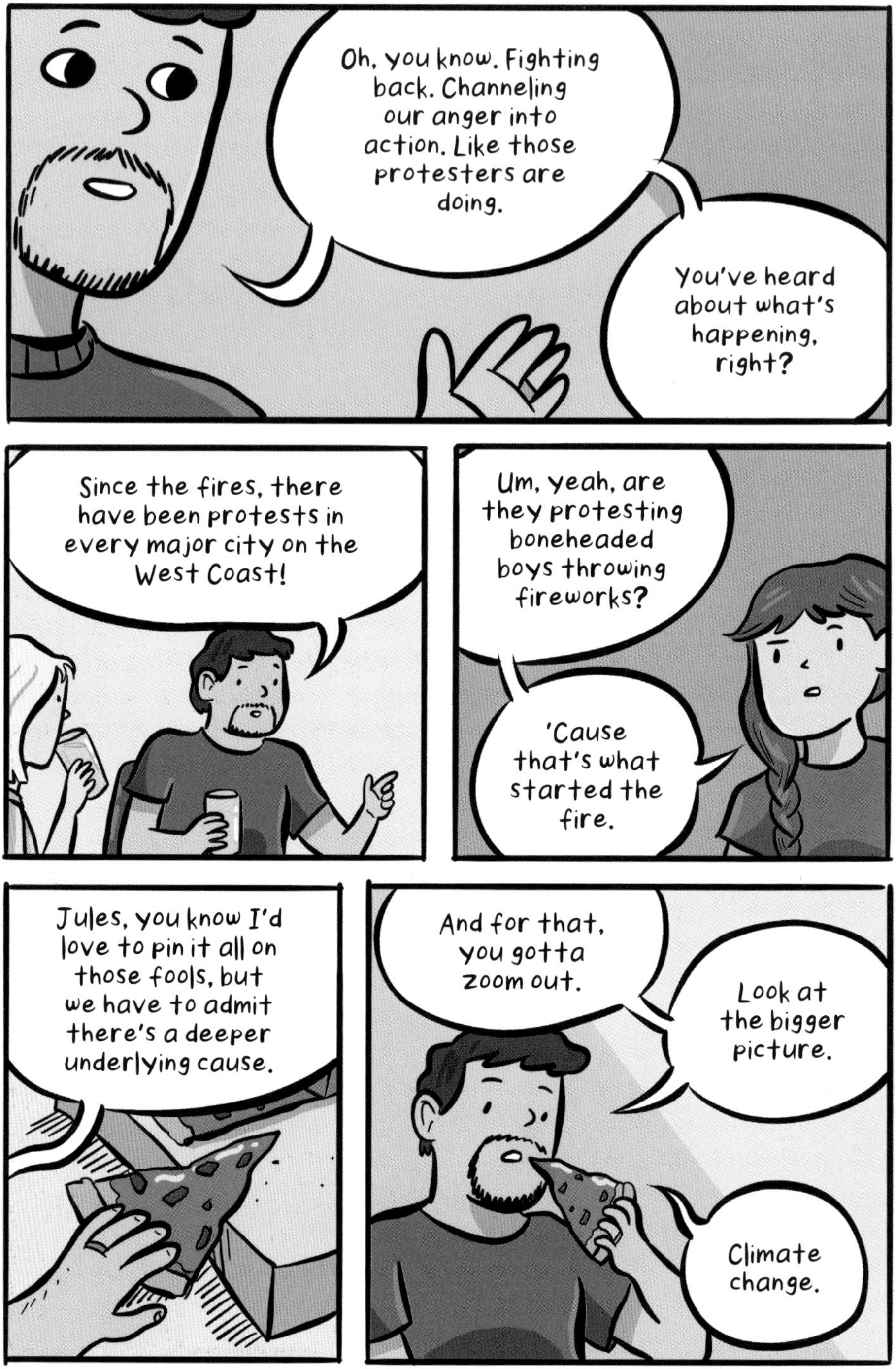
Oh, you know. Fighting back. Channeling our anger into action. Like those protesters are doing.
You've heard about what's happening, right?
Since the fires, there have been protests in every major city on the West Coast!
Um, yeah, are they protesting boneheaded boys throwing fireworks?
'Cause that's what started the fire.
Jules, you know I'd love to pin it all on those fools, but we have to admit there's a deeper underlying cause.
And for that, you gotta zoom out.
Look at the bigger picture.
Climate change.

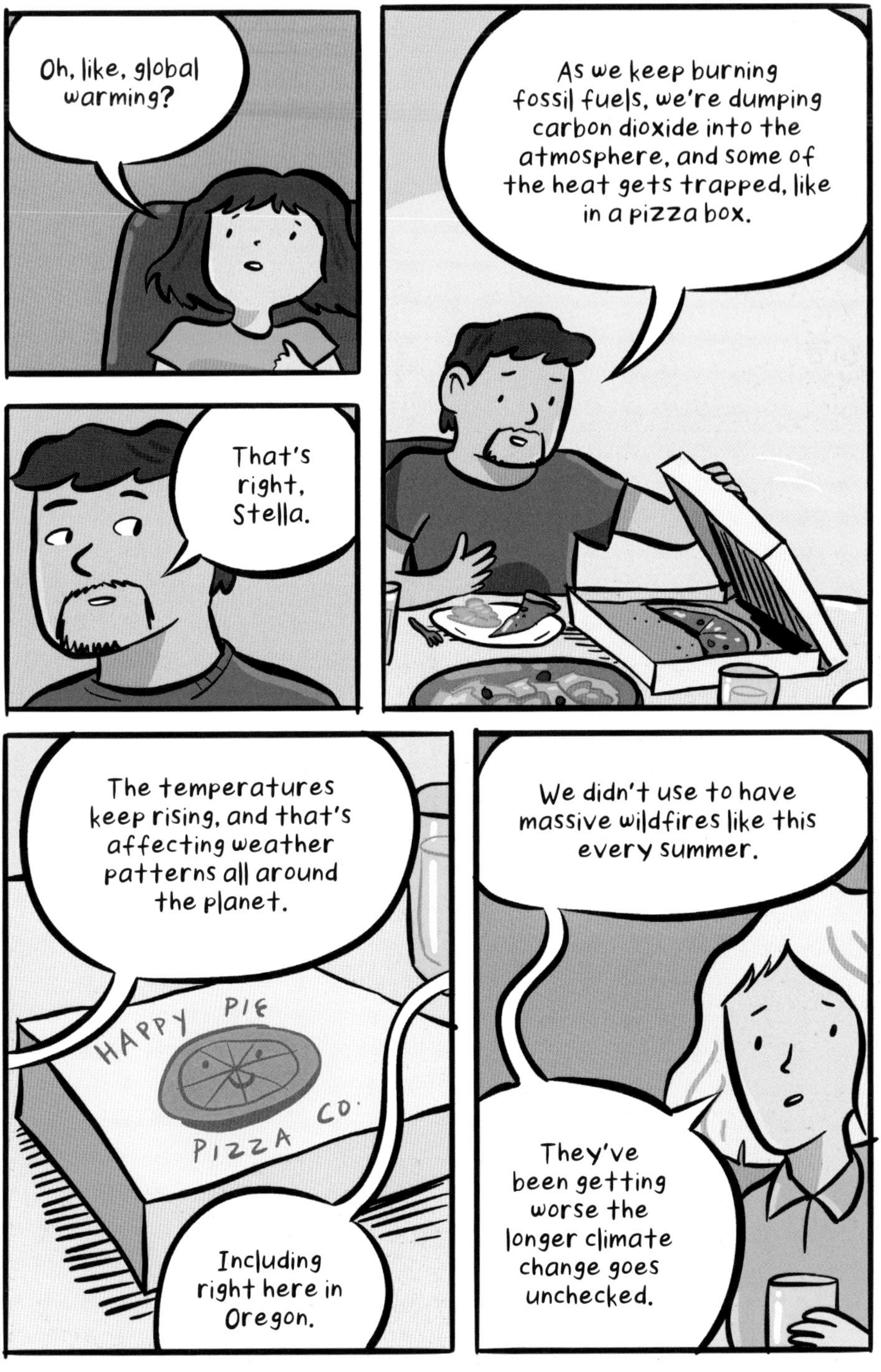
Oh, like, global warming?
As we keep burning fossil fuels, we're dumping carbon dioxide into the atmosphere, and some of the heat gets trapped, like in a pizza box.
That's right, Stella.
The temperatures keep rising, and that's affecting weather patterns all around the planet.
HAPPY PIE PIZZA CO.
Including right here in Oregon.
We didn't use to have massive wildfires like this every summer.
They've been getting worse the longer climate change goes unchecked.

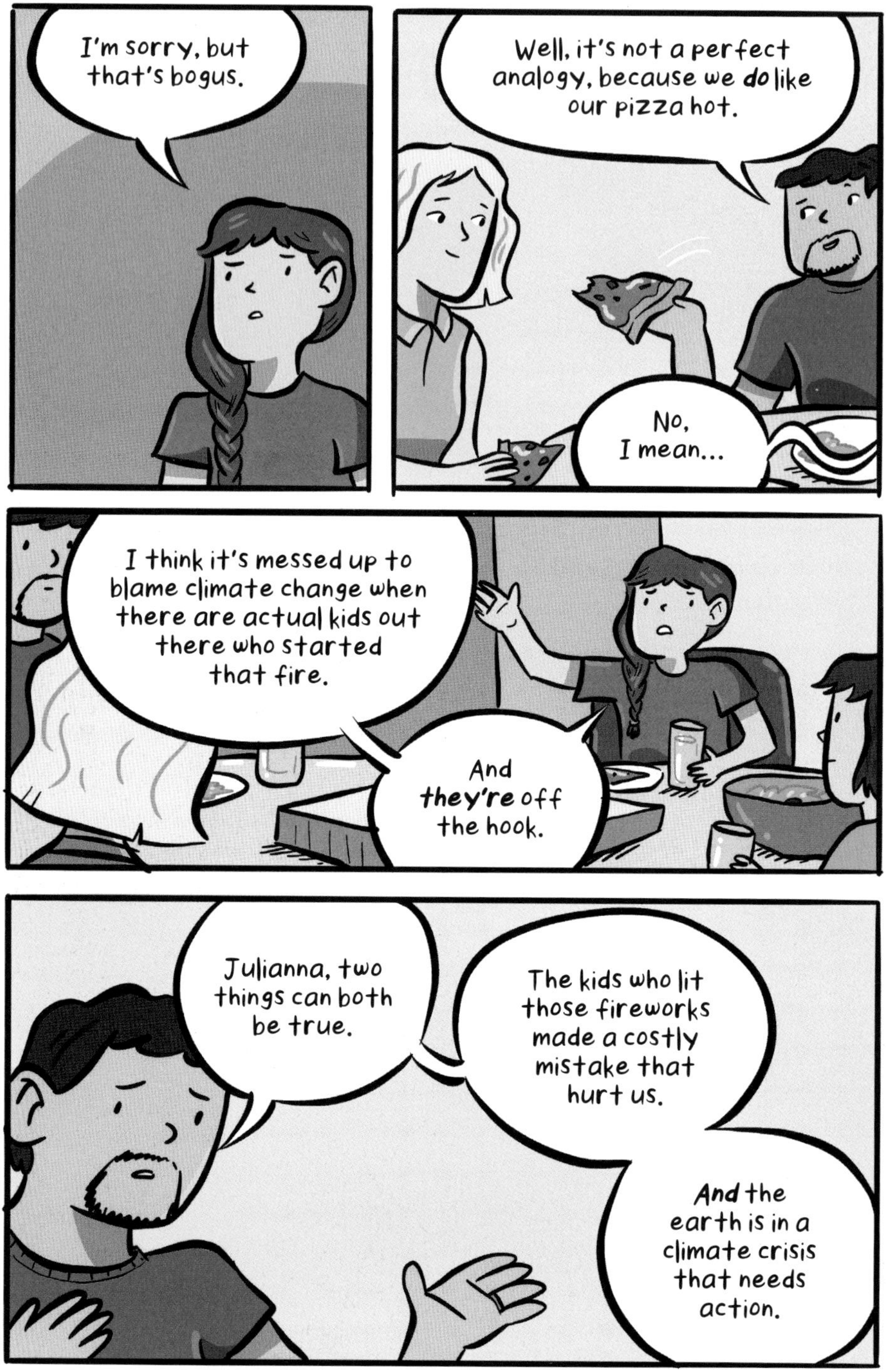
I'm sorry, but that's bogus.
Well, it's not a perfect analogy, because we **do** like our pizza hot.
No, I mean...
I think it's messed up to blame climate change when there are actual kids out there who started that fire.
And ***they're*** off the hook.
Julianna, two things can both be true.
The kids who lit those fireworks made a costly mistake that hurt us.
And the earth is in a climate crisis that needs action.

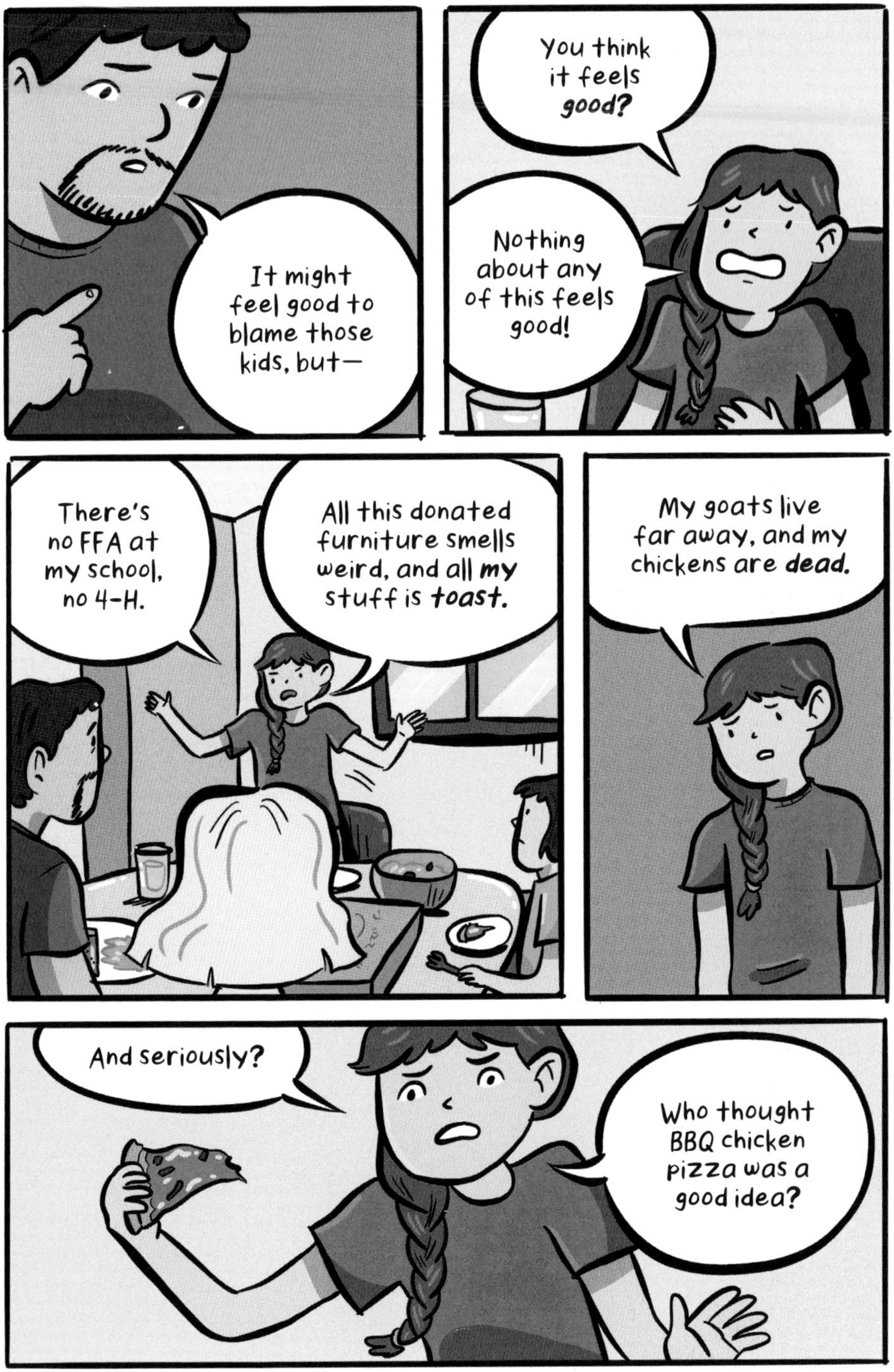
It might feel good to blame those kids, but—
You think it feels *good?*
Nothing about any of this feels good!
There's no FFA at my school, no 4-H.
All this donated furniture smells weird, and all *my* stuff is *toast.*
My goats live far away, and my chickens are *dead.*
And seriously?
Who thought BBQ chicken pizza was a good idea?

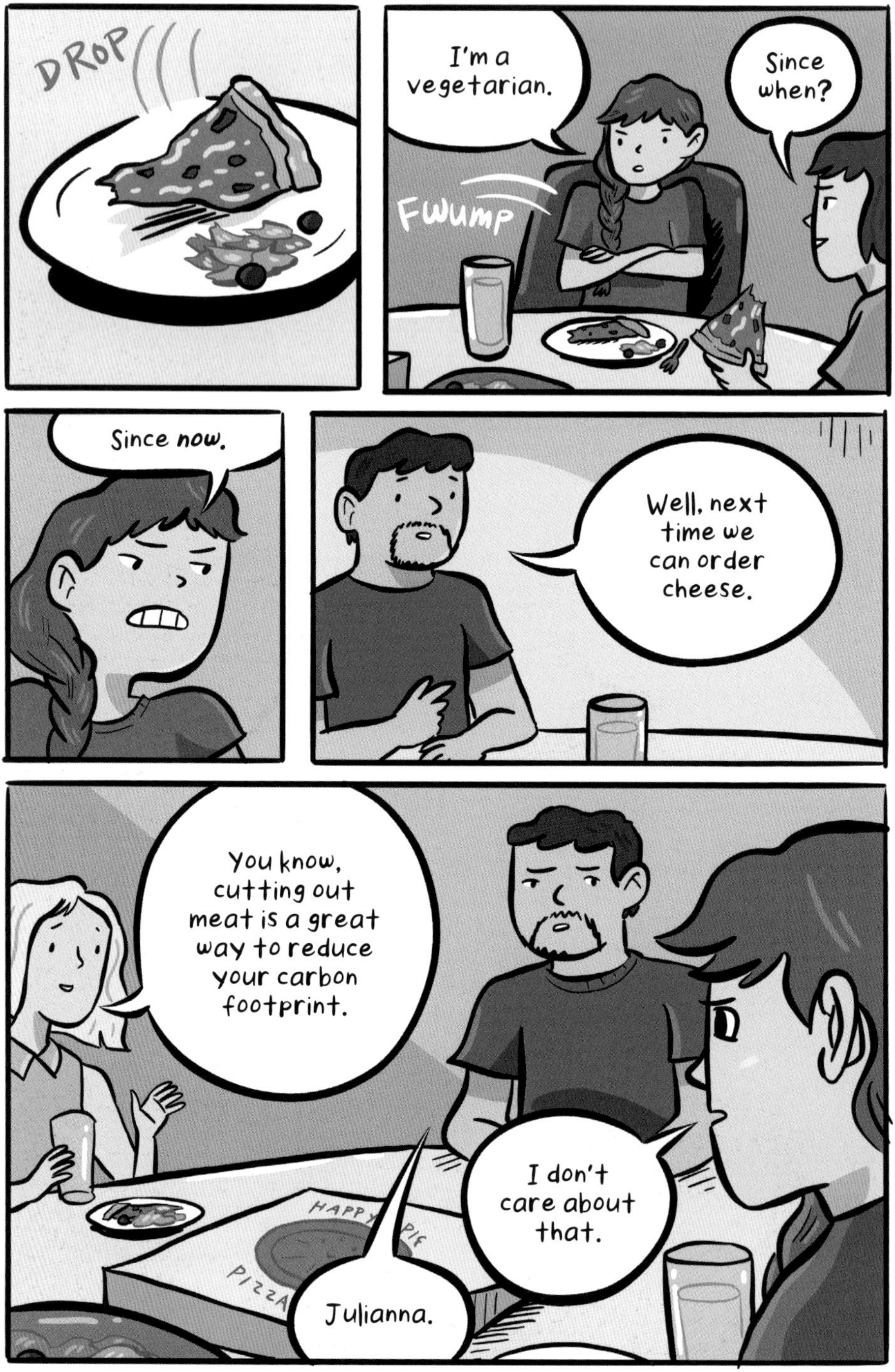
DROP
I'm a vegetarian.
Since when?
FWUMP
Since now.
Well, next time we can order cheese.
You know, cutting out meat is a great way to reduce your carbon footprint.
I don't care about that.
Julianna.
HAPPY PIE
PIZZA

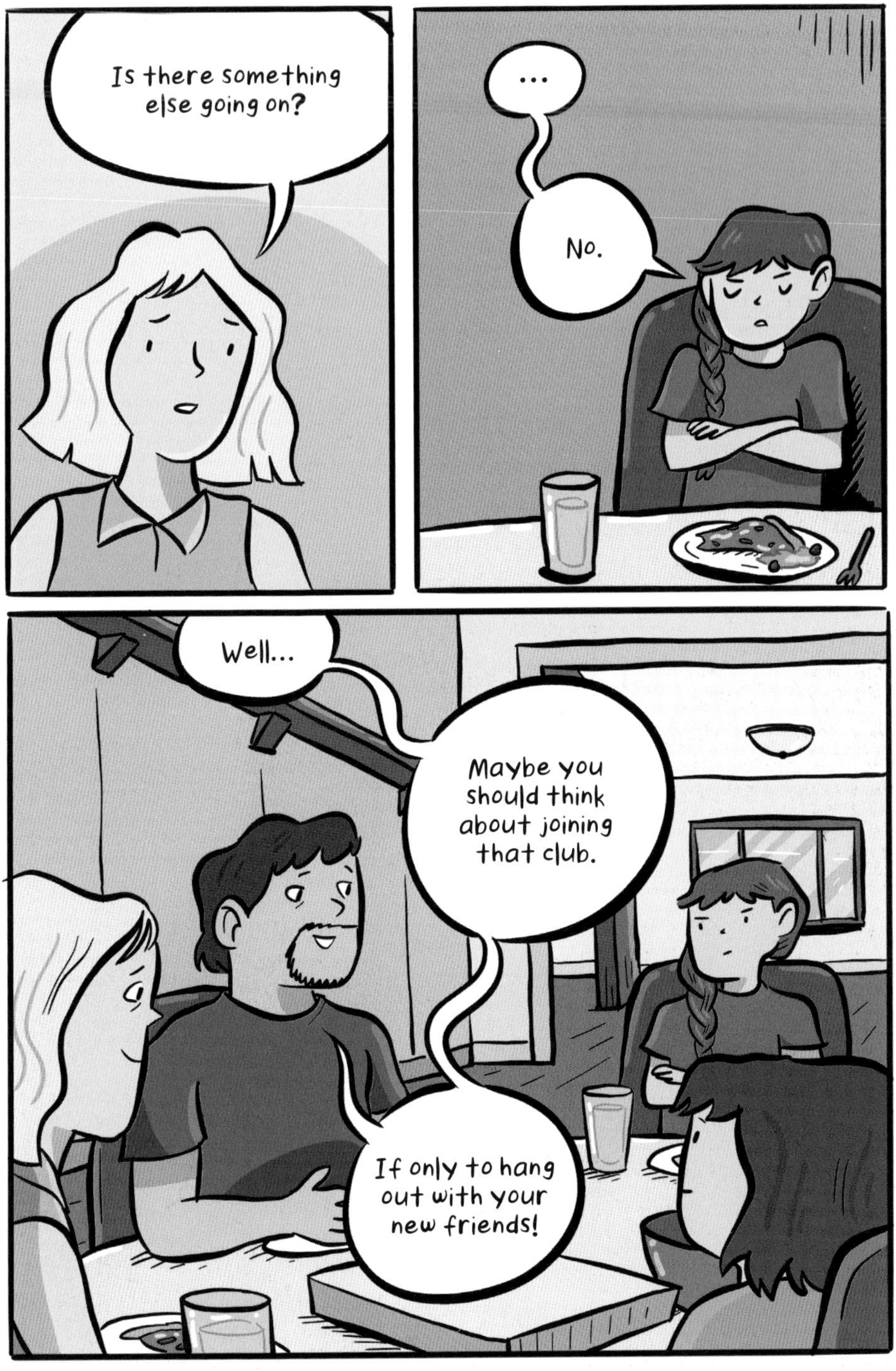
Is there something else going on?
...
No.
Well...
Maybe you should think about joining that club.
If only to hang out with your new friends!

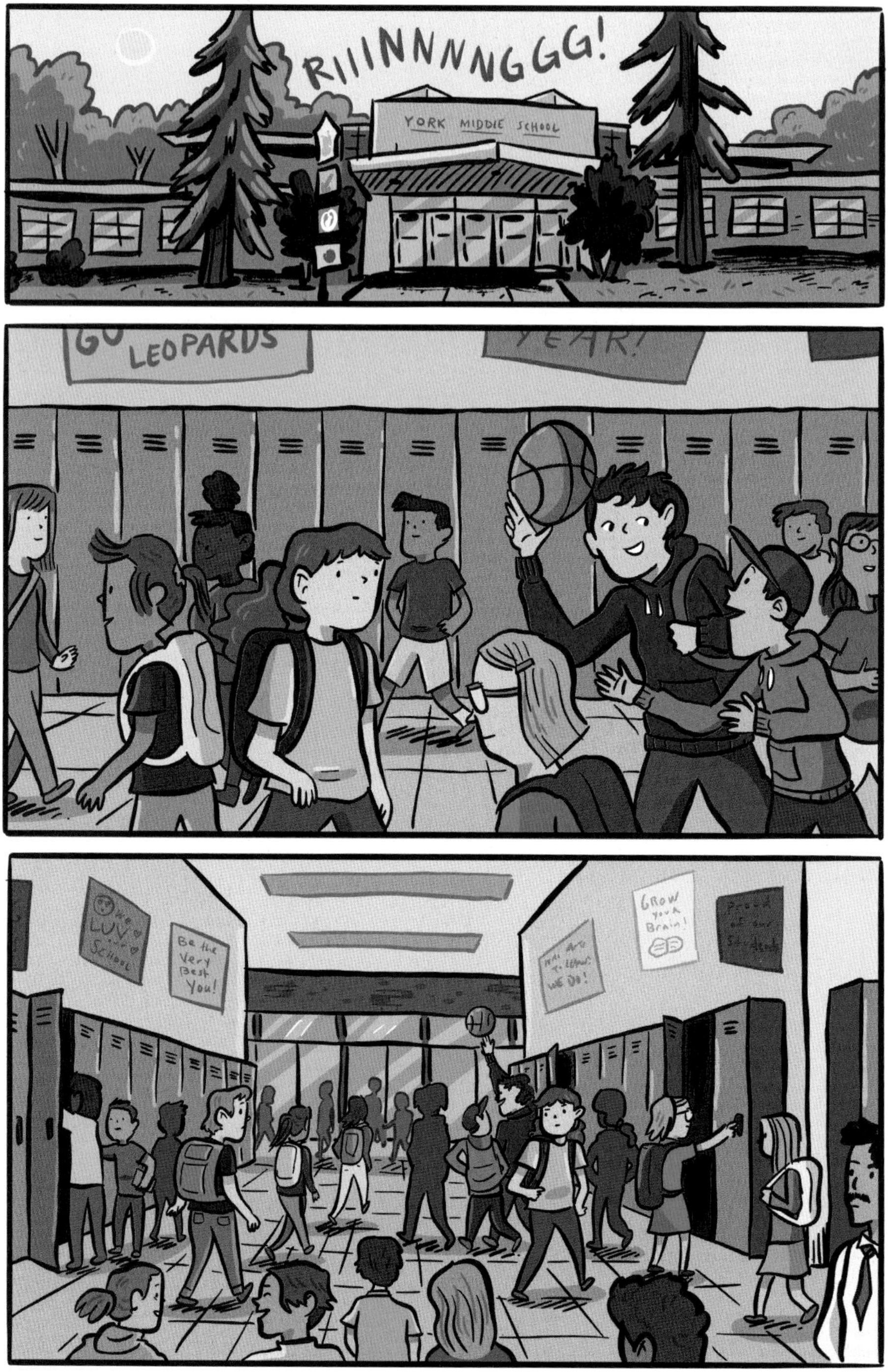
RIIINNNNGGG!
YORK MIDDLE SCHOOL
GO LEOPARDS
YEAR!
Be the Very Best You!
GROW your Brain!

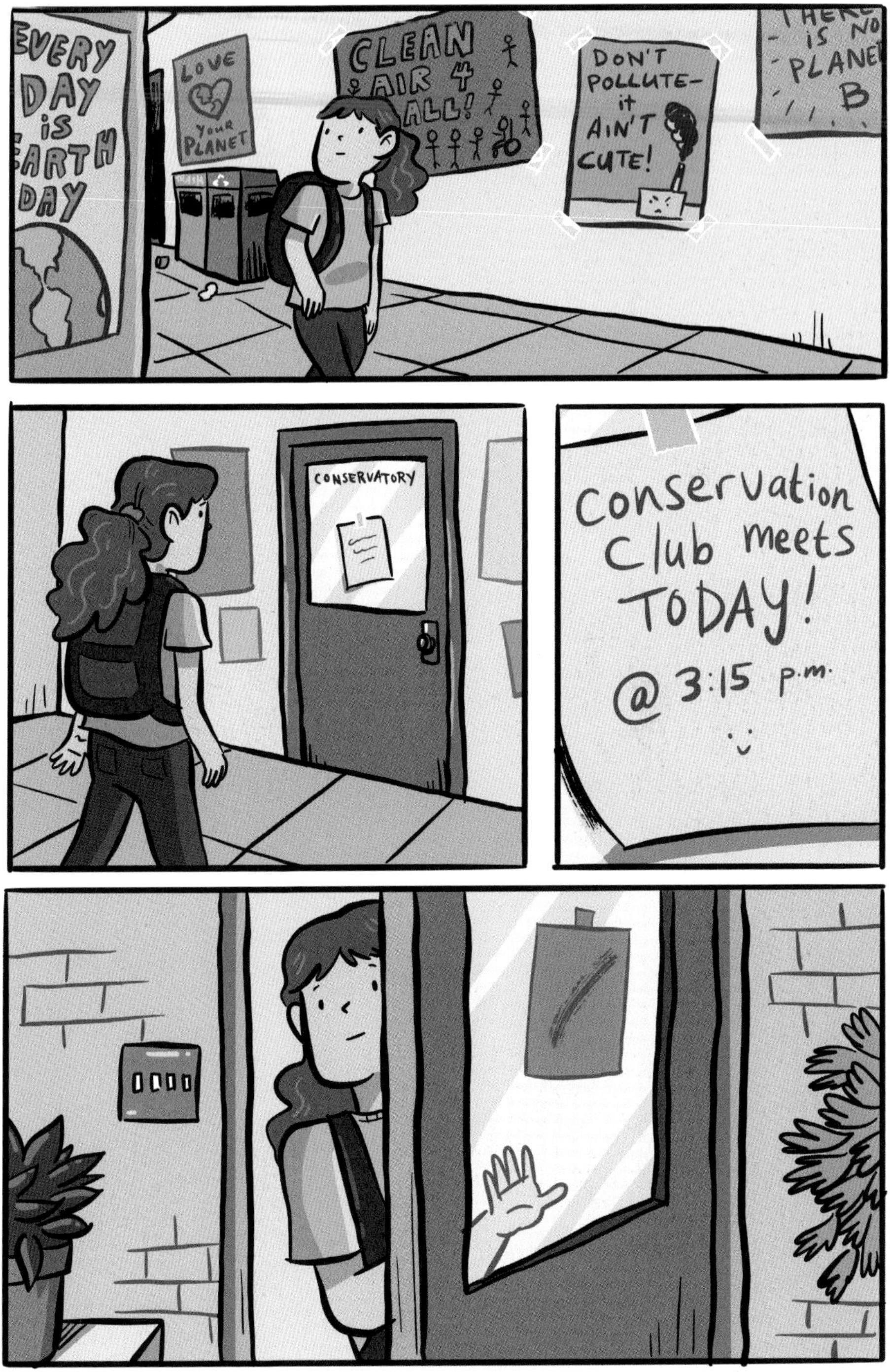
EVERY DAY IS EARTH DAY
LOVE YOUR PLANET
CLEAN AIR 4 ALL!
DON'T POLLUTE- it AIN'T CUTE!
IS NO PLANET B
CONSERVATORY
Conservation Club meets TODAY!
@ 3:15 p.m.

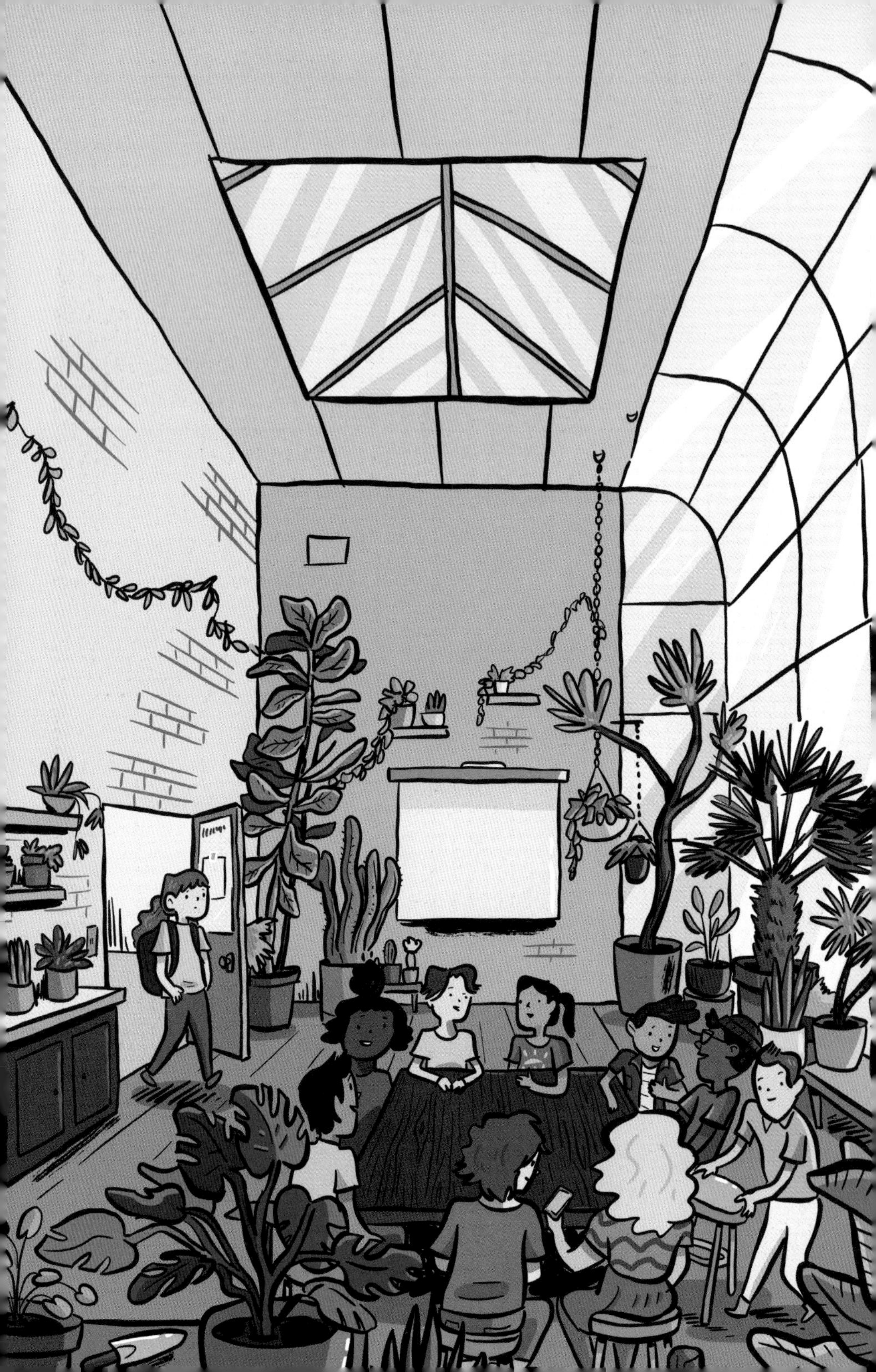

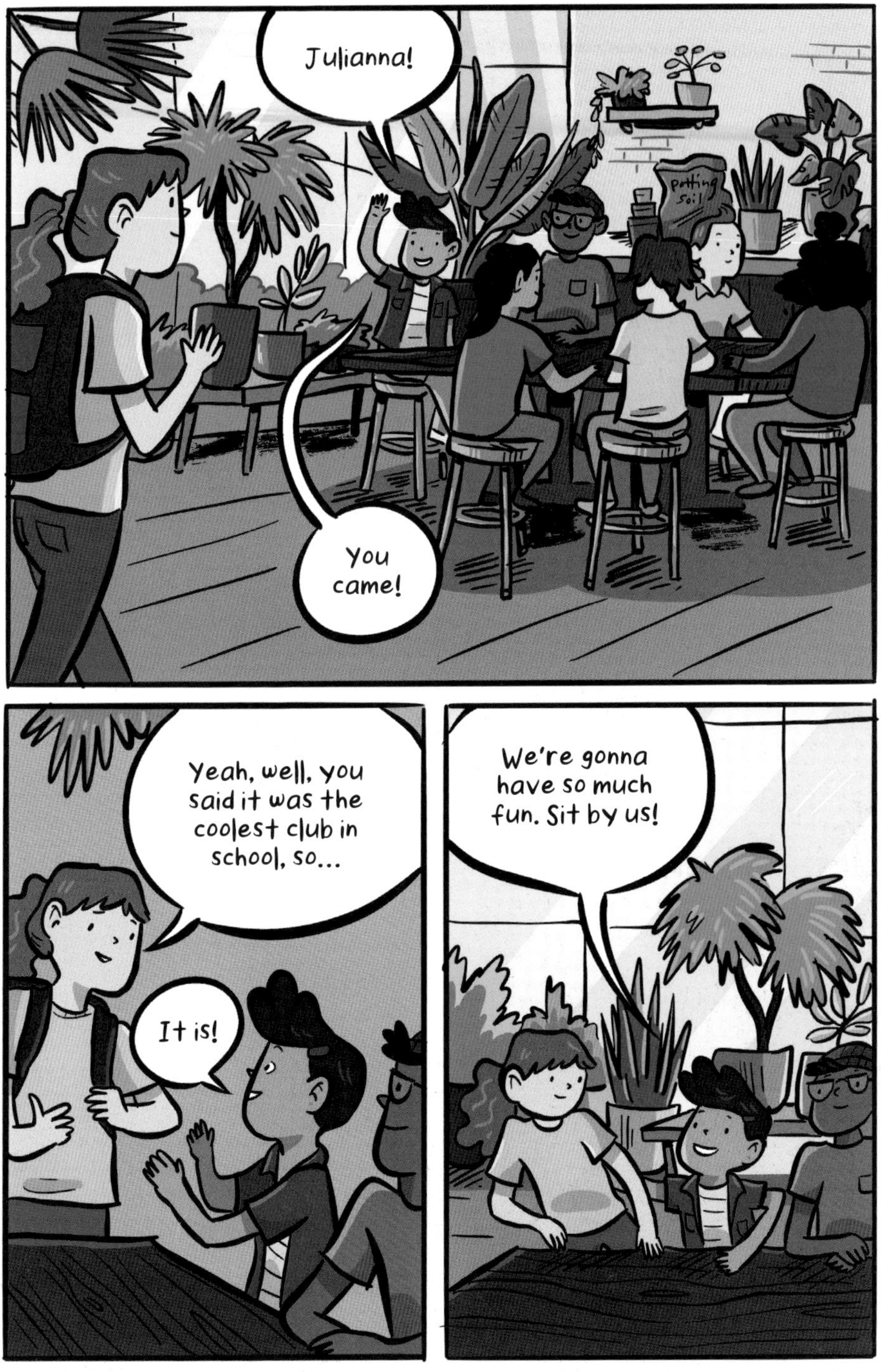
Julianna!
You came!
Yeah, well, you said it was the coolest club in school, so...
It is!
We're gonna have so much fun. Sit by us!

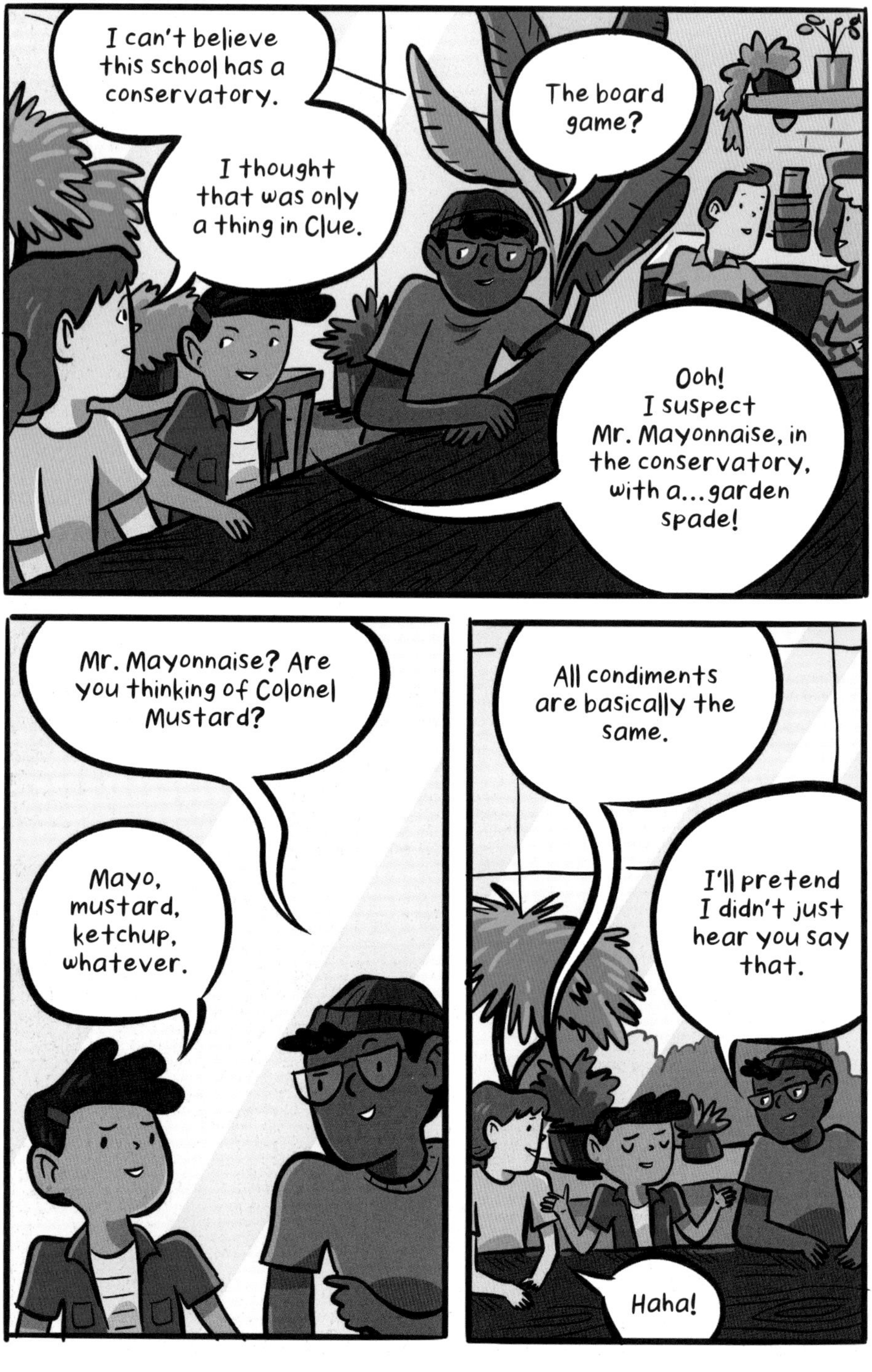
I can't believe this school has a conservatory.
I thought that was only a thing in Clue.
The board game?
Ooh! I suspect Mr. Mayonnaise, in the conservatory, with a...garden spade!
Mr. Mayonnaise? Are you thinking of Colonel Mustard?
Mayo, mustard, ketchup, whatever.
All condiments are basically the same.
I'll pretend I didn't just hear you say that.
Haha!

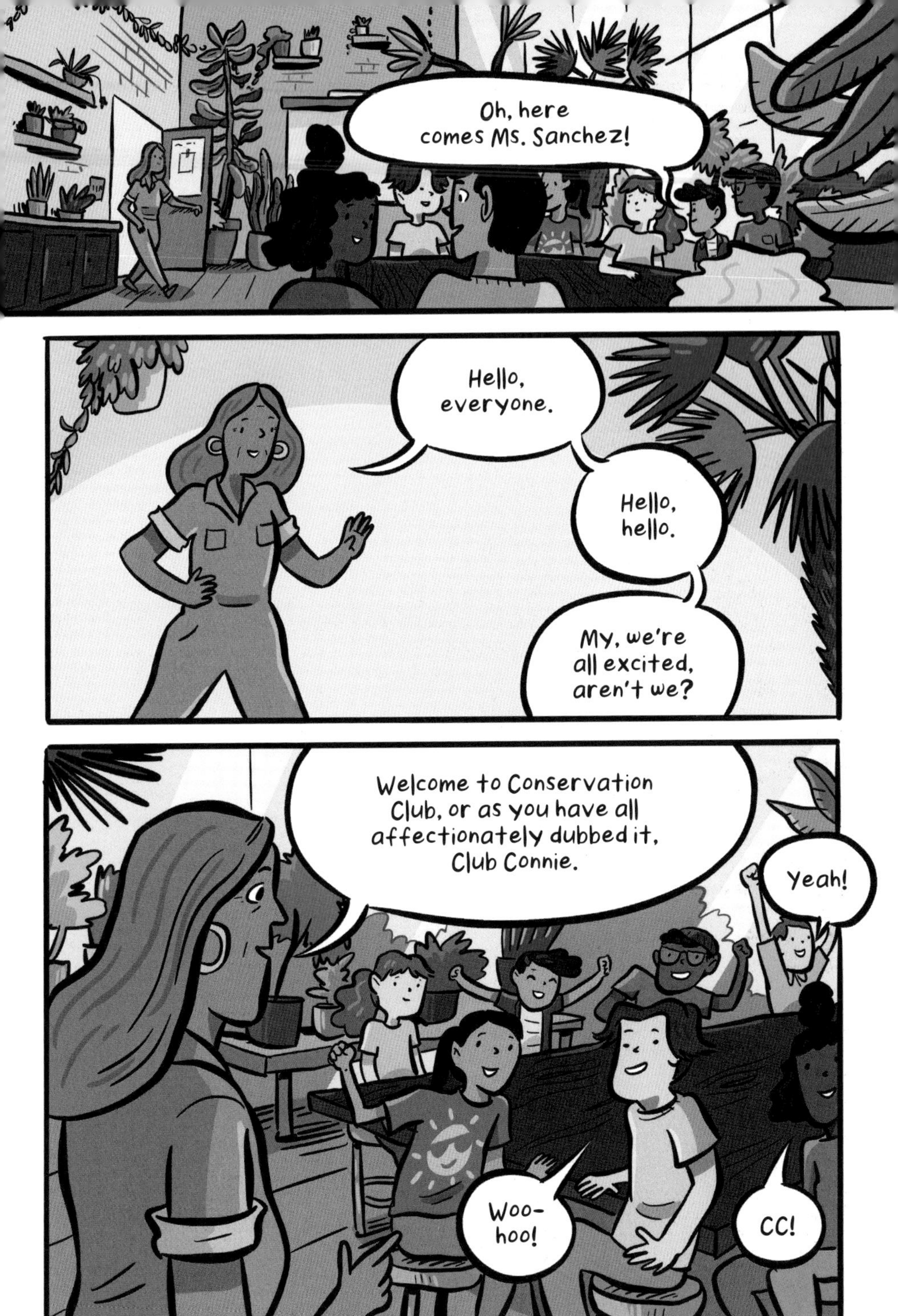

Oh, here comes Ms. Sanchez!
Hello, everyone.
Hello, hello.
My, we're all excited, aren't we?
Welcome to Conservation Club, or as you have all affectionately dubbed it, Club Connie.
Yeah!
Woo-hoo!
CC!

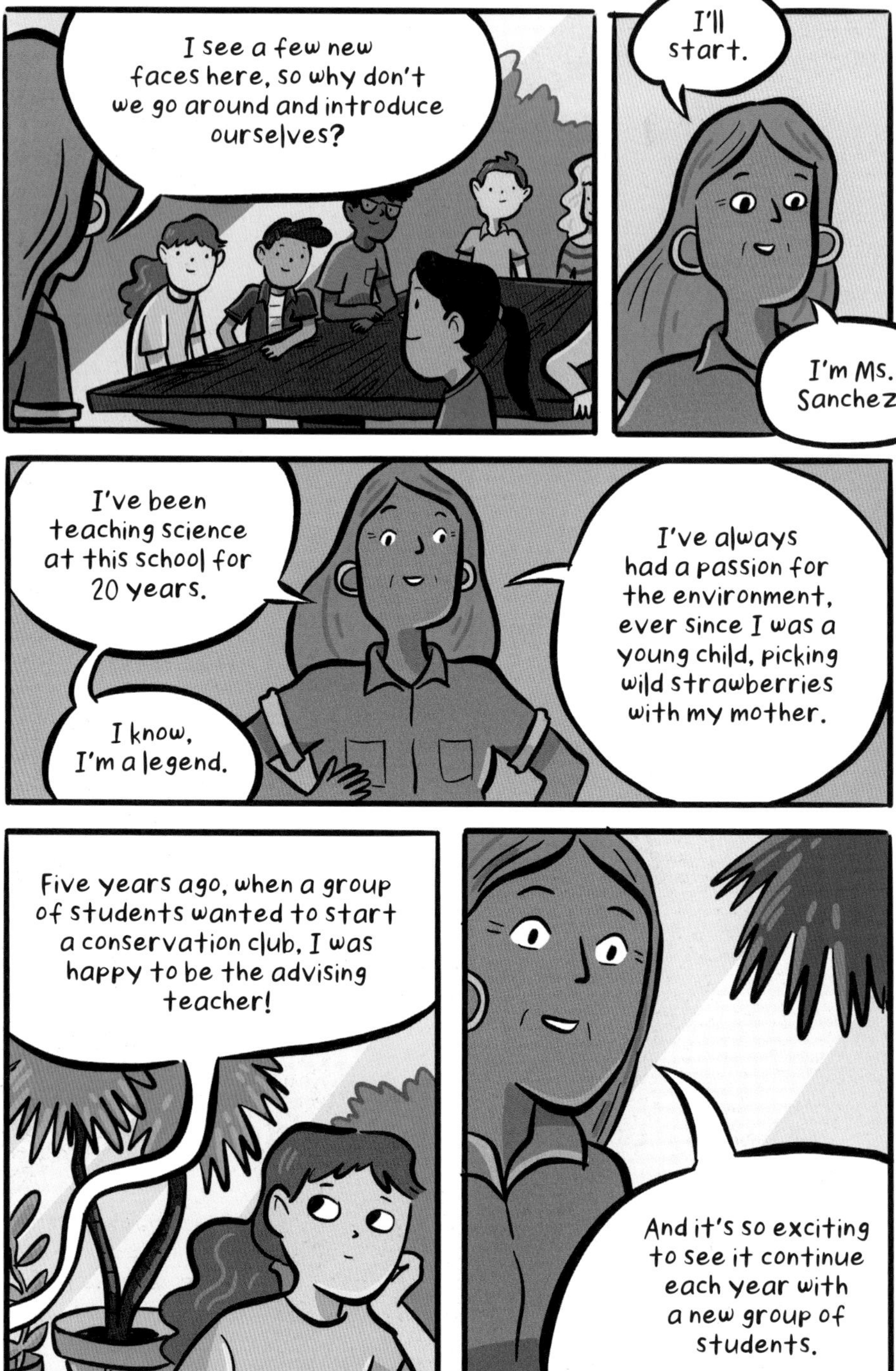
I see a few new faces here, so why don't we go around and introduce ourselves?
I'll start.
I'm Ms. Sanchez.
I've been teaching science at this school for 20 years.
I know, I'm a legend.
I've always had a passion for the environment, ever since I was a young child, picking wild strawberries with my mother.
Five years ago, when a group of students wanted to start a conservation club, I was happy to be the advising teacher!
And it's so exciting to see it continue each year with a new group of students.

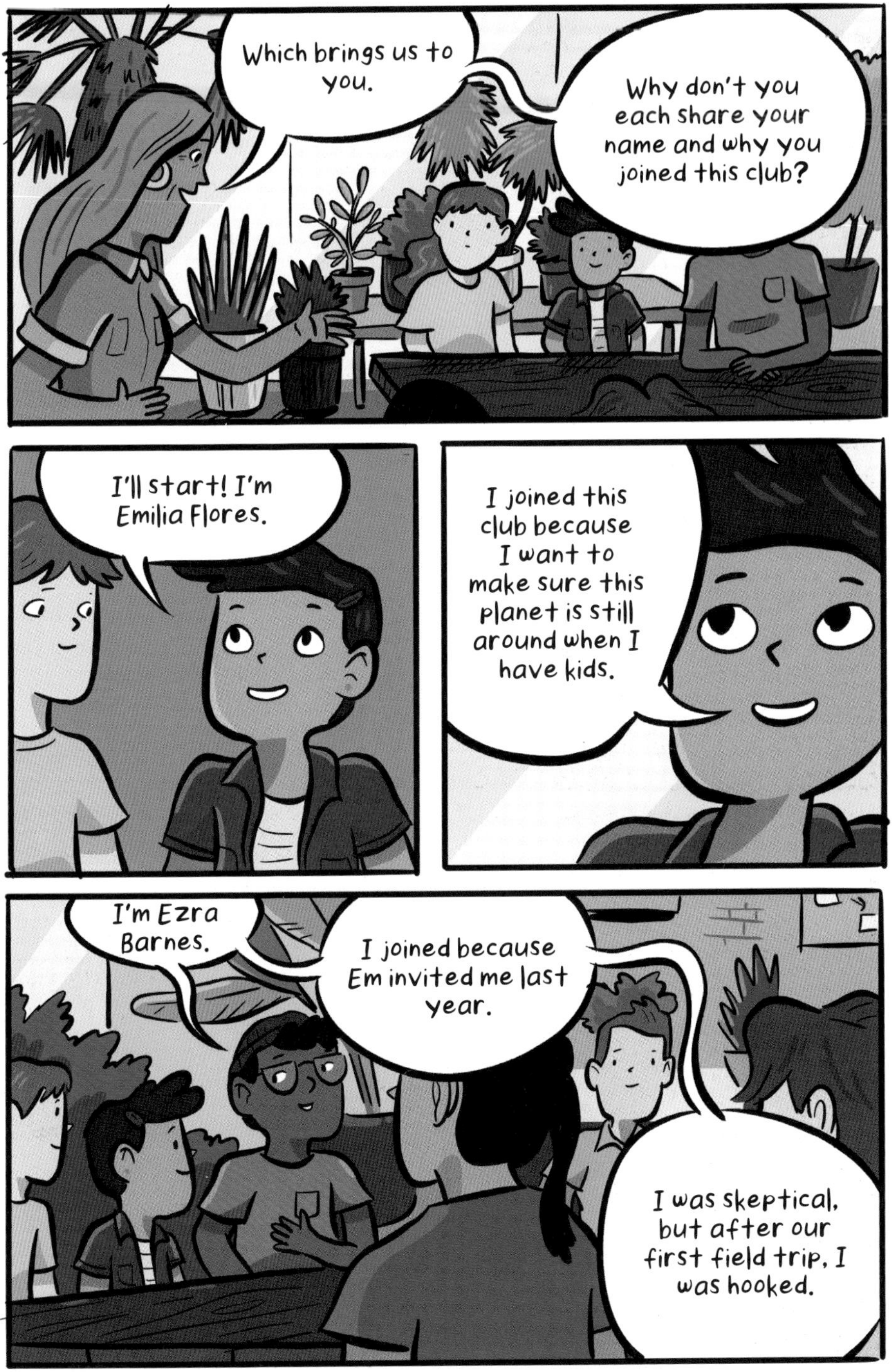
Which brings us to you.
Why don't you each share your name and why you joined this club?
I'll start! I'm Emilia Flores.
I joined this club because I want to make sure this planet is still around when I have kids.
I'm Ezra Barnes.
I joined because Em invited me last year.
I was skeptical, but after our first field trip, I was hooked.

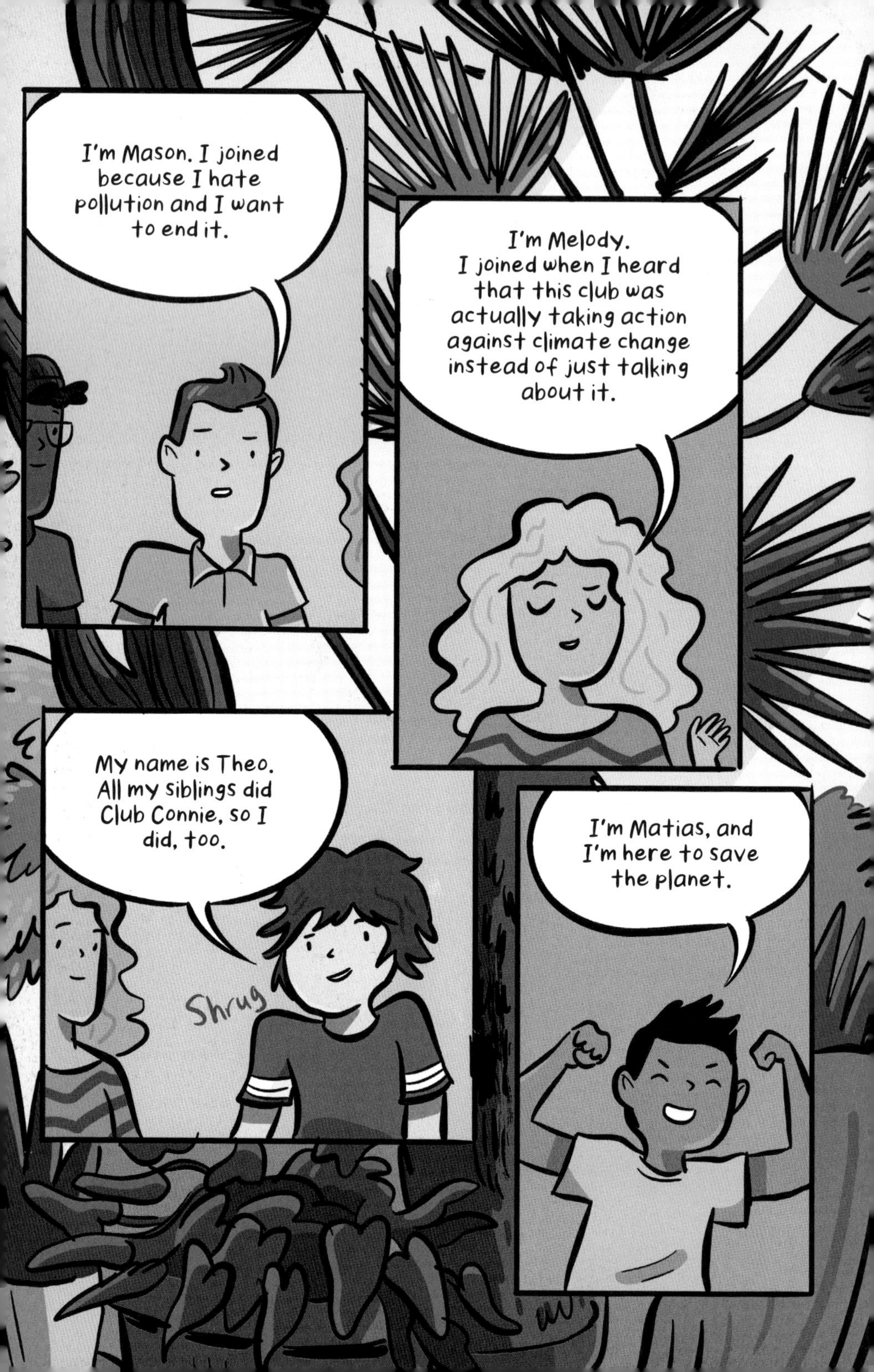
I'm Mason. I joined because I hate pollution and I want to end it.
I'm Melody. I joined when I heard that this club was actually taking action against climate change instead of just talking about it.
My name is Theo. All my siblings did Club Connie, so I did, too.
Shrug
I'm Matias, and I'm here to save the planet.

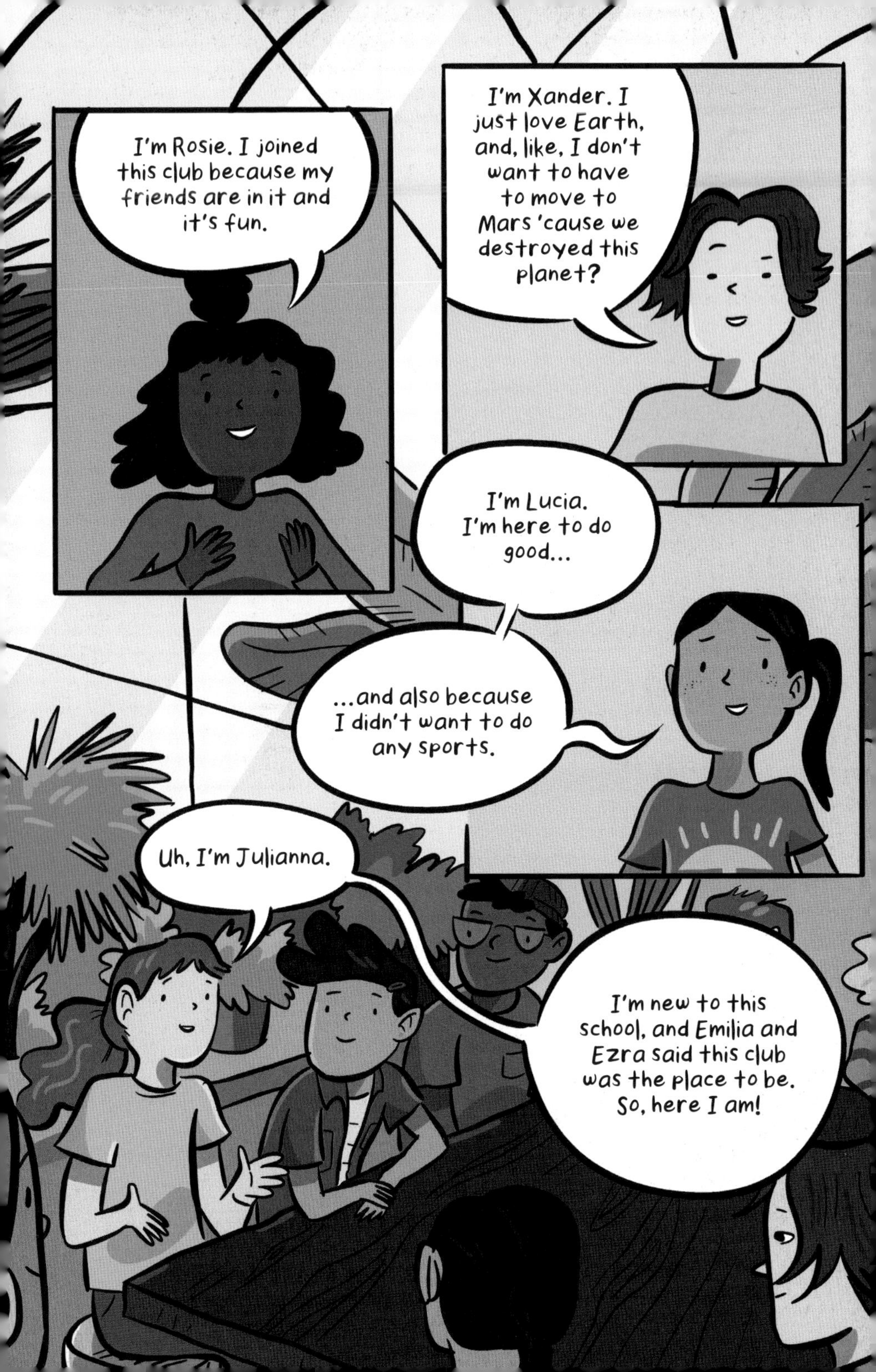
I'm Rosie. I joined this club because my friends are in it and it's fun.
I'm Xander. I just love Earth, and, like, I don't want to have to move to Mars 'cause we destroyed this planet?
I'm Lucia. I'm here to do good...
...and also because I didn't want to do any sports.
Uh, I'm Julianna.
I'm new to this school, and Emilia and Ezra said this club was the place to be. So, here I am!

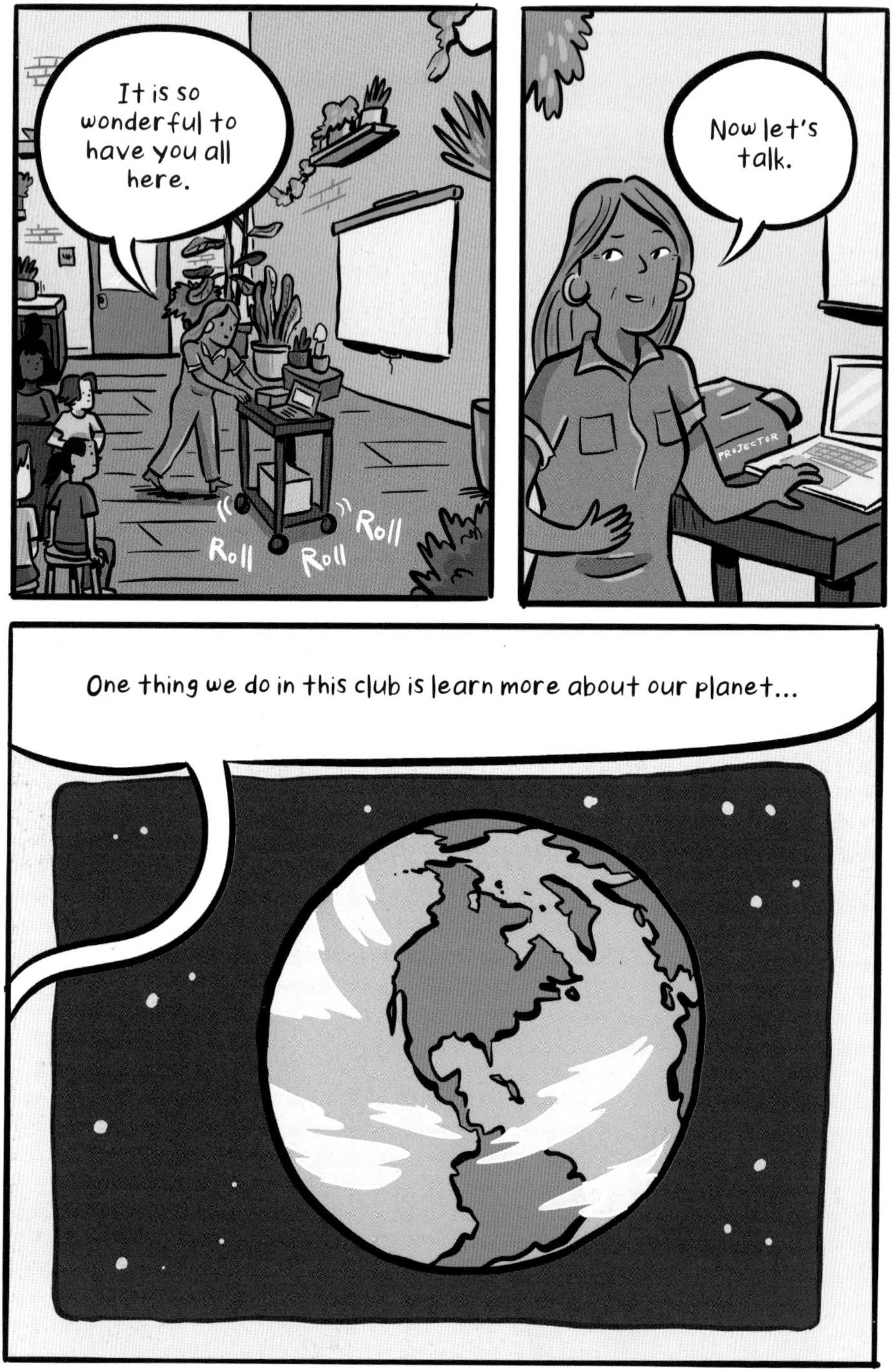
It is so wonderful to have you all here.
Roll
Roll
Roll
Now let's talk.
PROJECTOR
One thing we do in this club is learn more about our planet...

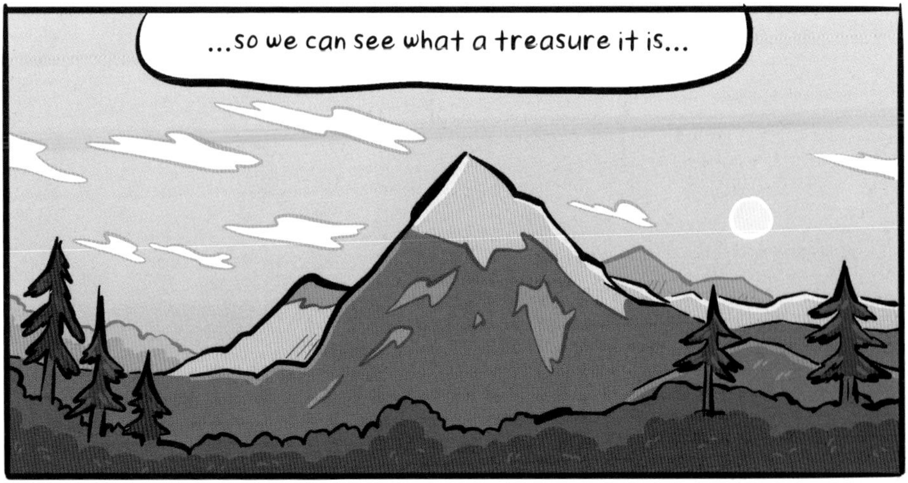
...so we can see what a treasure it is...

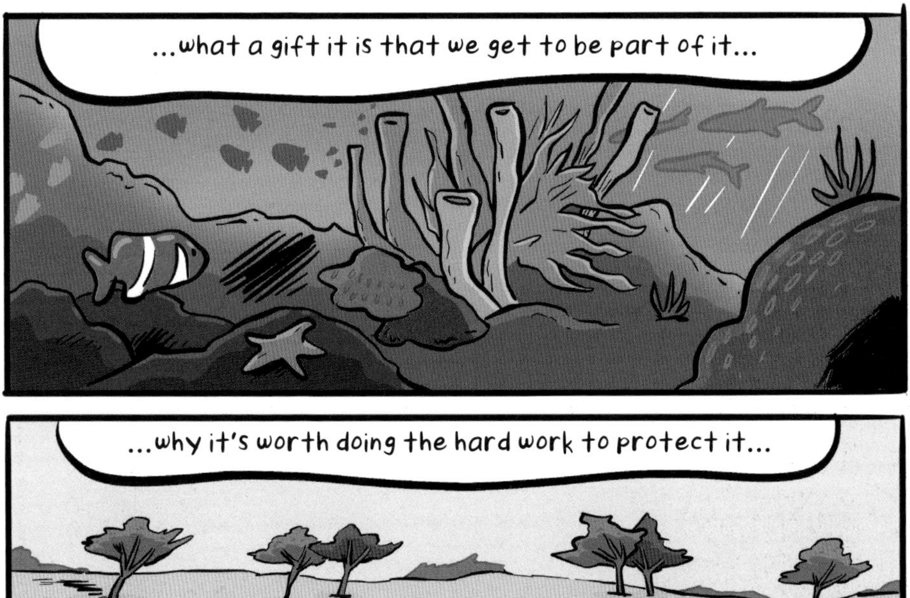
...what a gift it is that we get to be part of it...

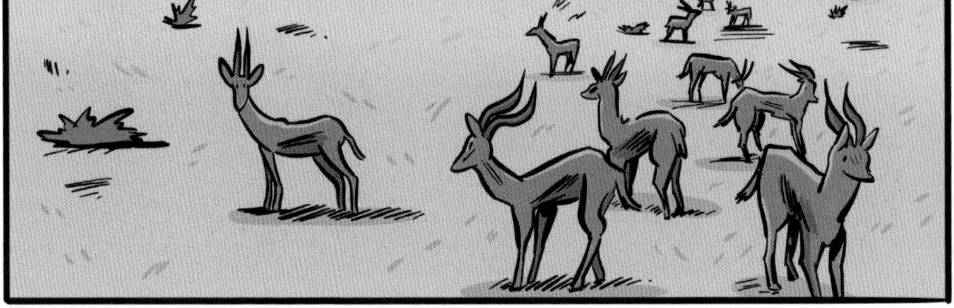
...why it's worth doing the hard work to protect it...

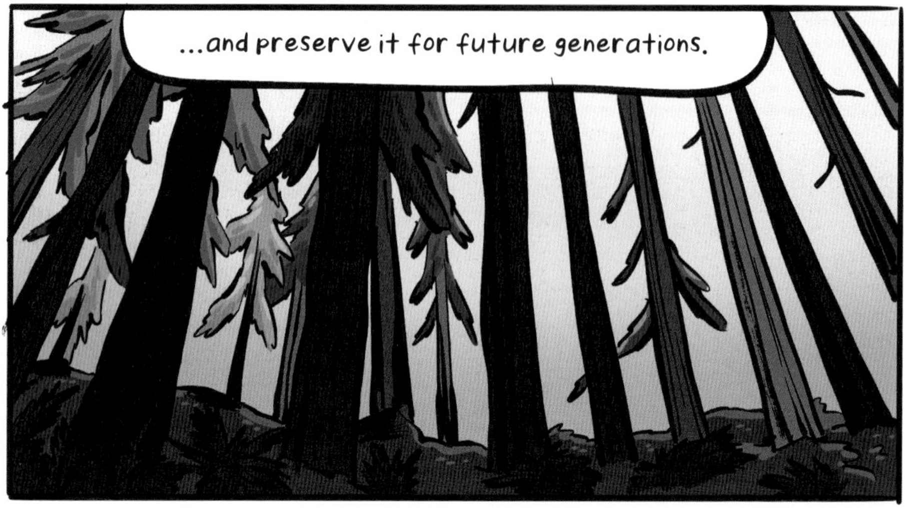
...and preserve it for future generations.

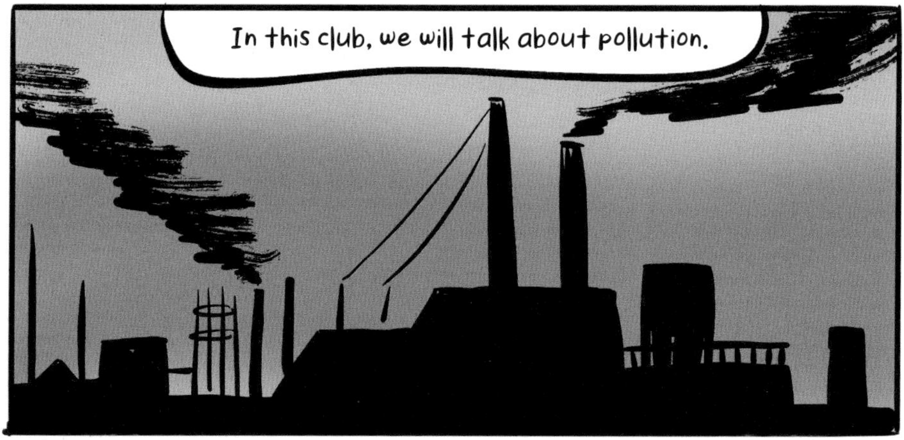
In this club, we will talk about pollution.

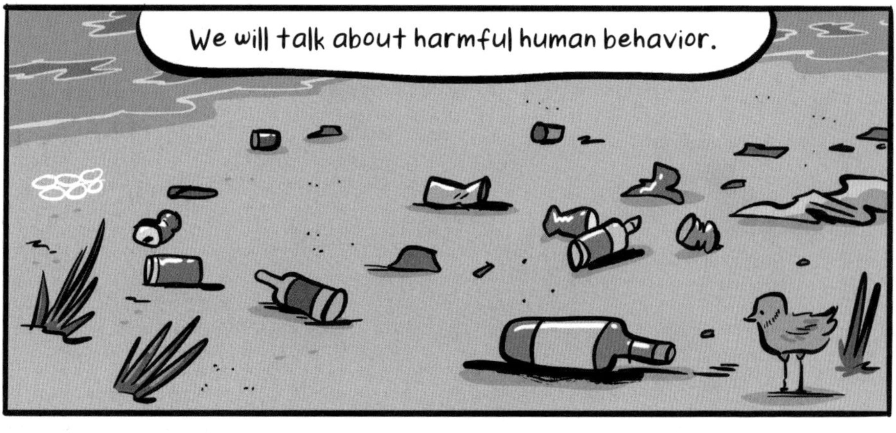
We will talk about harmful human behavior.

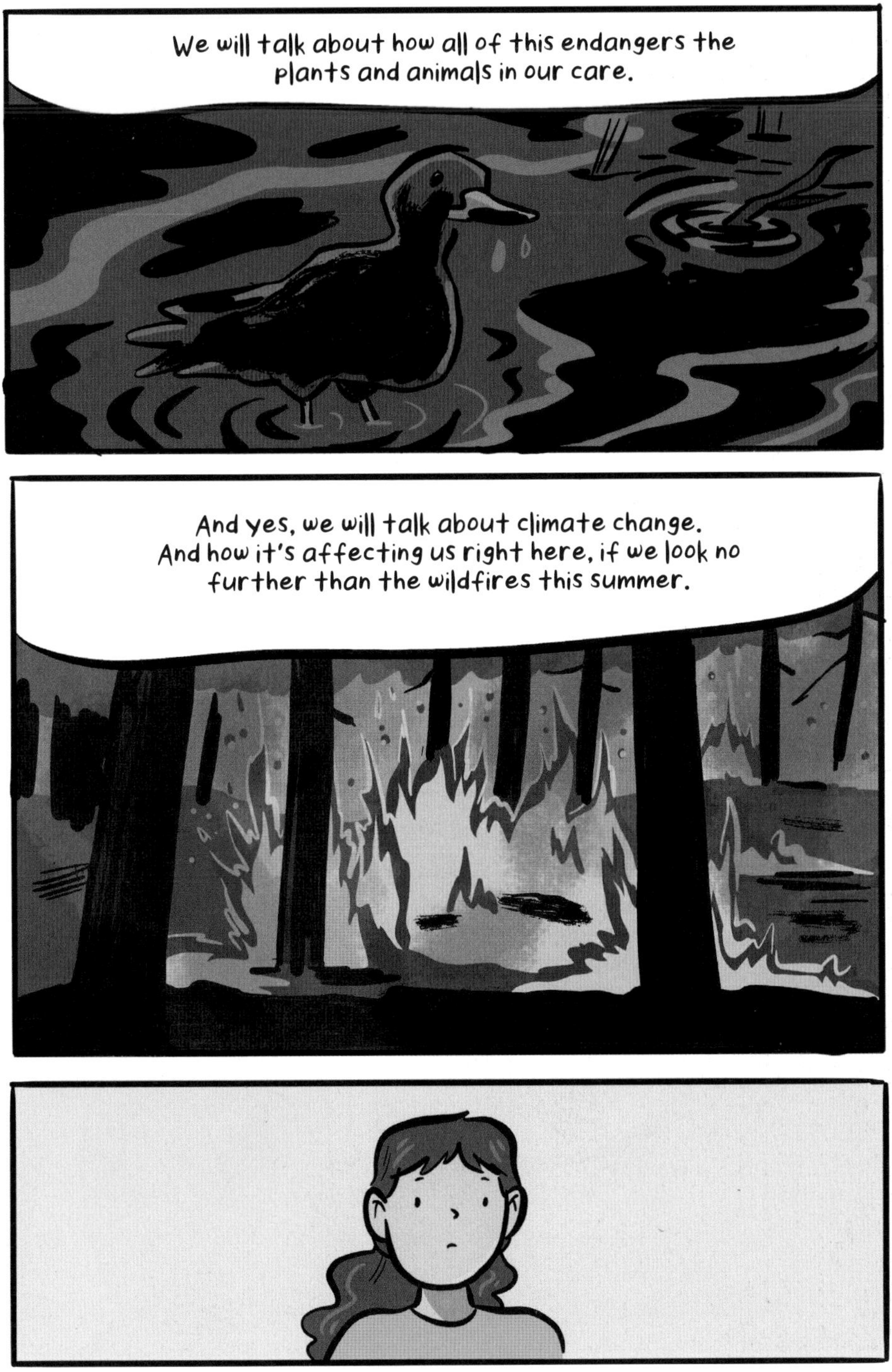
We will talk about how all of this endangers the plants and animals in our care.
And yes, we will talk about climate change. And how it's affecting us right here, if we look no further than the wildfires this summer.

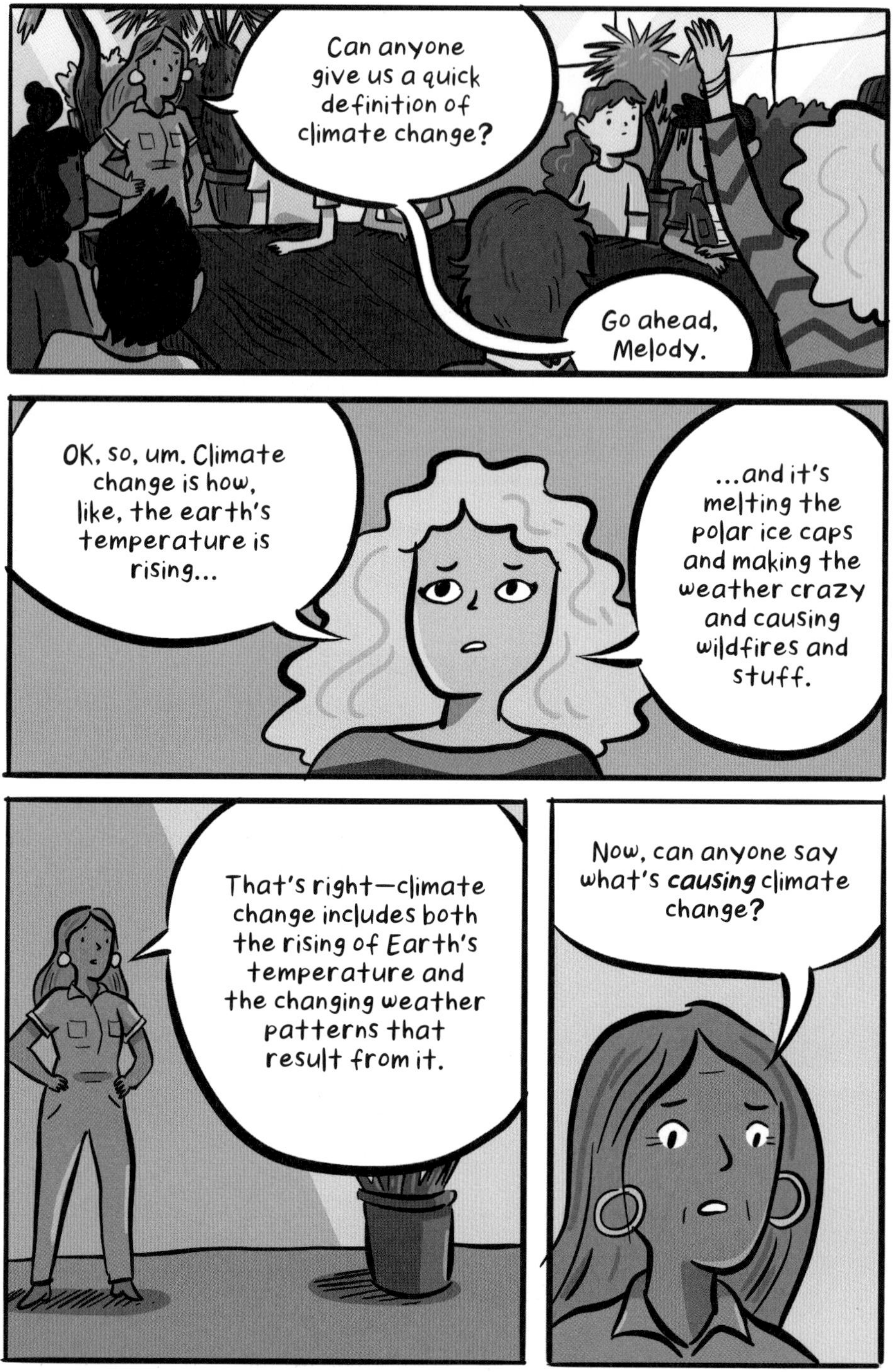
Can anyone give us a quick definition of climate change?
Go ahead, Melody.
OK, so, um. Climate change is how, like, the earth's temperature is rising...
...and it's melting the polar ice caps and making the weather crazy and causing wildfires and stuff.
That's right—climate change includes both the rising of Earth's temperature and the changing weather patterns that result from it.
Now, can anyone say what's *causing* climate change?

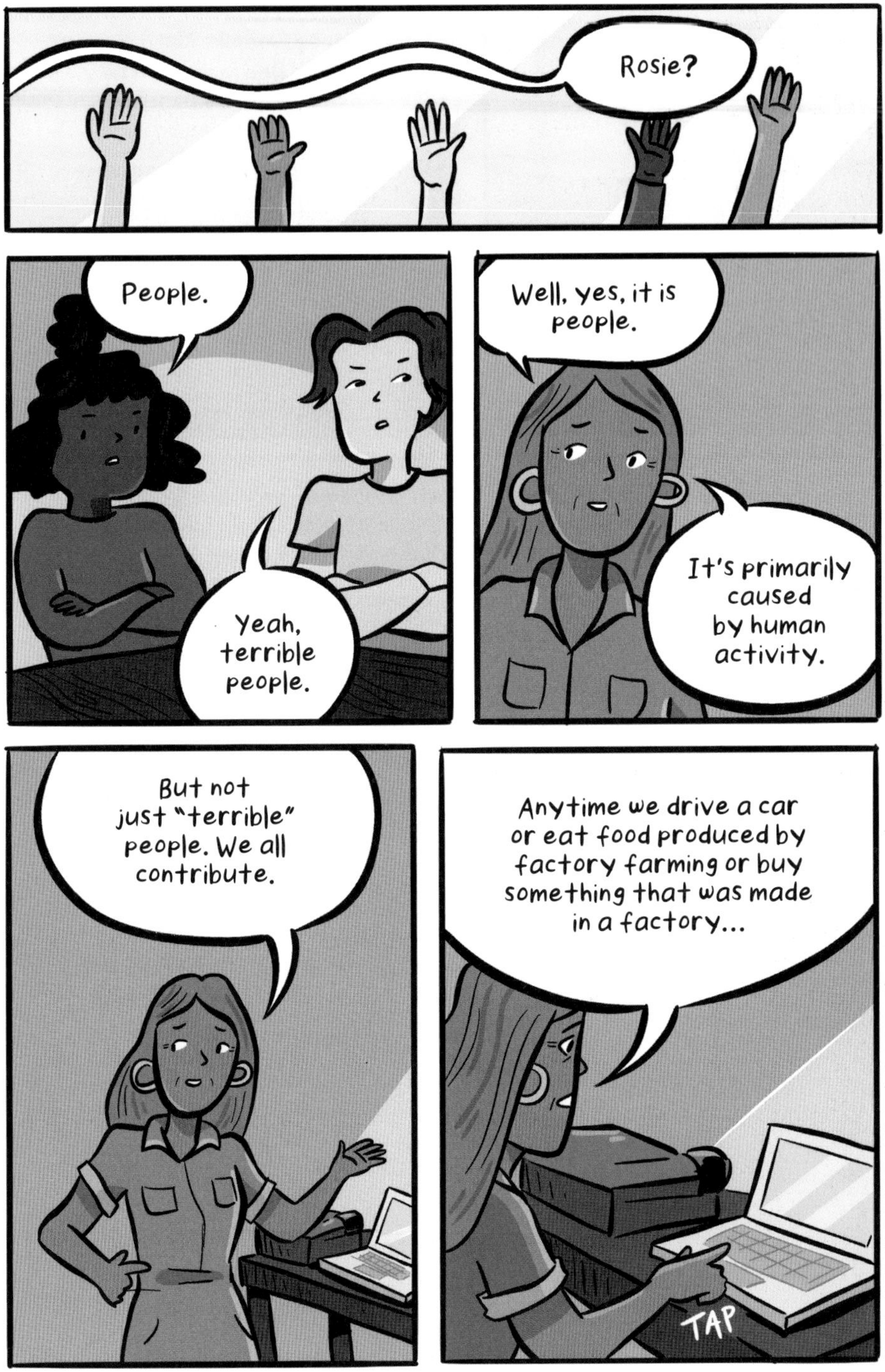
Rosie?
People.
Yeah, terrible people.
Well, yes, it is people.
It's primarily caused by human activity.
But not just "terrible" people. We all contribute.
Anytime we drive a car or eat food produced by factory farming or buy something that was made in a factory...
TAP

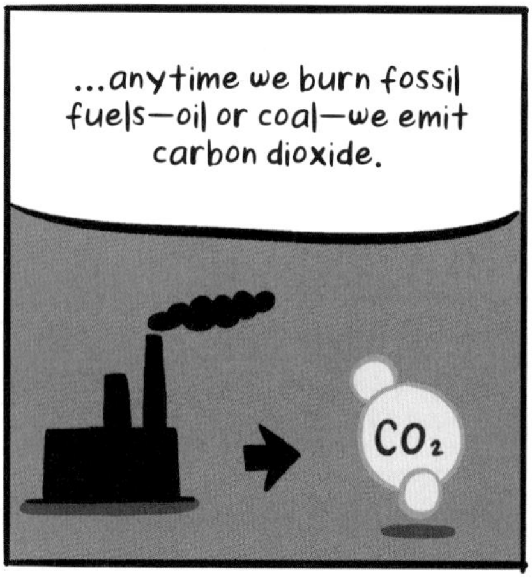
...anytime we burn fossil fuels—oil or coal—we emit carbon dioxide.
CO_2

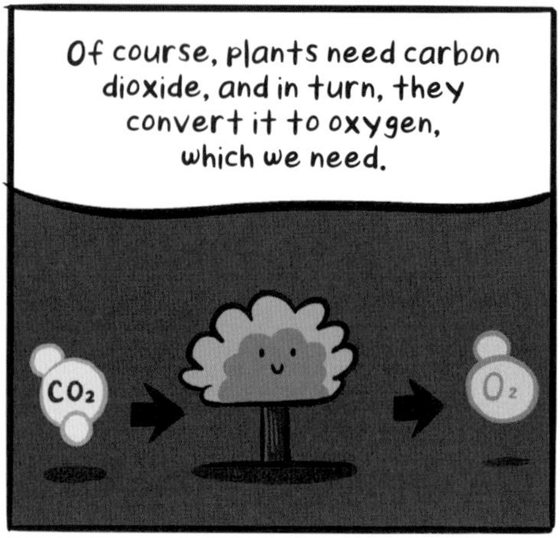
Of course, plants need carbon dioxide, and in turn, they convert it to oxygen, which we need.
CO_2
O_2

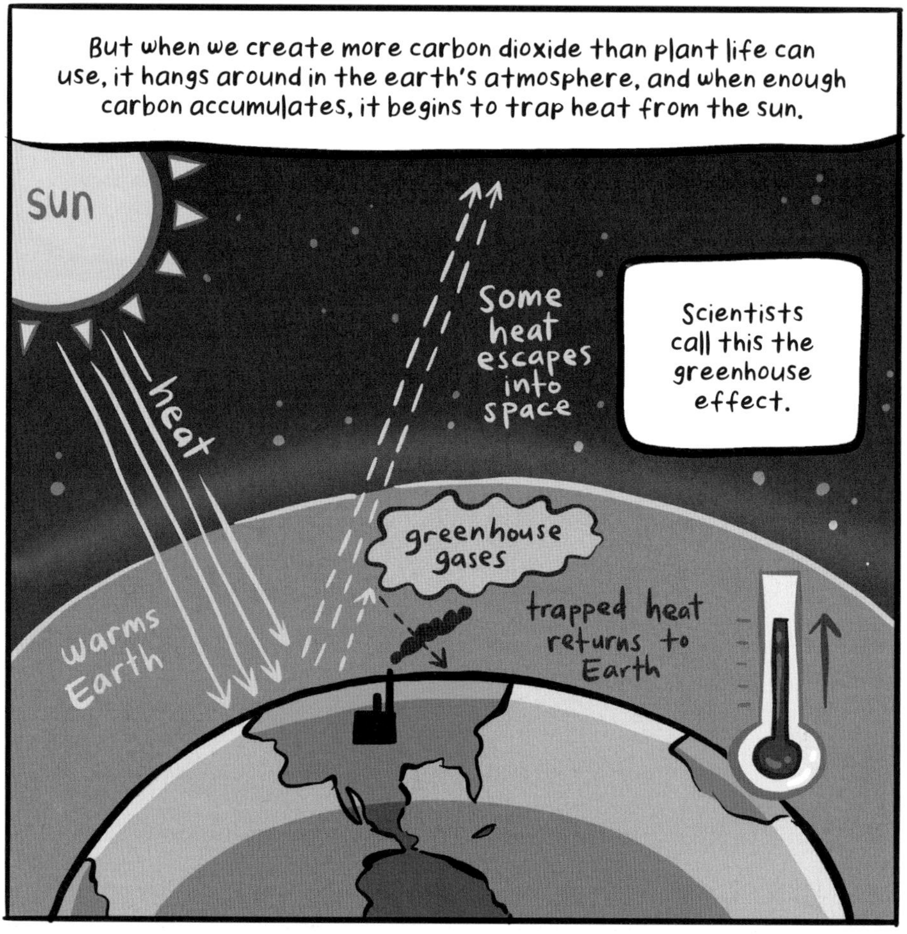
But when we create more carbon dioxide than plant life can use, it hangs around in the earth's atmosphere, and when enough carbon accumulates, it begins to trap heat from the sun.
sun
heat
Some heat escapes into space
Scientists call this the greenhouse effect.
greenhouse gases
warms Earth
trapped heat returns to Earth

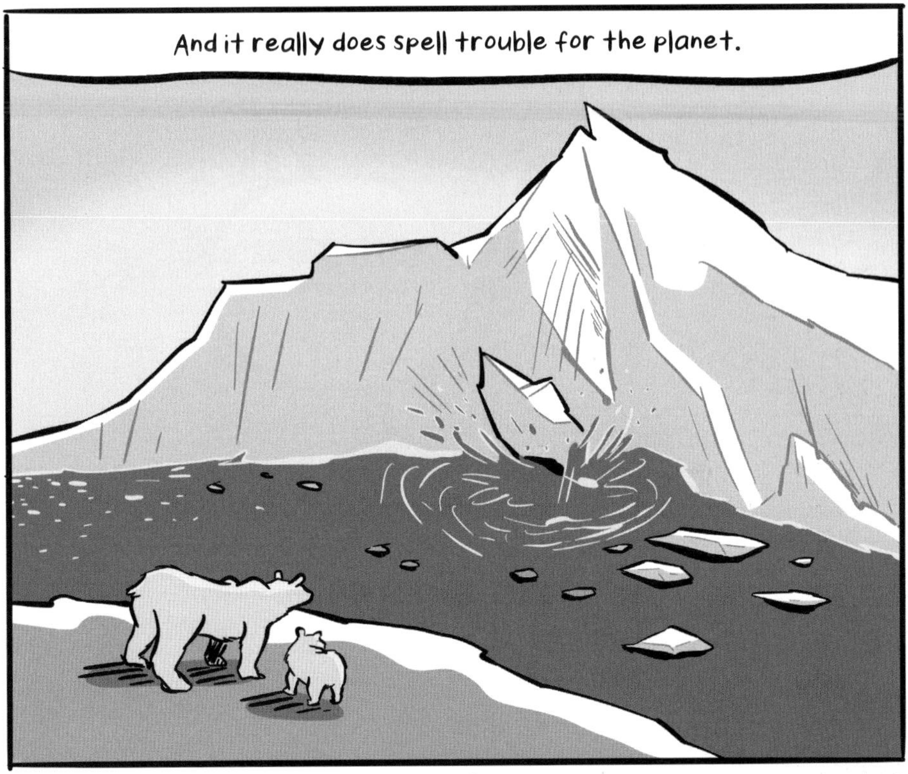
And it really does spell trouble for the planet.

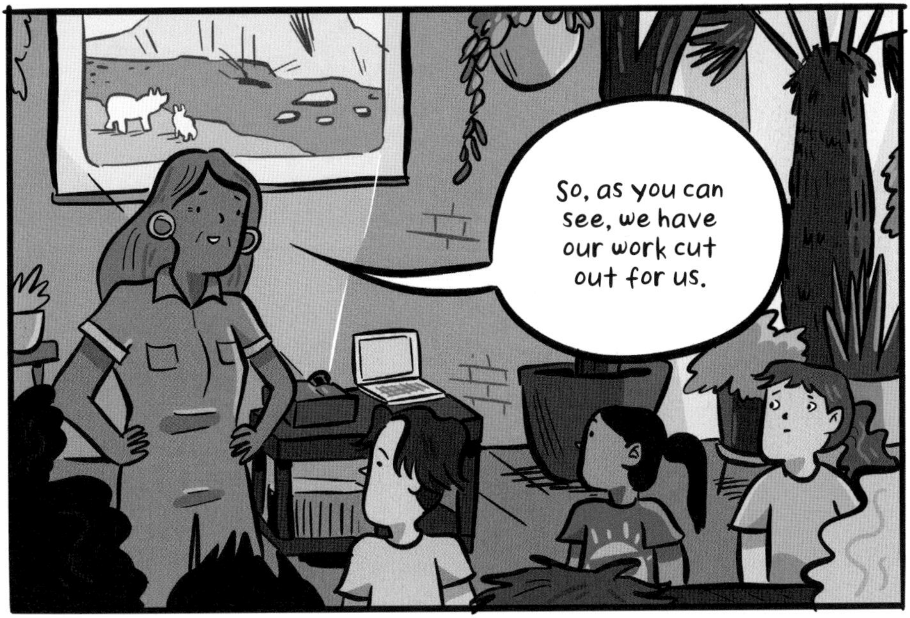
So, as you can see, we have our work cut out for us.

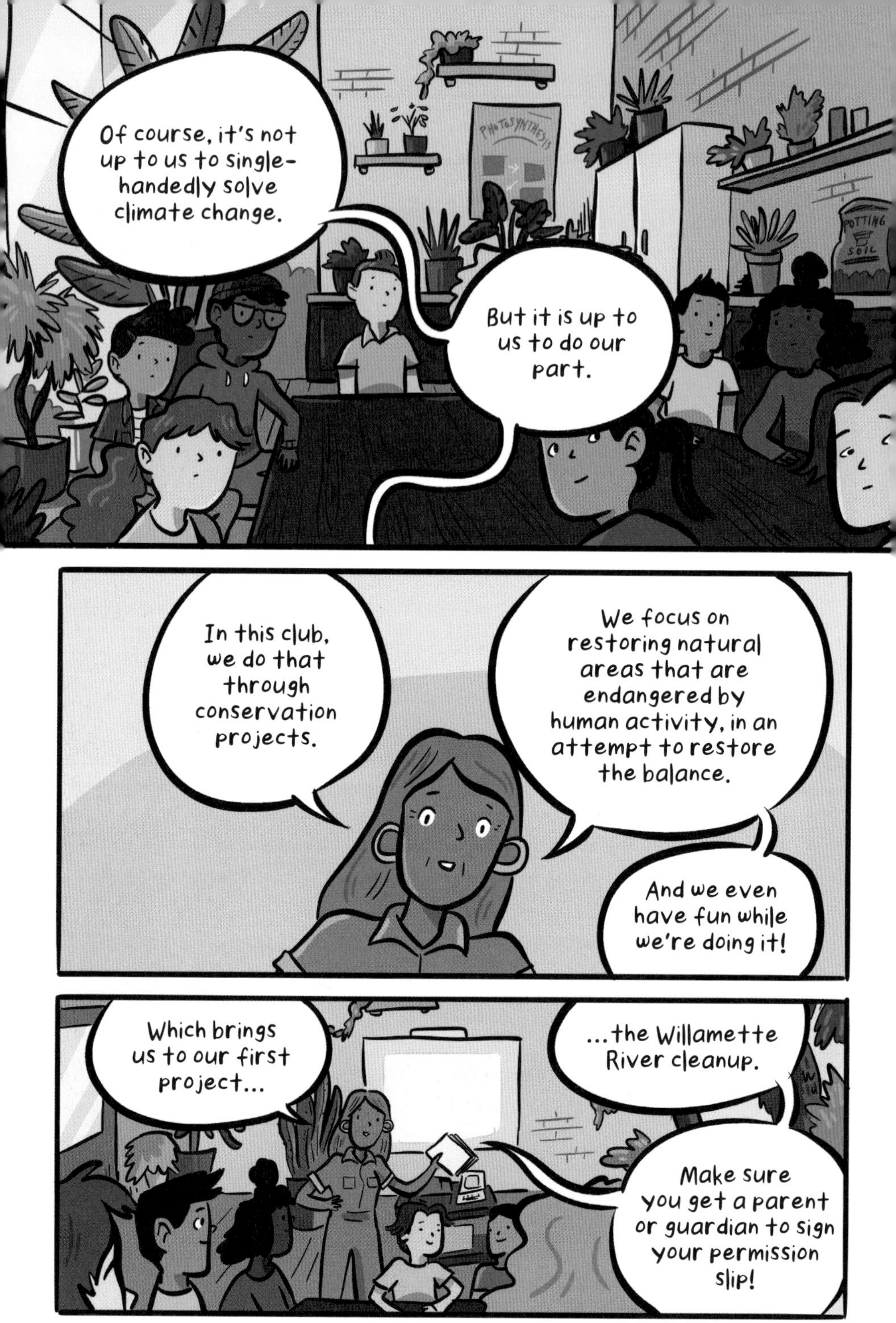
PHOTOSYNTHESIS
POTTING SOIL
Of course, it's not up to us to single-handedly solve climate change.
But it is up to us to do our part.
In this club, we do that through conservation projects.
We focus on restoring natural areas that are endangered by human activity, in an attempt to restore the balance.
And we even have fun while we're doing it!
Which brings us to our first project...
...the Willamette River cleanup.
Make sure you get a parent or guardian to sign your permission slip!

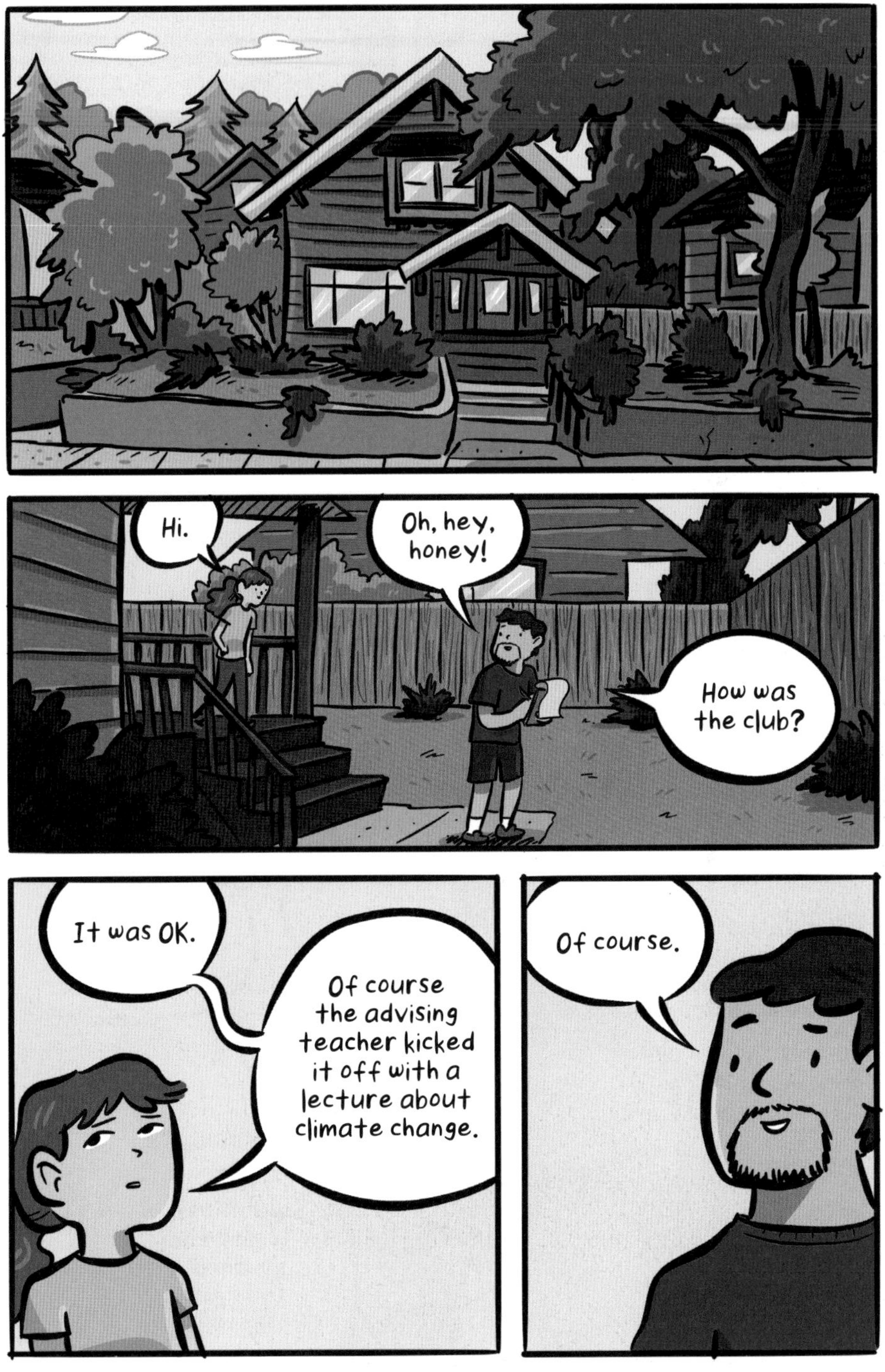
Hi.
Oh, hey, honey!
How was the club?
It was OK.
Of course the advising teacher kicked it off with a lecture about climate change.
Of course.

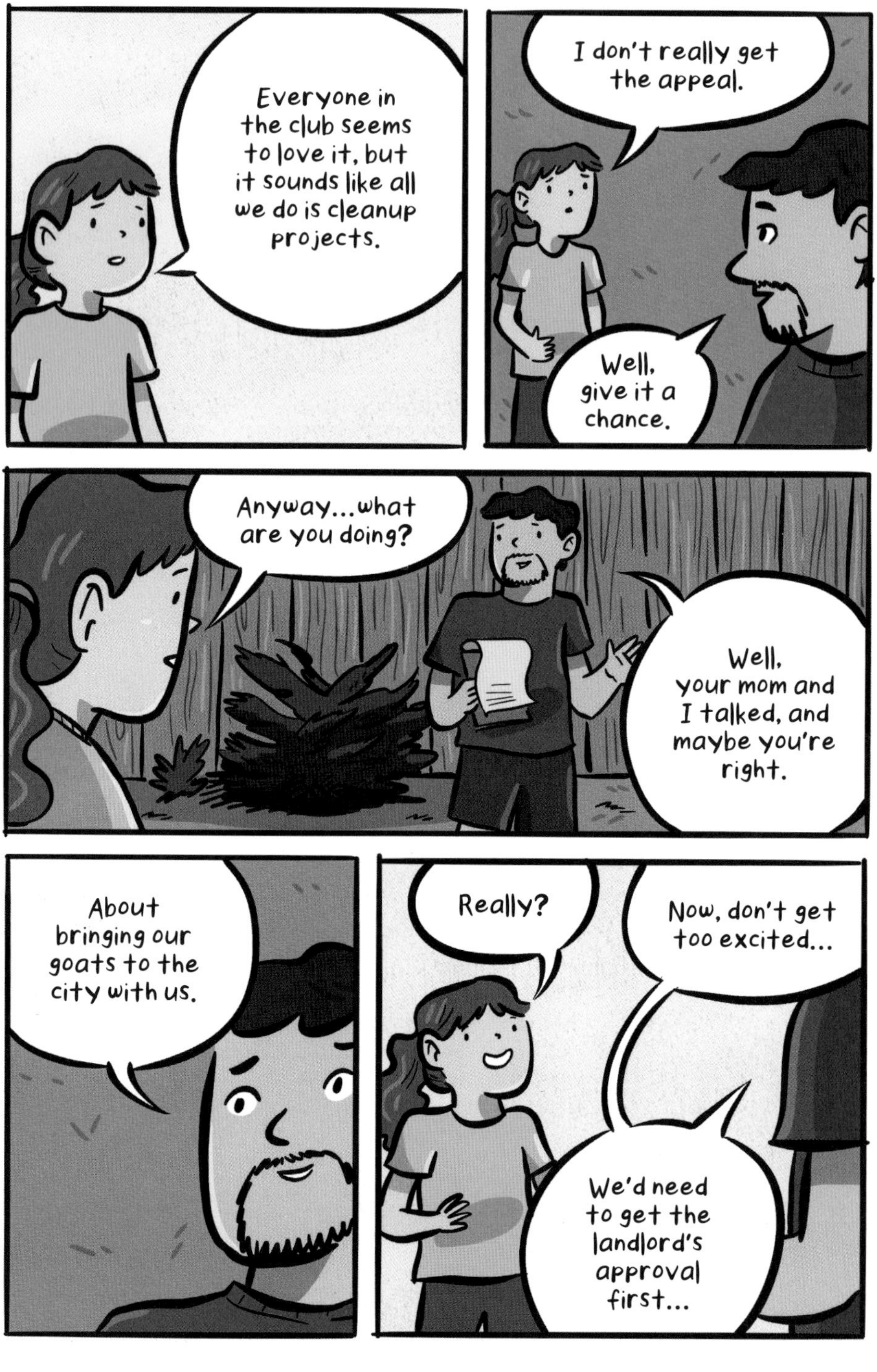
Everyone in the club seems to love it, but it sounds like all we do is cleanup projects.
I don't really get the appeal.
Well, give it a chance.
Anyway...what are you doing?
Well, your mom and I talked, and maybe you're right.
About bringing our goats to the city with us.
Really?
Now, don't get too excited...
We'd need to get the landlord's approval first...

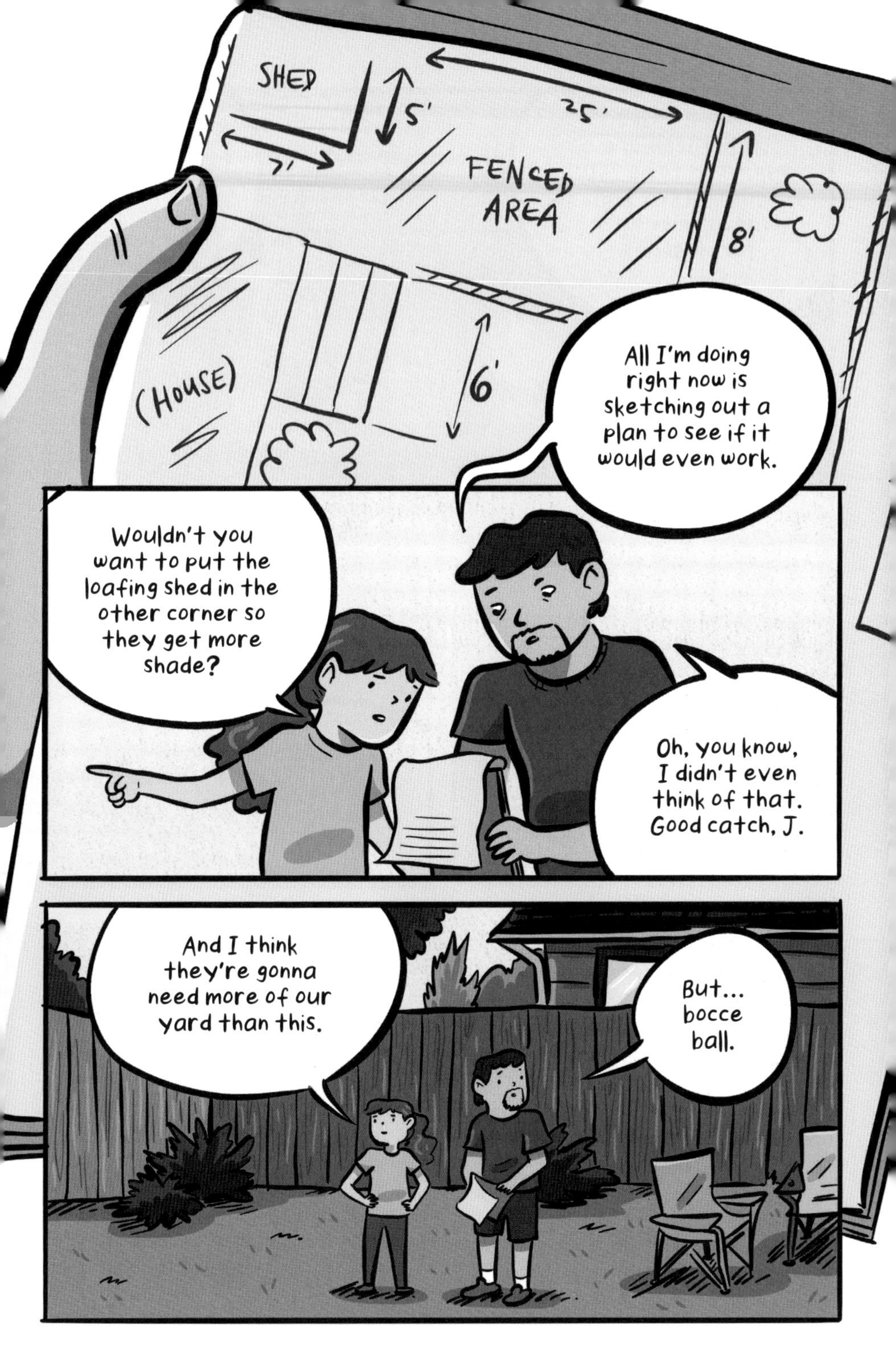
SHED
5'
25'
7'
FENCED AREA
8'
(HOUSE)
6'
All I'm doing right now is sketching out a plan to see if it would even work.
Wouldn't you want to put the loafing shed in the other corner so they get more shade?
Oh, you know, I didn't even think of that. Good catch, J.
And I think they're gonna need more of our yard than this.
But... bocce ball.

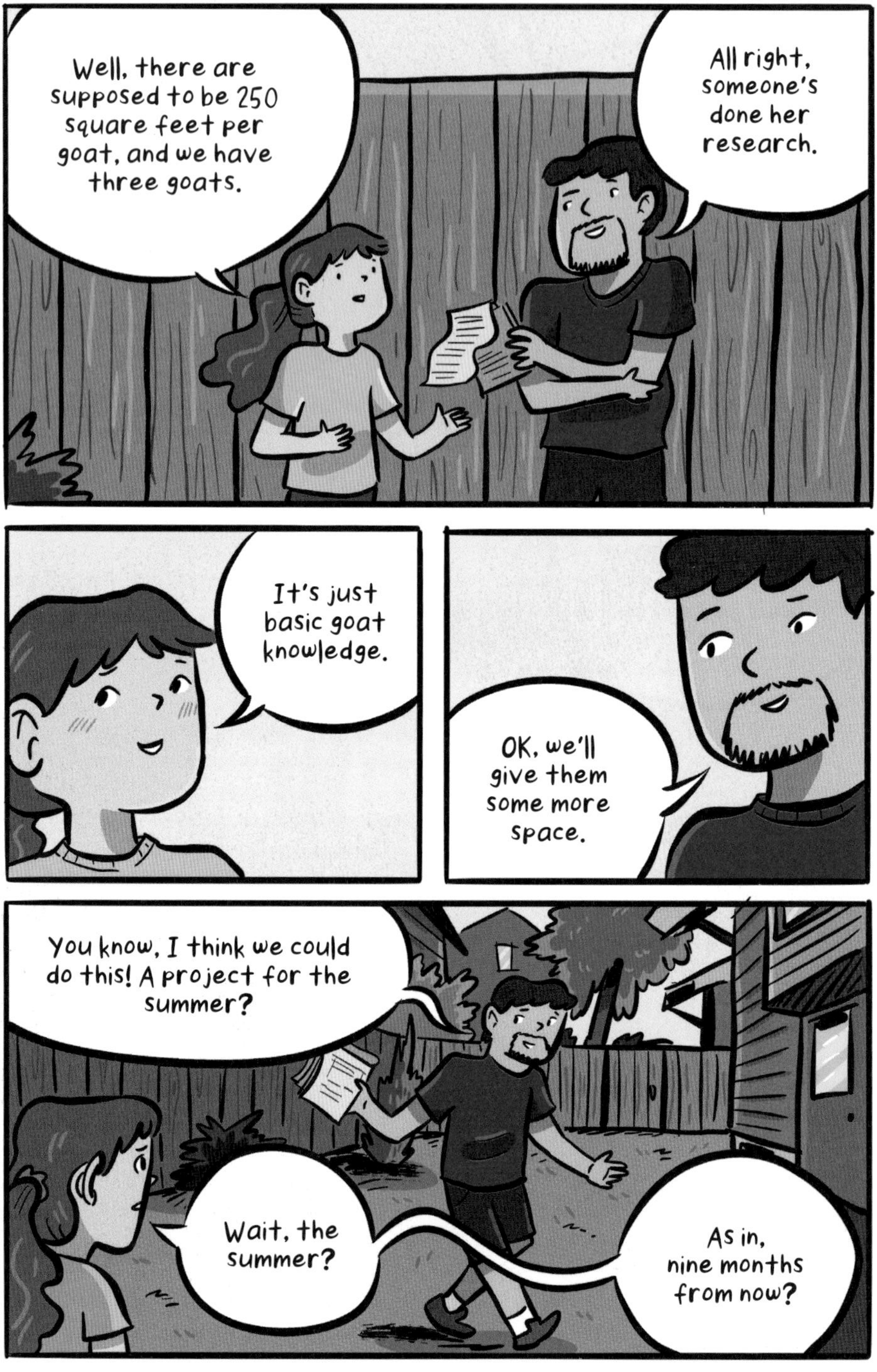
Well, there are supposed to be 250 square feet per goat, and we have three goats.
All right, someone's done her research.
It's just basic goat knowledge.
OK, we'll give them some more space.
You know, I think we could do this! A project for the summer?
Wait, the summer?
As in, nine months from now?

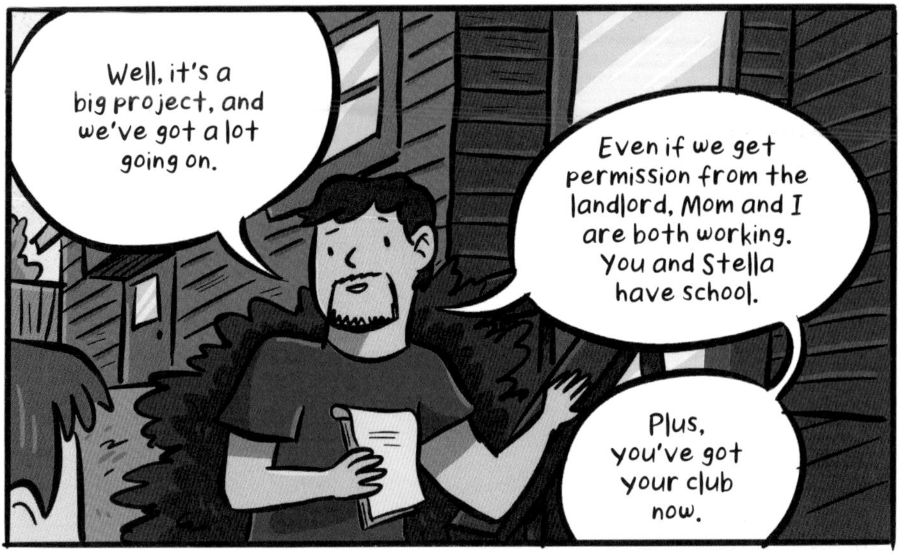
Well, it's a big project, and we've got a lot going on.
Even if we get permission from the landlord, Mom and I are both working. You and Stella have school.
Plus, you've got your club now.

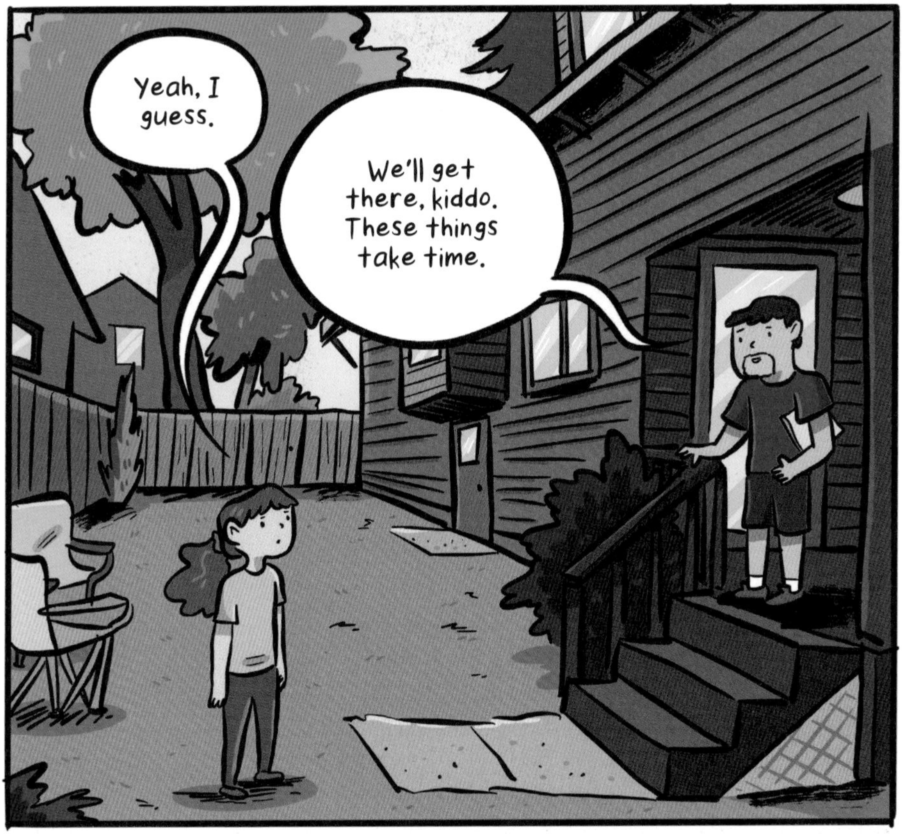
Yeah, I guess.
We'll get there, kiddo. These things take time.

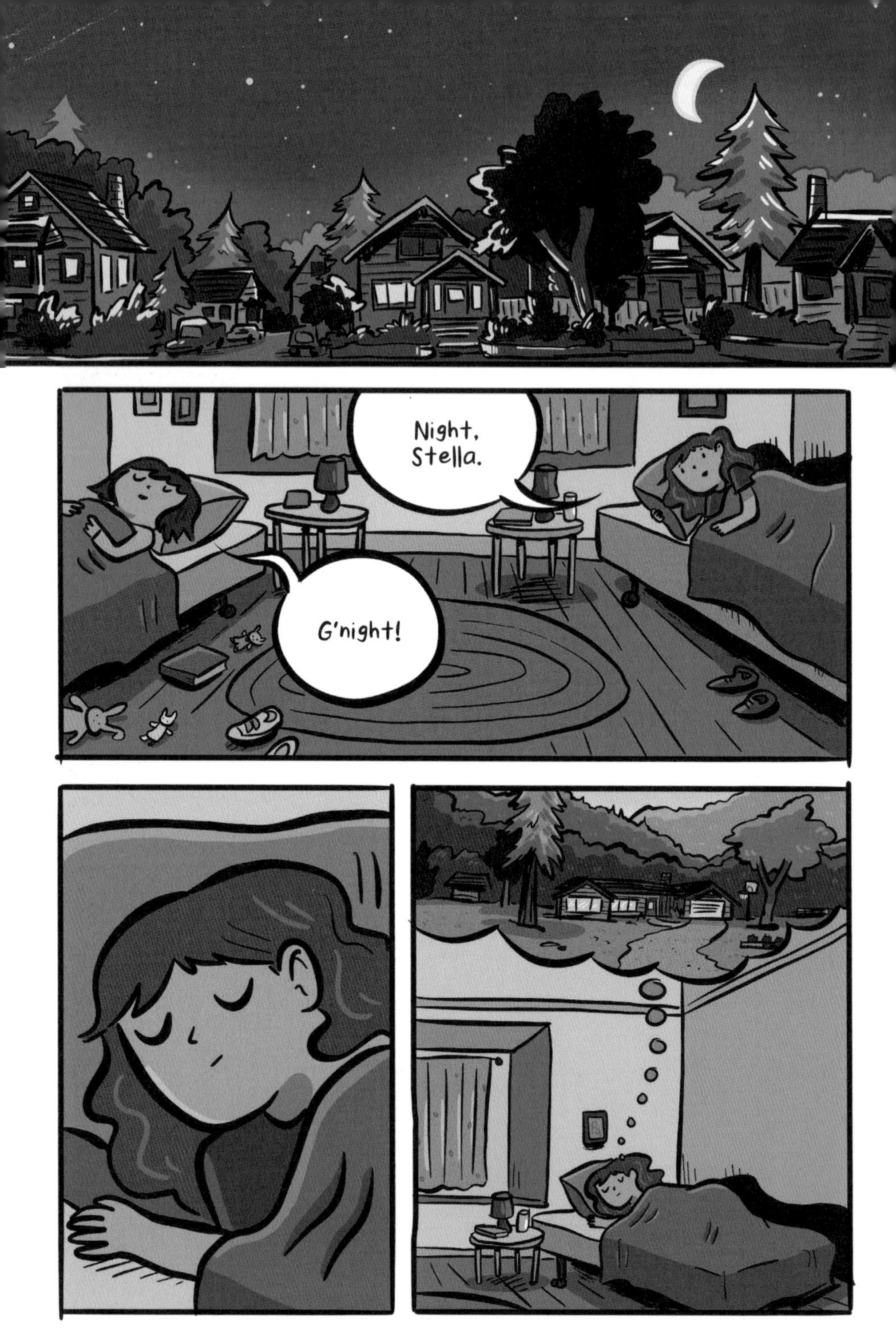
Night, Stella.
G'night!

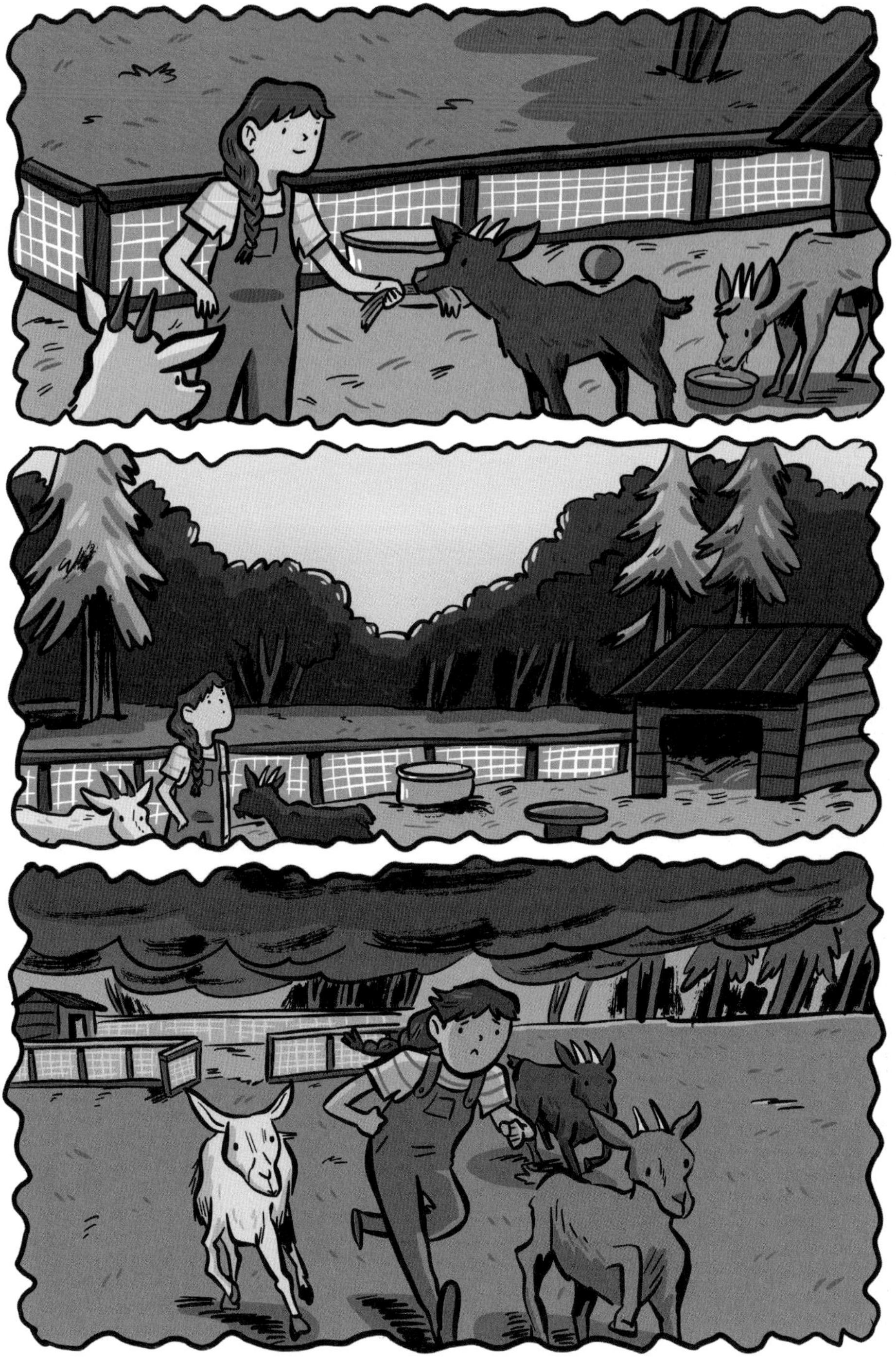

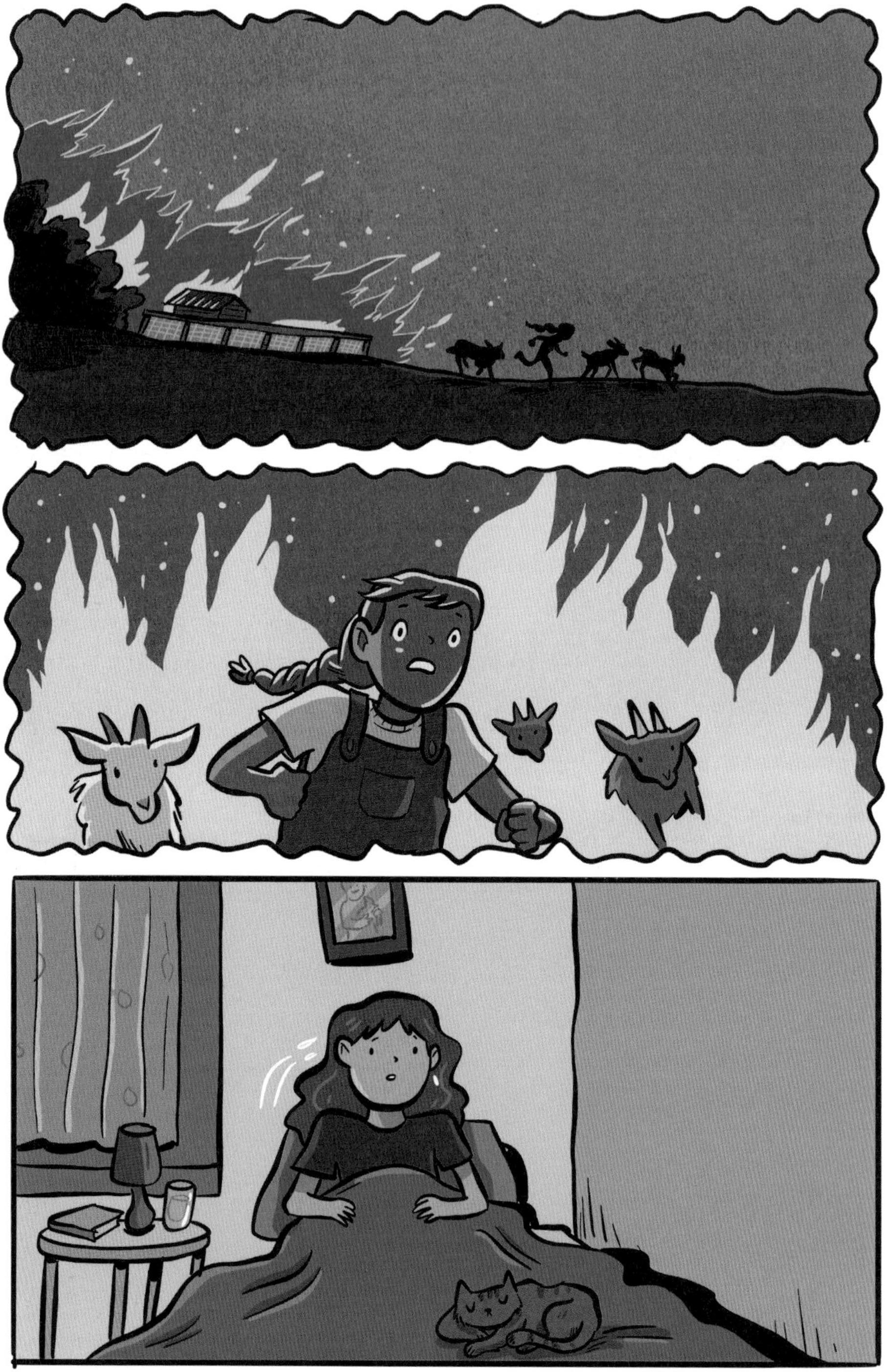

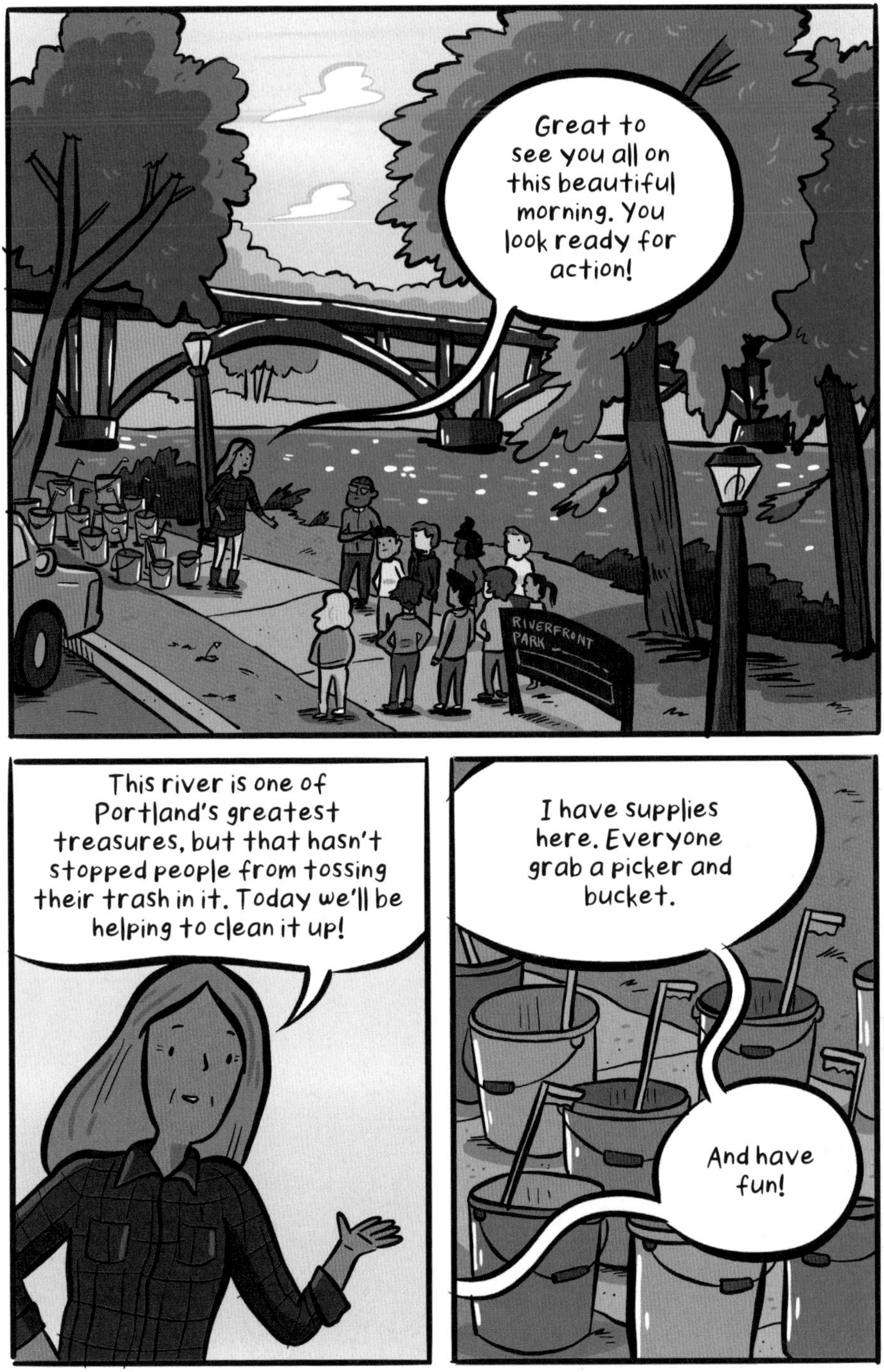
Great to see you all on this beautiful morning. You look ready for action!
RIVERFRONT PARK
This river is one of Portland's greatest treasures, but that hasn't stopped people from tossing their trash in it. Today we'll be helping to clean it up!
I have supplies here. Everyone grab a picker and bucket.
And have fun!

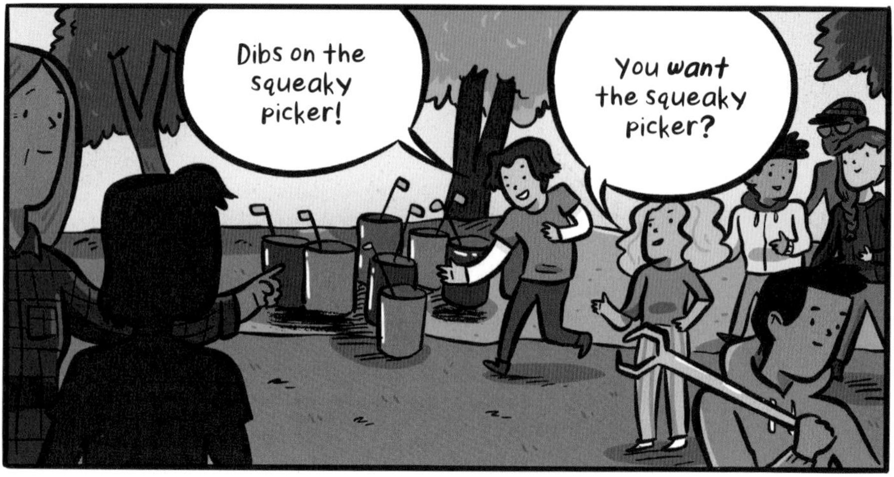
Dibs on the squeaky picker!
You *want* the squeaky picker?

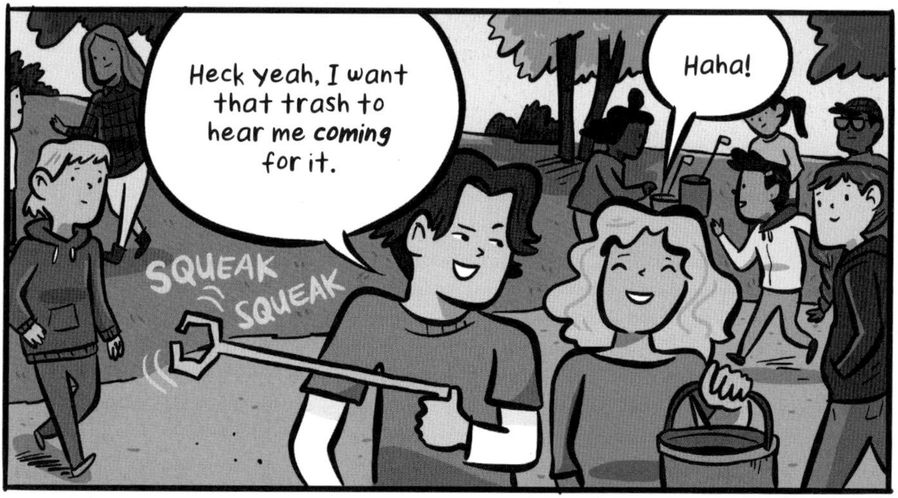
Heck yeah, I want that trash to hear me *coming* for it.
Haha!
SQUEAK SQUEAK

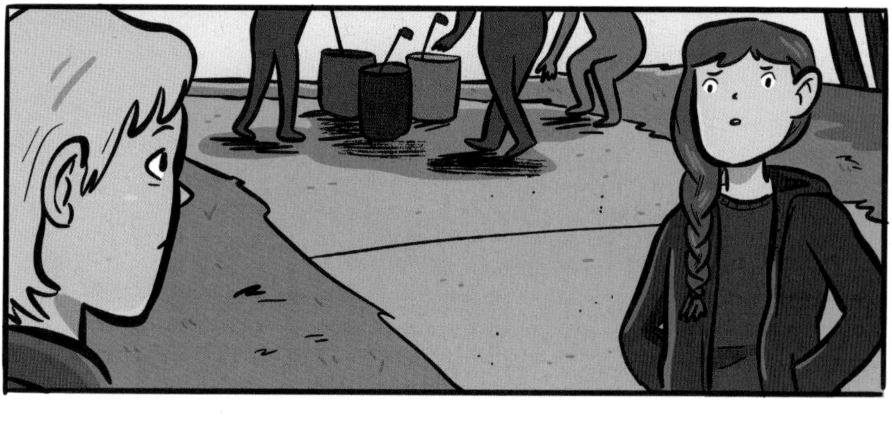

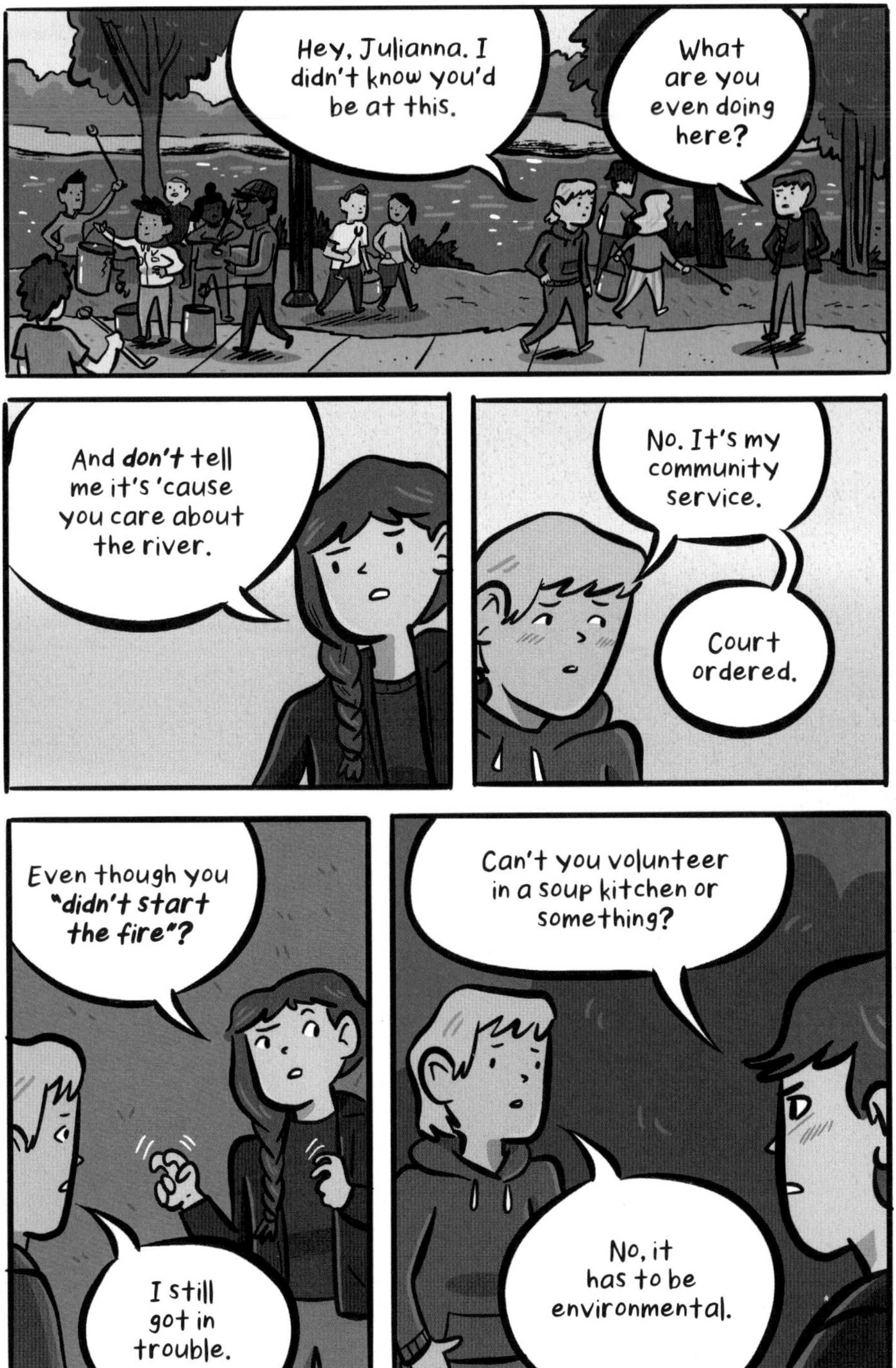
Hey, Julianna. I didn't know you'd be at this.
What are you even doing here?
And **don't** tell me it's 'cause you care about the river.
No. It's my community service.
Court ordered.
Even though you ***"didn't start the fire"***?
I still got in trouble.
Can't you volunteer in a soup kitchen or something?
No, it has to be environmental.

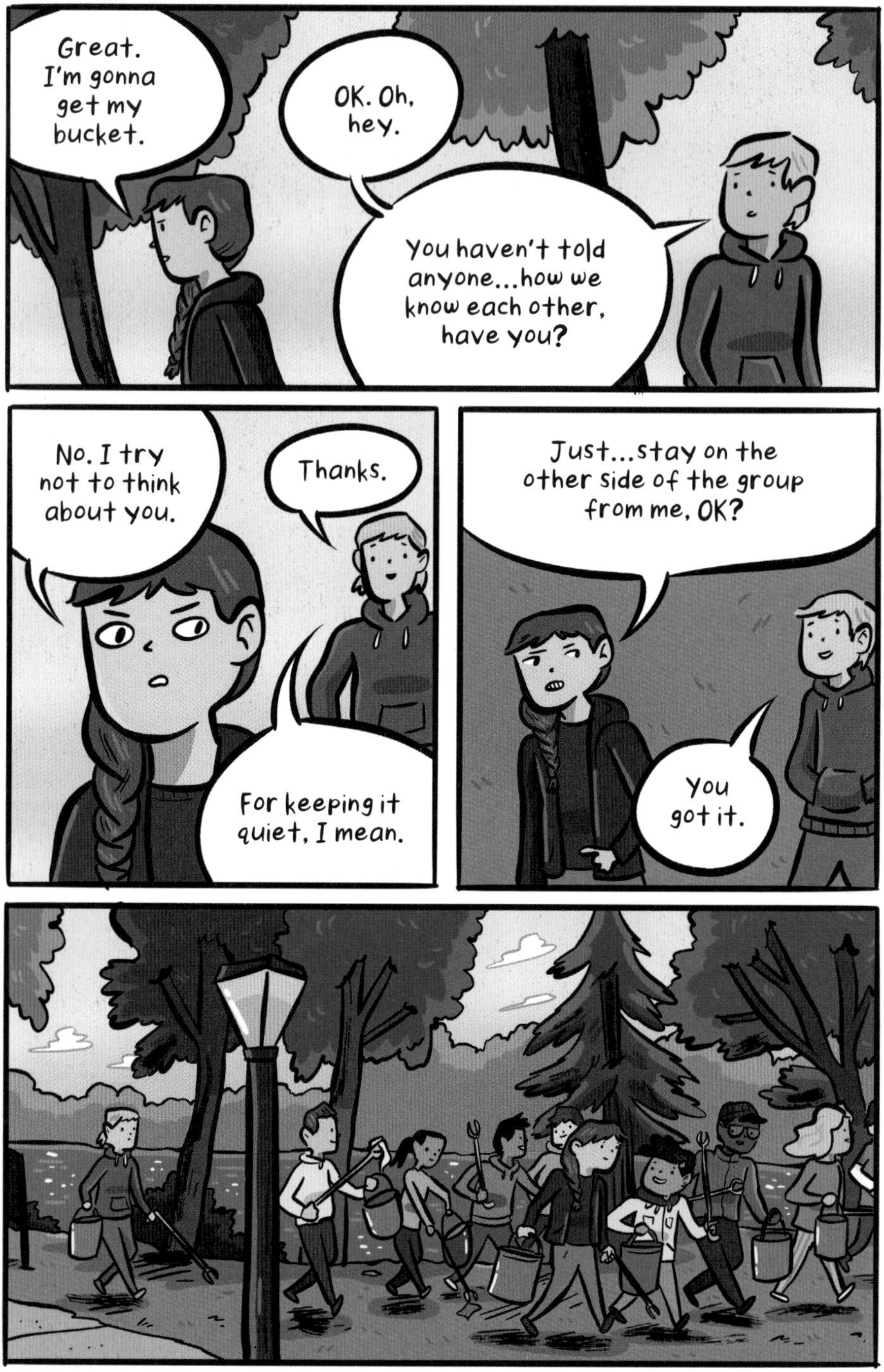
Great. I'm gonna get my bucket.
OK. Oh, hey.
You haven't told anyone...how we know each other, have you?
No. I try not to think about you.
Thanks.
For keeping it quiet, I mean.
Just...stay on the other side of the group from me, OK?
You got it.

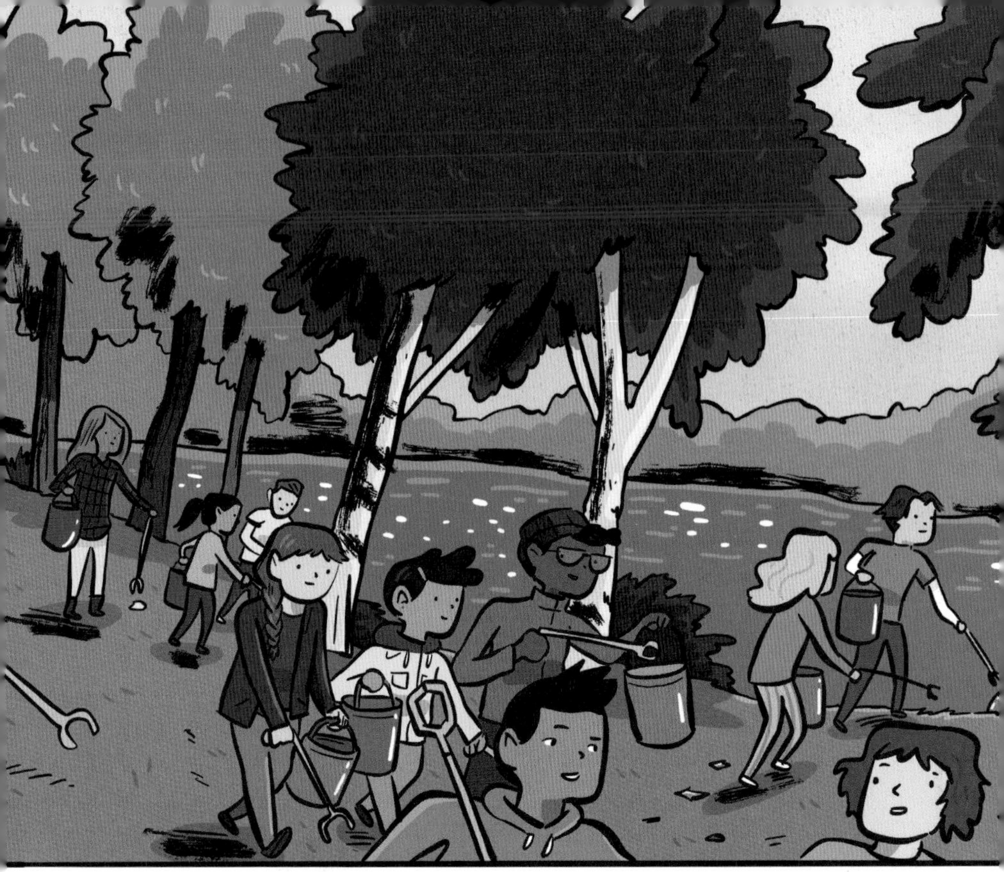

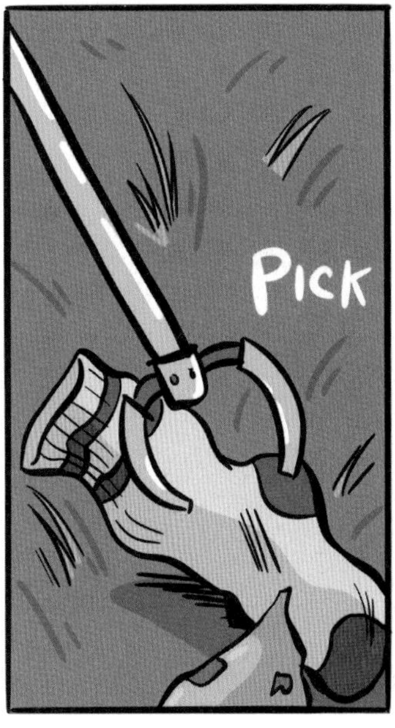
PICK

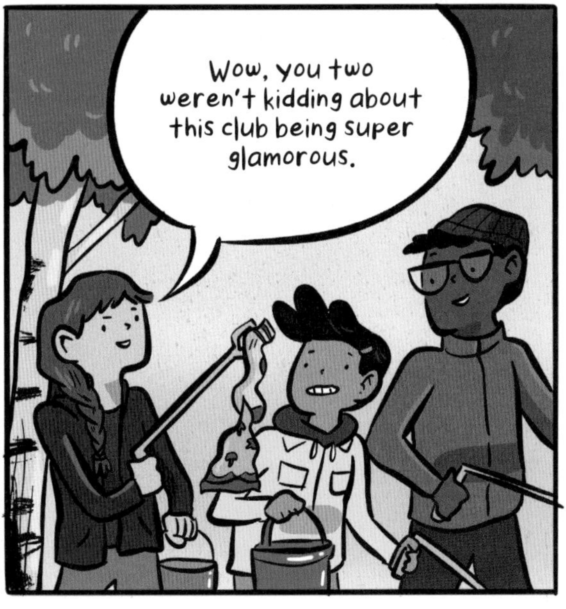
Wow, you two weren't kidding about this club being super glamorous.

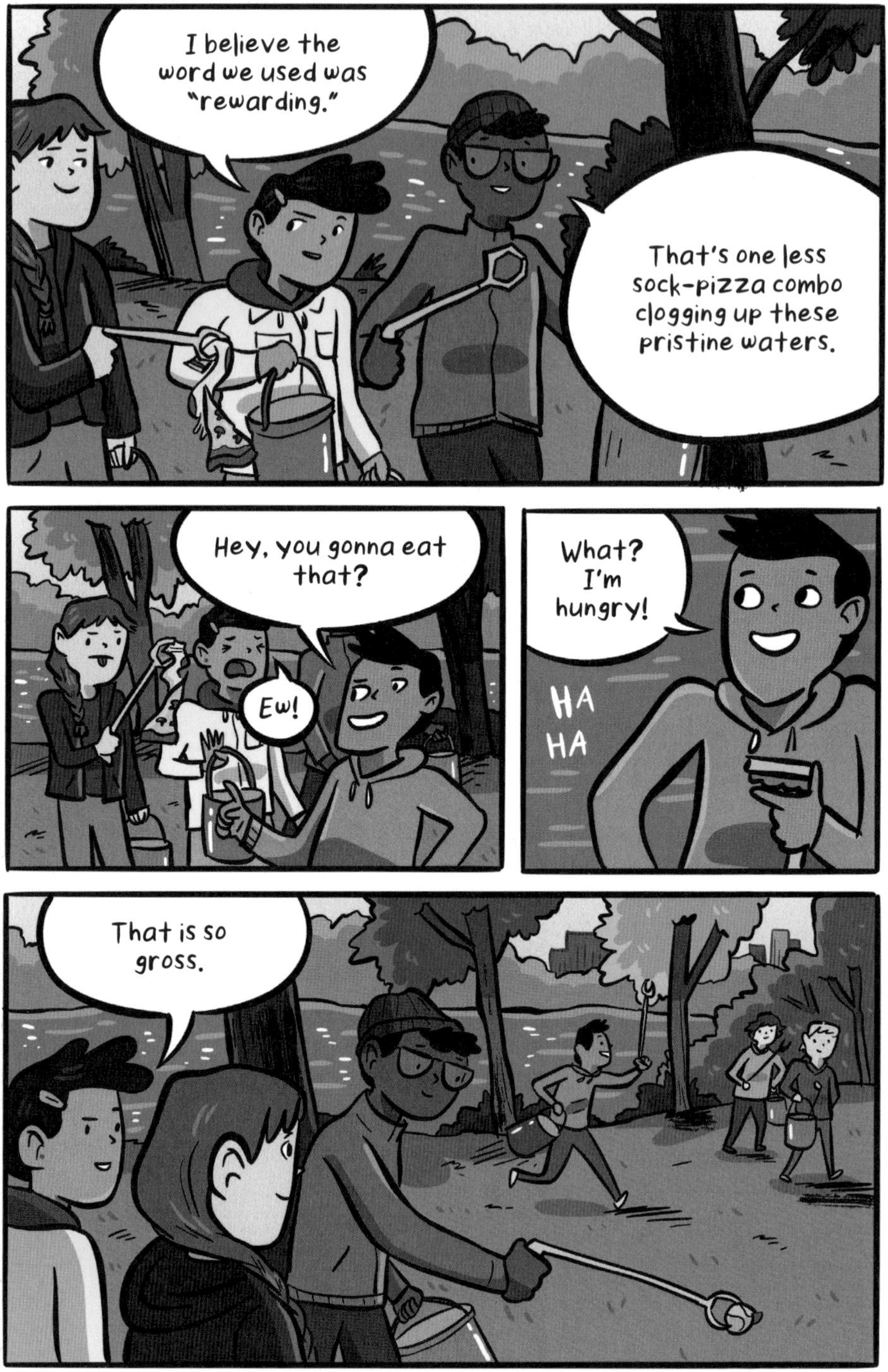
I believe the word we used was "rewarding."
That's one less sock-pizza combo clogging up these pristine waters.
Hey, you gonna eat that?
Ew!
What? I'm hungry!
HA HA
That is so gross.

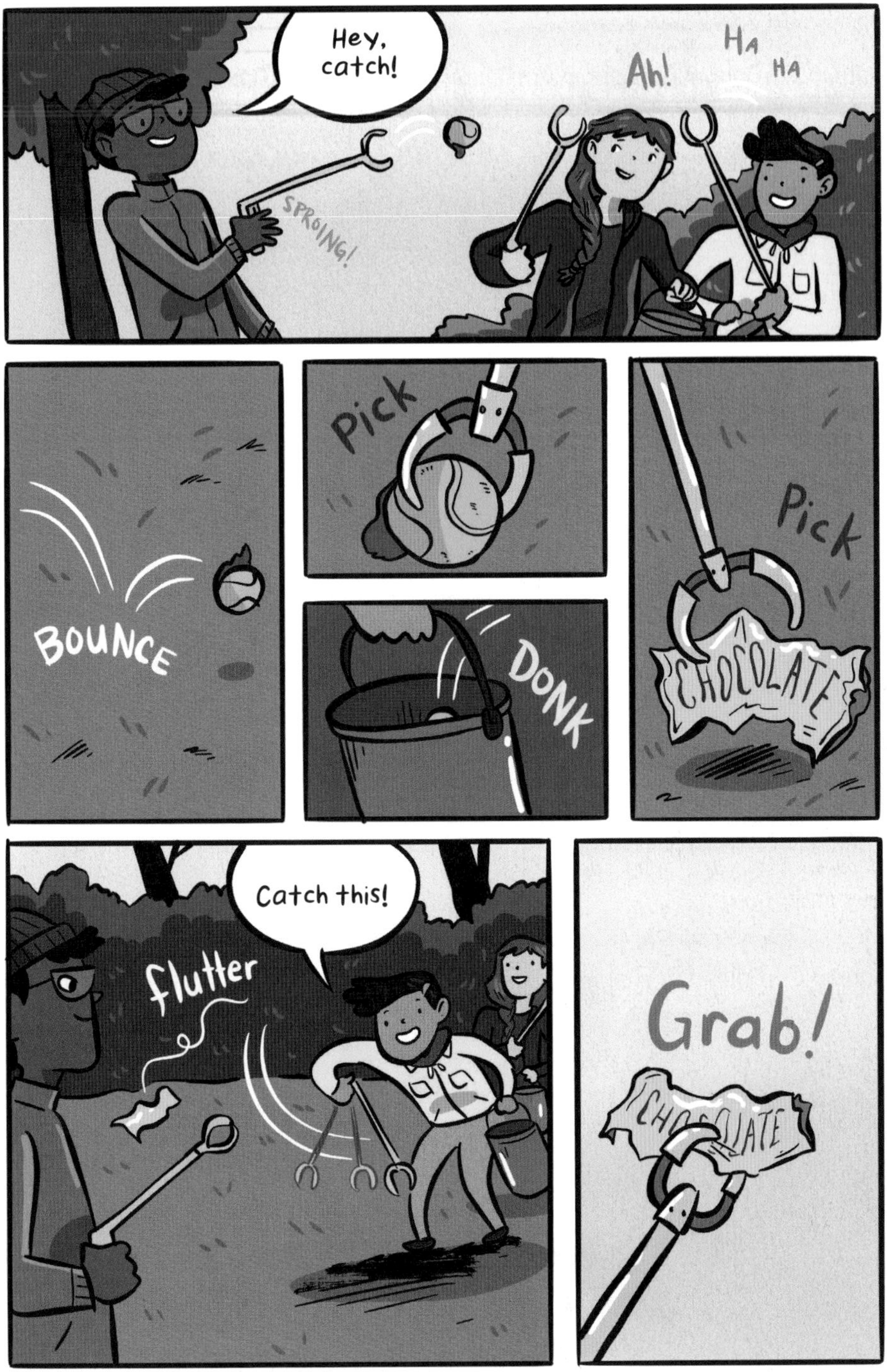
Hey, catch!
SPROING!
Ah!
HA HA HA
BOUNCE
Pick
DONK
Pick
CHOCOLATE
Catch this!
flutter
Grab!

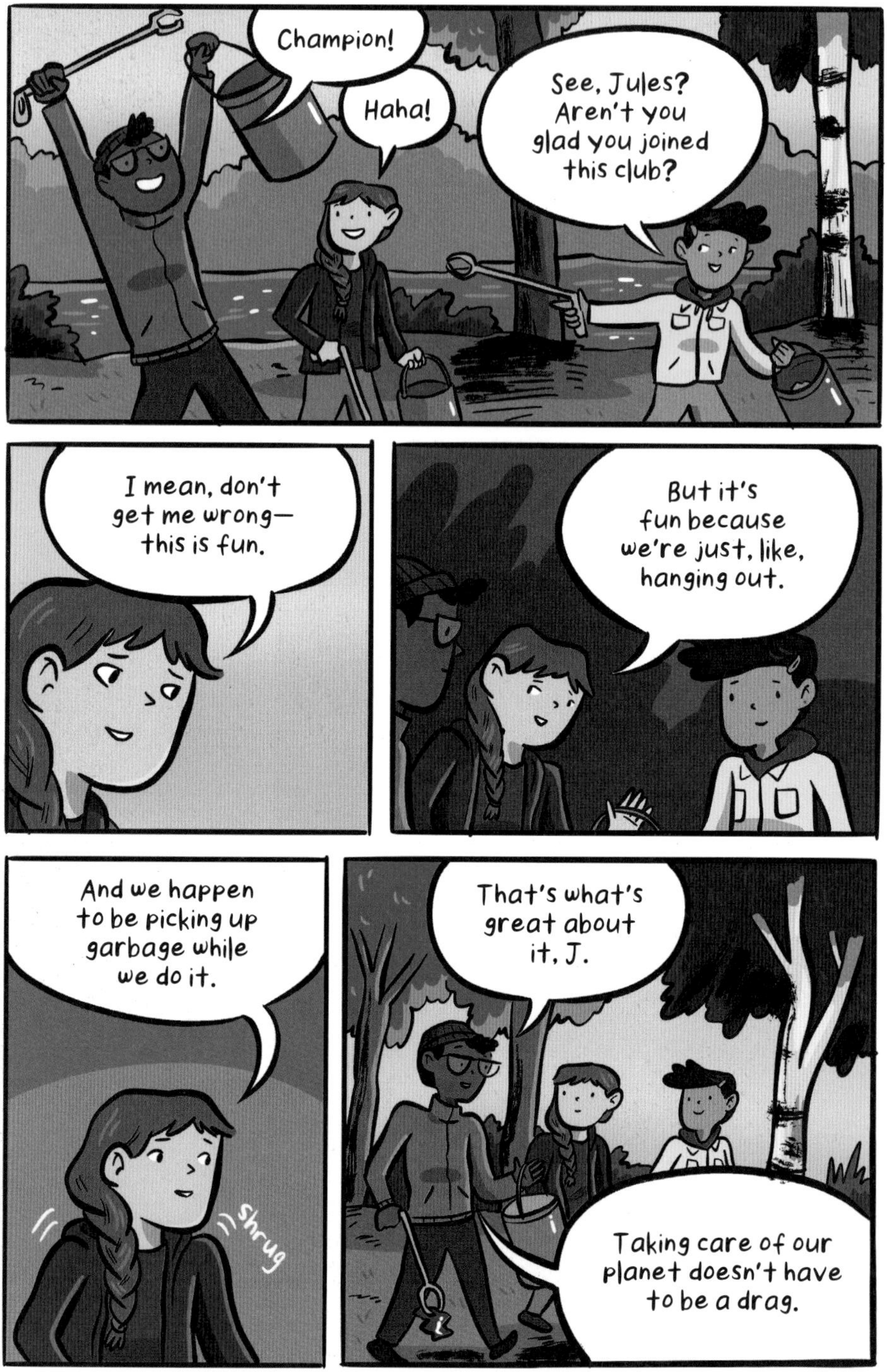
Champion!
Haha!
See, Jules? Aren't you glad you joined this club?
I mean, don't get me wrong— this is fun.
But it's fun because we're just, like, hanging out.
And we happen to be picking up garbage while we do it.
Shrug
That's what's great about it, J.
Taking care of our planet doesn't have to be a drag.

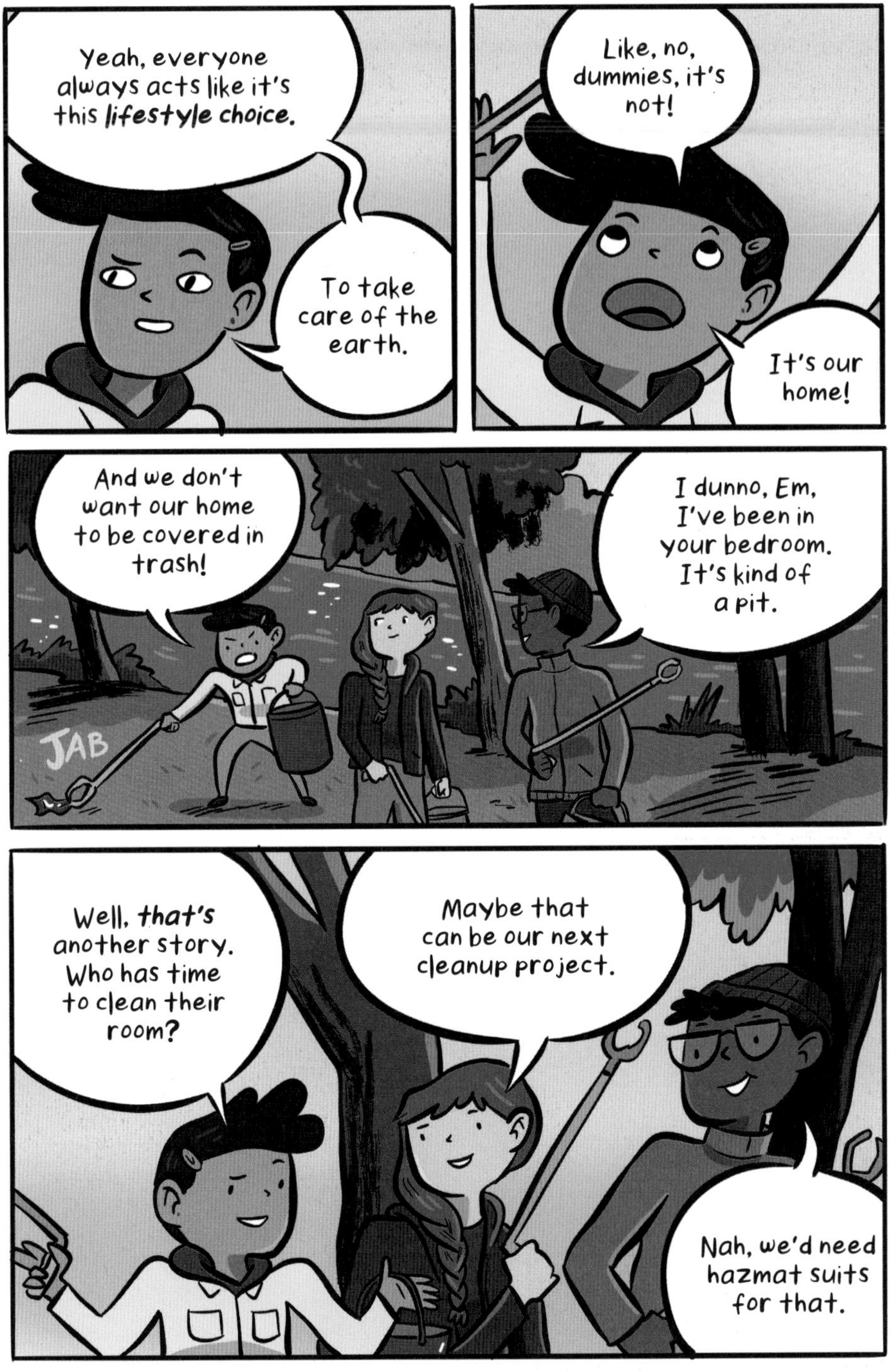
Yeah, everyone always acts like it's this *lifestyle choice.*
To take care of the earth.
Like, no, dummies, it's not!
It's our home!
And we don't want our home to be covered in trash!
I dunno, Em, I've been in your bedroom. It's kind of a pit.
JAB
Well, *that's* another story. Who has time to clean their room?
Maybe that can be our next cleanup project.
Nah, we'd need hazmat suits for that.

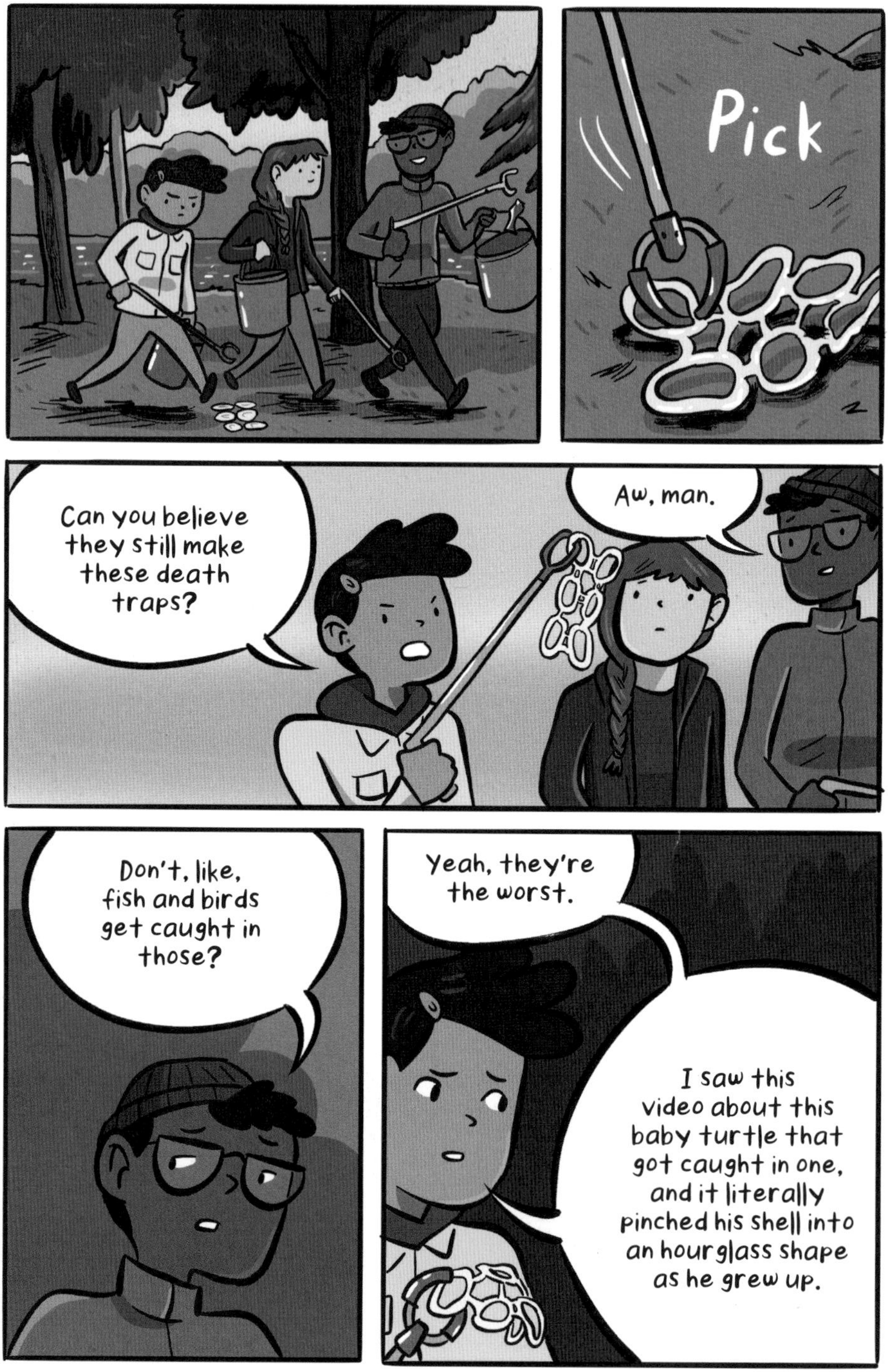
Pick
Can you believe they still make these death traps?
Aw, man.
Don't, like, fish and birds get caught in those?
Yeah, they're the worst.
I saw this video about this baby turtle that got caught in one, and it literally pinched his shell into an hourglass shape as he grew up.

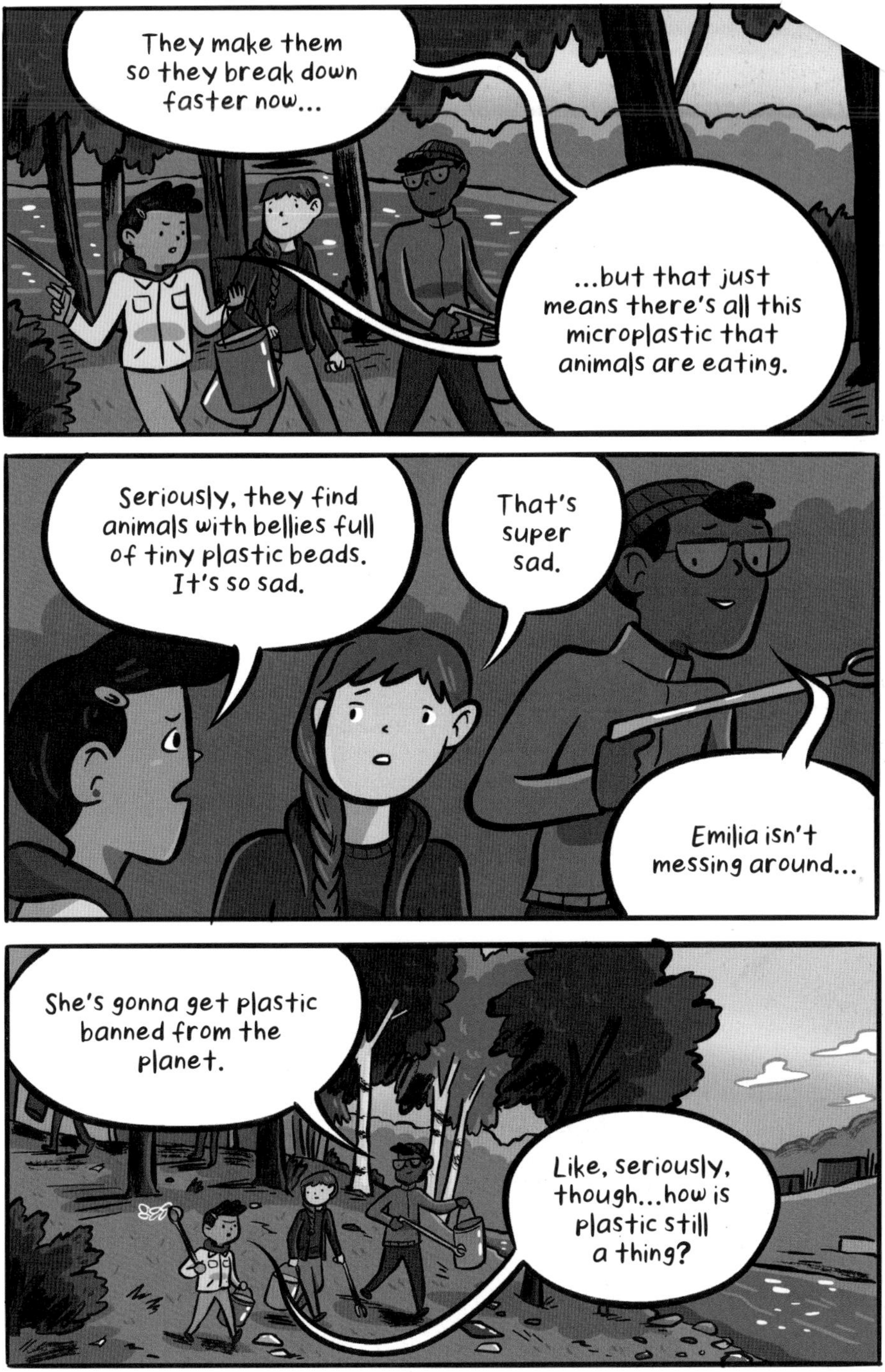
They make them so they break down faster now...
...but that just means there's all this microplastic that animals are eating.
Seriously, they find animals with bellies full of tiny plastic beads. It's so sad.
That's super sad.
Emilia isn't messing around...
She's gonna get plastic banned from the planet.
Like, seriously, though...how is plastic still a thing?

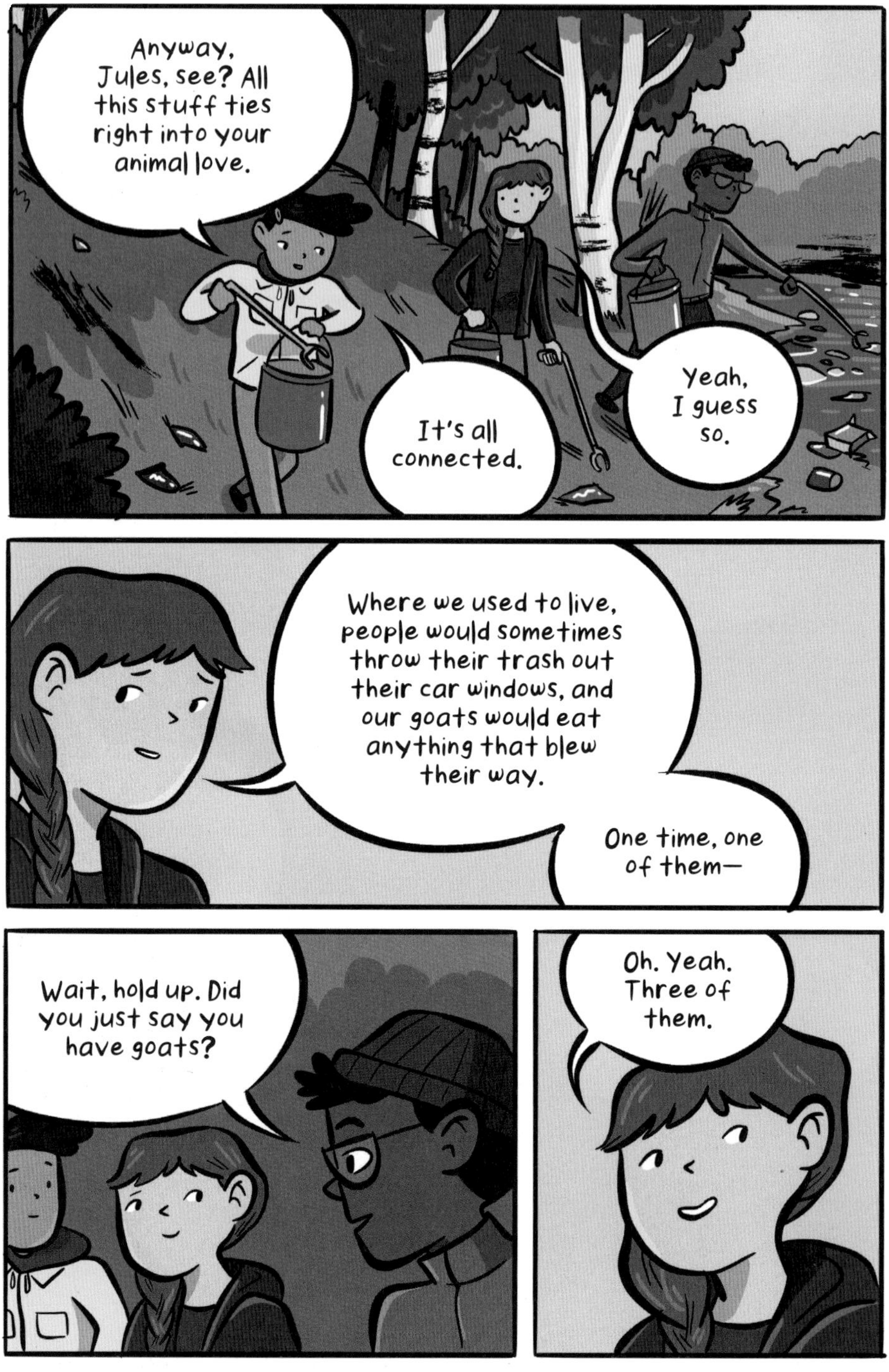
Anyway, Jules, see? All this stuff ties right into your animal love.
It's all connected.
Yeah, I guess so.
Where we used to live, people would sometimes throw their trash out their car windows, and our goats would eat anything that blew their way.
One time, one of them—
Wait, hold up. Did you just say you have goats?
Oh. Yeah. Three of them.

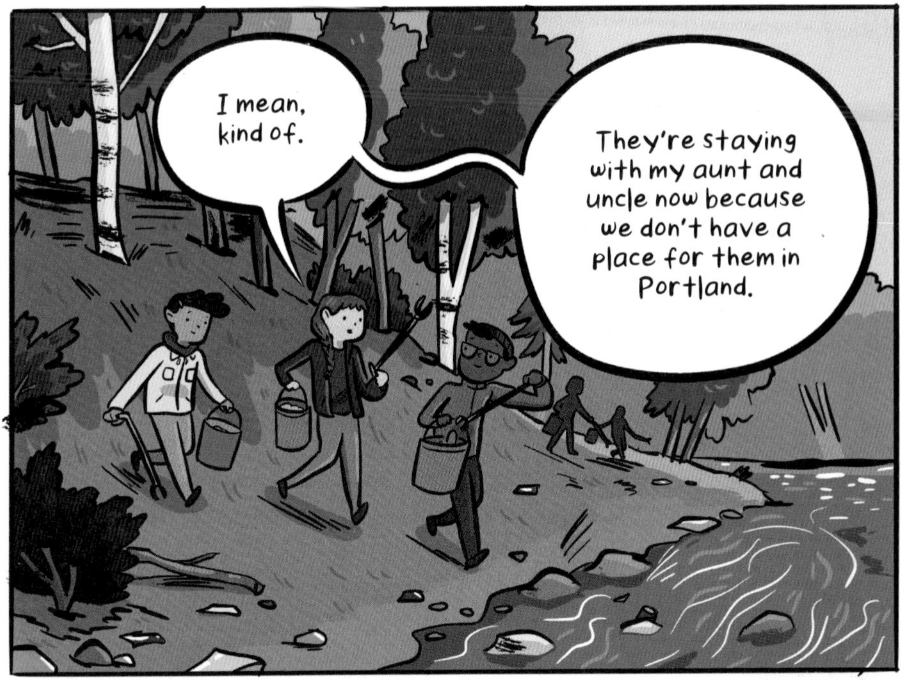
I mean, kind of.
They're staying with my aunt and uncle now because we don't have a place for them in Portland.

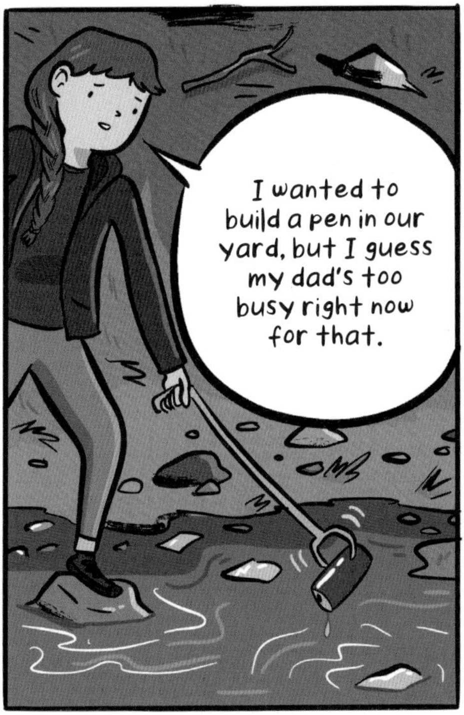
I wanted to build a pen in our yard, but I guess my dad's too busy right now for that.

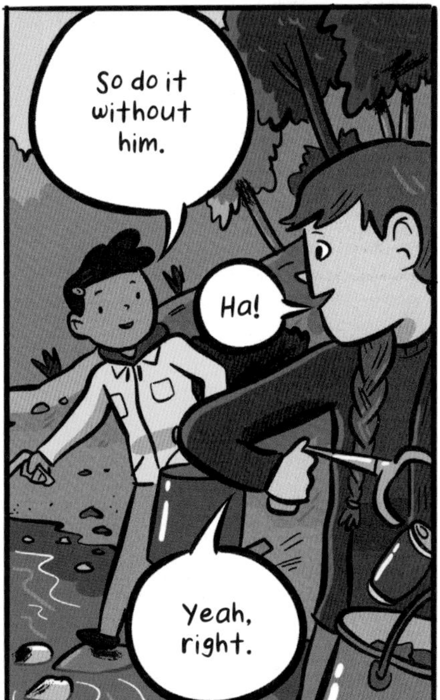
So do it without him.
Ha!
Yeah, right.

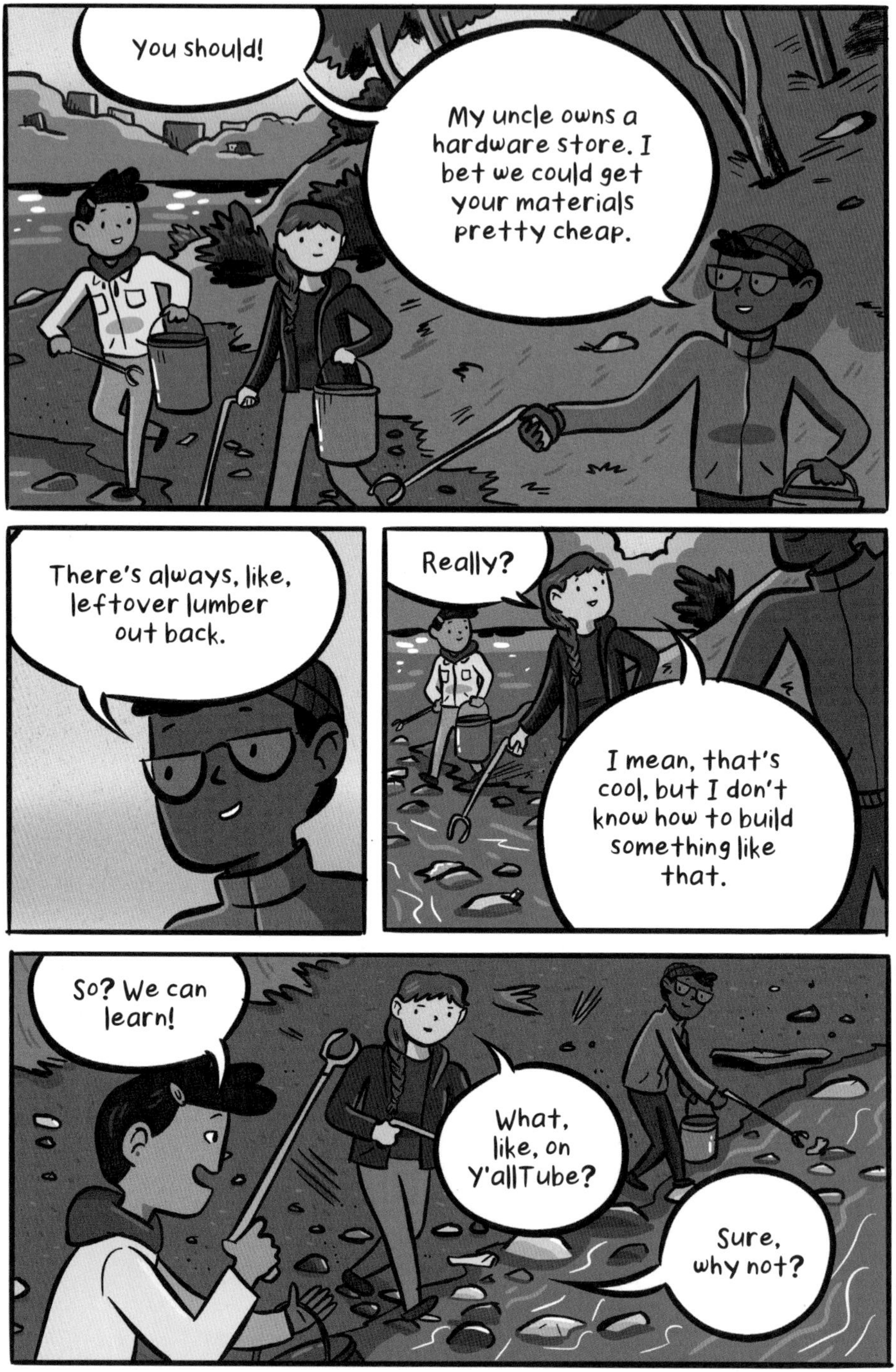
You should!
My uncle owns a hardware store. I bet we could get your materials pretty cheap.
There's always, like, leftover lumber out back.
Really?
I mean, that's cool, but I don't know how to build something like that.
So? We can learn!
What, like, on Y'allTube?
Sure, why not?

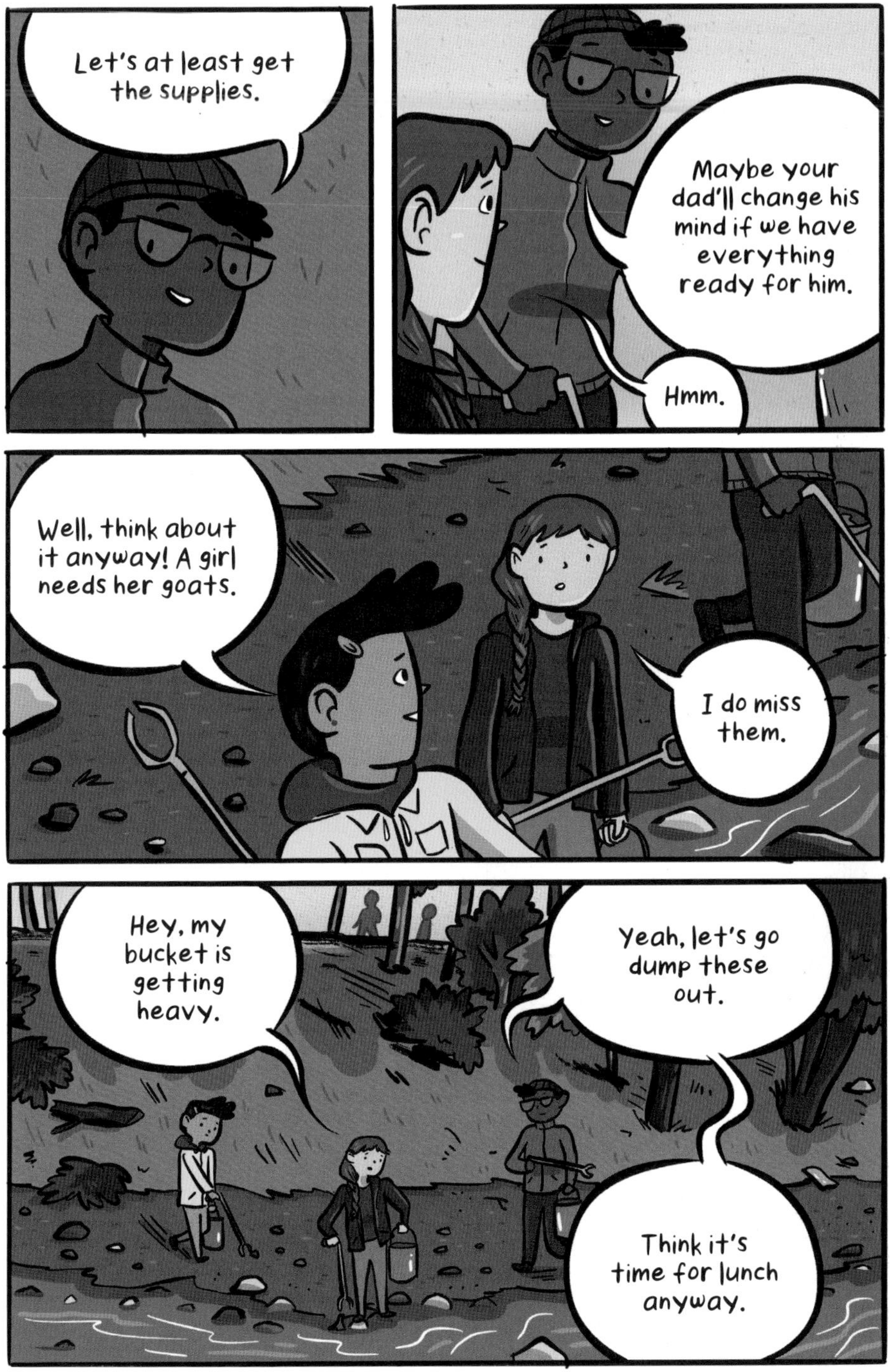
Let's at least get the supplies.
Maybe your dad'll change his mind if we have everything ready for him.
Hmm.
Well, think about it anyway! A girl needs her goats.
I do miss them.
Hey, my bucket is getting heavy.
Yeah, let's go dump these out.
Think it's time for lunch anyway.

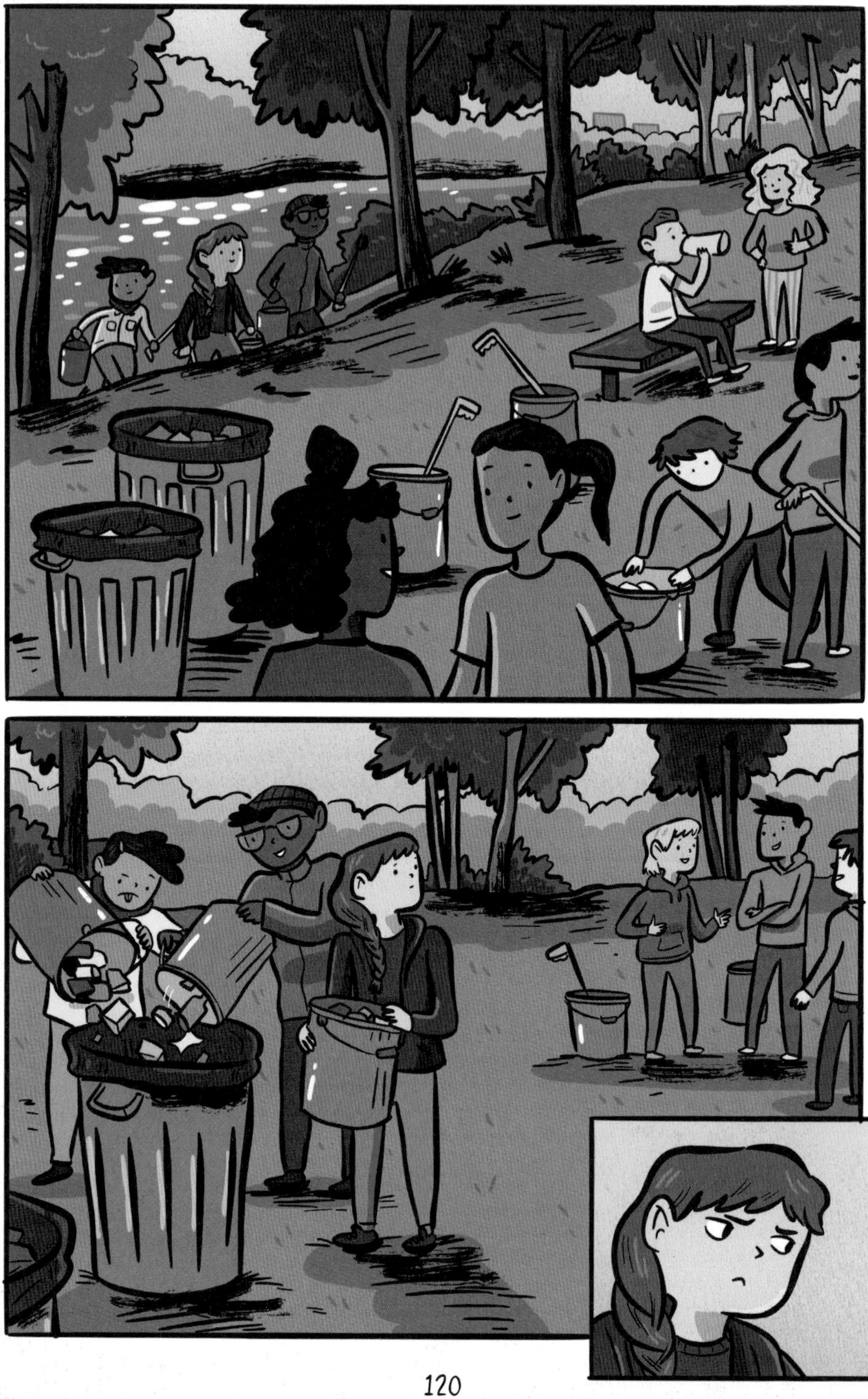

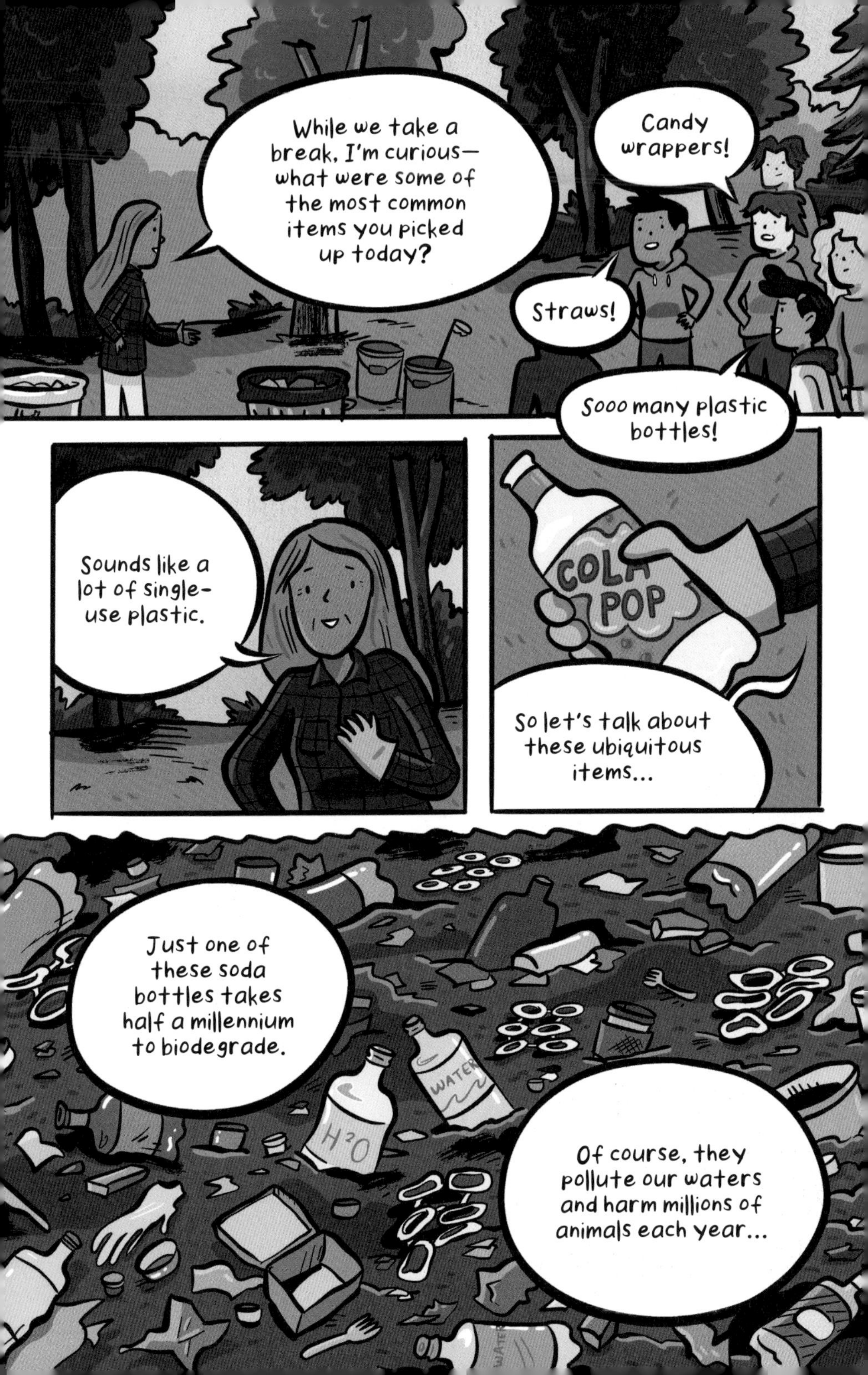
While we take a break, I'm curious—what were some of the most common items you picked up today?
Candy wrappers!
Straws!
Sooo many plastic bottles!
Sounds like a lot of single-use plastic.
COLA POP
So let's talk about these ubiquitous items...
Just one of these soda bottles takes half a millennium to biodegrade.
WATER
H2O
Of course, they pollute our waters and harm millions of animals each year...

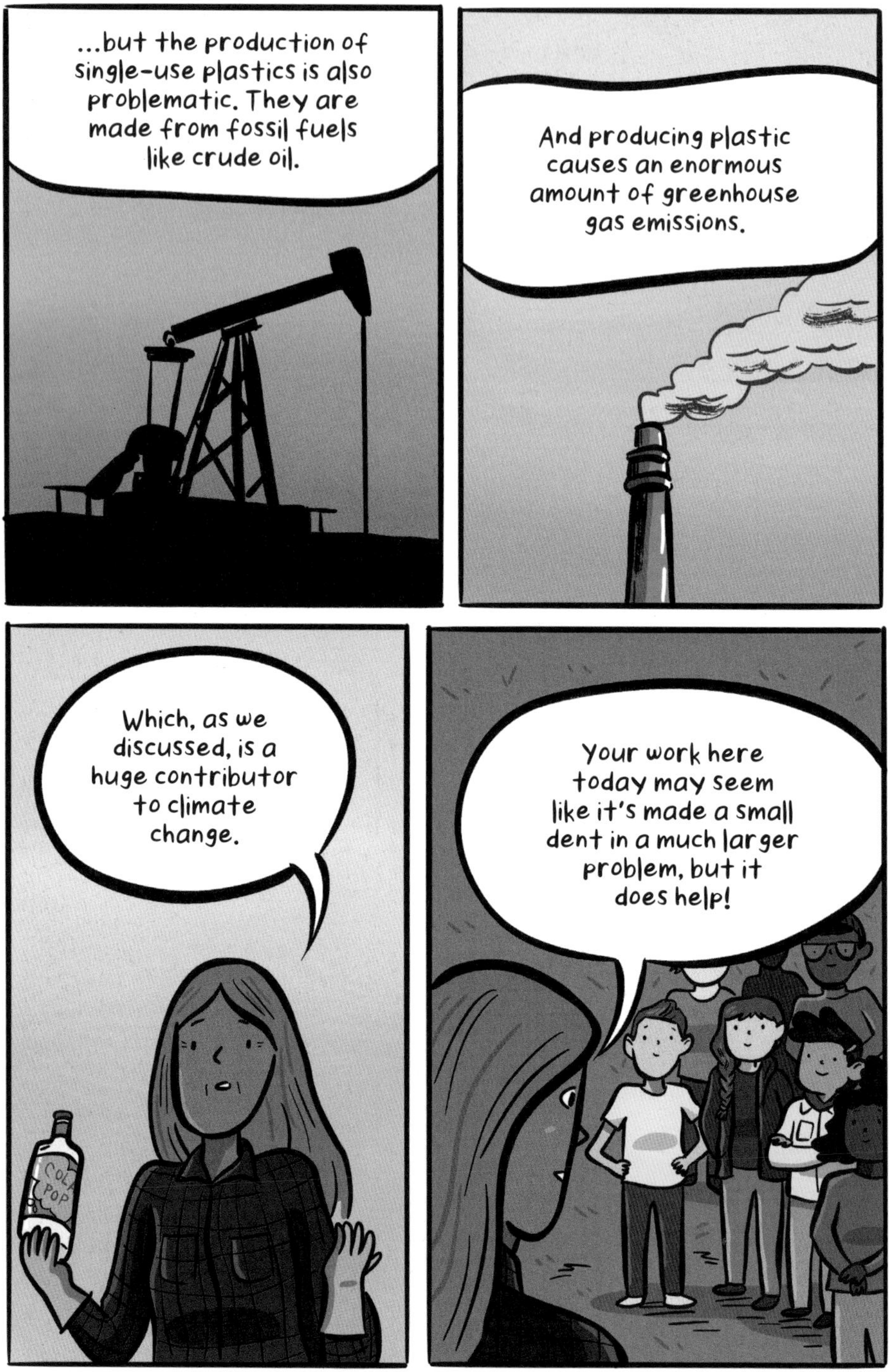
...but the production of single-use plastics is also problematic. They are made from fossil fuels like crude oil.
And producing plastic causes an enormous amount of greenhouse gas emissions.
Which, as we discussed, is a huge contributor to climate change.
COLA POP
Your work here today may seem like it's made a small dent in a much larger problem, but it does help!

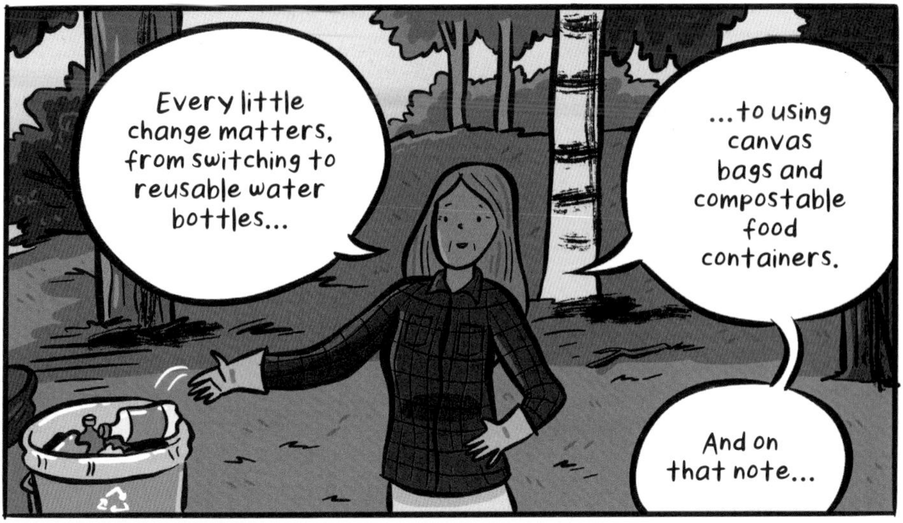
Every little change matters, from switching to reusable water bottles...
...to using canvas bags and compostable food containers.
And on that note...

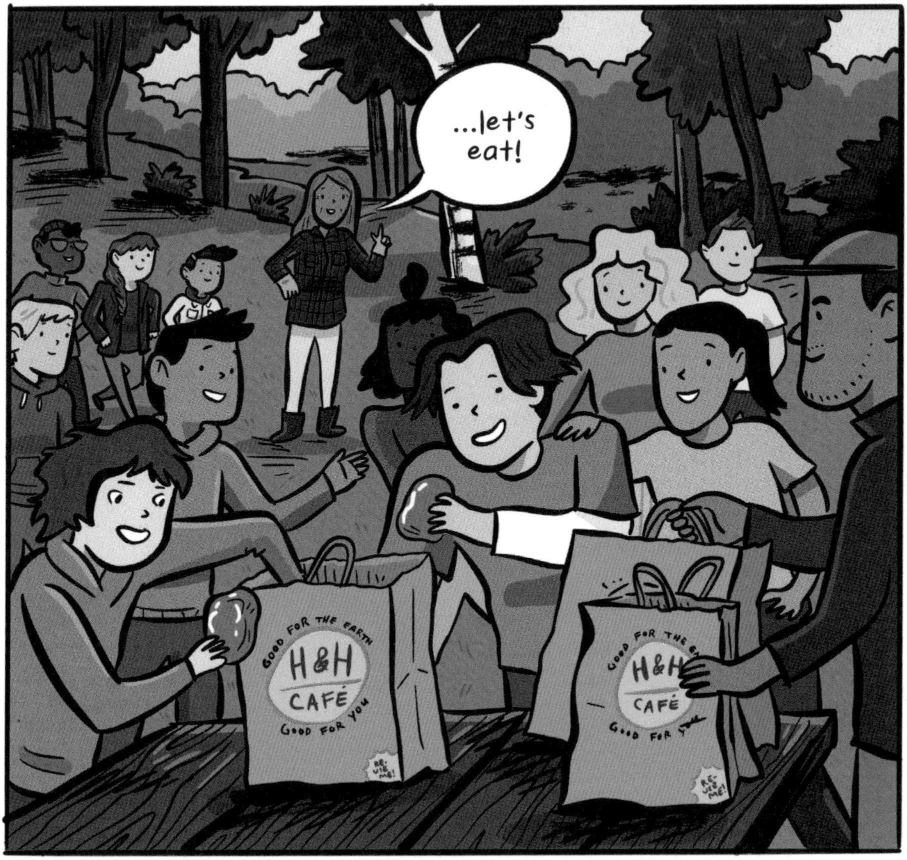
...let's eat!
GOOD FOR THE EARTH
H&H CAFÉ
GOOD FOR YOU
RE-USE ME!

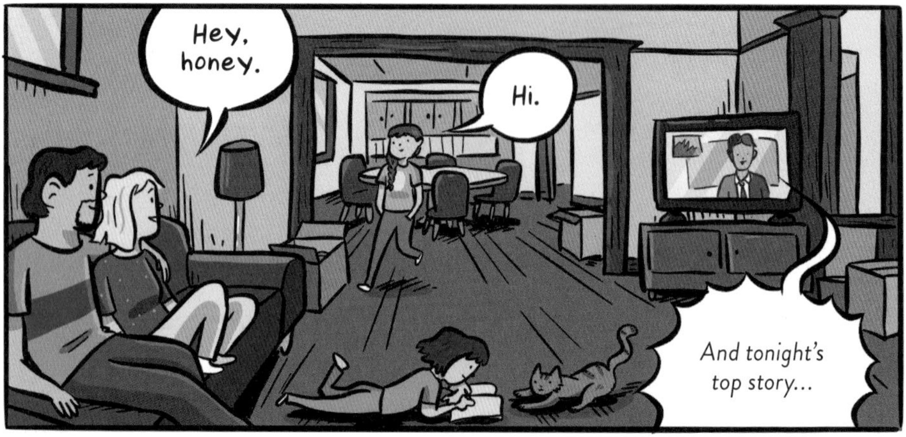
Hey, honey.
Hi.
And tonight's top story...

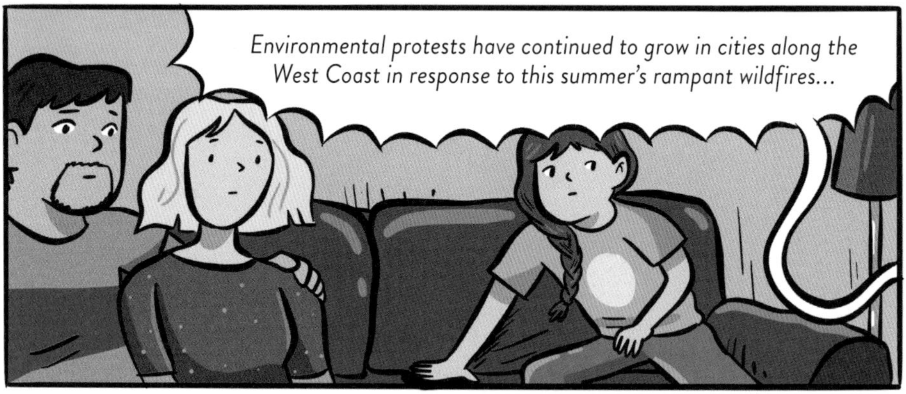
Environmental protests have continued to grow in cities along the West Coast in response to this summer's rampant wildfires...

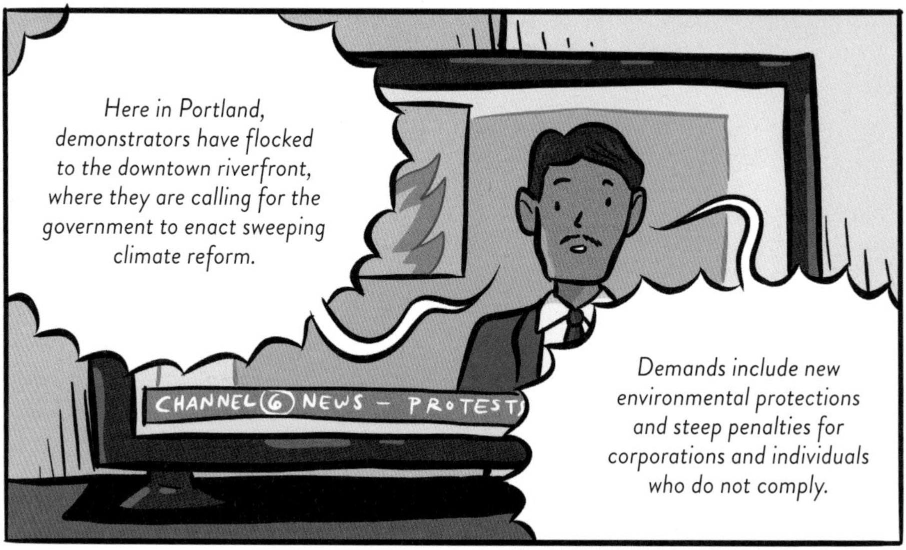
Here in Portland, demonstrators have flocked to the downtown riverfront, where they are calling for the government to enact sweeping climate reform.
CHANNEL 6 NEWS - PROTEST
Demands include new environmental protections and steep penalties for corporations and individuals who do not comply.

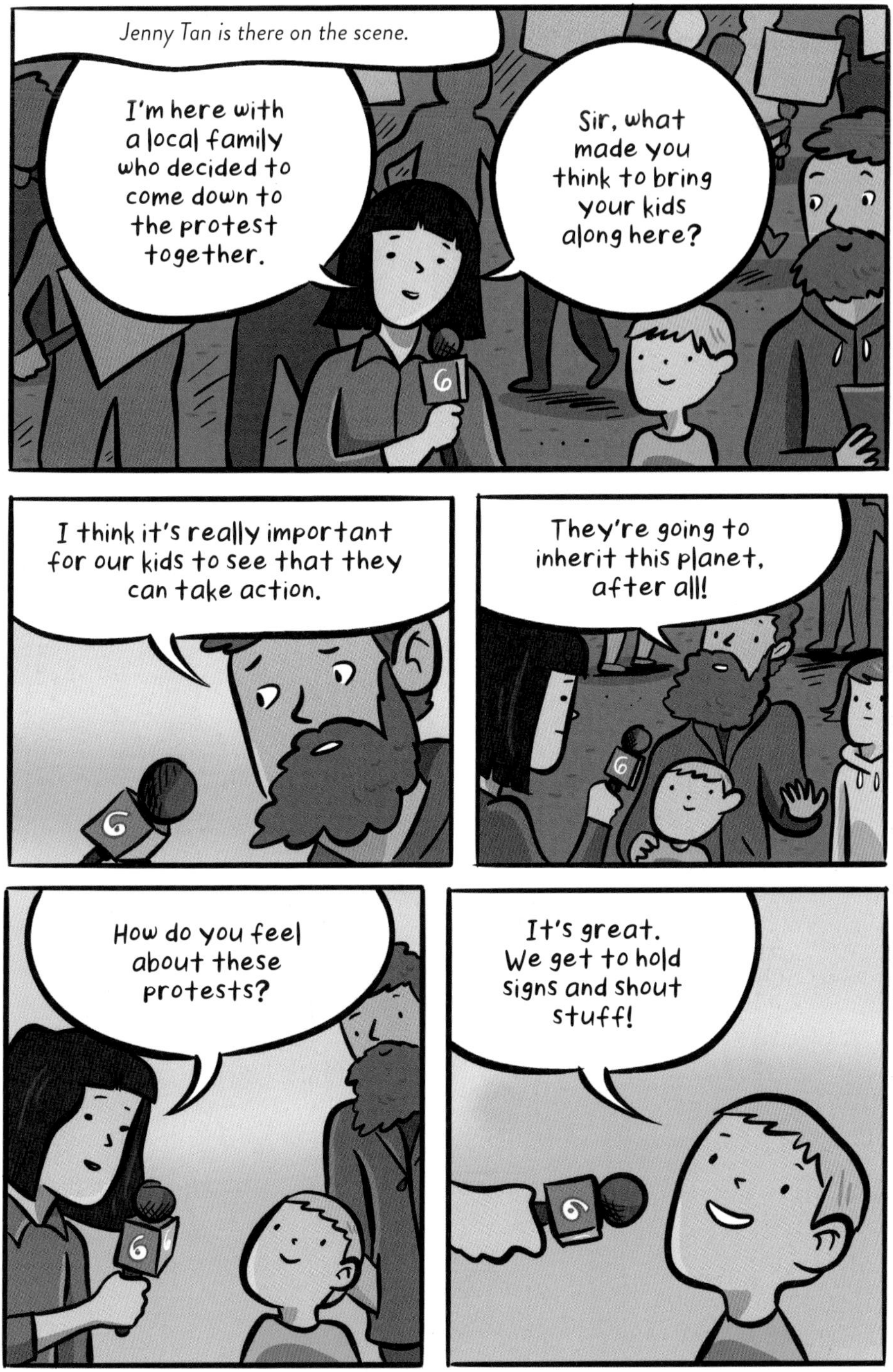
Jenny Tan is there on the scene.
I'm here with a local family who decided to come down to the protest together.
Sir, what made you think to bring your kids along here?
I think it's really important for our kids to see that they can take action.
They're going to inherit this planet, after all!
How do you feel about these protests?
It's great. We get to hold signs and shout stuff!

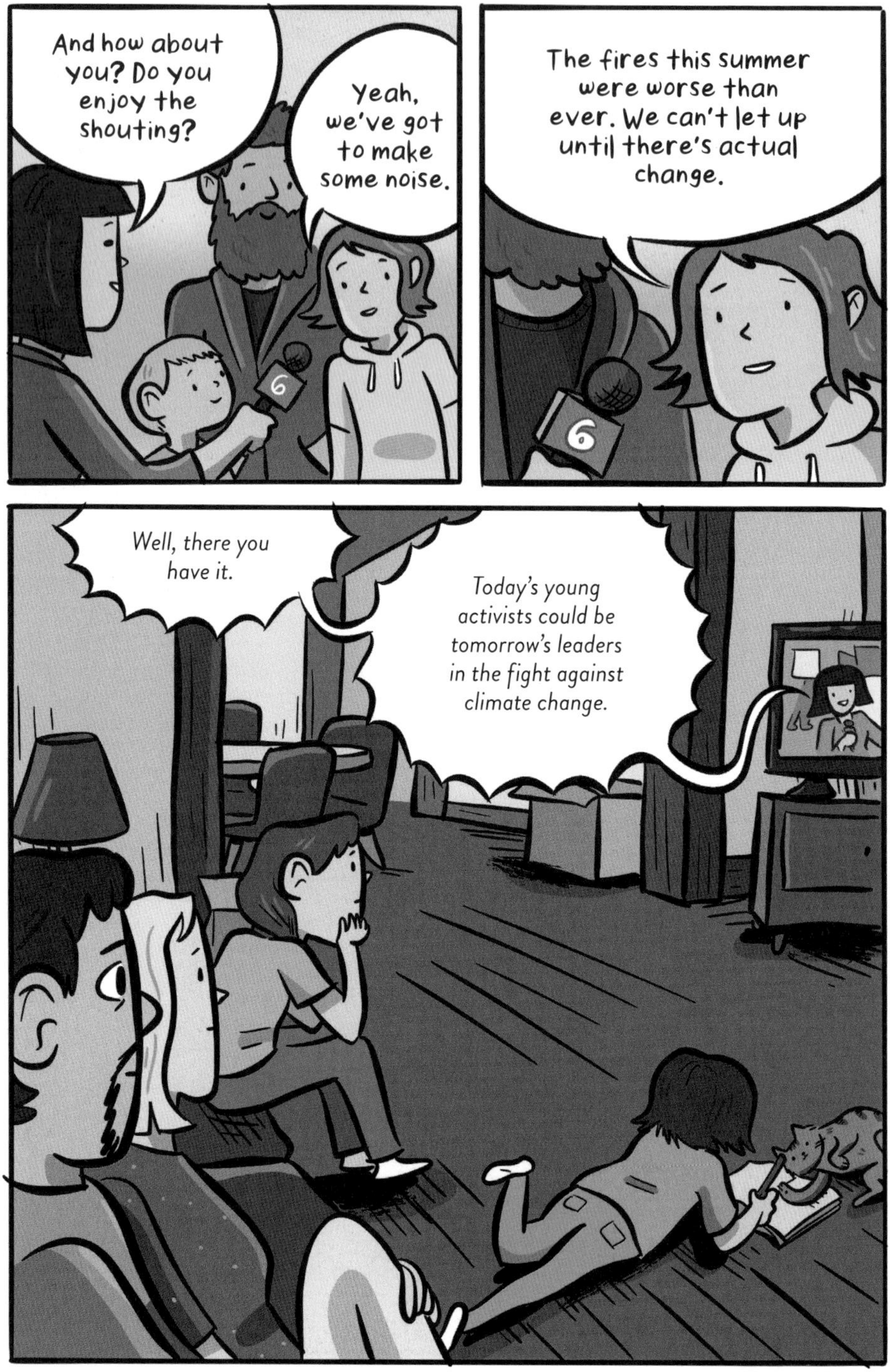

And how about you? Do you enjoy the shouting?
Yeah, we've got to make some noise.
The fires this summer were worse than ever. We can't let up until there's actual change.
Well, there you have it.
Today's young activists could be tomorrow's leaders in the fight against climate change.
6
6

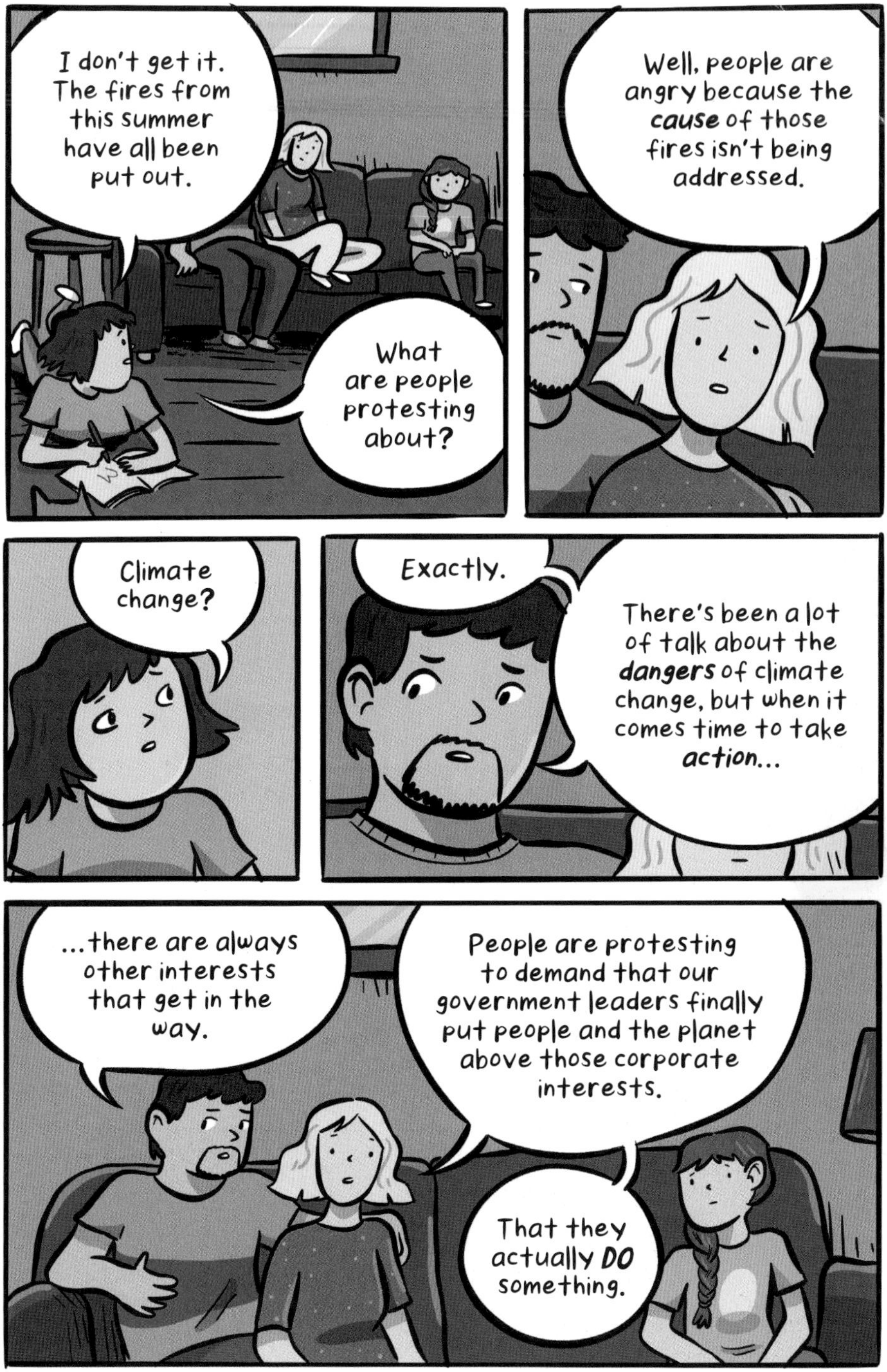
I don't get it. The fires from this summer have all been put out.
What are people protesting about?
Well, people are angry because the *cause* of those fires isn't being addressed.
Climate change?
Exactly.
There's been a lot of talk about the *dangers* of climate change, but when it comes time to take *action*...
...there are always other interests that get in the way.
People are protesting to demand that our government leaders finally put people and the planet above those corporate interests.
That they actually *DO* something.

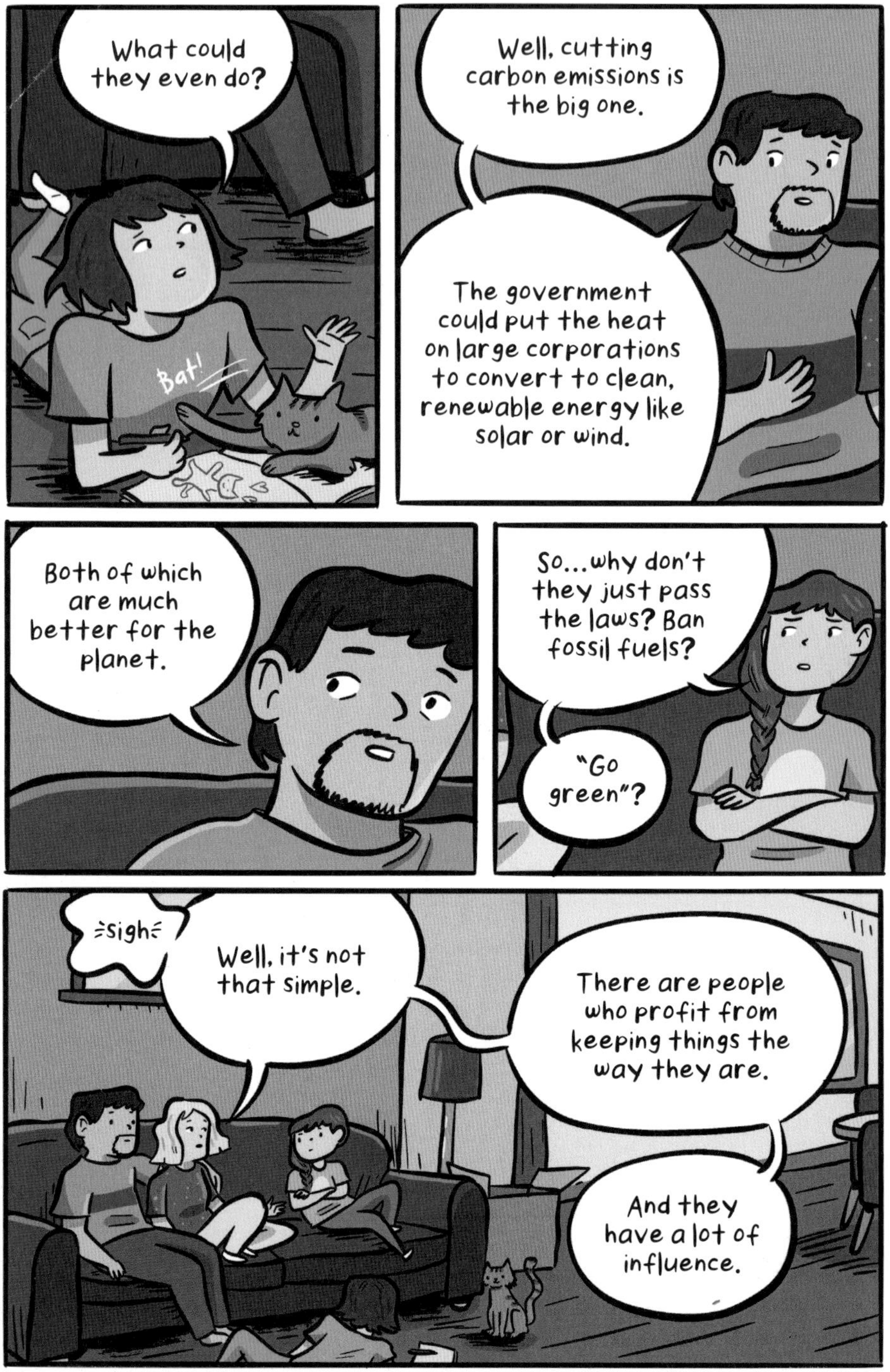
What could they even do?
Well, cutting carbon emissions is the big one.
The government could put the heat on large corporations to convert to clean, renewable energy like solar or wind.
Bat!
Both of which are much better for the planet.
So...why don't they just pass the laws? Ban fossil fuels?
"Go green"?
sigh
Well, it's not that simple.
There are people who profit from keeping things the way they are.
And they have a lot of influence.

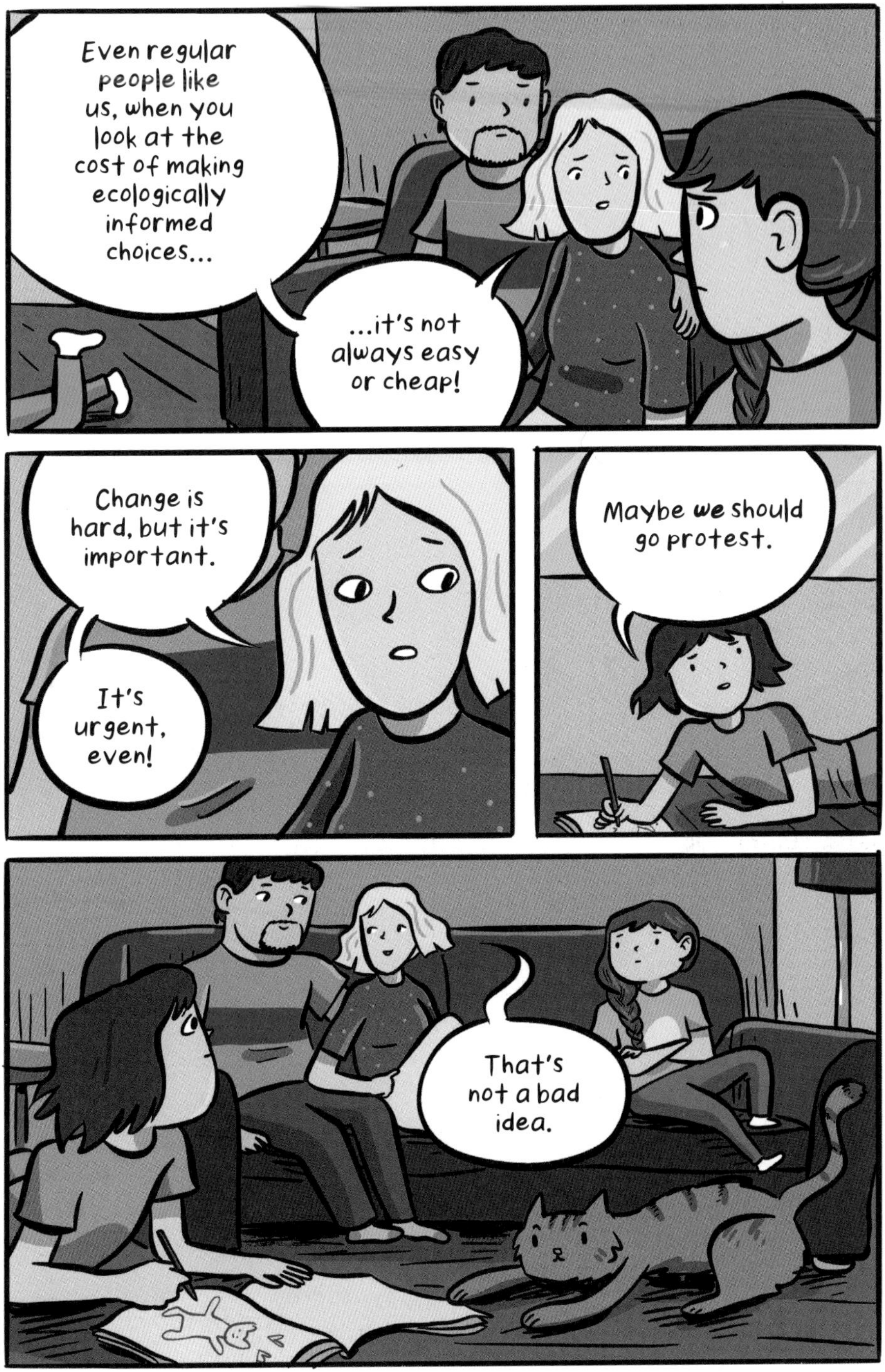
Even regular people like us, when you look at the cost of making ecologically informed choices...
...it's not always easy or cheap!
Change is hard, but it's important.
It's urgent, even!
Maybe *we* should go protest.
That's not a bad idea.

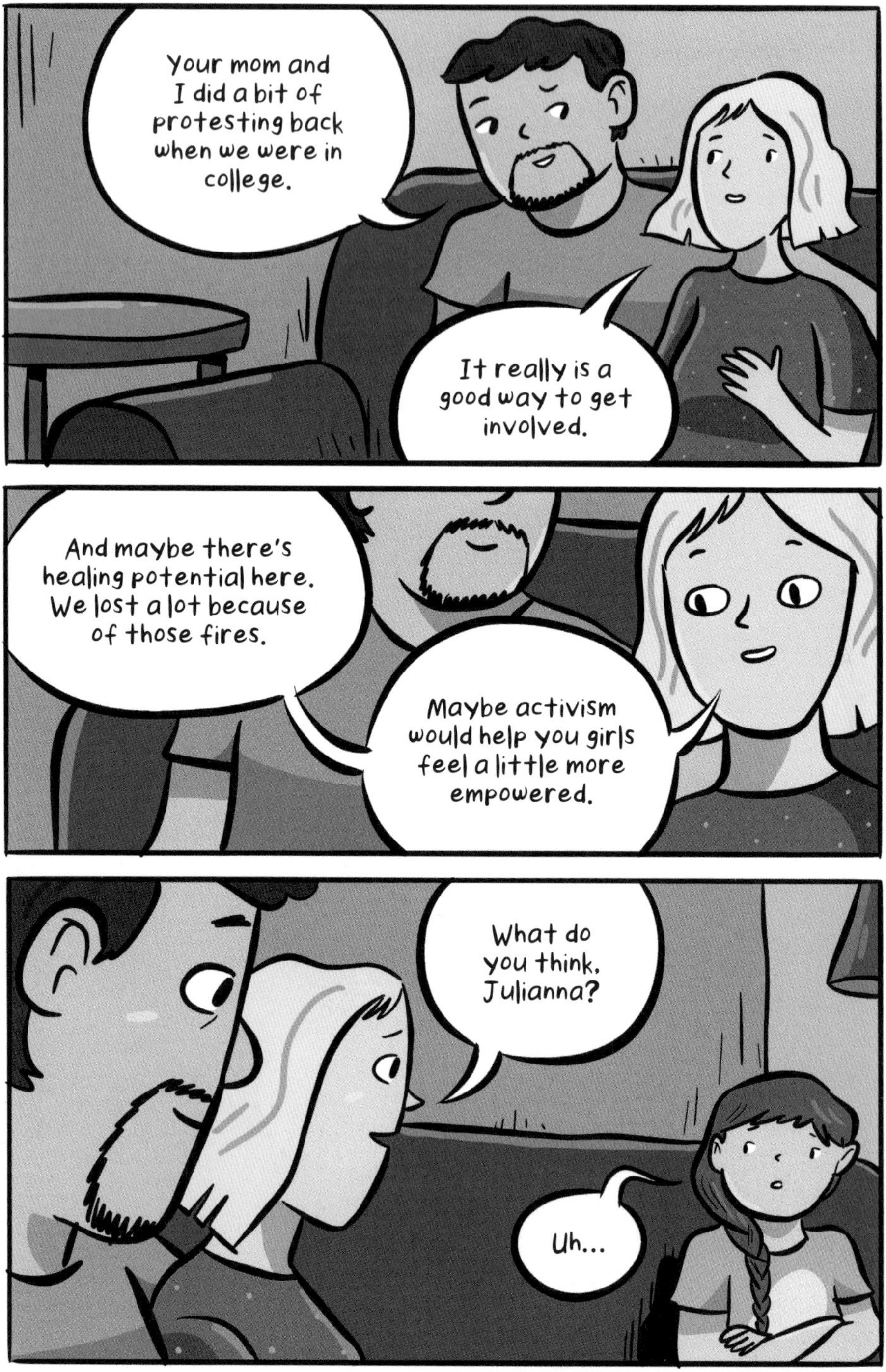
Your mom and I did a bit of protesting back when we were in college.
It really is a good way to get involved.
And maybe there's healing potential here. We lost a lot because of those fires.
Maybe activism would help you girls feel a little more empowered.
What do you think, Julianna?
Uh...

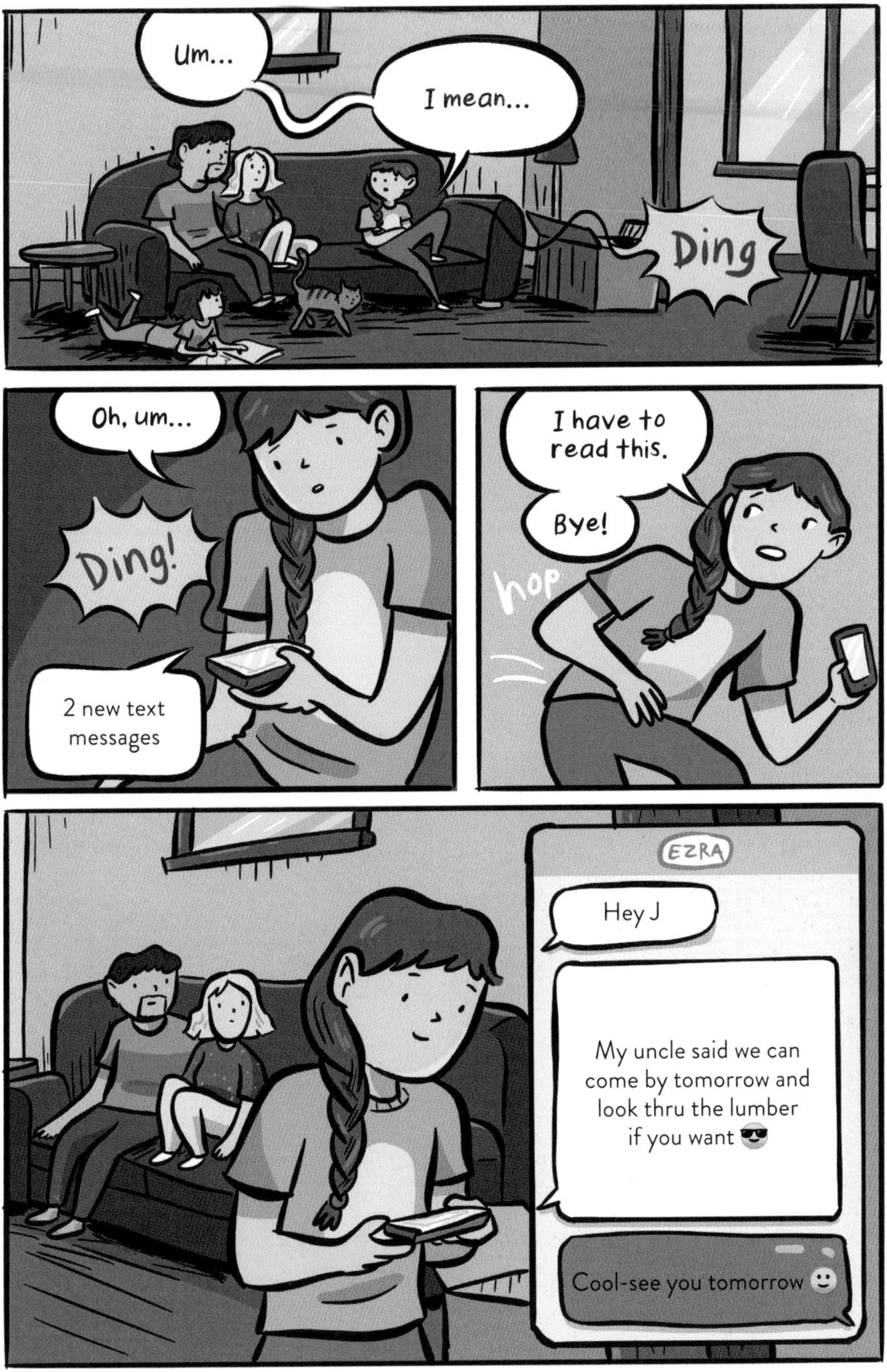
Um...
I mean...
Ding
Oh, um...
Ding!
2 new text messages
I have to read this.
Bye!
hop
EZRA
Hey J
My uncle said we can come by tomorrow and look thru the lumber if you want 😎
Cool-see you tomorrow 🙂

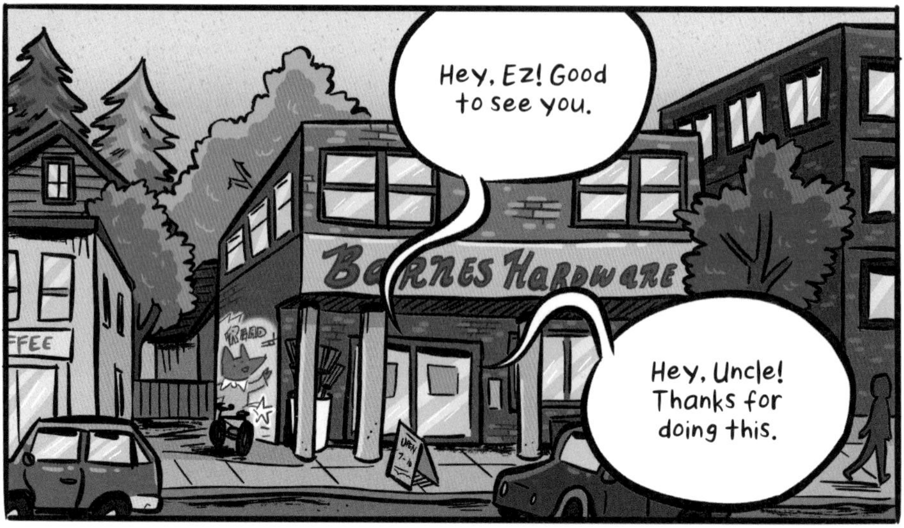
Hey, Ez! Good to see you.
Hey, Uncle! Thanks for doing this.

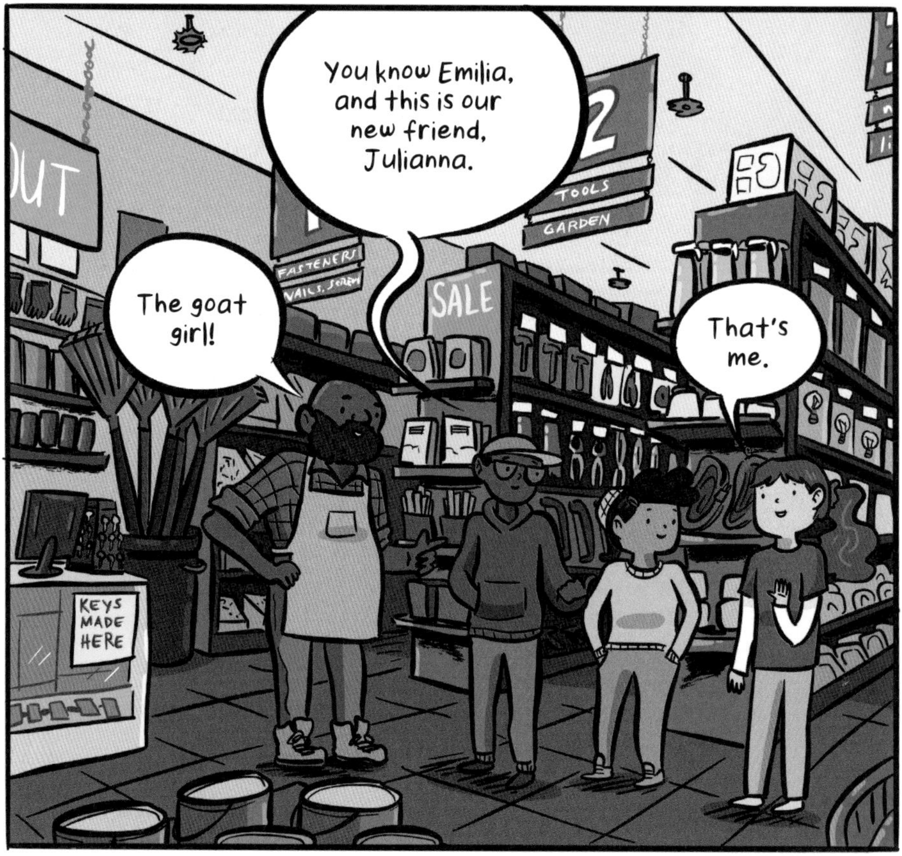
You know Emilia, and this is our new friend, Julianna.
The goat girl!
That's me.
TOOLS
GARDEN
FASTENERS
SALE
KEYS MADE HERE

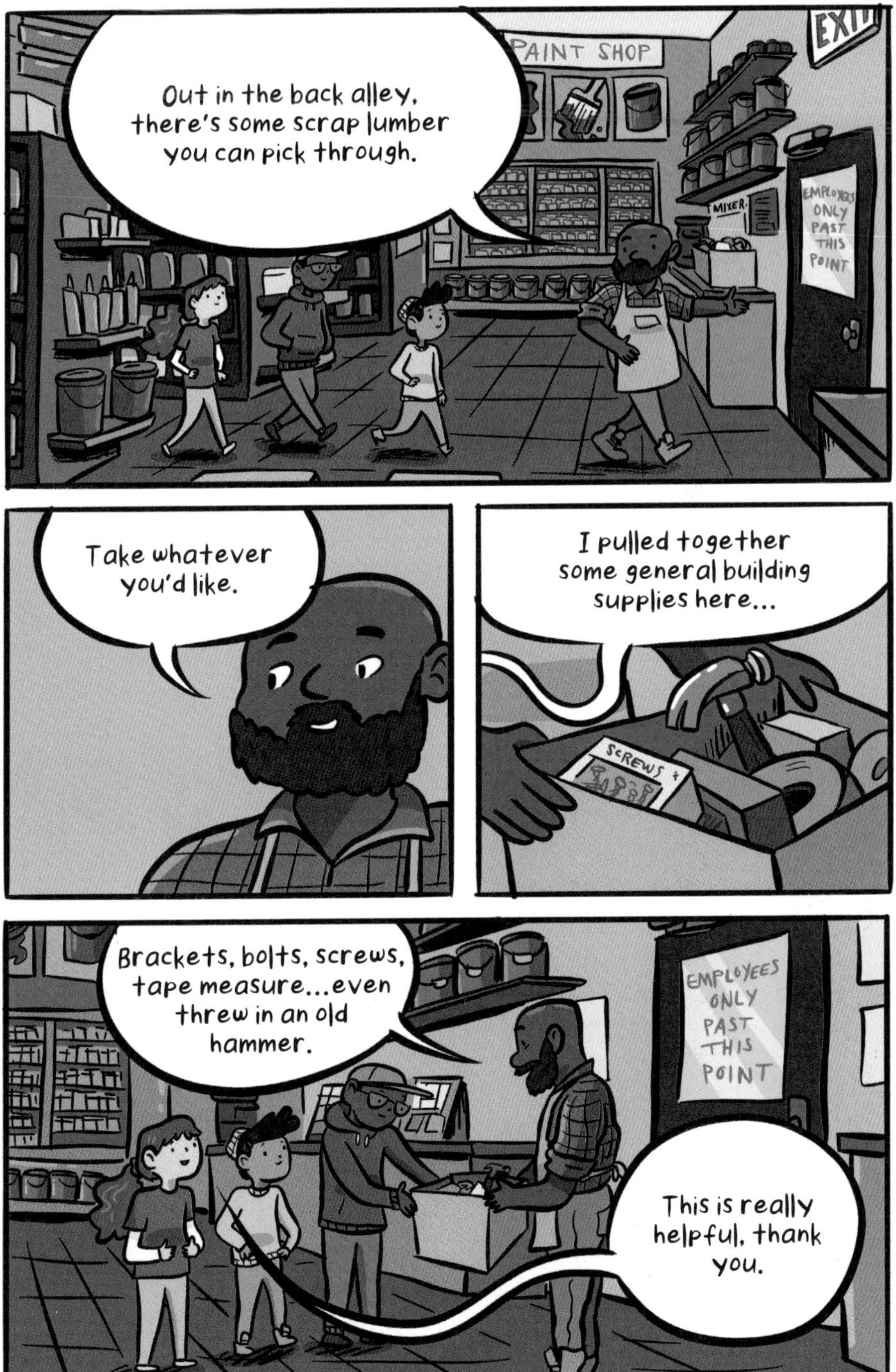
PAINT SHOP
EXIT
Out in the back alley, there's some scrap lumber you can pick through.
MIXER
EMPLOYEES ONLY PAST THIS POINT
Take whatever you'd like.
I pulled together some general building supplies here...
SCREWS
Brackets, bolts, screws, tape measure...even threw in an old hammer.
EMPLOYEES ONLY PAST THIS POINT
This is really helpful, thank you.

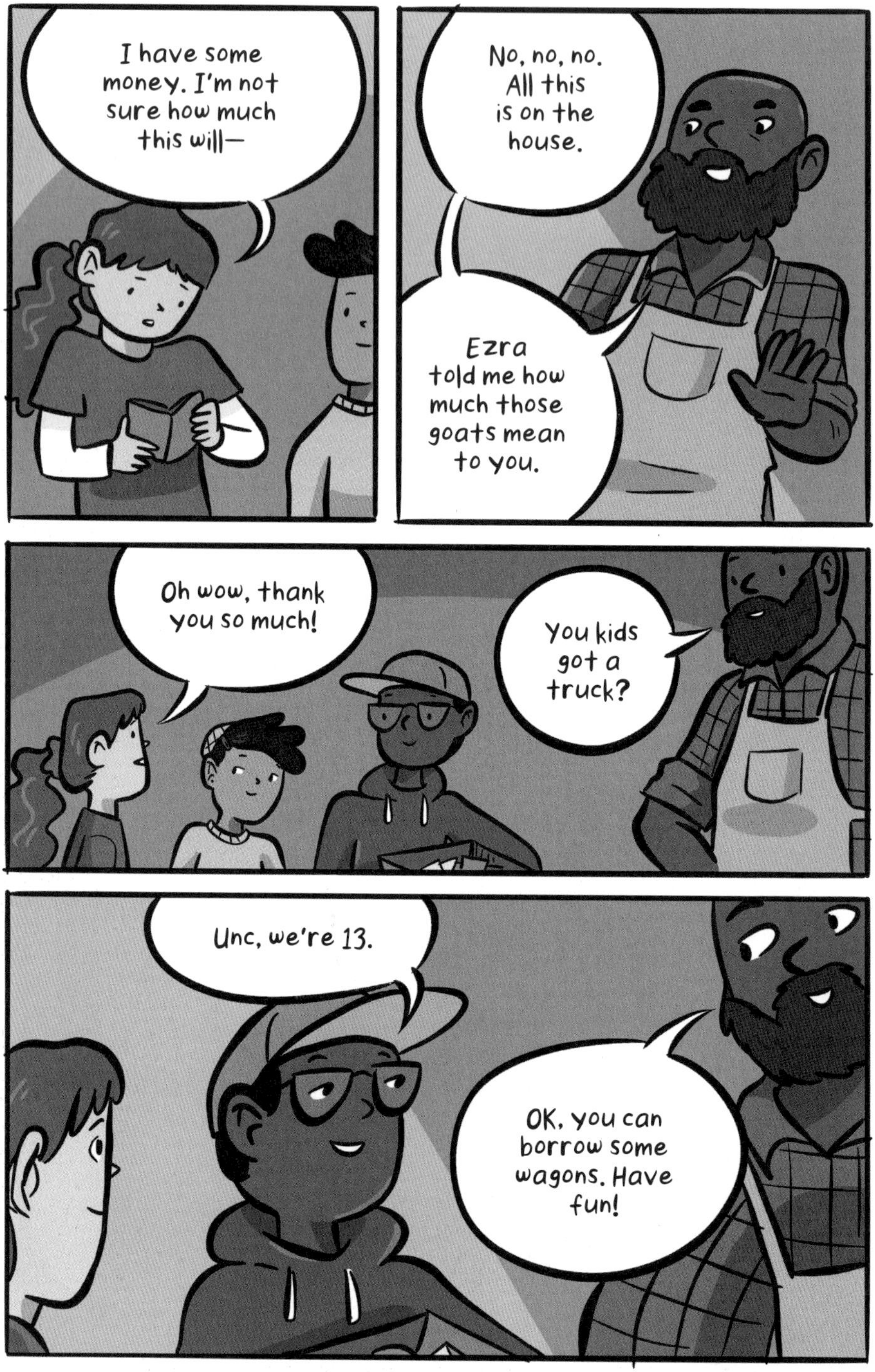
I have some money. I'm not sure how much this will—
No, no, no. All this is on the house.
Ezra told me how much those goats mean to you.
Oh wow, thank you so much!
You kids got a truck?
Unc, we're 13.
OK, you can borrow some wagons. Have fun!

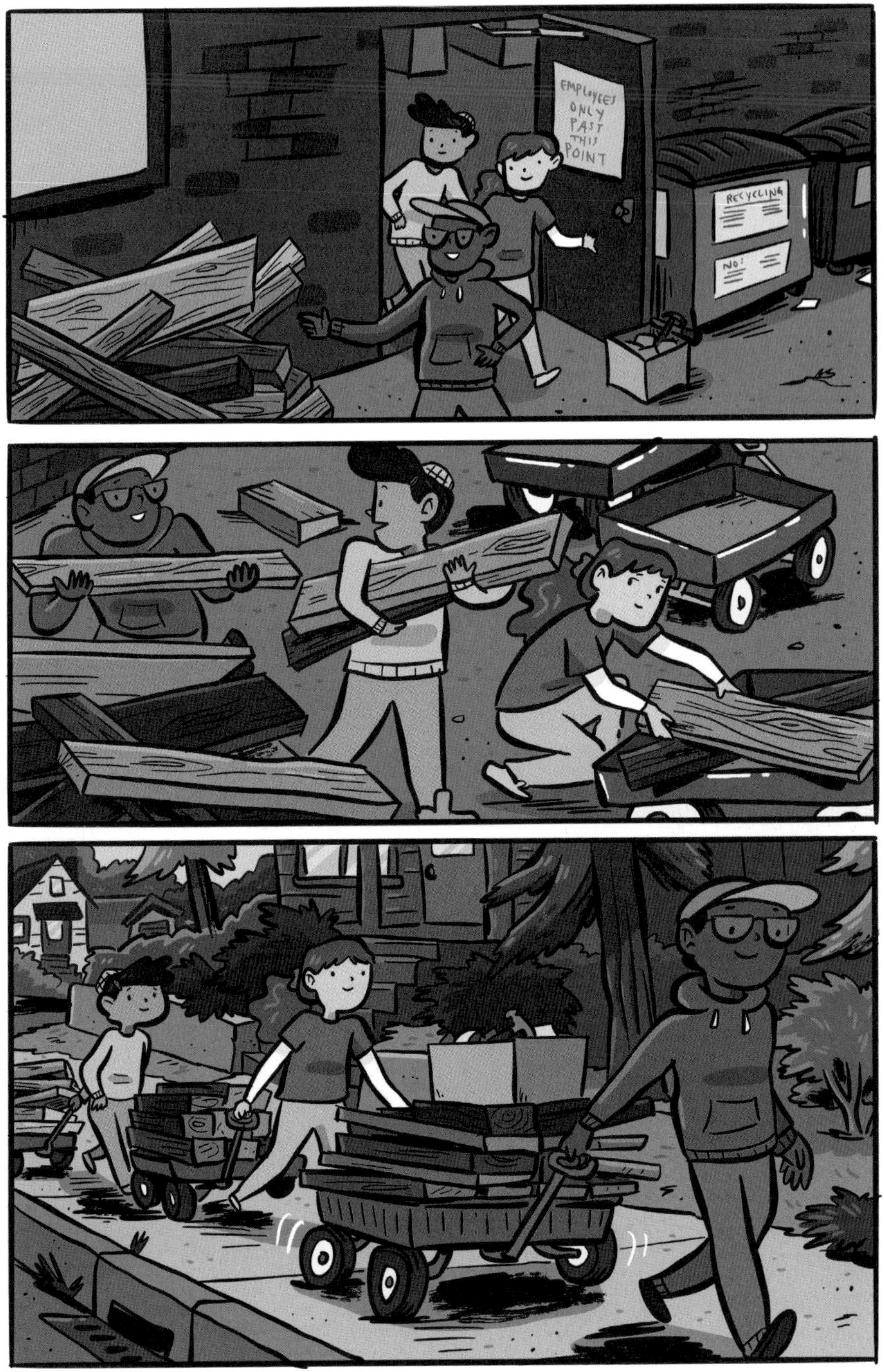
EMPLOYEES ONLY PAST THIS POINT
RECYCLING
NO!

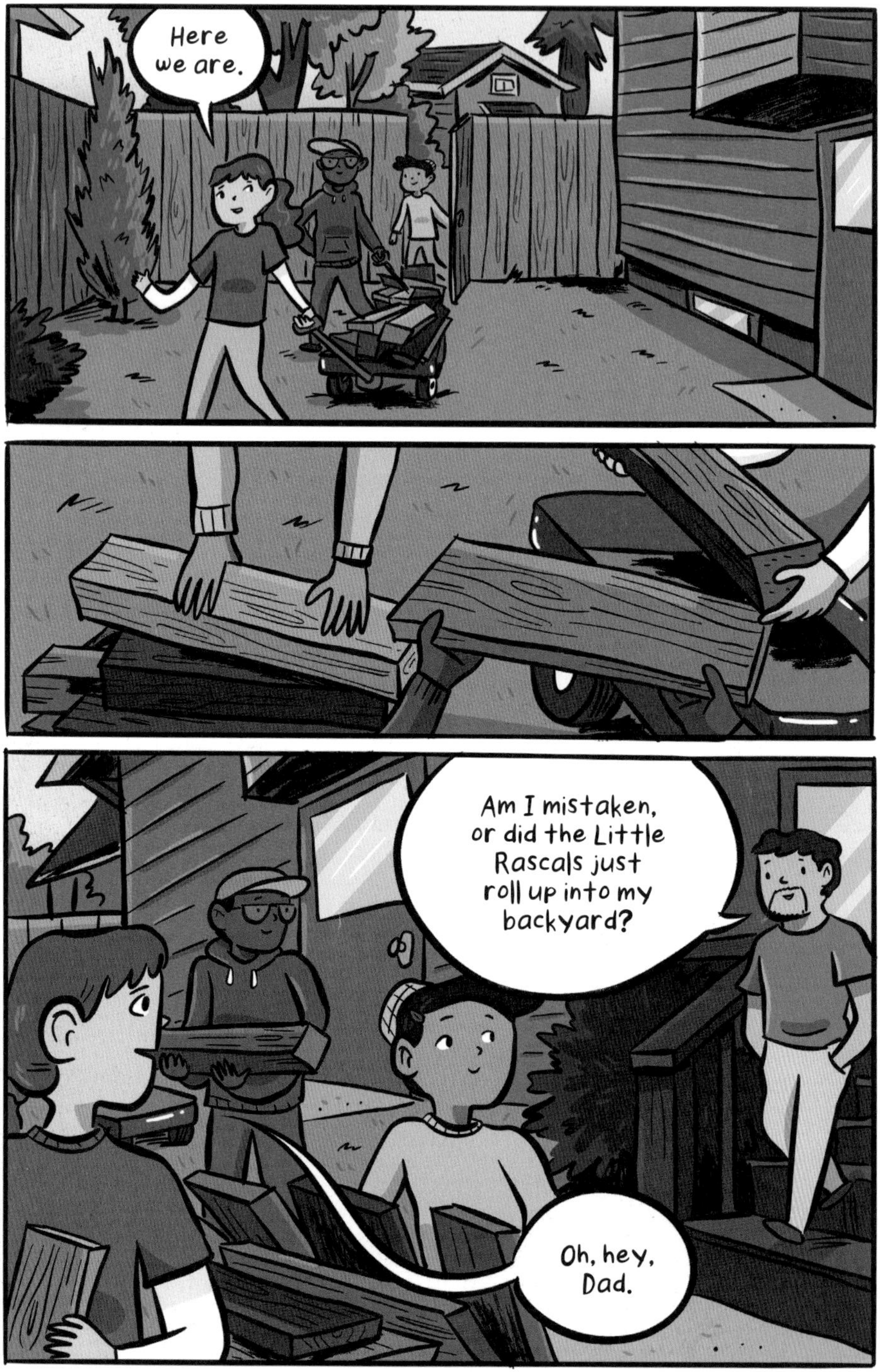
Here we are.
Am I mistaken, or did the Little Rascals just roll up into my backyard?
Oh, hey, Dad.

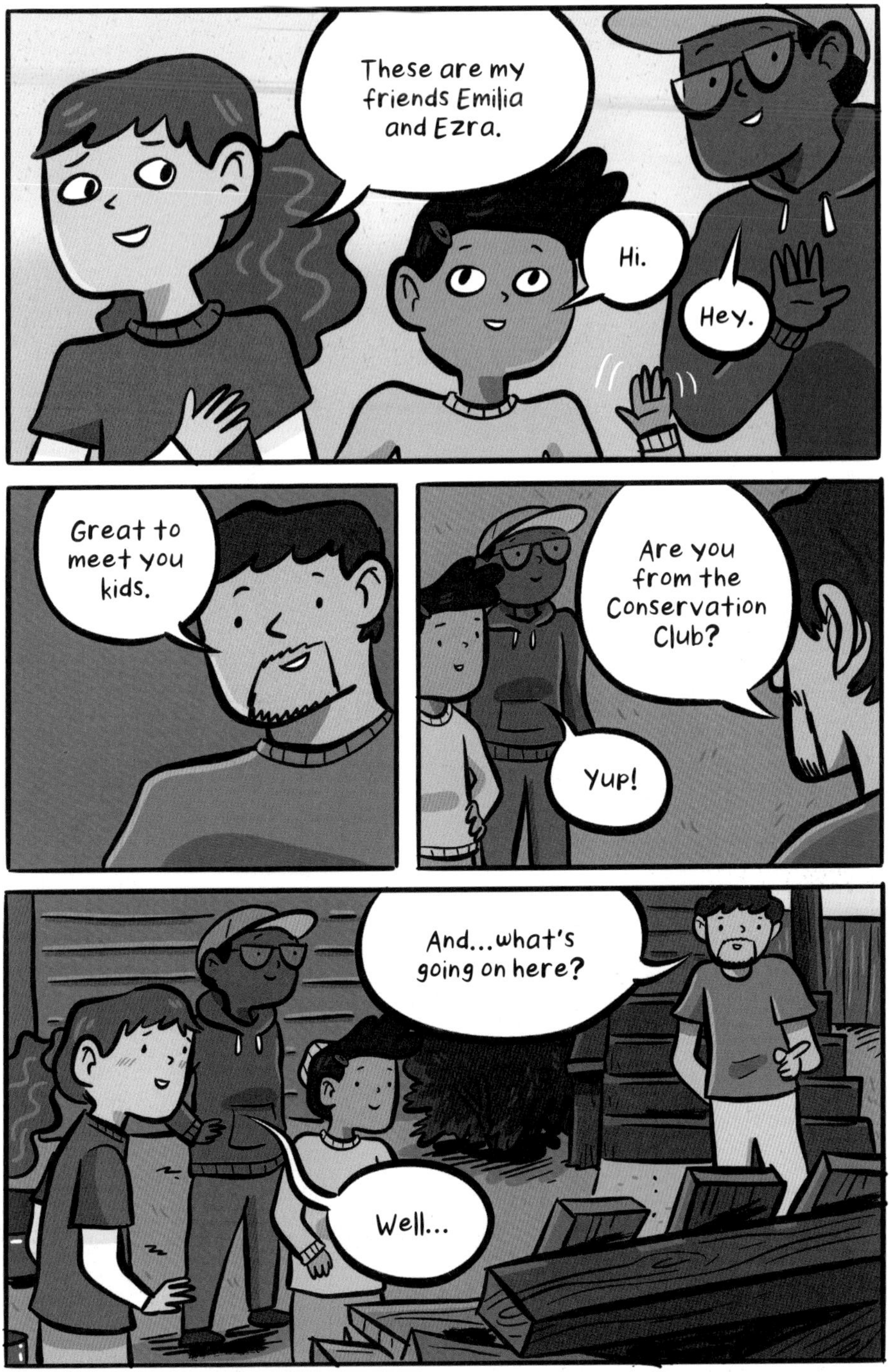
These are my friends Emilia and Ezra.
Hi.
Hey.
Great to meet you kids.
Are you from the Conservation Club?
Yup!
And...what's going on here?
Well...

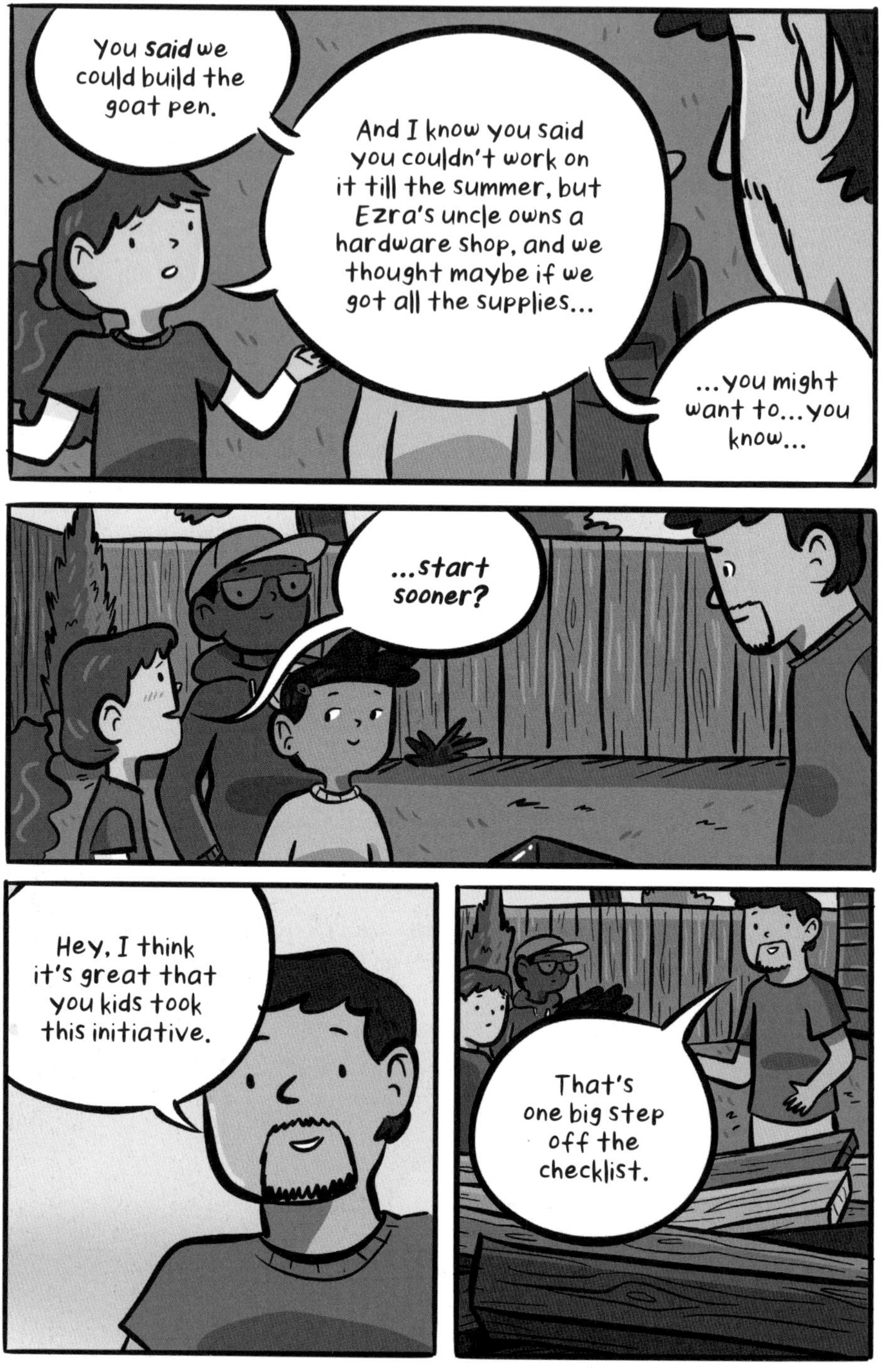
You **said** we could build the goat pen.
And I know you said you couldn't work on it till the summer, but Ezra's uncle owns a hardware shop, and we thought maybe if we got all the supplies...
...you might want to...you know...
...start sooner?
Hey, I think it's great that you kids took this initiative.
That's one big step off the checklist.

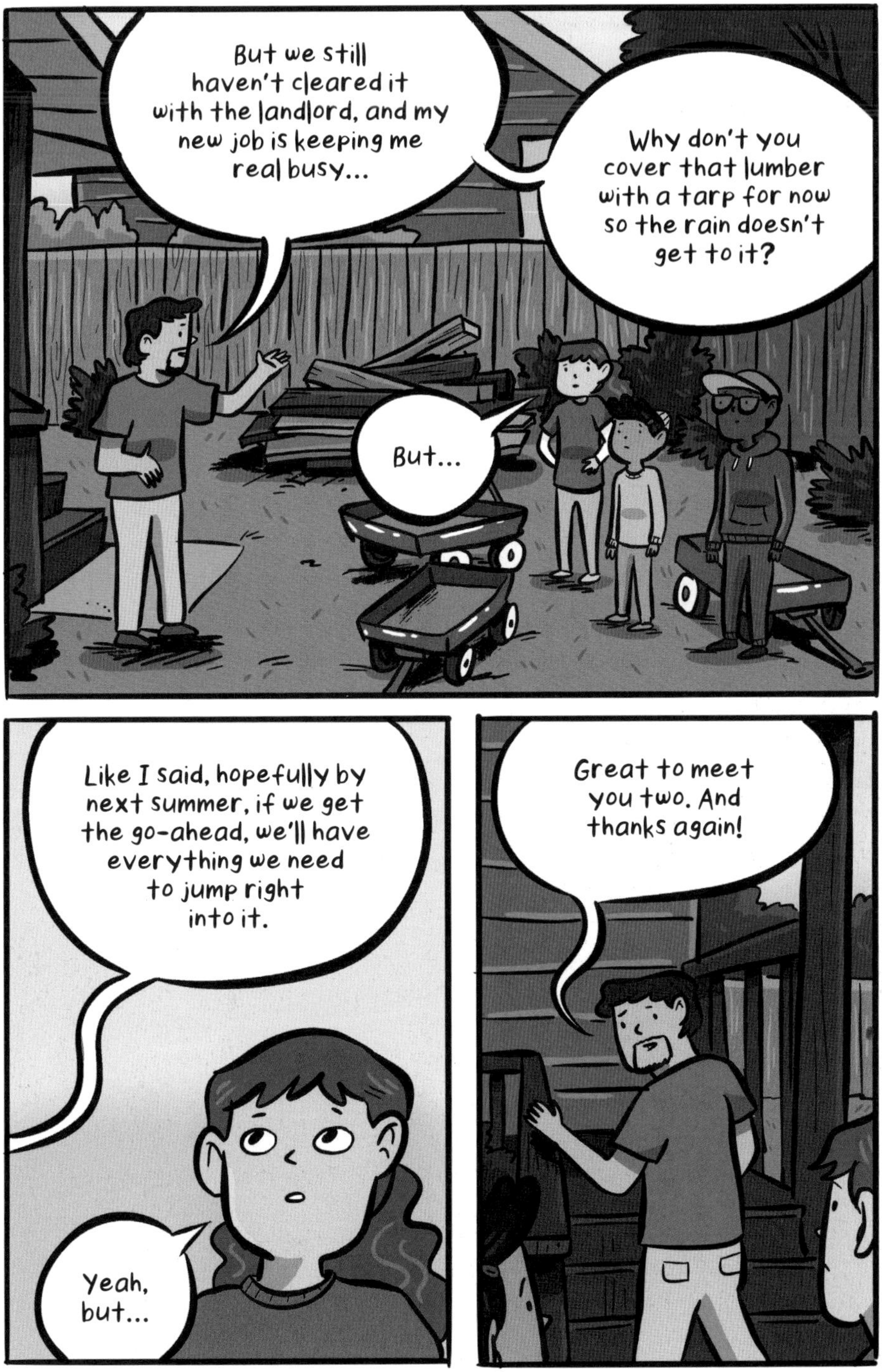
But we still haven't cleared it with the landlord, and my new job is keeping me real busy...
Why don't you cover that lumber with a tarp for now so the rain doesn't get to it?
But...
Like I said, hopefully by next summer, if we get the go-ahead, we'll have everything we need to jump right into it.
Yeah, but...
Great to meet you two. And thanks again!

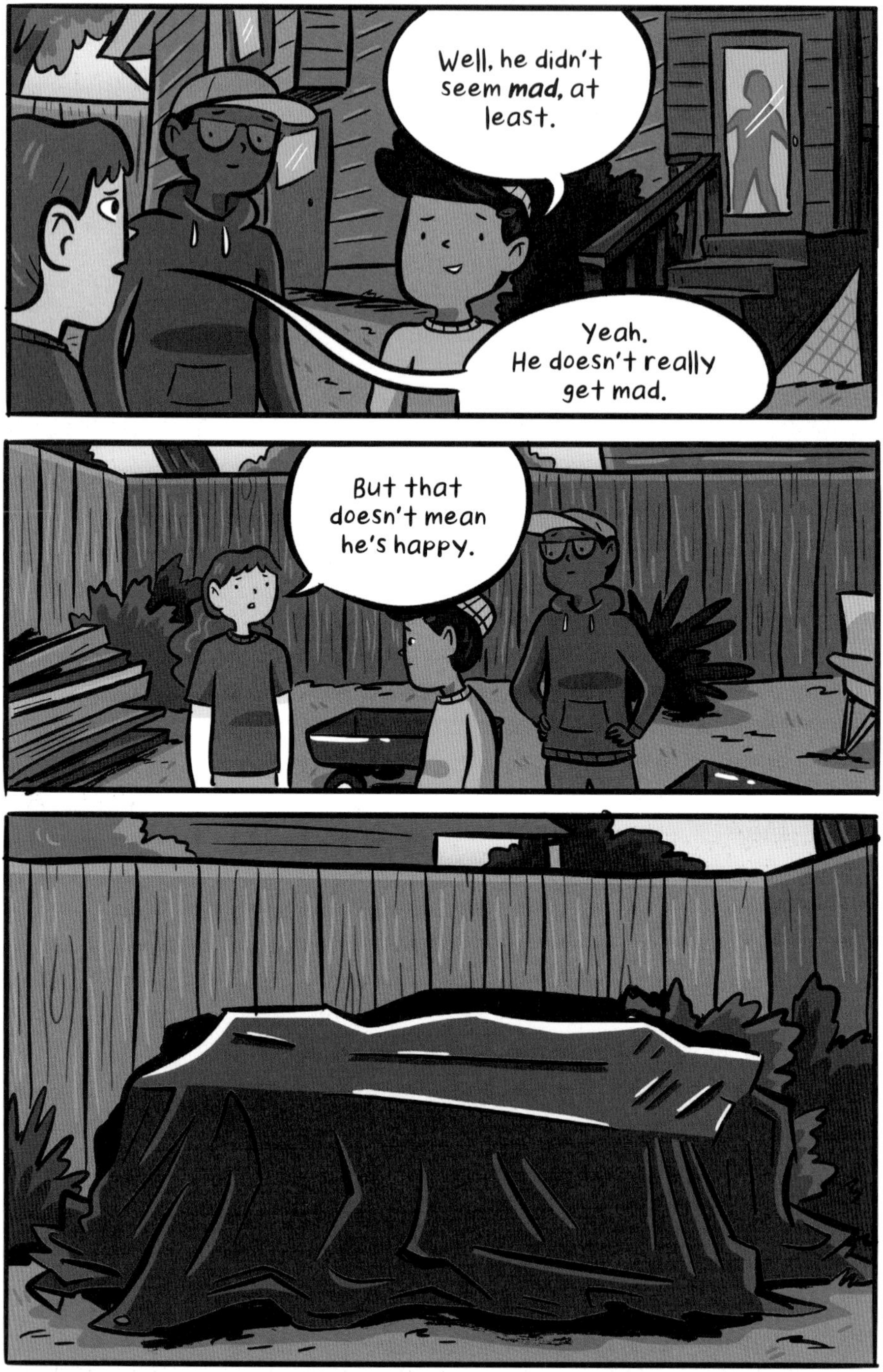
Well, he didn't seem **mad**, at least.
Yeah. He doesn't really get mad.
But that doesn't mean he's happy.

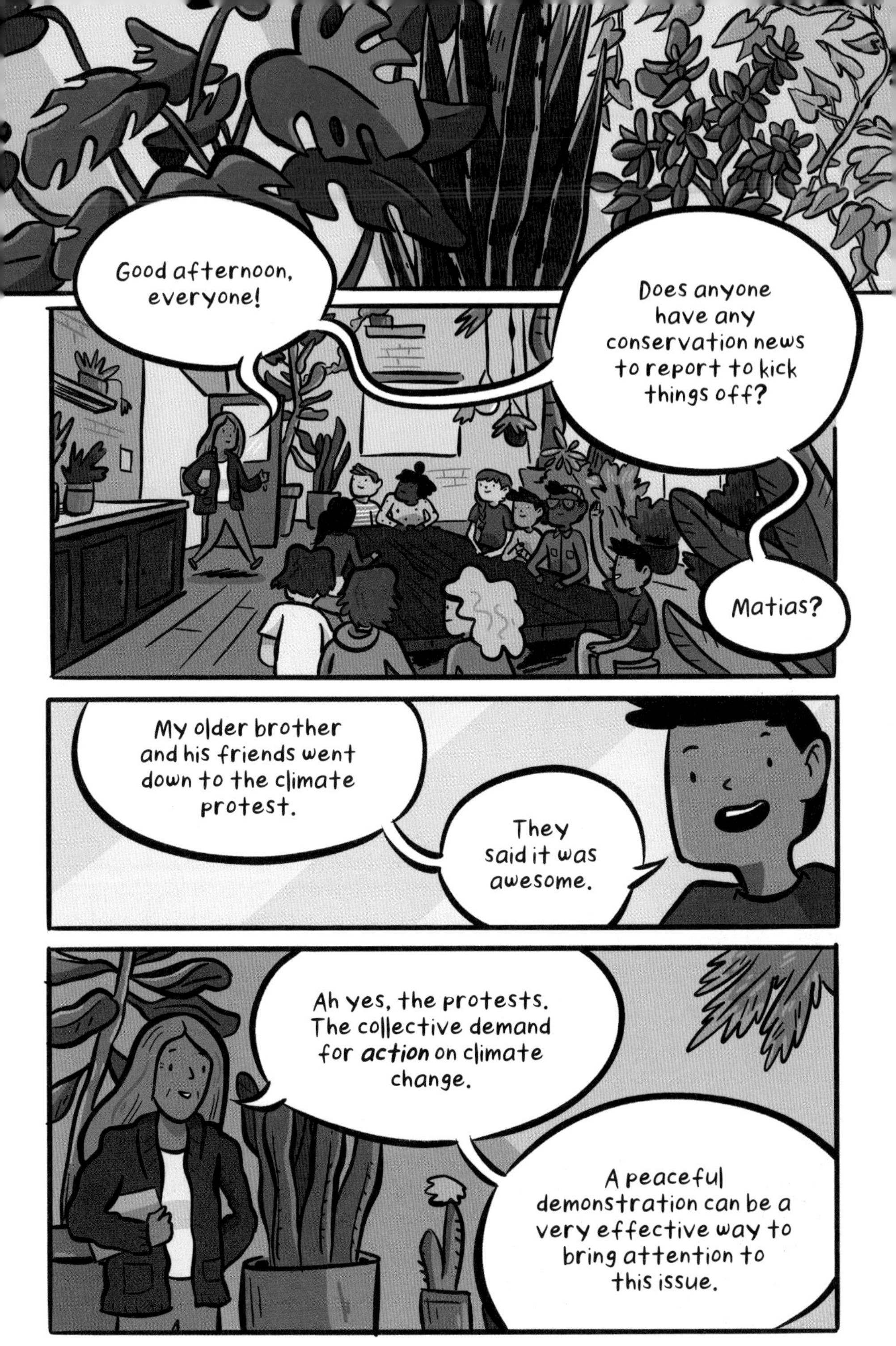
Good afternoon, everyone!
Does anyone have any conservation news to report to kick things off?
Matias?
My older brother and his friends went down to the climate protest.
They said it was awesome.
Ah yes, the protests. The collective demand for *action* on climate change.
A peaceful demonstration can be a very effective way to bring attention to this issue.

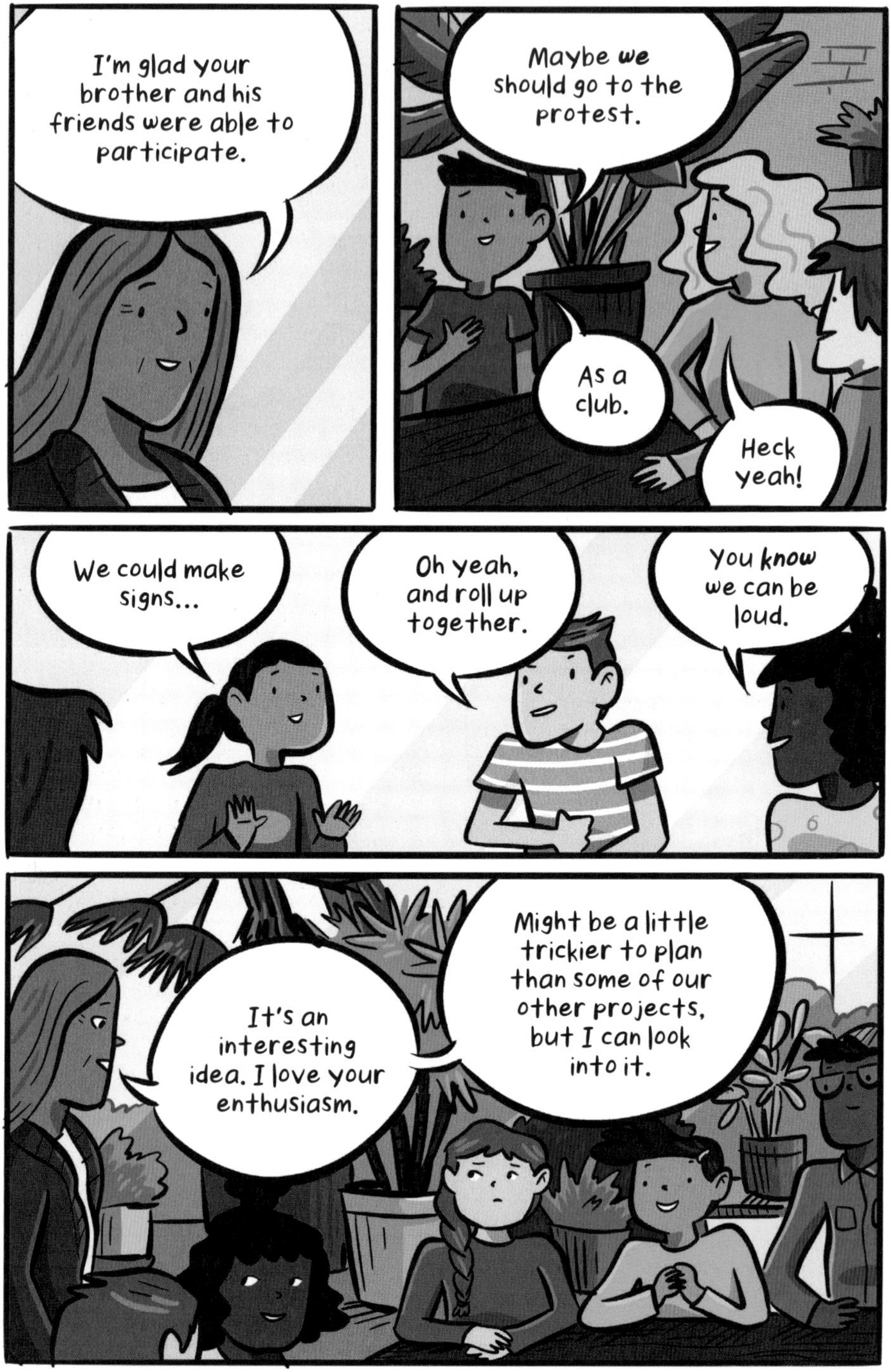
I'm glad your brother and his friends were able to participate.
Maybe we should go to the protest.
As a club.
Heck yeah!
We could make signs...
Oh yeah, and roll up together.
You know we can be loud.
It's an interesting idea. I love your enthusiasm.
Might be a little trickier to plan than some of our other projects, but I can look into it.

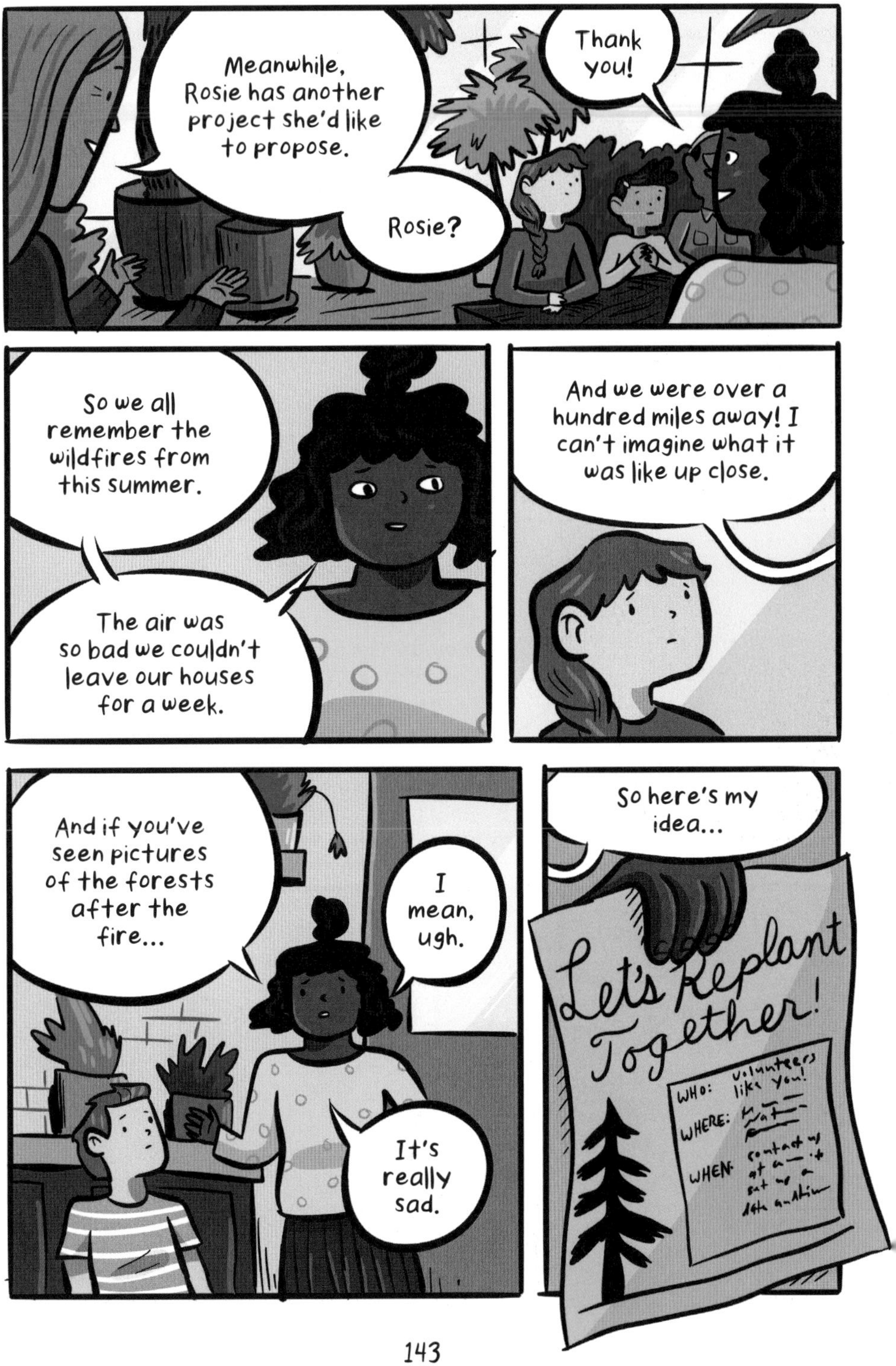
Meanwhile, Rosie has another project she'd like to propose.
Rosie?
Thank you!
So we all remember the wildfires from this summer.
The air was so bad we couldn't leave our houses for a week.
And we were over a hundred miles away! I can't imagine what it was like up close.
And if you've seen pictures of the forests after the fire...
I mean, ugh.
It's really sad.
So here's my idea...
Let's Replant Together!
WHO: volunteers like you!
WHERE:
WHEN:

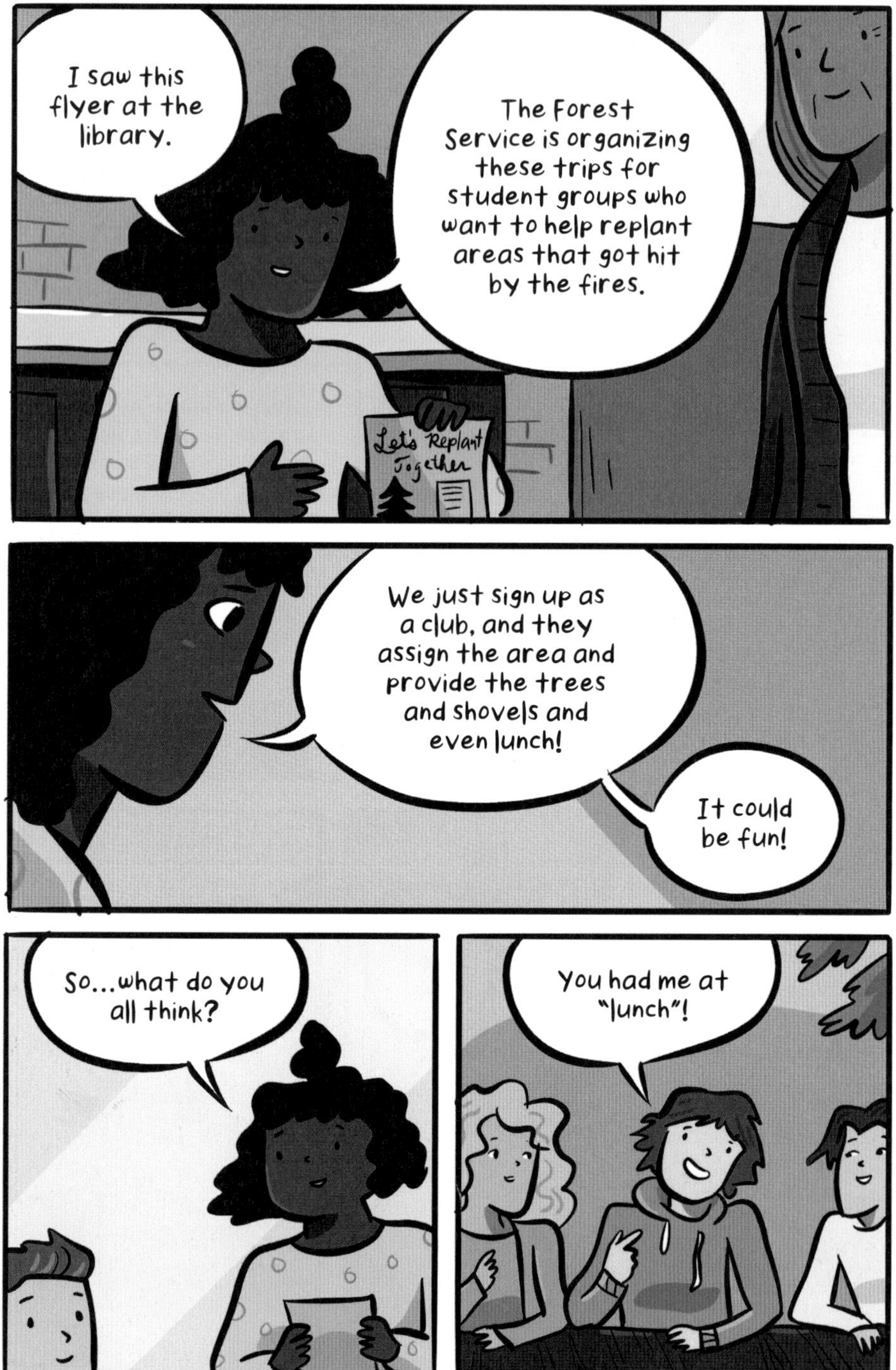
I saw this flyer at the library.
The Forest Service is organizing these trips for student groups who want to help replant areas that got hit by the fires.
Let's Replant Together
We just sign up as a club, and they assign the area and provide the trees and shovels and even lunch!
It could be fun!
So...what do you all think?
You had me at "lunch"!

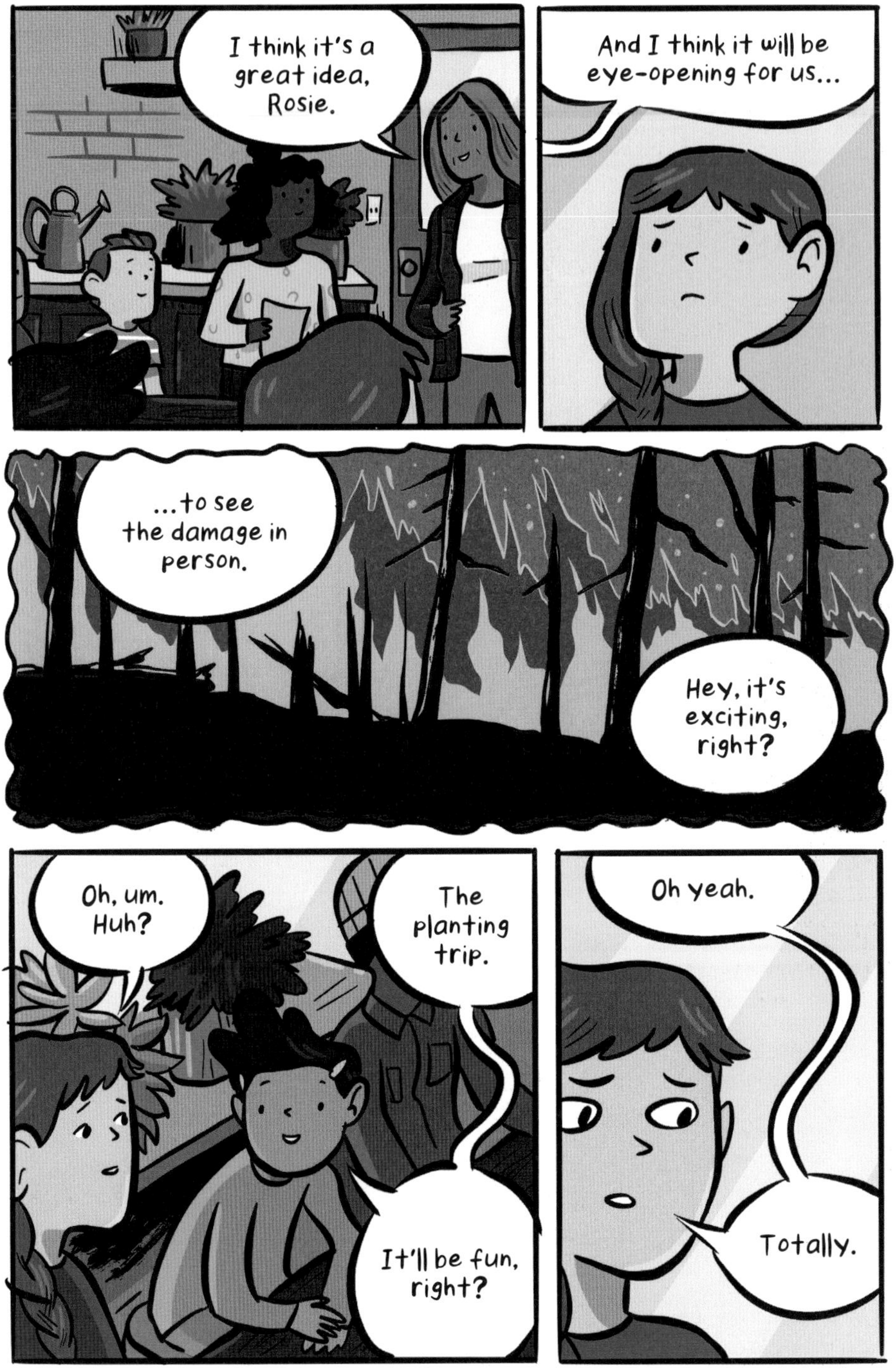
I think it's a great idea, Rosie.
And I think it will be eye-opening for us...
...to see the damage in person.
Hey, it's exciting, right?
Oh, um. Huh?
The planting trip.
It'll be fun, right?
Oh yeah.
Totally.

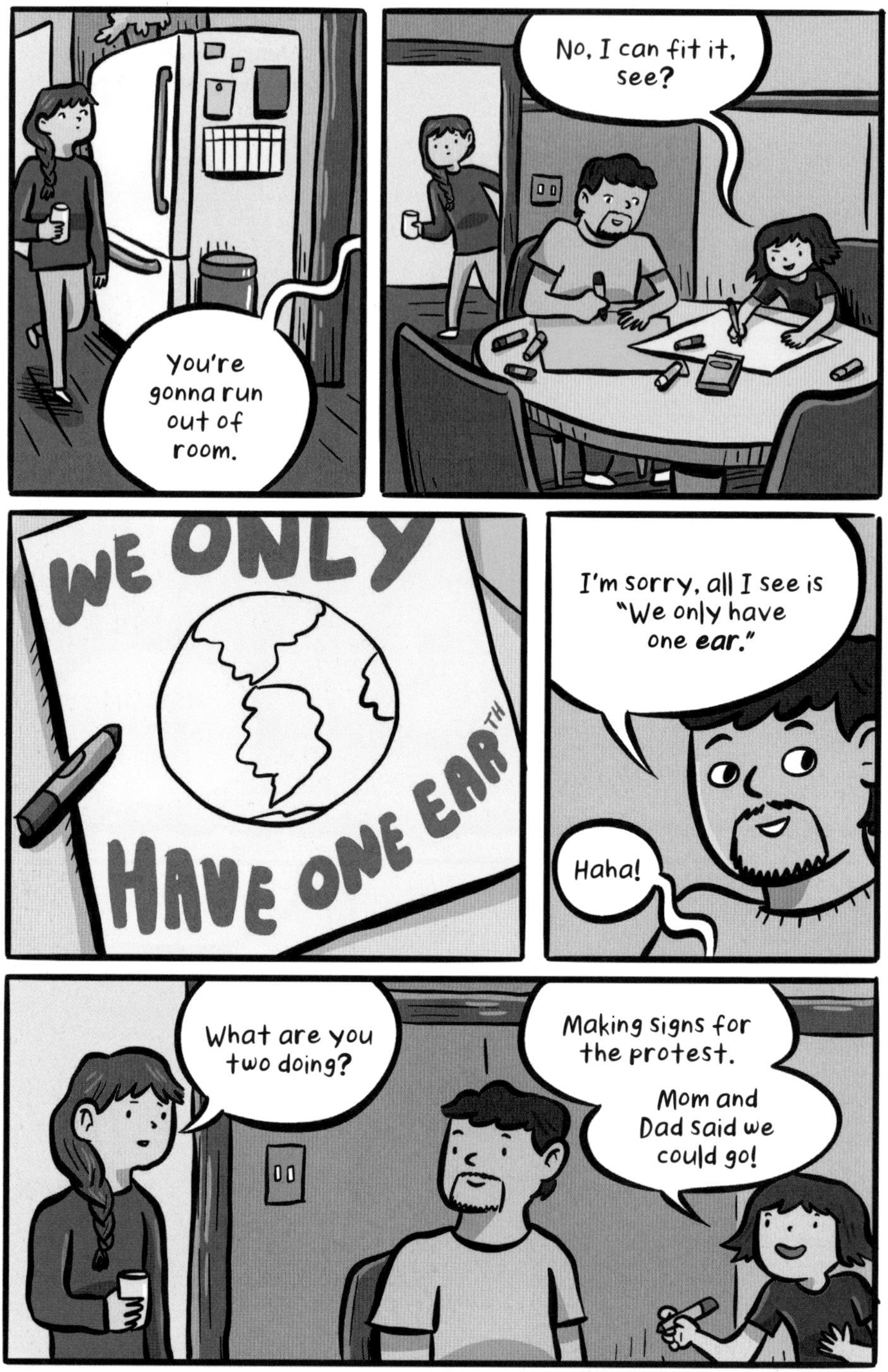
You're gonna run out of room.
No, I can fit it, see?
WE ONLY HAVE ONE EAR TH
I'm sorry, all I see is "We only have one ear."
Haha!
What are you two doing?
Making signs for the protest.
Mom and Dad said we could go!

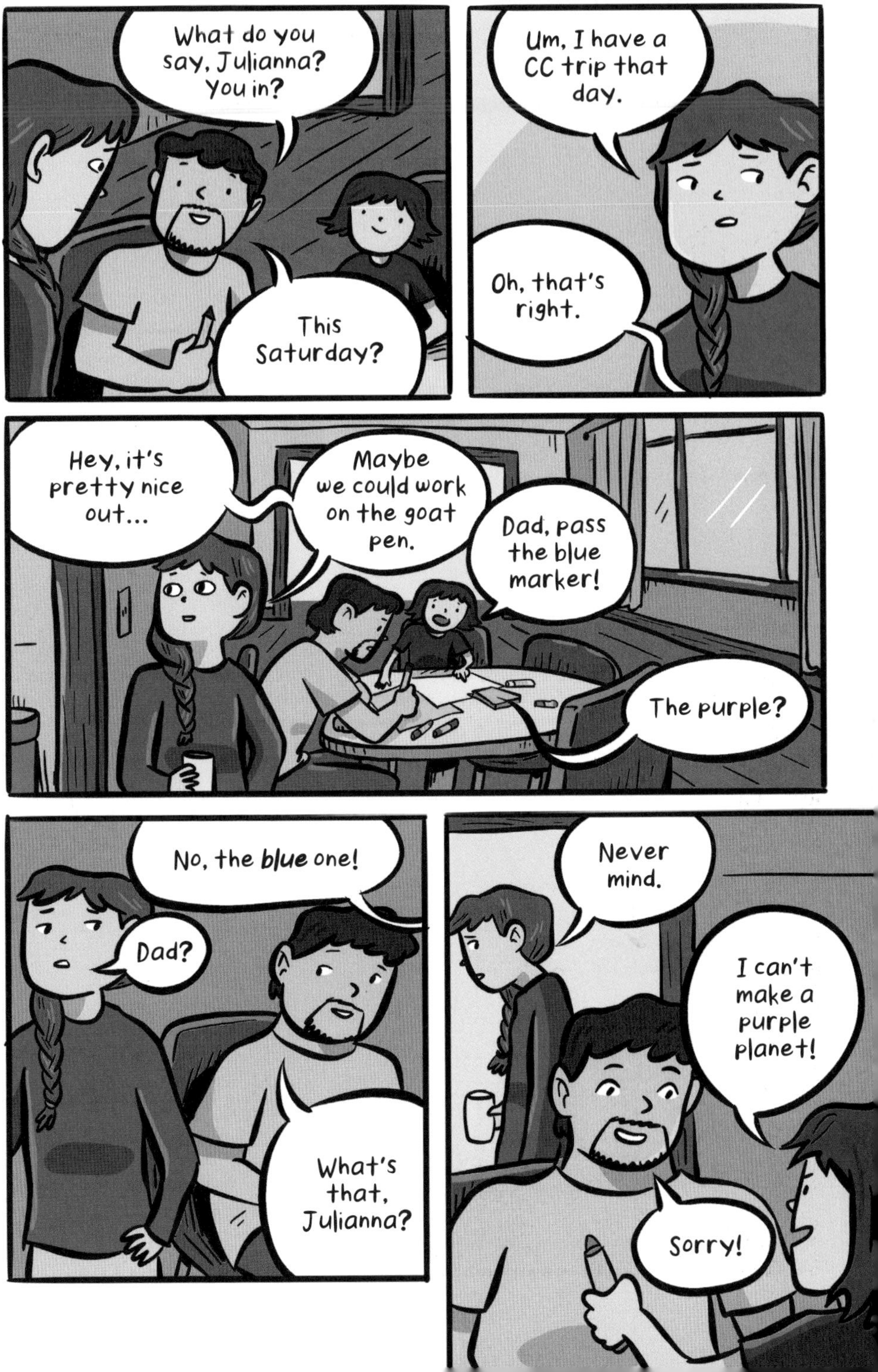
What do you say, Julianna? You in?
This Saturday?
Um, I have a CC trip that day.
Oh, that's right.
Hey, it's pretty nice out...
Maybe we could work on the goat pen.
Dad, pass the blue marker!
The purple?
No, the *blue* one!
Dad?
What's that, Julianna?
Never mind.
I can't make a purple planet!
Sorry!

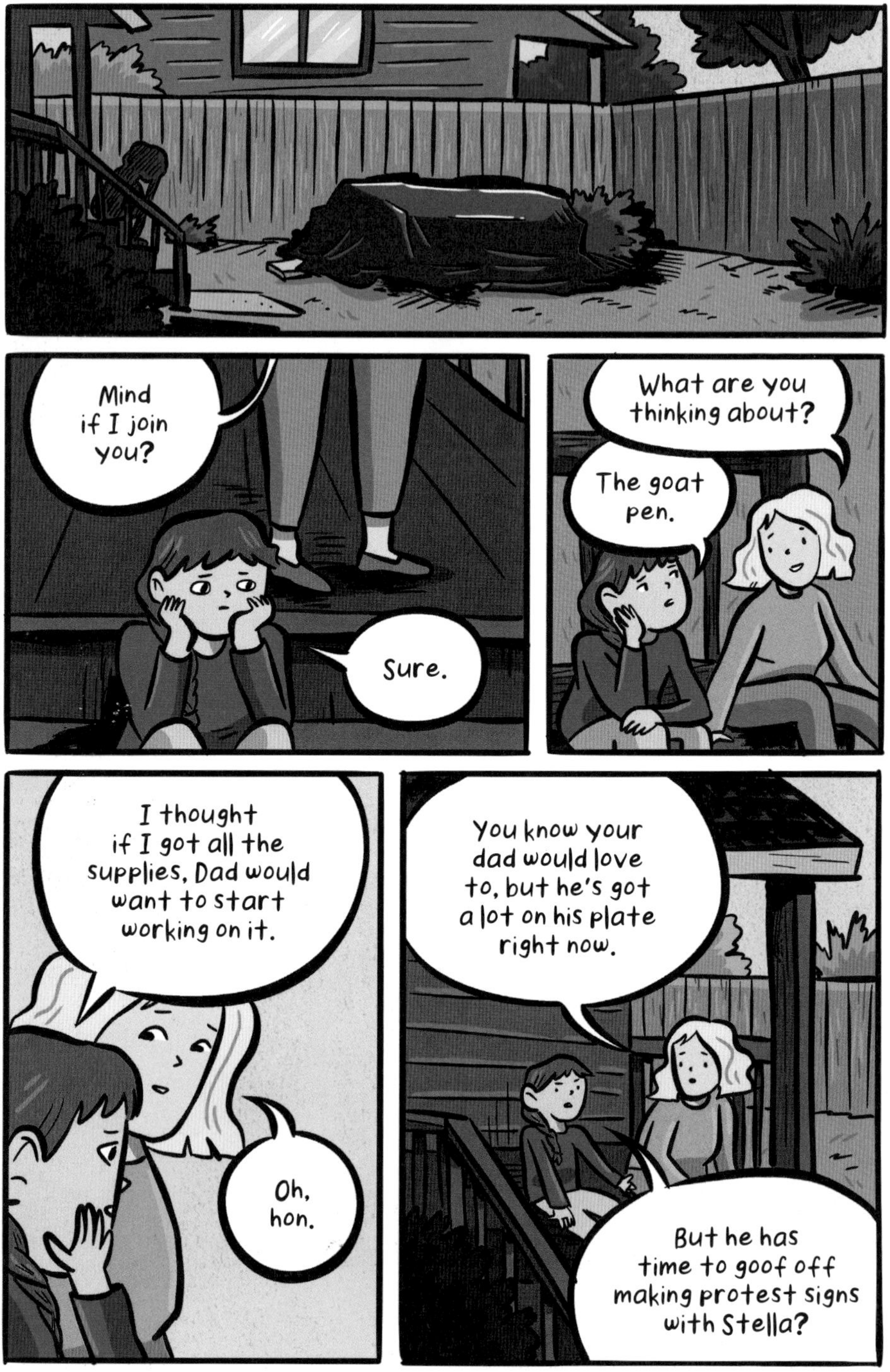
Mind if I join you?
Sure.
What are you thinking about?
The goat pen.
I thought if I got all the supplies, Dad would want to start working on it.
Oh, hon.
You know your dad would love to, but he's got a lot on his plate right now.
But he has time to goof off making protest signs with Stella?

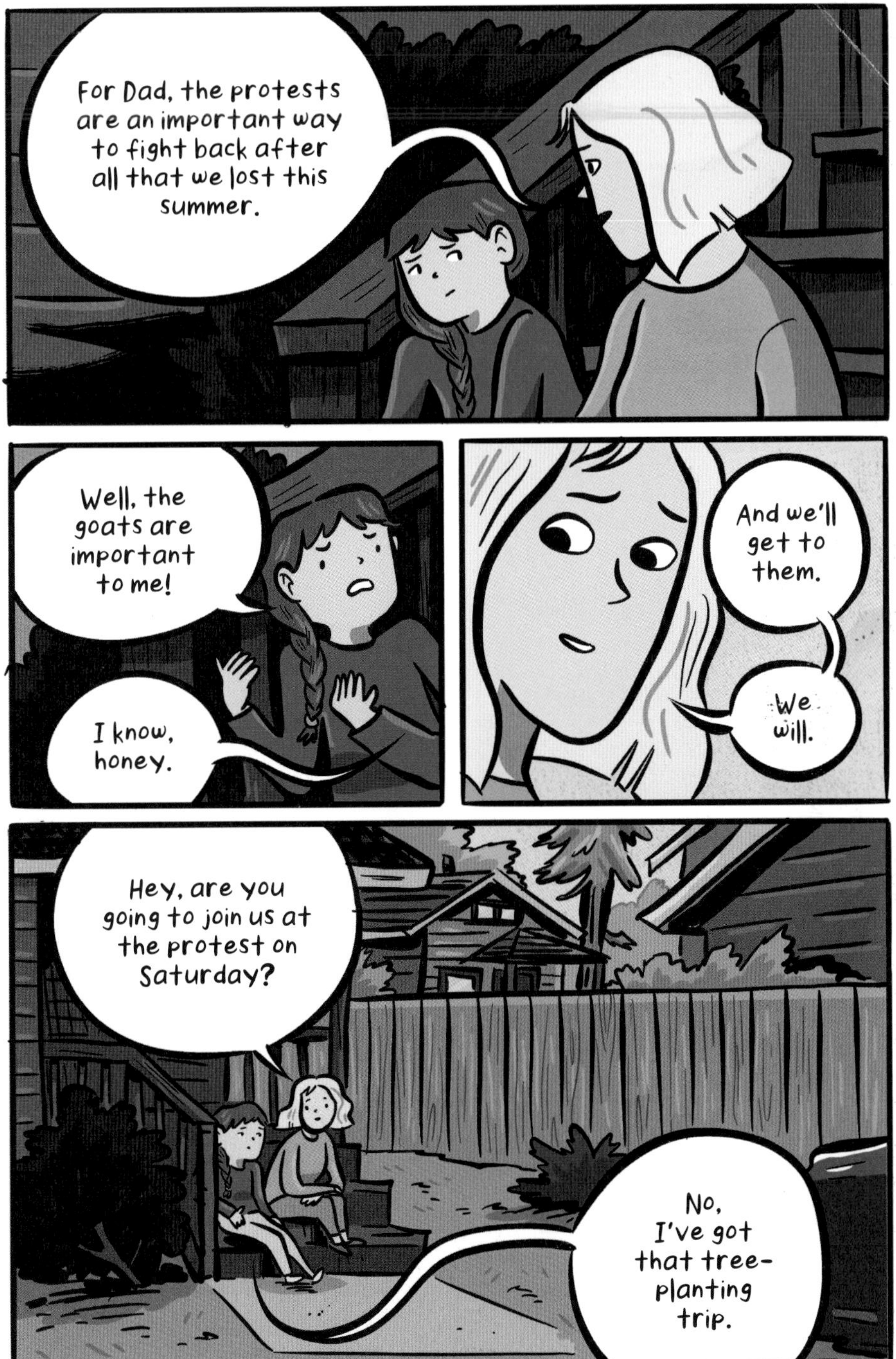
For Dad, the protests are an important way to fight back after all that we lost this summer.
Well, the goats are important to me!
I know, honey.
And we'll get to them.
We will.
Hey, are you going to join us at the protest on Saturday?
No, I've got that tree-planting trip.

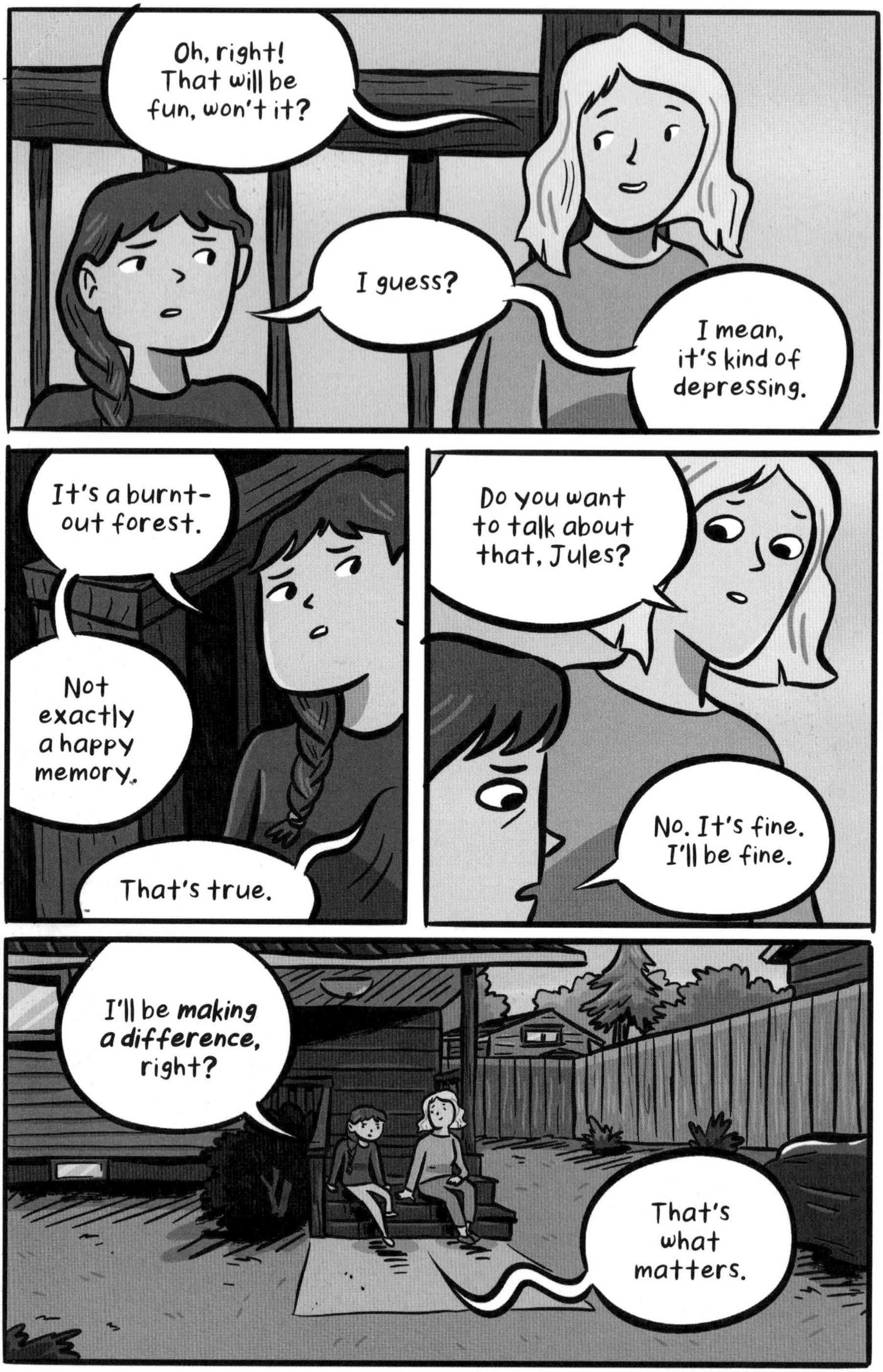
Oh, right! That will be fun, won't it?
I guess?
I mean, it's kind of depressing.
It's a burnt-out forest.
Not exactly a happy memory.
That's true.
Do you want to talk about that, Jules?
No. It's fine. I'll be fine.
I'll be *making a difference*, right?
That's what matters.

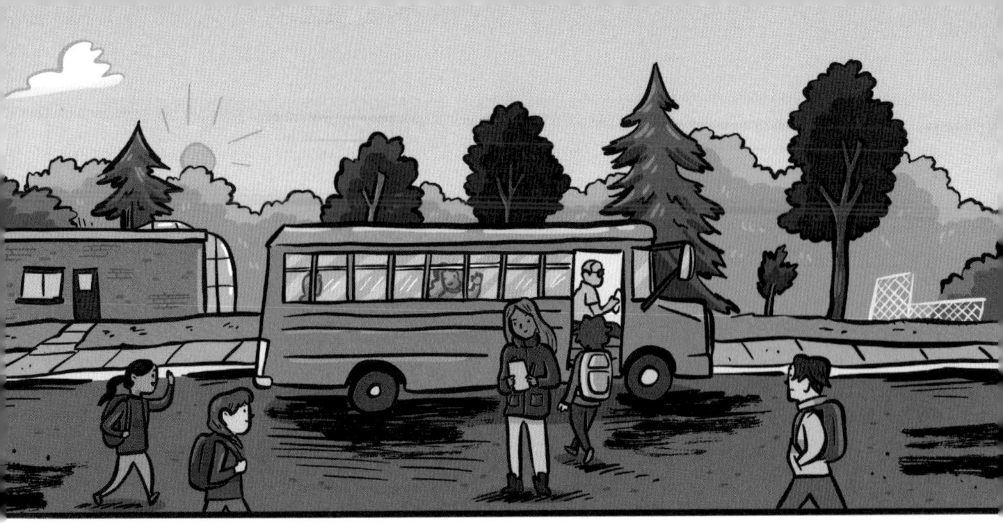

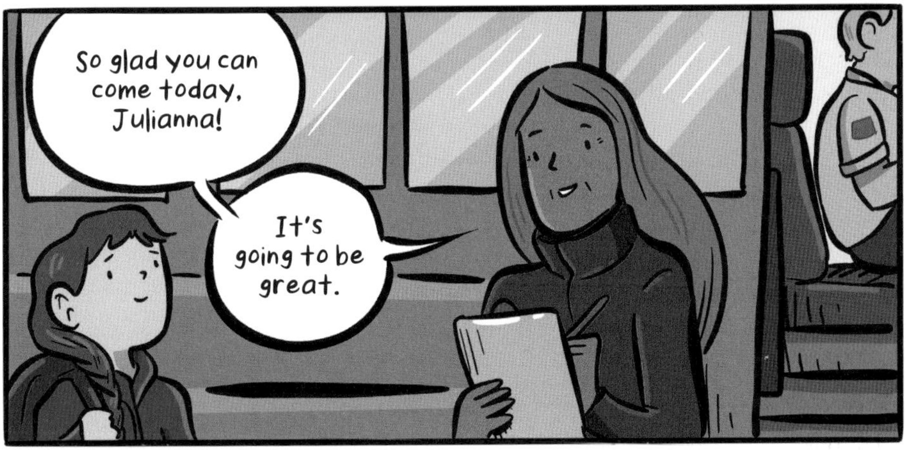
So glad you can come today, Julianna!
It's going to be great.

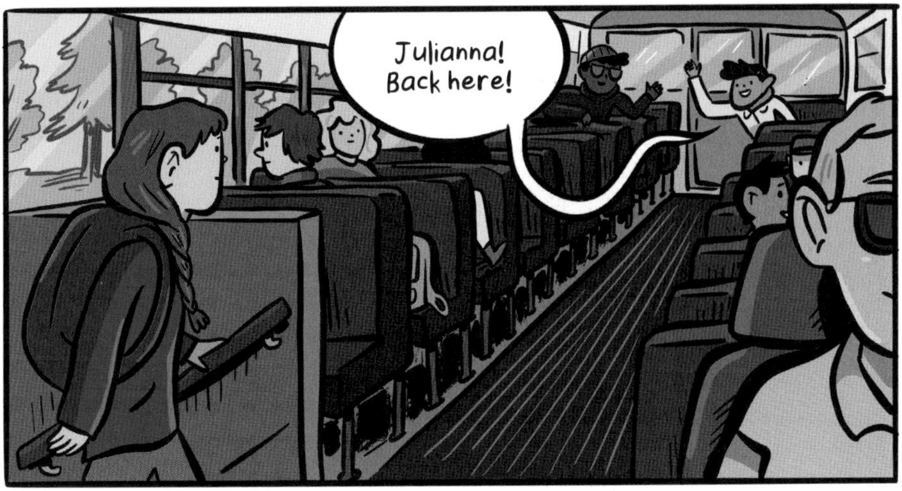
Julianna! Back here!

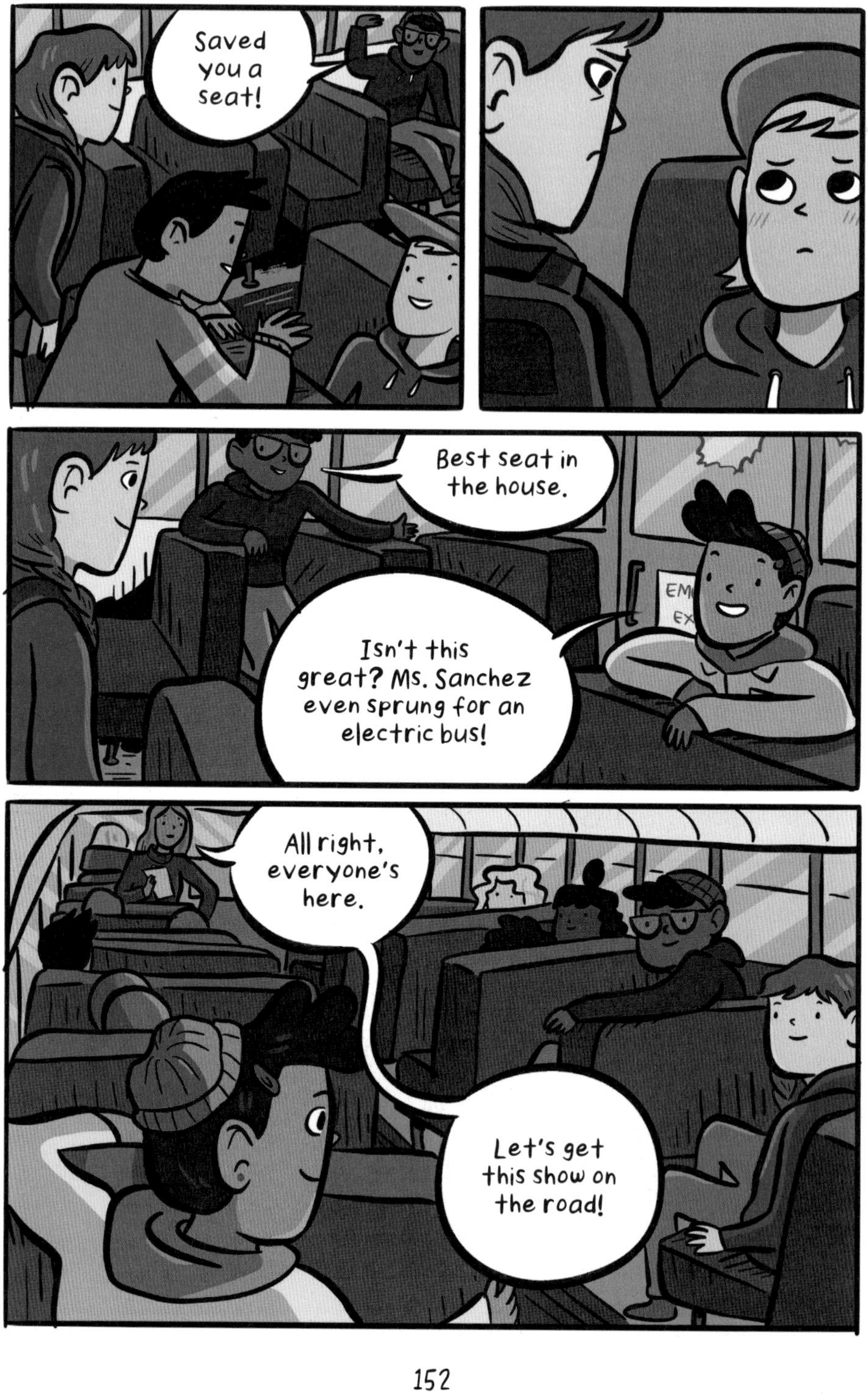
Saved you a seat!
Best seat in the house.
Isn't this great? Ms. Sanchez even sprung for an electric bus!
All right, everyone's here.
Let's get this show on the road!

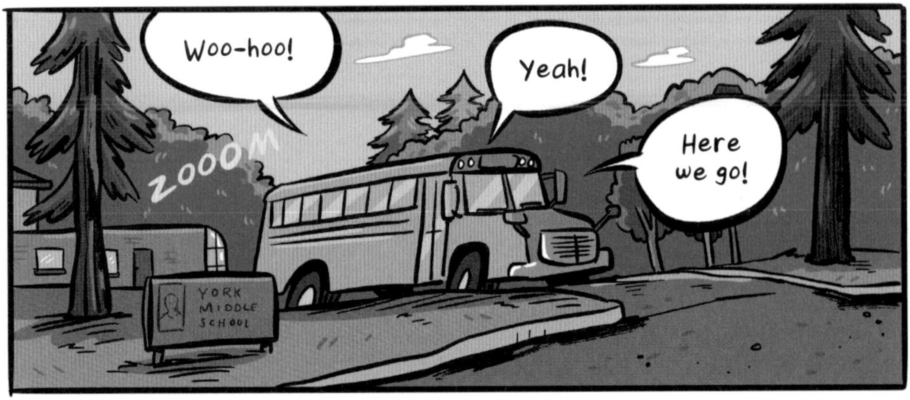
Woo-hoo!
Yeah!
ZOOOM
YORK MIDDLE SCHOOL
Here we go!

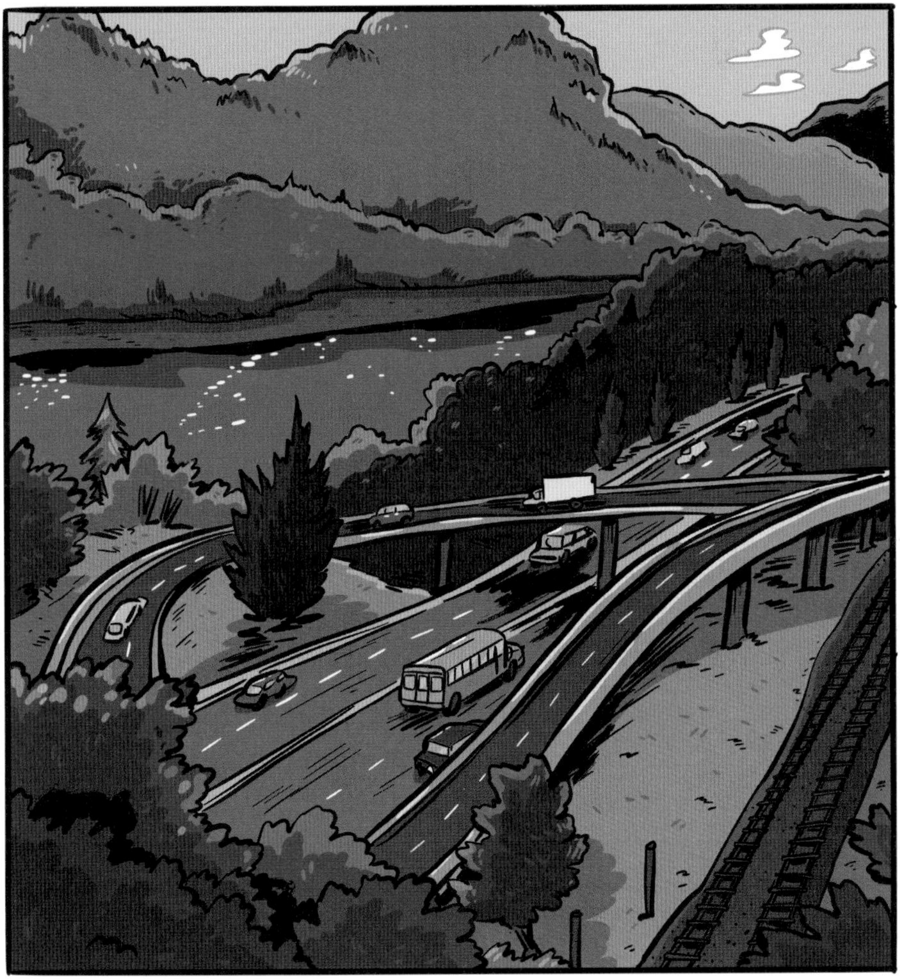

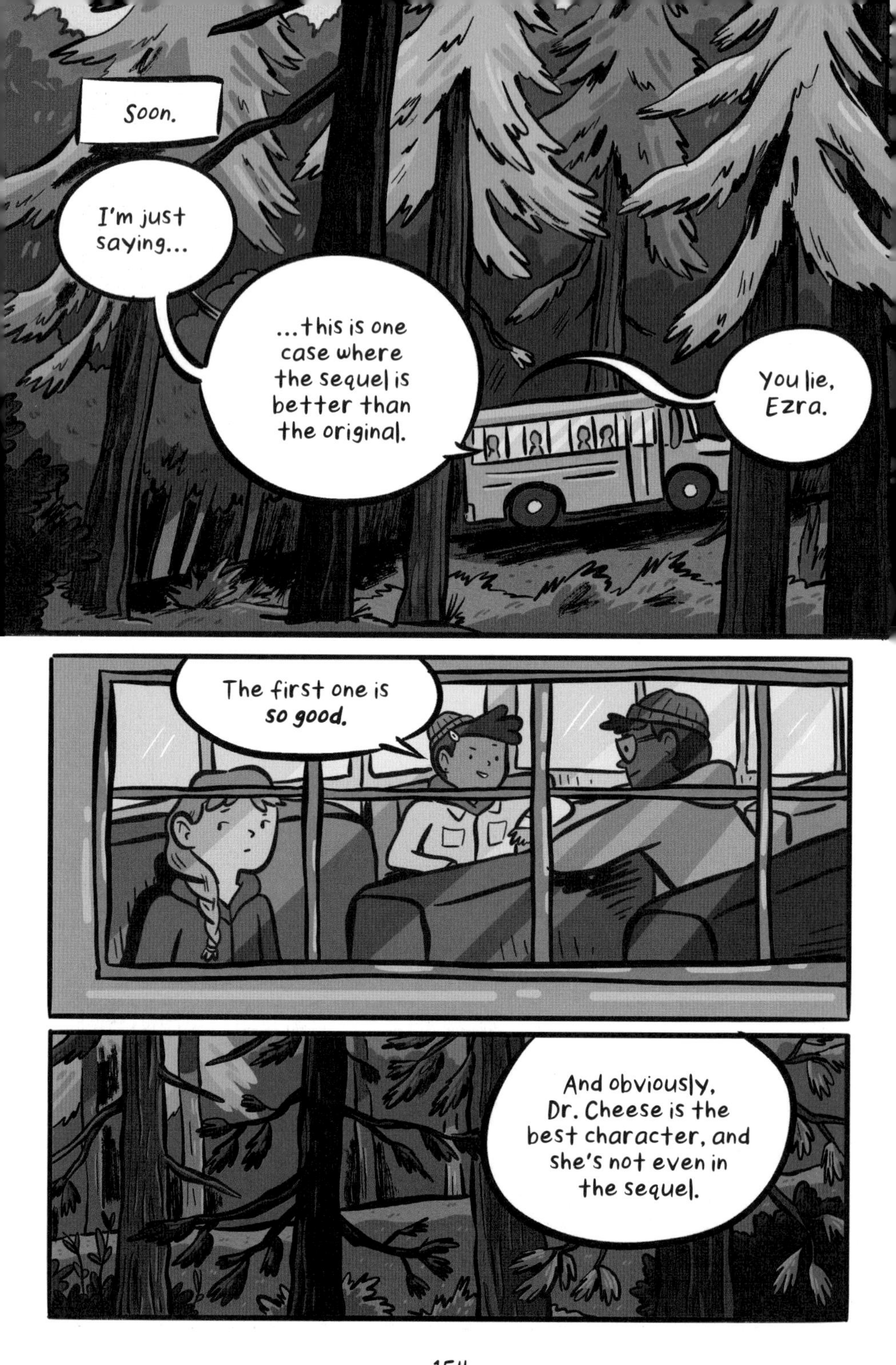
Soon.
I'm just saying...
...this is one case where the sequel is better than the original.
You lie, Ezra.
The first one is *so good.*
And obviously, Dr. Cheese is the best character, and she's not even in the sequel.

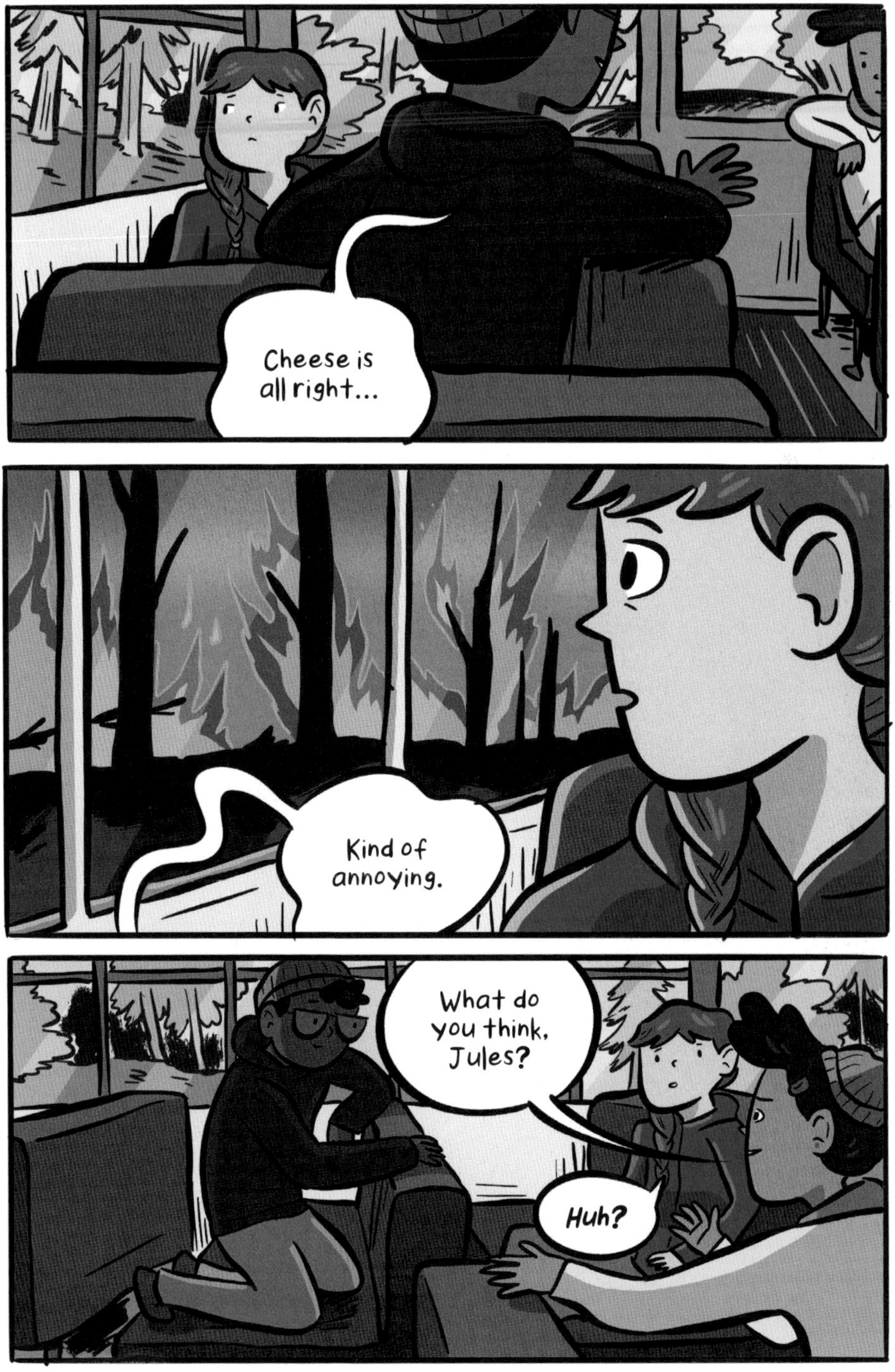
Cheese is all right...
Kind of annoying.
What do you think, Jules?
Huh?

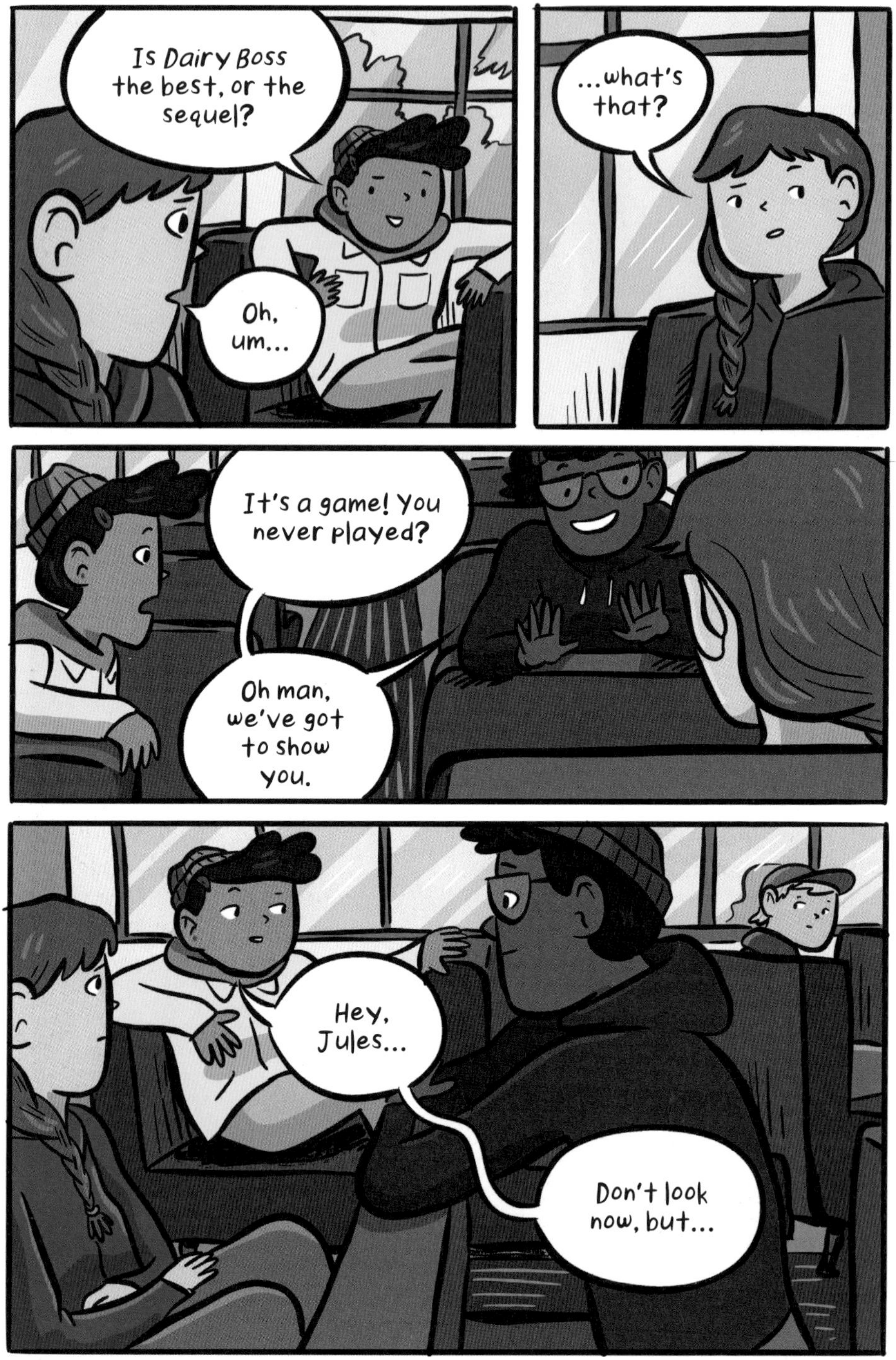
Is *Dairy Boss* the best, or the sequel?
Oh, um...
...what's that?
It's a game! You never played?
Oh man, we've got to show you.
Hey, Jules...
Don't look now, but...

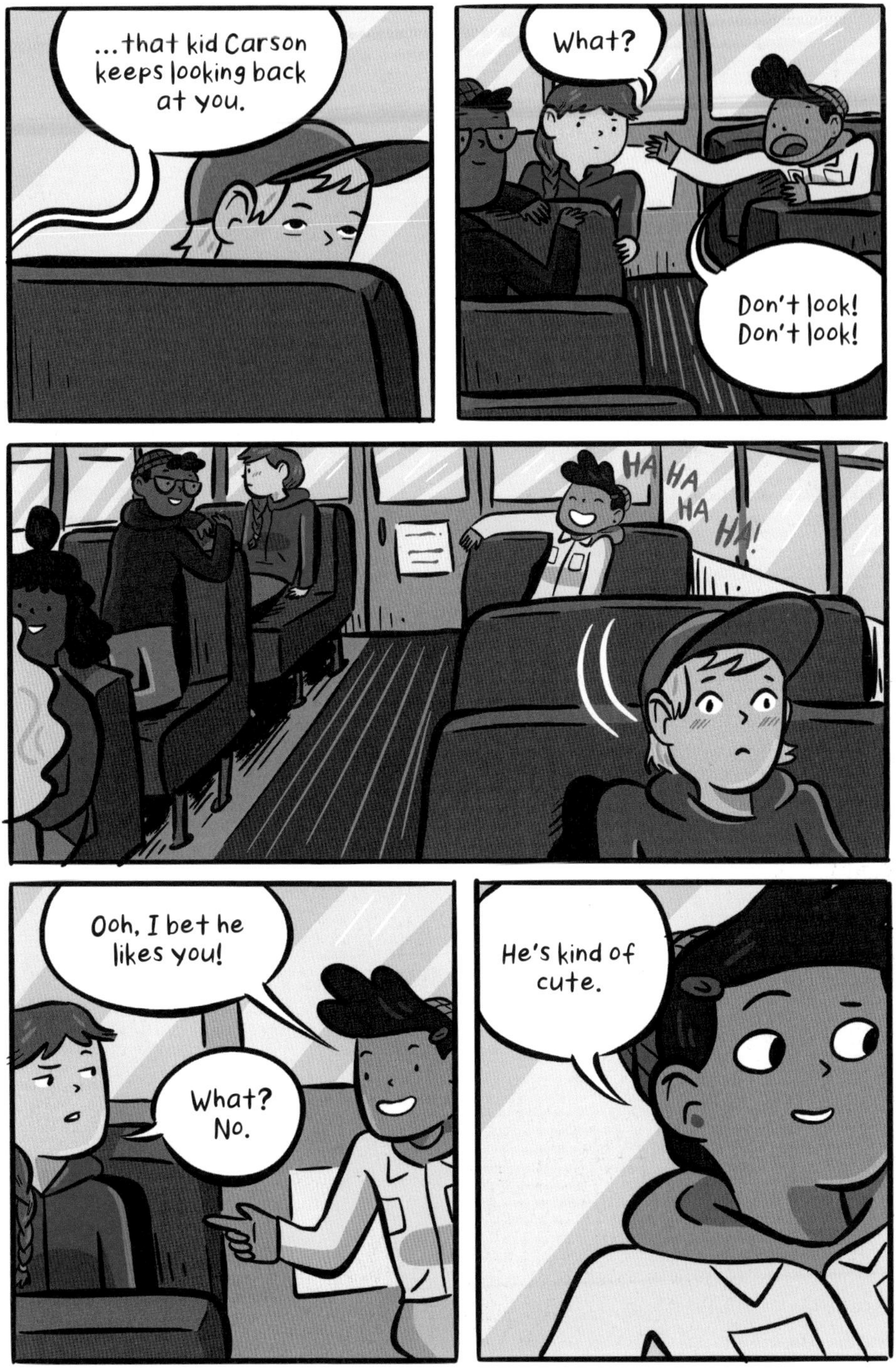
...that kid Carson keeps looking back at you.
What?
Don't look! Don't look!
HA HA HA HA!
Ooh, I bet he likes you!
What? No.
He's kind of cute.

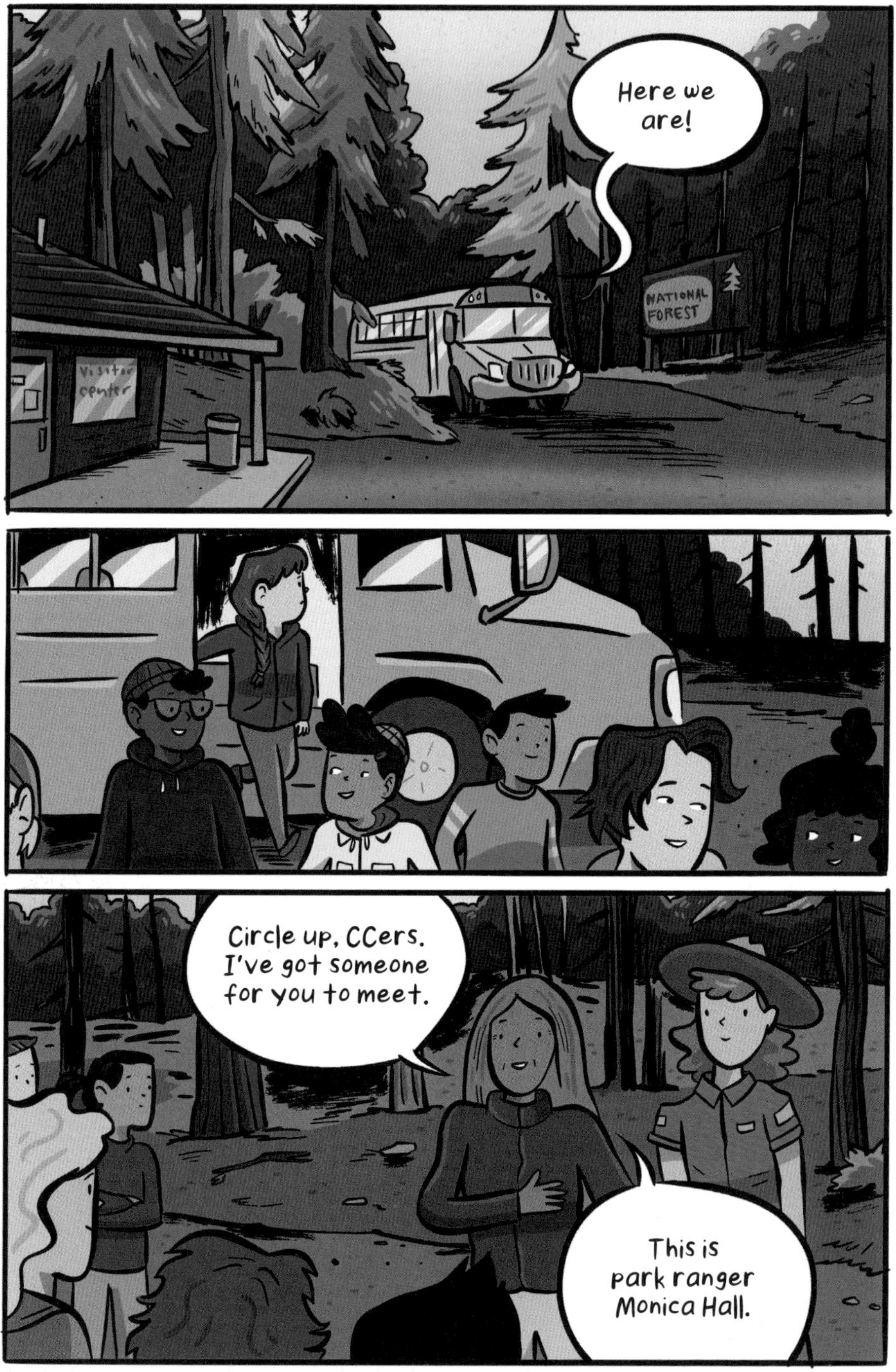
Here we are!
Visitor center
NATIONAL FOREST
Circle up, CCers. I've got someone for you to meet.
This is park ranger Monica Hall.

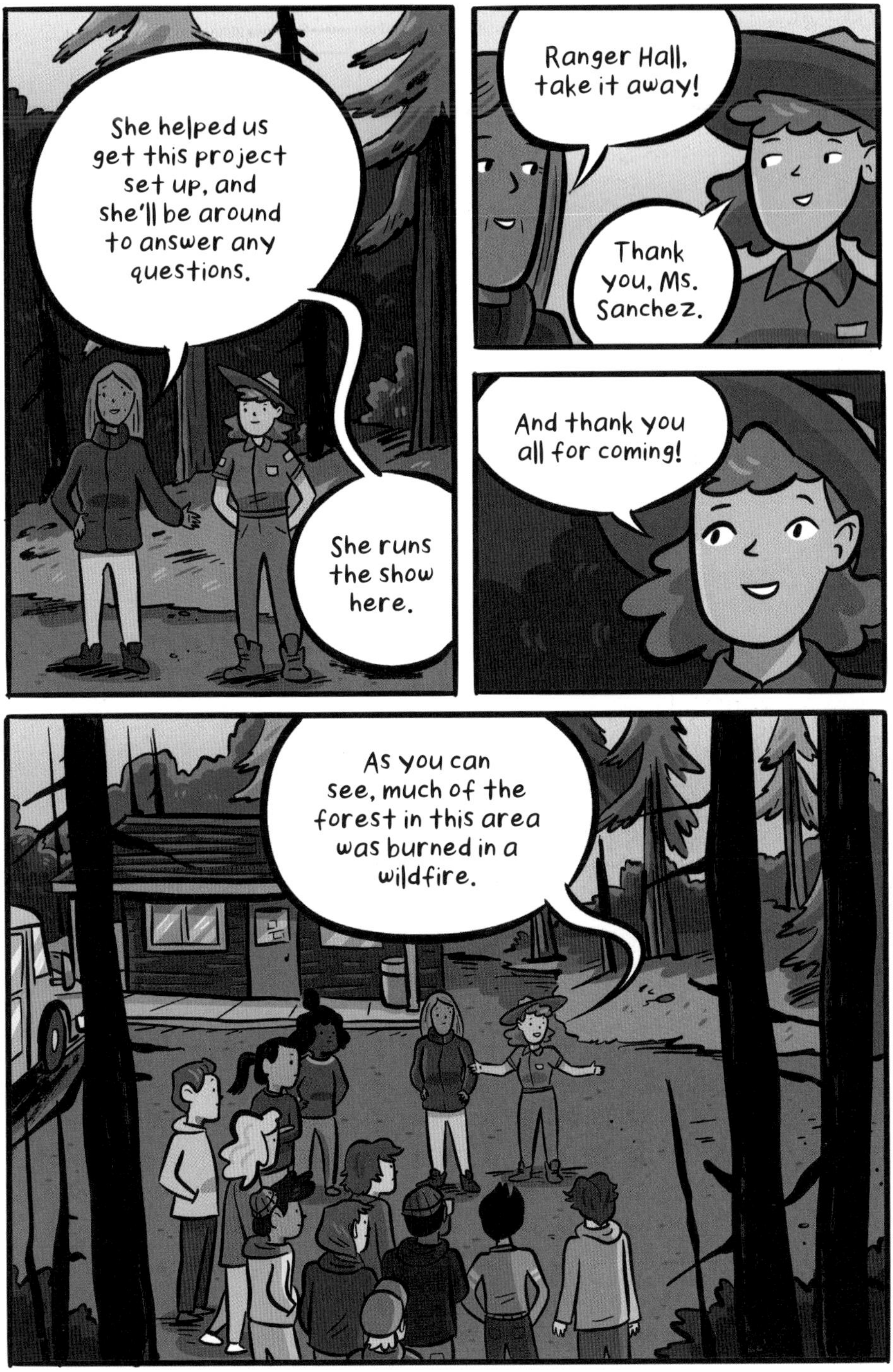
She helped us get this project set up, and she'll be around to answer any questions.
She runs the show here.
Ranger Hall, take it away!
Thank you, Ms. Sanchez.
And thank you all for coming!
As you can see, much of the forest in this area was burned in a wildfire.

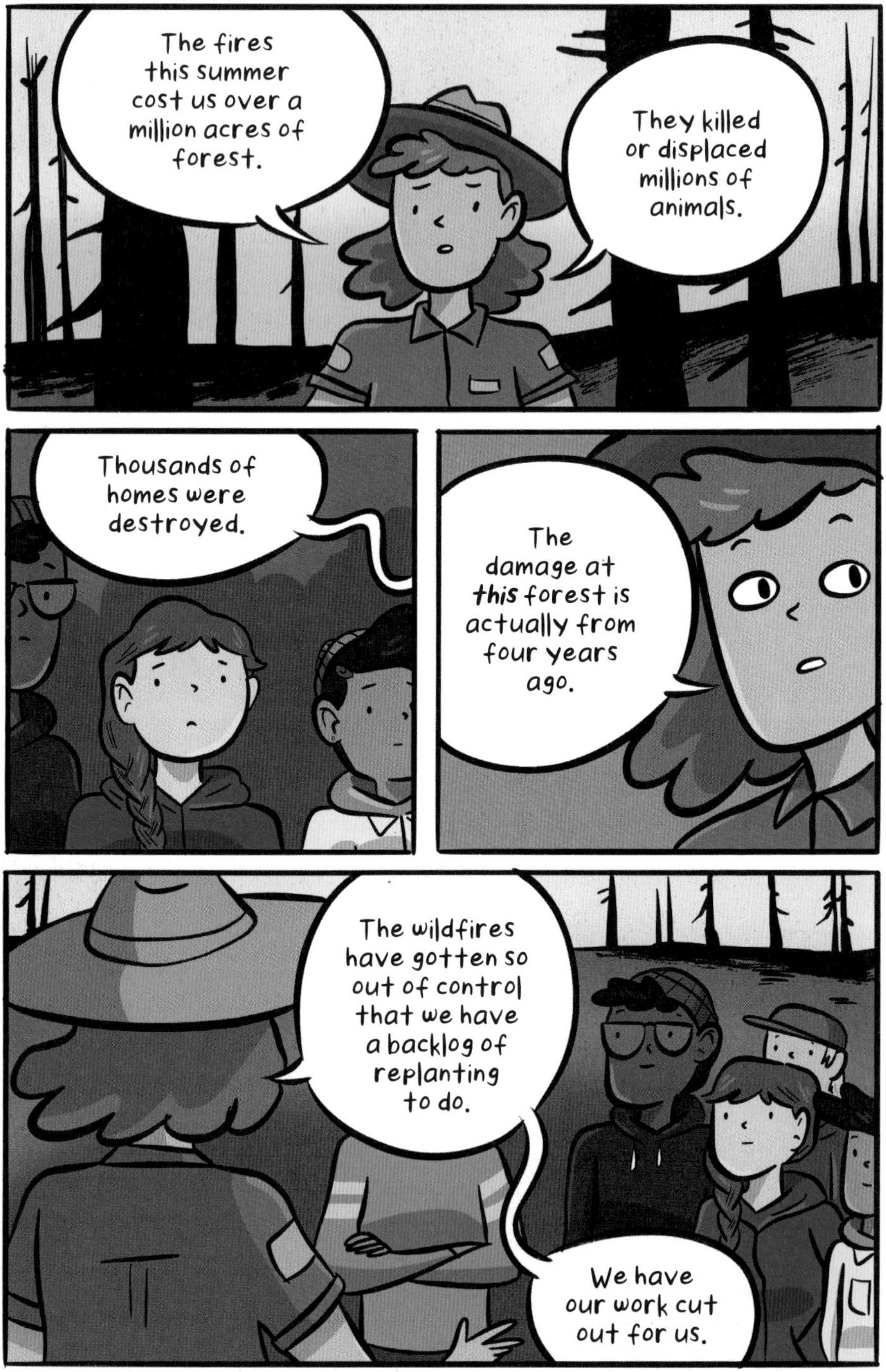
The fires this summer cost us over a million acres of forest.
They killed or displaced millions of animals.
Thousands of homes were destroyed.
The damage at *this* forest is actually from four years ago.
The wildfires have gotten so out of control that we have a backlog of replanting to do.
We have our work cut out for us.

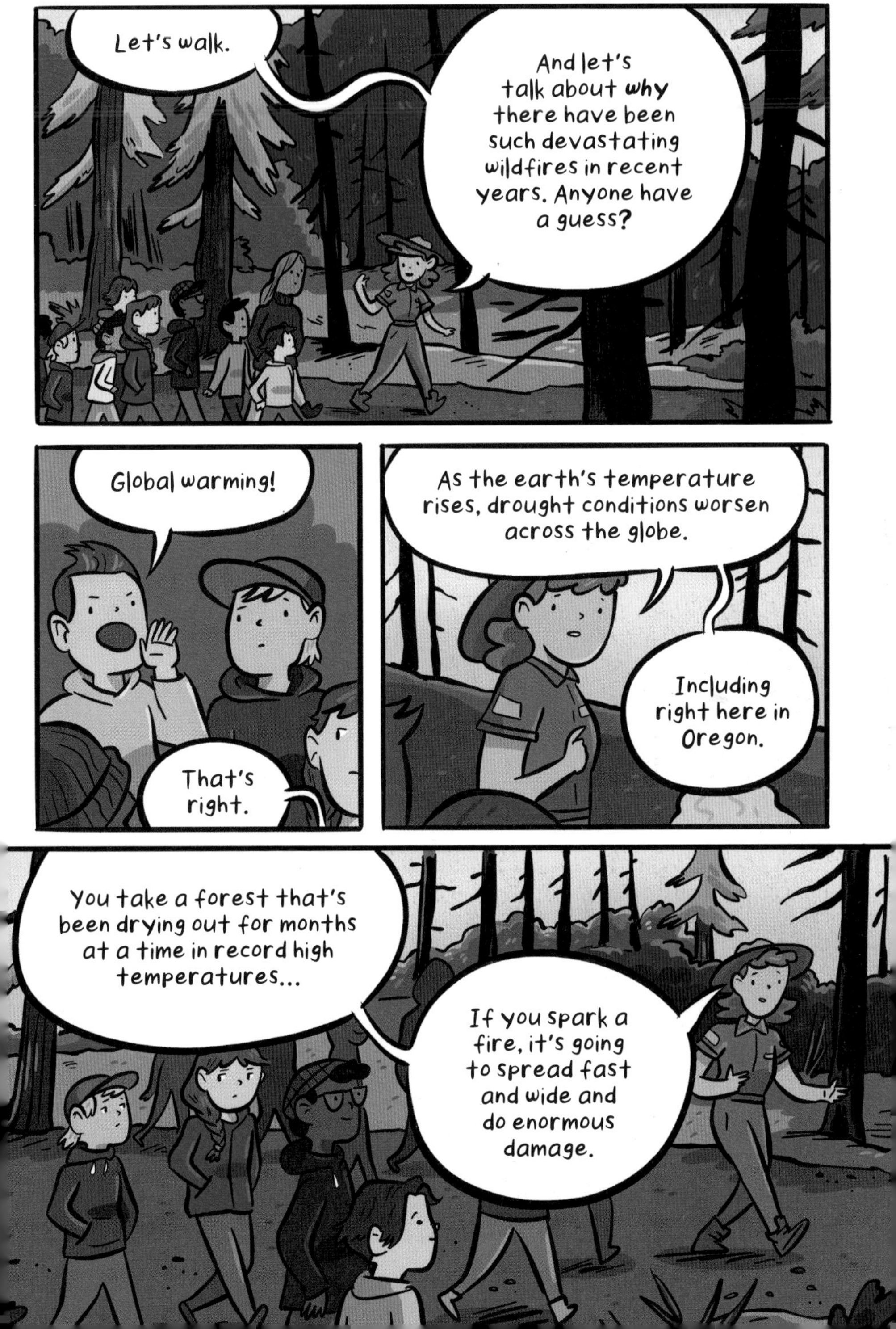
Let's walk.
And let's talk about **why** there have been such devastating wildfires in recent years. Anyone have a guess?
Global warming!
That's right.
As the earth's temperature rises, drought conditions worsen across the globe.
Including right here in Oregon.
You take a forest that's been drying out for months at a time in record high temperatures...
If you spark a fire, it's going to spread fast and wide and do enormous damage.

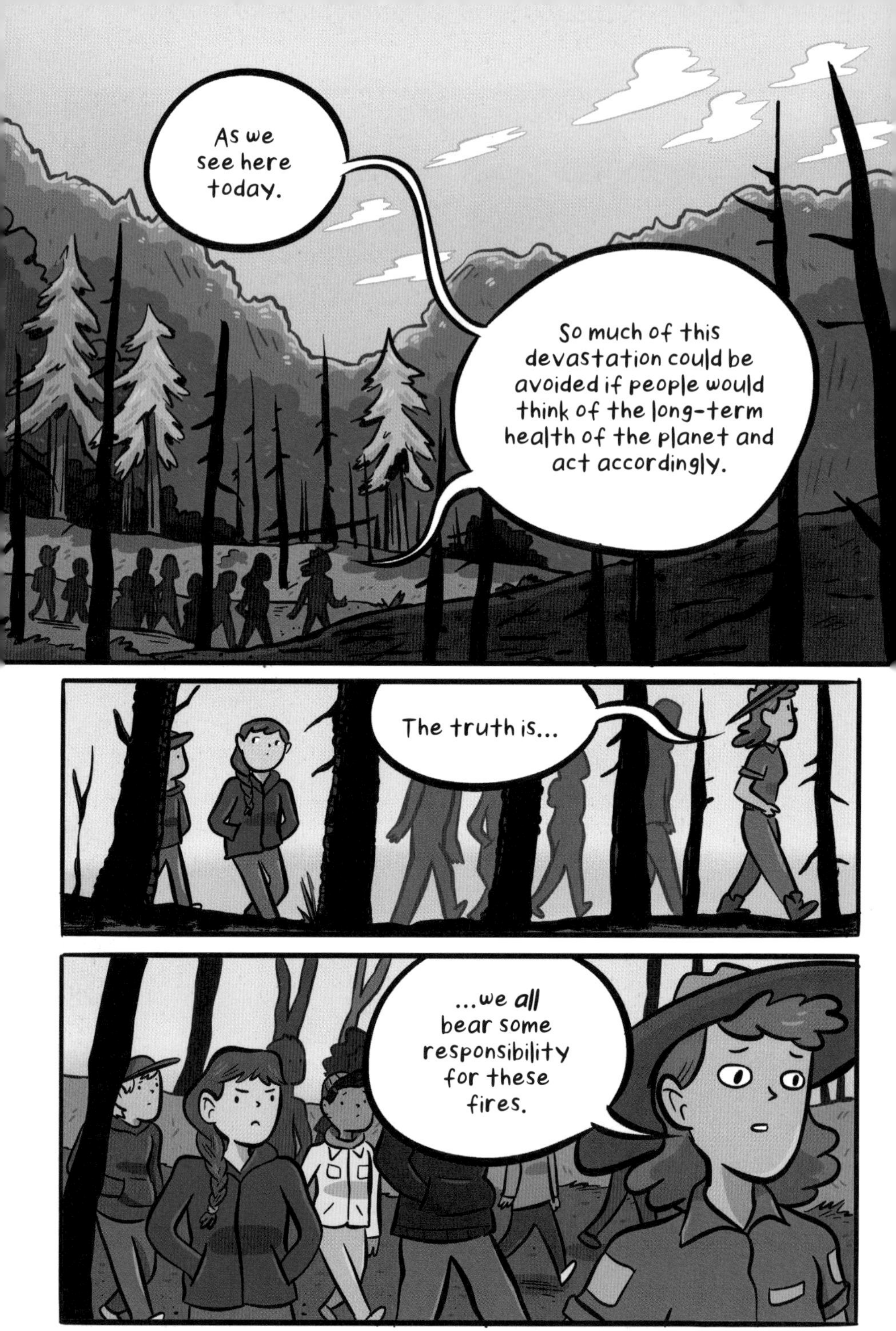
As we see here today.
So much of this devastation could be avoided if people would think of the long-term health of the planet and act accordingly.
The truth is...
...we *all* bear some responsibility for these fires.

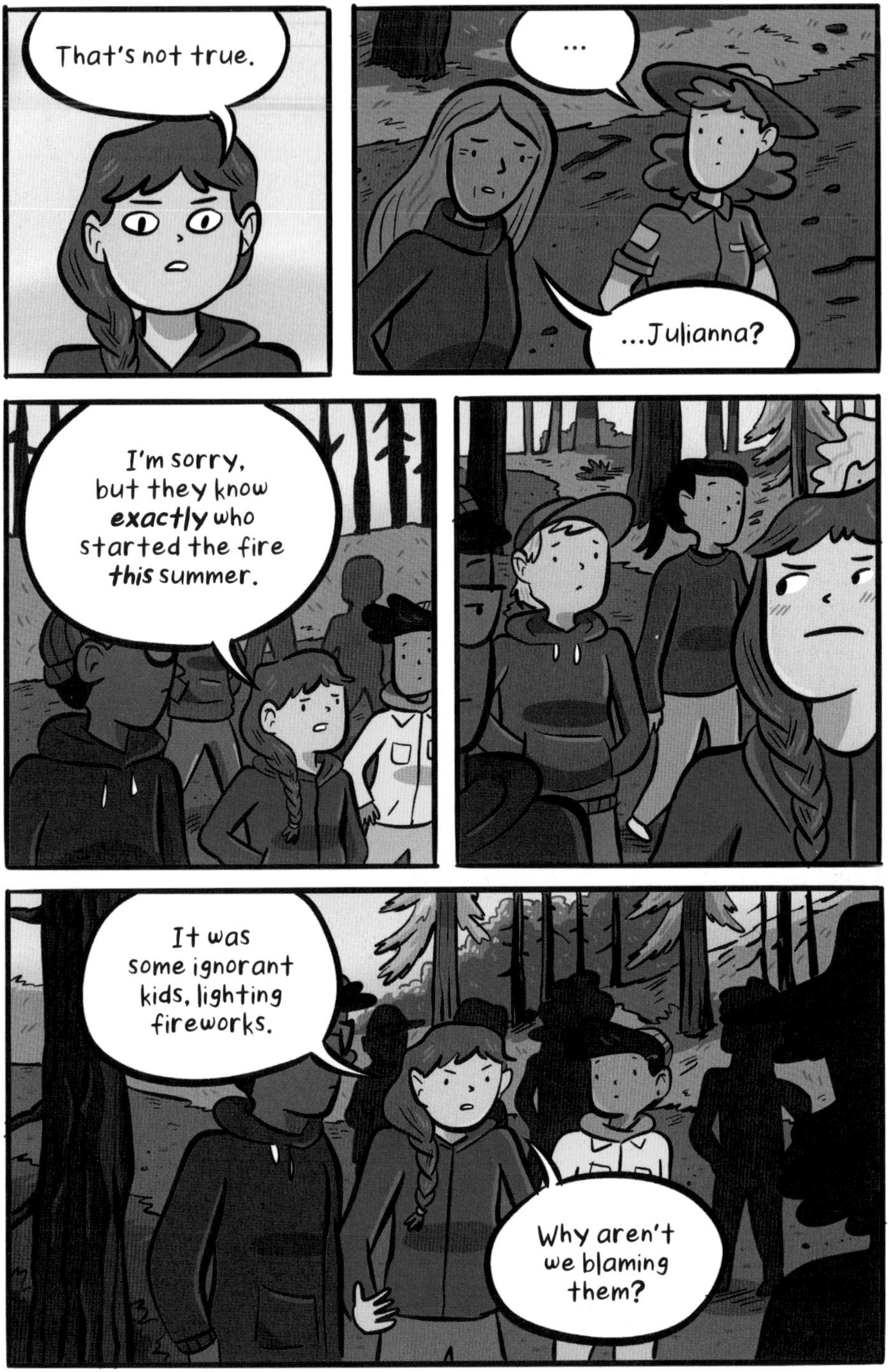
That's not true.
...
...Julianna?
I'm sorry, but they know **exactly** who started the fire **this** summer.
It was some ignorant kids, lighting fireworks.
Why aren't we blaming them?

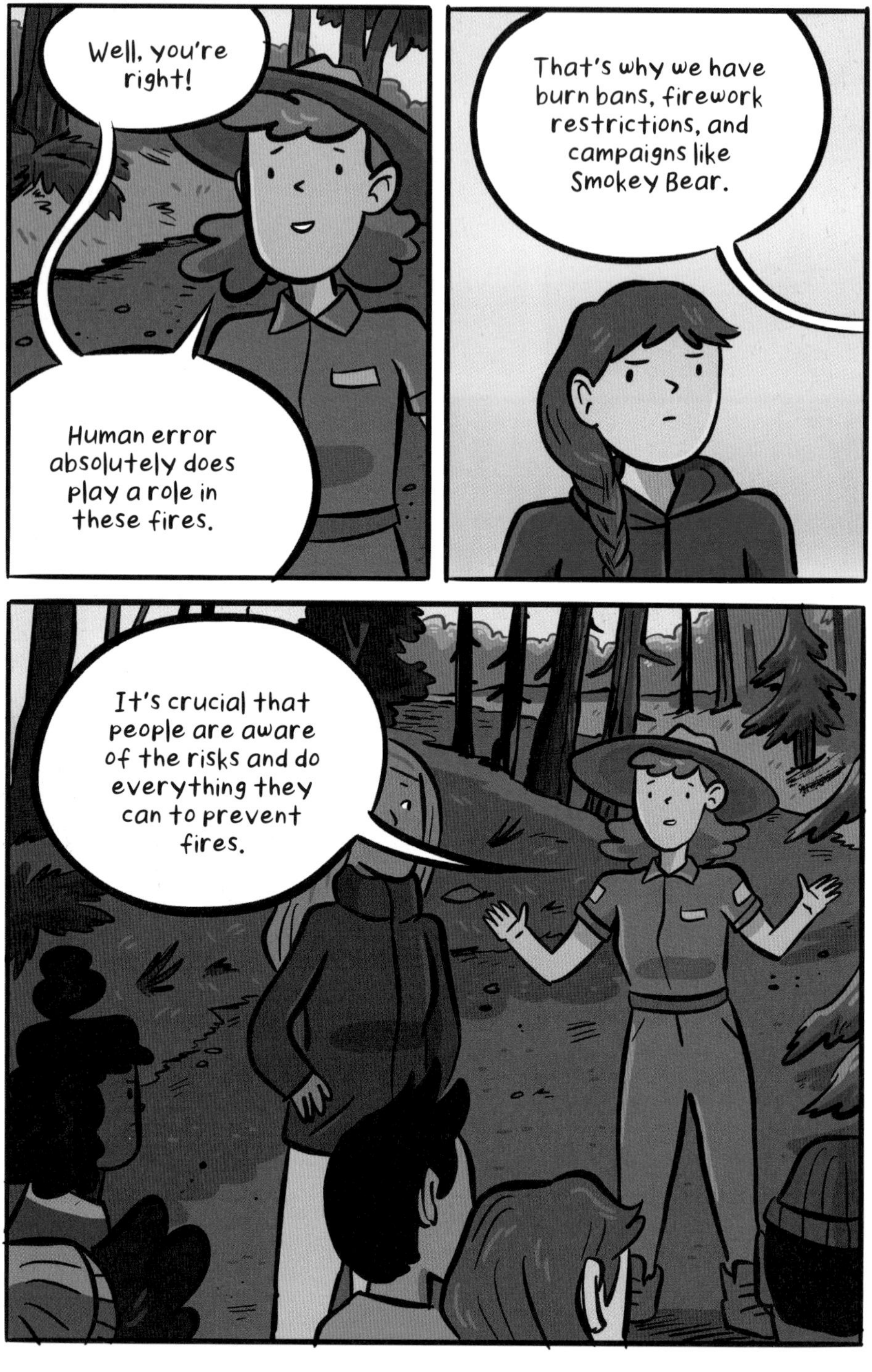
Well, you're right!
Human error absolutely does play a role in these fires.
That's why we have burn bans, firework restrictions, and campaigns like Smokey Bear.
It's crucial that people are aware of the risks and do everything they can to prevent fires.

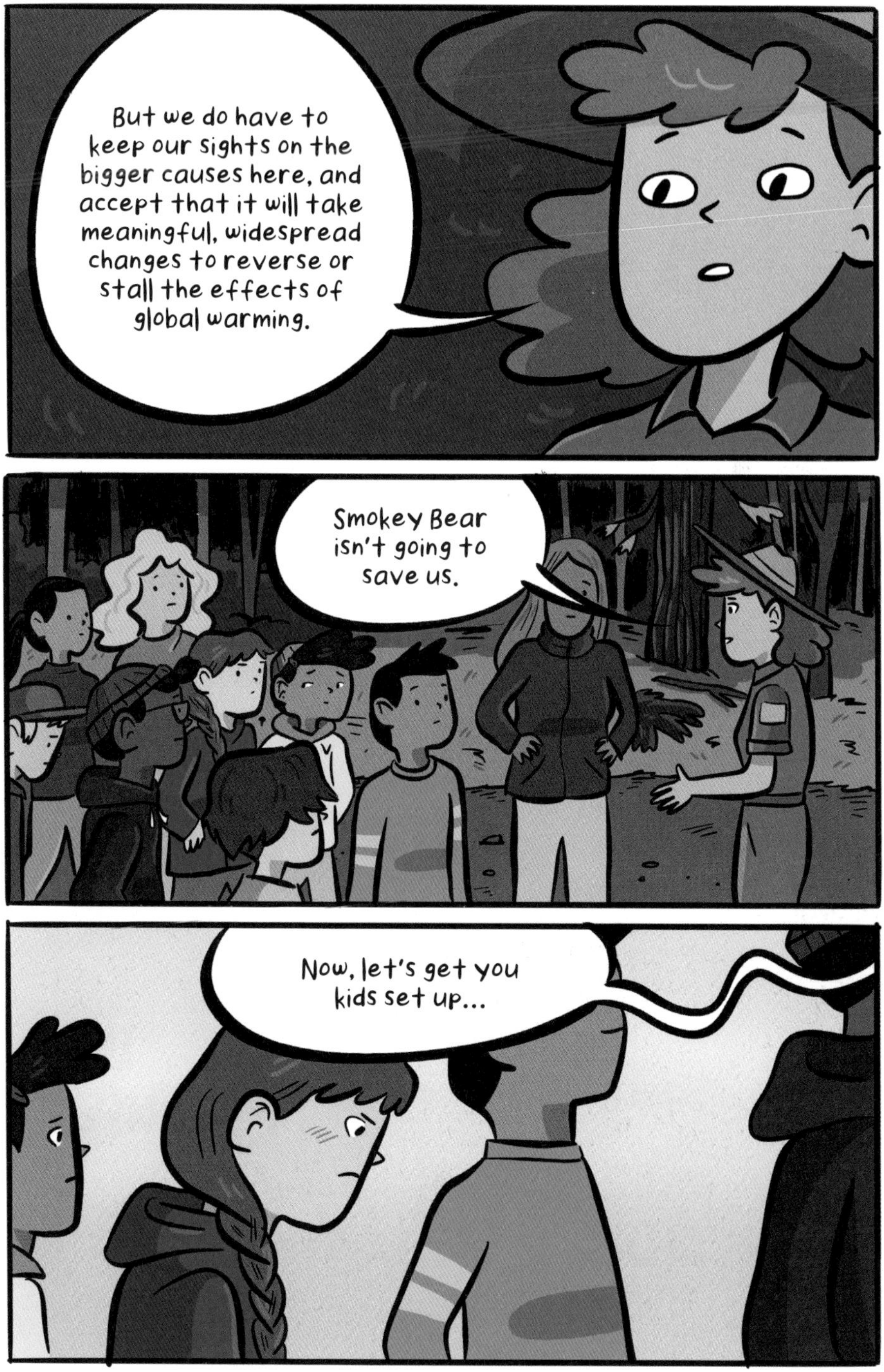
But we do have to keep our sights on the bigger causes here, and accept that it will take meaningful, widespread changes to reverse or stall the effects of global warming.
Smokey Bear isn't going to save us.
Now, let's get you kids set up...

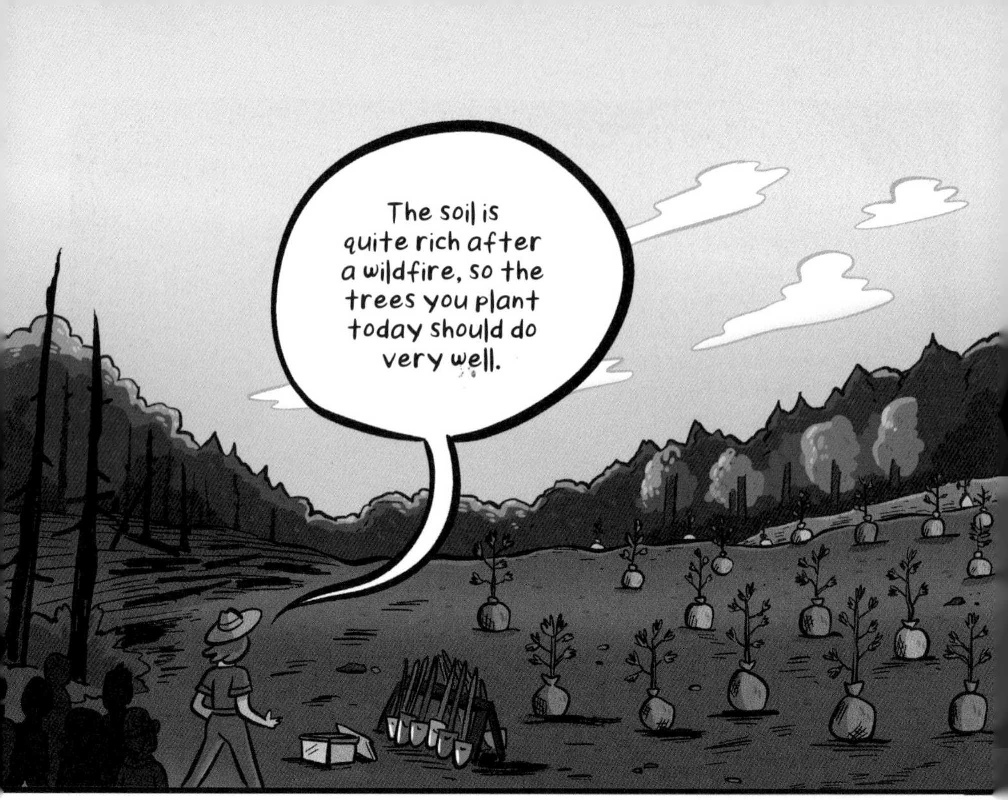
The soil is quite rich after a wildfire, so the trees you plant today should do very well.

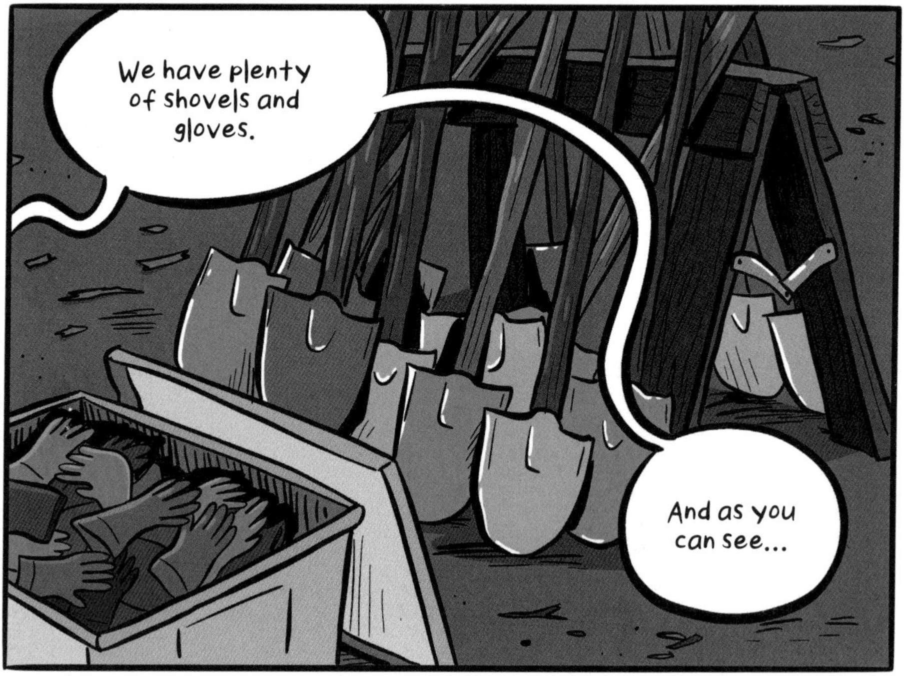
We have plenty of shovels and gloves.
And as you can see...

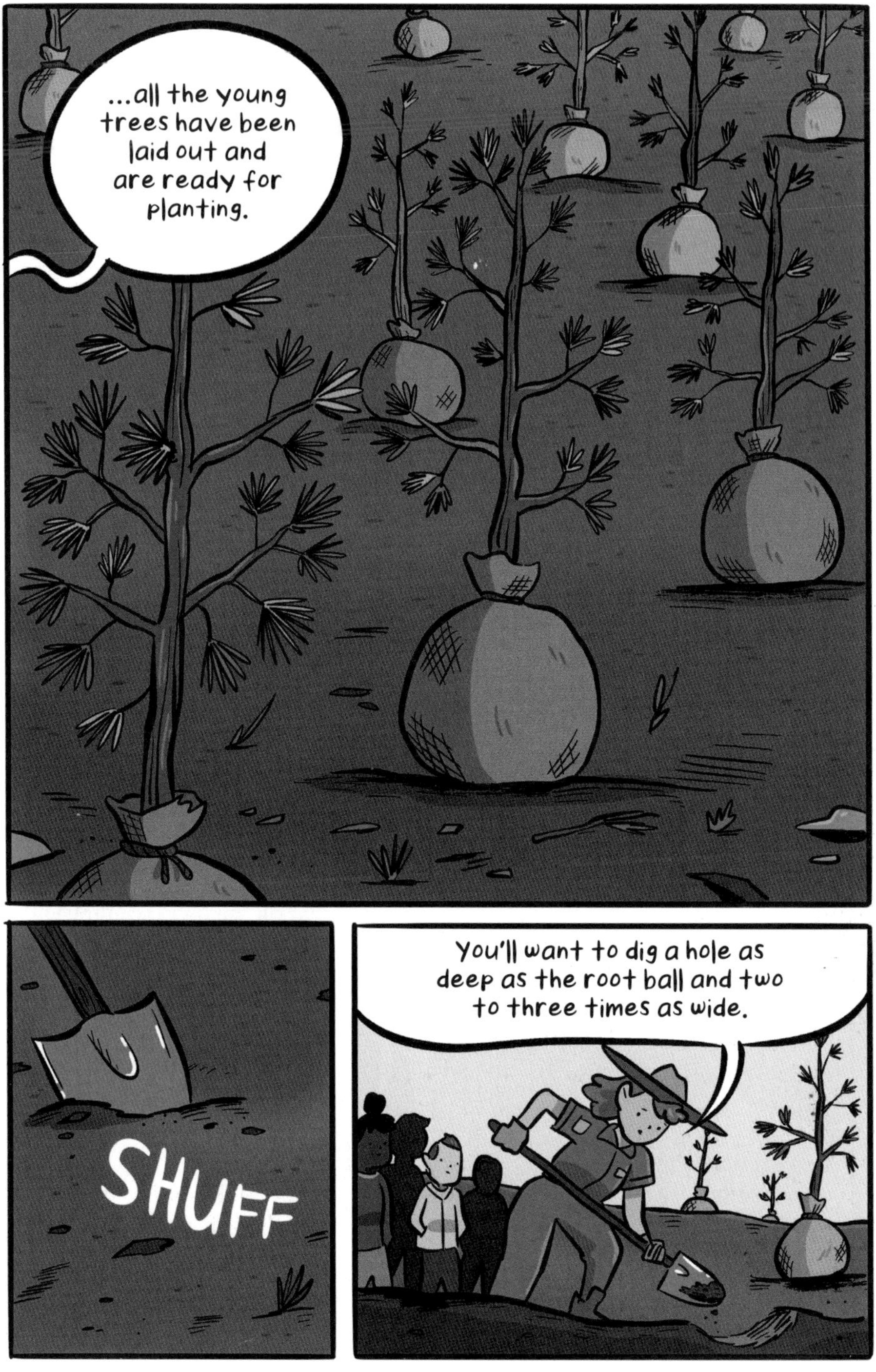
...all the young trees have been laid out and are ready for planting.
SHUFF
You'll want to dig a hole as deep as the root ball and two to three times as wide.

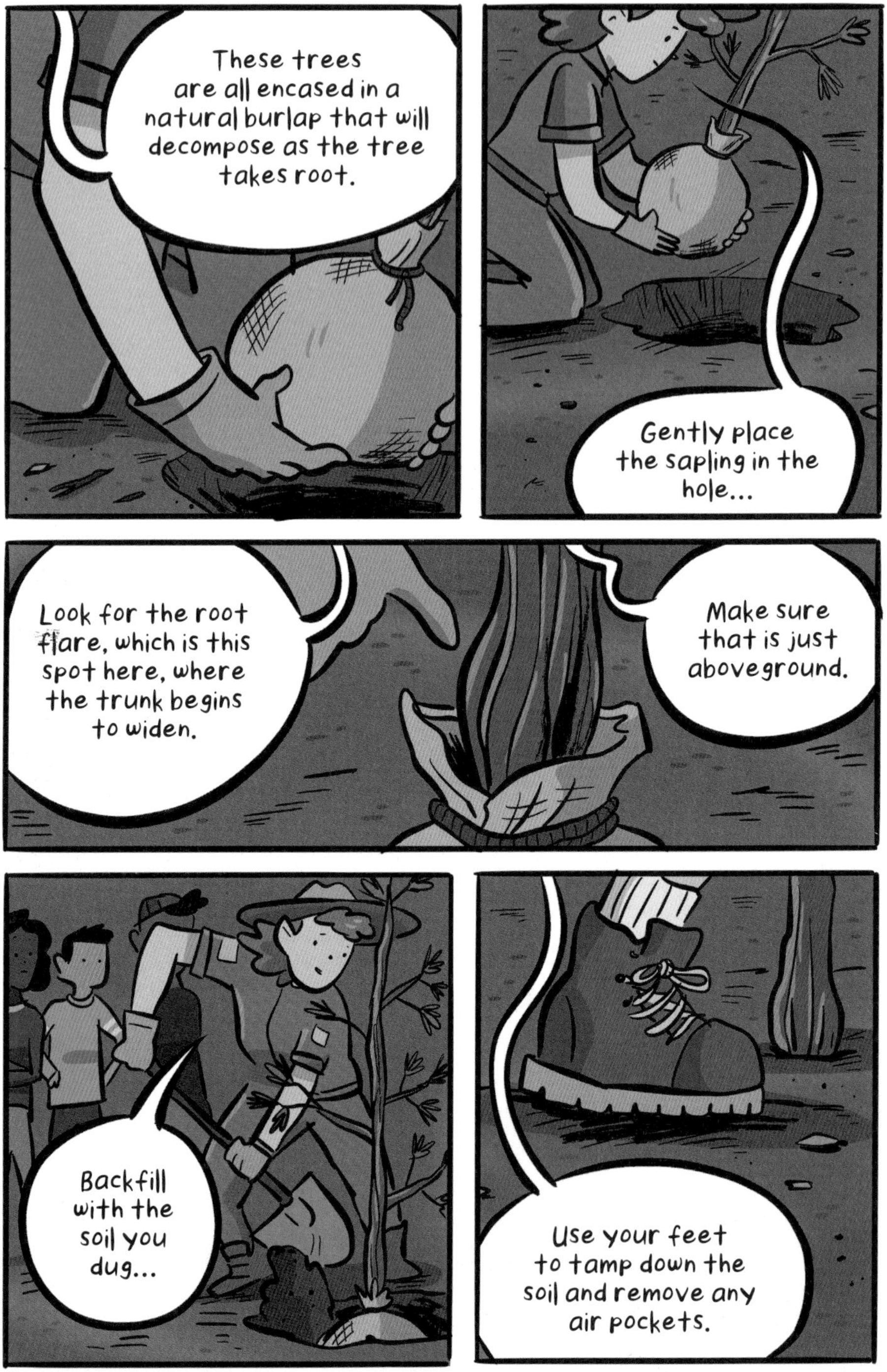
These trees are all encased in a natural burlap that will decompose as the tree takes root.
Gently place the sapling in the hole...
Look for the root flare, which is this spot here, where the trunk begins to widen.
Make sure that is just aboveground.
Backfill with the soil you dug...
Use your feet to tamp down the soil and remove any air pockets.

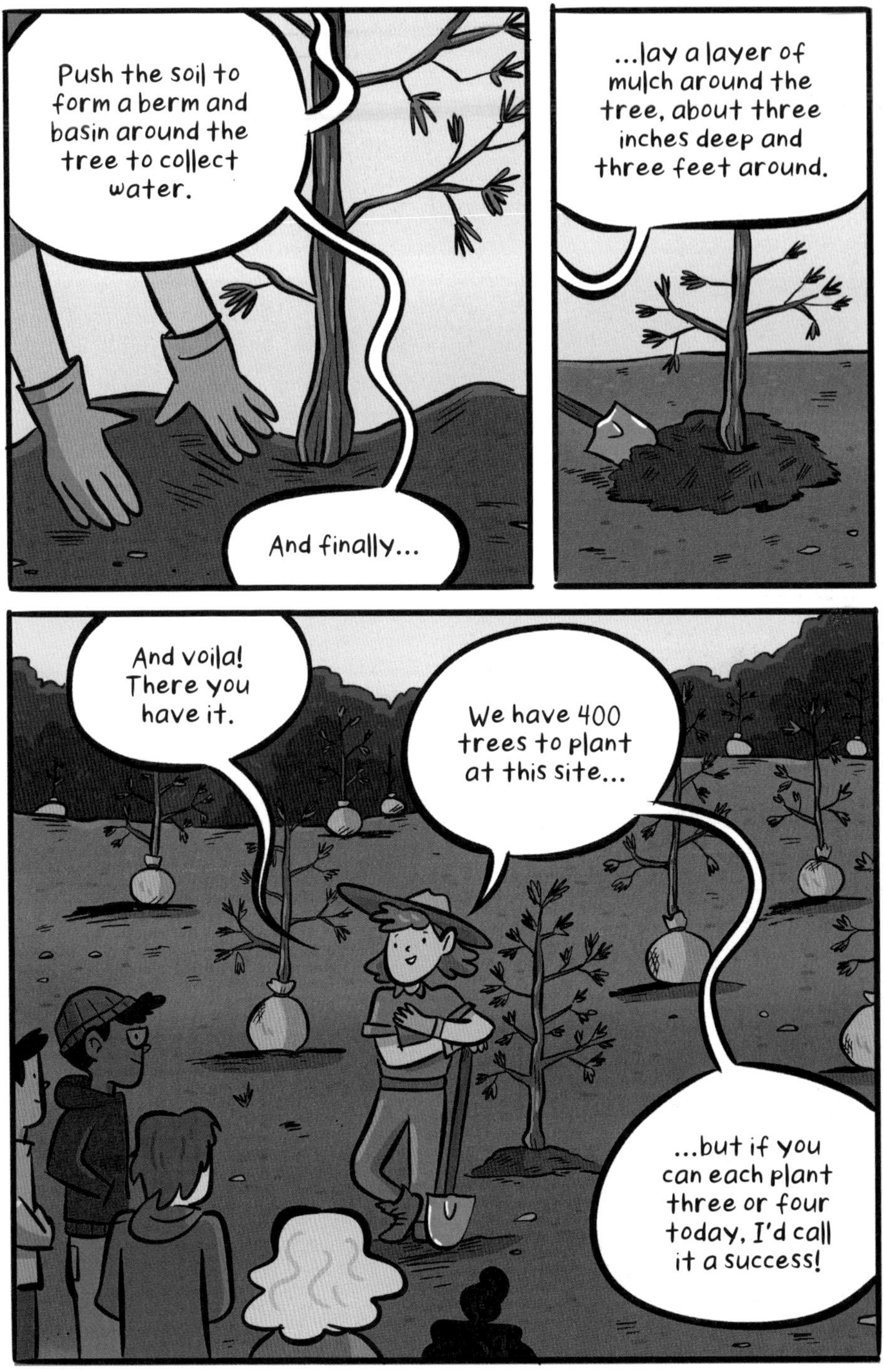
Push the soil to form a berm and basin around the tree to collect water.
And finally...
...lay a layer of mulch around the tree, about three inches deep and three feet around.
And voila! There you have it.
We have 400 trees to plant at this site...
...but if you can each plant three or four today, I'd call it a success!

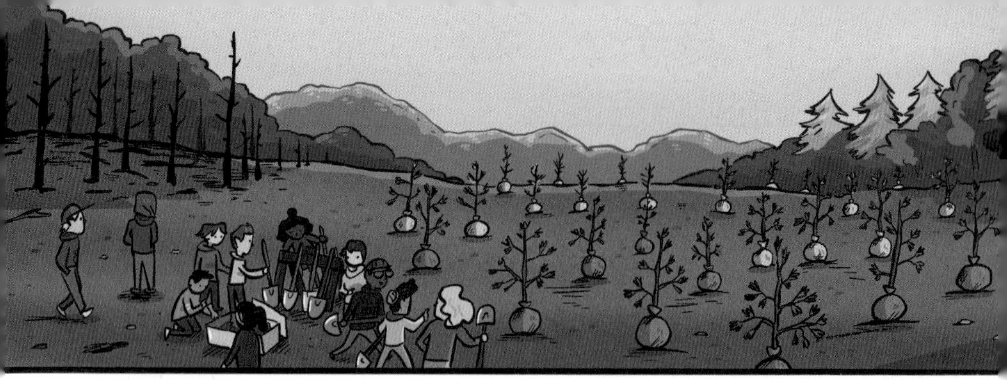

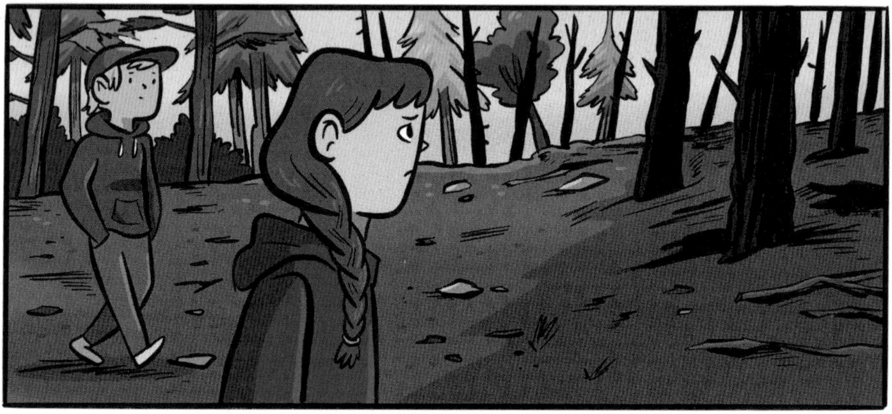

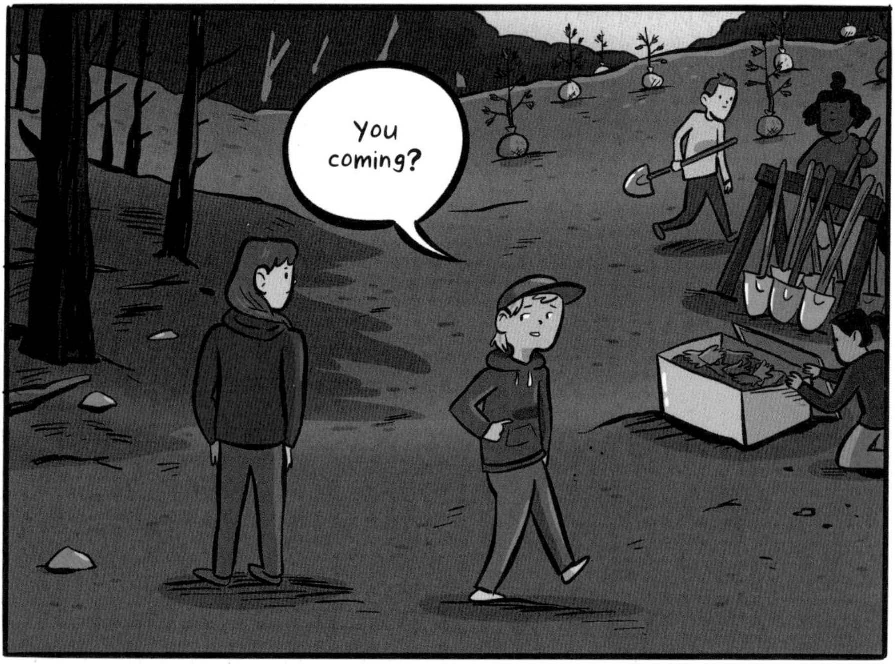
You coming?

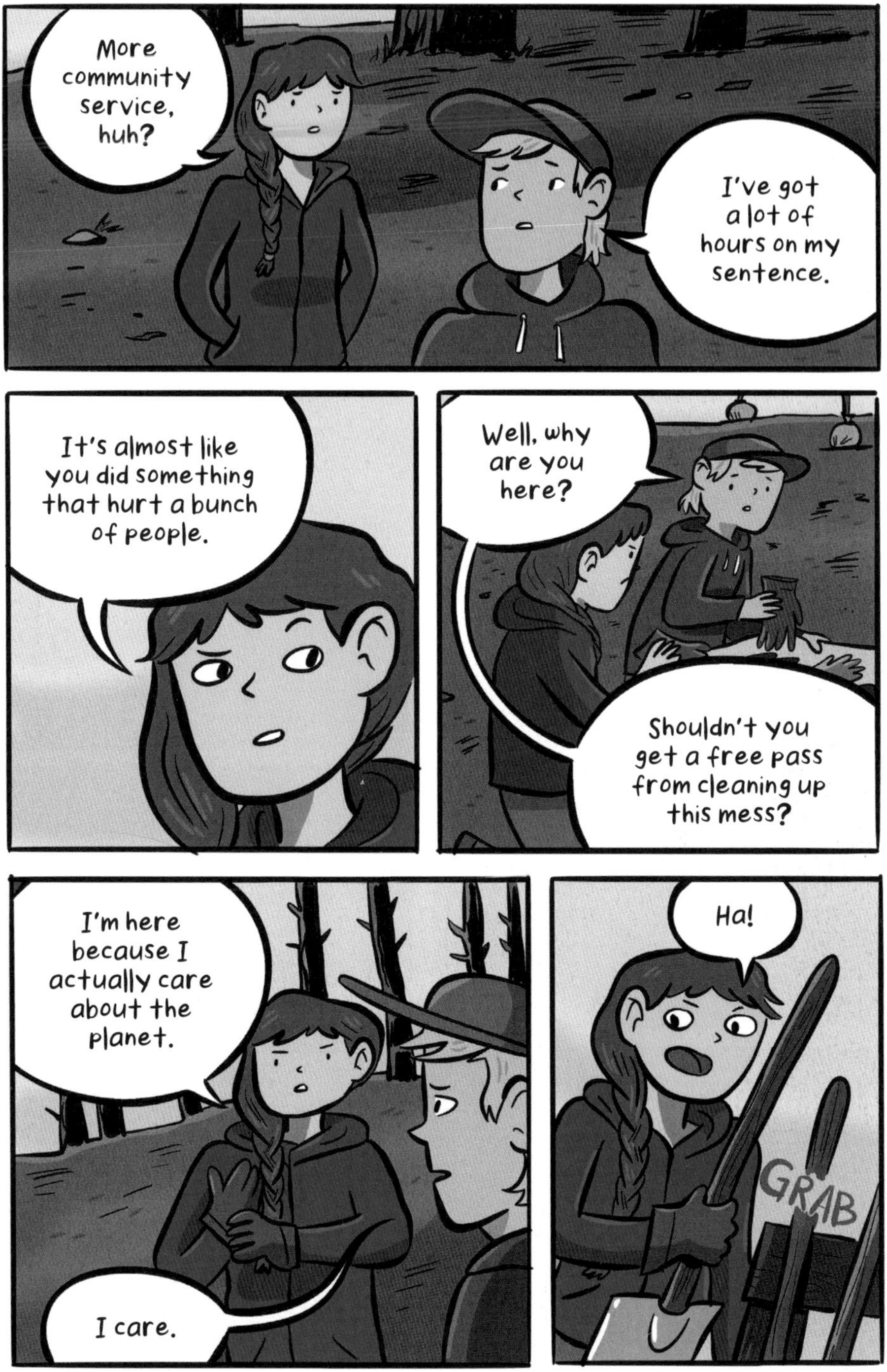
More community service, huh?
I've got a lot of hours on my sentence.
It's almost like you did something that hurt a bunch of people.
Well, why are you here?
Shouldn't you get a free pass from cleaning up this mess?
I'm here because I actually care about the planet.
I care.
Ha!
GRAB

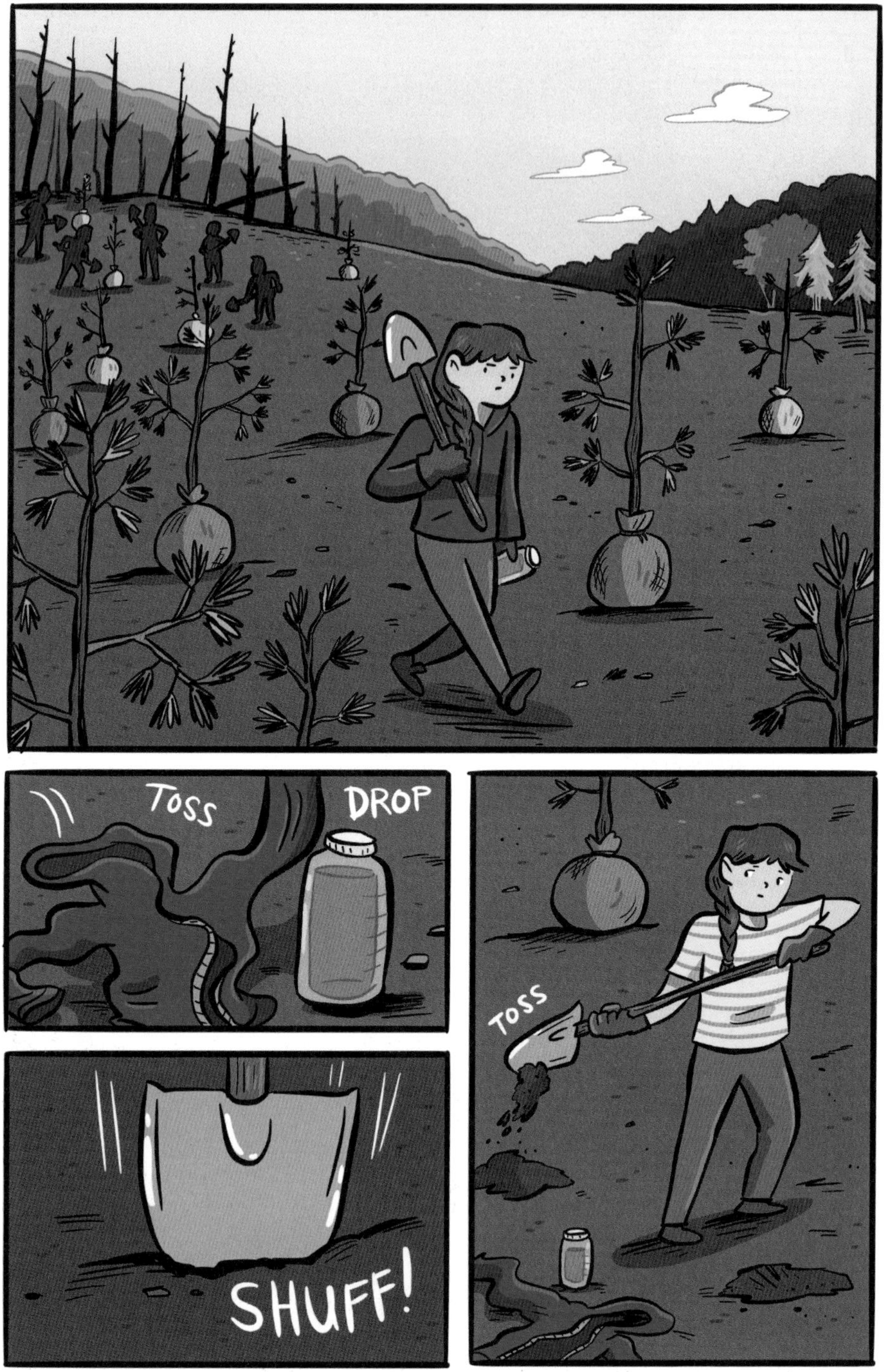
TOSS
DROP
TOSS
SHUFF!

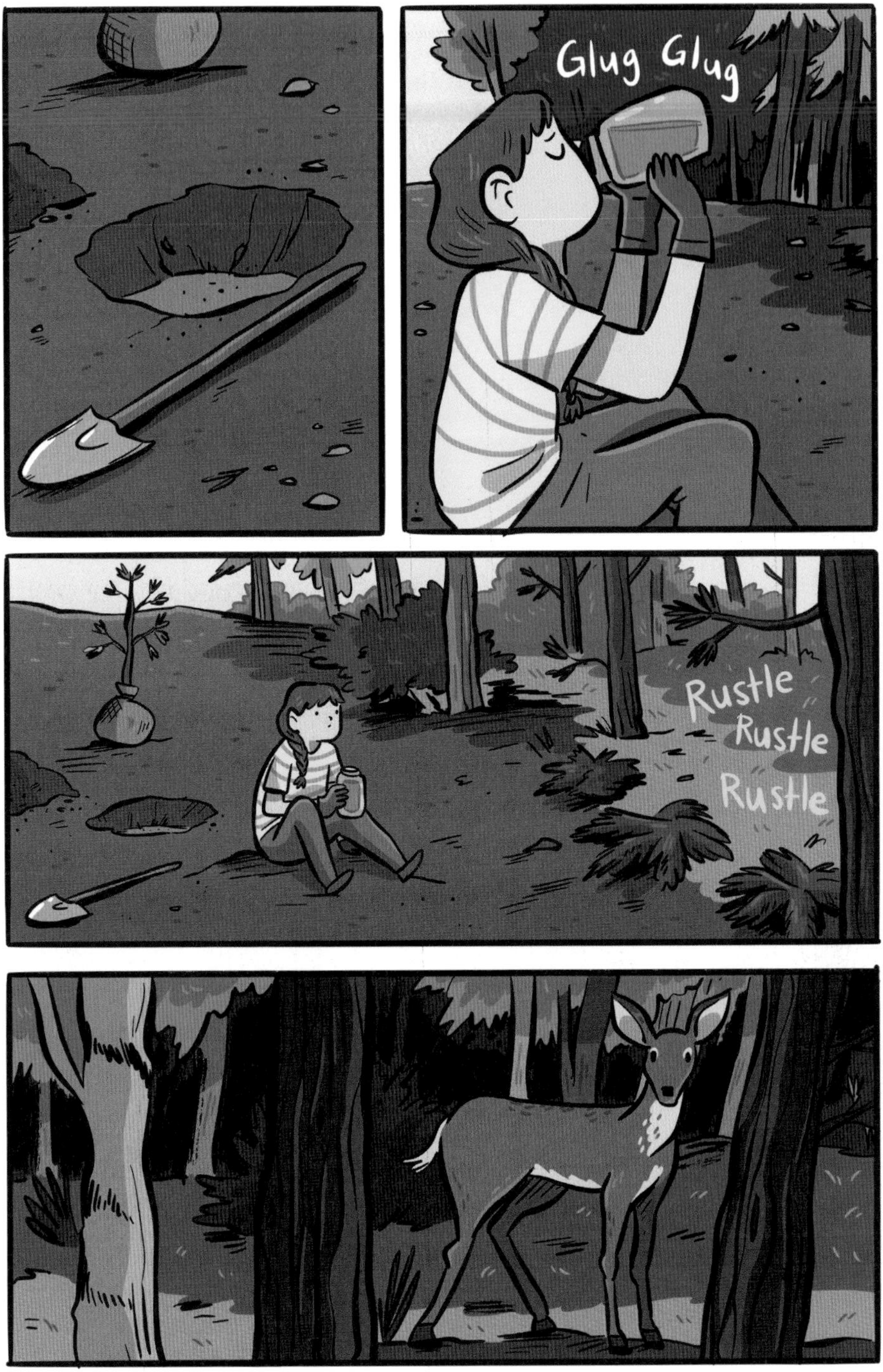
Glug Glug
Rustle
Rustle
Rustle

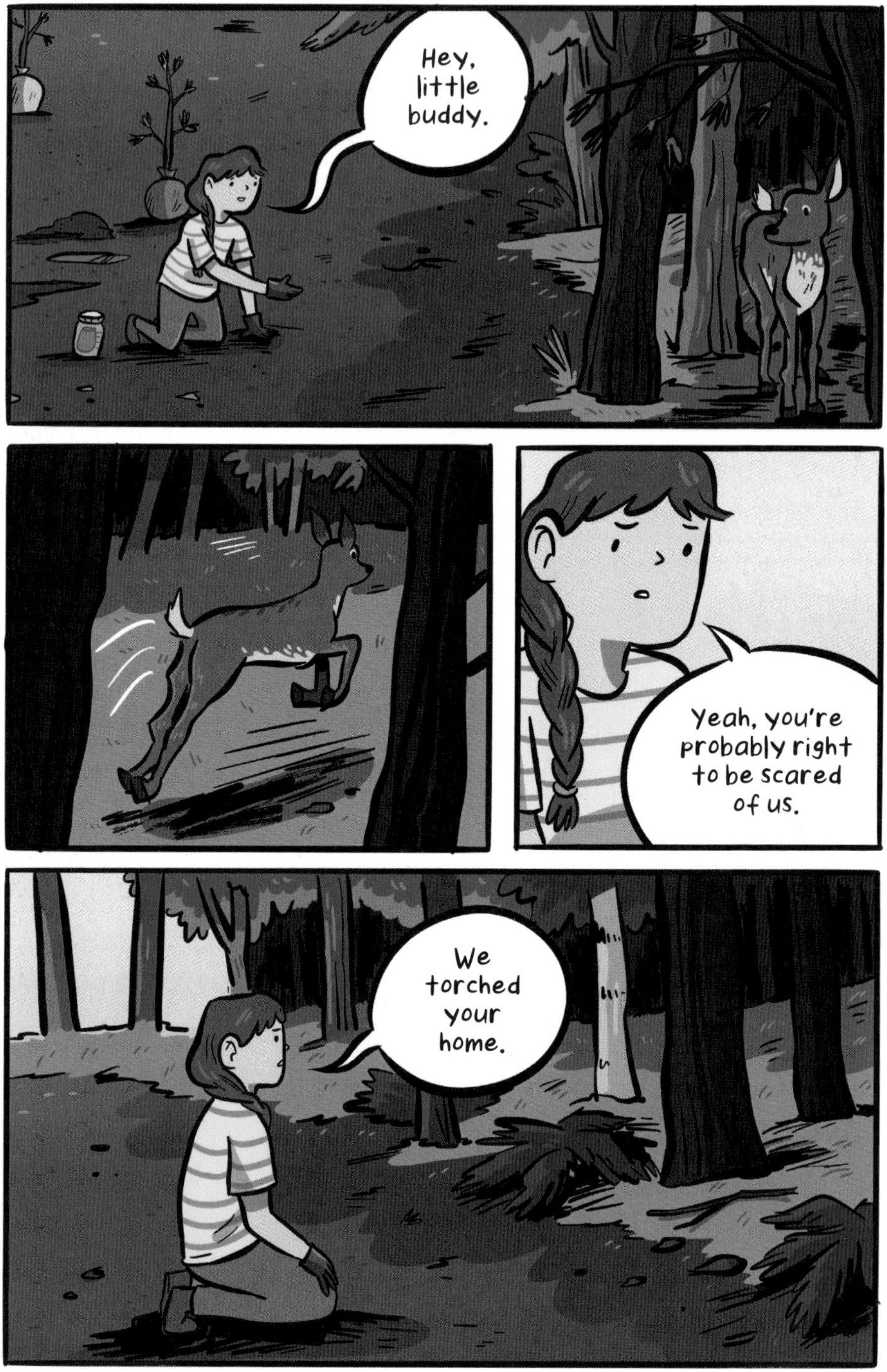
Hey, little buddy.
Yeah, you're probably right to be scared of us.
We torched your home.

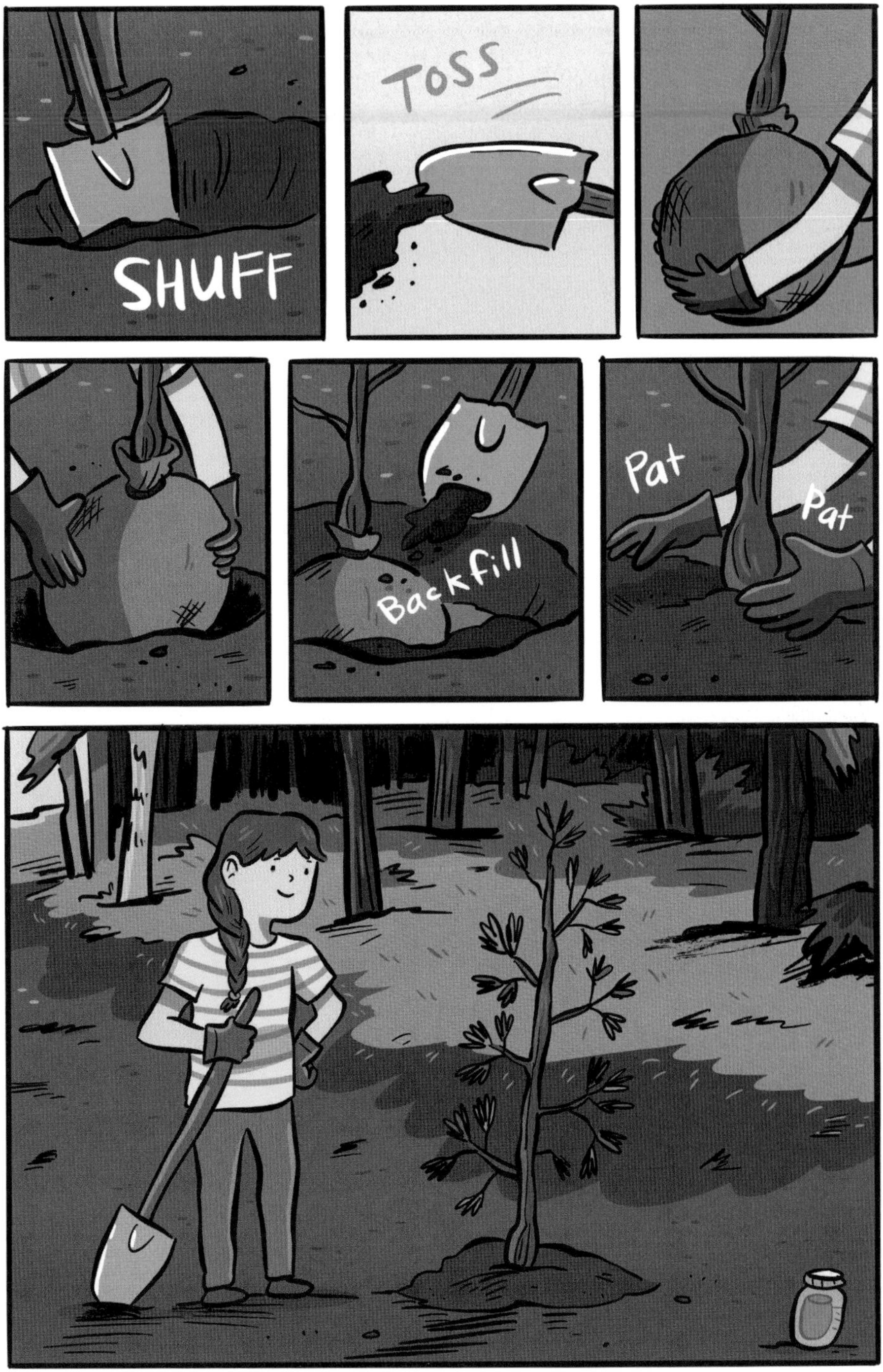
SHUFF
TOSS
Backfill
Pat
Pat

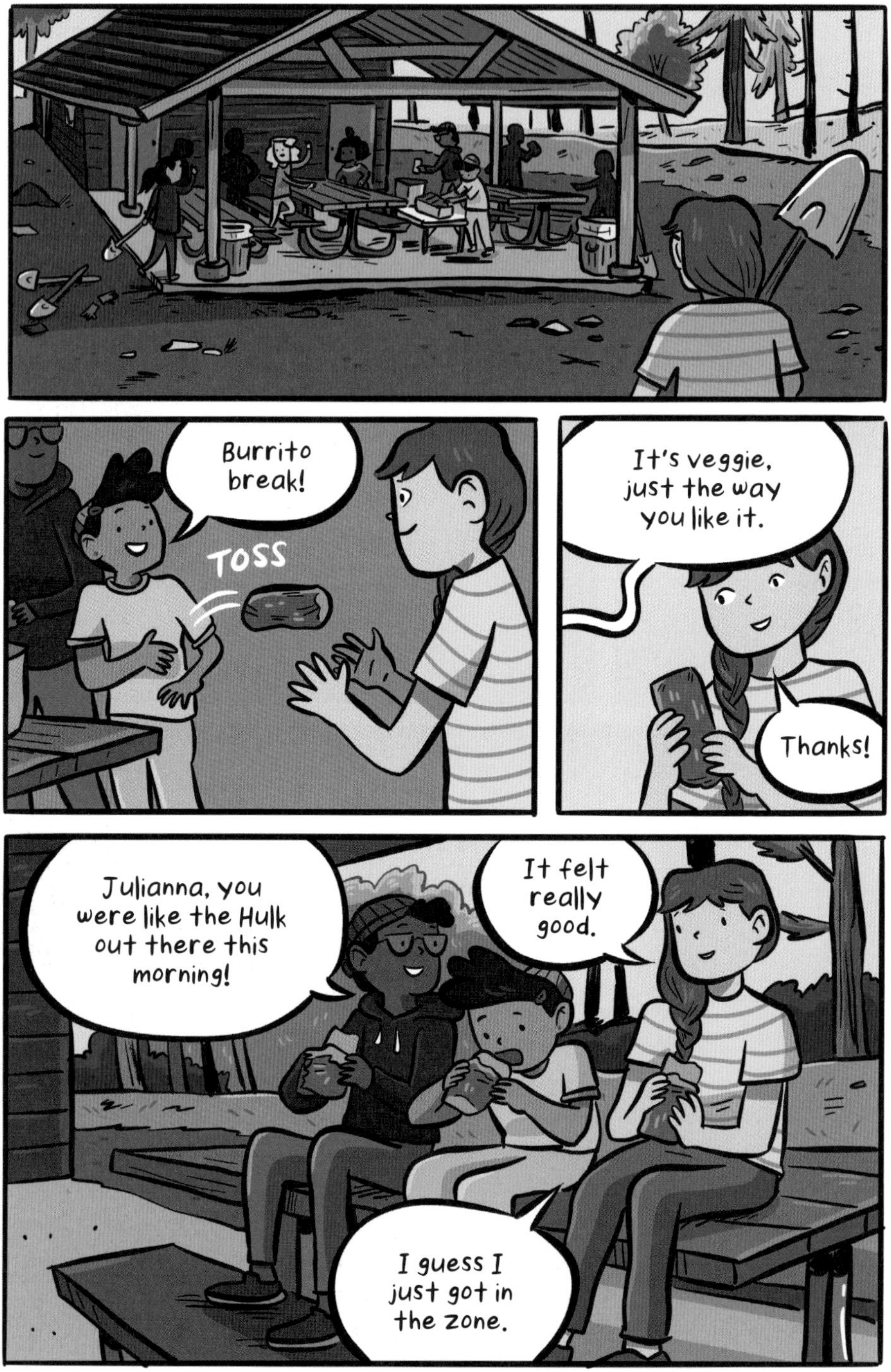
Burrito break!
TOSS
It's veggie, just the way you like it.
Thanks!
Julianna, you were like the Hulk out there this morning!
It felt really good.
I guess I just got in the zone.

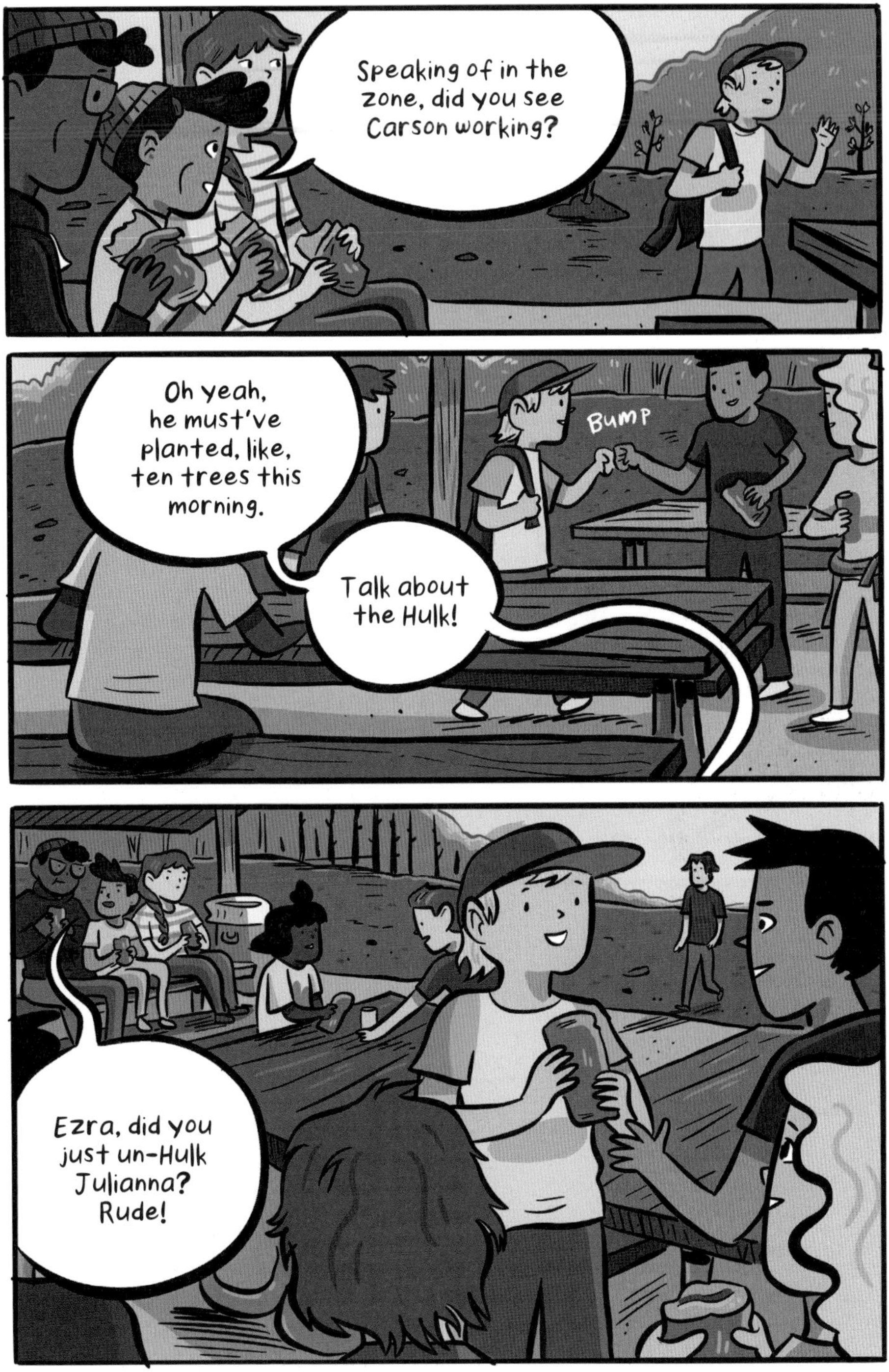
Speaking of in the zone, did you see Carson working?
Oh yeah, he must've planted, like, ten trees this morning.
BUMP
Talk about the Hulk!
Ezra, did you just un-Hulk Julianna? Rude!

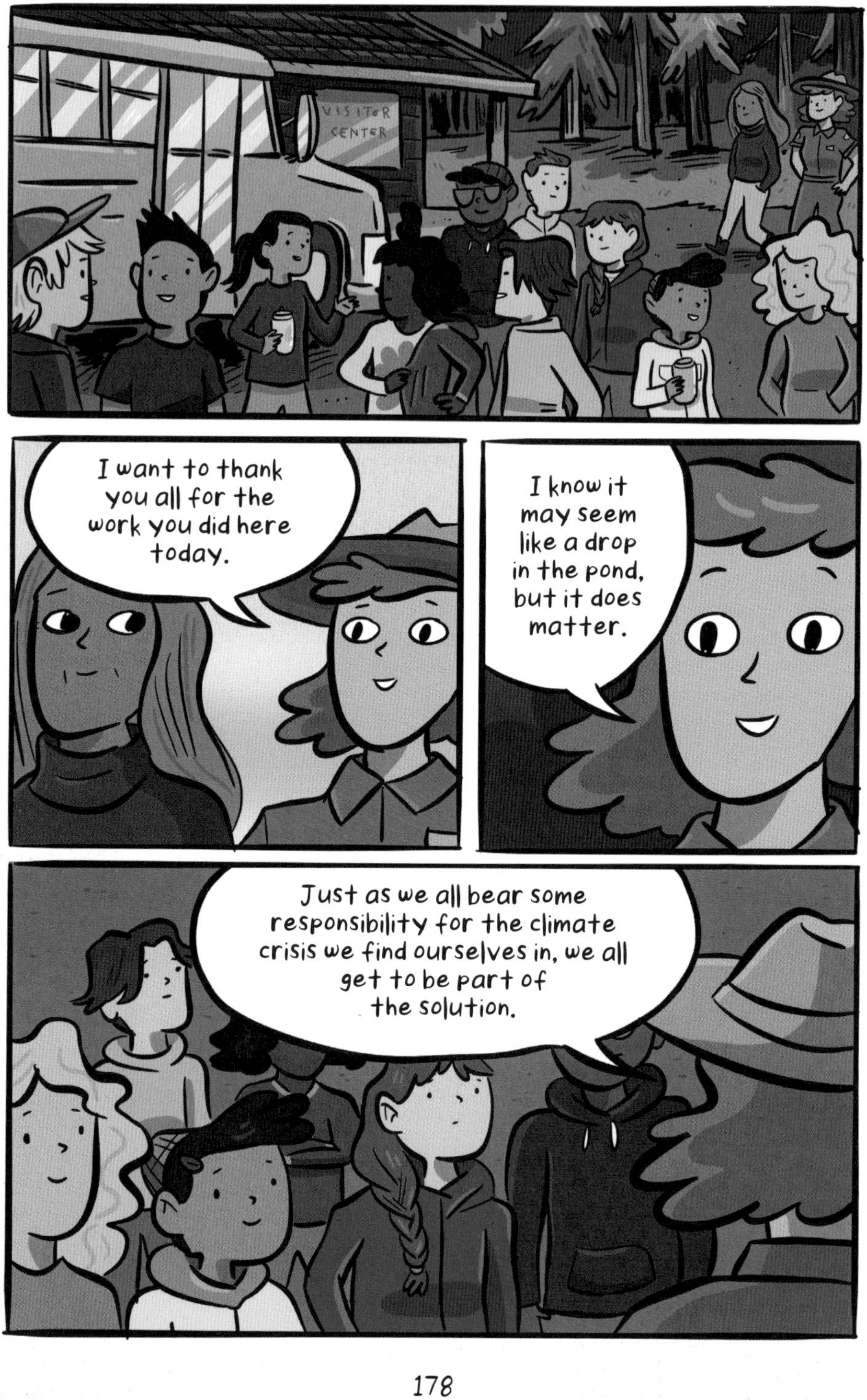
VISITOR CENTER
I want to thank you all for the work you did here today.
I know it may seem like a drop in the pond, but it does matter.
Just as we all bear some responsibility for the climate crisis we find ourselves in, we all get to be part of the solution.

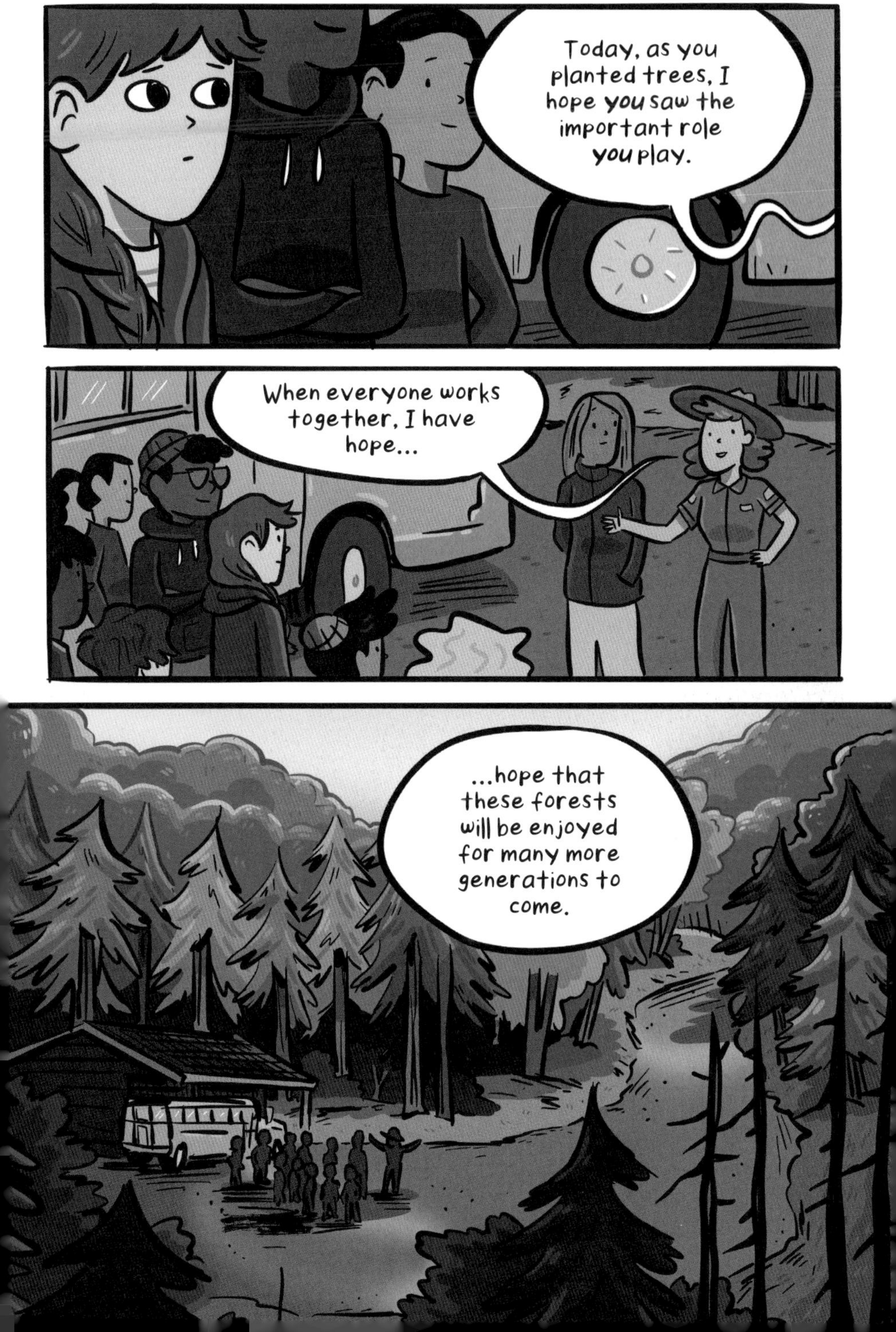
Today, as you planted trees, I hope you saw the important role you play.
When everyone works together, I have hope...
...hope that these forests will be enjoyed for many more generations to come.

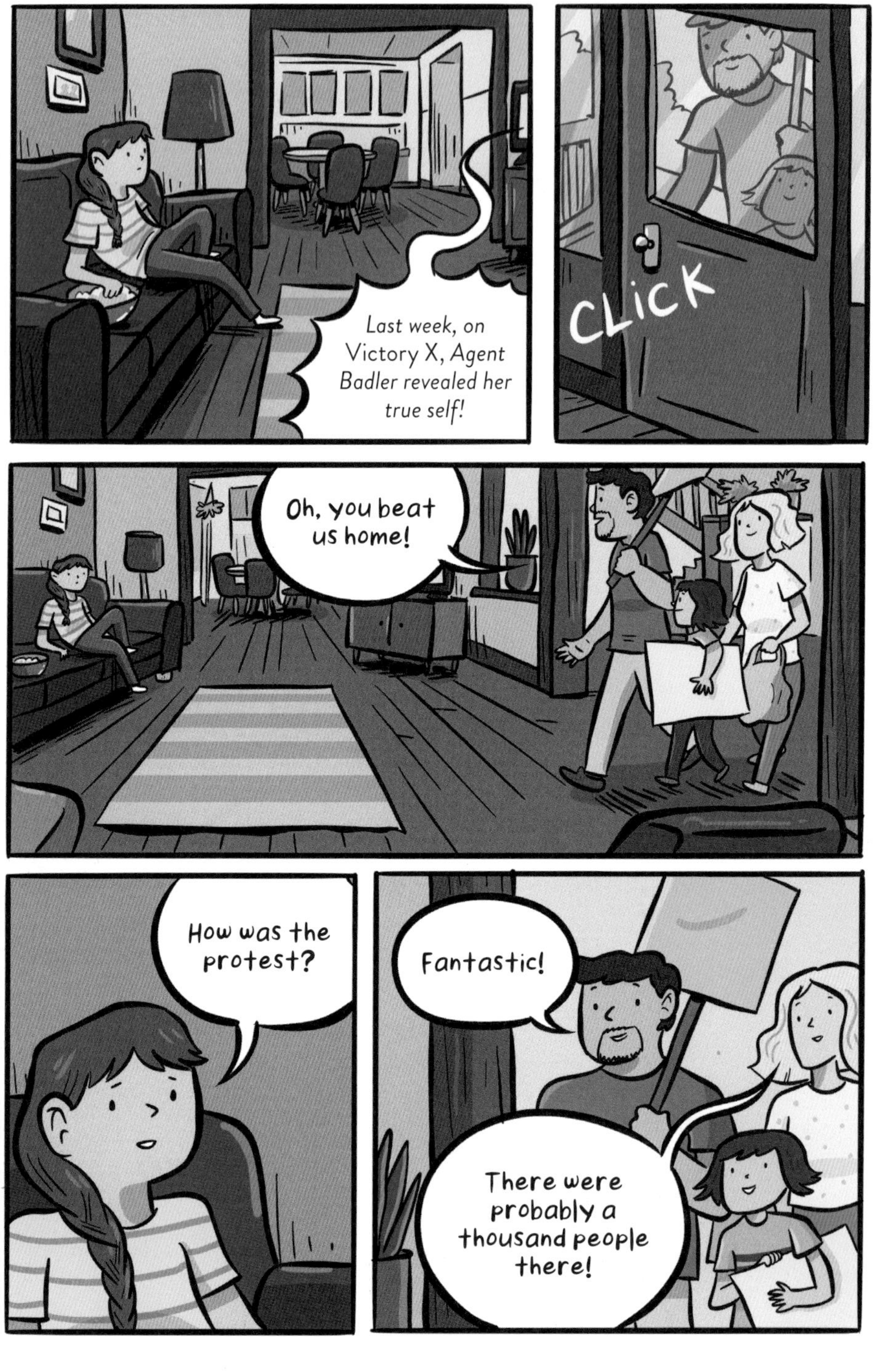
Last week, on Victory X, Agent Badler revealed her true self!
CLICK
Oh, you beat us home!
How was the protest?
Fantastic!
There were probably a thousand people there!

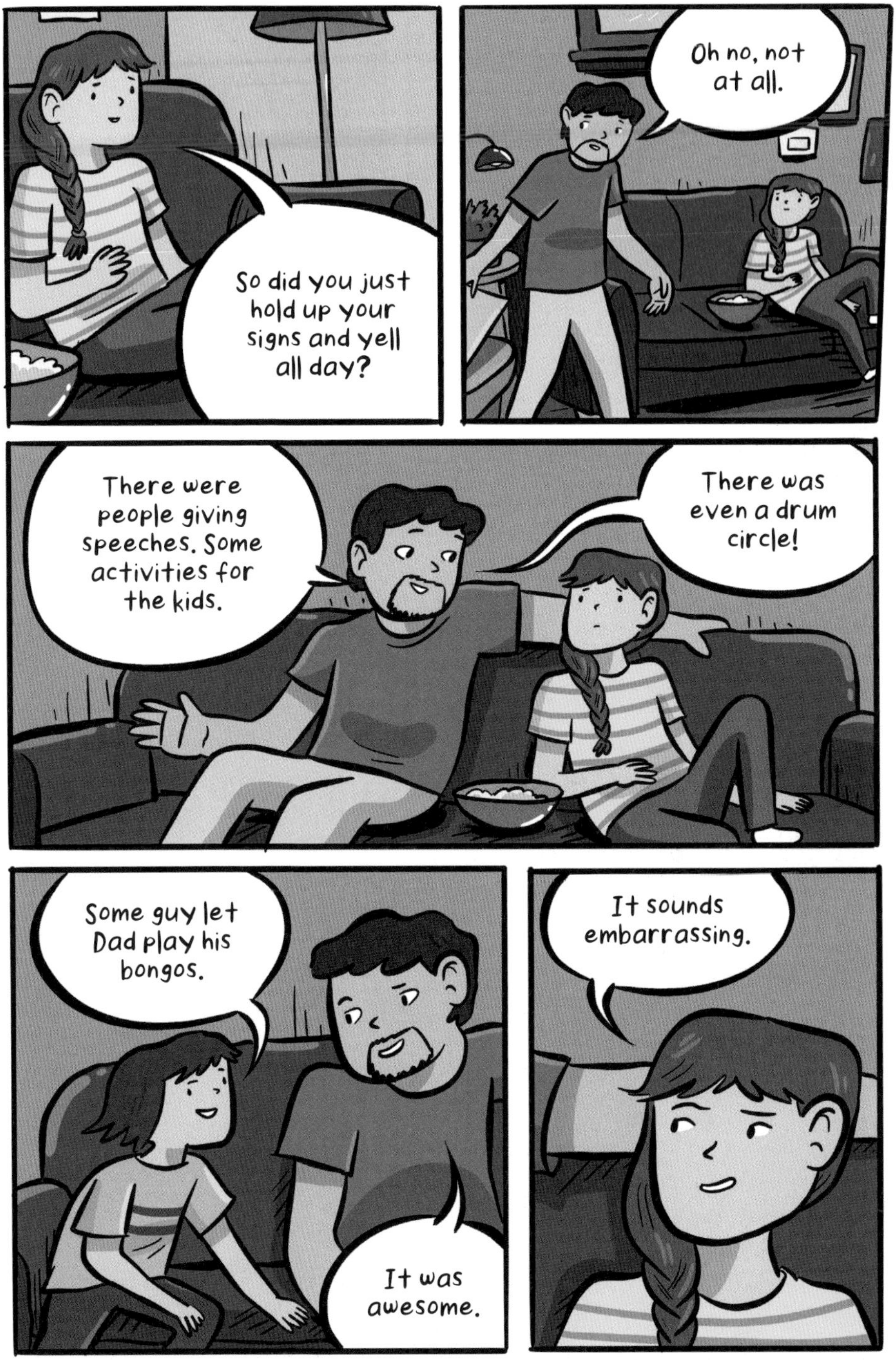
So did you just hold up your signs and yell all day?
Oh no, not at all.
There were people giving speeches. Some activities for the kids.
There was even a drum circle!
Some guy let Dad play his bongos.
It was awesome.
It sounds embarrassing.

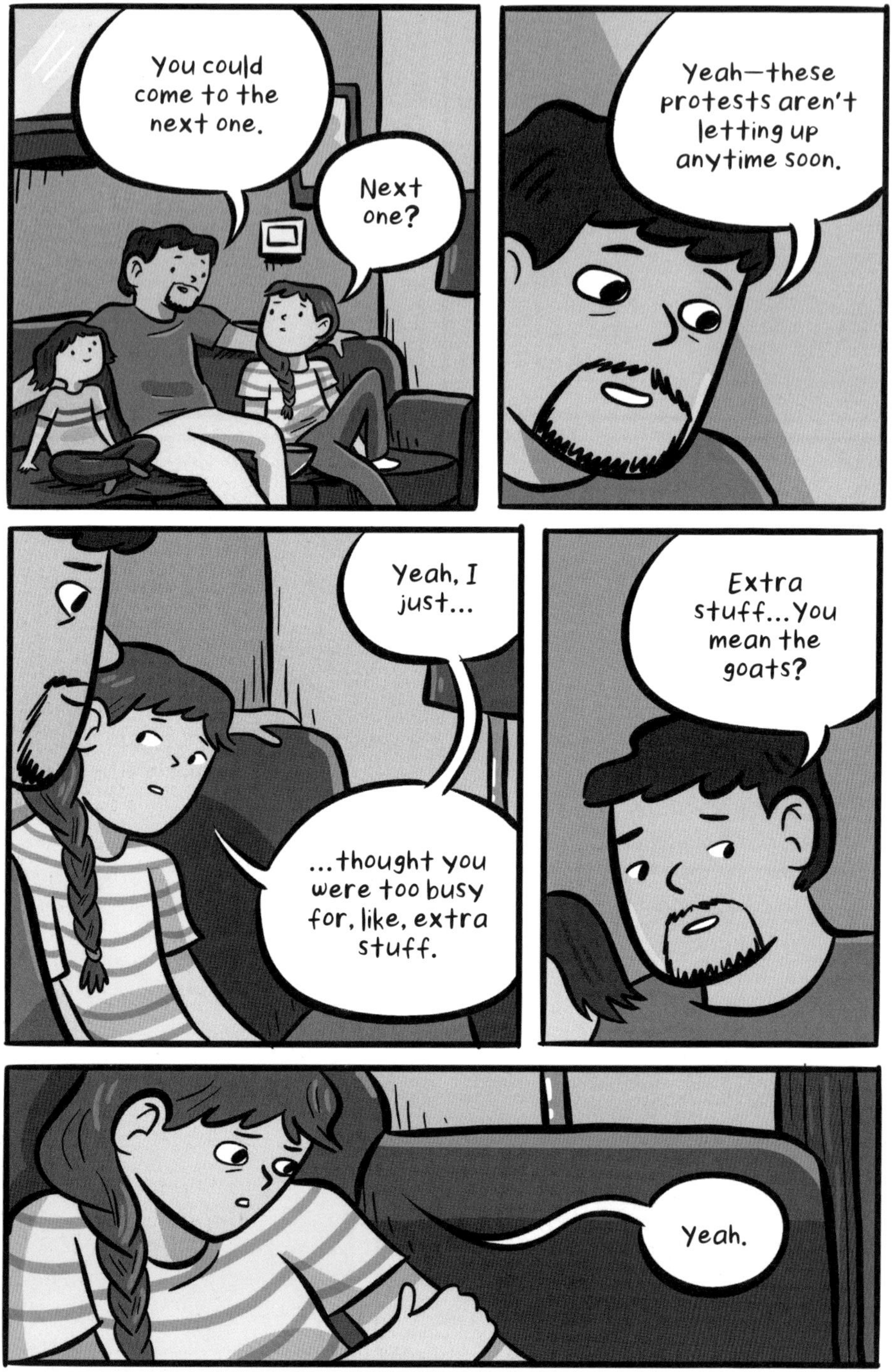
You could come to the next one.
Next one?
Yeah—these protests aren't letting up anytime soon.
Yeah, I just...
...thought you were too busy for, like, extra stuff.
Extra stuff...You mean the goats?
Yeah.

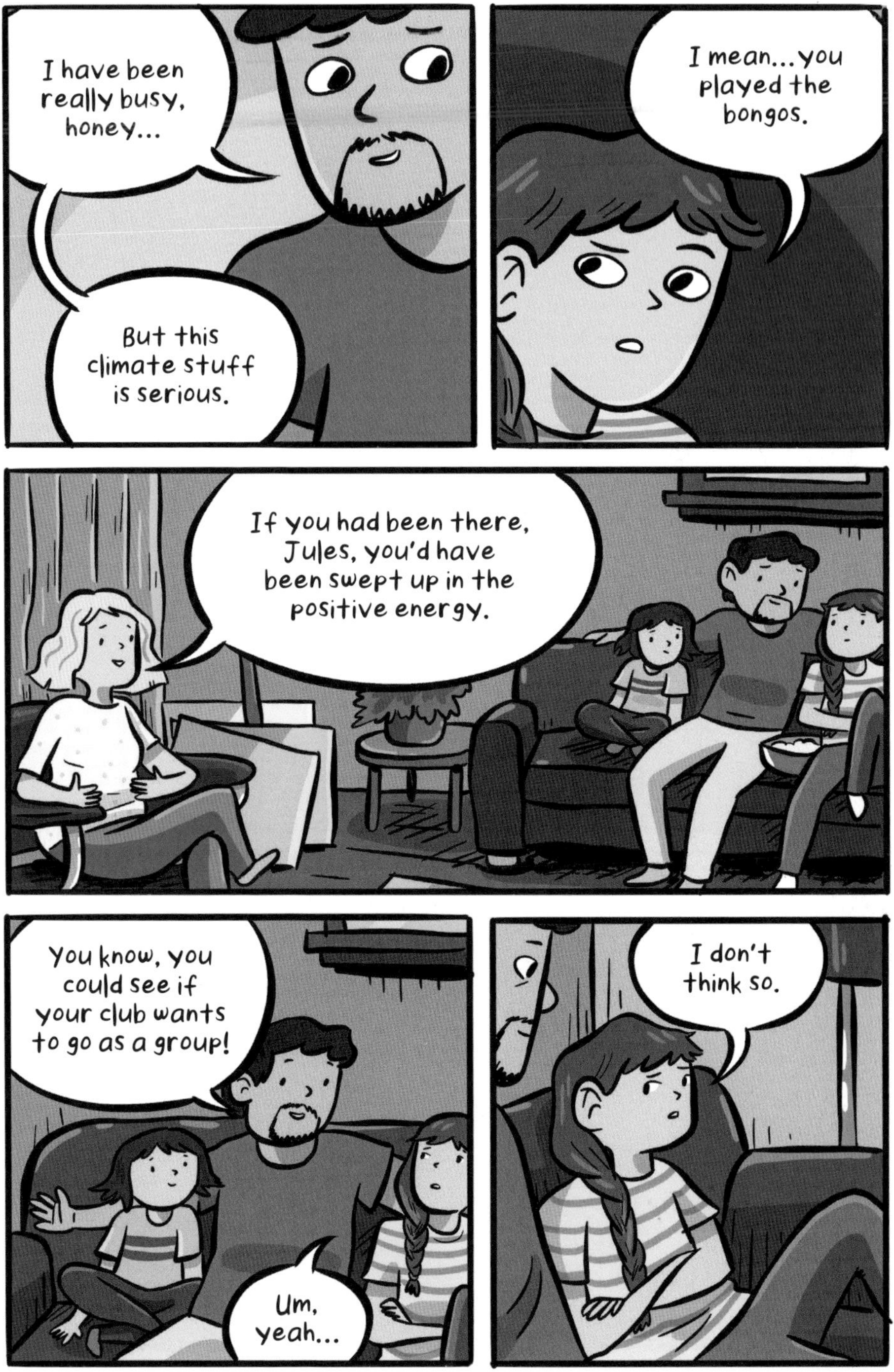

I have been really busy, honey...
But this climate stuff is serious.
I mean... you played the bongos.
If you had been there, Jules, you'd have been swept up in the positive energy.
You know, you could see if your club wants to go as a group!
Um, yeah...
I don't think so.

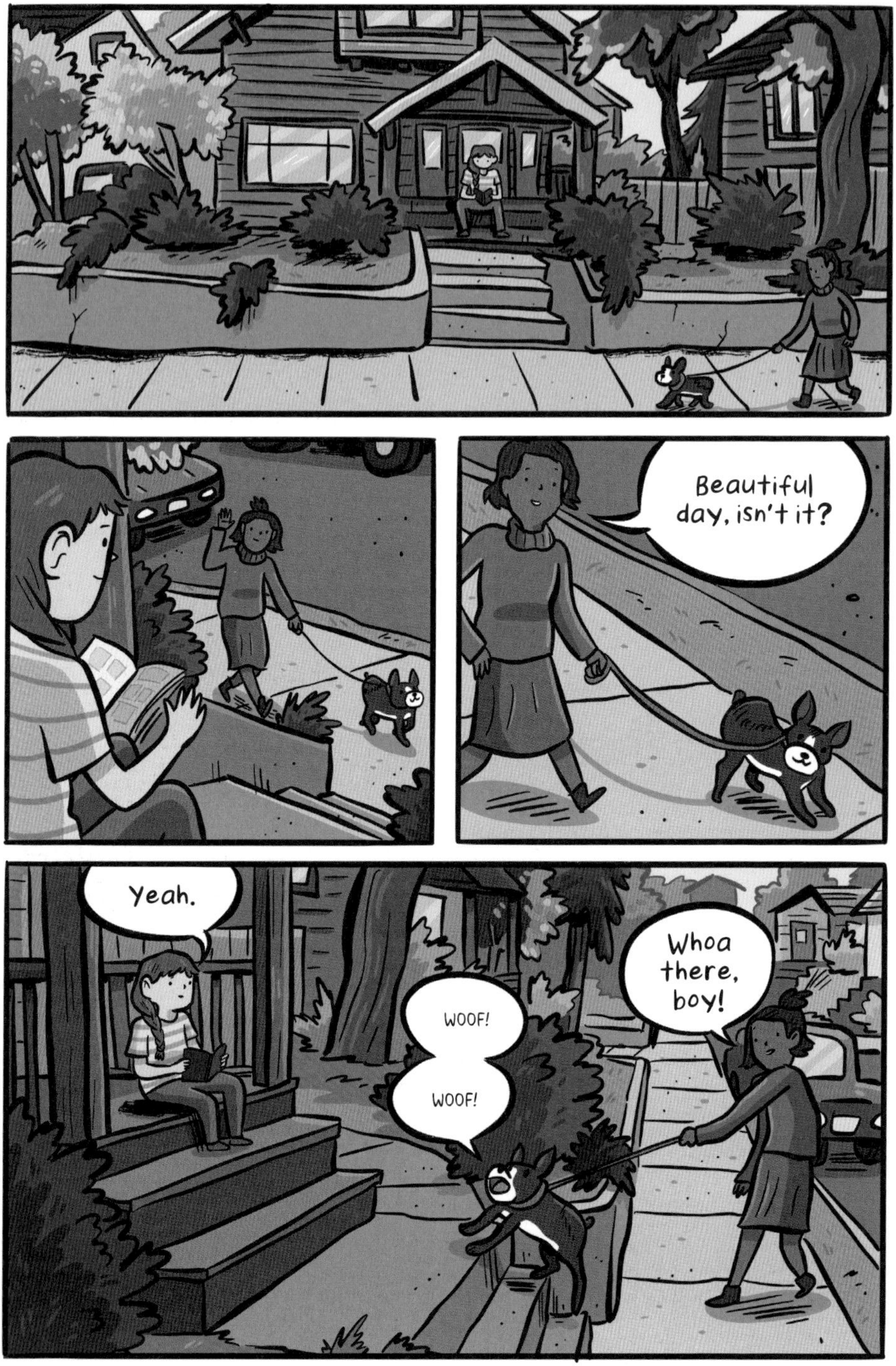
Beautiful day, isn't it?
Yeah.
Whoa there, boy!
WOOF!
WOOF!

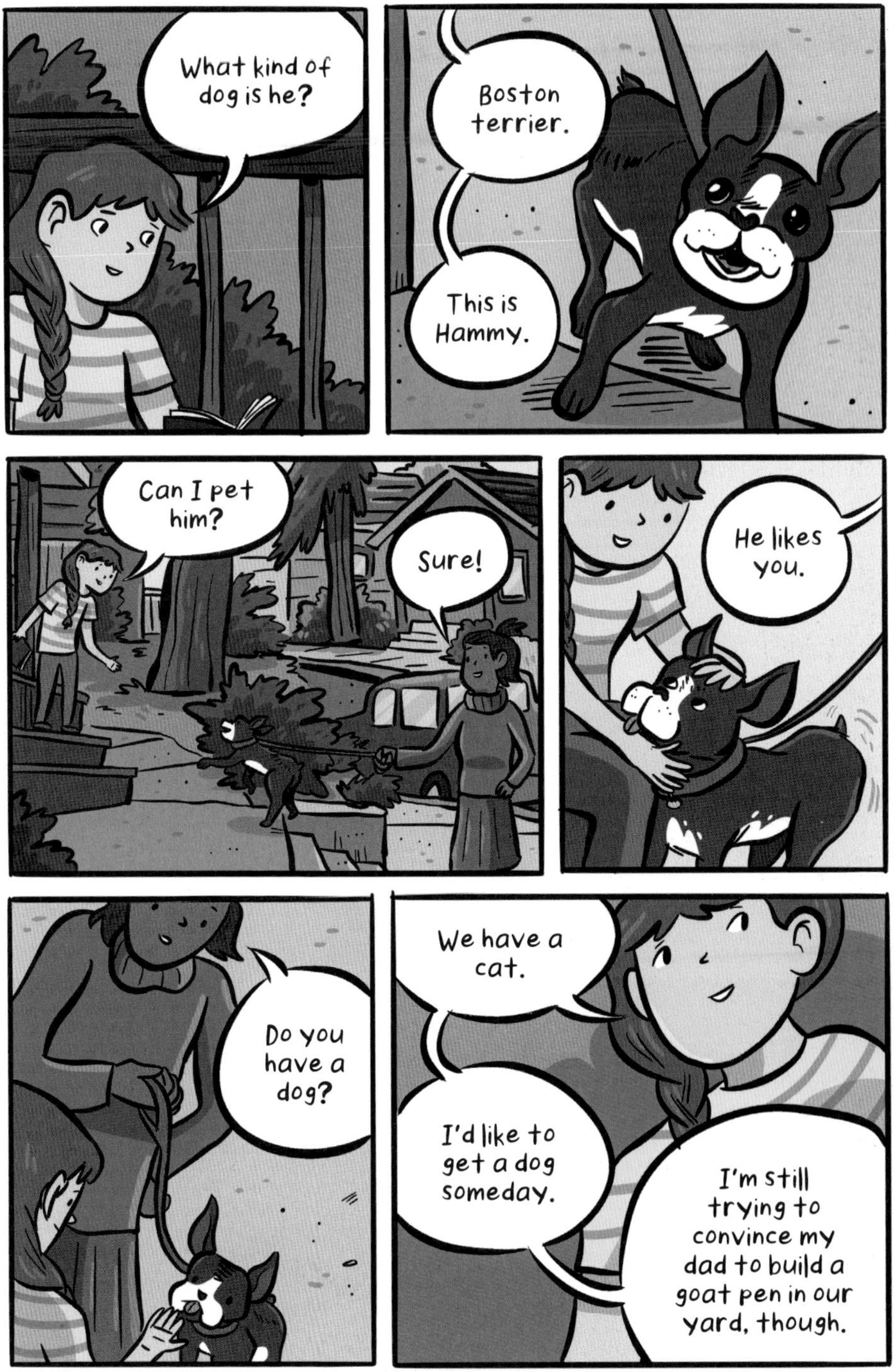
What kind of dog is he?
Boston terrier.
This is Hammy.
Can I pet him?
Sure!
He likes you.
Do you have a dog?
We have a cat.
I'd like to get a dog someday.
I'm still trying to convince my dad to build a goat pen in our yard, though.

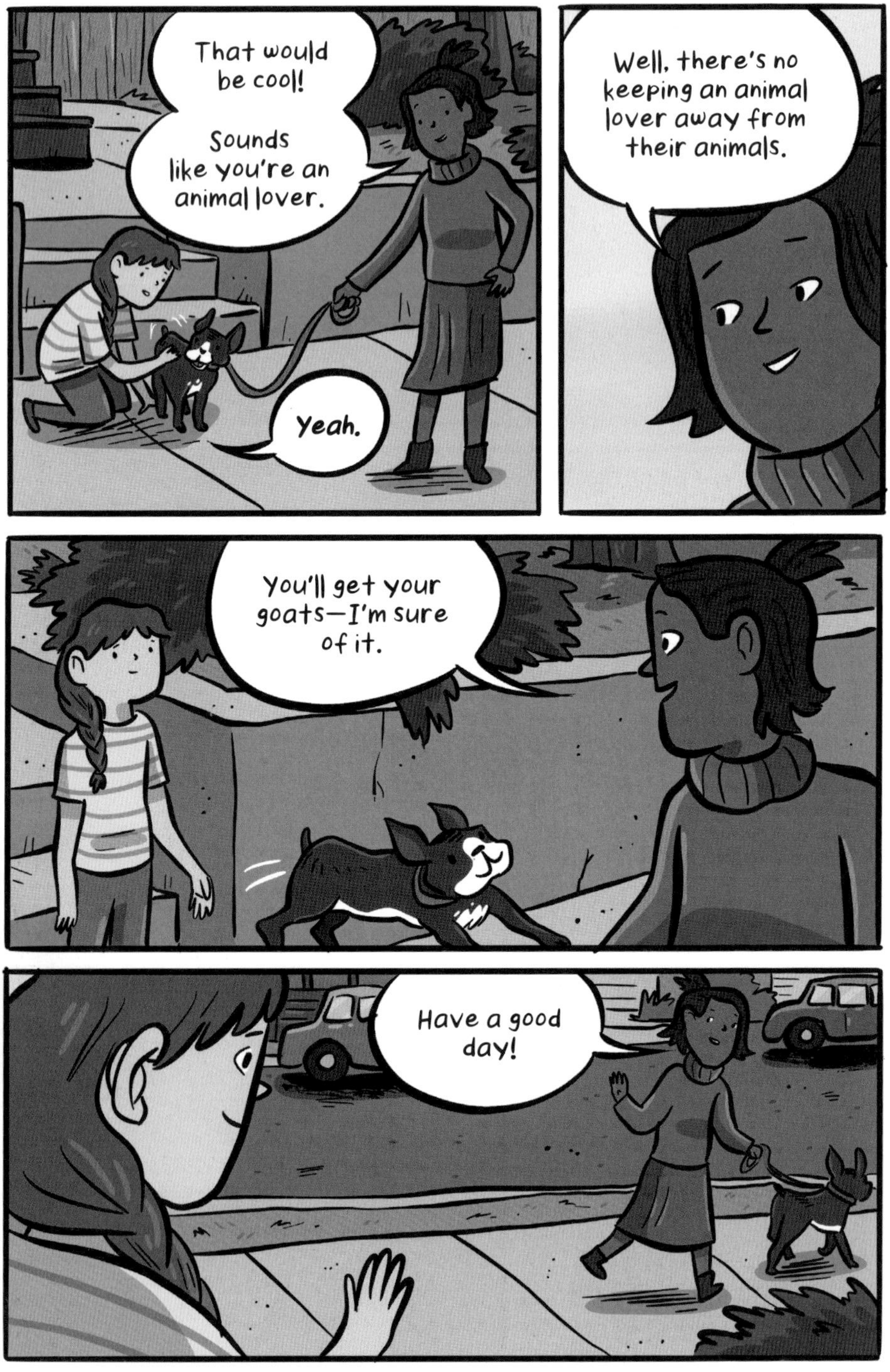
That would be cool!
Sounds like you're an animal lover.
Yeah.
Well, there's no keeping an animal lover away from their animals.
You'll get your goats—I'm sure of it.
Have a good day!

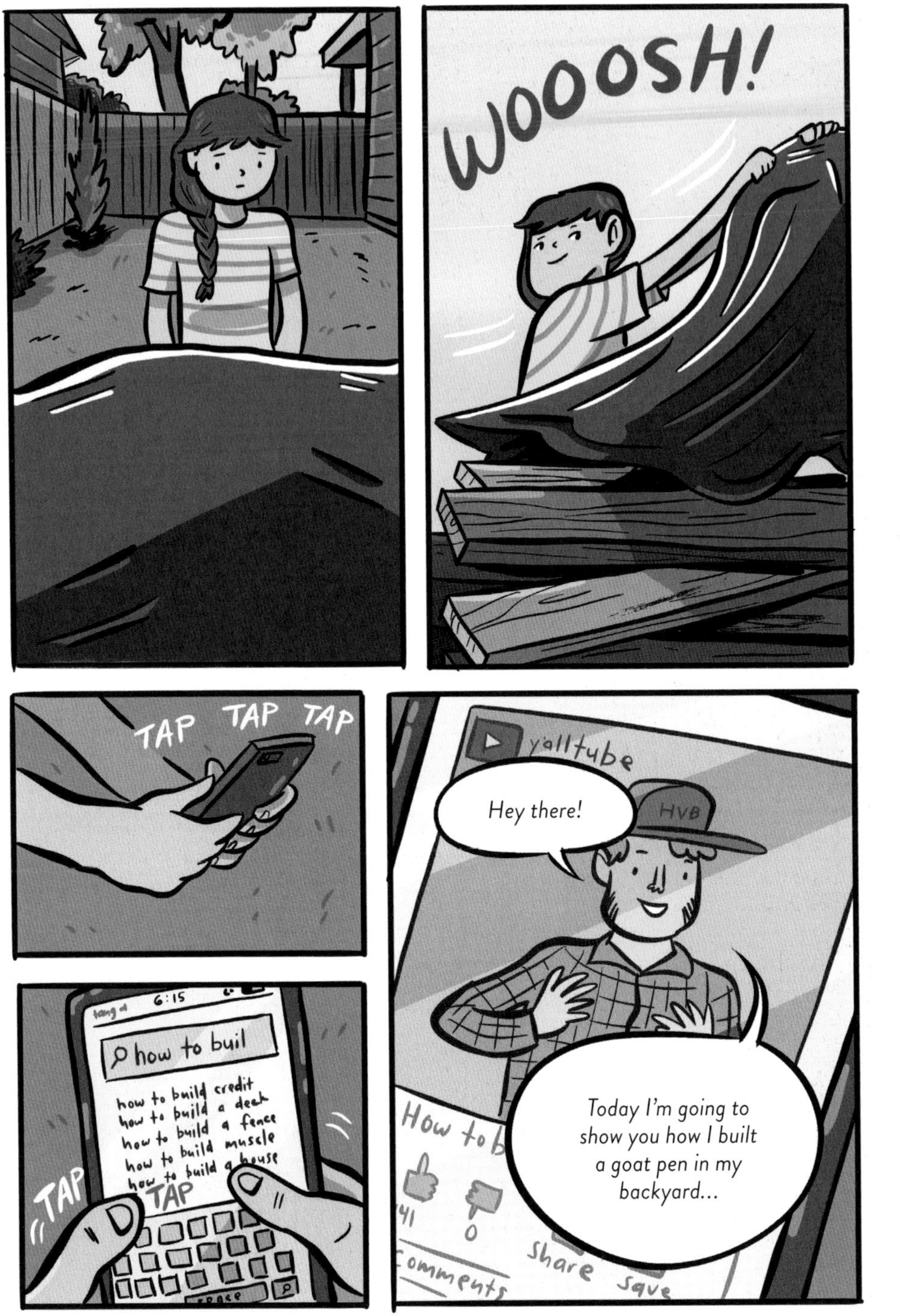
WOOOSH!
TAP TAP TAP
yalltube
Hey there!
HVB
6:15
how to buil
how to build credit
how to build a deck
how to build a fence
how to build muscle
how to build a house
TAP
TAP
Today I'm going to show you how I built a goat pen in my backyard...
How to b
0
share
save
comments

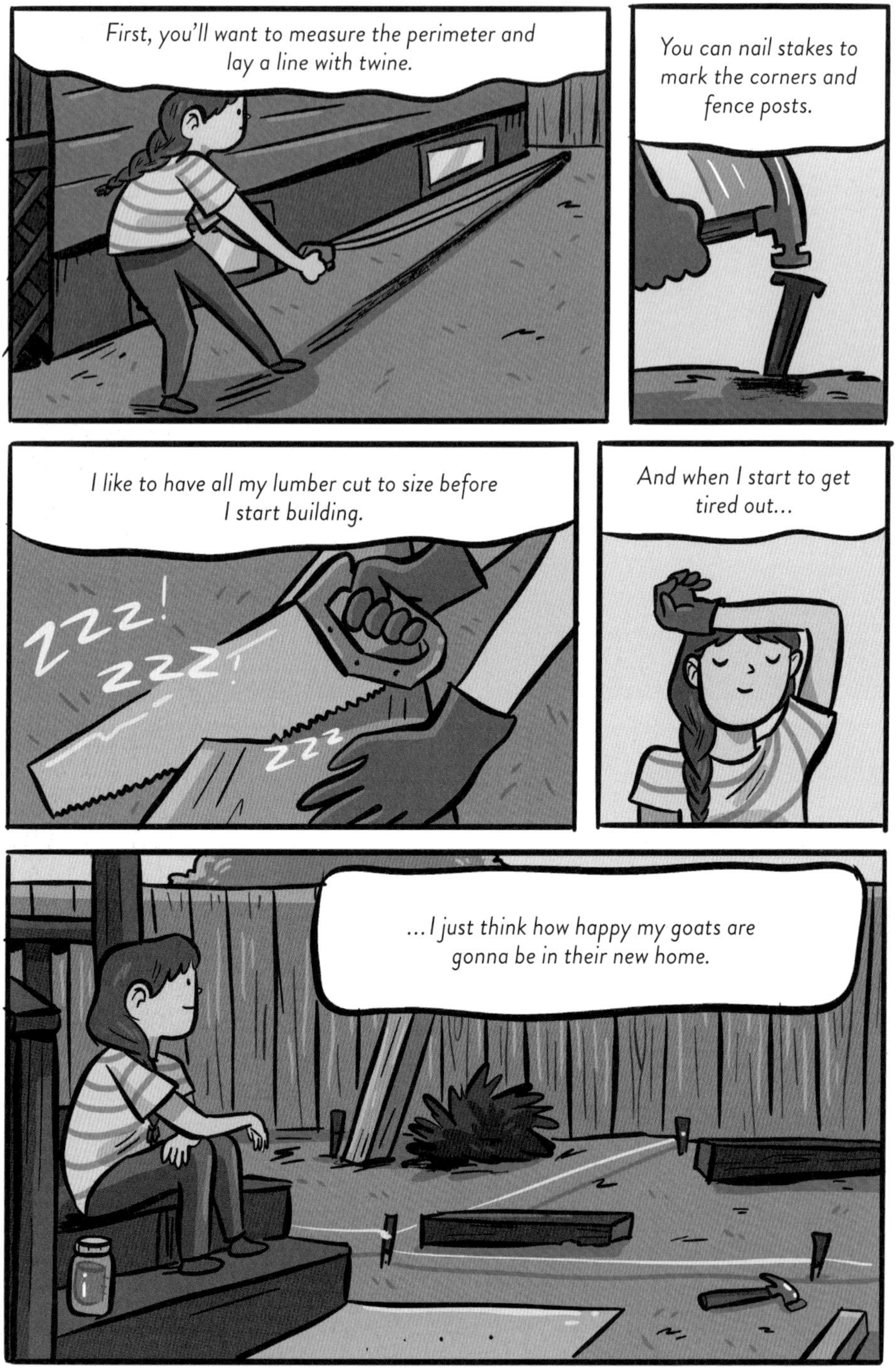
First, you'll want to measure the perimeter and lay a line with twine.
You can nail stakes to mark the corners and fence posts.
I like to have all my lumber cut to size before I start building.
ZZZ!
ZZZ!
ZZZ
And when I start to get tired out...
...I just think how happy my goats are gonna be in their new home.

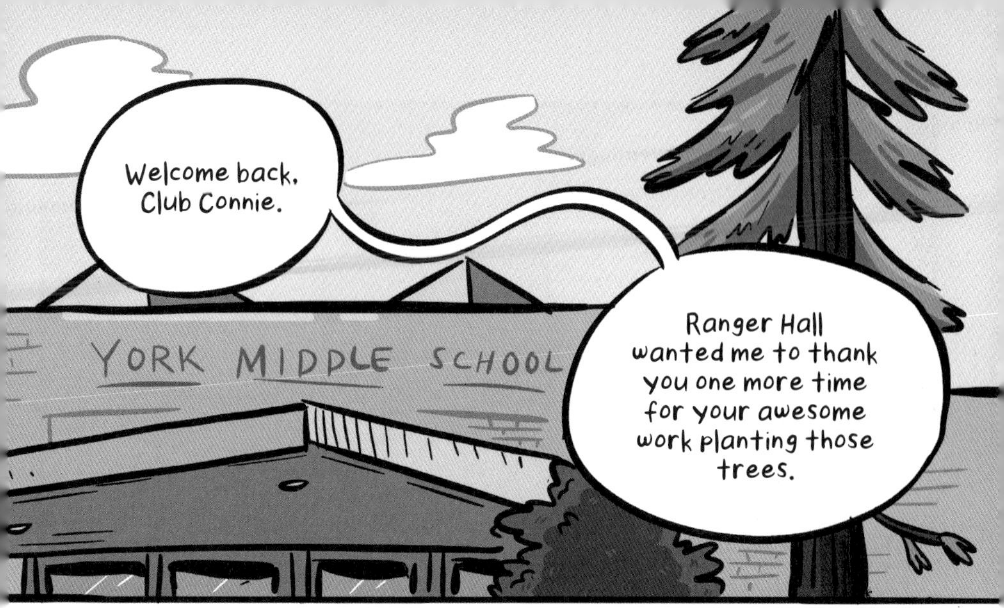
YORK MIDDLE SCHOOL
Welcome back, Club Connie.
Ranger Hall wanted me to thank you one more time for your awesome work planting those trees.

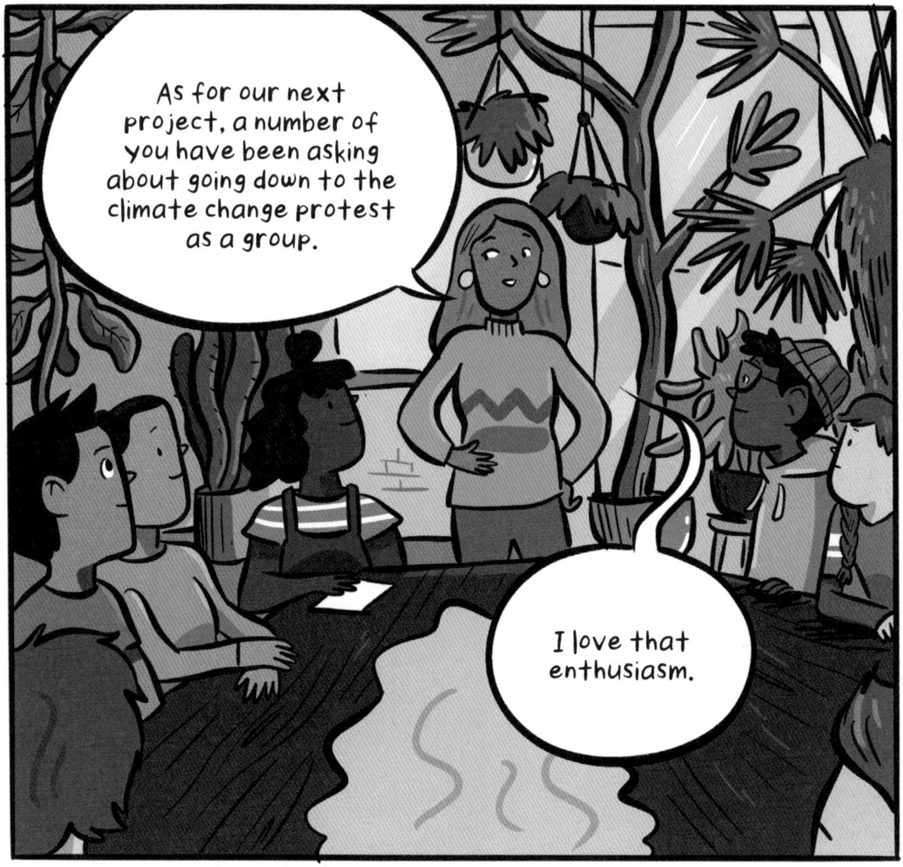
As for our next project, a number of you have been asking about going down to the climate change protest as a group.
I love that enthusiasm.

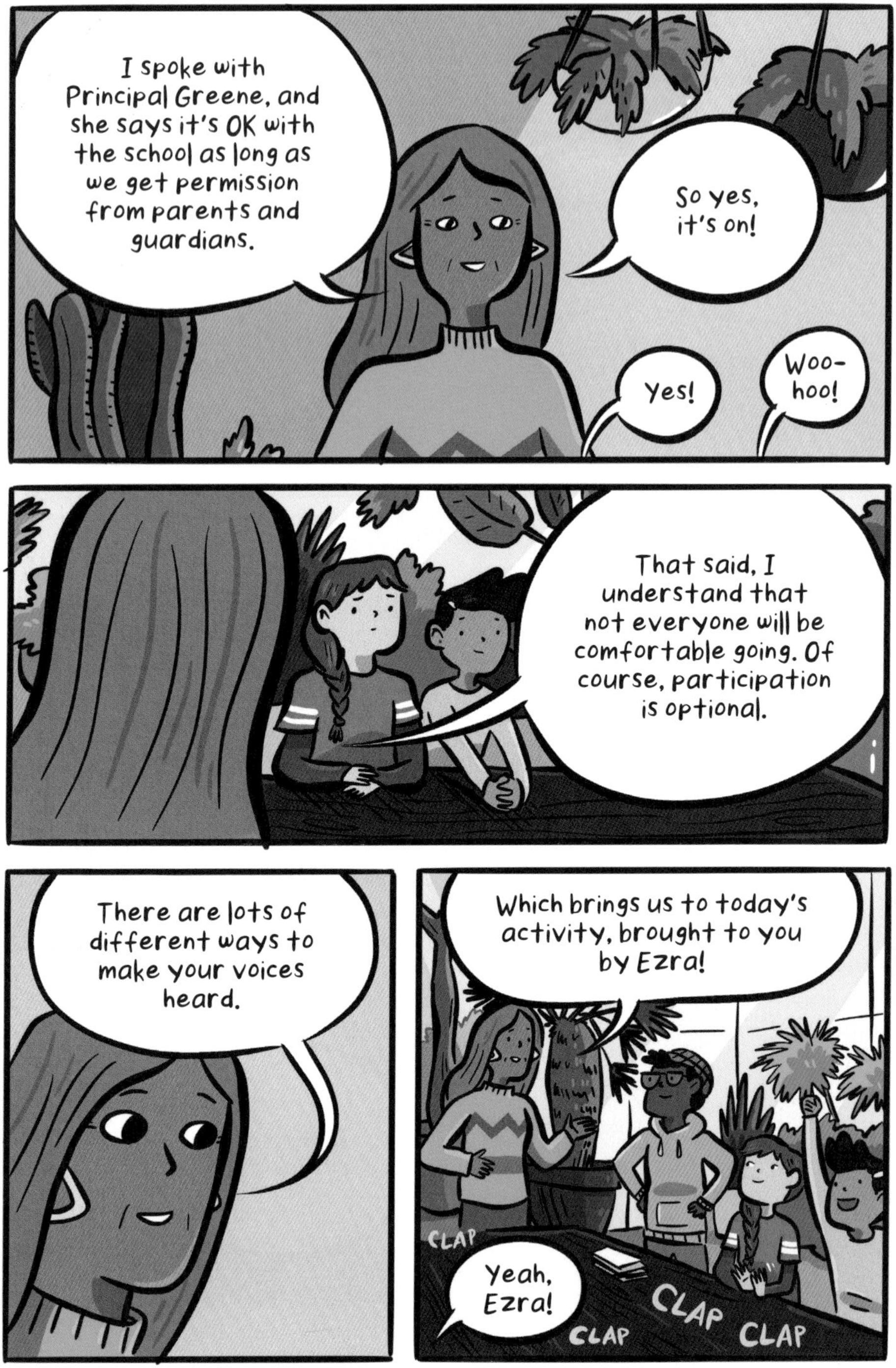
I spoke with Principal Greene, and she says it's OK with the school as long as we get permission from parents and guardians.
So yes, it's on!
Yes!
Woo-hoo!
That said, I understand that not everyone will be comfortable going. Of course, participation is optional.
There are lots of different ways to make your voices heard.
Which brings us to today's activity, brought to you by Ezra!
CLAP
Yeah, Ezra!
CLAP
CLAP
CLAP

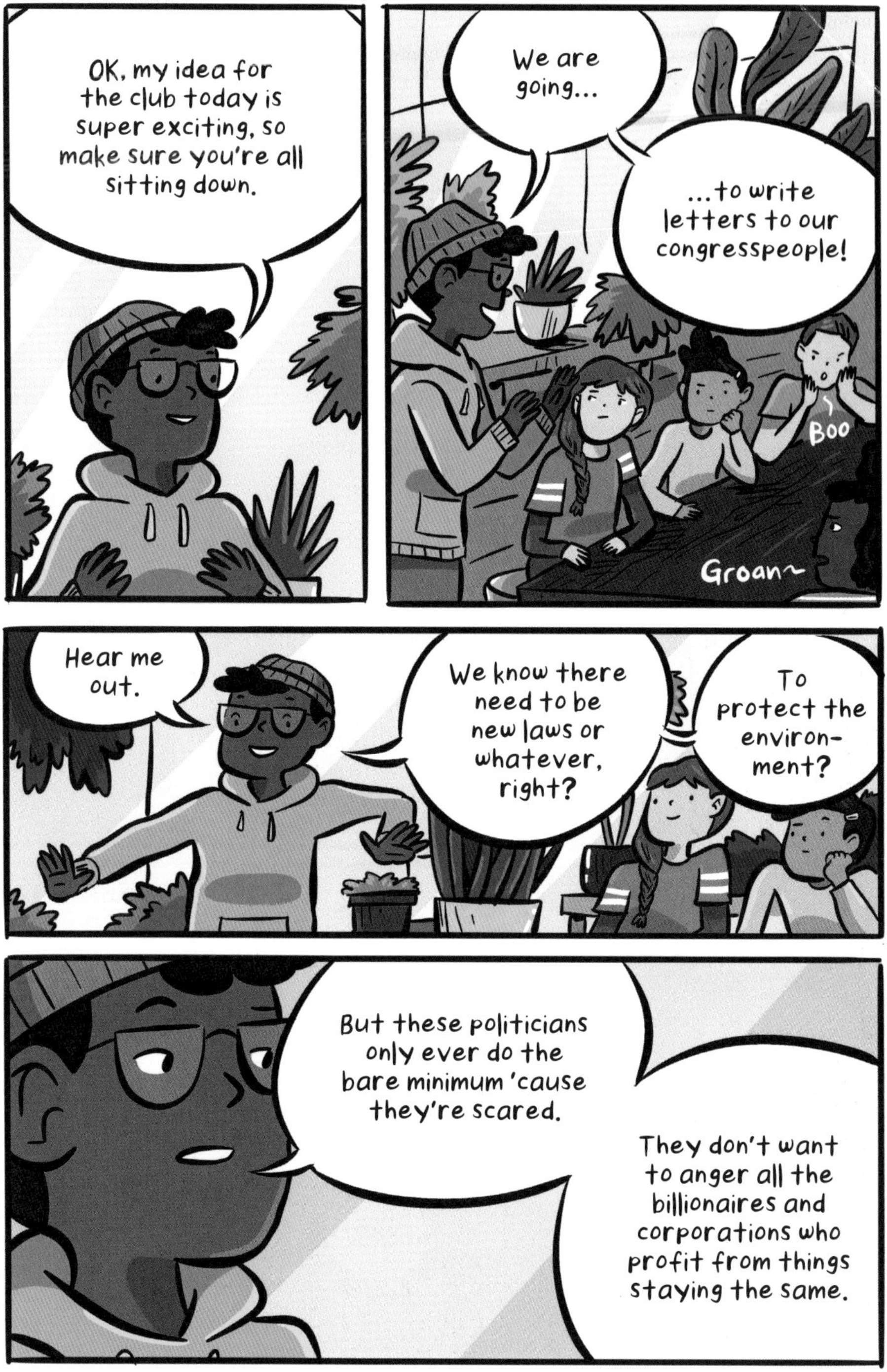
OK, my idea for the club today is super exciting, so make sure you're all sitting down.
We are going...
...to write letters to our congresspeople!
Boo
Groan~
Hear me out.
We know there need to be new laws or whatever, right?
To protect the environ-ment?
But these politicians only ever do the bare minimum 'cause they're scared.
They don't want to anger all the billionaires and corporations who profit from things staying the same.

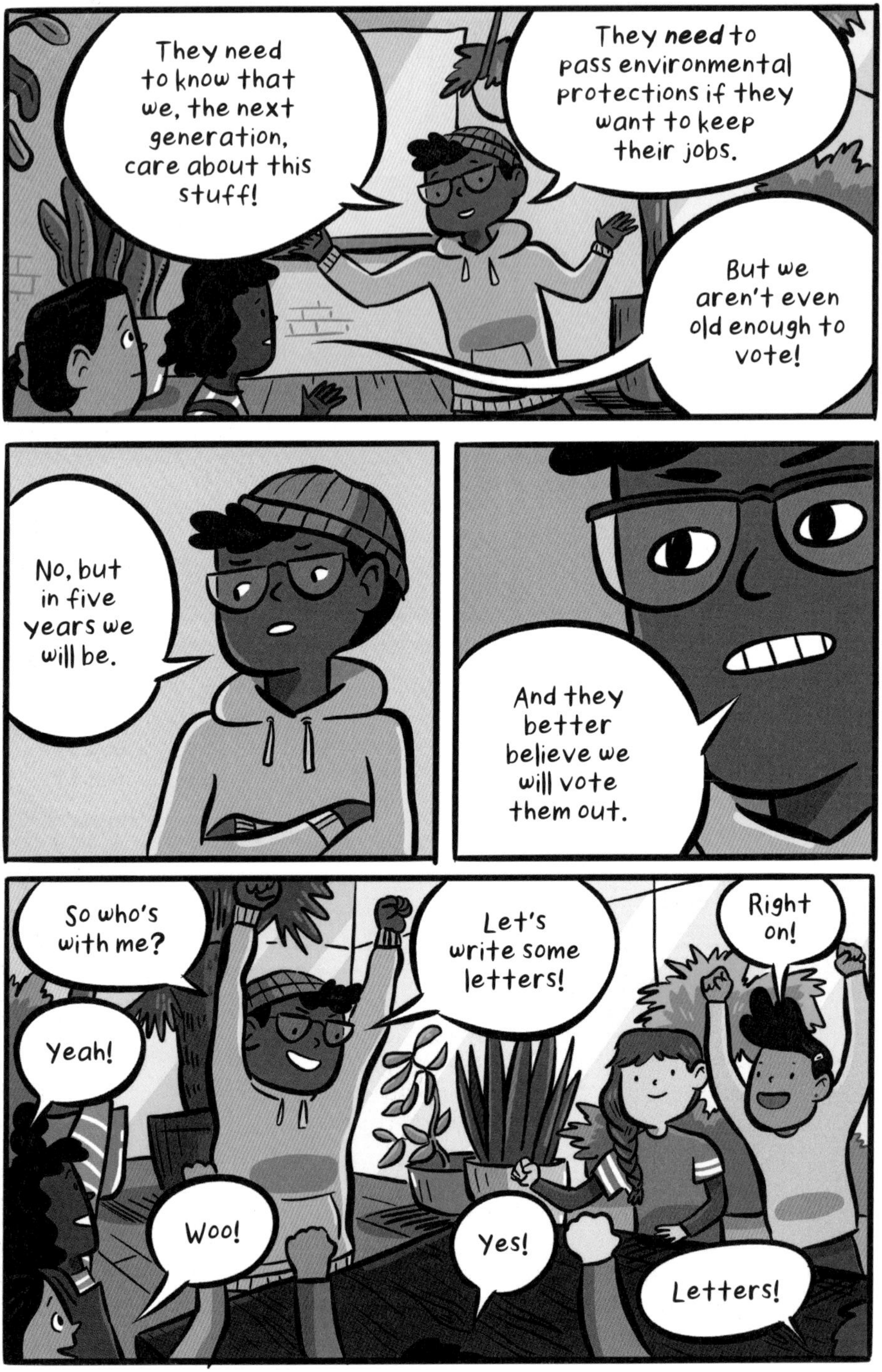
They need to know that we, the next generation, care about this stuff!
They **need** to pass environmental protections if they want to keep their jobs.
But we aren't even old enough to vote!
No, but in five years we will be.
And they better believe we will vote them out.
So who's with me?
Let's write some letters!
Right on!
Yeah!
Woo!
Yes!
Letters!

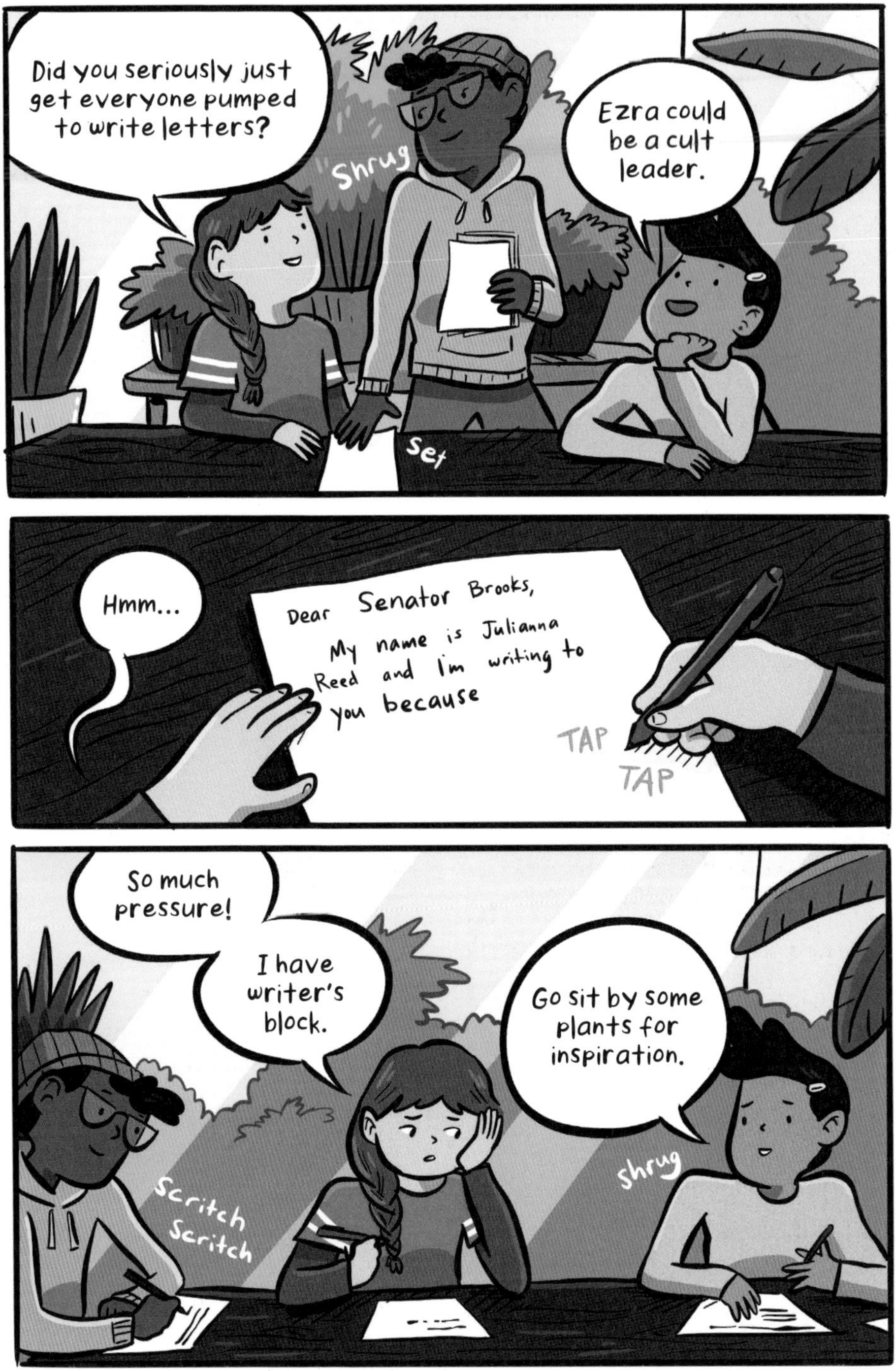
Did you seriously just get everyone pumped to write letters?
Shrug
Ezra could be a cult leader.
Set
Hmm...
Dear Senator Brooks,
My name is Julianna Reed and I'm writing to you because
TAP
TAP
So much pressure!
I have writer's block.
Go sit by some plants for inspiration.
Scritch
Scritch
shrug

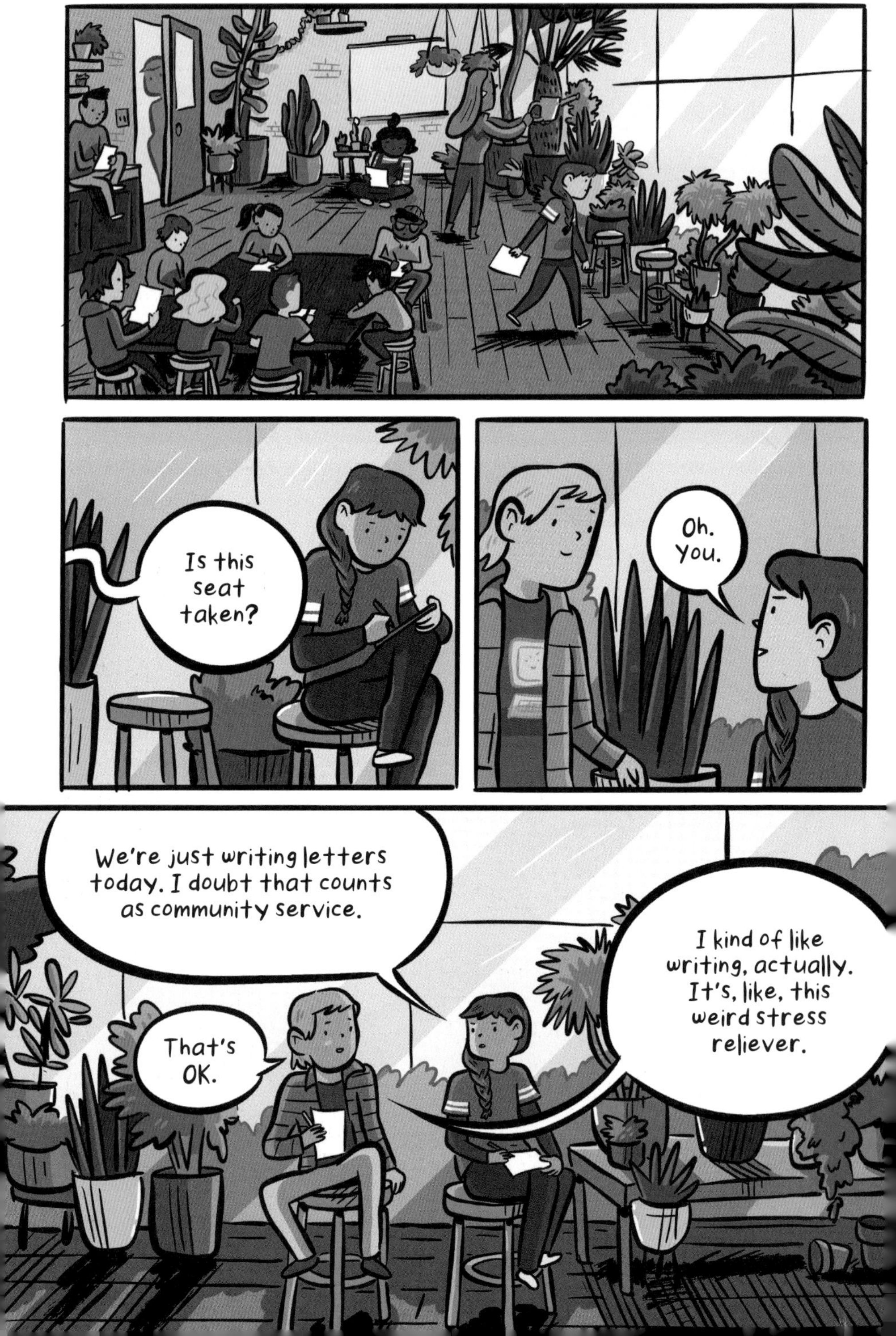
Is this seat taken?
Oh. You.
We're just writing letters today. I doubt that counts as community service.
That's OK.
I kind of like writing, actually. It's, like, this weird stress reliever.

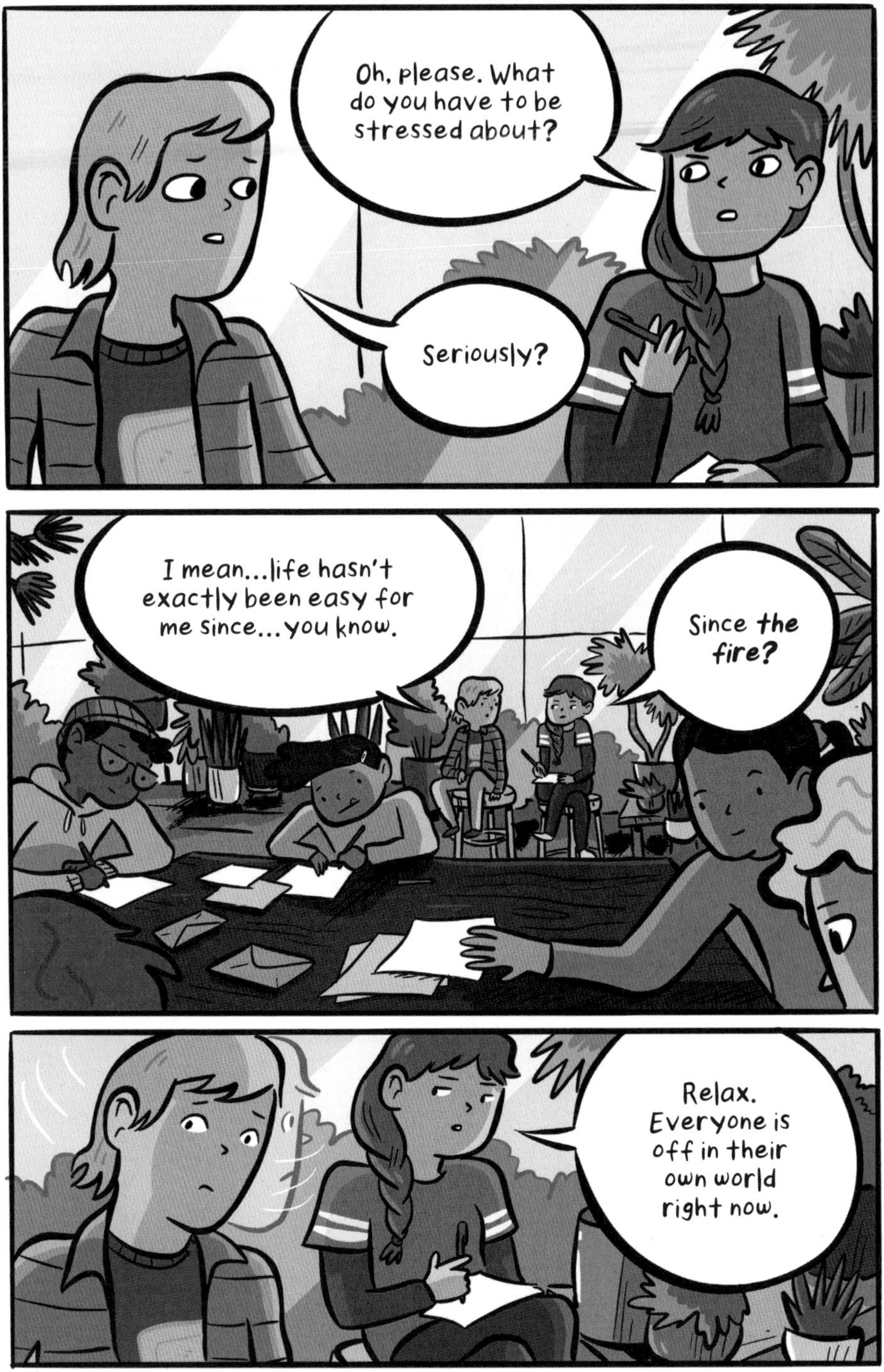
Oh, please. What do you have to be stressed about?
Seriously?
I mean...life hasn't exactly been easy for me since...you know.
Since the *fire?*
Relax. Everyone is off in their own world right now.

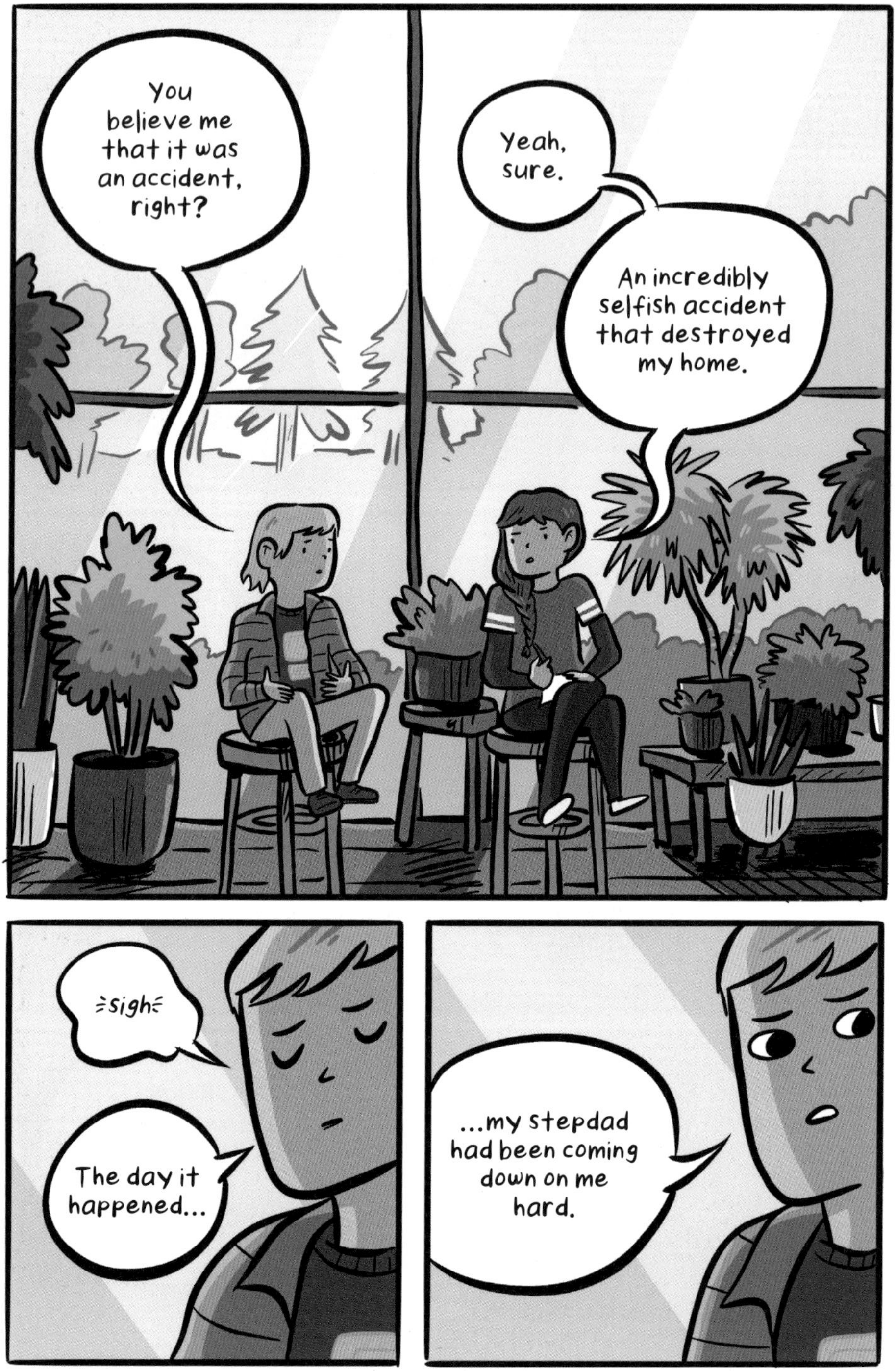
You believe me that it was an accident, right?
Yeah, sure.
An incredibly selfish accident that destroyed my home.
≈sigh≈
The day it happened...
...my stepdad had been coming down on me hard.

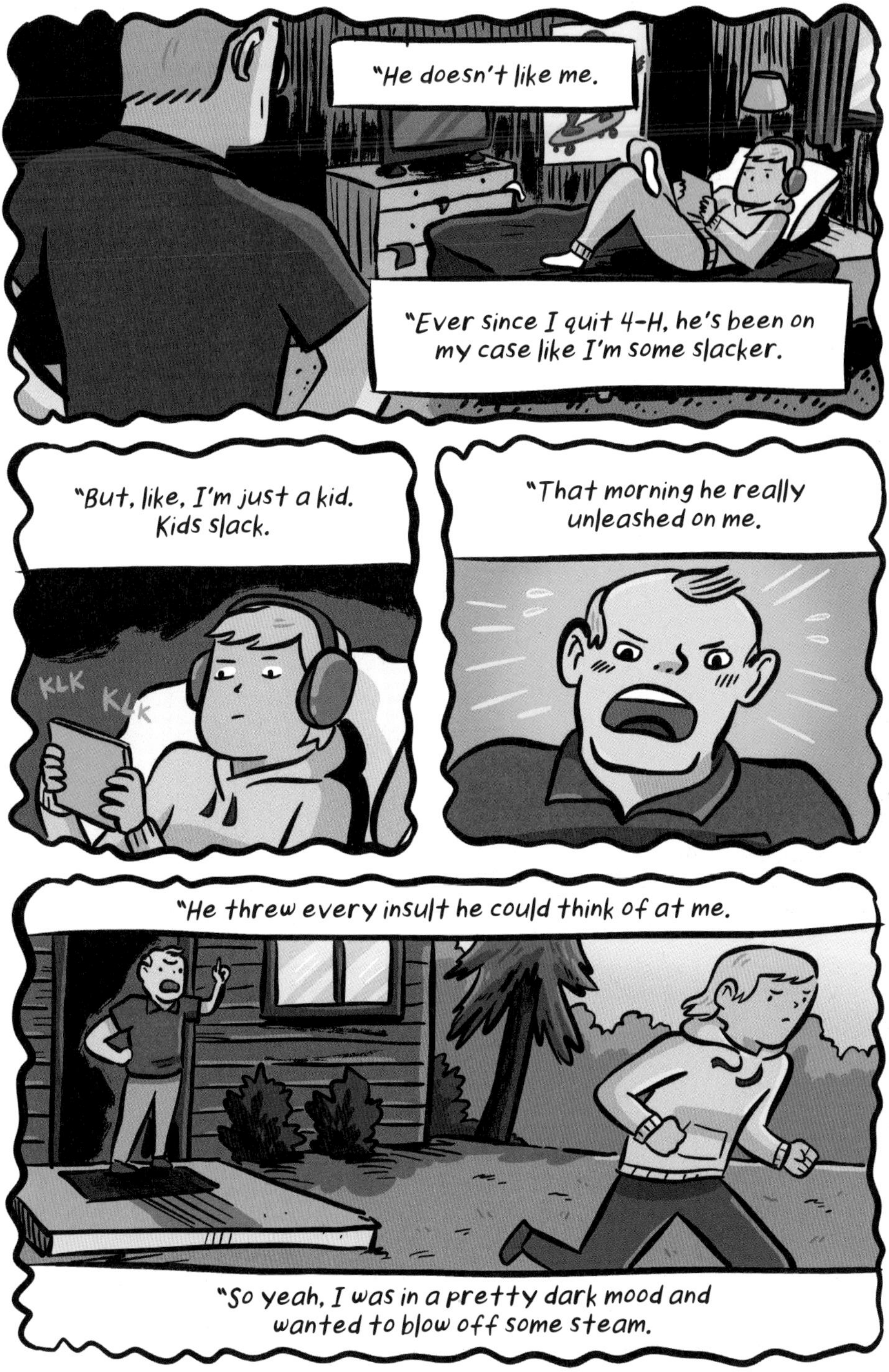
"He doesn't like me.
"Ever since I quit 4-H, he's been on my case like I'm some slacker.
"But, like, I'm just a kid. Kids slack.
KLK KLK
"That morning he really unleashed on me.
"He threw every insult he could think of at me.
"So yeah, I was in a pretty dark mood and wanted to blow off some steam.

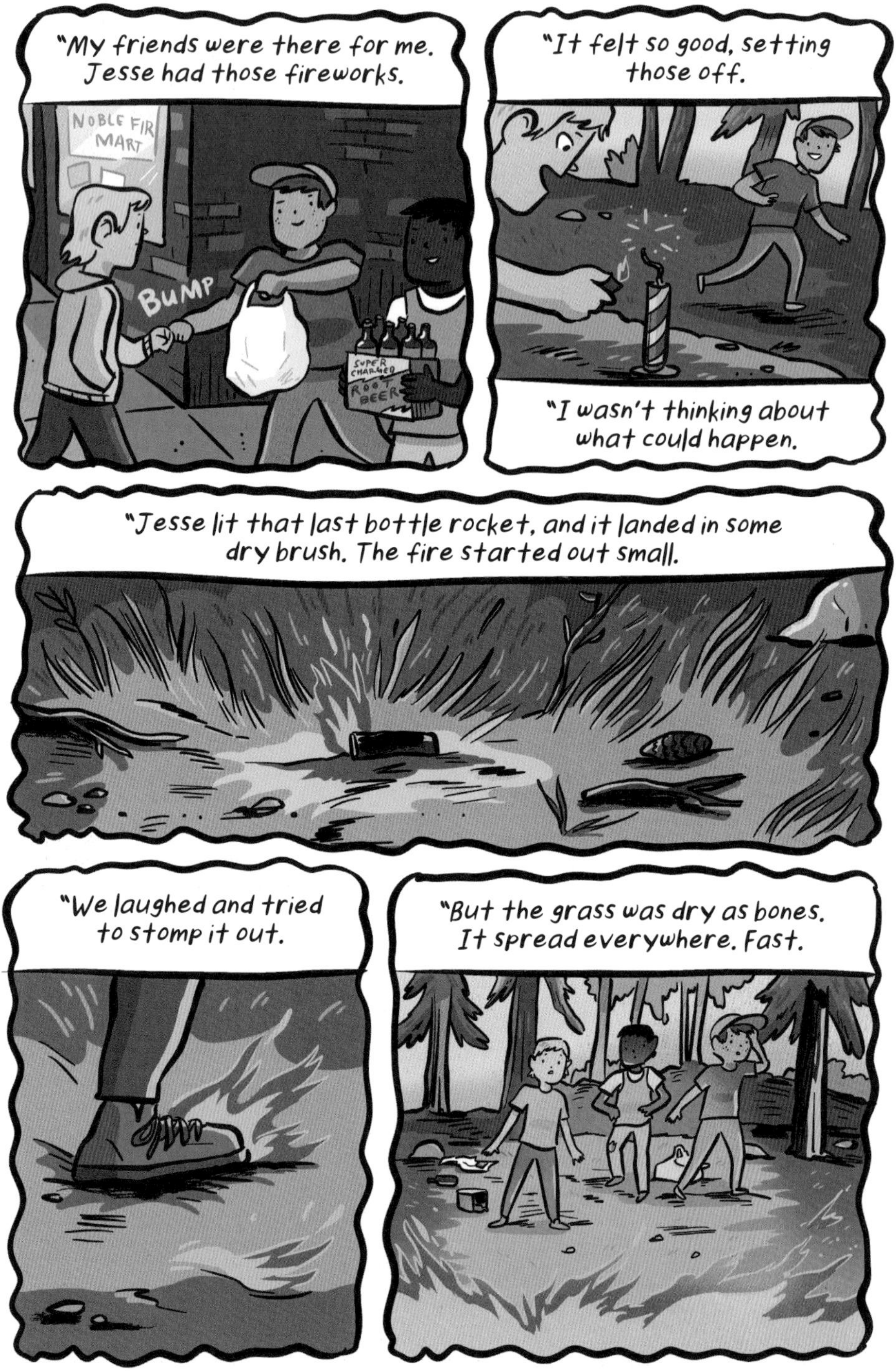
"My friends were there for me. Jesse had those fireworks.
NOBLE FIR MART
BUMP
SUPER CHARGED ROOT BEER
"It felt so good, setting those off.
"I wasn't thinking about what could happen.
"Jesse lit that last bottle rocket, and it landed in some dry brush. The fire started out small.
"We laughed and tried to stomp it out.
"But the grass was dry as bones. It spread everywhere. Fast.

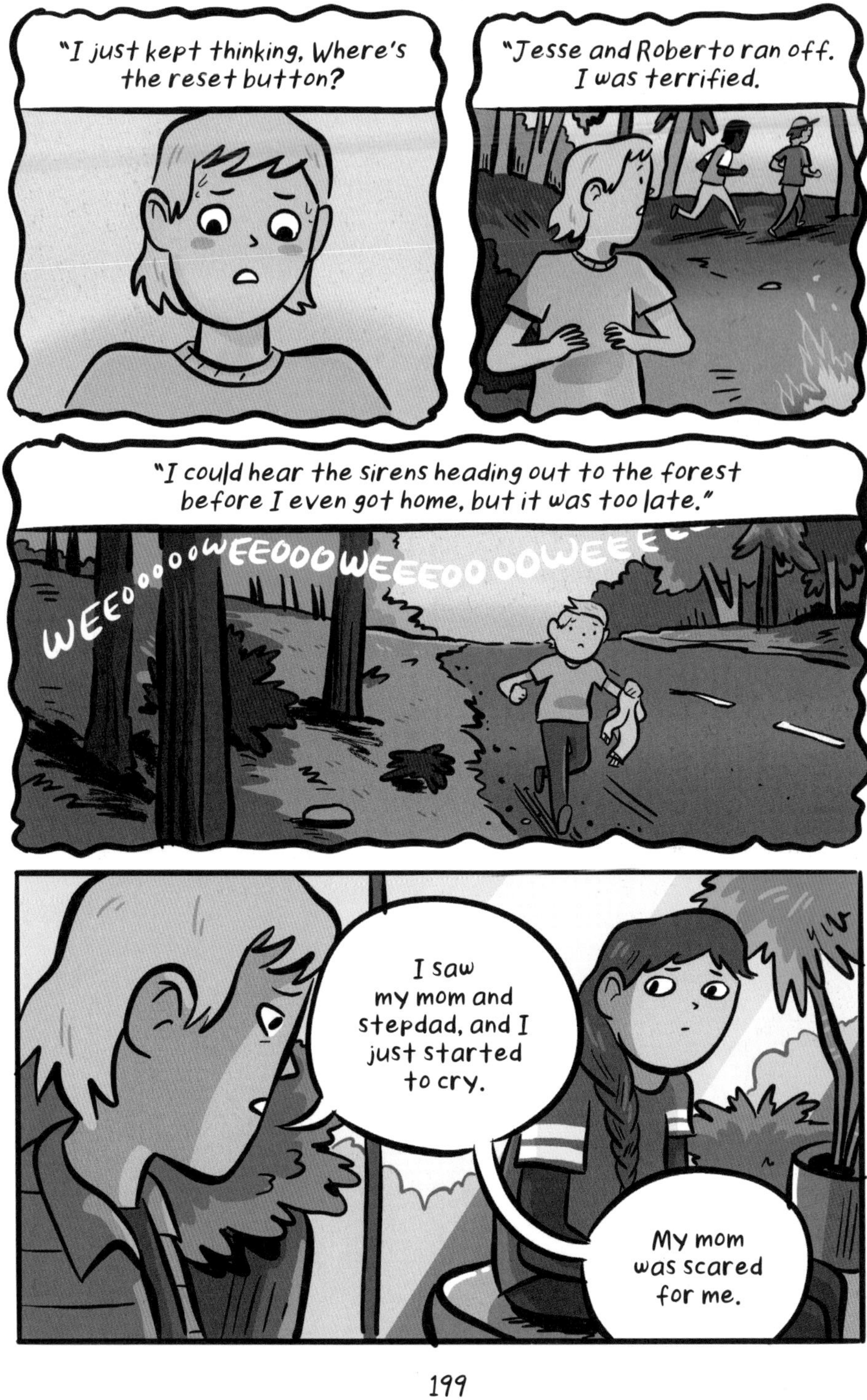
"I just kept thinking, Where's the reset button?
"Jesse and Roberto ran off. I was terrified.
"I could hear the sirens heading out to the forest before I even got home, but it was too late."
WEEoooooWEEOOOWEEEOO OOWEEE
I saw my mom and stepdad, and I just started to cry.
My mom was scared for me.

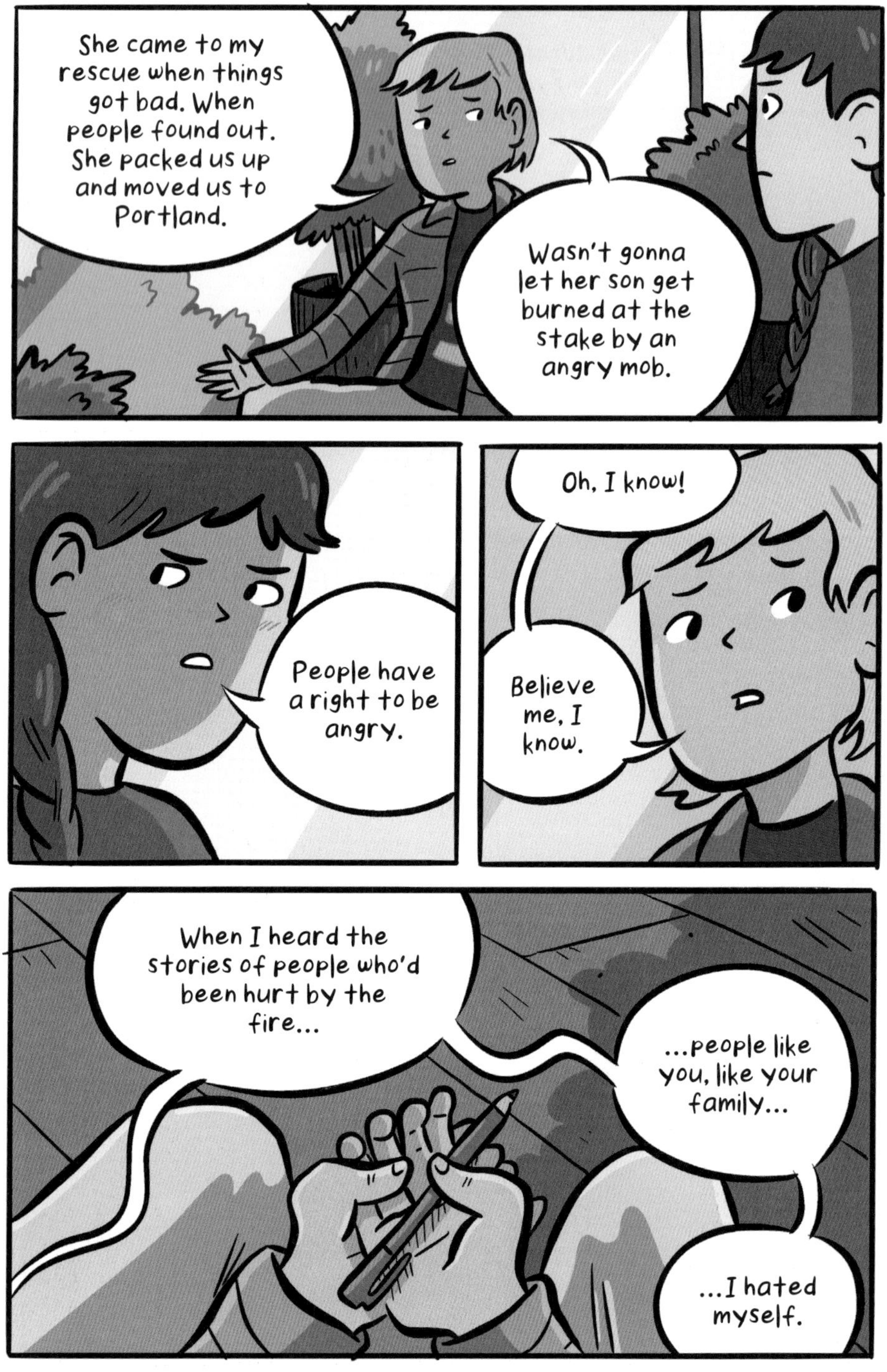
She came to my rescue when things got bad. When people found out. She packed us up and moved us to Portland.
Wasn't gonna let her son get burned at the stake by an angry mob.
People have a right to be angry.
Oh, I know!
Believe me, I know.
When I heard the stories of people who'd been hurt by the fire...
...people like you, like your family...
...I hated myself.

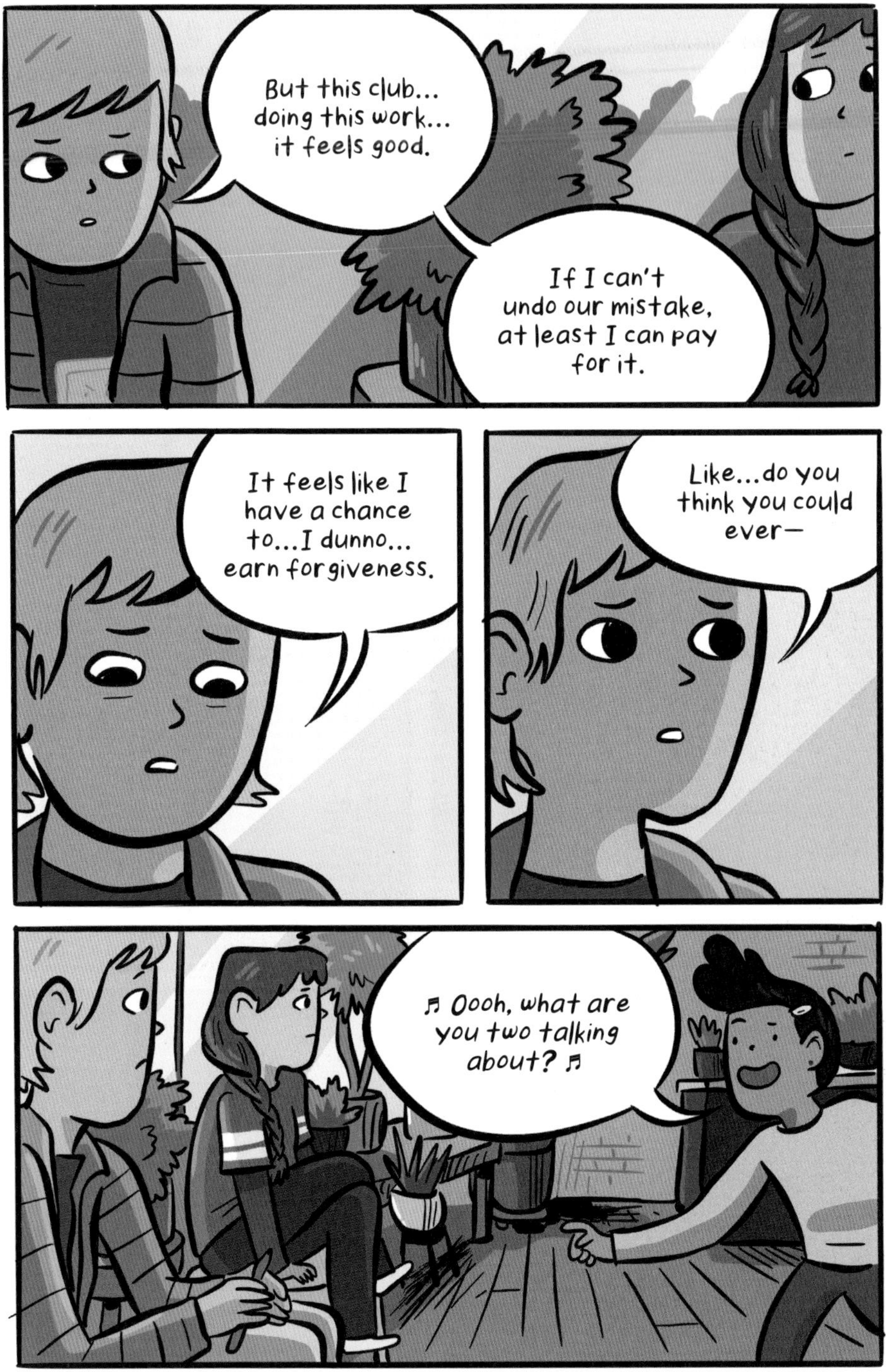
But this club... doing this work... it feels good.
If I can't undo our mistake, at least I can pay for it.
It feels like I have a chance to...I dunno... earn forgiveness.
Like...do you think you could ever—
♬ Oooh, what are you two talking about? ♬

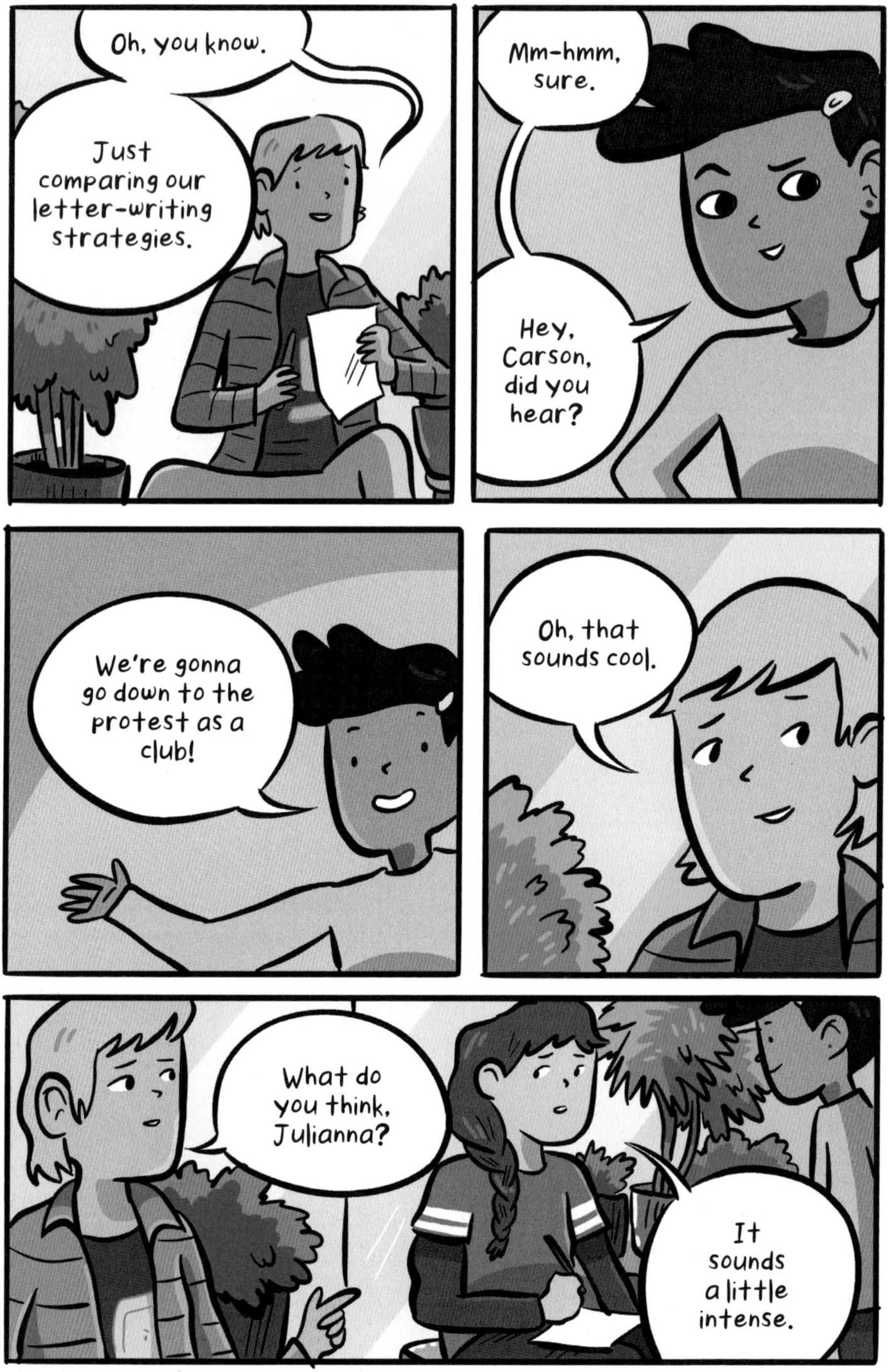
Oh, you know.
Just comparing our letter-writing strategies.
Mm-hmm, sure.
Hey, Carson, did you hear?
We're gonna go down to the protest as a club!
Oh, that sounds cool.
What do you think, Julianna?
It sounds a little intense.

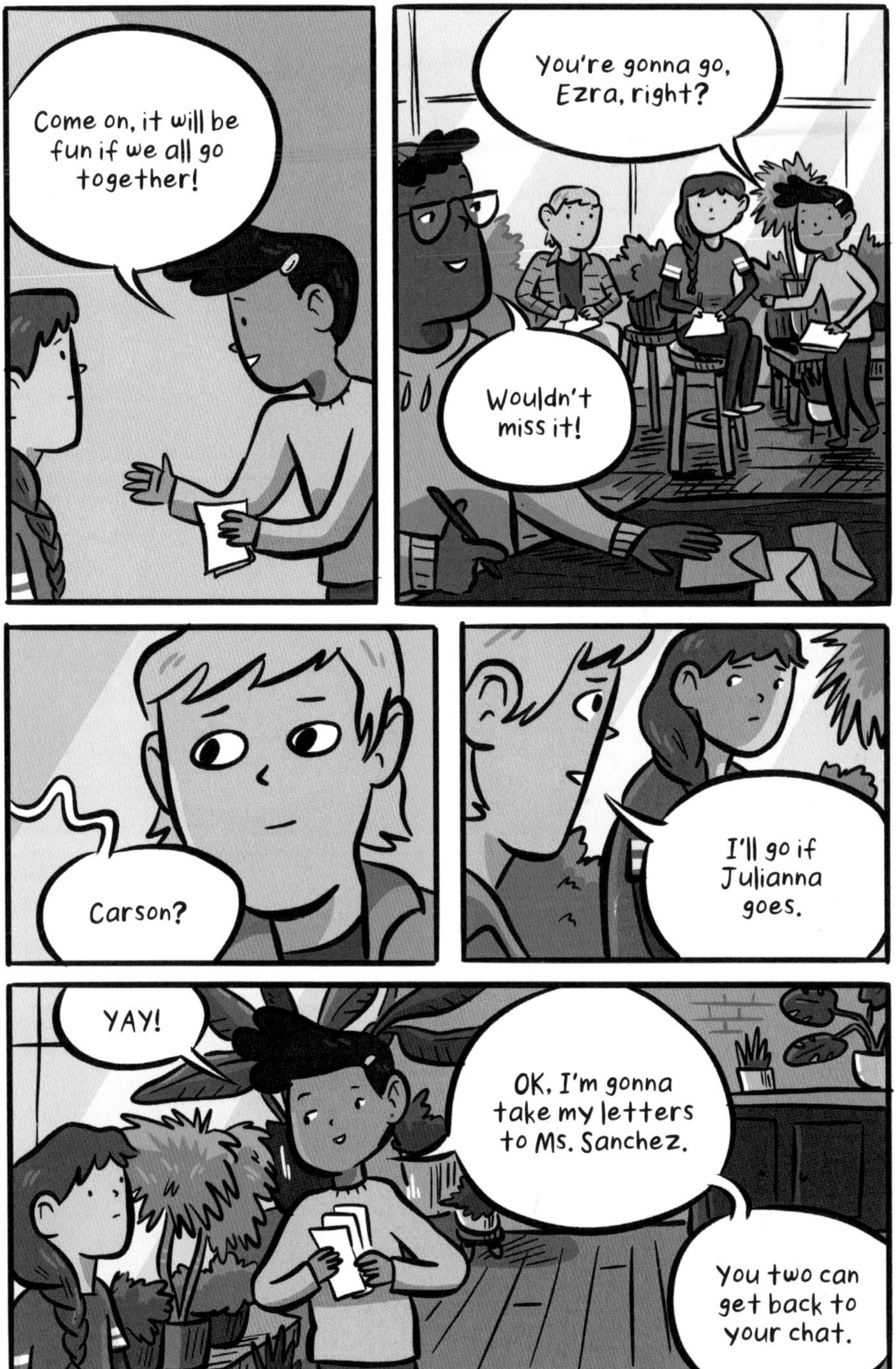
Come on, it will be fun if we all go together!
You're gonna go, Ezra, right?
Wouldn't miss it!
Carson?
I'll go if Julianna goes.
YAY!
OK, I'm gonna take my letters to Ms. Sanchez.
You two can get back to your chat.

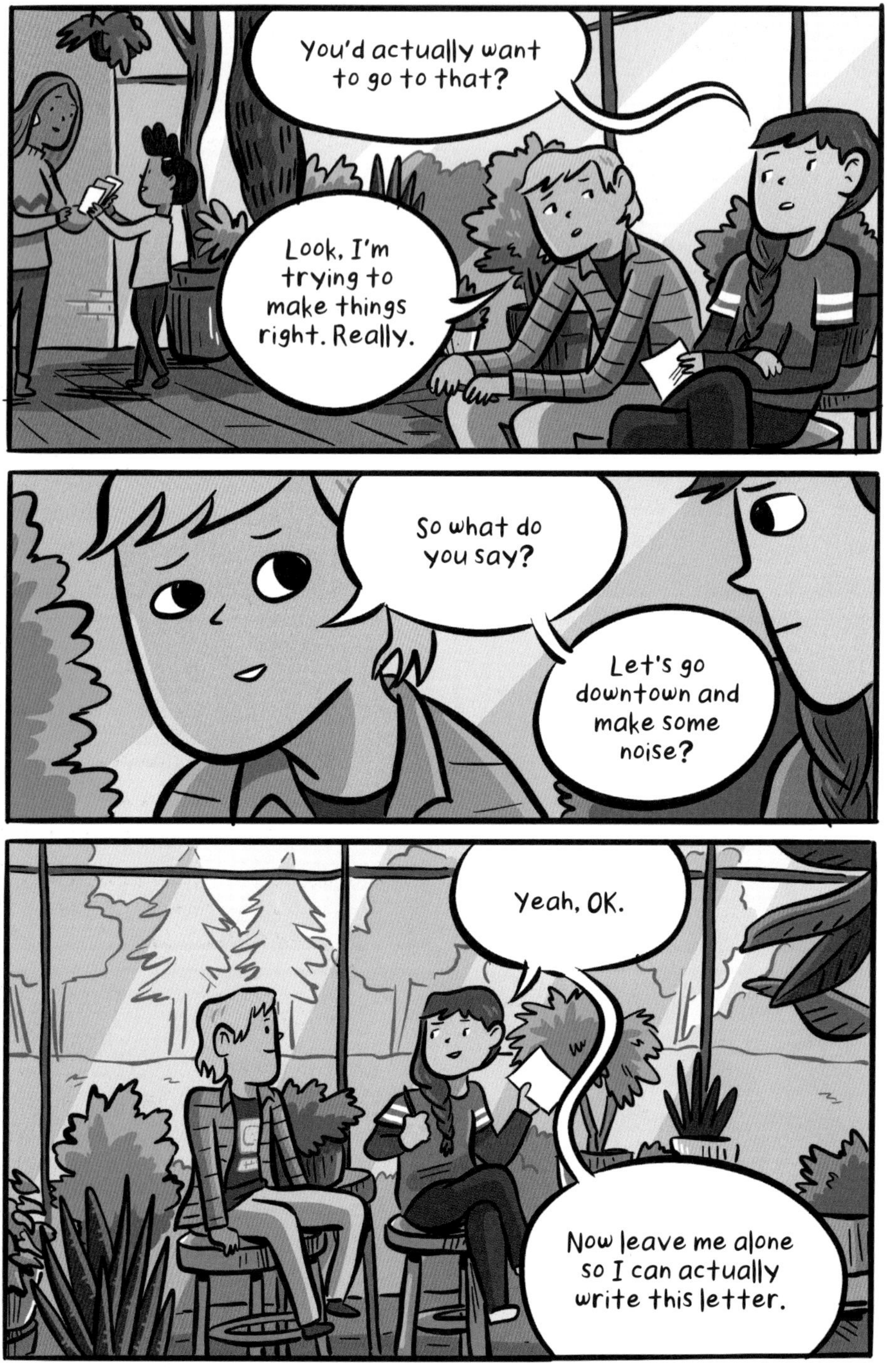
You'd actually want to go to that?
Look, I'm trying to make things right. Really.
So what do you say?
Let's go downtown and make some noise?
Yeah, OK.
Now leave me alone so I can actually write this letter.

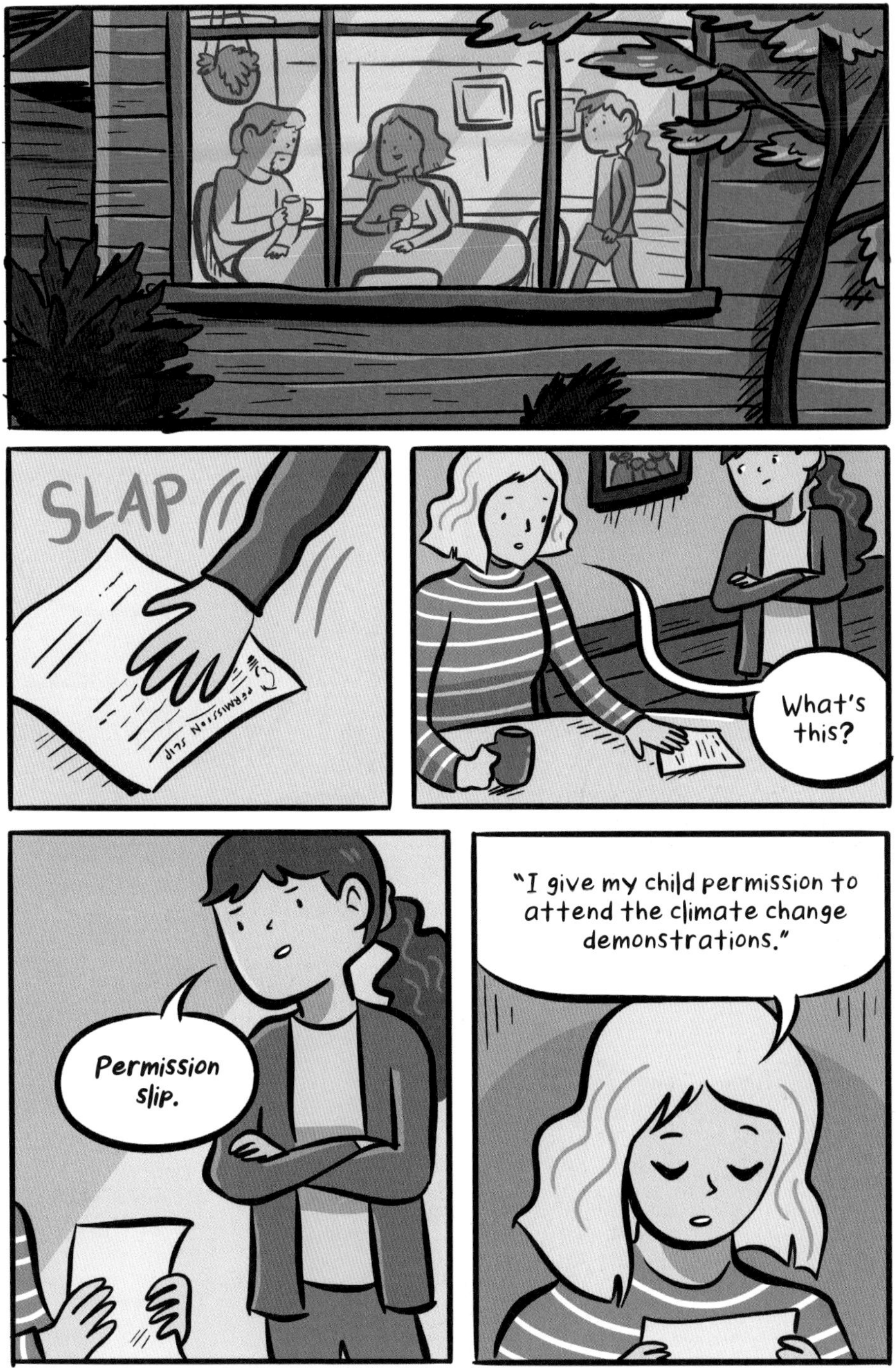
SLAP
PERMISSION SLIP
What's this?
Permission slip.
"I give my child permission to attend the climate change demonstrations."

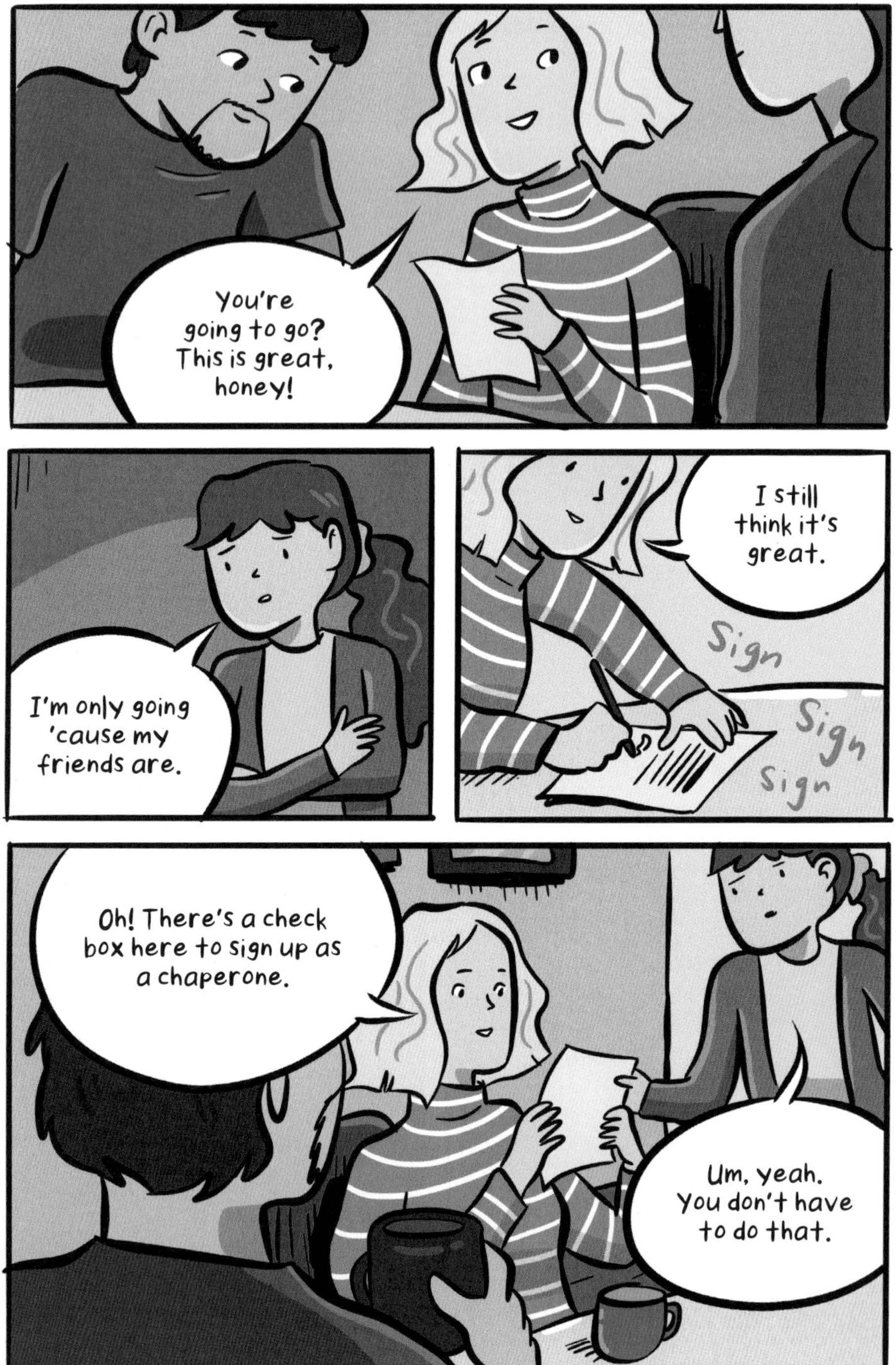
You're going to go? This is great, honey!
I'm only going 'cause my friends are.
I still think it's great.
Sign
Sign
Sign
Oh! There's a check box here to sign up as a chaperone.
Um, yeah. You don't have to do that.

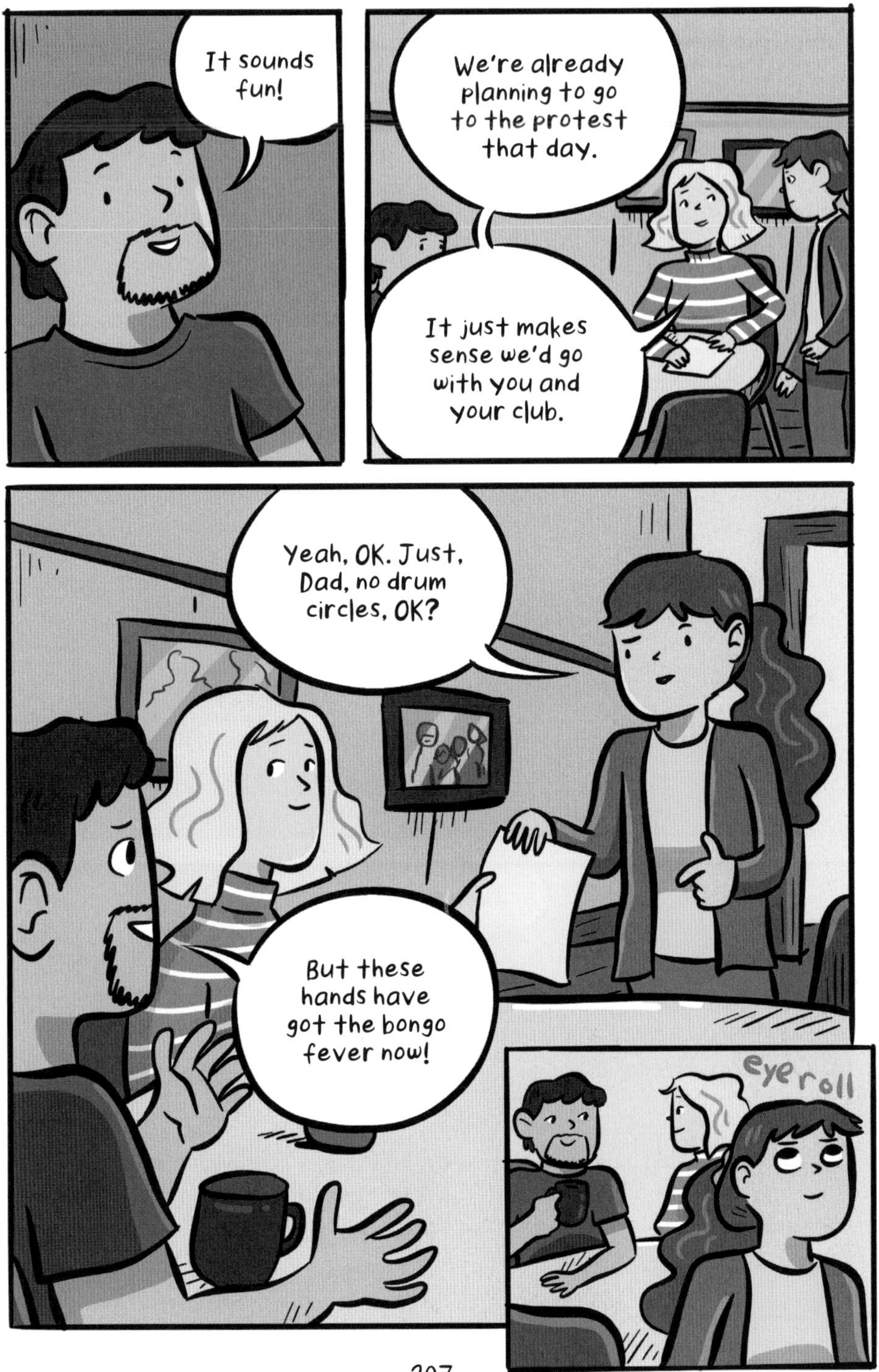
It sounds fun!
We're already planning to go to the protest that day.
It just makes sense we'd go with you and your club.
Yeah, OK. Just, Dad, no drum circles, OK?
But these hands have got the bongo fever now!
eye roll

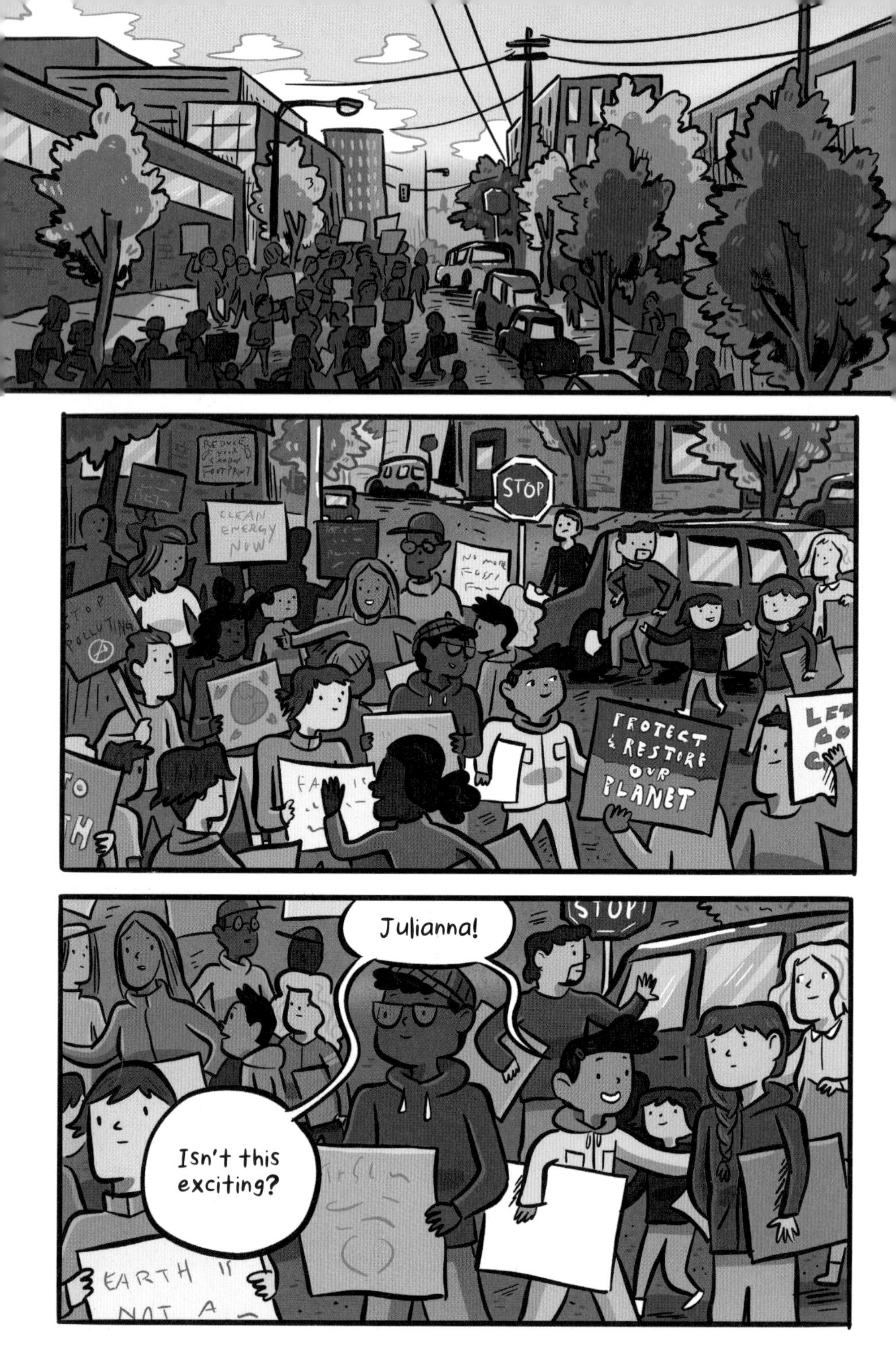
STOP
CLEAN ENERGY NOW
STOP POLLUTING
PROTECT & RESTORE OUR PLANET
Julianna!
Isn't this exciting?
EARTH IS
NOT A

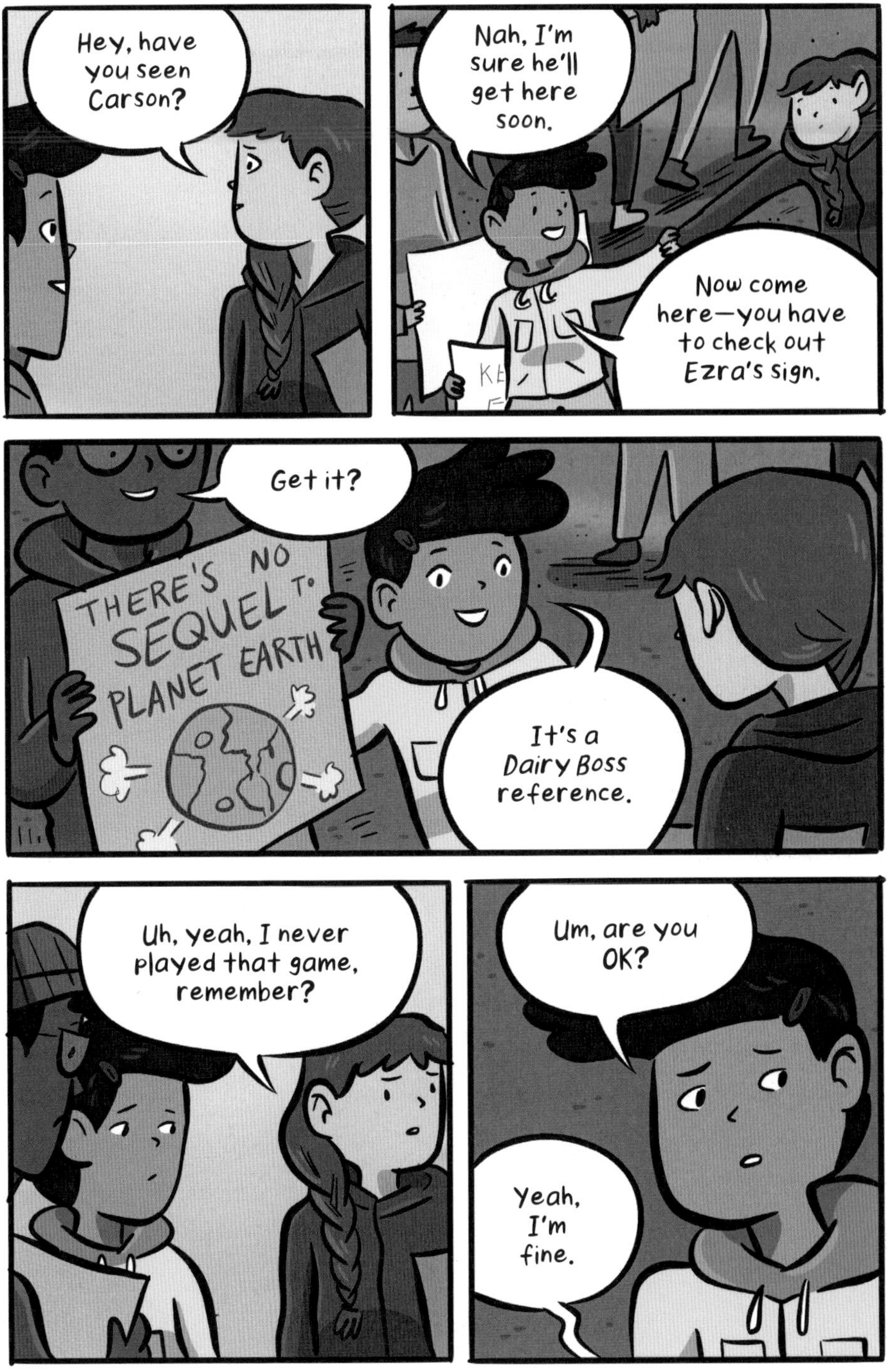
Hey, have you seen Carson?
Nah, I'm sure he'll get here soon.
Now come here—you have to check out Ezra's sign.
Get it?
THERE'S NO SEQUEL TO PLANET EARTH
It's a *Dairy Boss* reference.
Uh, yeah, I never played that game, remember?
Um, are you OK?
Yeah, I'm fine.

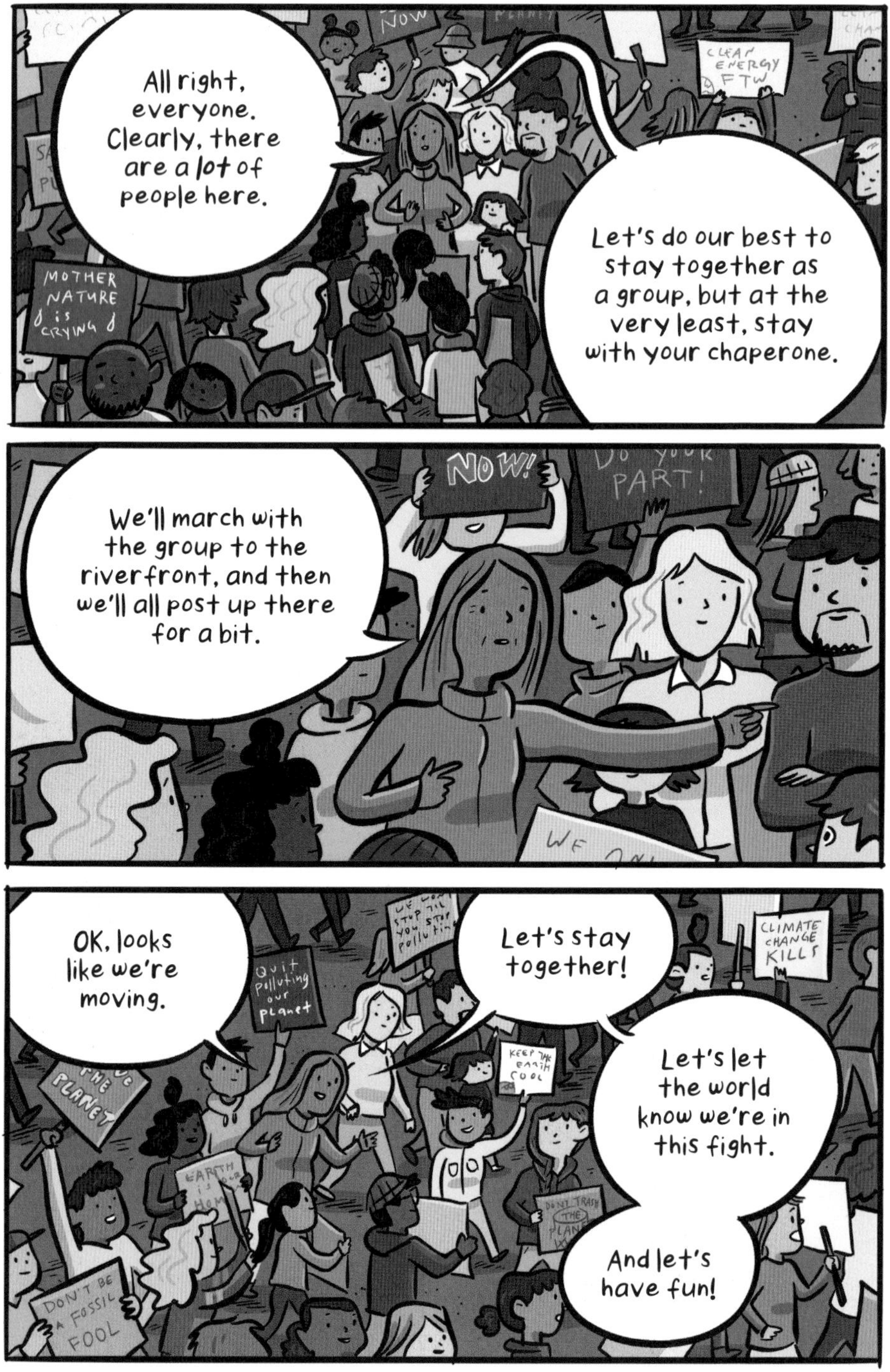
CLEAN ENERGY FTW
All right, everyone. Clearly, there are a lot of people here.
MOTHER NATURE is CRYING
Let's do our best to stay together as a group, but at the very least, stay with your chaperone.
NOW!
PART!
We'll march with the group to the riverfront, and then we'll all post up there for a bit.
OK, looks like we're moving.
Quit polluting our planet
Let's stay together!
CLIMATE CHANGE KILLS
KEEP THE EARTH COOL
PLANET
Let's let the world know we're in this fight.
And let's have fun!
DON'T BE A FOSSIL FOOL

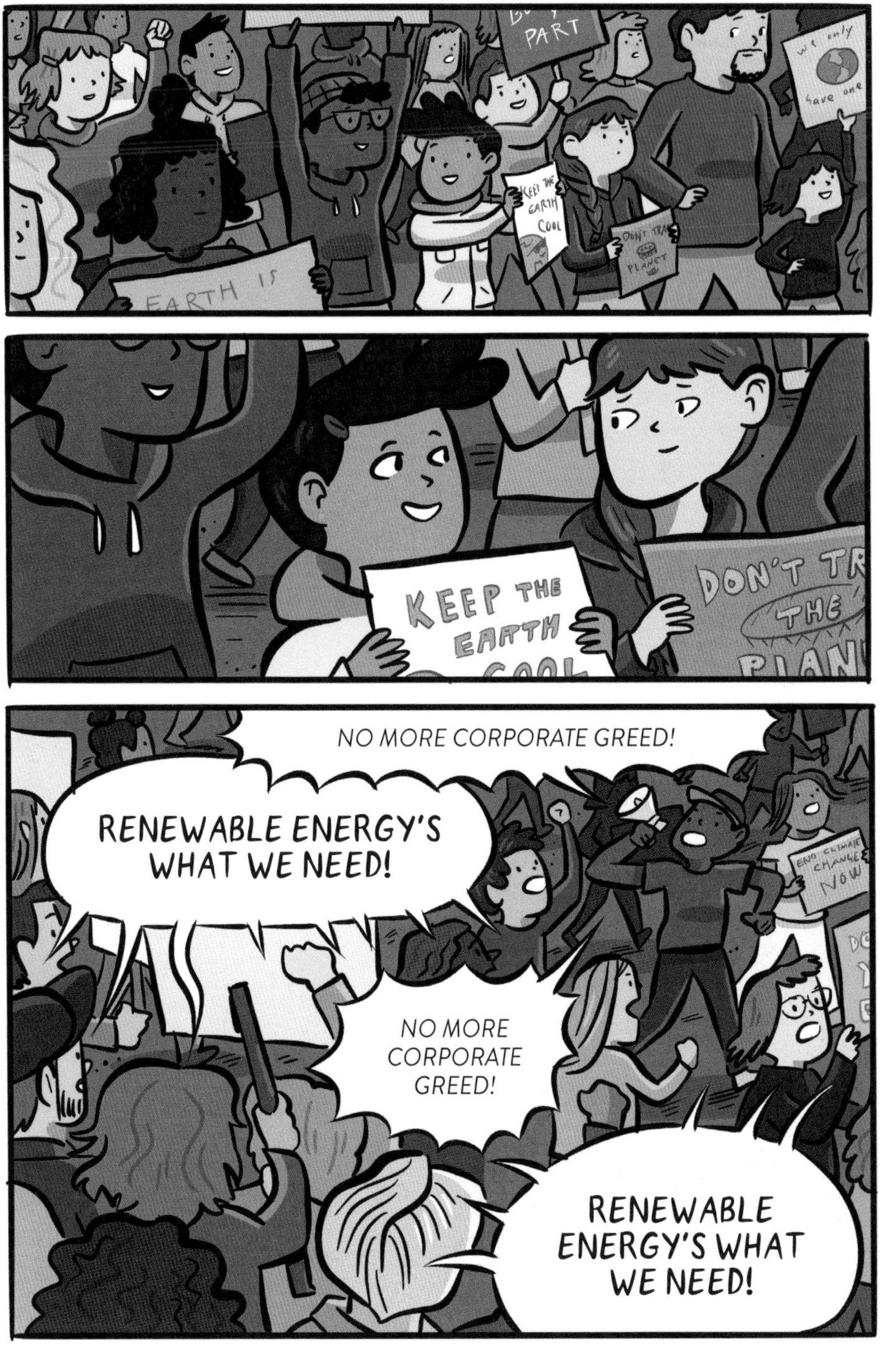
PART
we only
have one
KEEP THE EARTH COOL
EARTH IS
KEEP THE EARTH
NO MORE CORPORATE GREED!
RENEWABLE ENERGY'S WHAT WE NEED!
END CLIMATE CHANGE NOW
NO MORE CORPORATE GREED!
RENEWABLE ENERGY'S WHAT WE NEED!

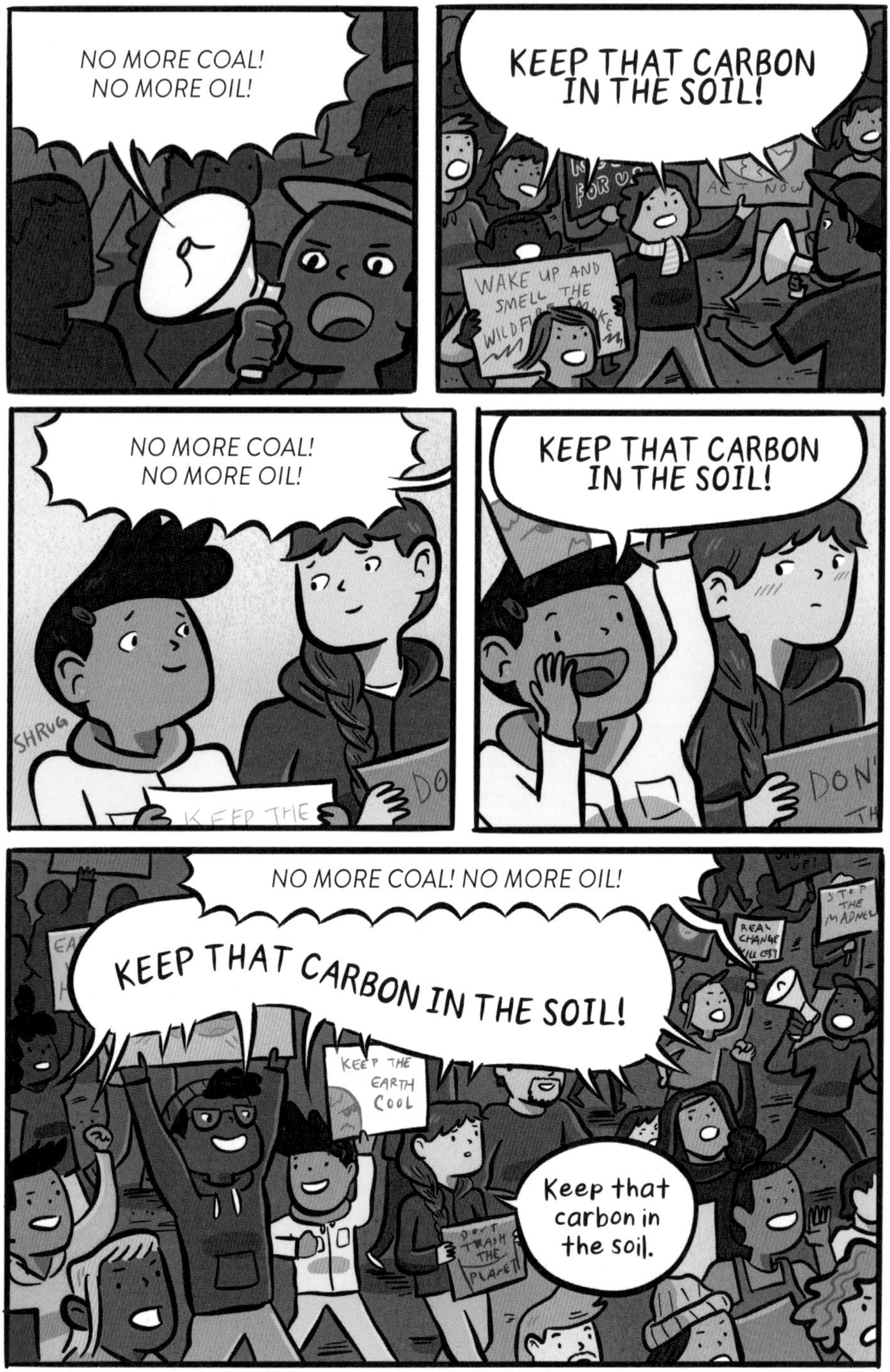
NO MORE COAL! NO MORE OIL!
KEEP THAT CARBON IN THE SOIL!
ACT NOW
WAKE UP AND SMELL THE WILDFIRE SMOKE
NO MORE COAL! NO MORE OIL!
SHRUG
KEEP THAT CARBON IN THE SOIL!
NO MORE COAL! NO MORE OIL!
KEEP THAT CARBON IN THE SOIL!
KEEP THE EARTH COOL
DON'T TRASH THE PLANET
Keep that carbon in the soil.

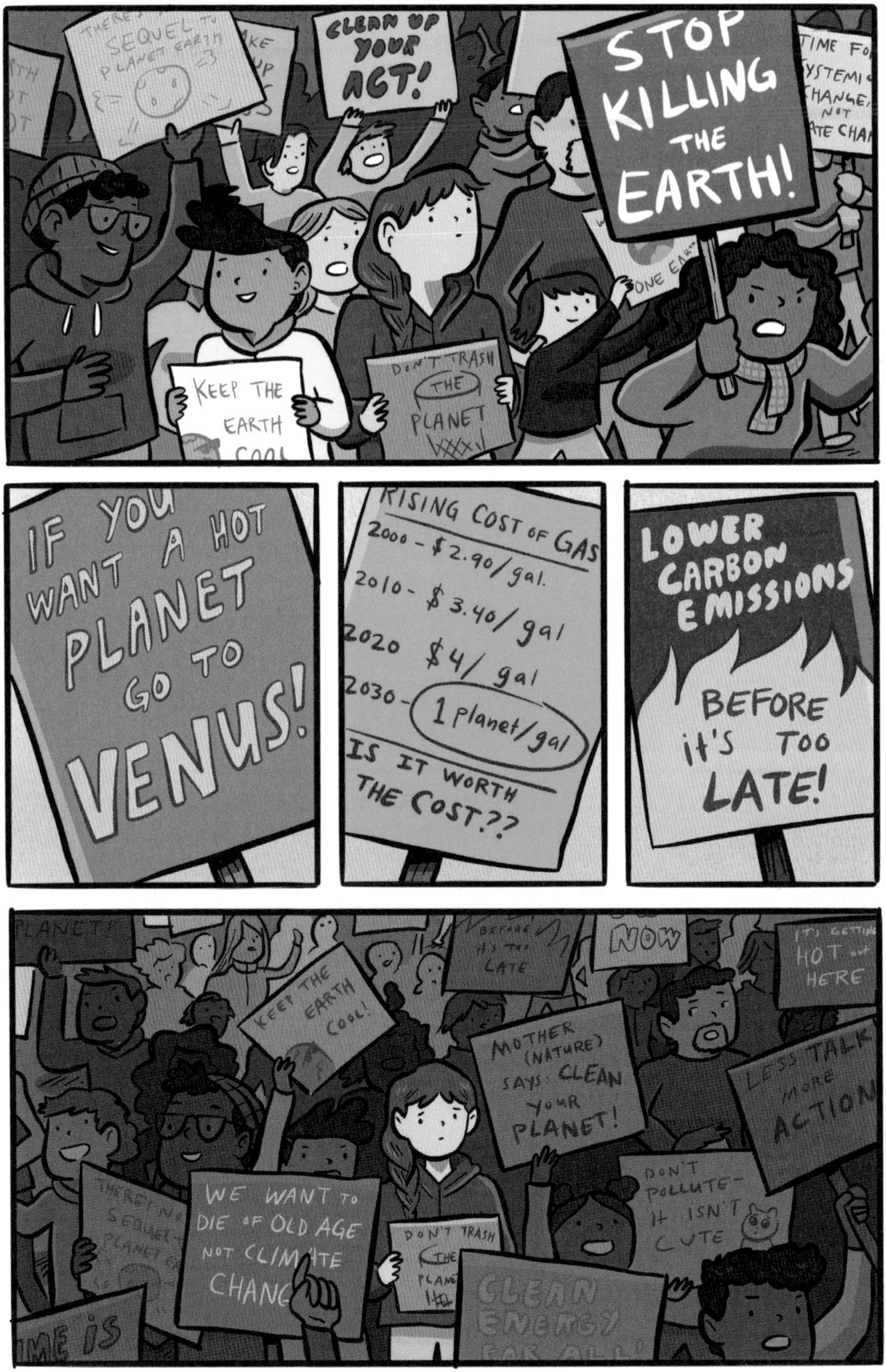
SEQUEL TO PLANET EARTH
CLEAN UP YOUR ACT!
STOP KILLING THE EARTH!
TIME FOR SYSTEMIC CHANGE, NOT ATE CHAN
ONE EAR
KEEP THE EARTH COOL
DON'T TRASH THE PLANET
IF YOU WANT A HOT PLANET GO TO VENUS!
RISING COST OF GAS
2000 - $2.90/gal.
2010 - $3.40/gal
2020 $4/gal
2030 - 1 planet/gal
IS IT WORTH THE COST??
LOWER CARBON EMISSIONS
BEFORE it's TOO LATE!
PLANET
BEFORE it's TOO LATE
NOW
IT'S GETTING HOT IN HERE
KEEP THE EARTH COOL!
MOTHER (NATURE) SAYS: CLEAN YOUR PLANET!
LESS TALK MORE ACTION
WE WANT TO DIE OF OLD AGE NOT CLIMATE CHANG
DON'T TRASH THE PLANE
DON'T POLLUTE - IT ISN'T CUTE
CLEAN ENERGY
ME IS

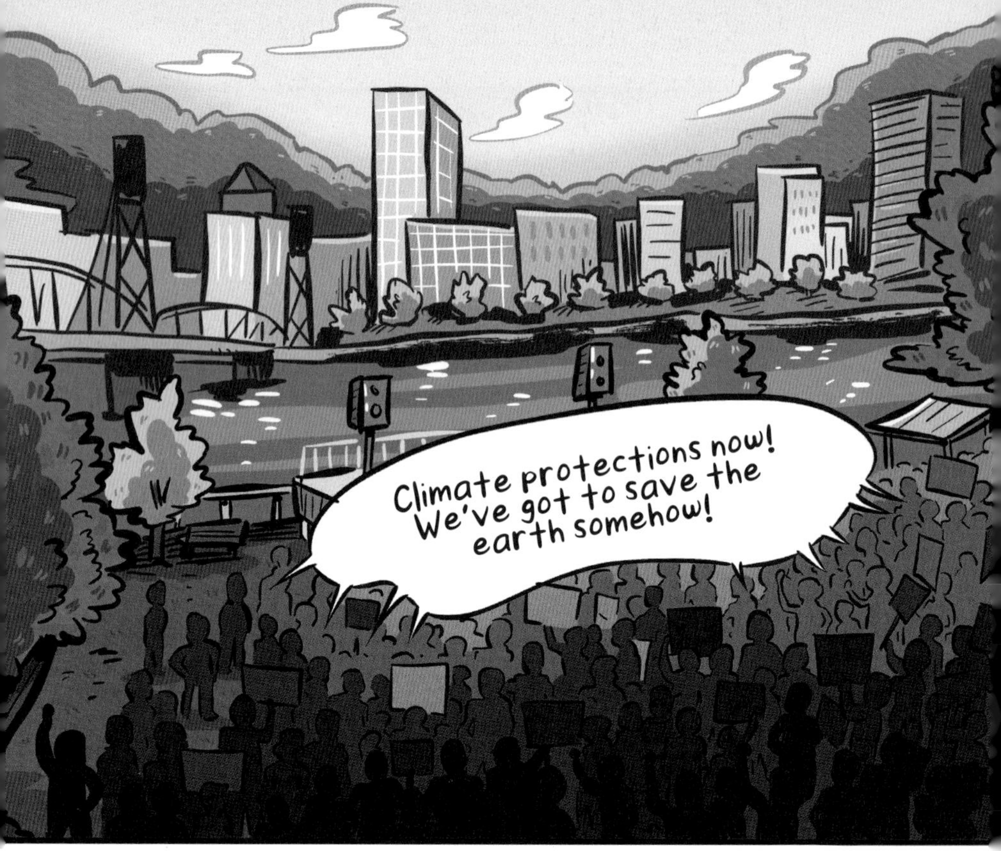
Climate protections now! We've got to save the earth somehow!

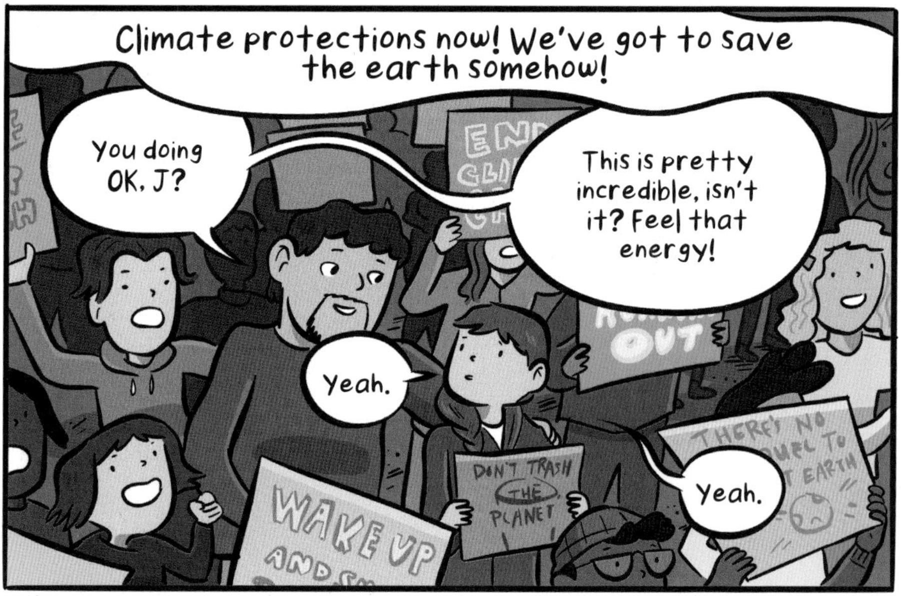
Climate protections now! We've got to save the earth somehow!
You doing OK, J?
This is pretty incredible, isn't it? Feel that energy!
Yeah.
WAKE UP
DON'T TRASH THE PLANET
Yeah.

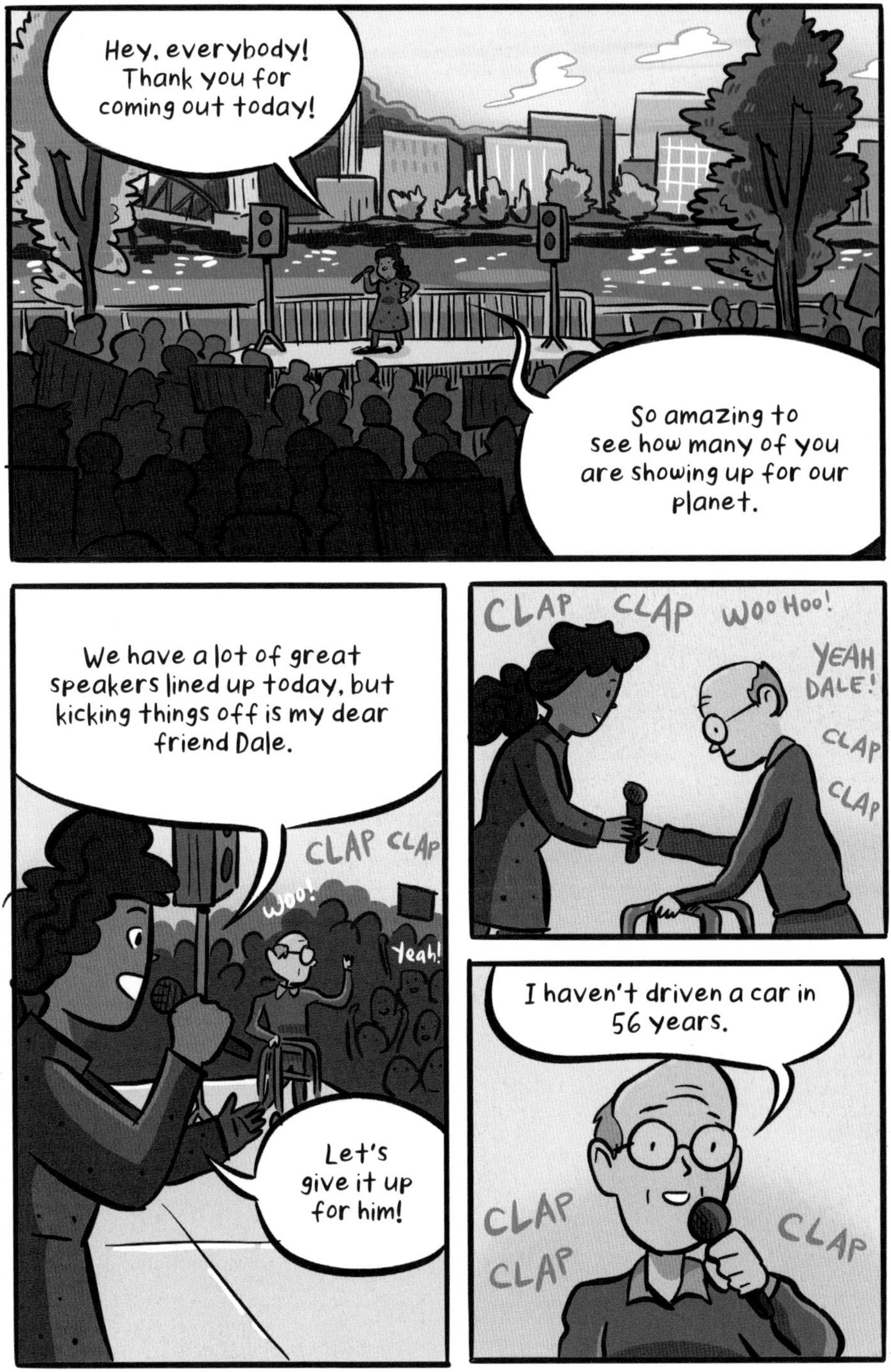
Hey, everybody! Thank you for coming out today!
So amazing to see how many of you are showing up for our planet.
We have a lot of great speakers lined up today, but kicking things off is my dear friend Dale.
CLAP CLAP
WOO!
Yeah!
Let's give it up for him!
CLAP CLAP WOO HOO!
YEAH DALE!
CLAP
CLAP
I haven't driven a car in 56 years.
CLAP CLAP
CLAP

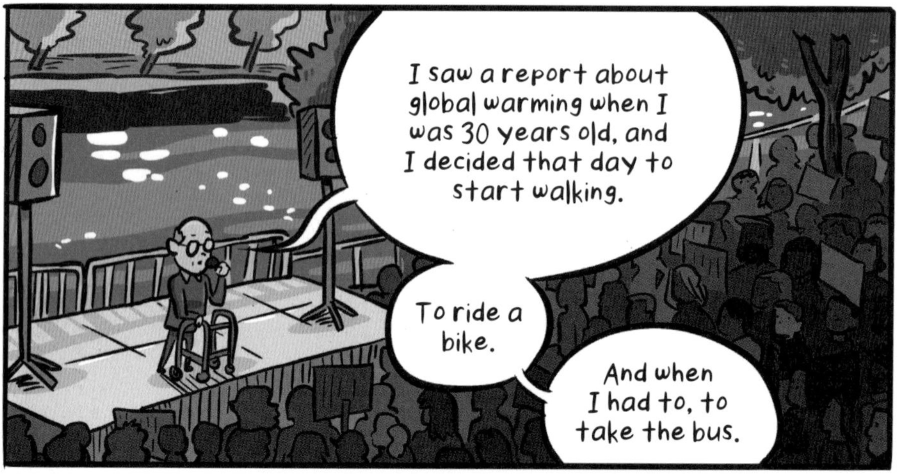
I saw a report about global warming when I was 30 years old, and I decided that day to start walking.
To ride a bike.
And when I had to, to take the bus.

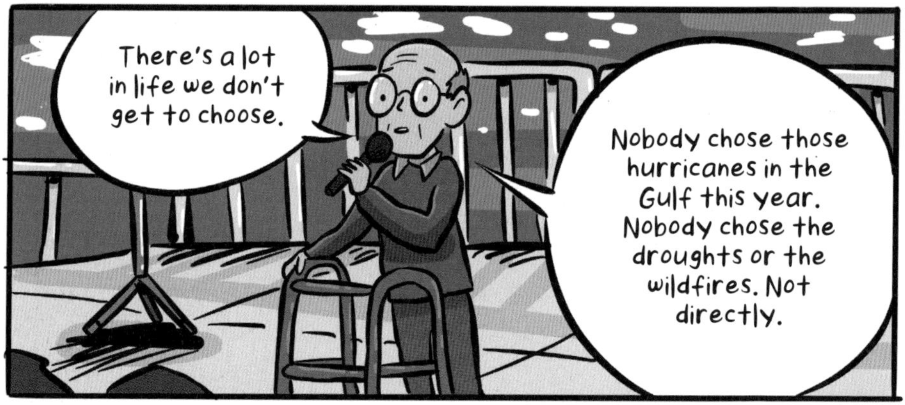
There's a lot in life we don't get to choose.
Nobody chose those hurricanes in the Gulf this year. Nobody chose the droughts or the wildfires. Not directly.

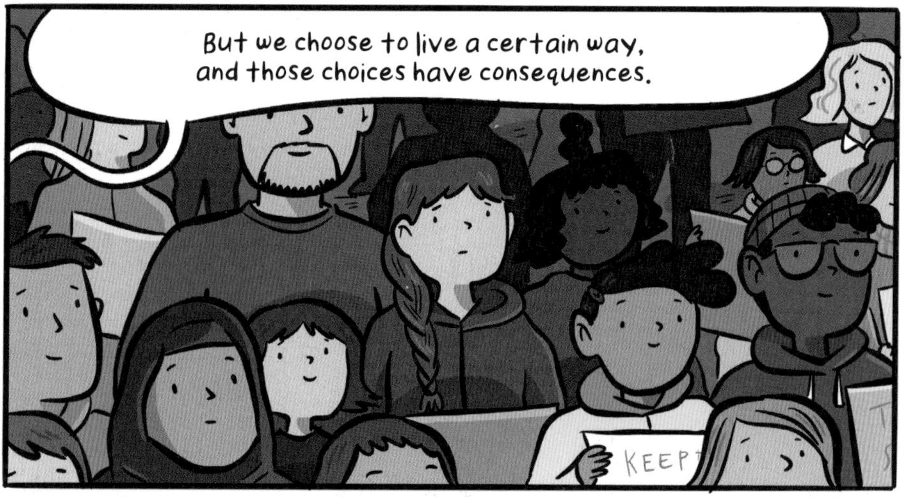
But we choose to live a certain way, and those choices have consequences.
KEEP

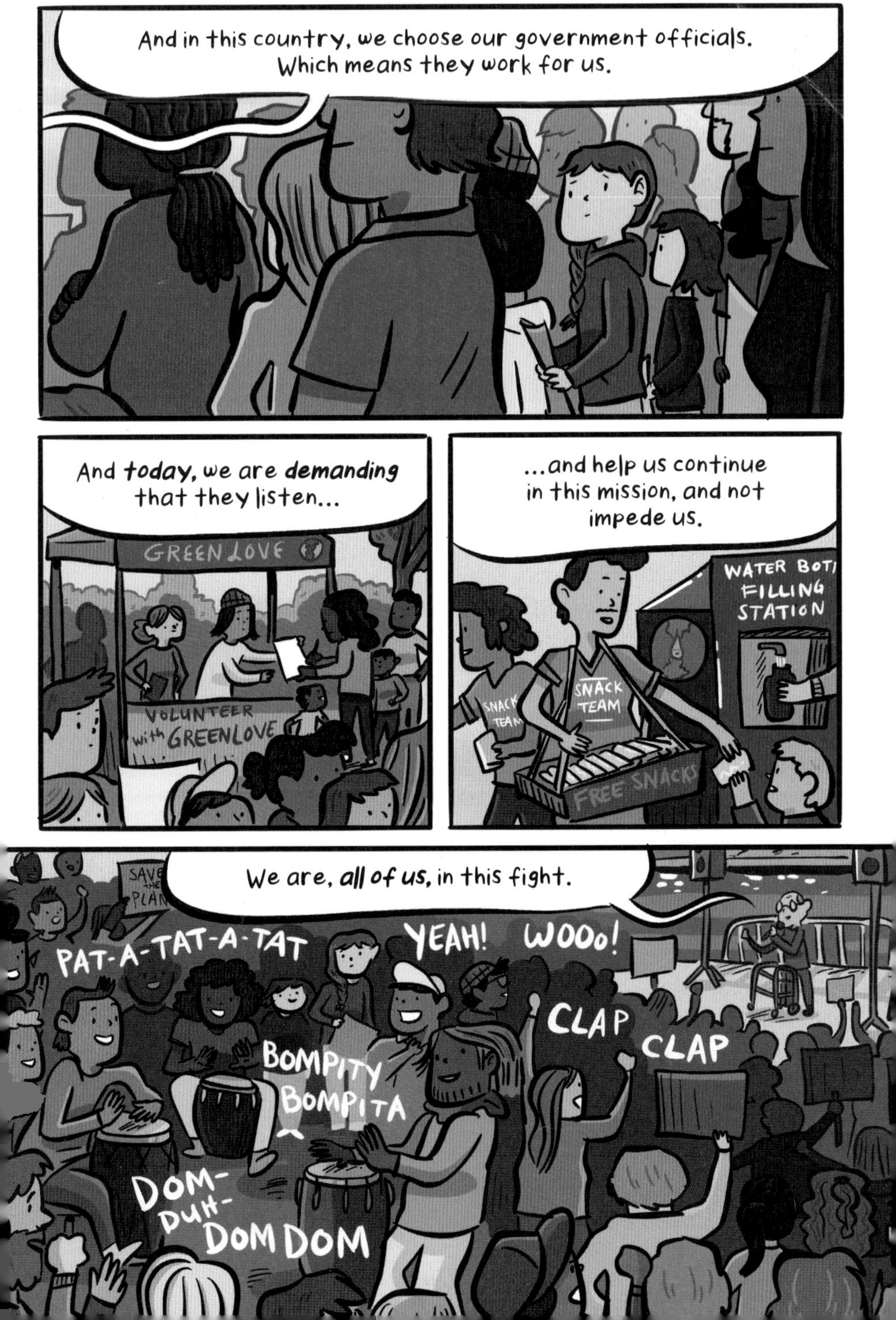
And in this country, we choose our government officials. Which means they work for us.
And *today*, we are *demanding* that they listen...
GREEN LOVE
VOLUNTEER with GREENLOVE
...and help us continue in this mission, and not impede us.
WATER BOT
FILLING STATION
SNACK TEAM
SNACK TEAM
FREE SNACKS
We are, *all of us*, in this fight.
PAT-A-TAT-A-TAT
YEAH!
WOOo!
CLAP
CLAP
BOMPITY BOMPITA
DOM-DUH-DOM DOM

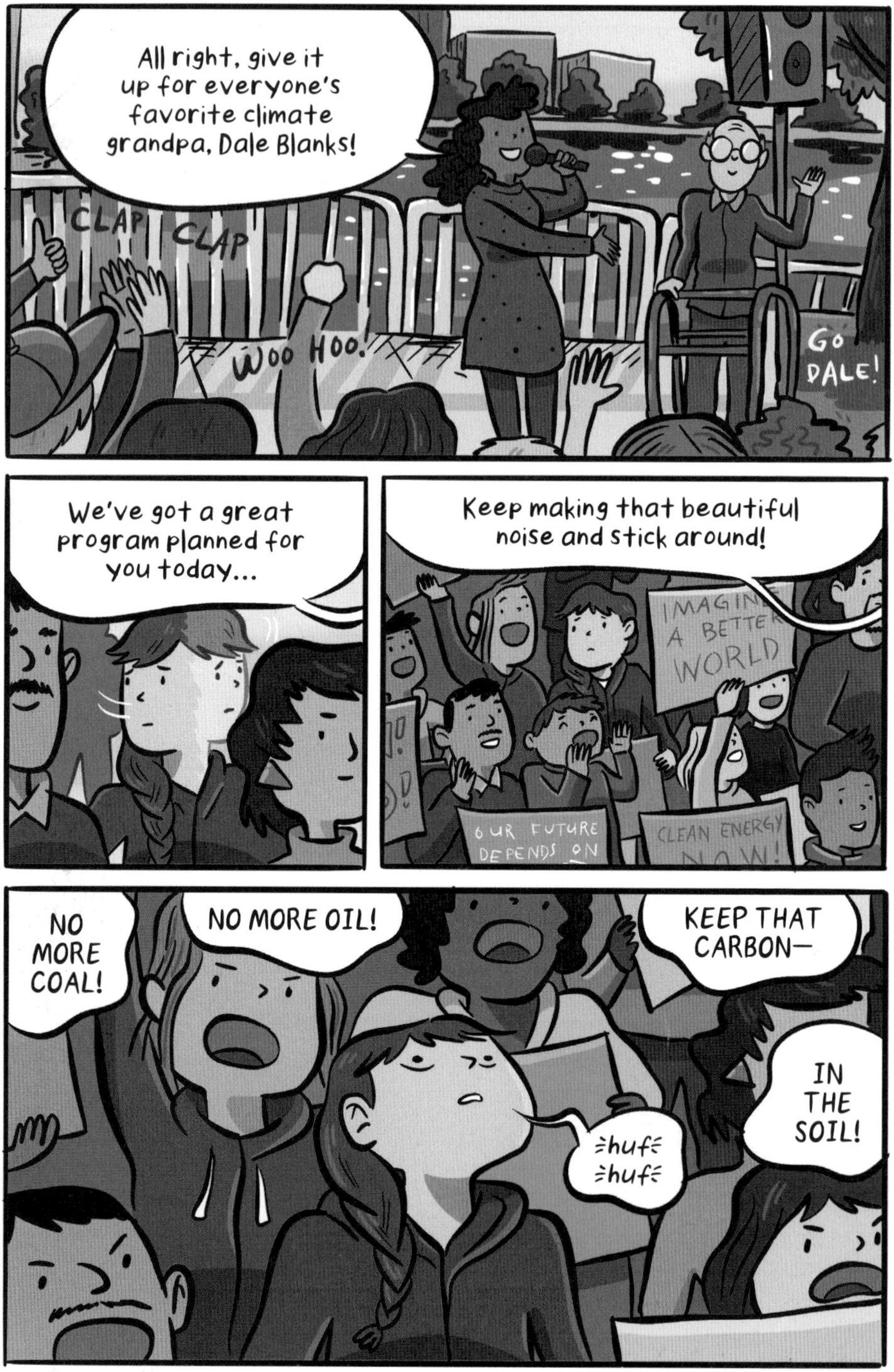
All right, give it up for everyone's favorite climate grandpa, Dale Blanks!
CLAP CLAP
WOO HOO!
GO DALE!
We've got a great program planned for you today...
Keep making that beautiful noise and stick around!
IMAGIN
A BETTE
WORLD
OUR FUTURE DEPENDS ON
CLEAN ENERGY
NO MORE COAL!
NO MORE OIL!
KEEP THAT CARBON—
IN THE SOIL!
huf huf

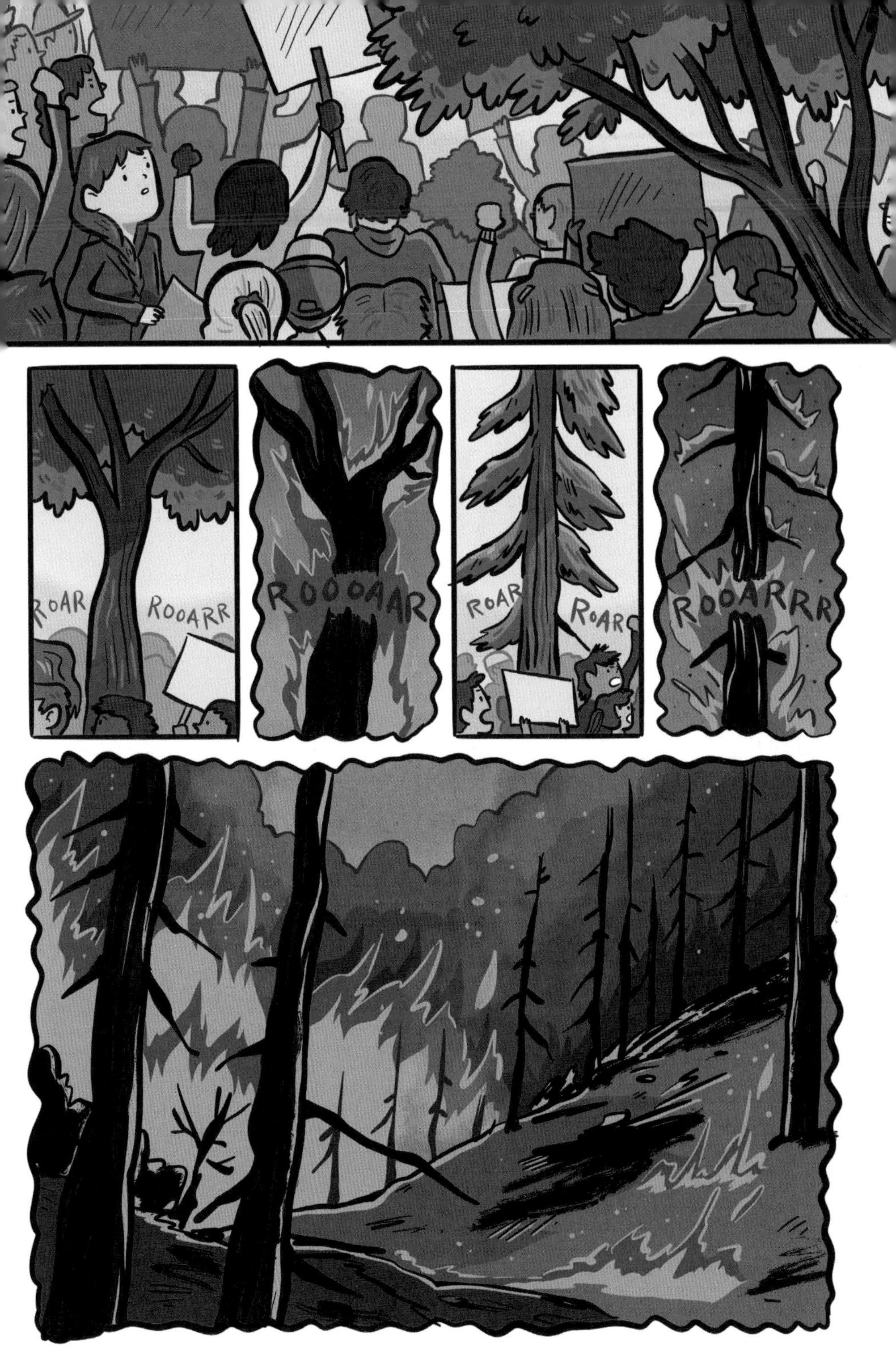
ROAR
ROOARR
ROOOAAR
ROAR
ROAR
ROOARRRR

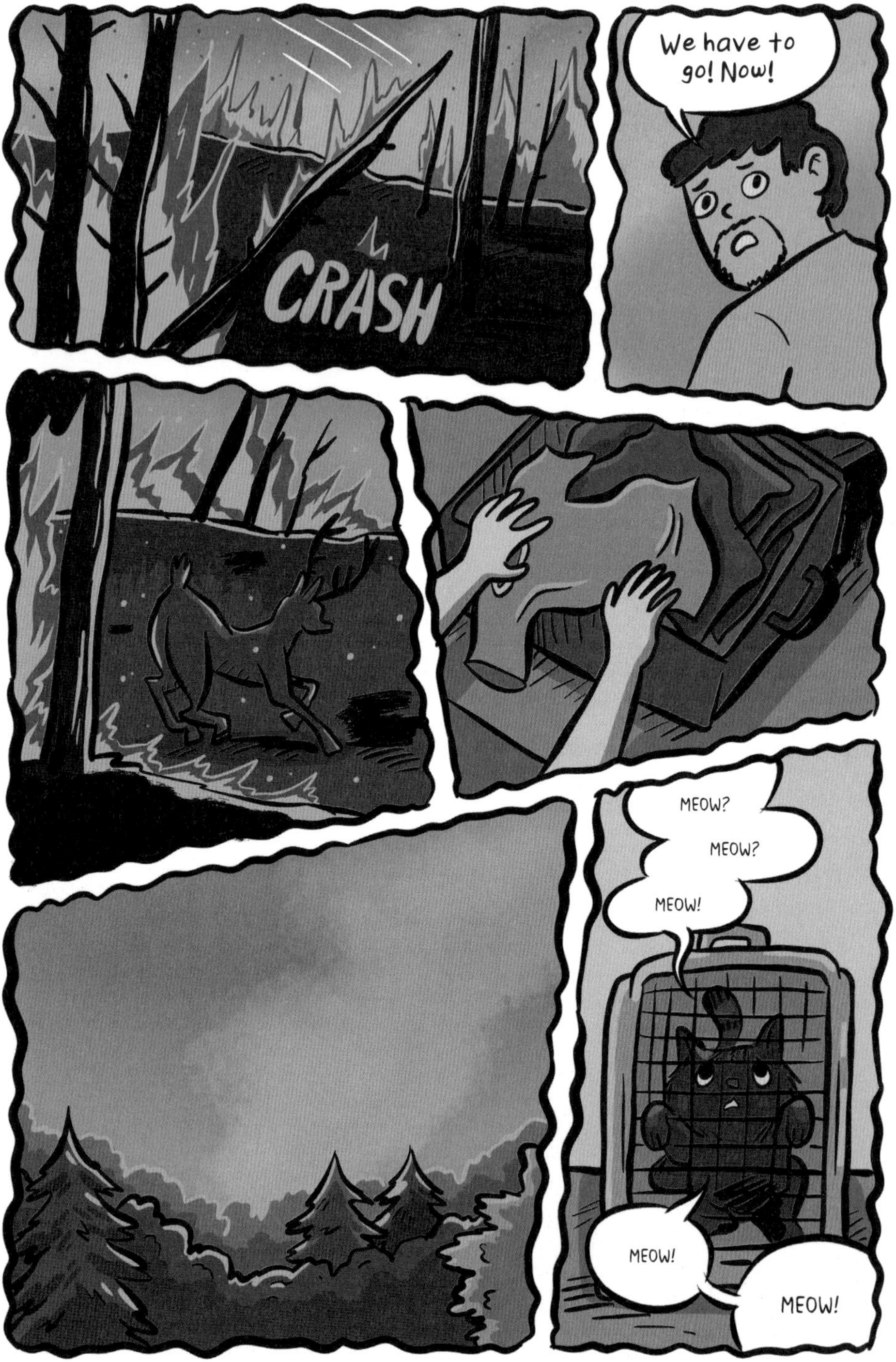
CRASH
We have to go! Now!
MEOW?
MEOW?
MEOW!
MEOW!
MEOW!

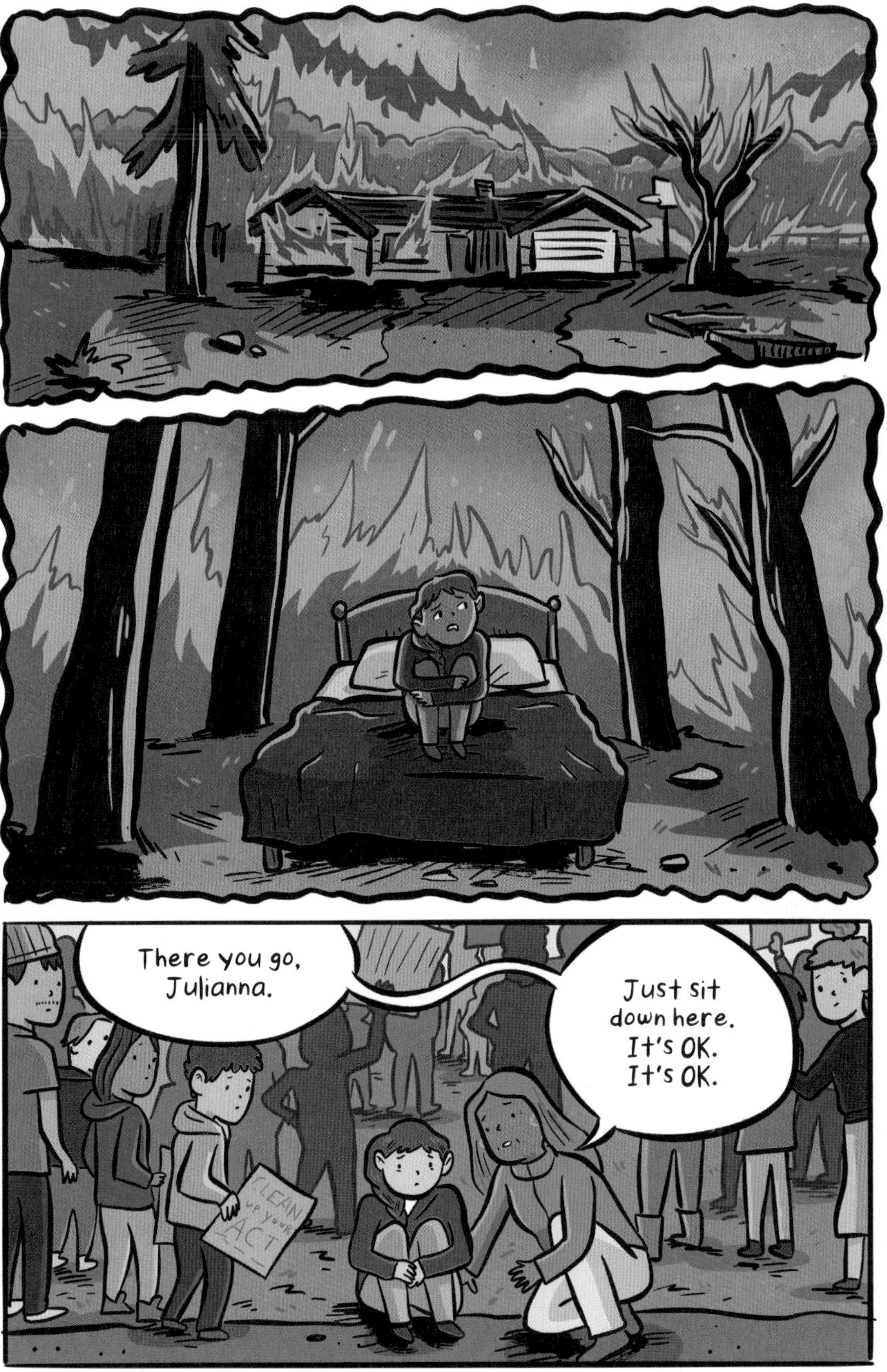
There you go, Julianna.
Just sit down here. It's OK. It's OK.
CLEAN up your ACT

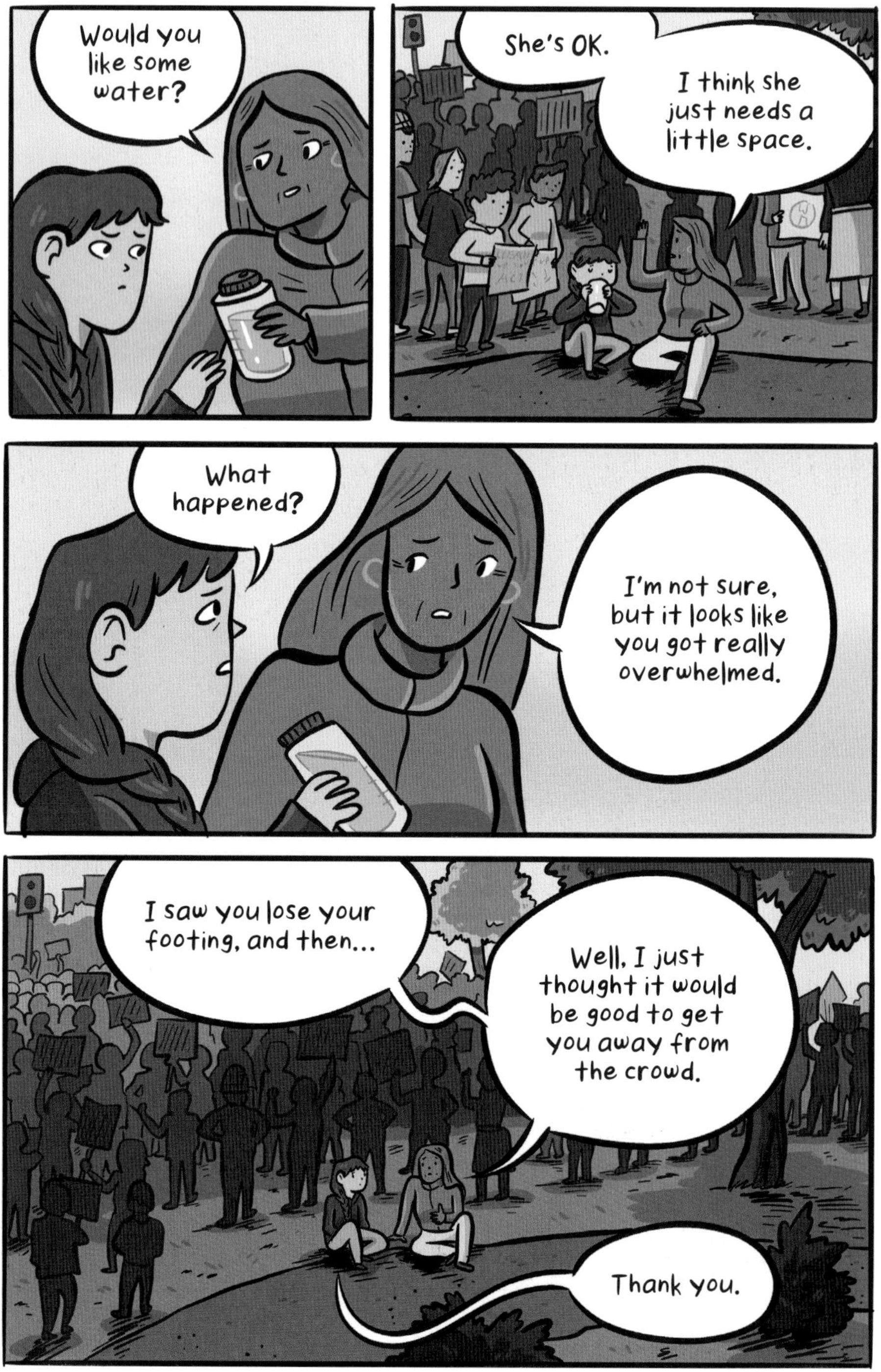
Would you like some water?
She's OK.
I think she just needs a little space.
What happened?
I'm not sure, but it looks like you got really overwhelmed.
I saw you lose your footing, and then...
Well, I just thought it would be good to get you away from the crowd.
Thank you.

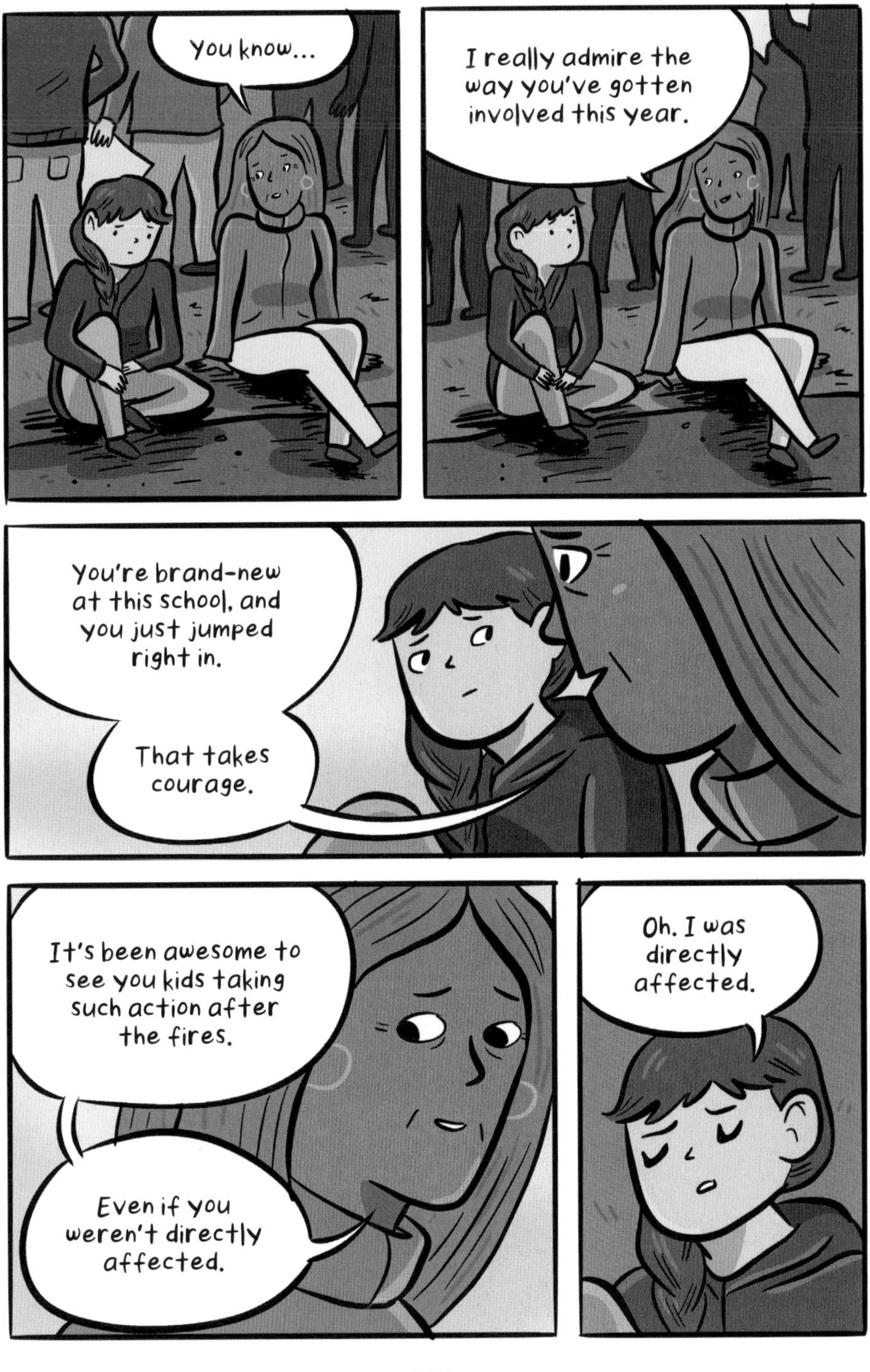

You know...
I really admire the way you've gotten involved this year.
You're brand-new at this school, and you just jumped right in.
That takes courage.
It's been awesome to see you kids taking such action after the fires.
Even if you weren't directly affected.
Oh. I was directly affected.

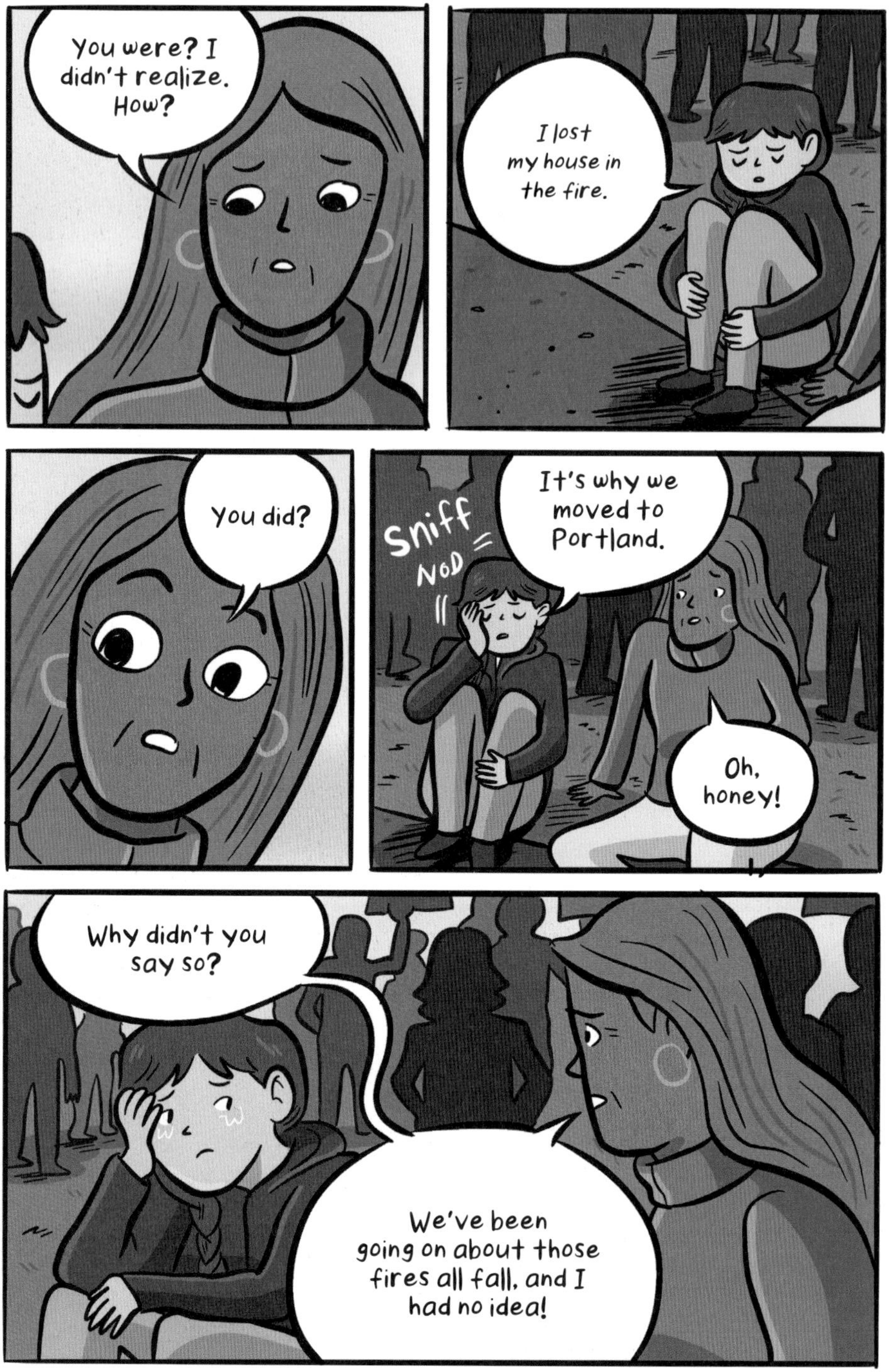
You were? I didn't realize. How?
I lost my house in the fire.
You did?
Sniff
NOD
It's why we moved to Portland.
Oh, honey!
Why didn't you say so?
We've been going on about those fires all fall, and I had no idea!

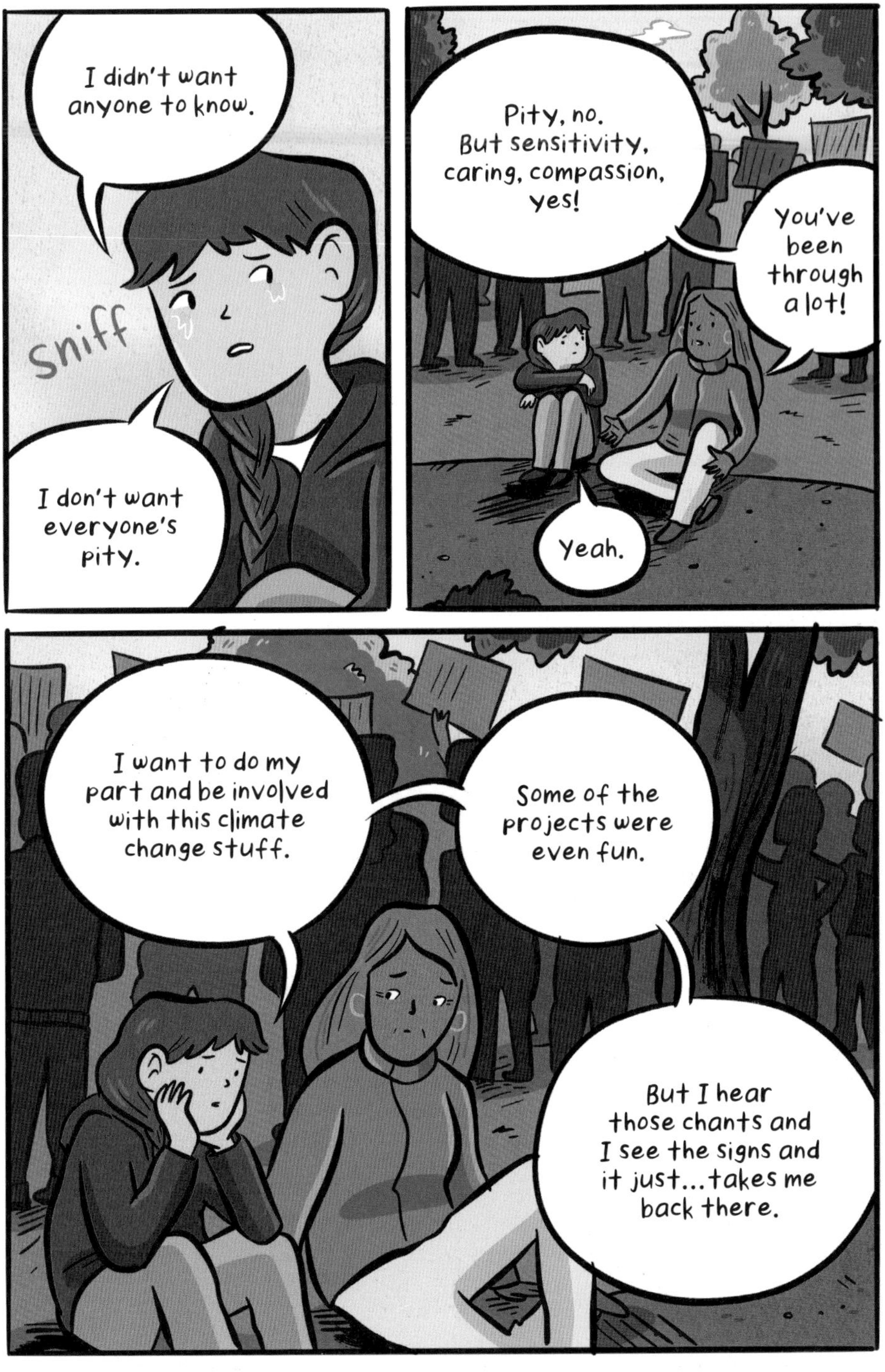
I didn't want anyone to know.
Sniff
I don't want everyone's pity.
Pity, no. But sensitivity, caring, compassion, yes!
You've been through a lot!
Yeah.
I want to do my part and be involved with this climate change stuff.
Some of the projects were even fun.
But I hear those chants and I see the signs and it just... takes me back there.

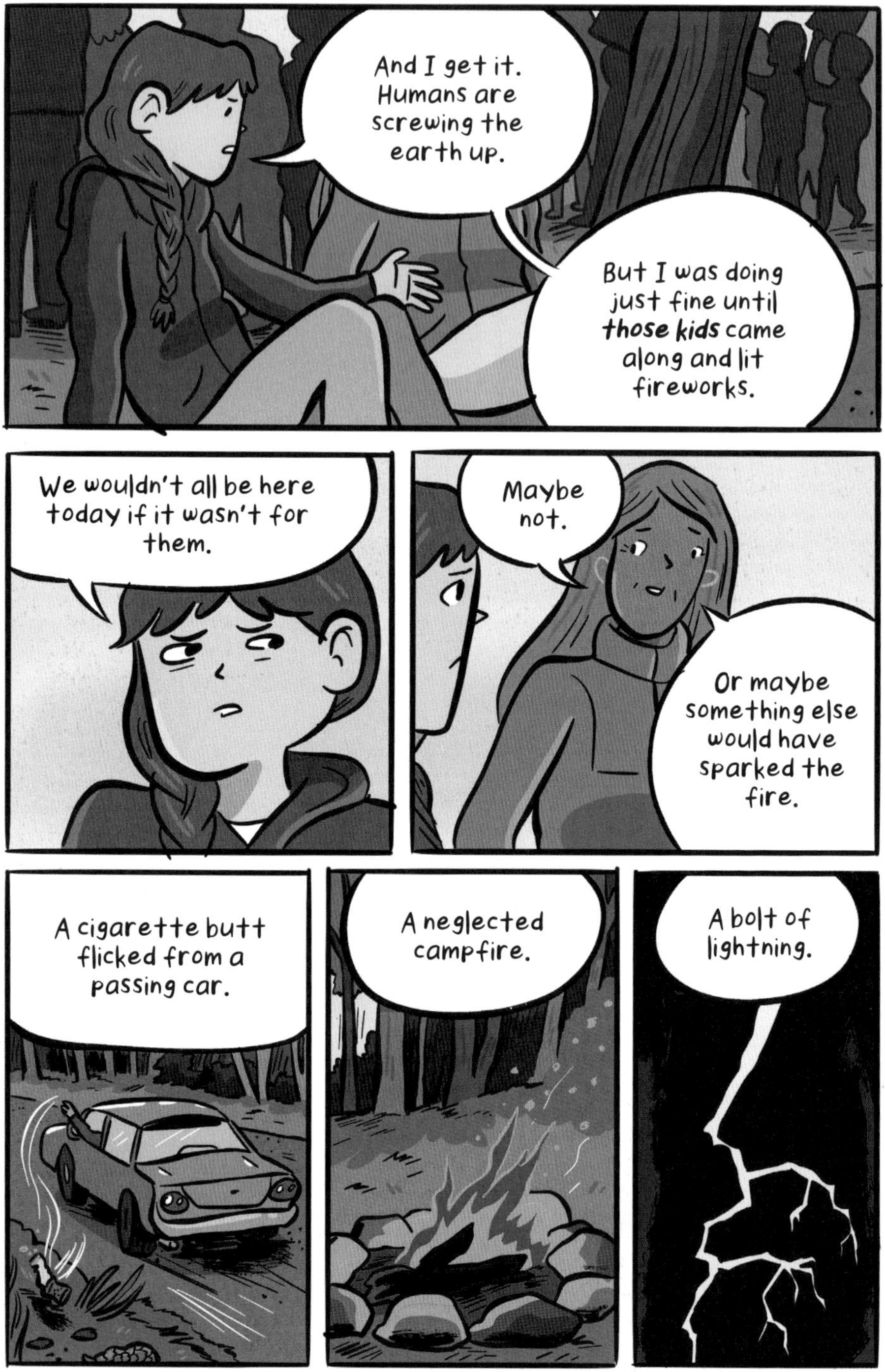
And I get it. Humans are screwing the earth up.
But I was doing just fine until **those kids** came along and lit fireworks.
We wouldn't all be here today if it wasn't for them.
Maybe not.
Or maybe something else would have sparked the fire.
A cigarette butt flicked from a passing car.
A neglected campfire.
A bolt of lightning.

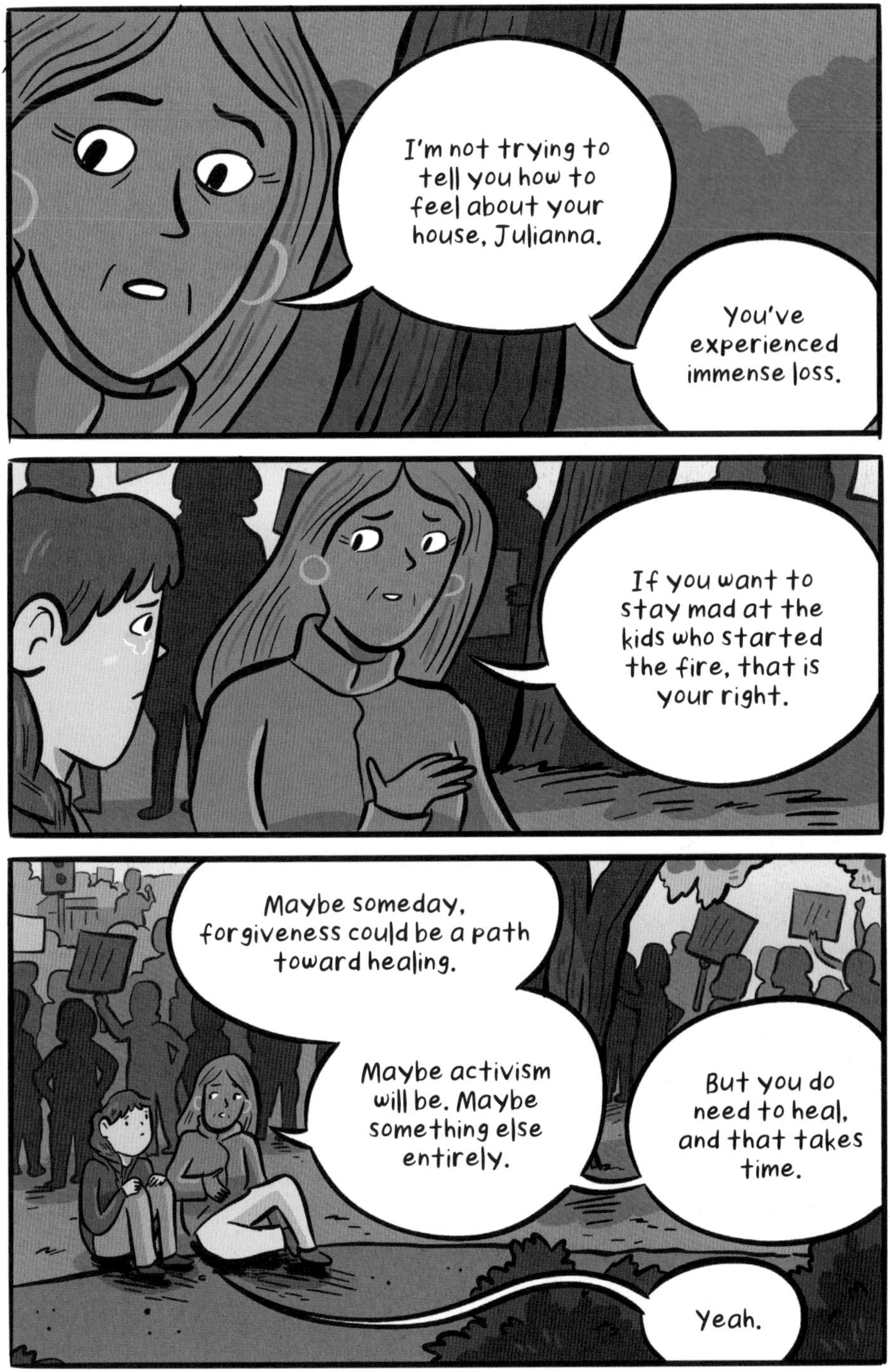
I'm not trying to tell you how to feel about your house, Julianna.
You've experienced immense loss.
If you want to stay mad at the kids who started the fire, that is your right.
Maybe someday, forgiveness could be a path toward healing.
Maybe activism will be. Maybe something else entirely.
But you do need to heal, and that takes time.
Yeah.

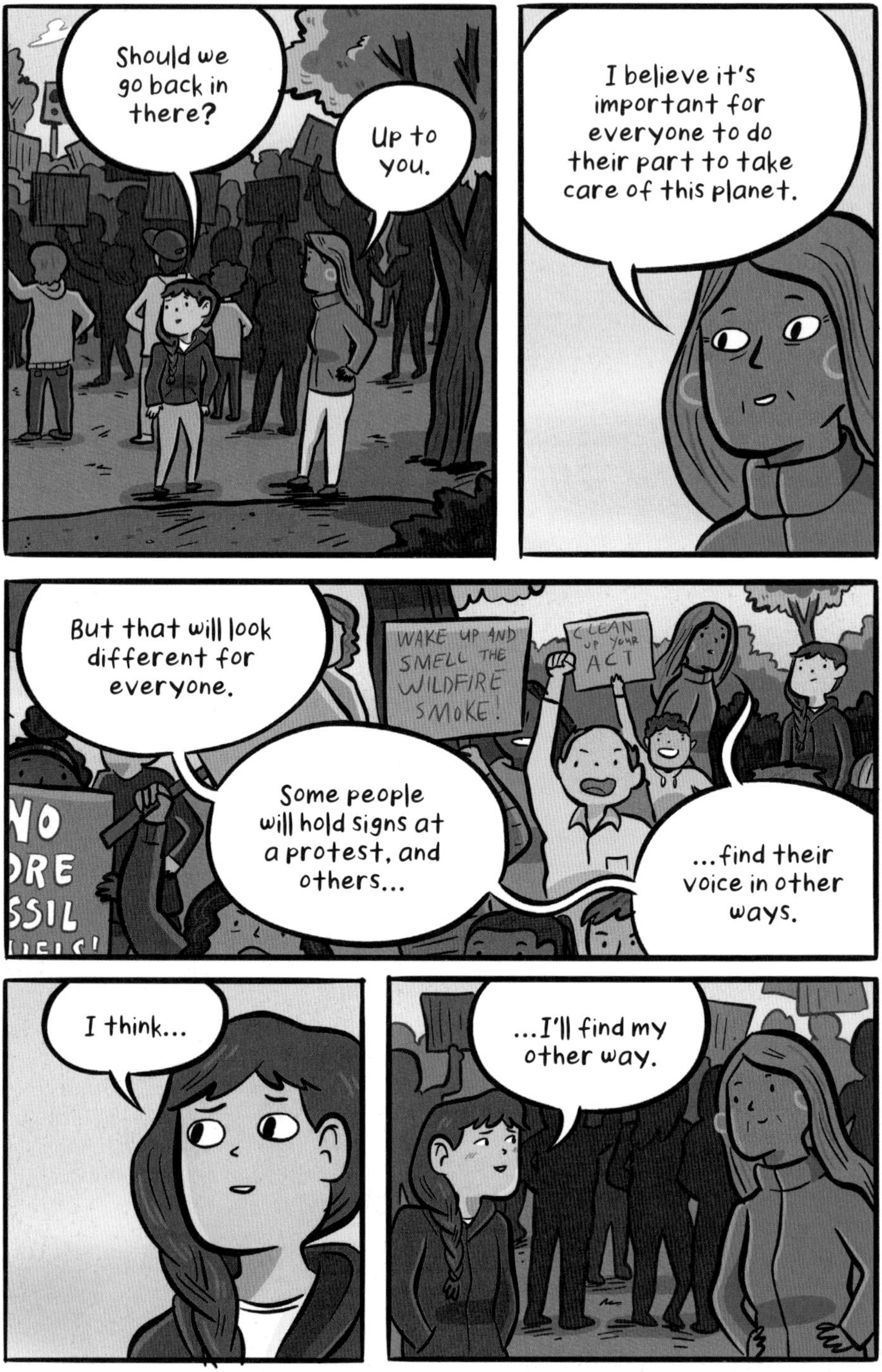

Should we go back in there?
Up to you.
I believe it's important for everyone to do their part to take care of this planet.
But that will look different for everyone.
WAKE UP AND SMELL THE WILDFIRE SMOKE!
CLEAN UP YOUR ACT
Some people will hold signs at a protest, and others...
...find their voice in other ways.
I think...
...I'll find my other way.

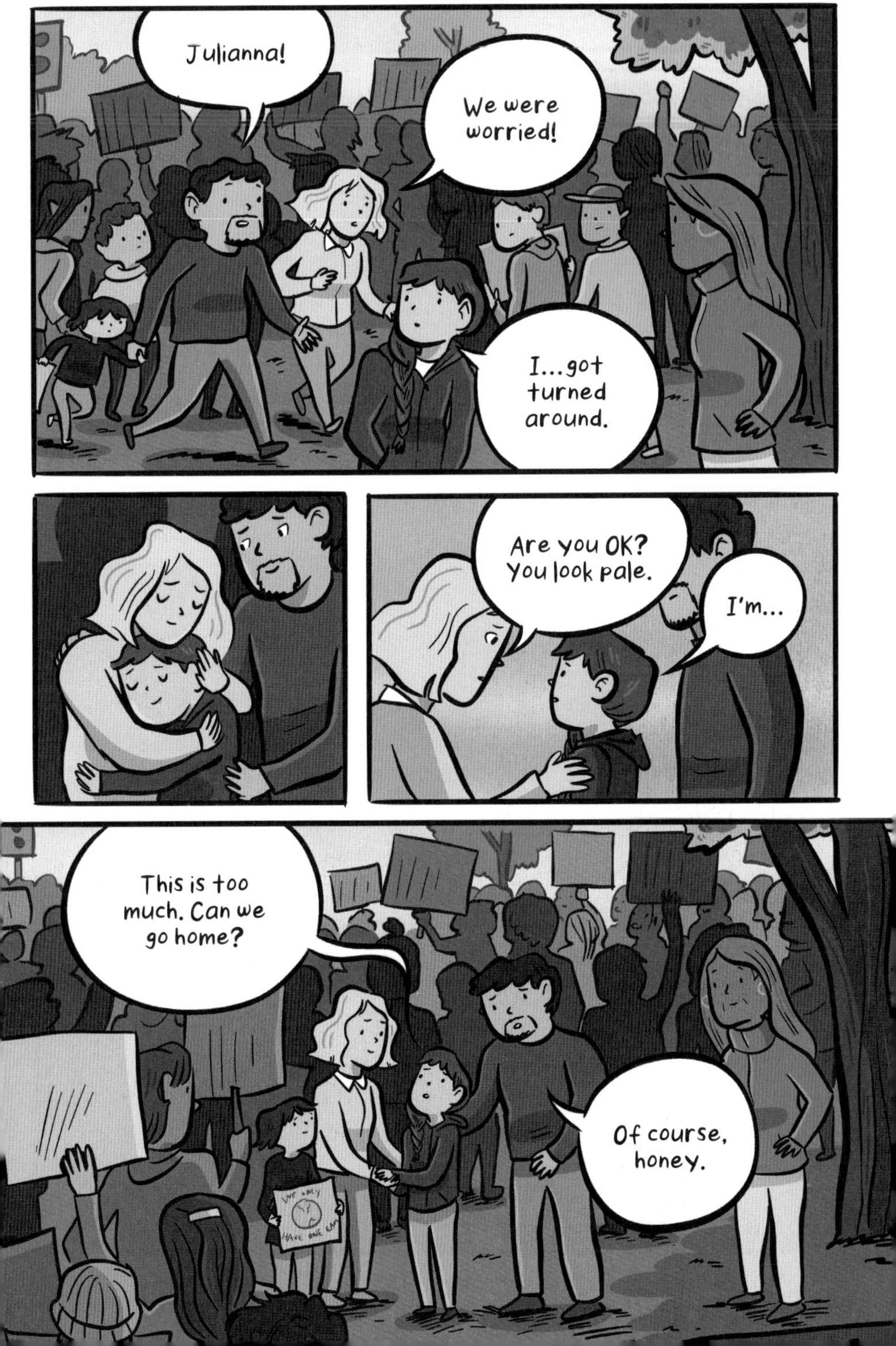
Julianna!
We were worried!
I...got turned around.
Are you OK? You look pale.
I'm...
This is too much. Can we go home?
Of course, honey.

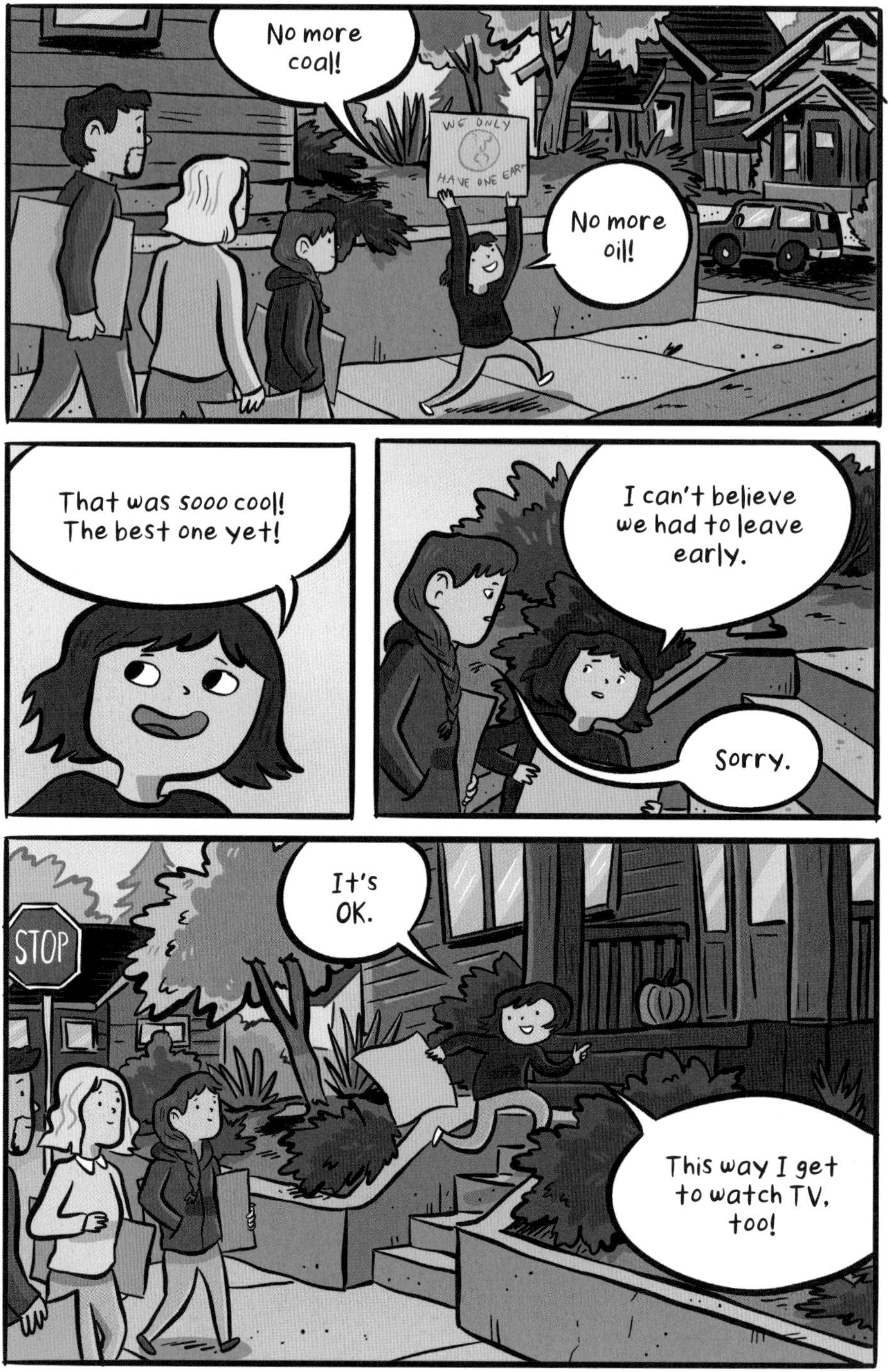

No more coal!
WE ONLY
HAVE ONE EAR
No more oil!
That was sooo cool! The best one yet!
I can't believe we had to leave early.
Sorry.
STOP
It's OK.
This way I get to watch TV, too!

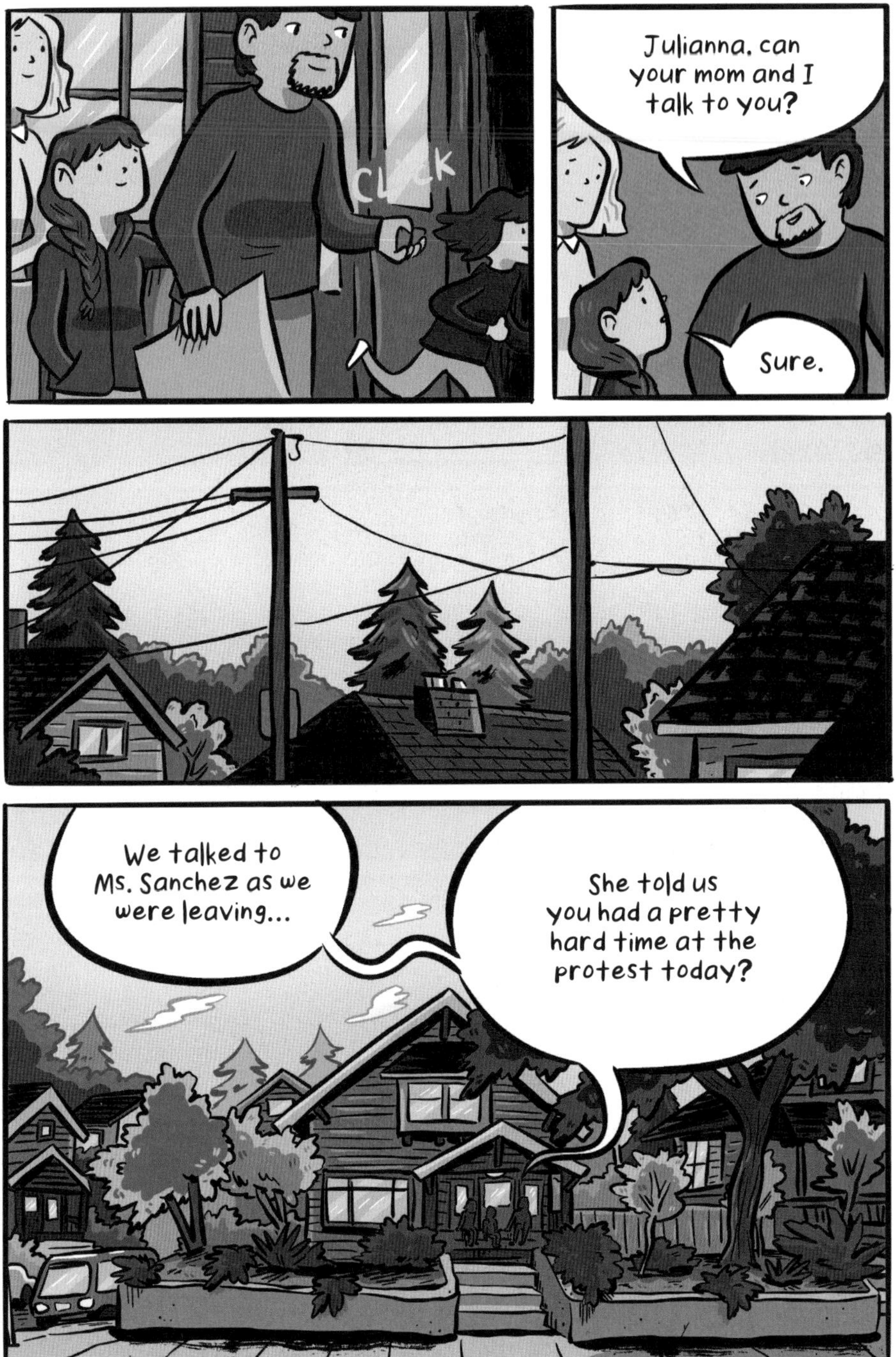
CLICK
Julianna, can your mom and I talk to you?
Sure.
We talked to Ms. Sanchez as we were leaving...
She told us you had a pretty hard time at the protest today?

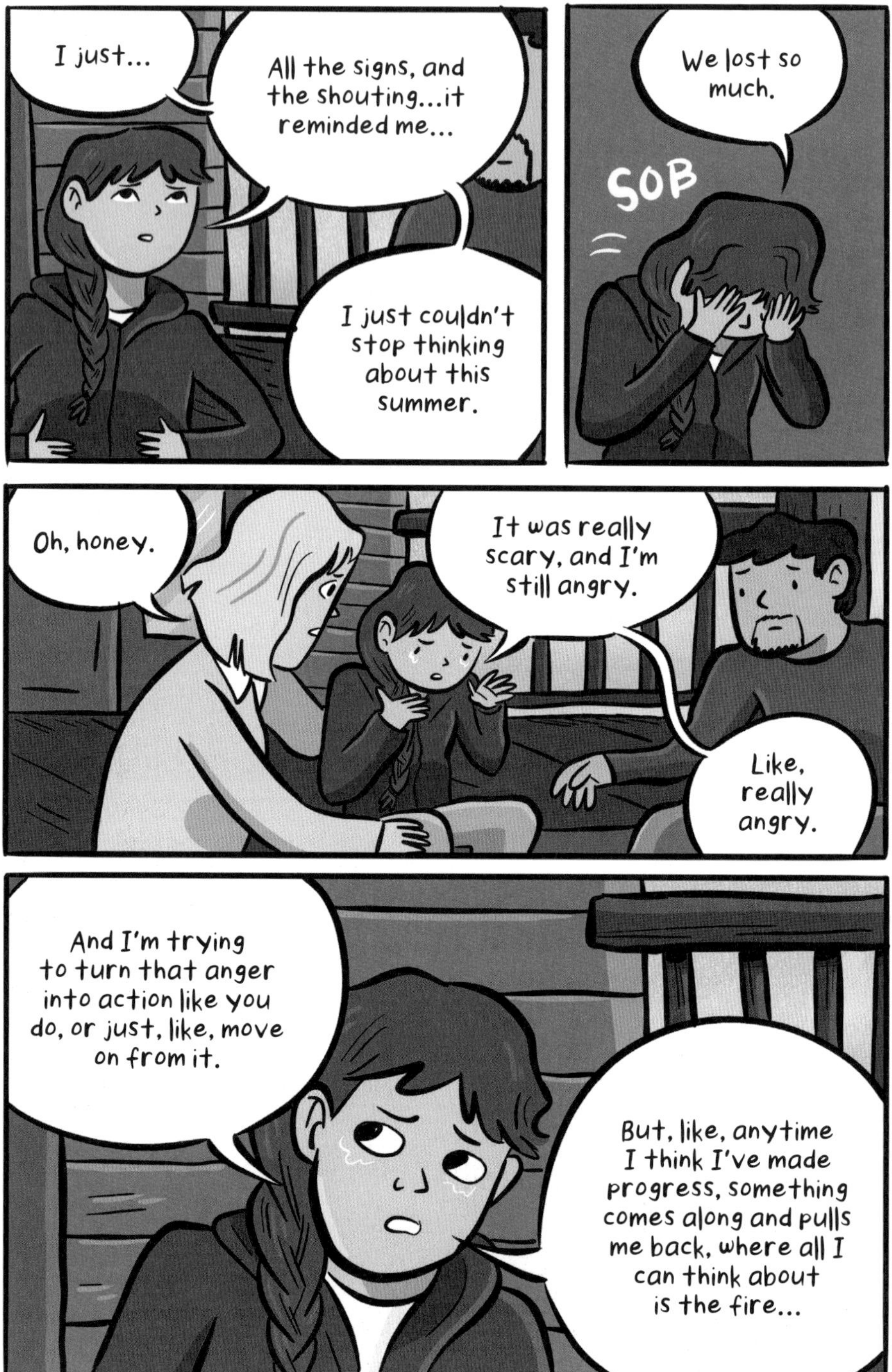
I just...
All the signs, and the shouting...it reminded me...
I just couldn't stop thinking about this summer.
We lost so much.
SOB
Oh, honey.
It was really scary, and I'm still angry.
Like, really angry.
And I'm trying to turn that anger into action like you do, or just, like, move on from it.
But, like, anytime I think I've made progress, something comes along and pulls me back, where all I can think about is the fire...

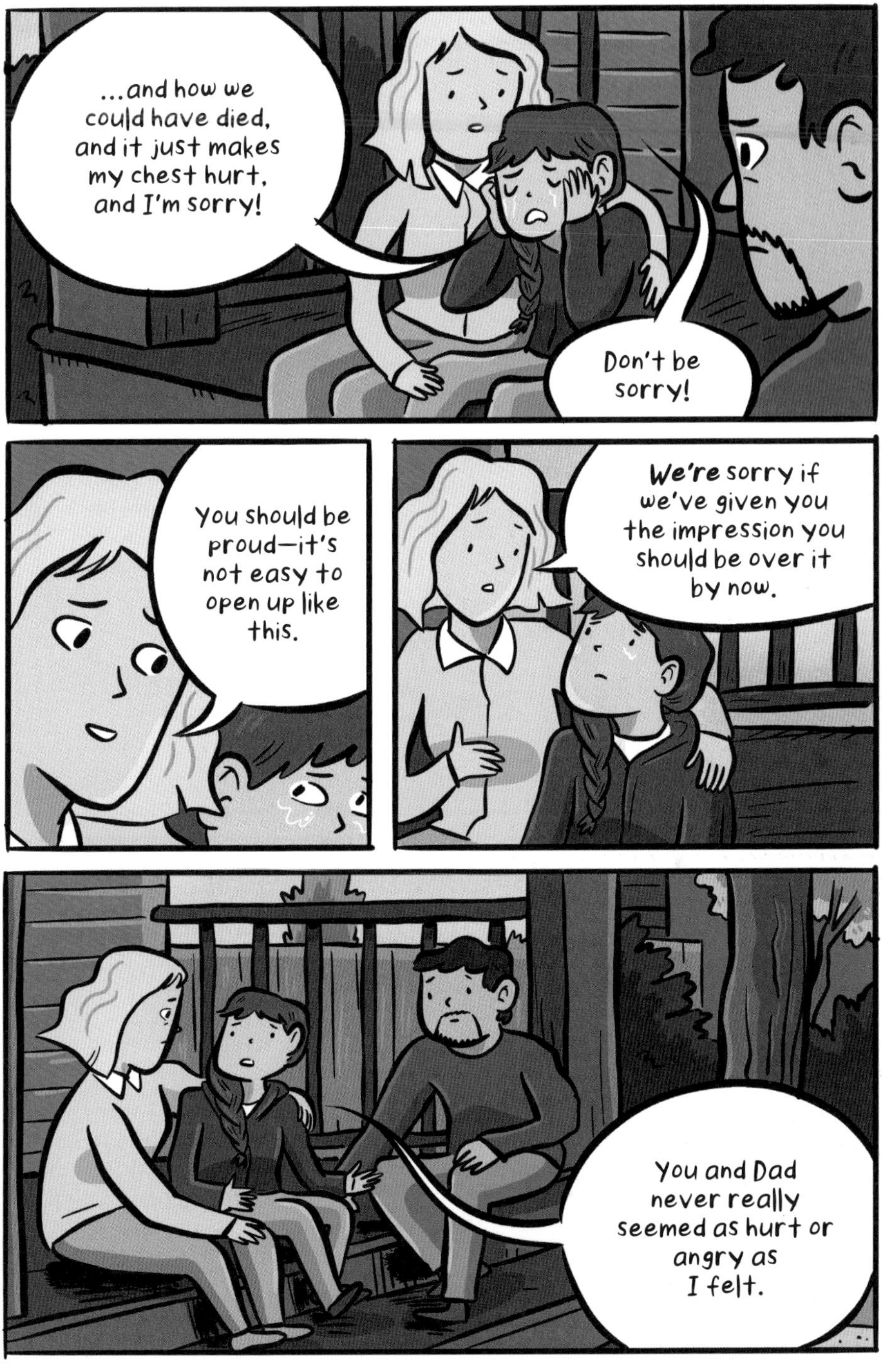
...and how we could have died, and it just makes my chest hurt, and I'm sorry!
Don't be sorry!
You should be proud—it's not easy to open up like this.
We're sorry if we've given you the impression you should be over it by now.
You and Dad never really seemed as hurt or angry as I felt.

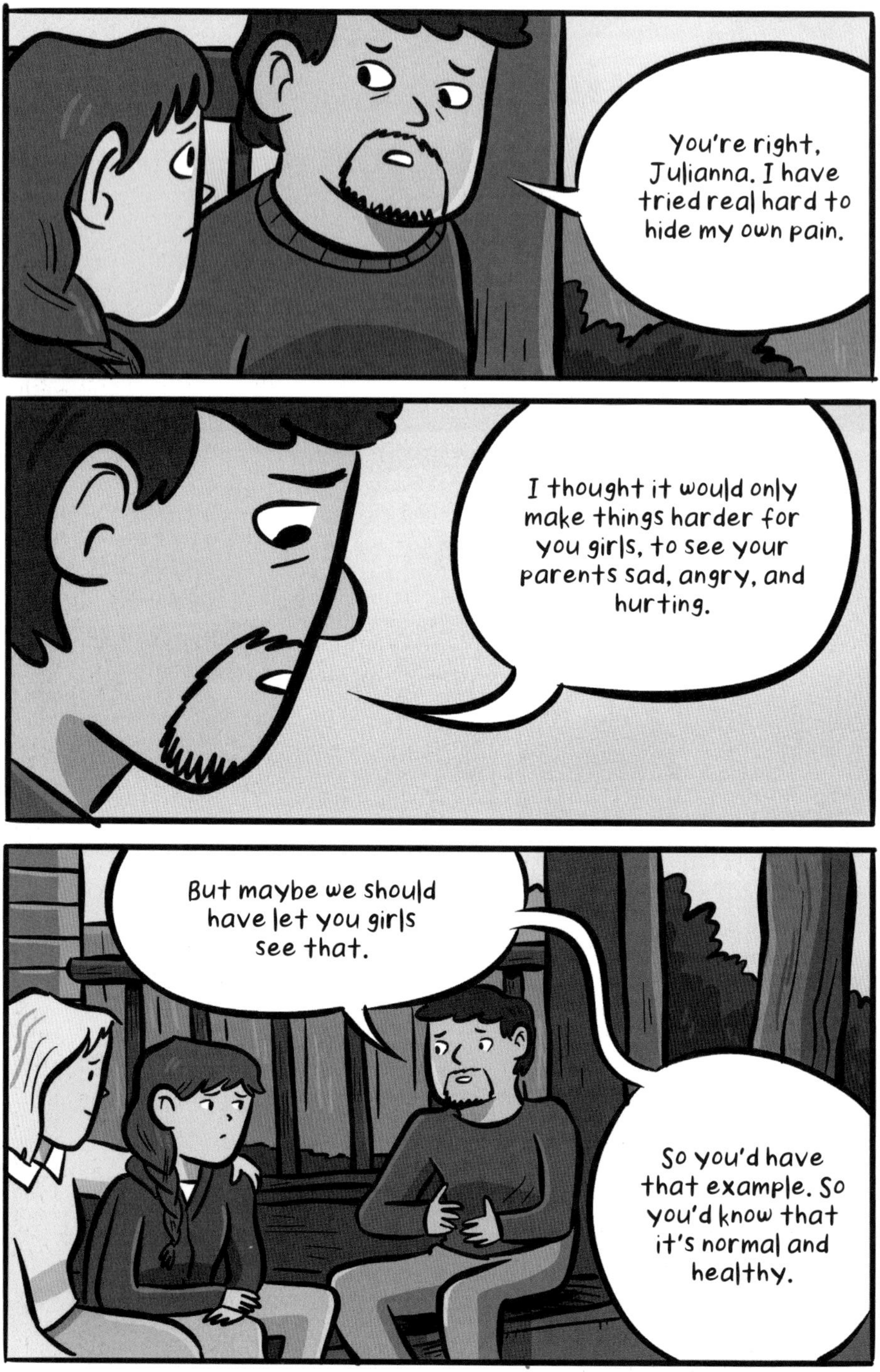
You're right, Julianna. I have tried real hard to hide my own pain.
I thought it would only make things harder for you girls, to see your parents sad, angry, and hurting.
But maybe we should have let you girls see that.
So you'd have that example. So you'd know that it's normal and healthy.

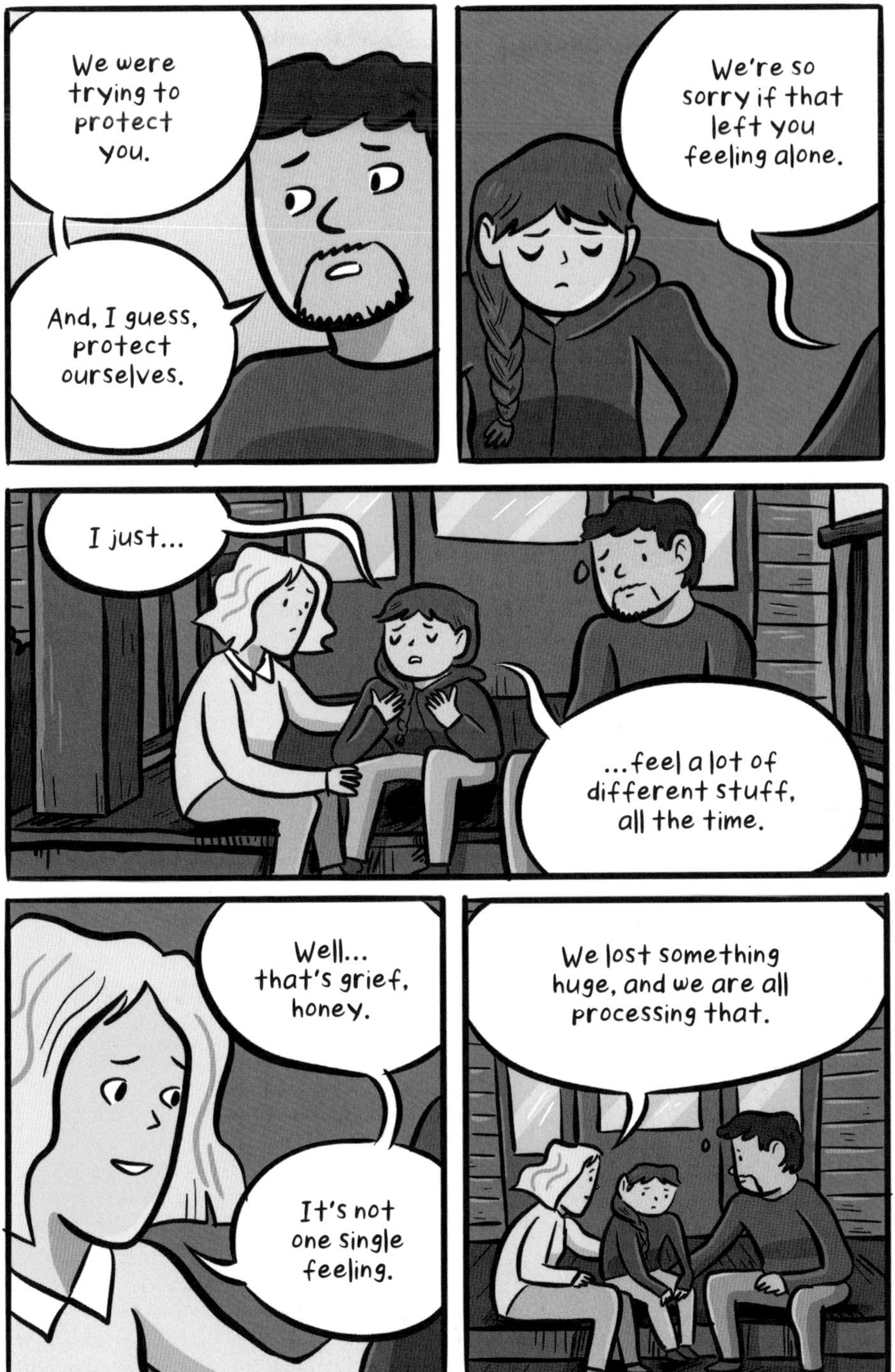
We were trying to protect you.
And, I guess, protect ourselves.
We're so sorry if that left you feeling alone.
I just...
...feel a lot of different stuff, all the time.
Well... that's grief, honey.
It's not one single feeling.
We lost something huge, and we are all processing that.

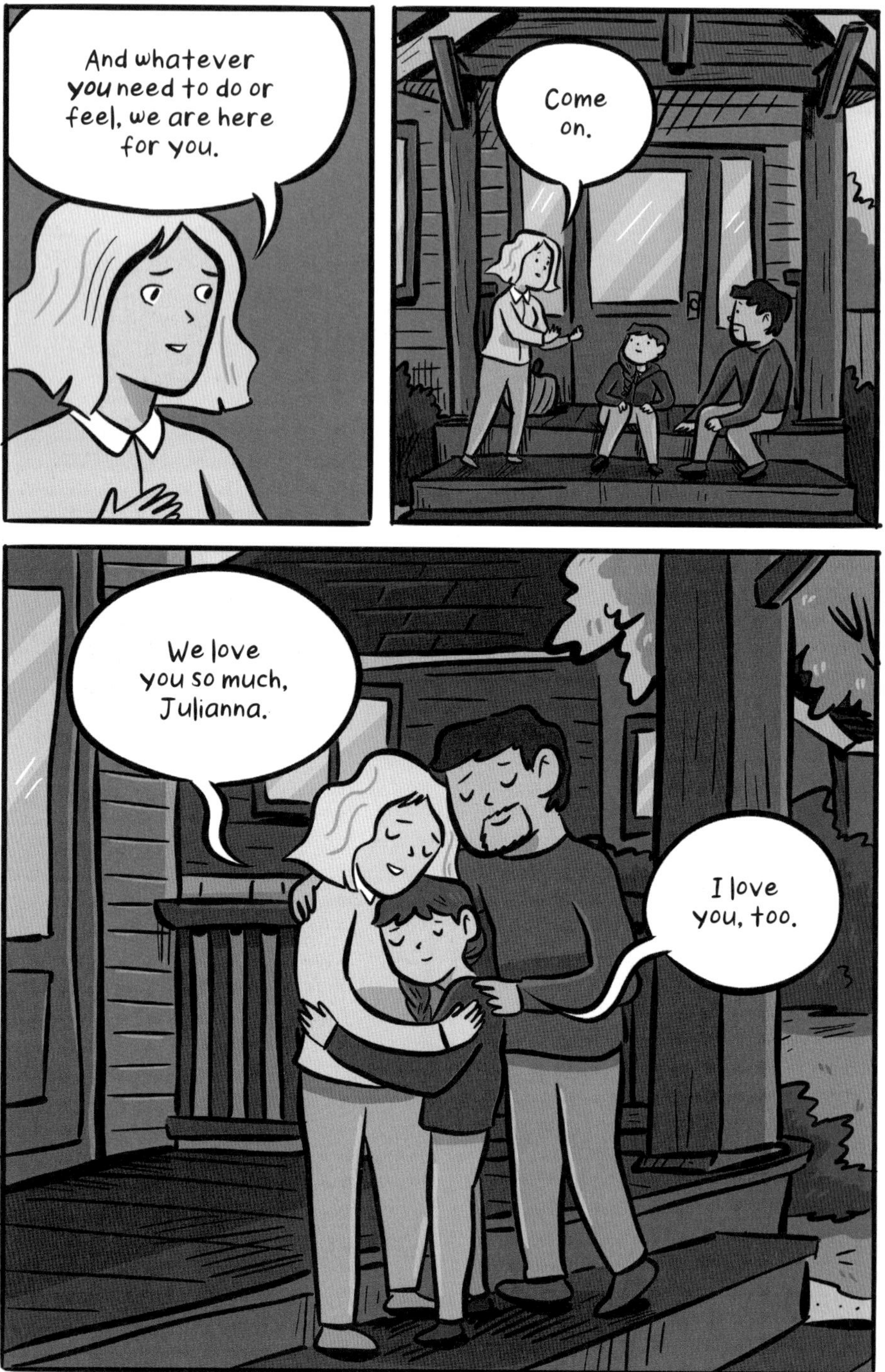
And whatever you need to do or feel, we are here for you.
Come on.
We love you so much, Julianna.
I love you, too.

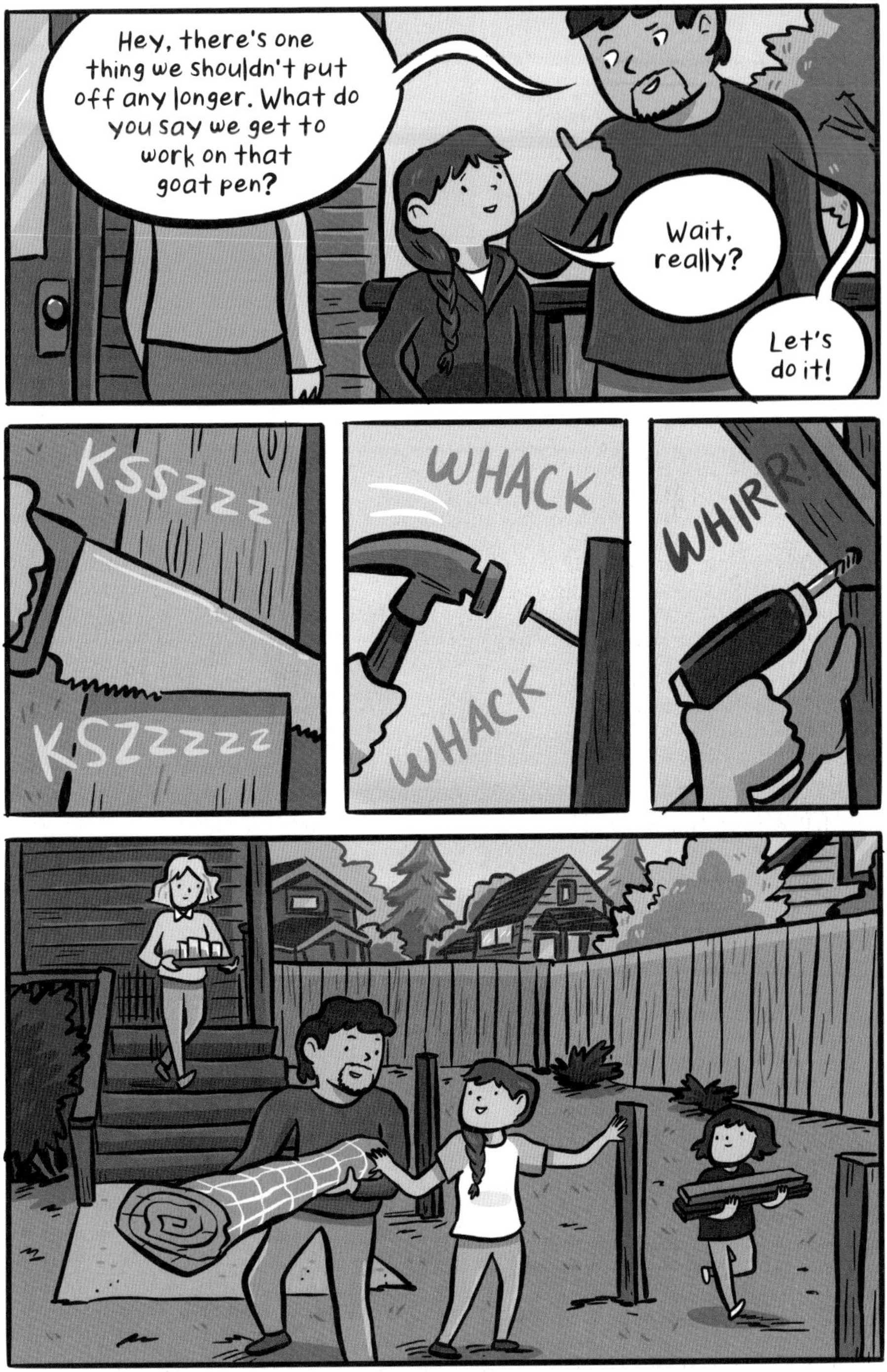
Hey, there's one thing we shouldn't put off any longer. What do you say we get to work on that goat pen?
Wait, really?
Let's do it!
KSSZZZ
KSZZZZZ
WHACK
WHACK
WHIRR!

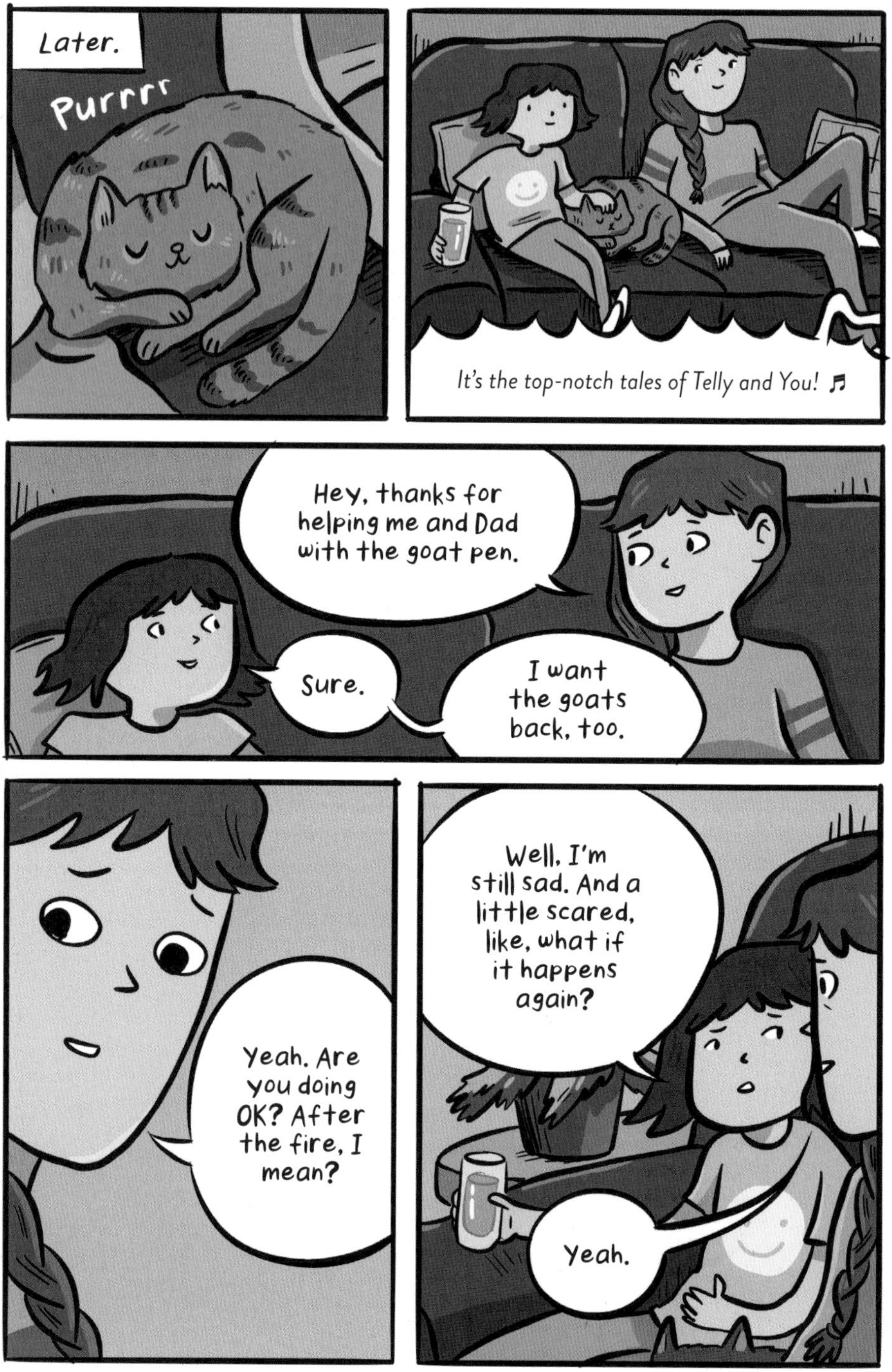
Later.
Purrrr
It's the top-notch tales of Telly and You! ♬
Hey, thanks for helping me and Dad with the goat pen.
Sure.
I want the goats back, too.
Yeah. Are you doing OK? After the fire, I mean?
Well, I'm still sad. And a little scared, like, what if it happens again?
Yeah.

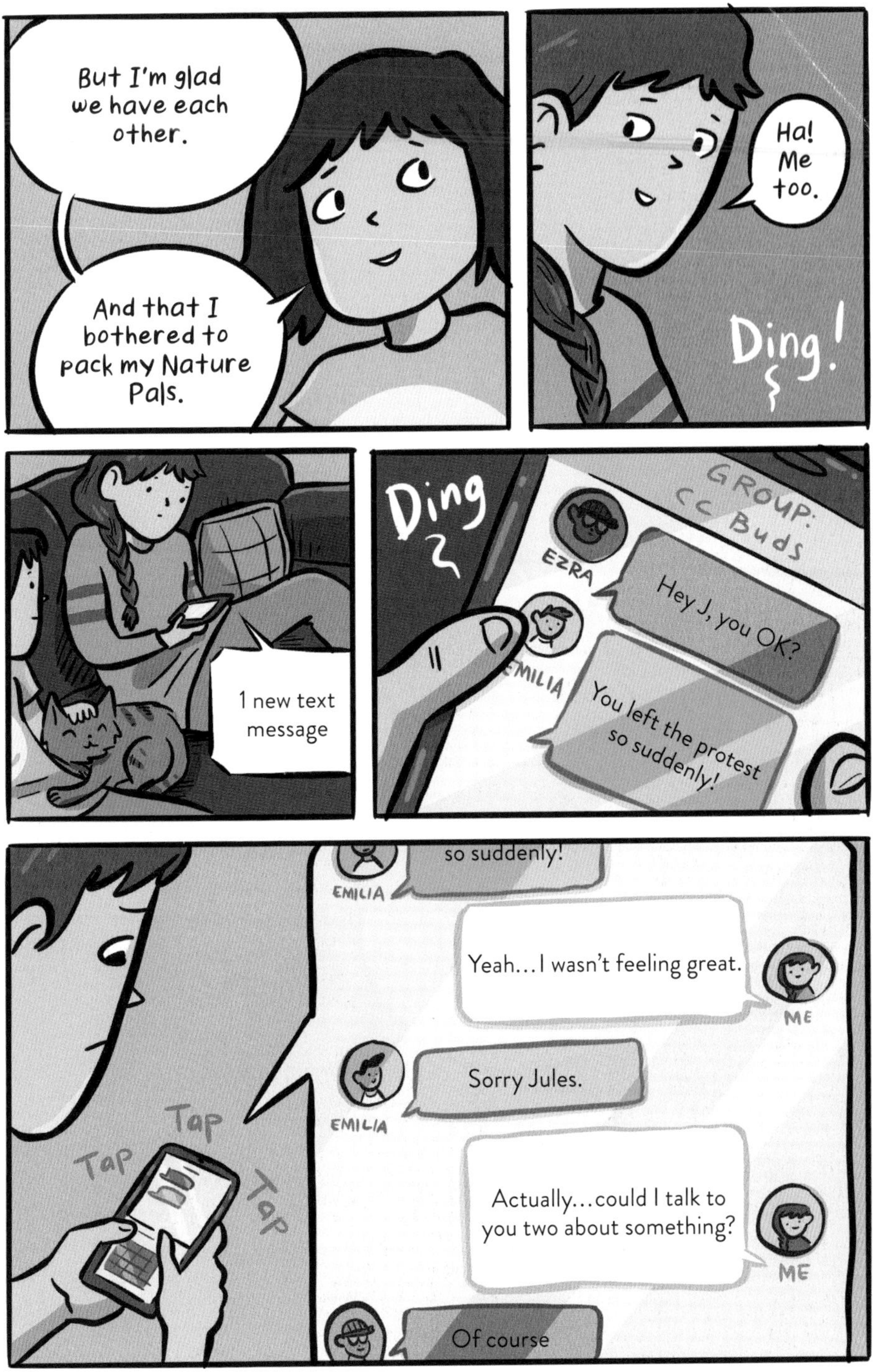
But I'm glad we have each other.
And that I bothered to pack my Nature Pals.
Ha! Me too.
Ding!
1 new text message
Ding
GROUP: CC Buds
EZRA
Hey J, you OK?
EMILIA
You left the protest so suddenly!
so suddenly!
EMILIA
Yeah...I wasn't feeling great.
ME
Sorry Jules.
EMILIA
Tap
Tap
Tap
Actually...could I talk to you two about something?
ME
Of course

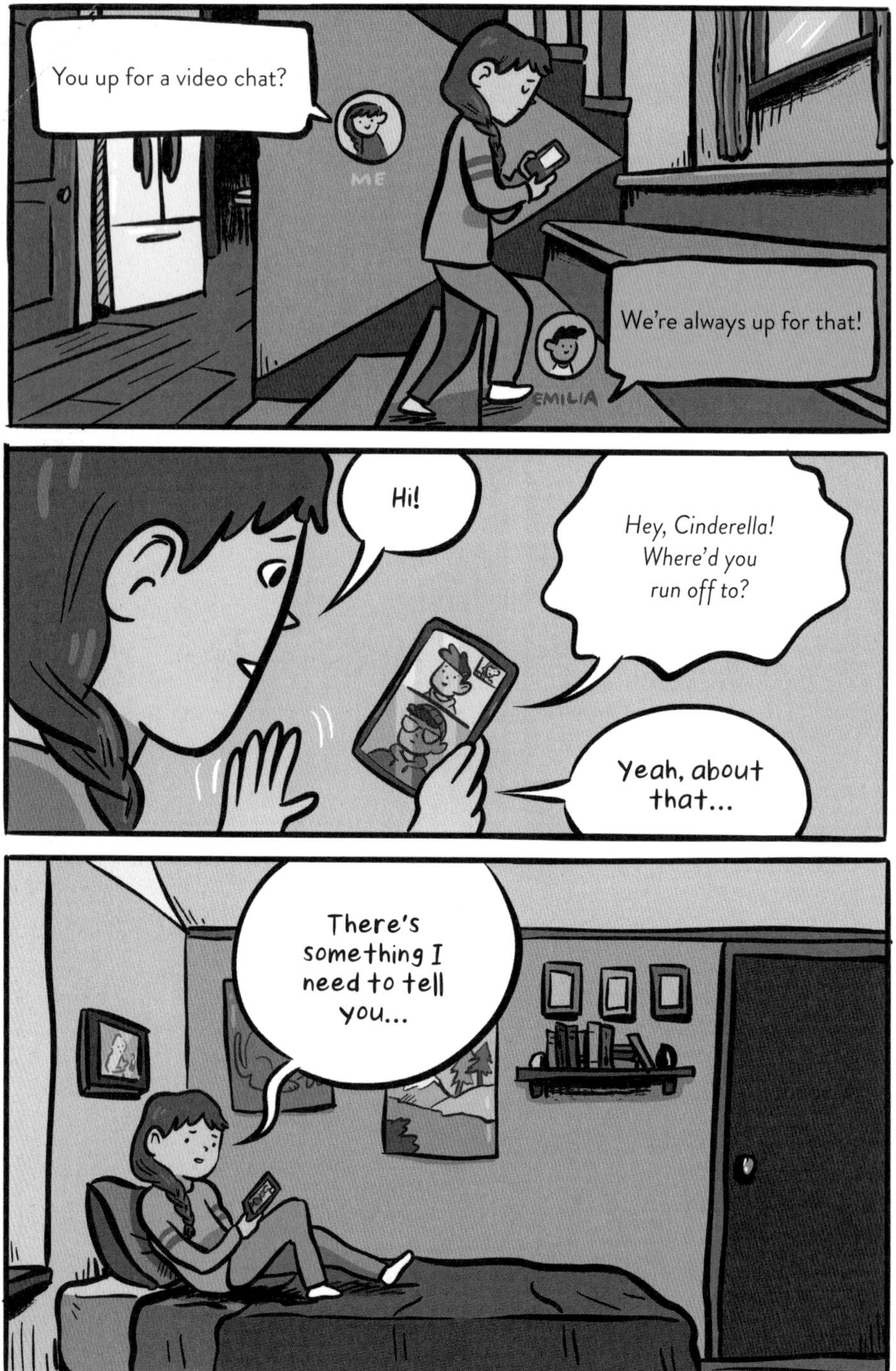
You up for a video chat?
ME
We're always up for that!
EMILIA
Hi!
Hey, Cinderella! Where'd you run off to?
Yeah, about that...
There's something I need to tell you...

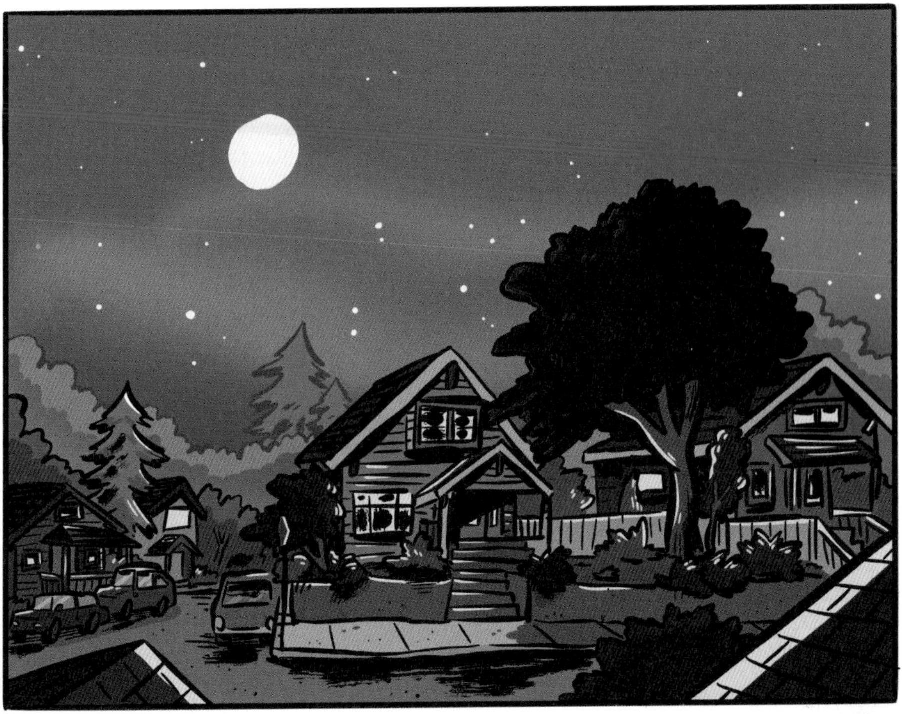

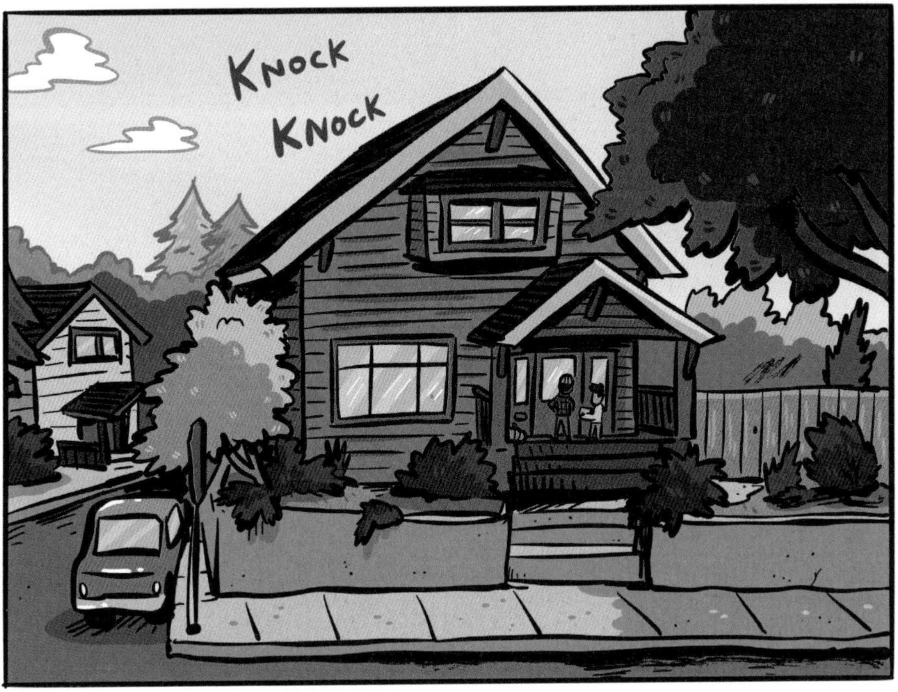
KNOCK
KNOCK

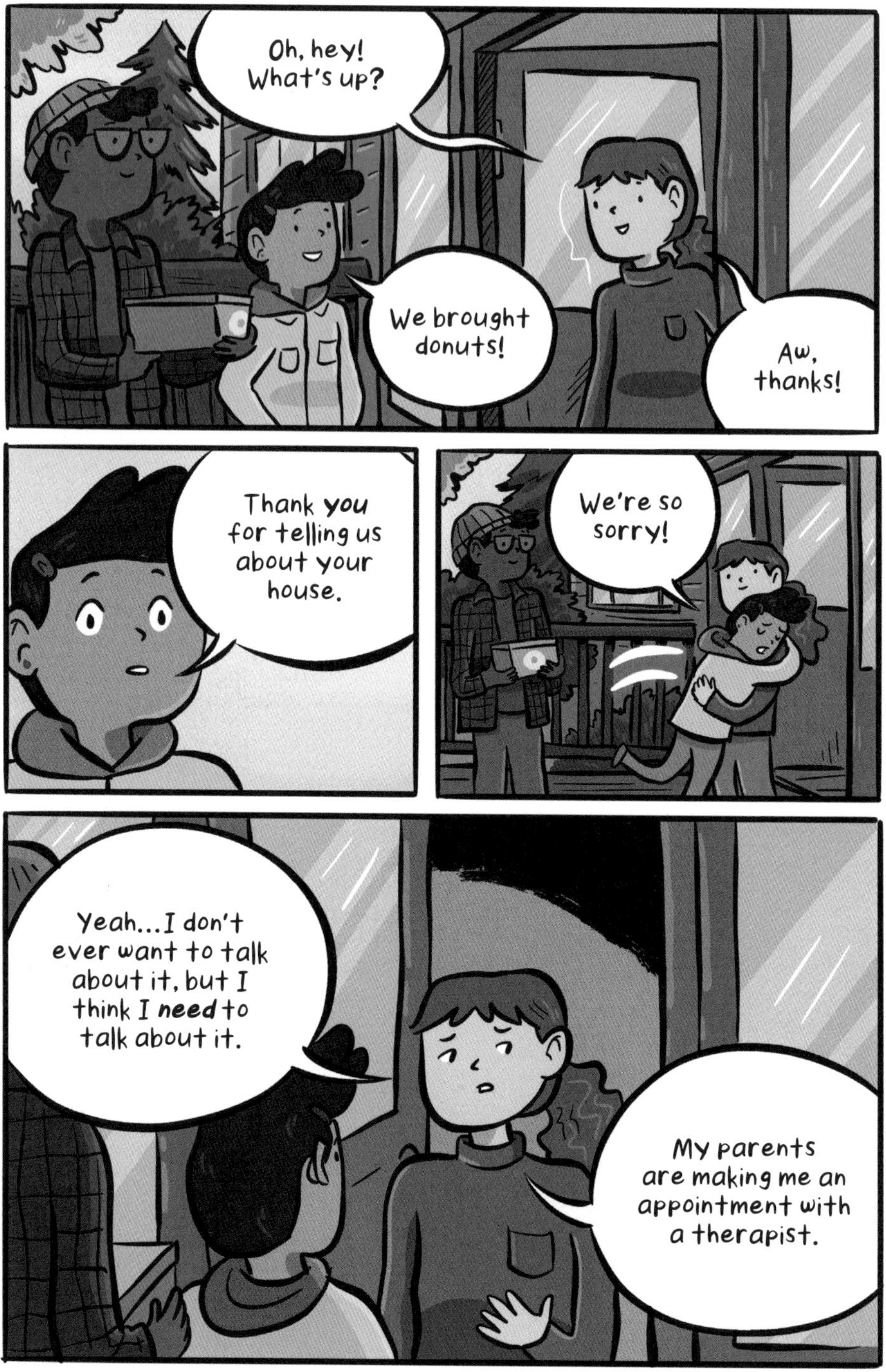
Oh, hey! What's up?
We brought donuts!
Aw, thanks!
Thank *you* for telling us about your house.
We're so sorry!
Yeah...I don't ever want to talk about it, but I think I *need* to talk about it.
My parents are making me an appointment with a therapist.

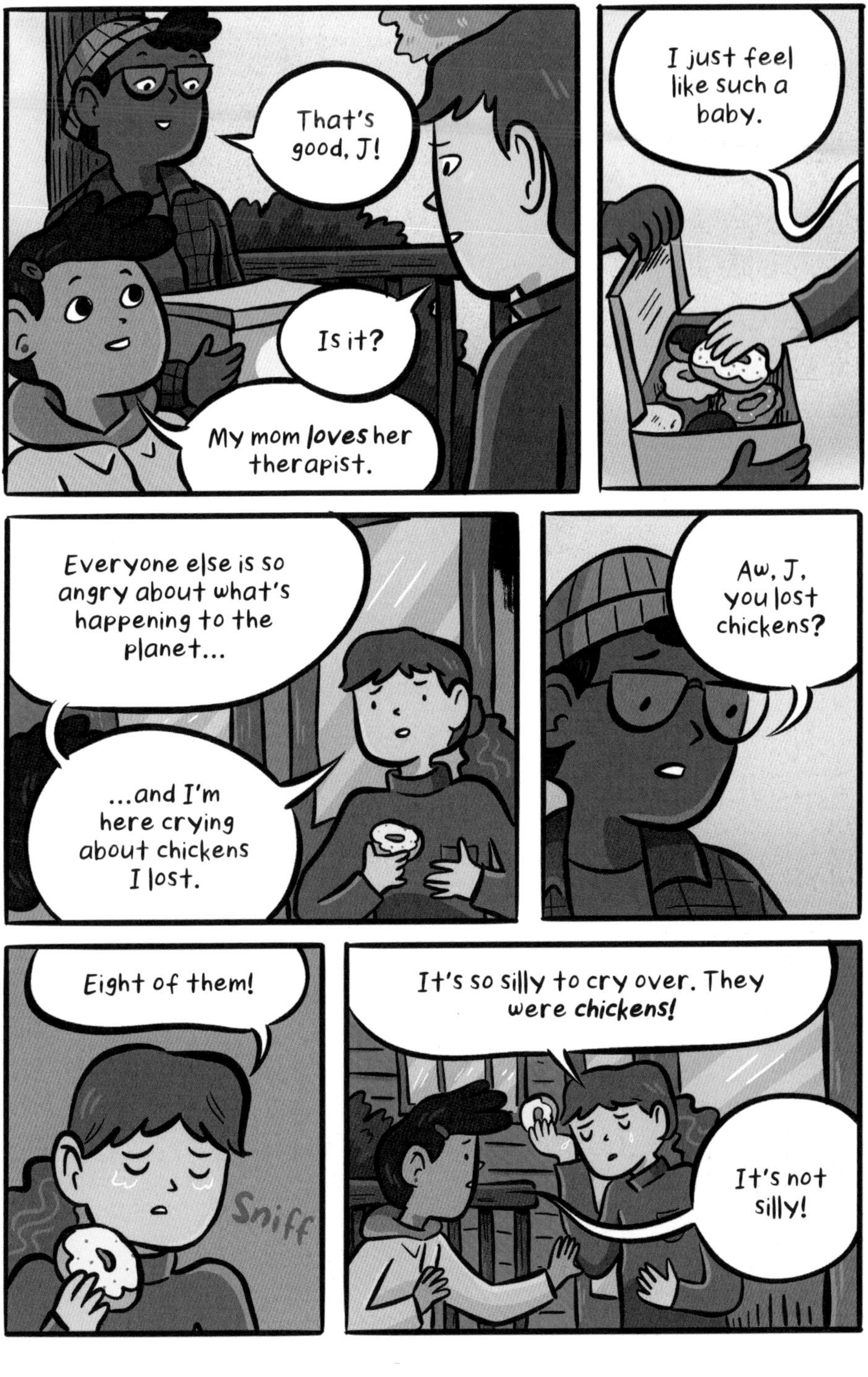
That's good, J!
Is it?
My mom *loves* her therapist.
I just feel like such a baby.
Everyone else is so angry about what's happening to the planet...
...and I'm here crying about chickens I lost.
Aw, J, you lost chickens?
Eight of them!
Sniff
It's so silly to cry over. They were **chickens!**
It's not silly!

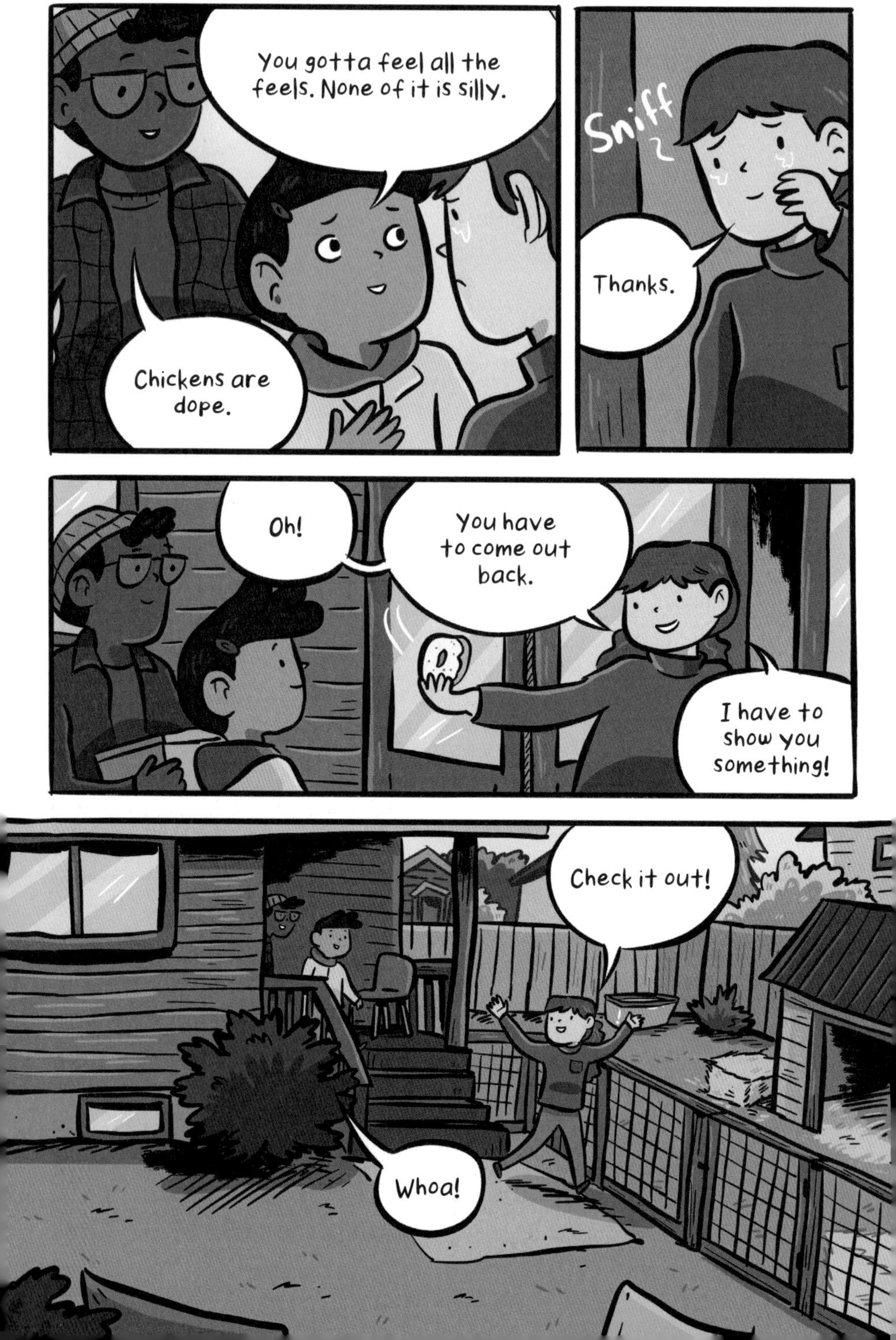
You gotta feel all the feels. None of it is silly.
Chickens are dope.
Sniff
Thanks.
Oh!
You have to come out back.
I have to show you something!
Check it out!
Whoa!

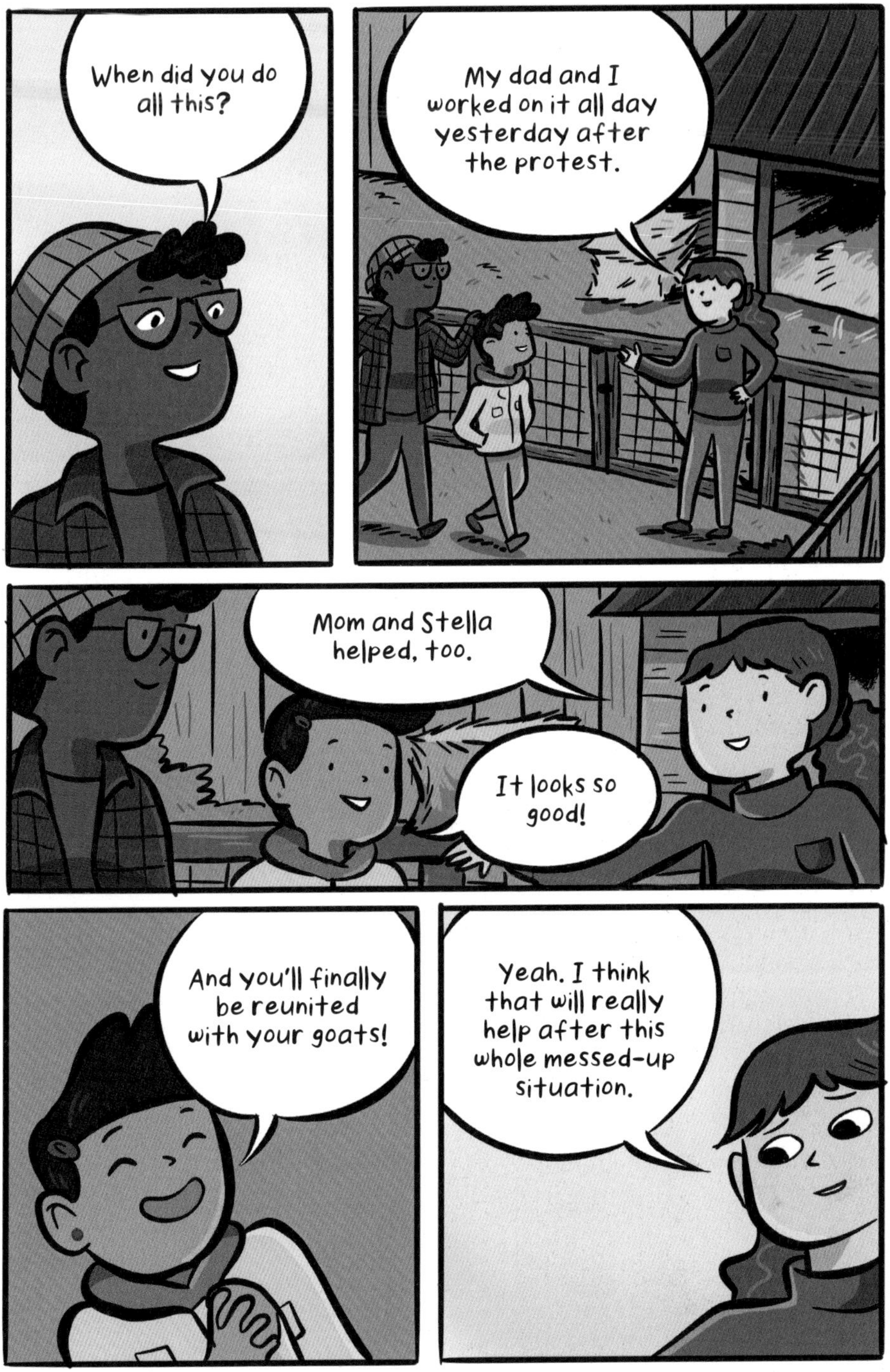
When did you do all this?
My dad and I worked on it all day yesterday after the protest.
Mom and Stella helped, too.
It looks so good!
And you'll finally be reunited with your goats!
Yeah. I think that will really help after this whole messed-up situation.

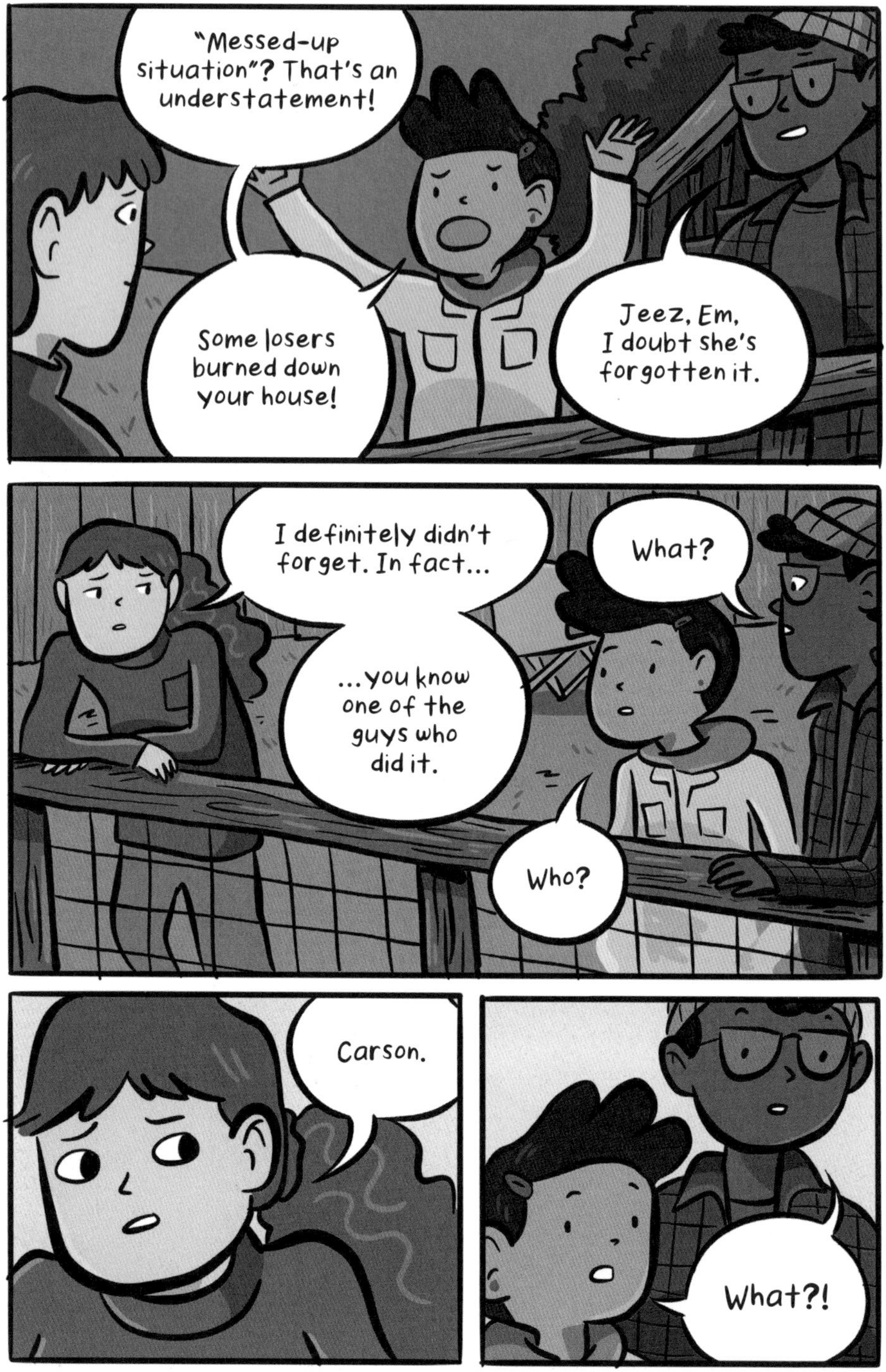
"Messed-up situation"? That's an understatement!
Some losers burned down your house!
Jeez, Em, I doubt she's forgotten it.
I definitely didn't forget. In fact...
What?
...you know one of the guys who did it.
Who?
Carson.
What?!

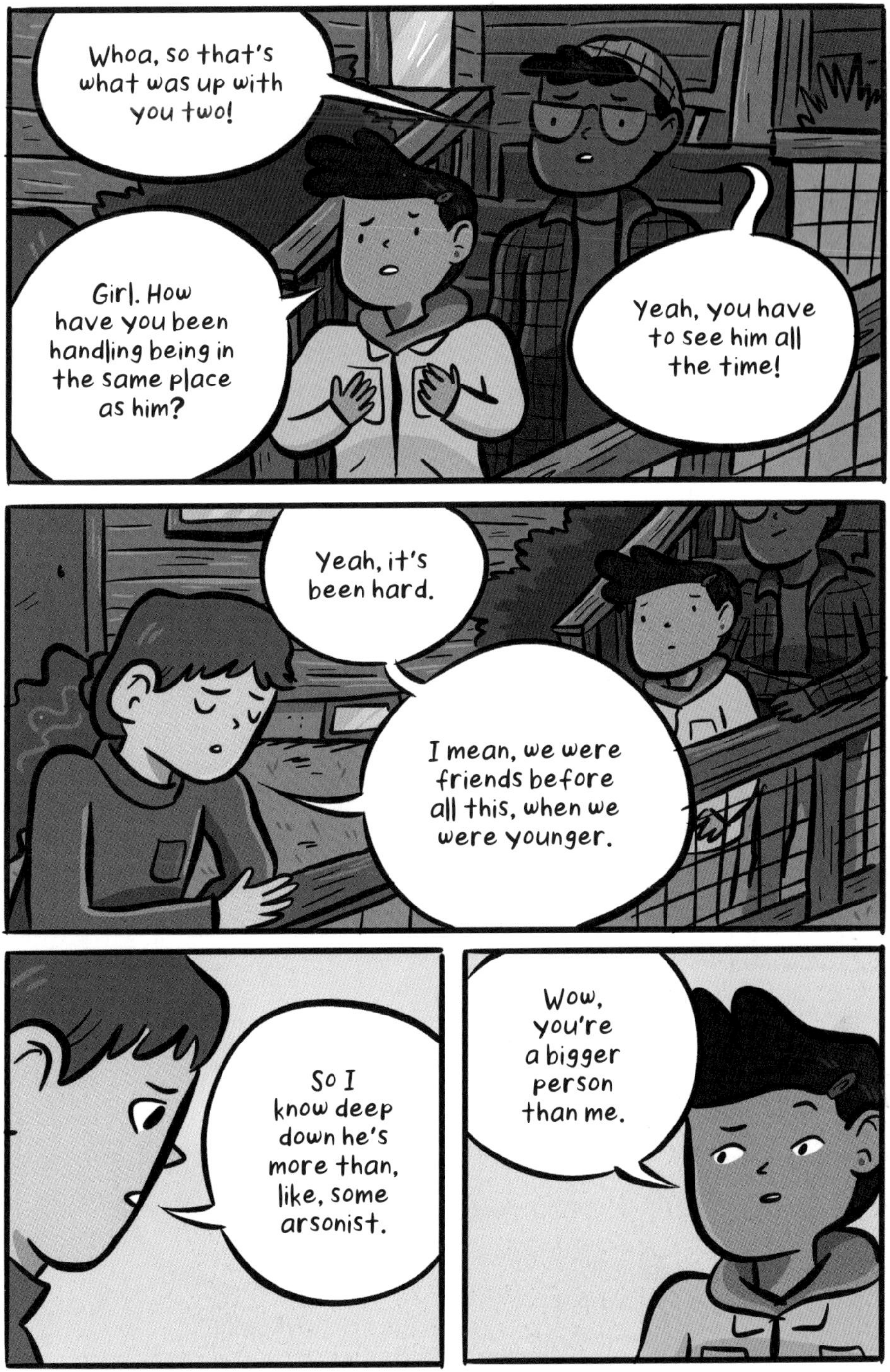
Whoa, so that's what was up with you two!
Girl. How have you been handling being in the same place as him?
Yeah, you have to see him all the time!
Yeah, it's been hard.
I mean, we were friends before all this, when we were younger.
So I know deep down he's more than, like, some arsonist.
Wow, you're a bigger person than me.

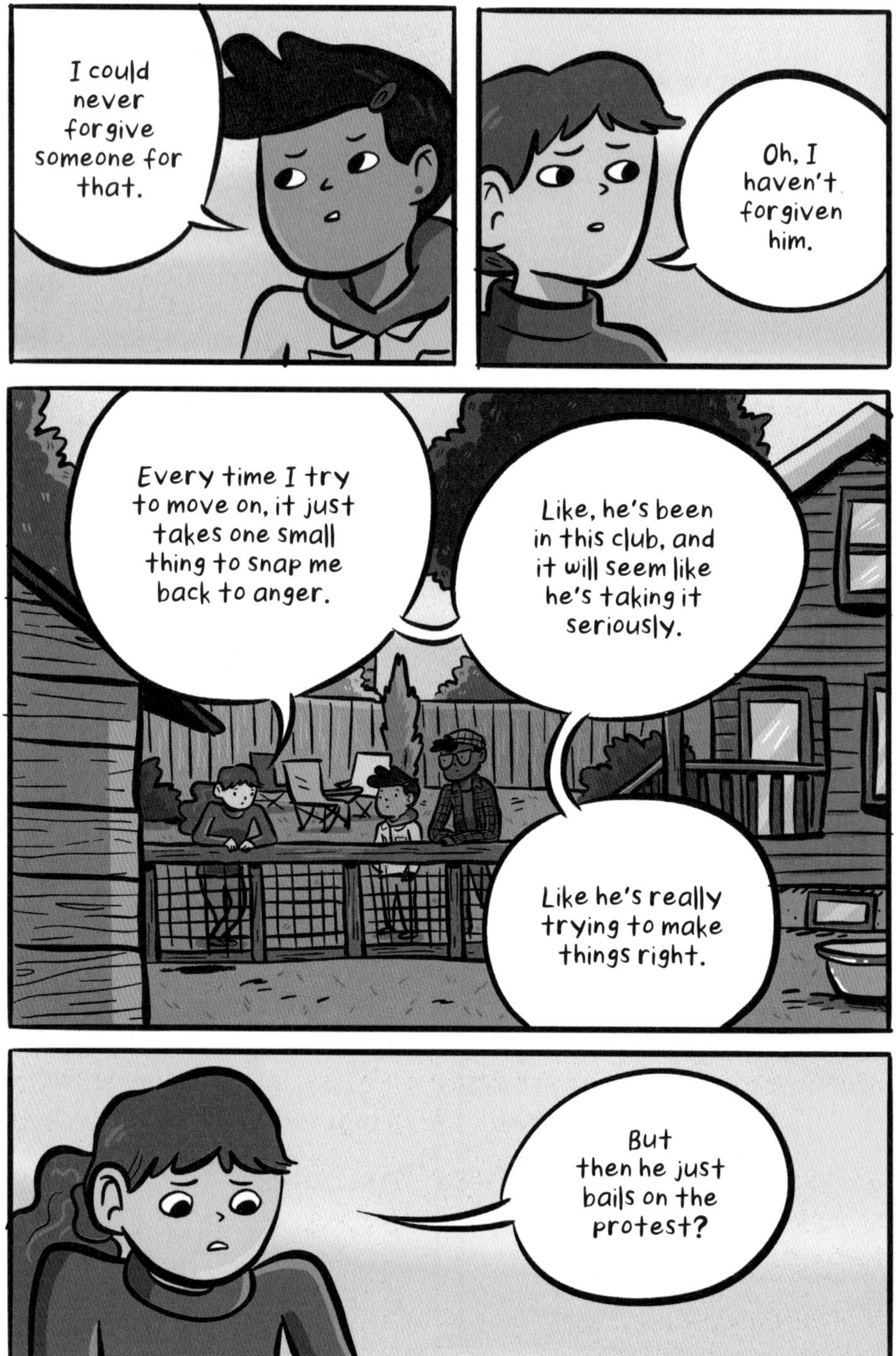
I could never forgive someone for that.
Oh, I haven't forgiven him.
Every time I try to move on, it just takes one small thing to snap me back to anger.
Like, he's been in this club, and it will seem like he's taking it seriously.
Like he's really trying to make things right.
But then he just bails on the protest?

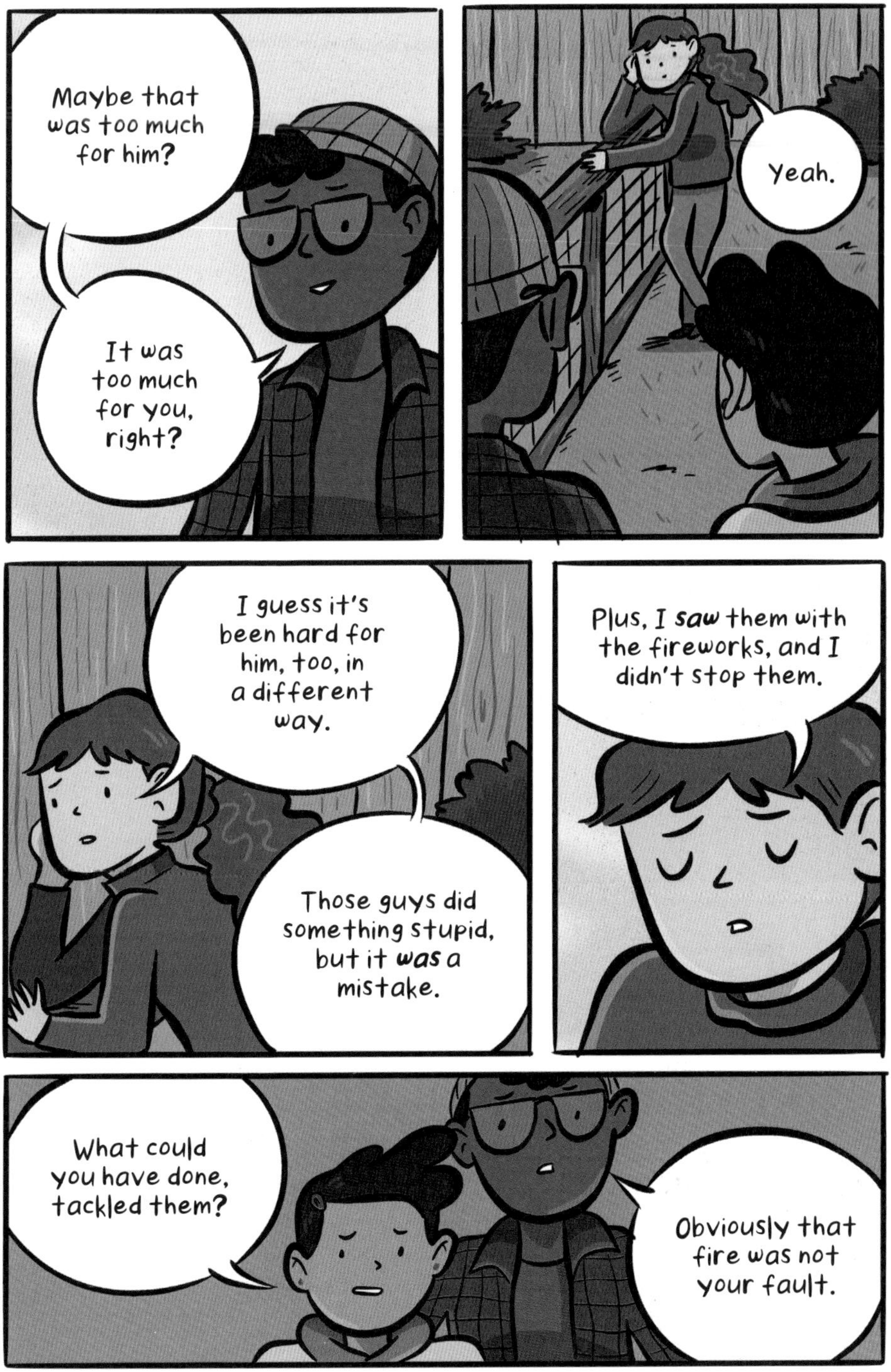
Maybe that was too much for him?
It was too much for you, right?
Yeah.
I guess it's been hard for him, too, in a different way.
Those guys did something stupid, but it *was* a mistake.
Plus, I *saw* them with the fireworks, and I didn't stop them.
What could you have done, tackled them?
Obviously that fire was not your fault.

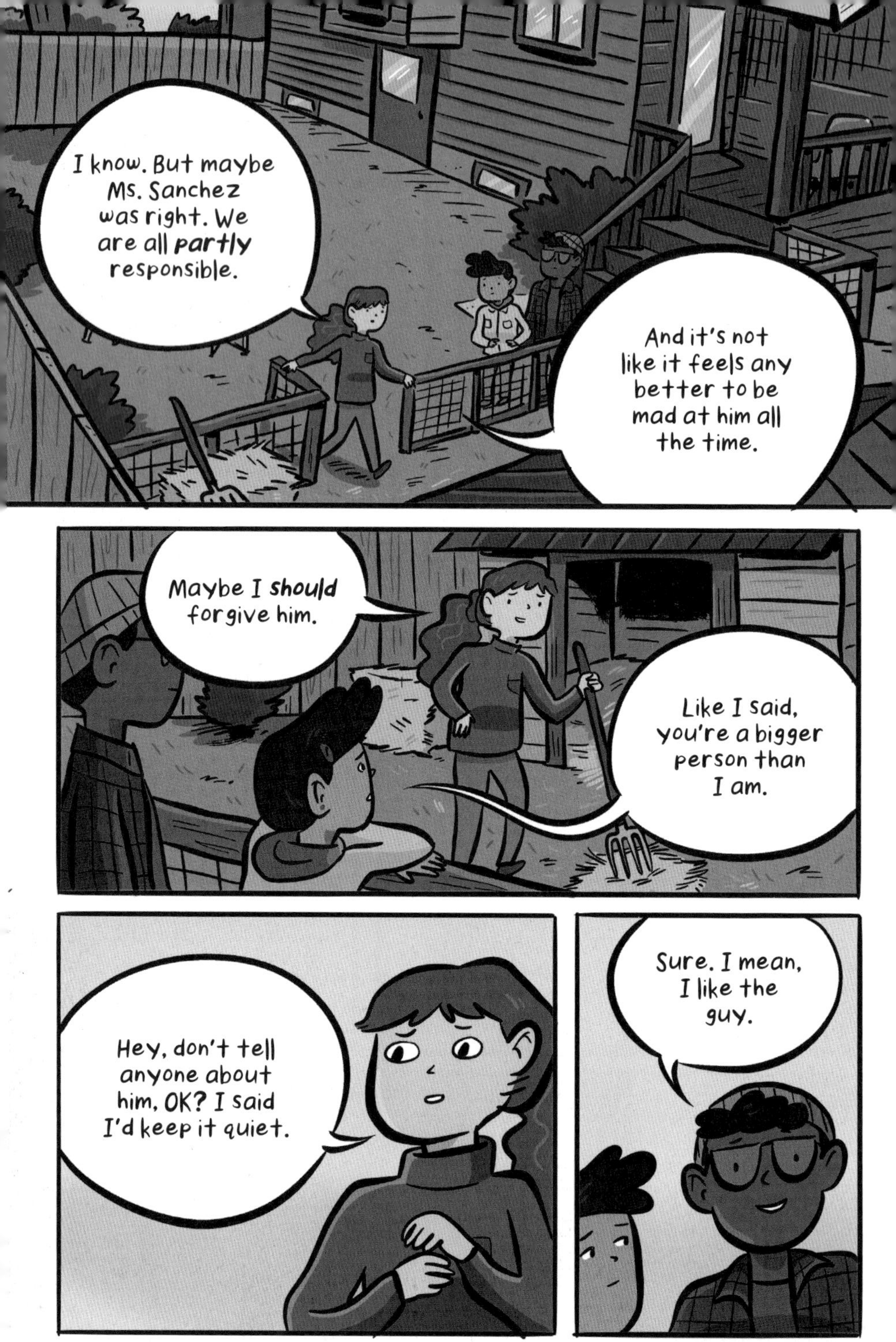

I know. But maybe Ms. Sanchez was right. We are all **partly** responsible.
And it's not like it feels any better to be mad at him all the time.
Maybe I **should** forgive him.
Like I said, you're a bigger person than I am.
Hey, don't tell anyone about him, OK? I said I'd keep it quiet.
Sure. I mean, I like the guy.

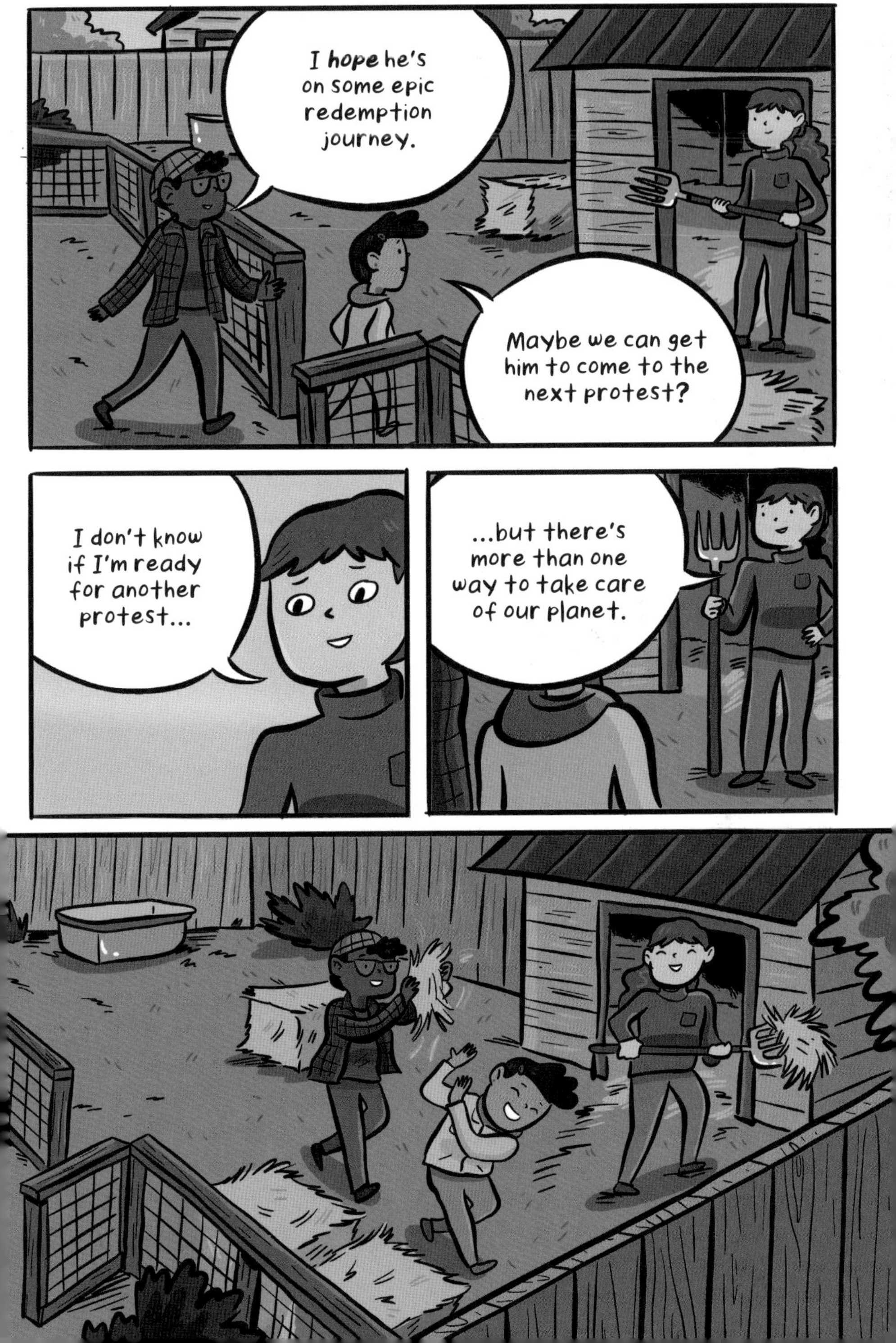
I hope he's on some epic redemption journey.
Maybe we can get him to come to the next protest?
I don't know if I'm ready for another protest...
...but there's more than one way to take care of our planet.

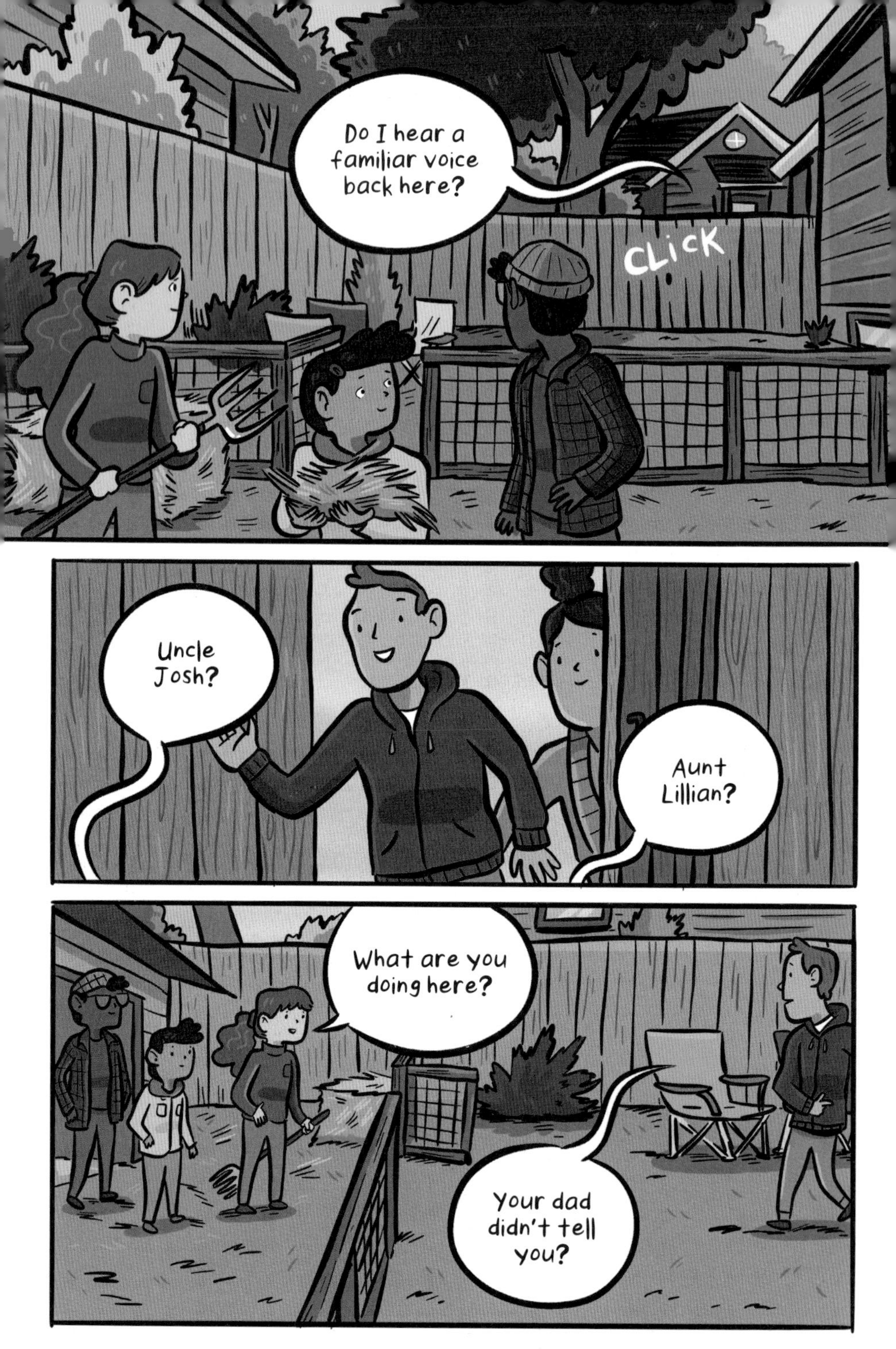
Do I hear a familiar voice back here?
CLICK
Uncle Josh?
Aunt Lillian?
What are you doing here?
Your dad didn't tell you?

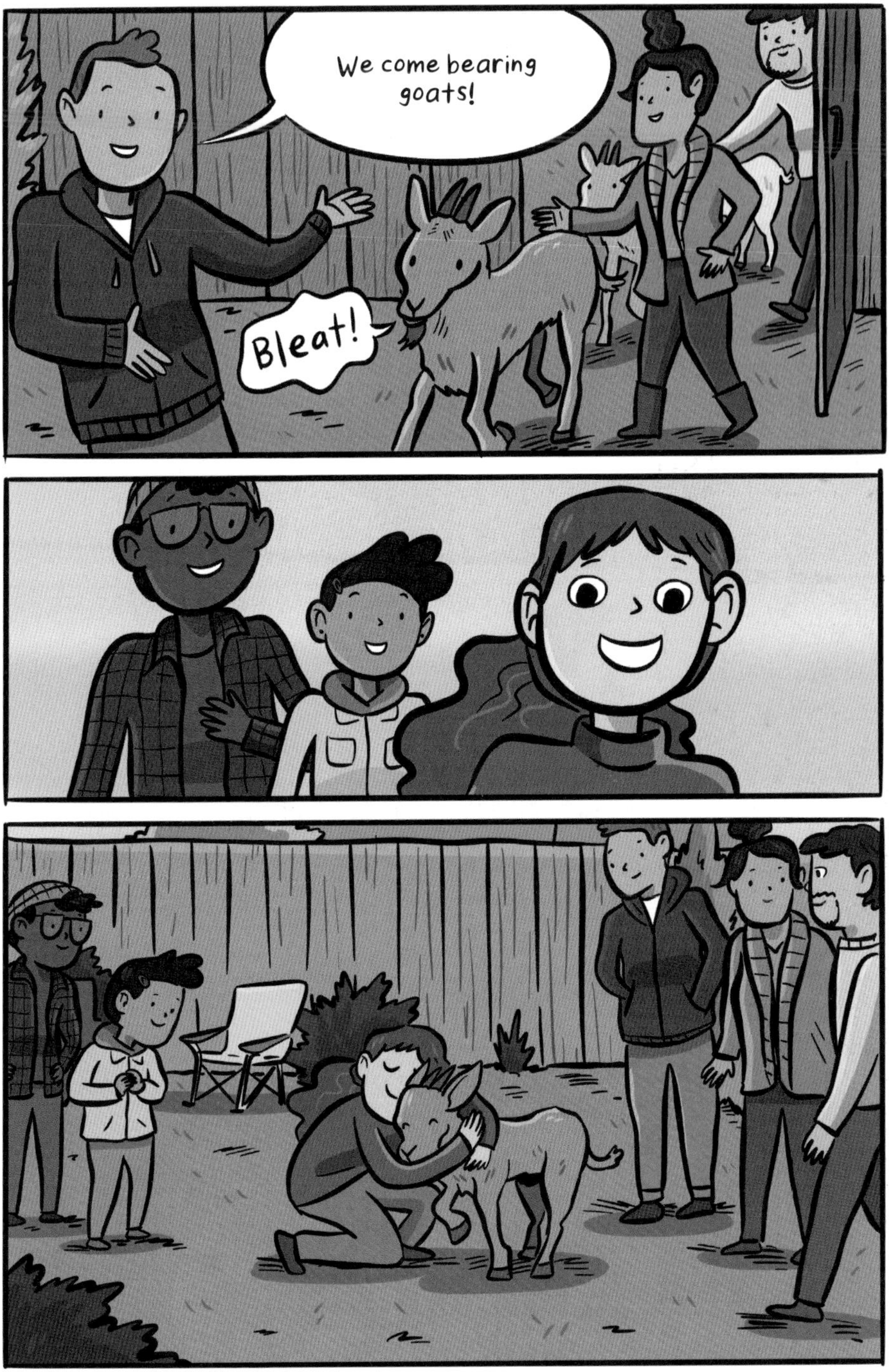
We come bearing goats!
Bleat!

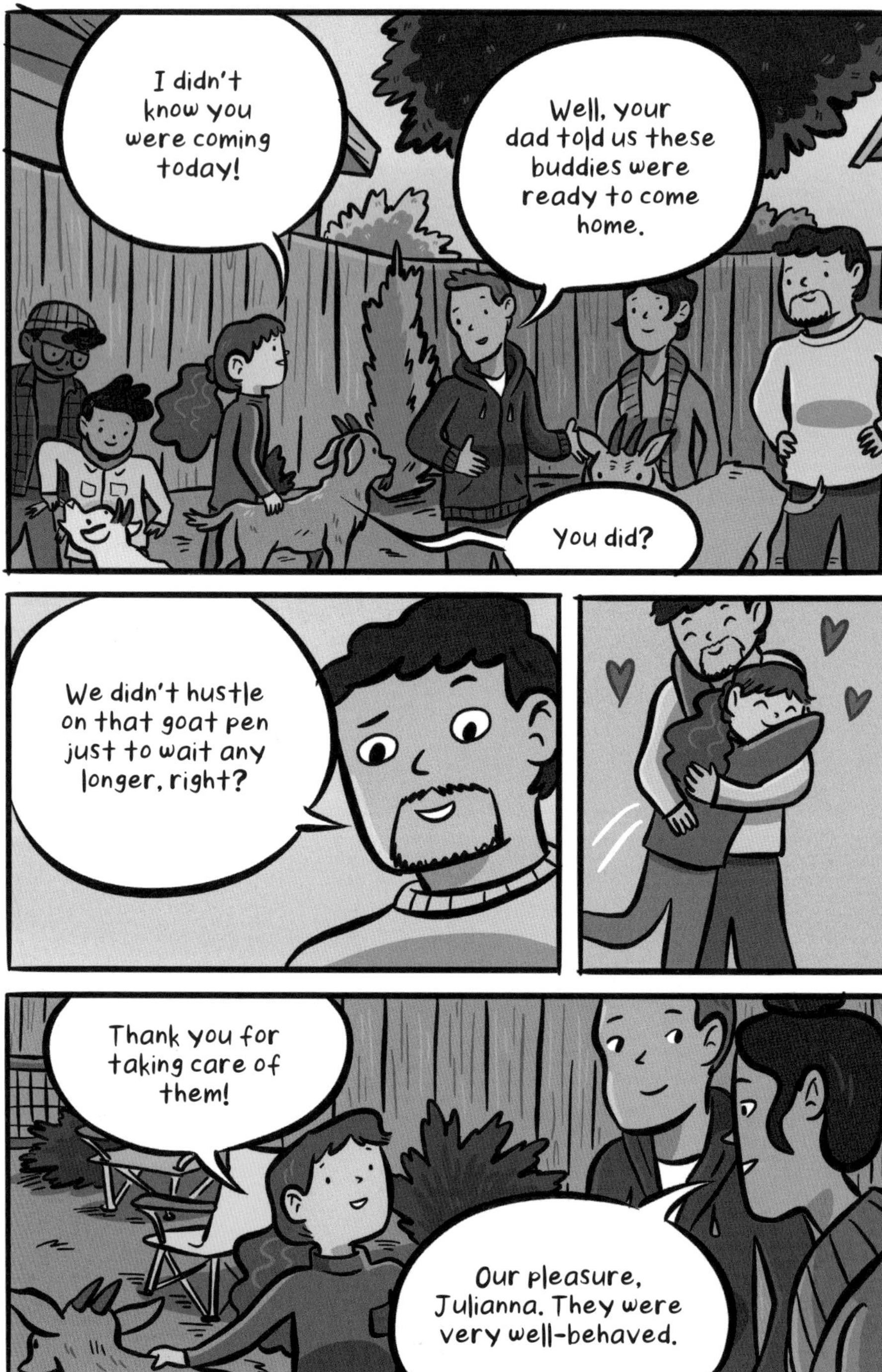
I didn't know you were coming today!
Well, your dad told us these buddies were ready to come home.
You did?
We didn't hustle on that goat pen just to wait any longer, right?
Thank you for taking care of them!
Our pleasure, Julianna. They were very well-behaved.

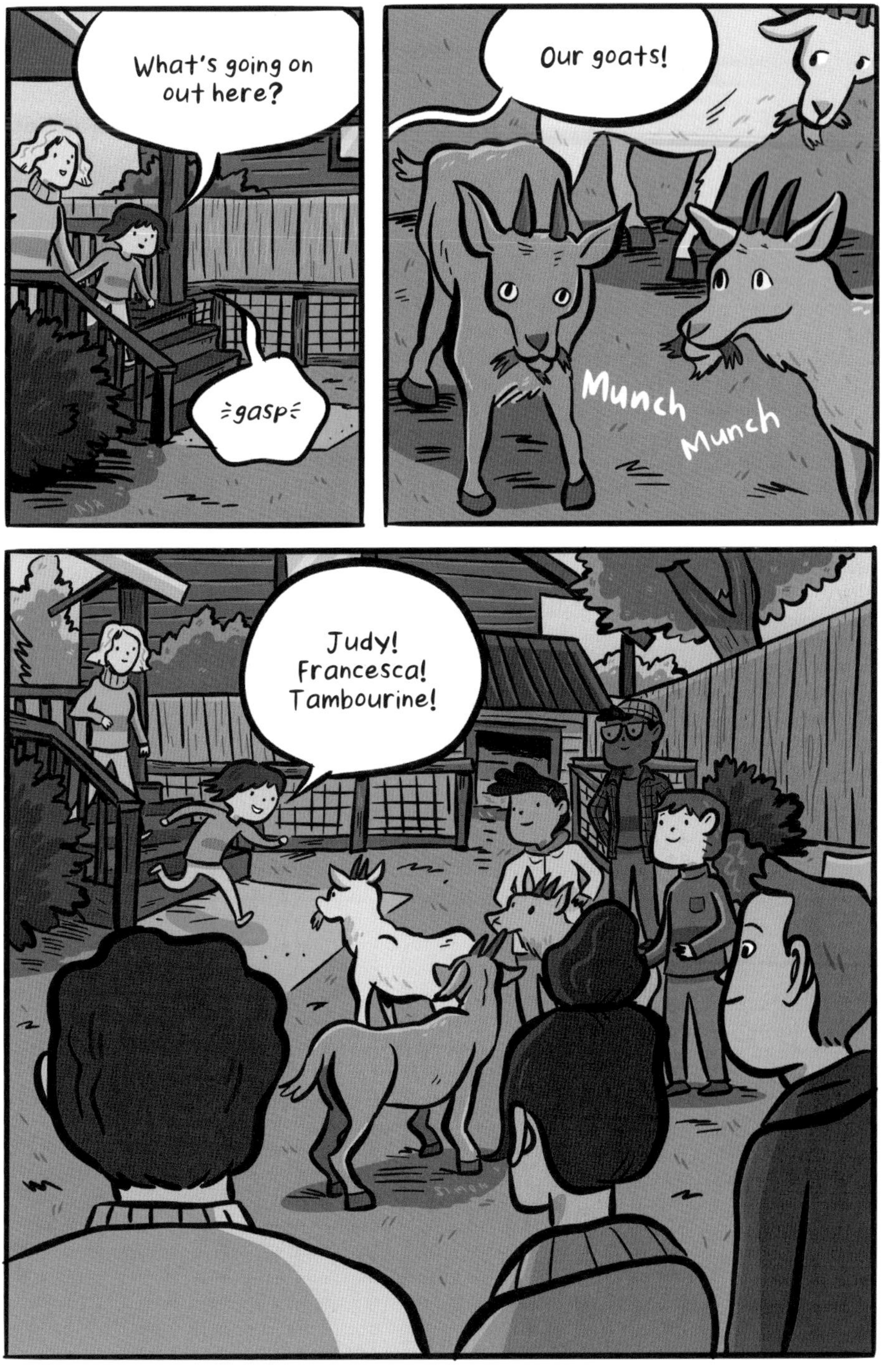
What's going on out here?
gasp
Our goats!
Munch
Munch
Judy! Francesca! Tambourine!

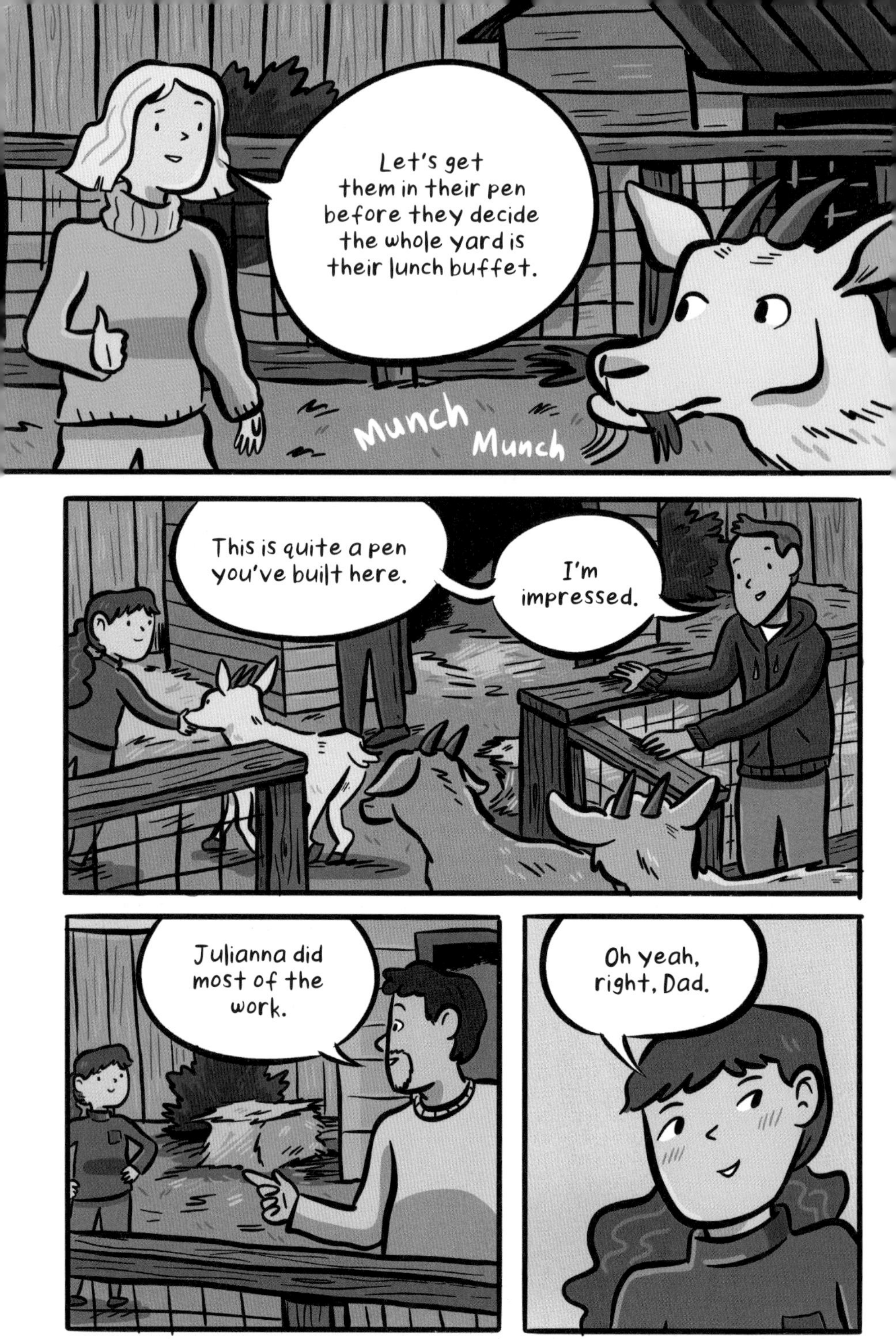
Let's get them in their pen before they decide the whole yard is their lunch buffet.
Munch
Munch
This is quite a pen you've built here.
I'm impressed.
Julianna did most of the work.
Oh yeah, right, Dad.

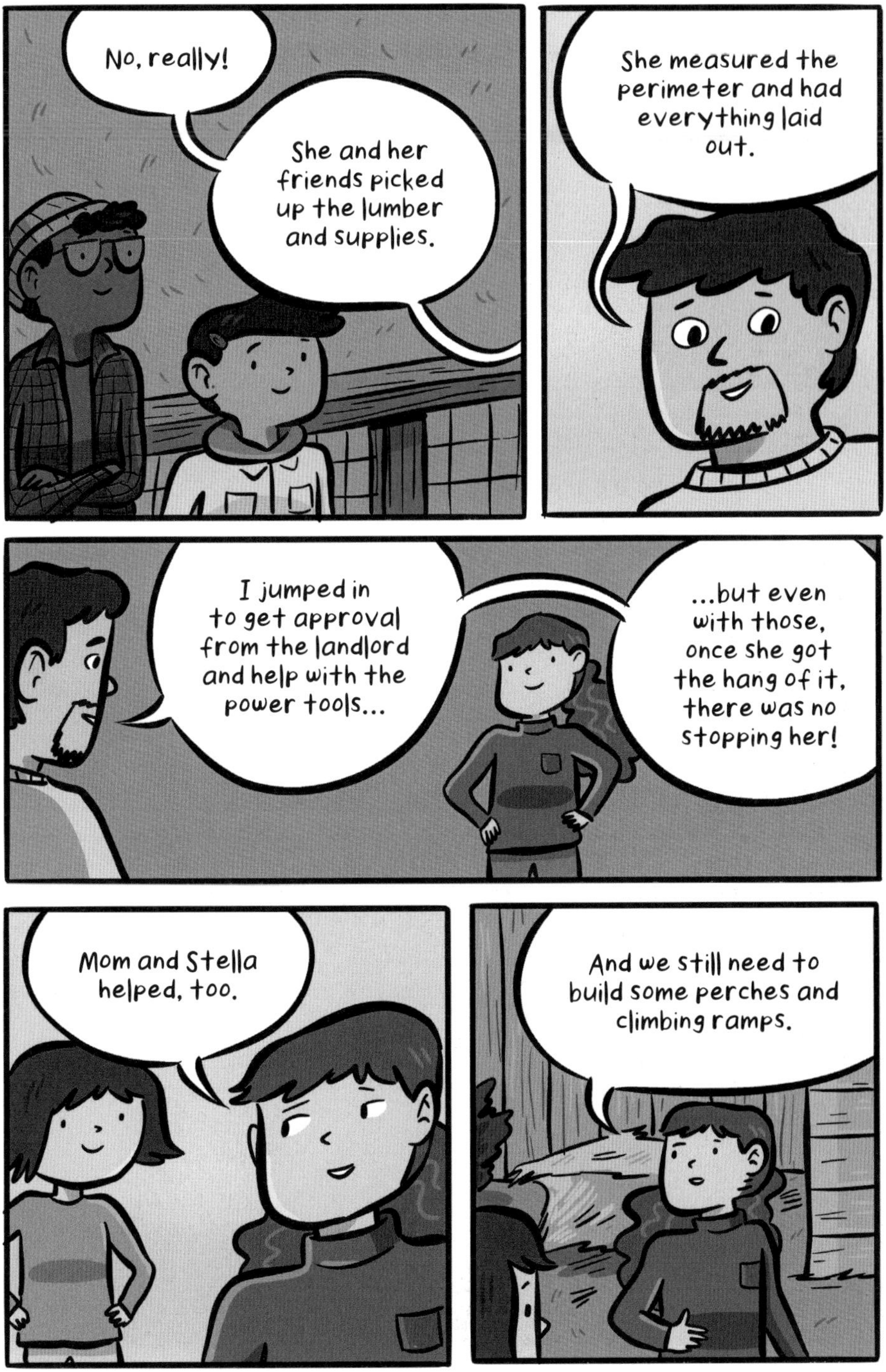
No, really!
She and her friends picked up the lumber and supplies.
She measured the perimeter and had everything laid out.
I jumped in to get approval from the landlord and help with the power tools...
...but even with those, once she got the hang of it, there was no stopping her!
Mom and Stella helped, too.
And we still need to build some perches and climbing ramps.

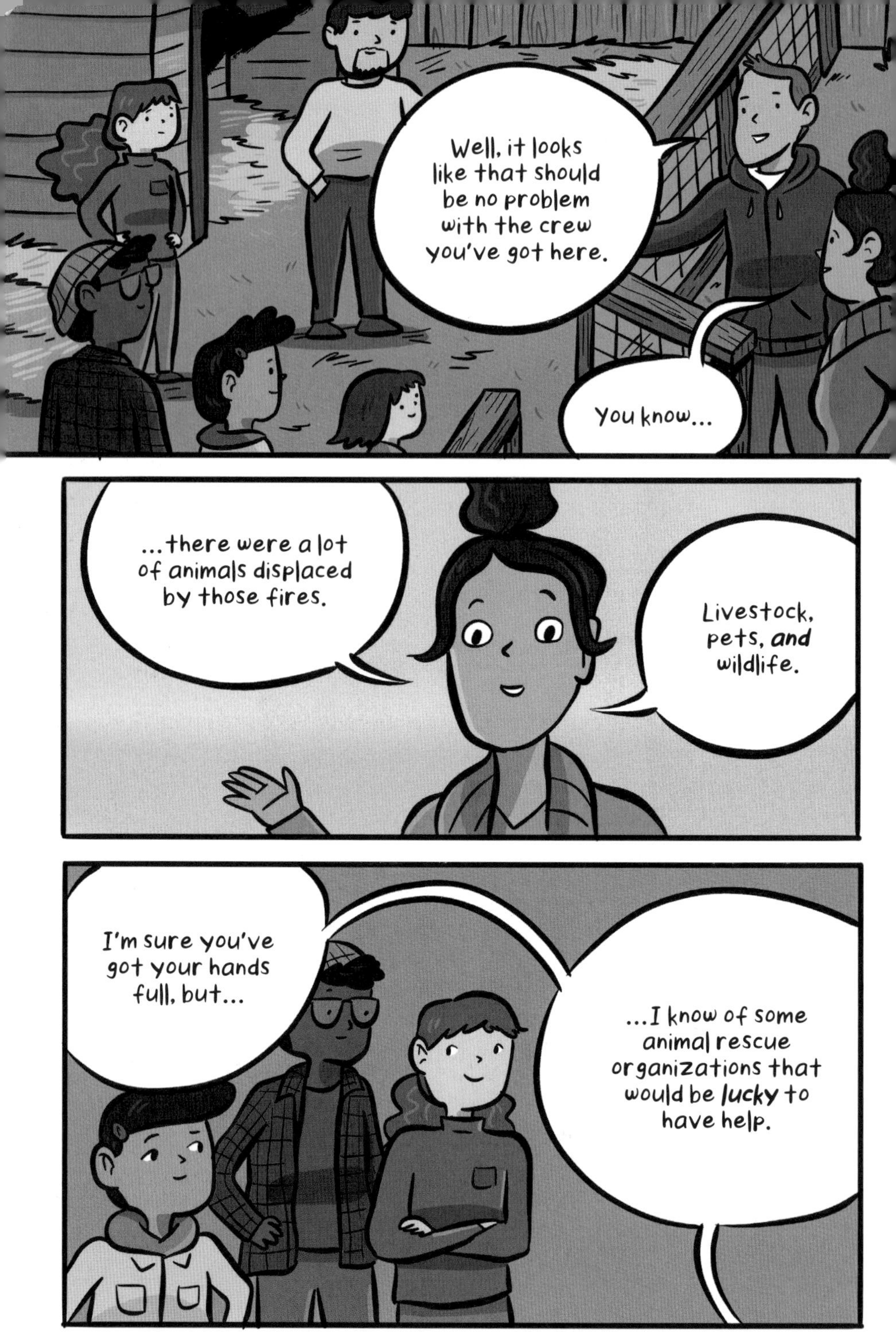
Well, it looks like that should be no problem with the crew you've got here.
You know...
...there were a lot of animals displaced by those fires.
Livestock, pets, *and* wildlife.
I'm sure you've got your hands full, but...
...I know of some animal rescue organizations that would be *lucky* to have help.

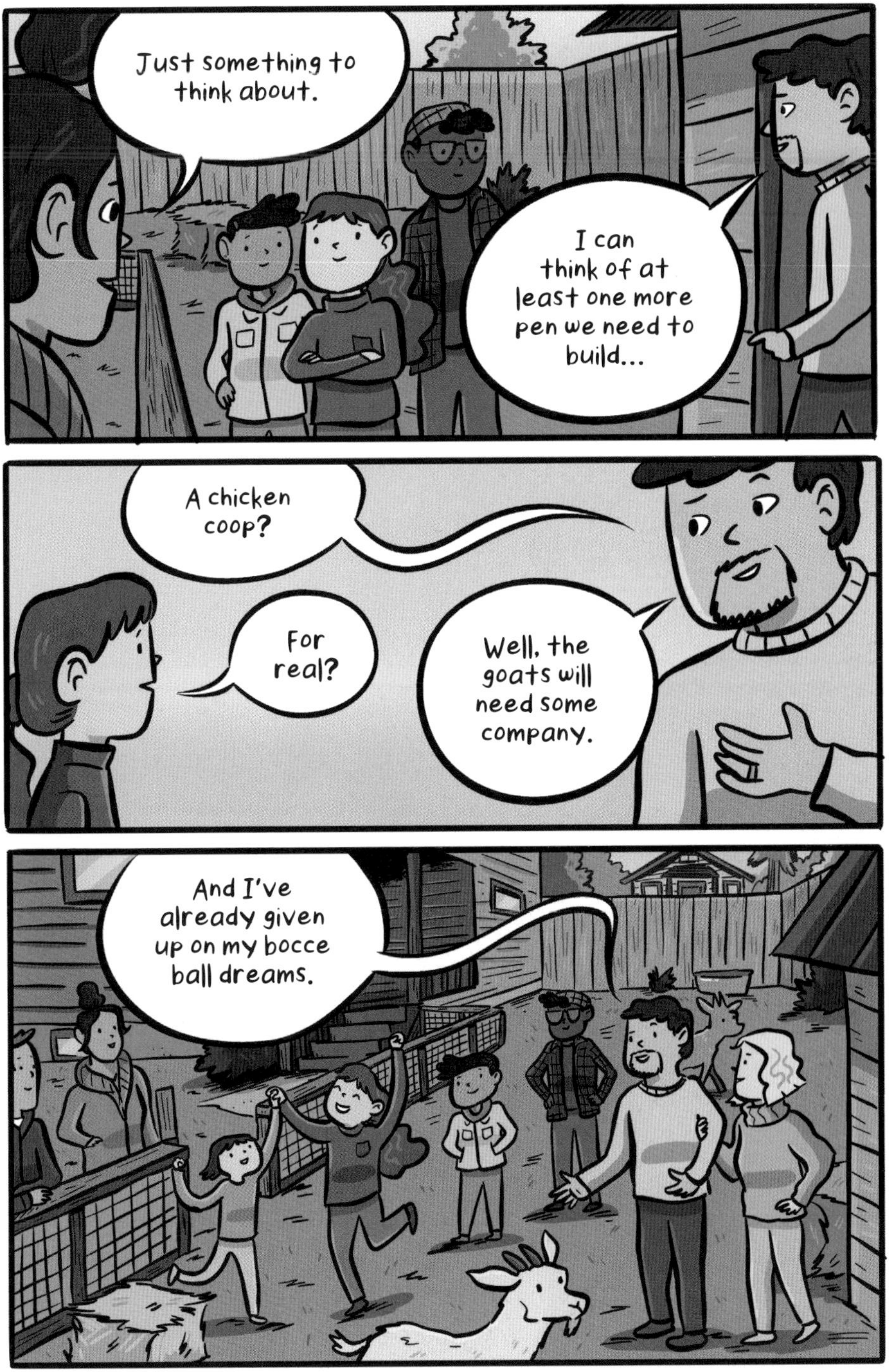
Just something to think about.
I can think of at least one more pen we need to build...
A chicken coop?
For real?
Well, the goats will need some company.
And I've already given up on my bocce ball dreams.

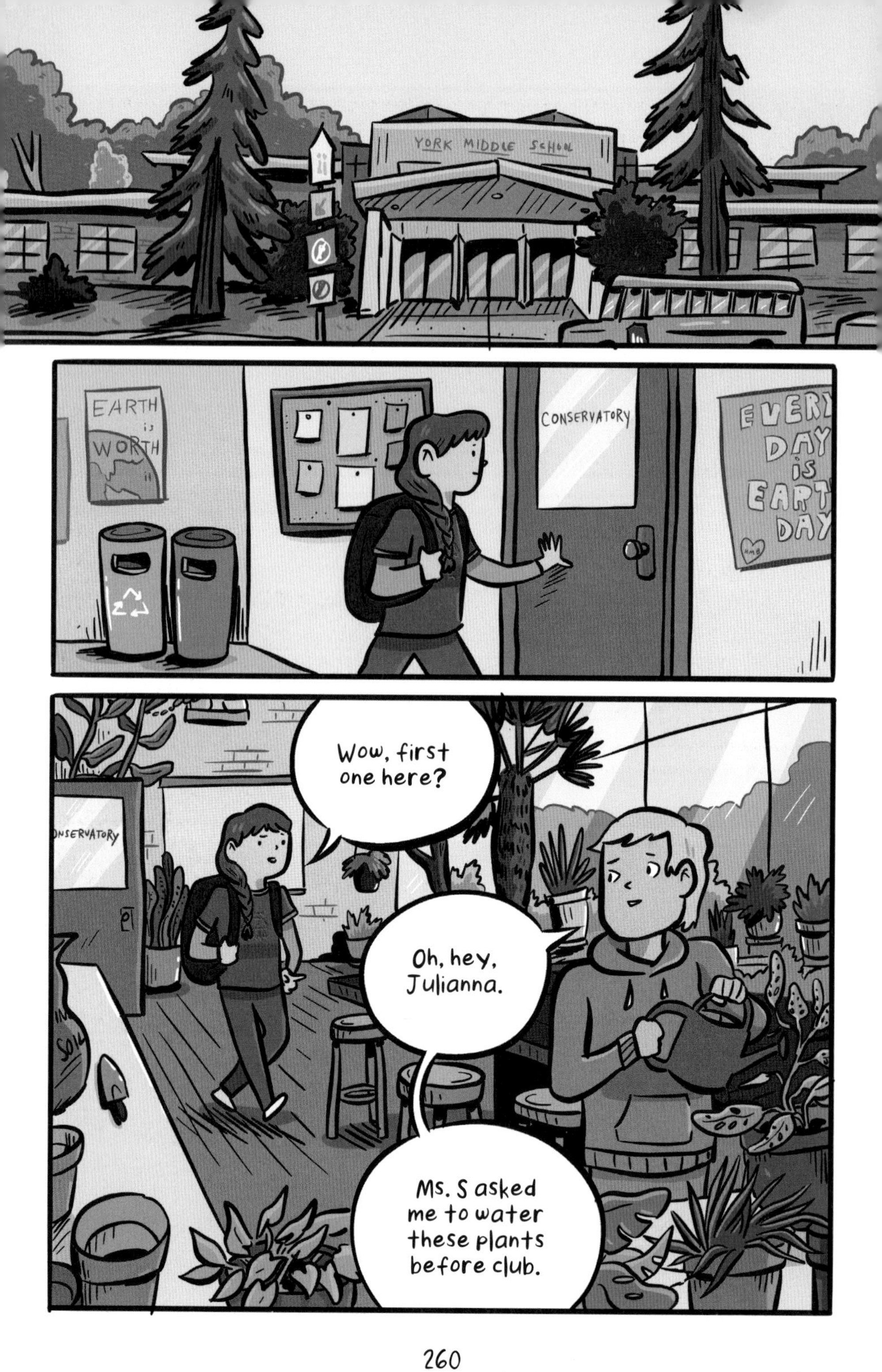
YORK MIDDLE SCHOOL
EARTH is WORTH
CONSERVATORY
EVERY DAY IS EARTH DAY
HMB
CONSERVATORY
Wow, first one here?
Oh, hey, Julianna.
Ms. S asked me to water these plants before club.
SOIL

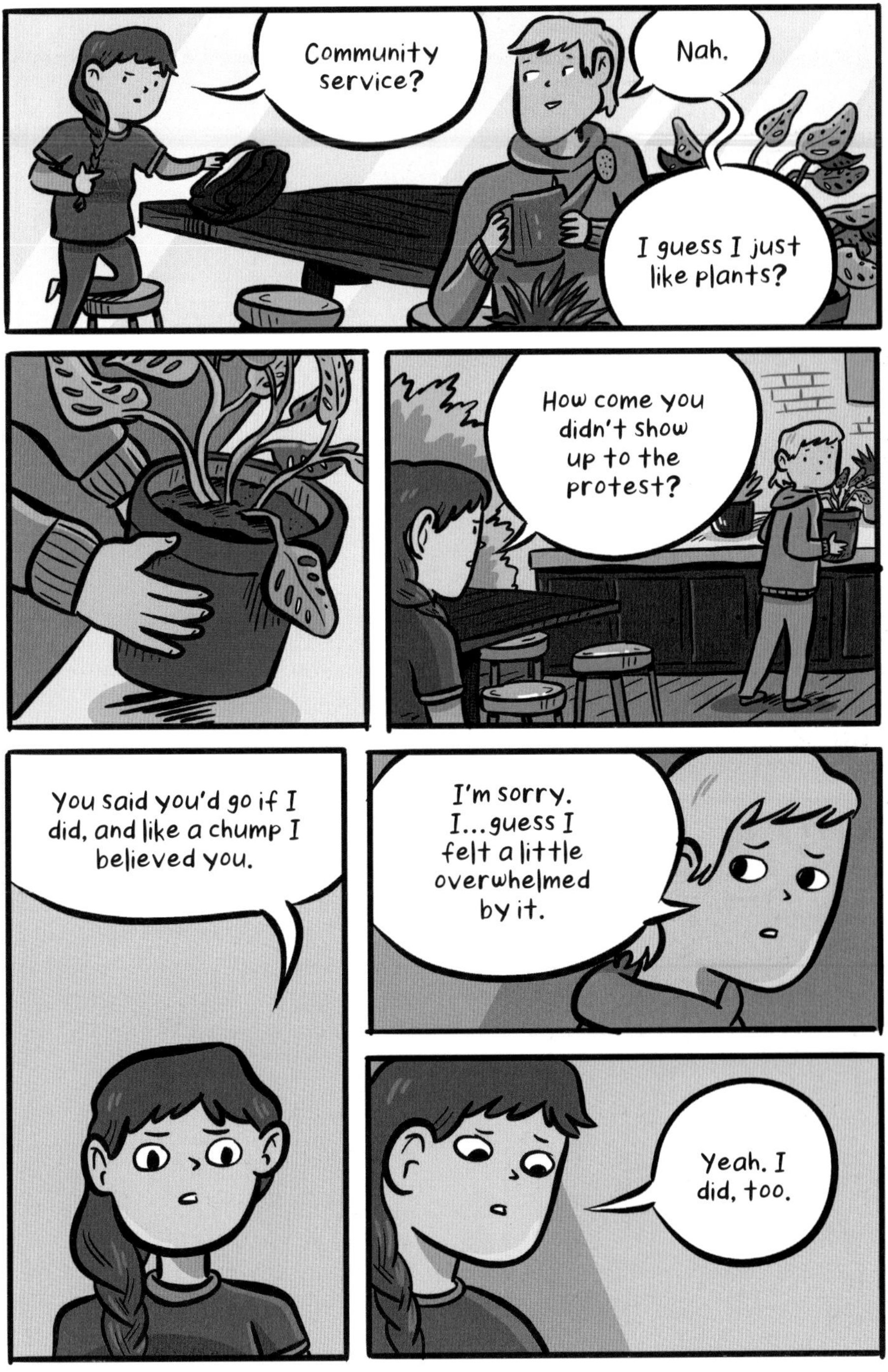
Community service?
Nah.
I guess I just like plants?
How come you didn't show up to the protest?
You said you'd go if I did, and like a chump I believed you.
I'm sorry. I...guess I felt a little overwhelmed by it.
Yeah. I did, too.

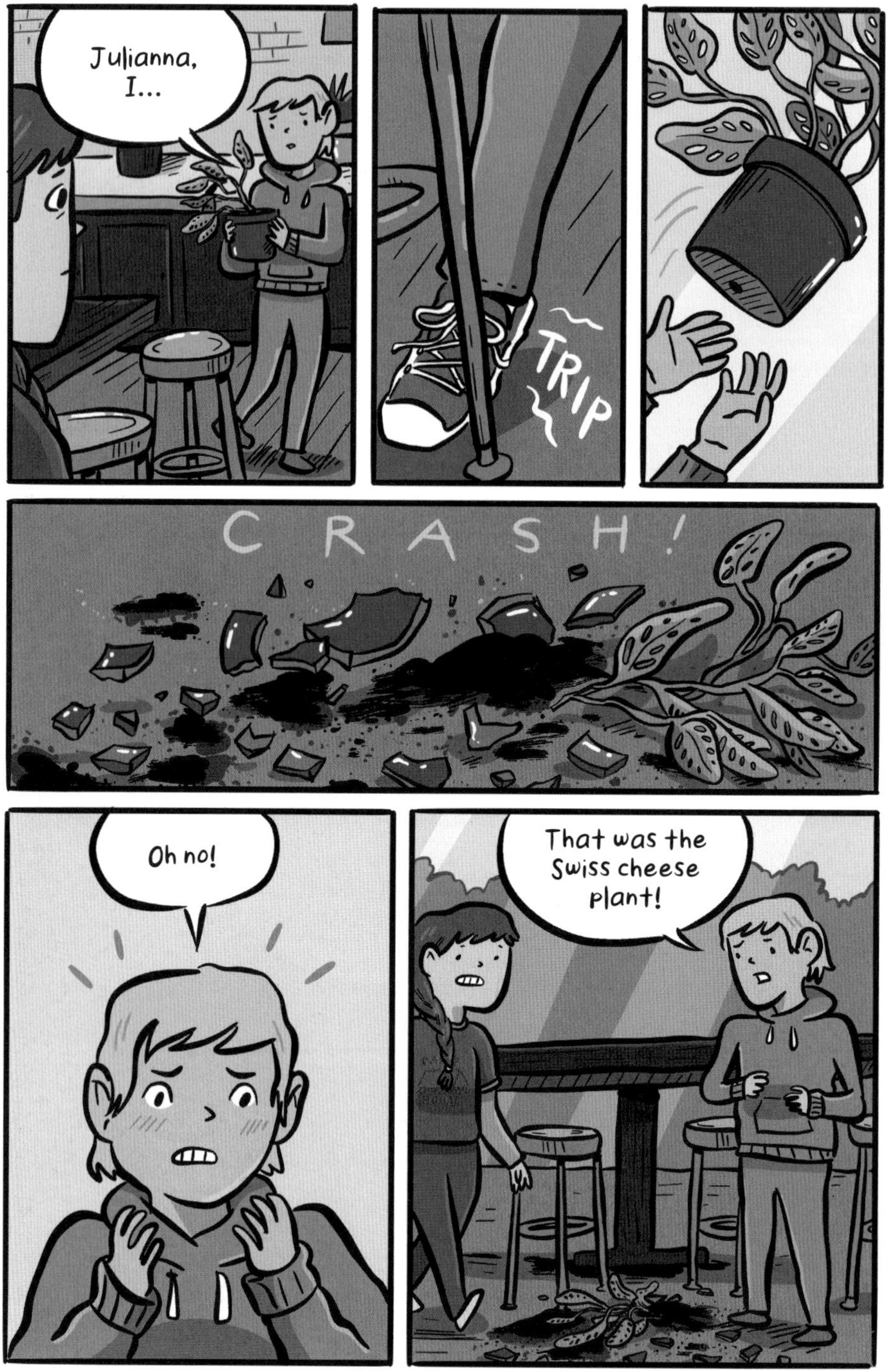
Julianna, I...
TRIP
CRASH!
Oh no!
That was the Swiss cheese plant!

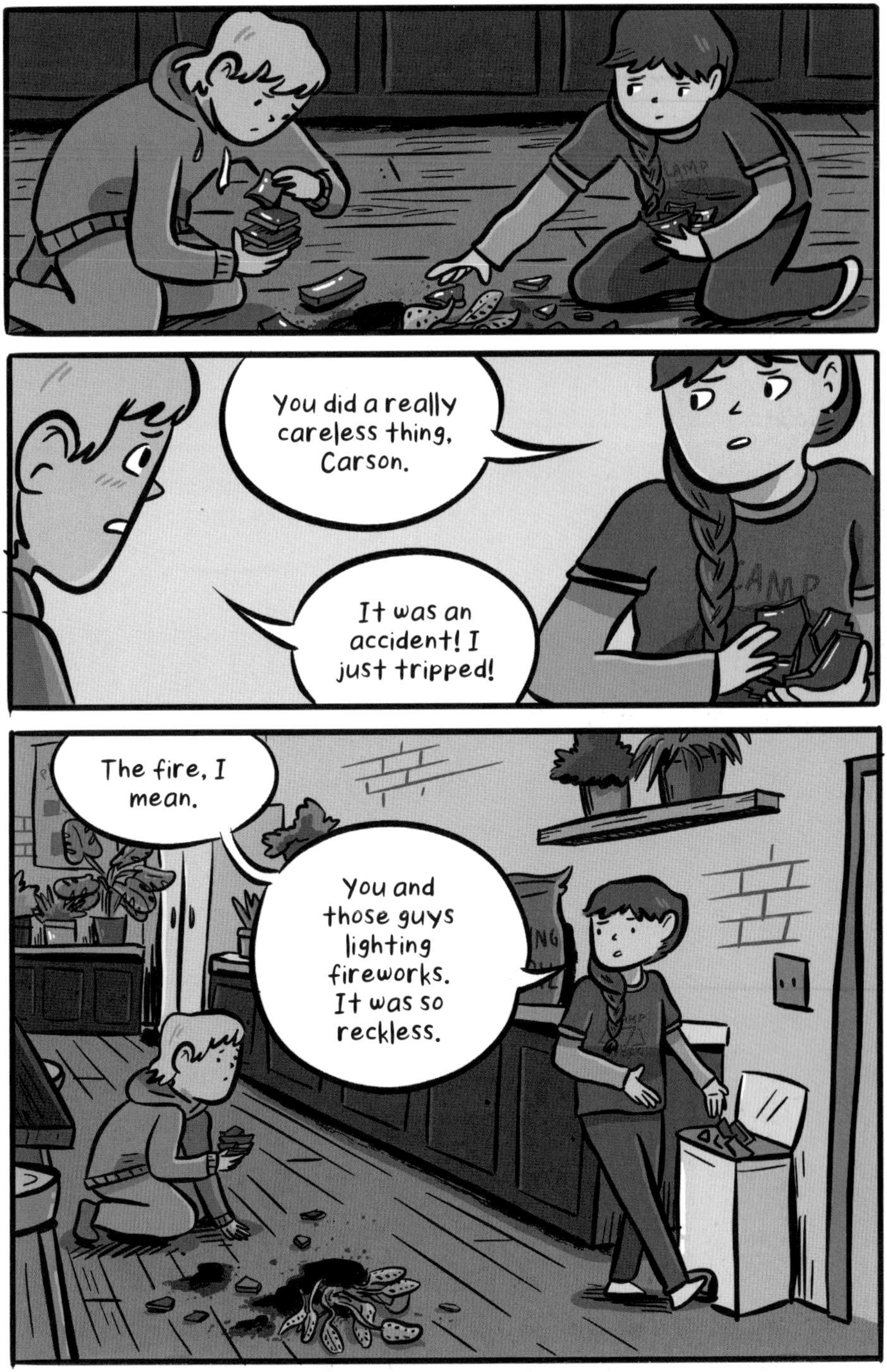
You did a really careless thing, Carson.
It was an accident! I just tripped!
The fire, I mean.
You and those guys lighting fireworks. It was so reckless.

But...

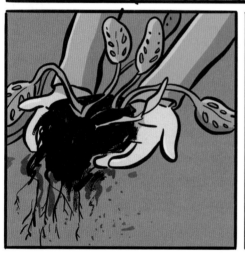

...you already know that.

Yeah...

I've been so sad and angry about all of it.

And all I've wanted to do was blame you.

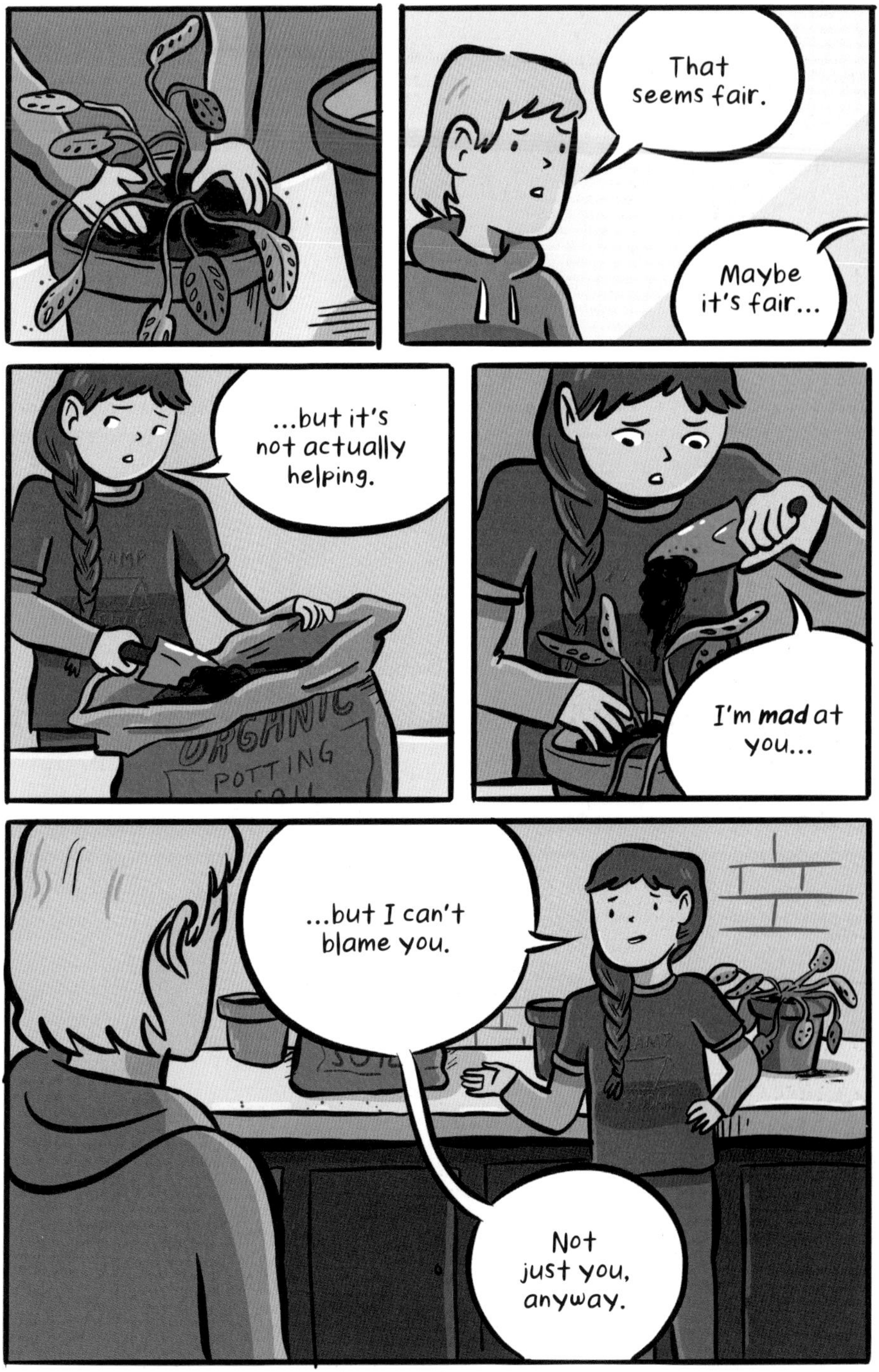
That seems fair.
Maybe it's fair...
...but it's not actually helping.
ORGANIC POTTING SOIL
I'm *mad* at you...
...but I can't blame you.
Not just you, anyway.

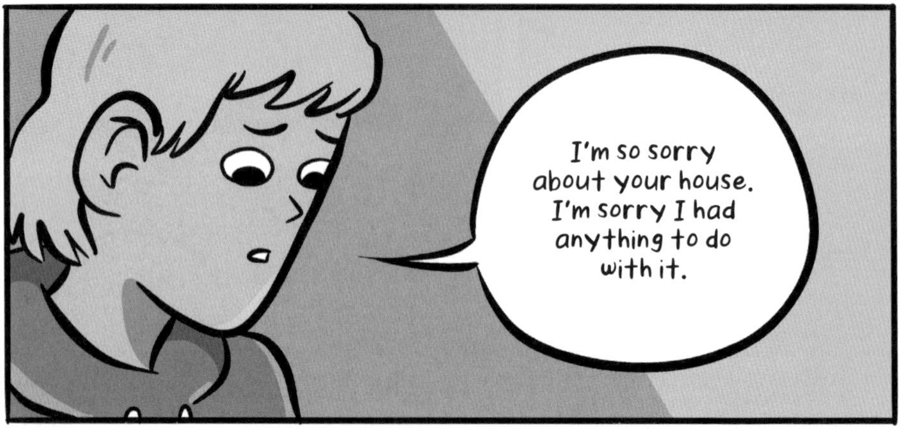
I'm so sorry about your house. I'm sorry I had anything to do with it.

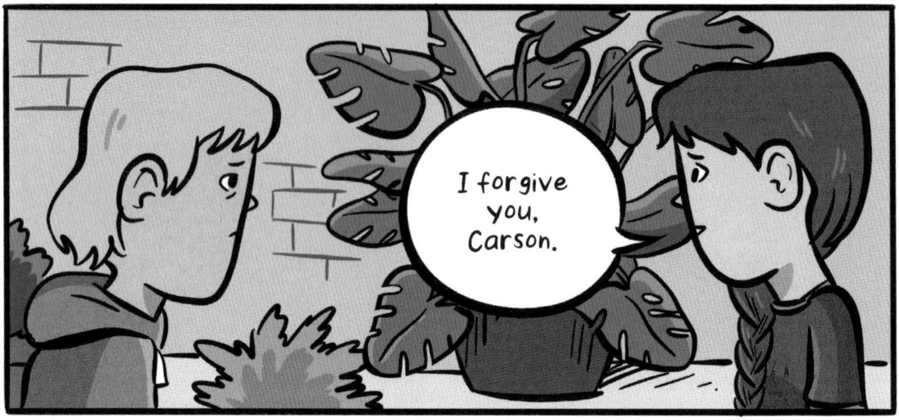
I forgive you, Carson.

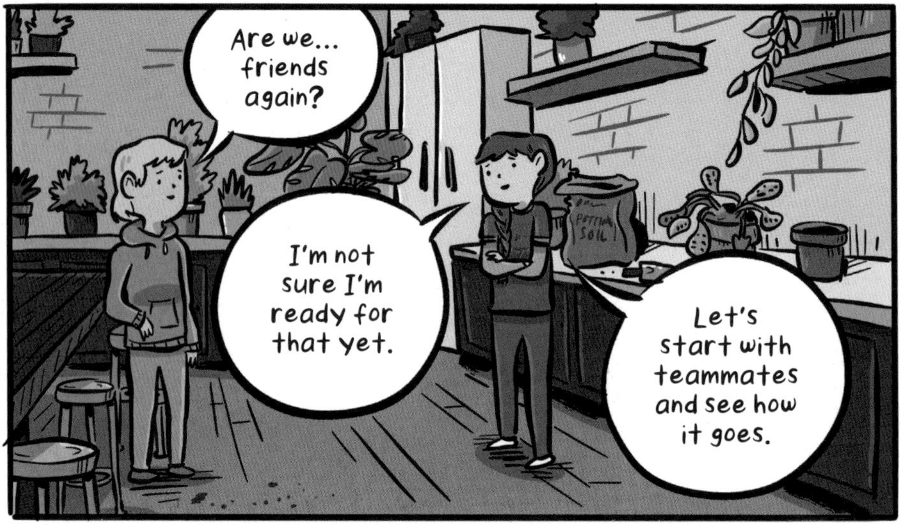
Are we... friends again?
I'm not sure I'm ready for that yet.
Let's start with teammates and see how it goes.
POTTING SOIL

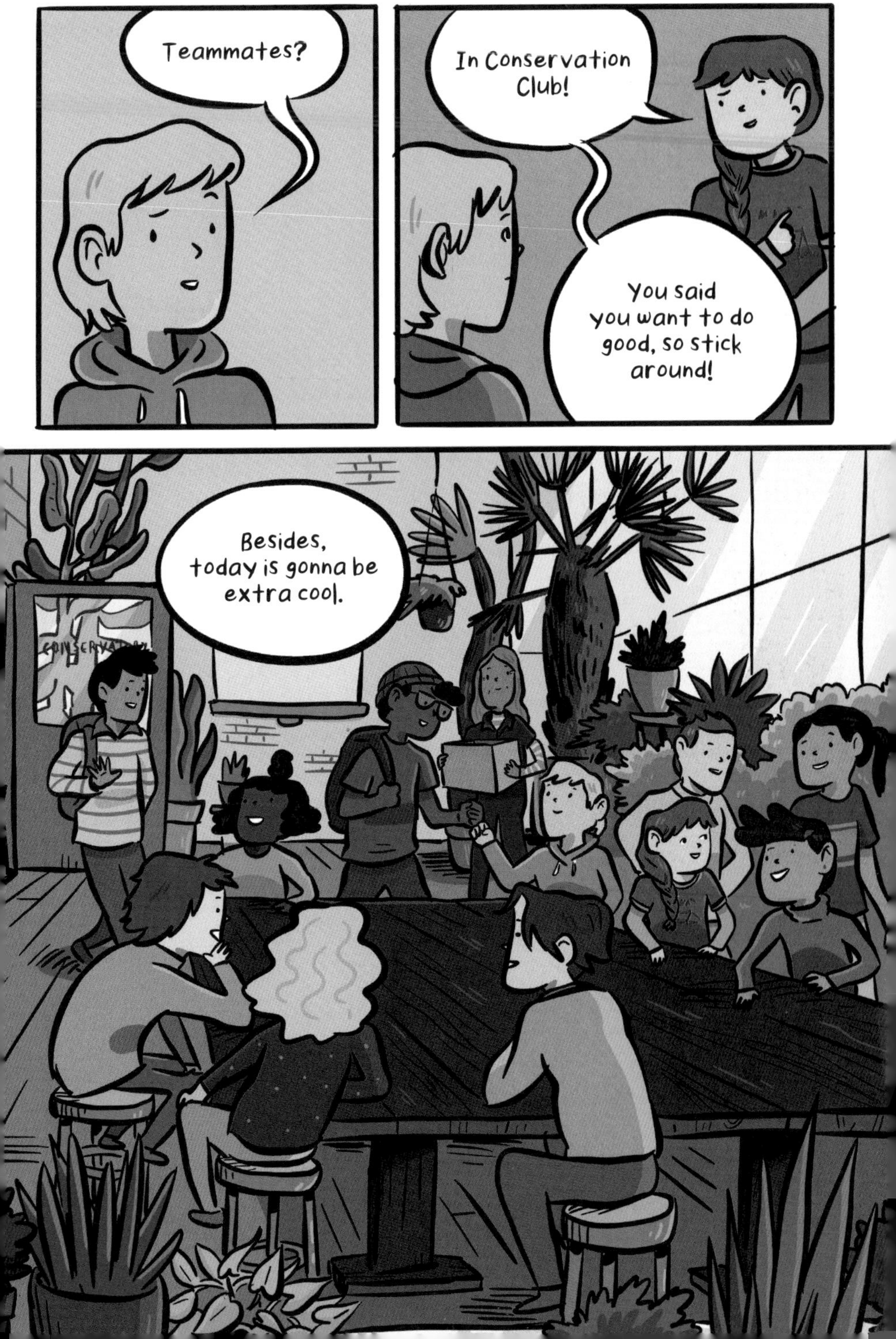
Teammates?
In Conservation Club!
You said you want to do good, so stick around!
Besides, today is gonna be extra cool.

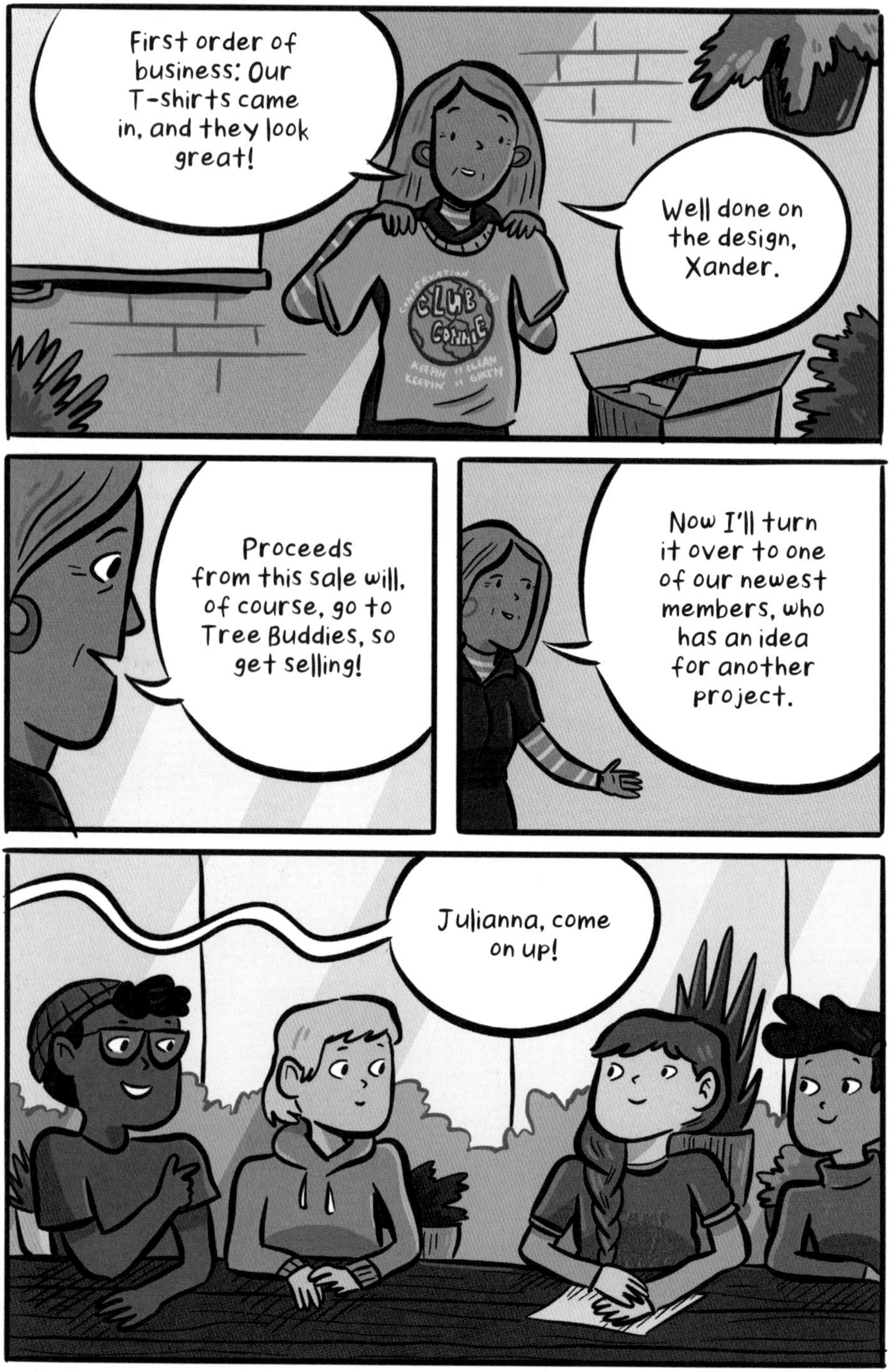
First order of business: Our T-shirts came in, and they look great!
Well done on the design, Xander.
CLUB CONNIE
Proceeds from this sale will, of course, go to Tree Buddies, so get selling!
Now I'll turn it over to one of our newest members, who has an idea for another project.
Julianna, come on up!

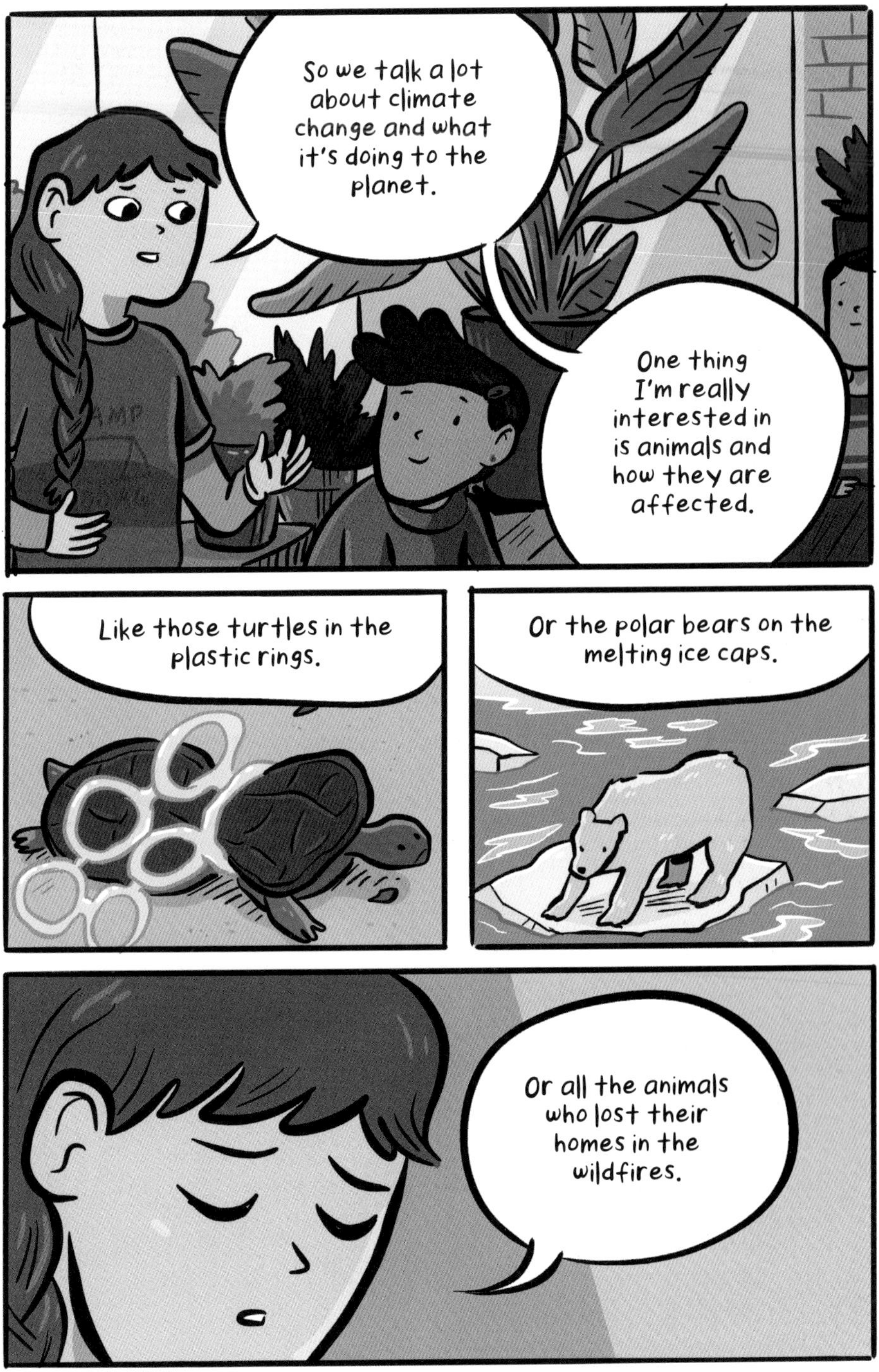
So we talk a lot about climate change and what it's doing to the planet.
One thing I'm really interested in is animals and how they are affected.
Like those turtles in the plastic rings.
Or the polar bears on the melting ice caps.
Or all the animals who lost their homes in the wildfires.

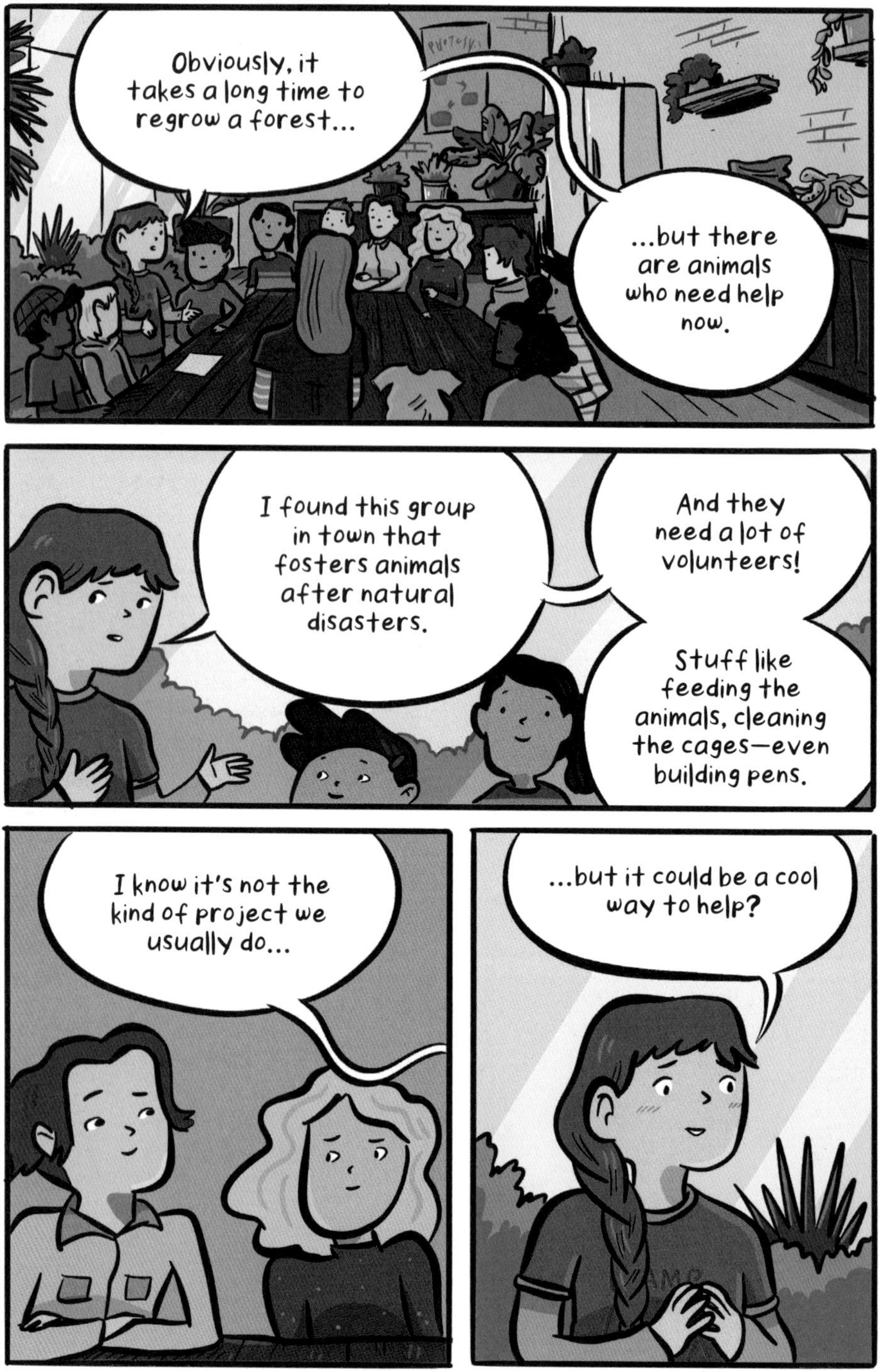

Obviously, it takes a long time to regrow a forest...
...but there are animals who need help now.
I found this group in town that fosters animals after natural disasters.
And they need a lot of volunteers!
Stuff like feeding the animals, cleaning the cages—even building pens.
I know it's not the kind of project we usually do...
...but it could be a cool way to help?

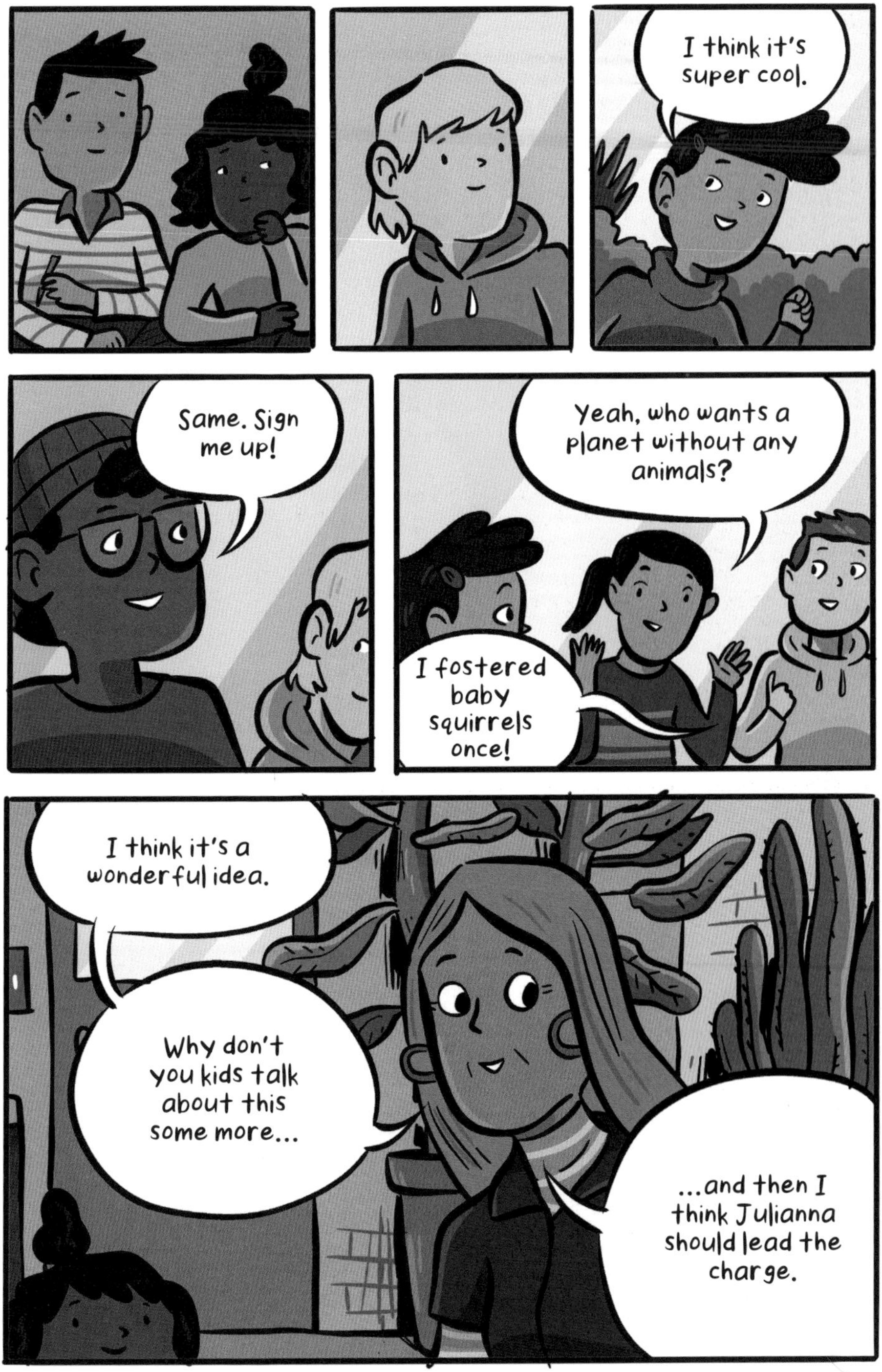
I think it's super cool.
Same. Sign me up!
Yeah, who wants a planet without any animals?
I fostered baby squirrels once!
I think it's a wonderful idea.
Why don't you kids talk about this some more...
...and then I think Julianna should lead the charge.

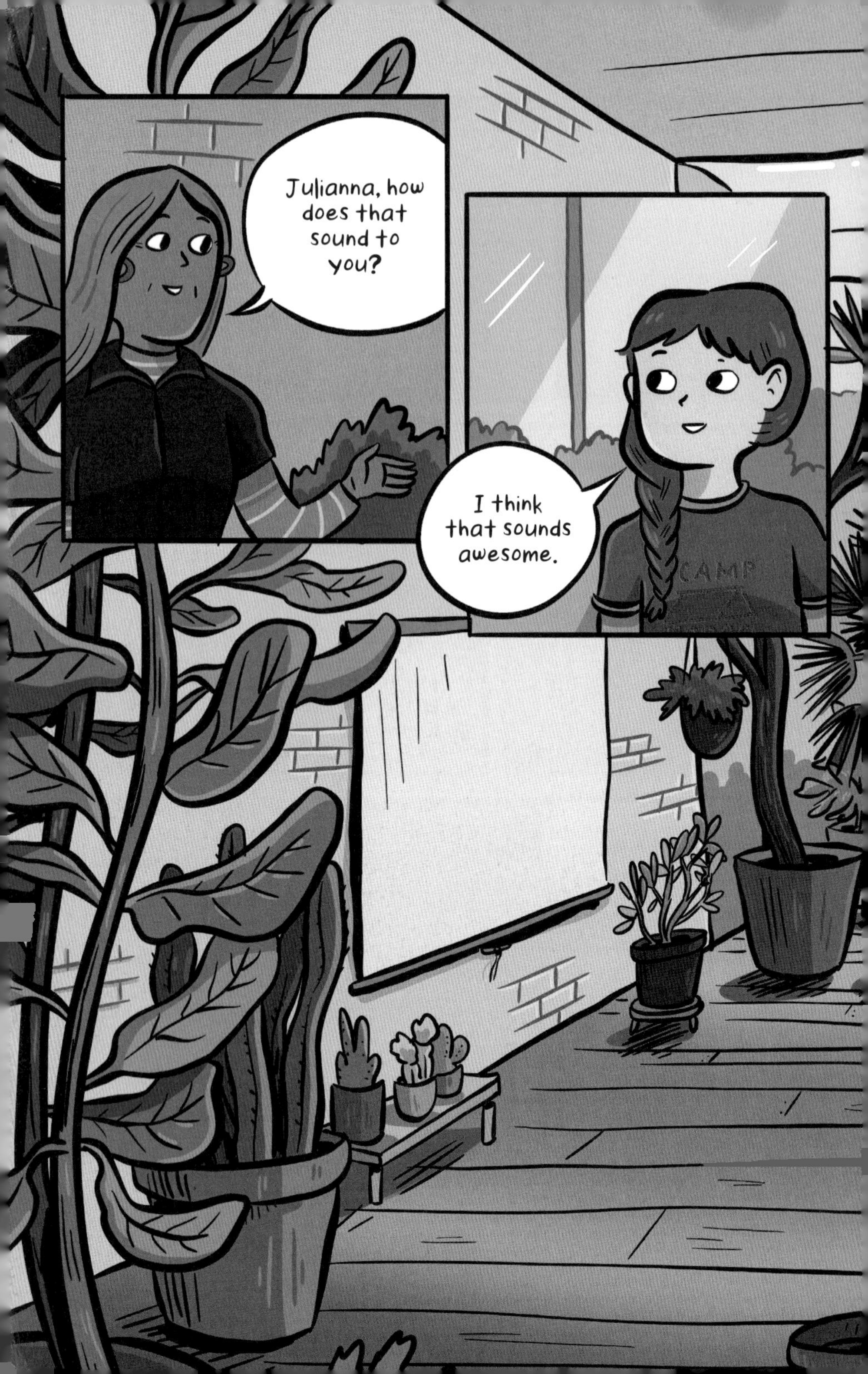
Julianna, how does that sound to you?
I think that sounds awesome.
CAMP

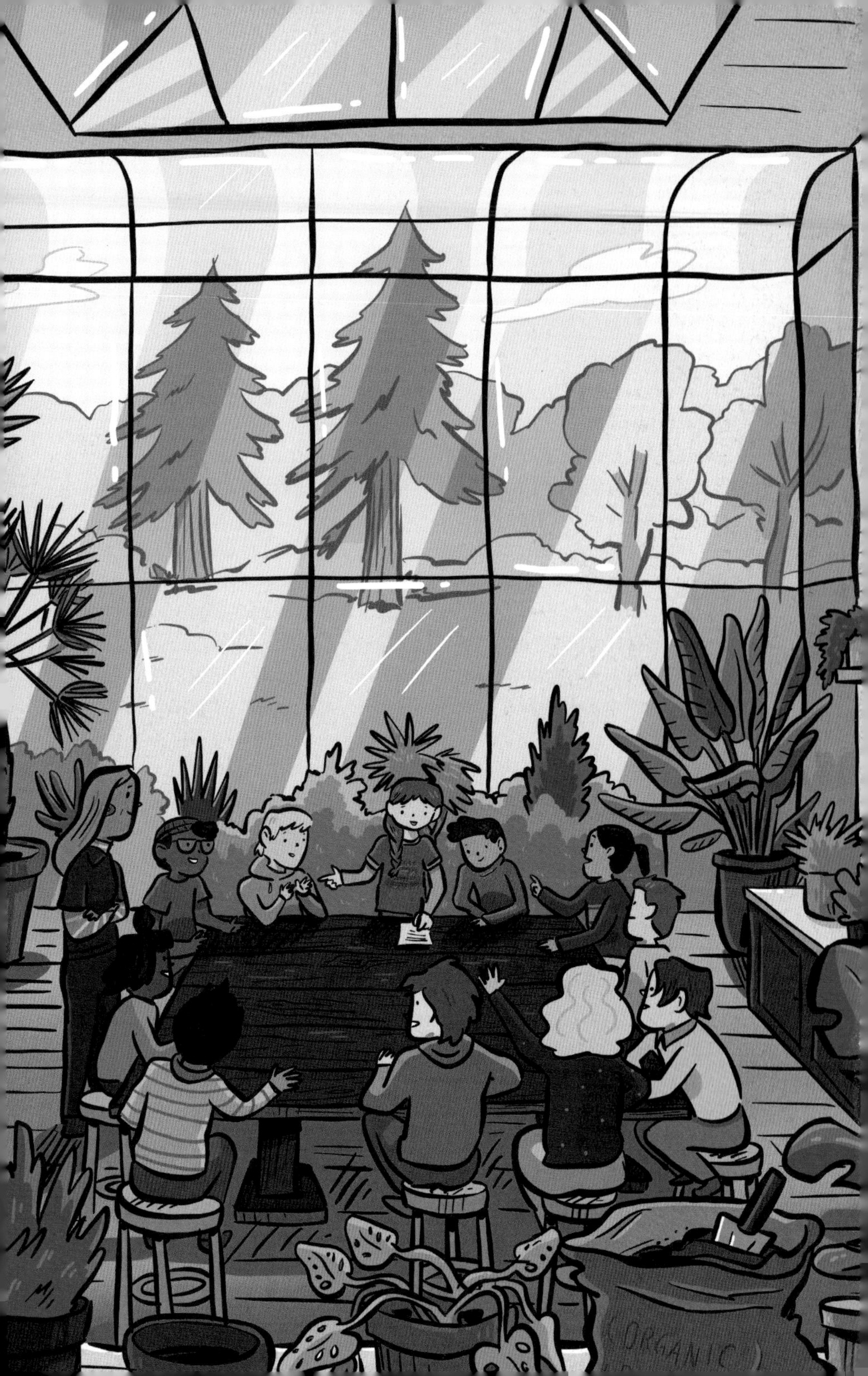
ORGANIC

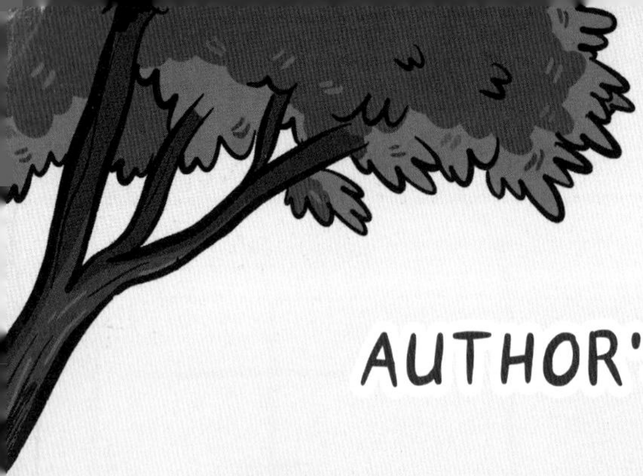

AUTHOR'S NOTE

Hi there,

Now that you've read *Wildfire*, I thought I would share a little bit about how this story came about. There was a week in the summer of 2020 when the wildfires were so bad in Oregon that my family and I (and hundreds of thousands of other people in the area) had to stay inside for a week, with even the small cracks in the doorways taped shut. The fires were heading our direction, and though they never reached us (fortunately!), the air quality had become toxic because of all the smoke. The sky was an eerie yellow. Everything outdoors, including all the plants, was covered in a layer of ash. We had our suitcases packed in case we got the order to evacuate. It was very scary, and it was sad to think about all the people and animals whose lives were being directly affected by the wildfires. It was sad to think of our beautiful forests and fields being burned.

In the middle of that week, I was trying to think of an idea for my next book. My editor suggested that I write a story about wildfires, and very quickly an idea began to take shape. A family who had lost their home to a wildfire must build a new life and come to terms with the cause of the destruction. Like Julianna, my first inclination in writing this story was to place all blame on Carson and the kids who sparked the fire. But I realized that the story goes deeper than one single, reckless mistake. The wildfires that affected us, like the wildfire that affects Julianna, were not the result of one person's actions but countless people's actions over many years. Almost as soon as I started writing, I realized there was no way to tell this story without digging into the underlying cause: climate change.

Wildfires have been around for a long, long time, and they actually play an important role in the cycles of life on our planet. But over the past fifty years, the frequency and severity of wildfires have increased. It's no coincidence that this is happening while the long-term average temperatures on the earth continue to rise. Rising temperatures cause worsening drought conditions, reduce mountaintop snowpack, and leave forests dryer for longer periods of time. All of these factors have contributed to longer and more intense wildfire seasons in recent years. Wildfires are not a new phenomenon, but they are getting worse because of climate change.

It can feel really hopeless and overwhelming to think and talk about climate change. Sometimes when adults talk about it, they can make it sound like the future is very dark. Who wants to think about that? Not me! But not thinking about something doesn't help change the situation. And that's a big part of why I decided it was important to look this issue in the face and call it out, because it's not too late to change things.

The good news for our planet is that we know some big ways to help slow or even stop climate change. The most impactful thing we can do is reduce our carbon emissions, which is a fancy way to say we can stop putting so much carbon dioxide into the air! There are lots of ways we can do this as individuals: Instead of driving, we can walk, ride a bike, or take public transit. We can use reusable containers for our lunches, drinking water, and shopping. We can conserve energy at home by turning off lights and devices when we aren't using them. We can cut back on eating red meat, and we can buy food that's grown close to where we live. All of these are important changes we can make in our own lives to help reduce our carbon footprint—that is, how much carbon we put into the atmosphere. It's very important that we each take responsibility to care for our planet in the ways that we can; it will help our planet, and it tends to benefit our own health as well!

But even with all of us making small changes in our own lives, there are some bigger changes that we as a society need to push for as well. The most common sources of carbon emissions are electricity and heat—two very necessary things! For a long time, the main fuel source for these industries has been coal and oil, which create a lot of energy when burned but unfortunately generate a lot of carbon dioxide as well. The good news is that humans have developed clean, renewable energy alternatives to the fossil fuels that have long powered us. Solar power, wind, and hydro energy are increasingly viable options. The more we can switch over to these energy sources, the cleaner our air will be. And one of the biggest things we can do to support our planet is push for leaders to make these larger changes!

As Julianna learned in this book, taking action will look different for everyone, but everyone can do their part. Whether by writing letters to politicians or business leaders, attending a climate rally, or volunteering in our communities, there are so many ways to make a difference. This planet has been our home for a long time, and each generation gets a chance to care for it the very best that they can. When we all work together, we can help ensure that it lasts for many, many, many generations to come.

Sincerely,
Breena Bard

ADDITIONAL RESOURCES

There are a lot of resources if you'd like to learn more about how to get involved with the environment. Here are a few that I've found helpful!

Artis, Zanagee, and Olivia Greenspan. *A Kids Book About Climate Change.* Portland, OR: A Kids Company About, 2020.

Citizens' Climate Lobby. "How to Write a Letter to Congress."
https://citizensclimatelobby.org/blog/advocacy/how-to-write-a-letter-to-congress/.

The Climate Museum. "Climate Art for Congress."
https://climatemuseum.org/climateartforcongress.

Fothergill, Alastair, and Keith Scholey, series prod. *Our Planet.* Season 1. Aired April 5, 2019, on Netflix.
https://www.netflix.com/title/80049832.

Fridays for Future.
https://fridaysforfuture.org/.

NASA. "Vital Signs of the Planet." Global Climate Change.
https://climate.nasa.gov/.

National Geographic Kids. "Save the Earth Tips."
https://kids.nationalgeographic.com/nature/save-the-earth/topic/save-the-earth-tips.

Union of Concerned Scientists. "Infographic: Western Wildfires and Climate Change."
https://www.ucsusa.org/resources/western-wildfires-and-climate-change.

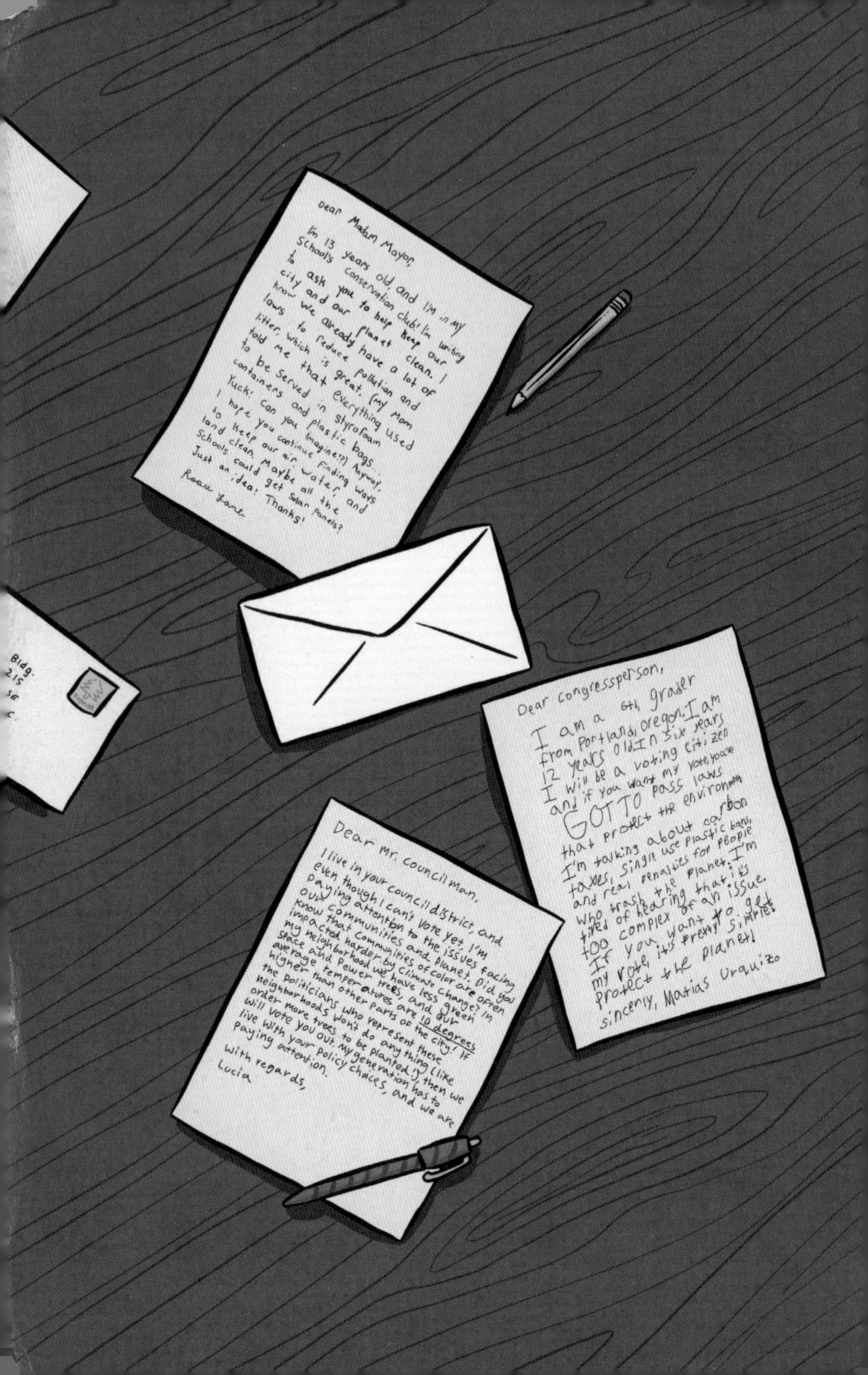
Dear Madam Mayor,
I'm 13 years old, and I'm in my School's conservation club. I'm writing to ask you to help keep our city and our planet clean. I know we already have a lot of laws to reduce pollution and litter, which is great. (My Mom told me that everything used to be served in styrofoam containers and plastic bags... Yuck! Can you imagine?!) Anyway, I hope you continue finding ways to keep our air, water, and land clean. Maybe all the Schools could get Solar Panels? Just an idea! Thanks!
Dear Congressperson,
I am a 6th grader from Portland, Oregon. I am 12 years old. In six years I will be a voting citizen and if you want my vote, you've GOTTO pass laws that protect the environment. I'm talking about carbon taxes, single use plastic bans, and real penalties for people who trash the planet. I'm tired of hearing that it's too complex of an issue. If you want to get my vote, it's pretty simple: protect the planet!
Sincenly, Matias Urquizo
Dear Mr. Councilman,
I live in your council district, and even though I can't vote yet, I'm paying attention to the issues facing our communities and planet. Did you know that communities of color are often impacted harder by climate change? In my neighborhood, we have less green space and fewer trees, and our average temperatures are 10 degrees higher than other parts of the city! If the politicians who represent these neighborhoods won't do anything (like order more trees to be planted!), then we will vote you out. My generation has to live with your policy choices, and we are paying attention.
With regards,
Lucia

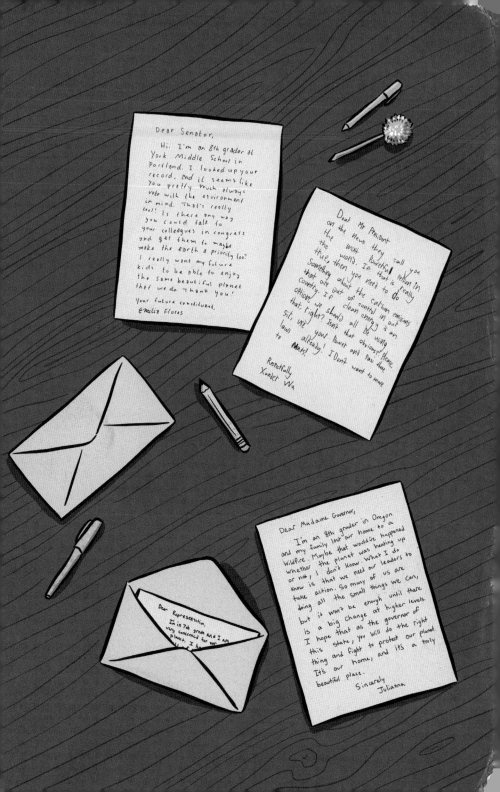

Dear Senator,

Hi. I'm an 8th grader at York Middle School in Portland. I looked up your record, and it seems like you pretty much always vote with the environment in mind. That's really cool! Is there any way you could talk to your colleagues in congress and get them to maybe make the earth a priority too? I really want my future kids to be able to enjoy the same beautiful planet that we do. Thank you!

Your future constituent,
Emilia Flores

Dear Mr President,

on the news they call you the most powerful person in the world. If that is really the, then you need to do something about the carbon emissions that are out of control in our country. If clean energy is an option, we should all be using it, right? Isnt that obviously, please, sir, use your power and pass those laws already! I Dont want to move to Mars!

Regretfully,
Xander Wu

Dear Madame Governor,

I'm an 8th grader in Oregon and my family lost our home to a wildfire. Maybe that would've happened whether the planet was heating up or not, I don't know. What I do know is that we need our leaders to take action. So many of us are doing all the small things we can, but it won't be enough until there is a big change at higher levels. I hope that as the governor of this state, you will do the right thing and fight to protect our planet. It's our home, and it's a truly beautiful place.

Sincerely,
Julianna

Dear Representative,

I'm in 7th grade And I am very concerned for our planet. I ho...

ACKNOWLEDGMENTS

I have a lot of people to thank for their help and support in bringing this book into the world:

To my agent, Alex Slater, for clearing a path through the thicket and guiding me along with so much care. To my editor, Andrea Colvin, who saw something in this story and nurtured it, just like she said she would. This book literally would not exist without the two of you! Thank you!

Thank you to Andrea Bell, who brought this book to life with magnificent color.

To everyone at Little, Brown Ink, especially designers Carolyn Bull and Ann Dwyer, art director Megan McLaughlin, and production editor Jake Regier.

To my heroes and pals Jonathan Hill, Aron Nels Steinke, Jen de Oliveira, Sam Wedelich, and Simone Lia.

To my friends Ash, Heidie, Nick, Michaela, Gena, Katia, Ashley, Holly, and everyone else who has been in my corner.

To Aunt Shirley and Uncle Dave as well as Jen and Ian—thank you for letting me put your homes in this story!

Thank you to Bruce Congdon, Divine Kickingbird, and all the scientists and activists who have shared their knowledge of—and passion for—the need to care for this planet.

Thank you to the firefighters everywhere.

And, of course, endless thanks to Mom, Dad, Meagan, Rodney, Shawn, Leona, Louie, all of the Bards, and every member of my family for their endless enthusiasm and support.

Finally, to my three favorite humans: Zech, Harvey, and Helen. You're the most patient, the most encouraging, the most inspiring, and the most fun. Thank you for always cheering me on!

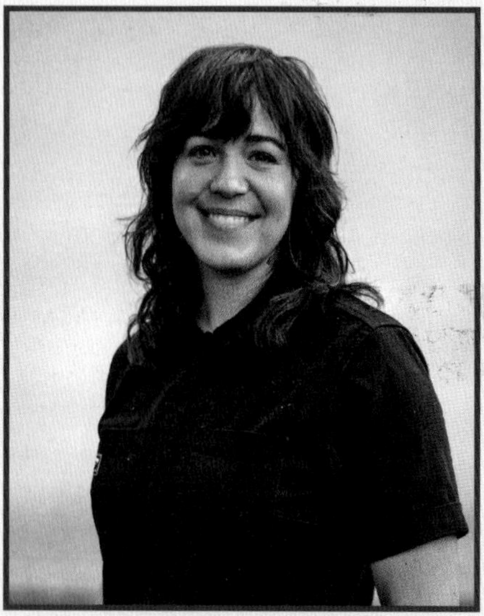

Weeno Photography

BREENA BARD

writes and illustrates comics for kids and kids at heart, drawing inspiration from the stacks of graphic novels on her bedside table. She lives in Portland, Oregon, with her husband and two kids. When she's not working on books, Breena enjoys eating pizza, watching movies, playing the drums, and exploring the outdoors with her family.